OF
LOVE
AND
LIFE

OF
LOVE
AND
LIFE

Three novels selected and condensed
by Reader's Digest

CONDENSED BOOKS DIVISION

The Reader's Digest Association Limited, London

With the exception of actual personages identified as such, the
characters and incidents in the fictional selections in this volume
are entirely the product of the authors' imaginations and have no
relation to any person or event in real life.

The Reader's Digest Association Limited
11 Westferry Circus, Canary Wharf, London E14 4HE

www.readersdigest.co.uk

CONTENTS

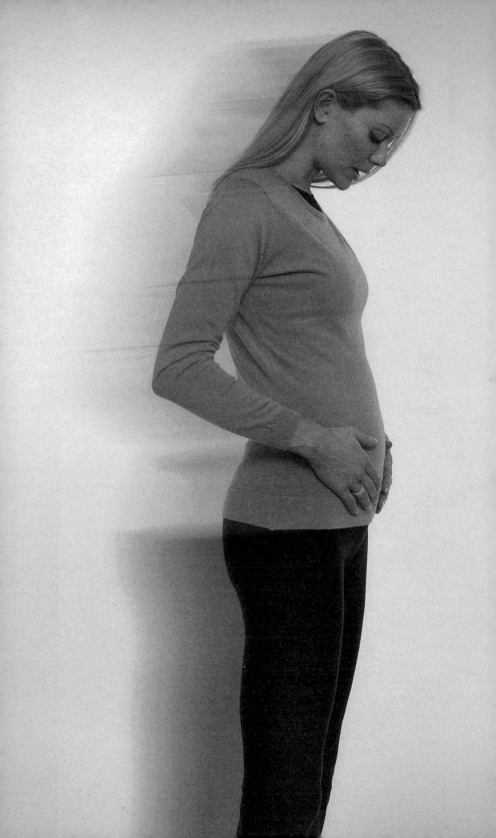

Linda Taylor

GOING AGAINST THE GRAIN

Louise isn't sure where her life took a wrong turn, but it's not shaping up as well as she might have hoped. Scatty, disorganised, bad at co-ordinating her ward-robe, Louise wishes she could be more like her dynamic, elder sister Rachel—or even like her Mum . . .
Heroically, Louise plans to make a new start, but first one disaster strikes and then another and another.

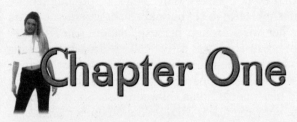# Chapter One

'OH MY GOD!'

It was Monday morning. But that wasn't the half of it. It was very *late* on Monday morning.

Louise squashed her face into the orange cushion, then the red one, then the rust one. She wriggled until she found the limp pillow buried underneath. She flattened her cheek against the cool cotton and opened one eye. The psychedelic yellow and green sunbursts on the pillowcase put a bomb under any lingering sensations of tranquillity. These colours were supposed to turn her into a positive thinker, according to an article she had read. This morning they were burning out the backs of her retinas. She groaned, pulled a face and struggled into a sitting position in bed. She pulled the duvet up round her shoulders, stuck an Ultra-Low cigarette between her lips and thought about lighting it.

Something else struck her as her arms waved around in front of her body. They ached. Not only that, her throat was raw, her nose was defunct as breathing apparatus, and her head was about to explode with pain. She gave the cigarette a regretful look before flinging it aside, collapsing back against her pile of cushions and closing her eyes. So the tickly nose, sore throat and hot head of the previous evening had not just been the usual Sunday night list of complaints brought on by the thought of Andrew and Jez's Monday morning faces, alight with manic cheer brought about by a frenetic need to keep Party Animals afloat. She really did have a cold. A horrible one.

She let out a low, earthy groan and let her eyelids droop. She groped for her radio alarm. What had she left it on? She hoped it was Virgin.

She needed to be rocked right out of bed. It was Classic FM. She clicked it off again quickly, lay still, and then frowned.

The finger of guilt prodding at her solar plexus was telling her that she had overslept by a lot this time. She wasn't going to be able to make up for it by bursting into the Party Animals office clutching scraps of paper covered with ideas that she had hastily scribbled down on the tube and pretending that she had spent the morning on 'project analysis'. There was no way she was going to make it in today.

She wanted a cup of tea, but the flat was freezing and she couldn't face getting out of bed. But she'd have to get out of bed any minute now and ring work to simper her way through her explanation. They'd never believe she'd overslept because she was actually ill. Andrew was looking for an opportunity to fire her, she felt sure of that after the last warning he gave her. It was her own fault. She'd just never felt at home in that company, just as she'd never felt at home anywhere else. She'd taken too much time off, despite knowing that it would rebound on her later.

She'd joined Party Animals as a project manager. They were an Exciting and Young company, Andrew and Jez explained. Great, she'd enthused, feeling neither exciting nor young, but overwhelmingly jobless. Everybody wanted parties, and was prepared to pay a great deal, they said. Especially in Cambridge, where they had been undergraduates together, and where they had both got the idea. At the time, the philistine thought had occurred to her that everybody in London was too knackered or too pissed off to go to parties, and that in Cambridge it might have been different, but she had smiled in an Exciting and Young sort of way and got the job. In practice, her job involved sitting in the office trying to sound like a receptionist if somebody rang before handing the phone over to one of her bosses. She was starting to think that the Exciting and Young company was a Not Very Well Thought Out company.

She wound the duvet round her body and slid her legs over the edge of the bed. Her feet flopped about until they met the carpet. She had a vision of herself melting into the floor like an ice cream. Perhaps she would stay there all day. Perhaps she would die of dehydration and nobody would know. Not until Harris upstairs smelt something funny coming from her flat, and then she'd be uncovered, rolled up in her duvet, her glassy eyes still fixed longingly on her unlit cigarette.

She paused while she planned her own funeral. She wondered what music they might play. Jon, wiping away a tear in the front pew, would be sorry that he was scared of commitment and had made her agree that what they really needed was space from each other. If he could only see the state that she was in, he would realise how much he loved her. The reality, though, was that none of those thoughts would sprint across his mind.

He didn't exactly want things to end between them completely, he'd explained, it was just that it wasn't healthy to live in each other's pockets. She'd been in this situation before, and the alarm bells were pealing melodiously. They had spent a year and a half on an association which she, at least, had thought of as a relationship, but which he'd seen as a cool and modern arrangement. It had jogged along, at first in a fairly sprightly manner, becoming somewhat red-faced and wheezing after a time, and had eventually suffered a coronary and collapsed in an ungainly fashion on a park bench. It was over. But what was really irritating Louise was that Jon hadn't had the courage to say this. Instead, he'd talked about space. You have that universe, and I'll just leap into my rocket and jet off to this one. Bye then.

With a pout, Louise inched herself in her duvet cocoon across the carpet towards the telephone, reached it and fell on top of it. She pulled up the receiver and poked her fingers at the buttons, then lay back and waited for Andrew to answer in his exhaustingly keen voice.

'Party Animals, this is Andrew speaking, how can I help you?'

'Andrew.' She paused, her breath coming in short rasps. 'Andrew, my aunt's dead.'

'Louise?'

'Yes,' she said.

'Louise, you told us your aunt died over a year ago. You can't come up with that one again. Where are you?'

'I'm at home, and it's a different aunt.'

'Look, we've had everything under the sun from you. I got in this morning, and do you know what Jez said? "Monday," he said. "What will Louise come up with today?" So what is it?'

'I've got the flu.' Louise rolled over and landed on her face. Unfortunately, it was where she'd left a hunk of uneaten nan bread. She nudged the plate to one side with her nose.

'Are you saying you can't come in?' Andrew sounded bored.

'I'm saying I can't even get to the kettle. I'm saying that I'm genuinely ill, and even saying it makes my throat hurt more, and makes me iller.' She coughed roughly, her eyes streaming.

'Sounds like you've had a night on the piss and sixty Marlboros,' Andrew said heartlessly. 'No point in expecting you in this afternoon, I suppose?'

There was a long, intolerant pause. Louise remembered that she'd once thought Andrew fancied her. If he had, he was certainly getting over it.

'I'm sorry,' she said.

'You always are, Louise. Will we see you tomorrow, or is this a three-day hangover?'

'I'll be in tomorrow. I promise. If I can just sleep this off, I'm sure I'll make it—'

Andrew hung up.

She lay back on the floor. It was a relief to have made the phone call. She was authentically off sick even if Andrew and Jez didn't believe her. They'd just have to survive without her. And now that she had freed herself for the day, she had a strong urge to fight the germs and do something more fun than lying in bed with the curtains closed.

She rang Sally at work.

'Louise Twigg?' Sally sounded ridiculously polite. She had someone with her. 'Could I possibly call you back?'

'It was only a quickie,' Louise raced on. 'I wondered what you're doing for lunch?'

'That would be a little tricky.'

'This evening then?'

'Er, I'm afraid I have a fairly full timetable for the immediate future.'

'Fergus,' Louise declared.

'Yes.'

Louise rolled her eyes to the ceiling. What was the matter with men these days? Didn't Fergus have a life of his own?

'Bye then, Sal.'

'You could call me later in the week if that's convenient.'

'And you'll pencil me in a window. I know. Talk to you soon.'

She hung up.

'Selfish cow,' she uttered into the air, and sniffed hard. She supposed that if Jon were as adoring as Fergus, she and Sally would have even fewer opportunities to meet up. As it was, whenever they squashed themselves into wine bars to discuss Jon, Sally always gave her a funny look. As if it were all Louise's own fault. But it wasn't just Fergus. It was also the fact that Sally was busy being a brilliant solicitor. She couldn't work out for the moment which of Sally's areas of total fulfilment she felt the most peevish about.

Perhaps later, she consoled herself, she'd go shopping on her own. Some new clothes would show Andrew and Jez that she meant business, and tomorrow she'd turn up at Party Animals with a fresh attitude. After she'd had another hour's sleep. She climbed back onto the bed, ran a hand vaguely through the tangled strands of her dark blonde hair, and collapsed onto her mountain of mismatched cushions.

When Louise woke up again, her first image was of Jon climbing over his desk and reaching for Kelly's breasts. It must have been a dream. One of those dreams that tells you what's really going on. For some reason, something was telling her that at this moment he was grabbing somebody's breasts. She knew, even in her state of semi-delirium, that they weren't hers.

With men, there had always been one casually dropped name that caused her palpitations and night-sweats. Jon's was Kelly. She was 'harmless', according to Jon. Louise knew that Jon slept with every woman he called 'harmless'. It was his code.

'Right!'

She cast herself out of bed and fiddled with the radio until she hit upon something loud, discordant and energetic. It was time to make some changes. And the first day of the rest of her life would start with a trip to the shops. Later, when she felt really good about herself, she would sort things out with Jon once and for all.

In Flickers, her favourite candle shop, she pondered over the aromatic oils. She'd heard the lavender was good for seduction. She put that one back. Lemon would be bracing. Cinnamon might be nice to burn when she was eating another takeaway from Aziz. And she could spread eucalyptus all over the cushions to clear her nose. She collected a range of tiny bottles before ambling towards the till. She smiled at the bemused face of the woman at the counter. She glanced down instinctively at her clothes. She'd wanted to wear the maroon sweater with this rather short pink skirt, but that had been at the bottom of the laundry basket, so she'd had to make do with the long cardigan she'd bought to wear with trousers. With her coat open to let some cool air make contact with her flushed skin, it probably looked as if she'd forgotten to put anything on the bottom at all. But the tights were opaque. And her boots came up to the knee. It wasn't that obscene, yet the woman's features were definitely crumpled with dismay. Louise smiled more broadly and was met with an overt frown.

'Is there a problem?'

'Don't move!' the assistant issued and slid from behind the counter.

Louise obediently froze.

'The belt of your coat, dear. It's caught on the candelabra. You'll bring the whole thing crashing down if you twitch a muscle.'

They smiled at each other while the woman worked slim, pointed fingers on the obstruction.

'You need to move the other way—slowly.'

Louise winced as the top of the candelabra made contact with her head. The mobile above the shop door tinkled. She cast an idle glance at the figure that had just strode in and wriggled back to yank at the belt of her coat.

'It's a nice coat,' the assistant said. 'These long ones are quite fashionable, aren't they?'

'Are they?'

'Oh yes. I think you're supposed to wear something underneath, though.'

Louise managed a laugh and flipped up her cardigan to reveal the pink pleated skirt. She glanced down and realised that she was flashing her tights and a pair of hip-hugging white knickers to the customer who was waiting patiently at the till.

'Louise?' a naggingly familiar voice queried.

She winced, and made full eye contact with the man who was now leaning on the counter and drumming his fingers.

'Andrew?' she breathed, as if there could possibly be some doubt. He raised an auburn eyebrow at her in reply.

'Andrew, this isn't what it looks like. I came shopping to get some oil. For my nose.' He seemed uninterested in her, and as the assistant trotted back to the counter, began a conversation about outside lanterns.

'So—so what are you doing here?' Louise shuffled forward, her face reddening, her collection of bottles rattling in her hand. He looked over his shoulder at her with a studied lack of urgency that was ominous.

'You recommended Flickers. Remember? For all our lighting needs? It was a shame you were too ill to come to work today, because I was going to ask you to come down here and check out the range we could use for garden parties. And obviously, in your depleted state, you'd never have managed it. Would you?'

Louise opened her mouth and prayed for a sneeze. Nothing happened. She closed her mouth again.

He eyed the carrier bags by her feet. 'Been shopping?'

She decided that braving it out was the safest option. 'If you must know, Andrew, I've been buying myself a new outfit for work. I should be more professional about the way I do my job. So despite the fact that I feel dreadful, I dragged myself out so that I could turn over a new leaf. And I was on my way to the counter to ask about outside lighting when you walked in. It's just that I got my belt caught on the candelabra.'

She realised it didn't justify showing him her knickers, but that would have to go unexplained for now.

'Whatever you say, Louise.' He sounded bored as he glanced over a folder which the shop assistant had handed him and tucked it under his arm. He turned to go, then stopped and looked her up and down.

'Just a hint, Louise. Save the Miss Whiplash look for the bedroom.'

He nodded at the assistant, assured her he would be in touch and left the shop. Louise let out a long breath.

'Sadistic swine.'

'Oh dear.'

Louise slammed the bottles down onto the counter with a crash. 'I have decided that things are no longer going to go wrong.'

'That's seven pounds forty, then, dear.'

'And I'll take the candelabra too. We seem to have bonded.'

Later that evening, Louise was treated to the sight of Harris leaning against her door frame. She didn't know much about him even though he'd lived in the flat upstairs for a good few months, but she did know he was an actor. He had managed to mention his moment of fame in *Casualty* each time they'd banged into each other. She was never quite sure whether his range of expressions displayed genuine emotion, or if he was getting himself into character. This evening, though, he was doing thunderous quite convincingly. She pulled a rueful face.

'I'm sorry, Harris, is it the piano? Is it too loud?'

He was attractive, she had to admit. She hadn't really appreciated him before. Each time they'd met, he'd had a woman on his arm, or was on his way out to meet one. But it wasn't just that he was clamoured for that put her off. It was that he knew he was attractive. His clothes shouted it. Tonight he was in crisp chinos and a powder-blue shirt with the collar flipped up. And she could bet that the shirt had been chosen because it was exactly the same colour as his eyes.

'No, Louise. There's a small village in Venezuela that can't hear you. They've emailed me to ask you to sing louder.'

'You don't like it then?' She opened her eyes appealingly.

'It's not possible to do it *without* the singing, I suppose?' He folded his arms. She took a moment to admire his biceps covertly.

'It wouldn't be the same without the lyrics. The chorus is too repetitive.'

'But it's repetitive anyway,' he explained patiently. 'You've played "I'm Going to Wash That Man Right Out of My Hair" six times in a row. I know. I counted.'

She let out a hefty sigh. Her nose started to run, and before she could stop herself, she sneezed violently at him. She grappled with a tissue.

'You see the problem?' she said in a muffled voice. 'I'm ill. My ears are bunged up too. I can't tell what volume I'm playing at.'

He paused to assess her. She squirmed under his gaze. She hadn't bothered to change when she'd got home, and the short pink skirt was still hidden somewhere inside the long cardigan. He seemed to have only just noticed, and had visibly brightened.

'I'd say bed was the best cure,' he said slowly.

'Oh yes, I'm going there in a minute,' she nodded. 'Once I've done a few things.'

'Like washing your hair?'

'Oh, is it that bad?' She raked her hands through the limp strands.

'No, Louise, I was referring to the song. Your hair looks delicious.'

She eyed him over her tissue. Delicious? Her hair? What had got into him tonight?

'Well, if that was all, Harris, I'd better get back to—'

'What's that wonderful smell?' He poked his head through the doorway.

'Search me. I can't smell a thing.'

'Something's very . . .' He savoured his words. 'Erotic in here.'

He was edging himself inside her flat. Attractive or not, she wasn't in the mood for this. She had been planning a letter to Jon while she thumped away on her secondhand upright. 'It's lemony and fresh. Very stimulating.' He flared his nostrils at her.

'Are you rehearsing for a washing powder commercial?'

'Sharp, like you, madam. Have you been buying smelly candles?'

'It's the oil burner. Don't tell me you can actually smell it?'

'I expect the village in Venezuela can smell it as well. You're only supposed to put a few drops in, you know.'

'I know.' She grabbed his elbow and nudged him back to the door.

'You know what's good for colds?' He popped his head round the door as she began to close it on him.

'Enlighten me.'

'Sex,' he said without blinking.

'Sex?'

'It's all the sweating you do. One of the extras on *Casualty* had a stinking cold when we were filming the accident scene. She said—'

'Good night, Harris. Thank you for your concern.'

She shut the door firmly, leaned back against it, and drew in a noseful of lemony fresh air. She remained unstimulated. She gazed fondly at her new candelabra. At some point, she would go back to the shop and buy candles to go in it too, but money was tighter than she was admitting. There was the unpaid phone bill to contemplate. She wandered over to the piano and gently shut the lid over the keys. She would return to *South Pacific* tomorrow evening, perhaps with a little less gusto.

She dragged herself through into the kitchen. Didn't they say 'Feed a cold, starve a fever?' She yanked open the fridge door and squatted while she assessed the contents. A half-drunk bottle of South African white, the leftover sag aloo from Sunday, a jar of pizza topping, some mature cheddar cheese, four wilted spring onions.

She tutted, pulled out the mature cheddar, and took a bite out of the side. Today may have been the first day of the rest of her life, but there was always tomorrow. Then she would wow them at work, and what's more, go to the supermarket and buy some things that she could actually eat. And all this she would do in a skirt that was visible below the line of her jumper. She was in too good a mood to write to Jon tonight. Tomorrow she'd flash off the letter without a second thought.

She smiled, flicked the kitchen radio on to Classic FM and waltzed around until she was exhausted and knew she would sleep like a baby.

'**W**e've got to let you go, Louise.'

'Oh no, Andrew, you can't mean it!' Louise followed Andrew round the table in the middle of the office. 'I'm committed. I'm sorry. I'm here, aren't I? Jez, talk some sense into Andrew, will you?'

Jez cleared his throat nervously and looked down at the brochure he was flicking through on his lap as he lolled in his chair. Louise could tell he was agitated.

'I can't believe you'd do this to me without any warning!' Louise turned back to Andrew, who had paused on the opposite side of the table to rearrange his tie and deliver his most managerial glare. 'It's just because you saw me in Flickers yesterday, isn't it?'

'Stop it, Louise,' Andrew said in a cutting voice. 'We've been thinking about letting you go for a while. Yesterday just helped us to make up our minds.'

'Please don't fire me.' Louise abandoned her pursuit of Andrew. 'If you fire me, I won't even be able to sign on. Can't you at least give me notice so that I can find another job? A month?' Jez looked at Andrew. His eyes were sympathetic. He kept silent. That was the way it usually worked. Andrew was the bombastic one. Jez was the quiet one. When it came to nasty, management business, like firing unreliable employees, it would be up to Andrew to make the pronouncement.

'I'm sorry, Louise,' Andrew said, holding out his hands as if he was trying to persuade a psychopath to give him the gun. 'It's not just the way you've done the job. It's to do with our turnover as well. Things aren't going brilliantly.'

'That's an understatement,' Jez murmured.

'OK, things are awful. The bank's going to call in the loan unless we come up with something drastic.'

'I'm with you so far,' Louise said. 'Firing me is drastic. For me, anyway.'

'It's not just that.' Andrew glanced at Jez, who obviously wasn't going to help.

'What is it?' Louise asked, standing up straight again. 'There's something you're not telling me. It's not just my salary, is it?'

'Spit it out, Andrew,' Jez said under his breath.

'We're going back to Cambridge. We should have stayed there in the first place. We're going to rent a house and run the business from the ground floor. London isn't right for our type of business. We can't afford the overheads here. We know the demand in Cambridge, and we've already discussed it with the bank. There won't be a need for a project manager there.'

'Oh,' Louise said.

'It makes perfect sense.'

'Yes, it does. No doubt you've been worried about this for a while.'

Jez looked up. He blinked at her.

'I mean, I can see your point.' She sat on the window-ledge and gazed across the tiny room. It was piled high with rubbish. Paperwork was balanced on boxes of coloured lights, champagne glasses, party balloons by the hundred. There seemed little point in arguing.

She smiled at Andrew. 'All I'm asking is that you make me redundant. If you fire me I'll find getting another job almost impossible. And I won't have anything to fall back on until I do. Just let me go nicely and give me a reference when I need one. Then we'll all part on good terms, won't we?'

'Sounds fair enough.' Jez looked at Andrew again.

Andrew bristled, and sniffed. 'I don't want it to rebound on us if I write you a reference,' he said.

'How could it? You don't have to tell any lies. Just say you've let me go because you're relocating. That's true, isn't it?'

'I'm not sure if we have to do this, legally, I mean,' Andrew said.

'I'm not sure if you can let me go without any notice, legally, I mean,' she replied pleasantly. 'Just give me a break, and write me a decent reference when I need it.' She eyed him firmly. 'Please?'

Andrew looked from her to Jez, who had his eyebrows raised, and nodded a reluctant yes.

'Thanks. I wish you both luck in Cambridge. I'll keep checking the FT. I'm sure I'll be buying shares in you one day.'

'Ah, Louise! How are you?'

Louise wasn't sure if being recognised on sight by the senior consultant in her old temping agency was an insult or a compliment, but she seated herself comfortably and prepared a willing smile.

'I'm really well, Judy. And how are you?'

'OK.' Judy was already at the computer keys. Louise had prepared a speech, but for the moment she kept it to herself. Judy tutted through pursed lips as she scrolled through the screen, deep in thought.

'The problem is . . .' Judy began, her eyes on the screen. 'That—'

'They're relocating Party Animals. It's not my fault.'

'Hmmn?'

Judy raised middle-aged eyes from her computer screen and dropped them on Louise. It was liked being sized up by a teacher. She resigned herself to the truth.

'It's your record, Louise. We have our own reputation to think of. It's no good us sending a temp if we have to send another one in her place in a matter of days. Do you see my point?'

'Yes,' Louise considered carefully. 'But I'm older now. I'm thirty-two, you see, and my attitude to so many things has changed. I really do want a chance in a proper job now.' A vision of her phone bill tangoed through her brain. 'And I'd like that chance as soon as possible.'

'Let's see. Drunk on reception, timekeeping, timekeeping,' Judy heartlessly read from her screen. 'Insolence to the managing director?' She looked at Louise quizzically. 'What on earth happened there?'

'She accused me of fondling her husband's bottom at the Christmas party.' Louise was defensive. 'She was completely wrong.'

'Ah.' Judy looked sympathetic.

'Look, is there any chance for me here or not? I'm so broke it would make you cry if you knew the whole story.'

'This is just the attitude that causes you problems.' For a moment Louise thought that Judy looked motherly. 'You need to sort out your priorities. You *are* good with people, but you're too chaotic.'

'Not any more.' Louise sat up efficiently. 'I've made some important decisions about my life, and from now on nothing's going to take me by surprise. And once I've made a decision, then, well, that's it.' She nodded affirmatively.

'All right, Louise, because I like you I'll probably be fired myself for this, but I'll give you another chance.'

'You will?' Now she seemed more motherly than ever.

'I'll put you on the books and let you know as soon as something comes up. You're a fast typist, good admin skills, and yes, I have to admit, among your misdemeanours you have managed to impress a few people with your communication skills.'

'Judy, you rock!' Louise stood up and grabbed the older woman in a hug. 'I don't suppose you could find me something that's just a tiny bit creative too?'

'I'll see what I can do. But don't expect it to be tomorrow.'

That was fine, Louise thought at home that evening. It meant she could kill off her remaining germs with a snifter of brandy without worrying about having a hangover the next day. And a glass or two of brandy was helping her to compose the perfect letter to Jon.

'Dear Jon,' she began, and stopped to giggle. She pulled a straight face, took another sip of brandy and tried to continue. She wrote another line, and stretched back in her chair. She could remember the very first time she'd seen Jon.

She'd stood next to him in the Punch and Judy in Covent Garden to order a drink, and he'd turned round lazily to assess her. She'd looked away, her pulse thumping, her skin glowing. It had been a lust-at-first-sight moment, and she'd known, from the way his pupils had widened when he'd seen her, that it had been mutual. He'd said it was all in her eyes. Come-to-bed eyes, he'd said, in a husky, come-to-bed-*with-me* sort of voice. It had melted her knees into pools of water. Of course, they hadn't that night. He'd asked her out for a drink the following Friday, and they *had* that night. That had been the beginning.

Louise stood up and paced round her kitchen. Maybe, just maybe, he might be wondering if she would phone. After all, did men these days want to do all the running? She lit a cigarette, downed another glass of brandy, and before she knew it was yanking the phone through from the bedroom on its extended lead and pressing out Jon's number.

As soon as it began to ring, she froze in horror at her own actions.

'My God!' she whispered to herself. 'What am I doing?'

Jon had asked for space. But he could have been lying. She was drunk. She didn't care. After several rings he picked up the phone.

'Hi,' she breathed at him. 'It's me. How's life?'

'Kelly! I was wondering where you'd got to!'

It could have been the result of her cold, the brandy and the cigarettes that had fatefully disguised her voice. It didn't have to be that he'd completely forgotten who she was.

'No, it's Louise.'

'God, Louise, I'm sorry. I'm expecting Kelly to ring about a customer. She's got some details that I need.'

'I bet she has.'

'What is it you wanted?'

Louise thought for a moment. What did she want? Right now she wanted to dig his heart out with a frozen chicken drumstick.

'Just to tell you that it's completely over. Whatever we had. Which wasn't anything. So I don't expect either of us will notice, will we?'

There was a long pause.

'Louise? Are you sure about this? I didn't exactly say that I wanted us to finish.'

'Piss off,' she said and hung up.

As soon as she'd put the phone down she thought of a string of fine insults that she could have thrown his way. She hopped across the kitchen and returned to her letter with renewed enthusiasm. Once she'd finished it, she dribbled another measure of brandy into her glass and drank it. Drinking a lot of brandy seemed like a very good idea.

Then she flicked through her battered Filofax to find his address. Other names and addresses jumped out at her like old photographs.

She continued her survey, and after another fortifying glass of brandy decided that she'd write to Lenny the disc jockey and Giles the accountant too. Well, she was single now, wasn't she? What did it matter if she reunited with a couple of old flames? And just to make sure she didn't change her mind about any of it, she decided she would go out and post the letters right now.

As she stomped out to the postbox in her boots and overcoat, her breath coming in vicious rasps, she couldn't help wishing that her last words to her boyfriend of nearly a year and a half hadn't been 'piss off'.

'Oh no, no, no.' She jammed the letters into the box and zigzagged back to her flat. She paused for breath in the hall before she put her keys into her flat door. There were muted sounds coming from Harris's flat.

Instinctively she climbed up the stairs and stood outside his door. She pulled off her gloves and rapped sharply.

He opened it an inch. His eyebrows shot up at the sight of her.

'Hi!' she hiccupped at him. 'Can you turn the music down, please?'

'It's really low already, Louise. It can't be disturbing you, can it?'

'Oh, OK. Then shall I turn mine down?'

'I can't hear anything.'

'So, um. Do you want to borrow some bubble bath?'

She gave him a lopsided smile. Just why she had floated up the stairs and decided to pester him right now she wasn't exactly sure, but the word 'rebound' shot into her mind and shot out again. She batted her eyelashes at him.

'Louise . . .' Harris slipped outside onto the landing and pulled the door to behind him. She realised that he was wearing nothing but a towel. His chest was damp. And very hairy. She stared at it fixedly.

'Louise, shall we talk about this tomorrow?'

'That's a nice chest you've got there. Nice amount of hair. A sprinkling, but not shagpile. If you see what I mean.' She slapped her hand over her mouth and giggled. 'Ooops, I said—'

'Look, why don't I pop down to see you tomorrow night?' He smiled, but he looked tense. He was hopping from one foot to the other as if he needed the loo.

''Snot a problem, Harris. I'll just go away. Tomorrow will do fine.'

'Big Boy?' a female voice called from inside his flat. Louise frowned and then hiccupped again, but it came out as a belch.

'Oh, I see.' She tapped the side of her nose. 'You've got company, Big Boy.'

'Yes! It's, er, an old friend.' He seemed happy that she'd worked it out, while still in some sort of pain. She turned to go, then glanced back.

'Big Boy? Is that your real name? Does that mean that Harris is only a stage name?'

'Bugger off, Louise.'

'Blimey. Must be an old friend.' She began her descent of the stairs. 'I know where I'm not wanted. Never mind.'

She nodded at him understandingly, maintaining a fixed smile as he slunk back into his flat and closed the door. She was grateful that he'd disappeared before she fell down the last two steps. She lay in a heap in the hall and wondered what she should do next. She should go to bed, of course.

She let herself into her flat, threw off her coat and headed straight for the bathroom. She started to hum. Being single was great. She could join a club. Or something. She was a free agent. Maybe she could even live her life like Harris did. She paused to chew on the bristles of her toothbrush. She looked devastatingly attractive tonight, she assured her own reflection in the bathroom mirror. Hadn't Jon fancied her once? And Harris? And a few others? She wouldn't be alone for long. Oh no.

She sat on the side of the bath and gazed around contentedly. Her eyes fell on a stock of Tampax under the basin. She chewed harder on the bristles. She was late, yes. Quite late. But not that late.

She did a fuddled calculation. Actually, she was that late. She stood up and fiddled around in the biscuit tin she used for embarrassing medical supplies. If she wasn't deluding herself she had half of a test left somewhere. It would just clear things up. She pulled out the box, and from it a plastic wand wrapped in foil. She tried to concentrate. Ah, yes. She knew what she had to do next.

After she'd managed to aim almost straight, she put the wand on the edge of the bath and continued with her ablutions. It was difficult not to sing when she was in such a good mood. And, as usual when she was poleaxed, the songs of the musicals her mother had taught her at the piano were the first to spring to mind.

She picked up the wand from the side of the bath and examined it carefully. Then she threw it in the bin with relief. She yawned at herself and rolled out several yards of dental floss. She made a cat's cradle with it while she sang the opening lines to 'Getting to Know You'. Then she remembered she was supposed to be doing something with her teeth. As she flicked the cotton strand in and out of her mouth and tried to hum at the same time, a thought occurred to her.

'Blue line, good; no line, bad. No, hang on—no line, good; blue line, bad.'

She stared at her flushed face in the mirror, a knotted mass of dental floss hanging from her front teeth.

'What was it again?'

She dropped to her knees and pulled the instructions on the box out of the bin. She read them aloud, this time with forced concentration.

'No line, good; blue line, bad.'

She retrieved the plastic wand from the bin.

'Oh shit.'

There could be no doubt about it. She was pregnant.

Chapter Two

'GOD, LOUISE. YOU LOOK a bit odd.'

Louise gave Sally Birlington, her best friend since she was eight, a withering look.

'What did you expect, Sal? I've got a streaming cold and I'm three and a half weeks pregnant.'

'Blimey. I still can't believe it.' Sally pulled her jacket lapels together in front of a thin silk blouse as they wandered into the flat together.

'What the hell is that?' asked Sally, pointing at the candelabra.

'Oh, it doesn't matter any more. It was only an idea anyway. Come through.'

'You're going to have to stop impulse buying, Lou. You know you always get it wrong. And it's chilly in here. You've got to keep warm, you know. I'll put the kettle on for you. You go and put your feet up.'

'Well, if you will walk around in evening wear in November, of course you'll be chilly.'

'What, this?' Sally plucked at her blouse. 'I have to look the part.'

'I know, ignore me. I'm just jealous.'

'So tell me all the gory details.' Sally fumbled around in the washing-up bowl for mugs, pausing just to inch up her sleeves. She ran the mugs under the tap and frowned as she tried to find a clean tea cloth.

'I'm really grateful you rushed round, Sal. You'd better not stay long, though. You don't want to get into trouble at work.'

'Hey, I'm a partner now, remember? I can fiddle my timetable if I want.'

'Oh yes.' Louise shuffled around in her daisy leggings, rollneck jumper and thick socks, undecided about whether to sit down or not. Since her pregnancy had been confirmed by the doctor, she had lost all capacity to make decisions. She felt as if her thought processes had left her head and were zooming around with the clouds earning air miles. She remembered that Sally would think she was a disaster area. Sally, who had done law at King's, way back then when she herself was dawdling through the biological science degree she hated. Sally, who had gone to university at eighteen, ginger and unexceptional, had apparently literally worked her freckles off and come out the other side stunningly beautiful, while Louise had sped in and out of Leicester in a revolving door. Sally, who was now a solicitor. A very good one. A partner, in fact. Sally, who at school had worn a brace and red hair in bunches, but now had perfect teeth and hair clamped in a delicious auburn ponytail by a stylish gold clasp. In a figure-hugging suit and neat heels, she looked fantastic. Louise suddenly wished that she hadn't rung Sally up and begged her to rush round.

'What did Jon say? Is he coming round? I don't want to be here when he arrives. You'll have so much to talk to him about.'

'I haven't told Jon yet.'

Sally raised an eyebrow and set the mugs next to the kettle.

'I swore you'd lost the ability to surprise me, but you've gone and done it again. It's just so . . . amazing.'

Louise decided to sit down before she fell down.

'How can I be pregnant? It was only because I did a test, just to reassure

24

myself. If I hadn't done the test, I wouldn't be pregnant at all.'

Sally slid herself into a chair and gave Louise a funny look.

'How did you feel when that thin blue line actually appeared?'

'That's the thing, Sal.' Louise shook her head, stunned. 'Up until now, I swore those bloody things didn't work.'

'Can I see it?'

Louise struggled up, trotted out to her bathroom and picked up the wand from the basin where she had left it. She placed it on the table in front of Sally. The blue line was more blurred than it had been when she'd first realised it was there, but it was still, undoubtedly, there.

'Wow,' Sally breathed. 'It really is true, then.'

'Yep.' Louise threw her hands in the air. 'But God Almighty, Sal, I feel exactly the same. Not sick, or hungry, or fat, or any of those things.'

'Shit.'

'Exactly. So what I want to know is, why have women been lying to us all these years? They always say you know when it happens. But you don't know. It's a lie. Take it from me.'

Sally turned her attention back to the blue line. 'And the doctor says it's definite.'

'Absolutely.'

'So now what?'

Louise sat back in her chair feeling hot and cold again. When she didn't answer the question, Sally got up and made them both tea, sniffing at the milk and pulling a face before slopping a millimetre into the mugs. She delivered Louise a mug and looked down at her with a sympathetic expression.

'You are going to have to tell Jon. You know that, don't you?'

'Of course I do. He's got to know.'

'And what about your mum? Have you told her?'

'Mum?' Louise gazed at Sally. 'I can't tell Mum. It's only just over a year since Dad died. She's too wrapped up in her own problems at the moment. I'm not likely to see her for a while anyway, and by that time I'll have done something about it.'

'What *are* you going to do about it, Lou?'

Louise sipped the tea. Sally was a loyal, wonderful friend. She and Sally had their differences. In fact, they hadn't got anything in common, but maybe that was why they'd remained friends. What they usually did was each try very hard to understand what the other was doing, even if privately she thought it was insane. But now, for the first time, Louise was in a situation that Sally couldn't understand even if she strained until she went purple. Only someone who'd never found herself pregnant could ask somebody else who just had what she was going to do about it.

'God, I don't know what I'm going to do, Sally. It's the most incredible, appalling, unbelievable, unearthly thing that has ever happened to me in my whole life!' She stood up and flapped her hands in the air.

'You've got to wash your hair before you see Jon,' Sally said cautiously. 'You don't want to look like a disaster area when you deliver a piece of news like this, do you?'

Louise thought about it all again as she lay in the bath. She had rung Jon at work. She told him she wanted to meet him. She didn't say why but had been so firm that he'd agreed. She'd suggested a pub in Kensington. It was neutral territory, and it would do.

What she would say when she got there was another thing. How did one announce something like this? Whatever she said, he would have to deal with the same volcano of reaction as she was. But let him erupt too. Then, when she had sent him away to distribute molten lava all over East Putney, she could get on with deciding what she was going to do.

She wallowed in the water for another ten minutes. It wasn't until she tried to sit up that she realised that she had put her hands on her stomach. It wasn't bulging, wobbling, growing, or any of the things she had imagined it might be. And yet, underneath all that pointless flesh was a little hive of activity, stirring itself, becoming something.

Jon was already in the Churchill Arms when she arrived. He was leaning on the bar and had already ordered himself a pint.

He looked gorgeous from behind. Slim, but tall, and elegant. Full of promise. And look where it had got them both. But she had to deal with this maturely. She stuck her tongue out at his back and made her way over to the bar. She ordered herself a drink and paid for it, only realising as she put her purse away that she hadn't bothered to say hello first. She turned to find Jon giving her a curious look.

It hadn't occurred to her to plan everything in advance, including instructions for her facial muscles. Whenever she met Jon, she always, always, broke into a bright smile. But this evening, she just stared at him, because she felt a strange tug inside that had nothing to do with lust. It was something to do with union. Jon shifted his elbow on the bar to look at her properly. She blinked back into his eyes. Lovely eyes. A sort of dark tawny shade with little brown flecks. Would the baby have them too? But he was talking to her.

'You look nice tonight. You've got a good colour. You must be keeping yourself well.'

There was no answer to that. Instead she said, 'Shall we sit down?'

'Sure.'

He seemed very calm considering that she'd told him to piss off less than twenty-four hours ago. She sat down and shrugged her thick coat onto the back of her chair, pulling at her jumper to reveal her shape. She wanted to remind him that she was a woman. Not that he'd be in doubt for much longer. He settled himself down, pulled out his cigarettes, and offered her one.

'Er, I'm not sure.' He shrugged, and took one for himself. 'No, I will,' she said, taking one from the box.

He held out his lighter for her, but she delved into her bag and found her own, not looking at him. She blew a plume of smoke away from them, and rested her hand round her glass. For the moment it was nice just to sit away from the bustle of the bar, to feel warm. Jon sipped at his beer and waited. She shouldn't really be smoking, she mused. But then again, she shouldn't really be pregnant either. She realised that Jon was watching her and swivelled her eyes to look at him.

'Last night I said we were finished,' she began, leaning forward.

'I remember.' He looked far too calm to be told that he was a father. Even if only for a week or two, she qualified quickly in her head, thoughts seesawing.

'Why did you want to meet up, Louise? I guess you've got some things to say to me. Just shoot. I probably deserve it all.'

She searched his eyes. He was so charming, laconic, at ease with himself. She suddenly had the desire to put a bomb under his complacency and dive for cover.

'I'm pregnant.'

She was pleased with herself. It came out without a tremor. He had stopped with his glass halfway to his mouth. If it wasn't for his cigarette burning away in the ashtray, he would look at that precise moment like one of the exotic butterflies framed on the wall, captured in a moment of life, pinned down, mounted and framed.

'Are you sure?' he asked eventually.

'Yep.'

'Oh God,' he said.

Well, at least he hadn't asked her who the father was, she consoled herself as she pecked at her beer.

'Don't get me wrong, Louise—but, are you sure who the father is?'

Ah well. So far, apart from a temporary blip, it was all going as she had imagined it.

'I don't think I'm even going to answer that,' she said. 'Except to say that you always make the mistake of assuming I'm like you.'

'Sorry,' he said. 'It's just that I thought you and Andrew had a thing.'

'What?' She almost spat her cigarette across the room.

'Well, he's a handsome bloke. I assumed that's why he employed you.'

'What? Because he's handsome?'

'Because he fancied you. It's what I thought.' He gave a half-laugh. 'Well, it wasn't on account of your organisational skills, was it?'

He puffed on his cigarette. 'So, er. How pregnant are you, Louise?'

'Completely.' She was confused by the question.

'No, how far gone—I mean, when did it happen?'

Perhaps he wasn't checking out her dates to see that they coincided with his, but it certainly felt like it.

'Three and a half weeks. The last time we had conjugal relations.'

He looked unenlightened.

'We went to the pictures in Leicester Square and back to Ealing for a curry. Is that any help?' He still looked blank. 'My name's Louise. Is that the clincher? You know, five foot eight, dark blonde hair, blue eyes, size twelve? Mother you disapprove of because she's common, sister you approve of because she's not.'

'But how, Louise? I mean, why that night?'

She stopped to count to ten. She got to ten, and went on to twenty.

'You knew I had come off the pill. You knew that the doctor had advised it. That's why, if you remember, we were using other methods.'

'Jesus Christ. Why the hell didn't you stay on the pill?'

'Because the doctor said I'd been on it too long. Why the hell didn't you know how to put a condom on properly?'

'Pack it in, Louise.'

'No, you pack it in. I assumed you knew what you were doing. If you hadn't known you should have said so, and we both could have practised on a banana until you got the hang of it.' She sat up. 'Why don't you start saying the right things. Or is it too much to ask?'

'Like what, for God's sake? You've just blown my world apart. I was going to tell you tonight that the bank's agreed to grant me an MBA loan. I can get a place next year at Cranfield, and my whole career begins properly from there. And then you land this on me.' He shook his head at her. 'It's just that your sense of timing is almost sadistic. If I didn't know you better, I'd think that you enjoyed telling me. Especially after last night.'

'Why?' She mouthed the question, stunned by his monologue.

'Because you knew damned well that this relationship was bogging me down. I needed to be free to think about leaving London, without any ties. So please explain why you rang me last night to finish, then brought me here tonight to tell me this. Why not tell me on the phone?'

'The answer to that is completely bloody obvious,' she yelled at him. 'I didn't know until today.'

She watched him crush his cigarette in agitation and immediately light another. She'd never seen him behave like this. She realised that by comparison she was stronger than him, but that hadn't occurred to her before.

'I'm getting another drink. Want one?' She nodded.

Jon returned and set a beer down for her. He took a deep breath as he sat down again. He seemed more peaceful. She wondered if he'd downed a triple whisky at the bar.

'I've just realised something,' he said in a more pleasant voice. 'I'd got you all wrong for a moment there. I'm sorry I was harsh. It's been a long day, and I was so excited about the loan. But you're obviously going to deal with it, aren't you? You wouldn't be drinking and smoking like this if you were thinking about keeping it.'

She sipped the froth from the top of her beer. Jon gave a short laugh.

'God, for a moment I thought you were going to demand marriage and security and all that crap.'

'Crap?' She raised her eyes to his.

'C'mon. You've got the same view of all that baggage as I have.'

'You're wrong, actually,' she said quietly. 'I would like nothing better at this moment than to know that I had someone to rely on.'

'Well, don't think I can be that person.' Then, as if regretting his abruptness, he softened momentarily. 'Look, I know I've been harsh, but this has come as a real shock to me. I've told you what's happening in my life. You've got to respect that. We had some good times together but neither of us was really committed. And certainly nothing like this was ever meant to happen.' He took a deep breath. 'I'm sorry, but if you go ahead with it, you'll be on your own. I want to make that perfectly clear.'

She paused for a moment to stub out the cigarette she had just lit.

'I didn't say I wanted to go ahead with it. All I said was that I wished I had someone to rely on.'

His shoulders slumped with relief.

'You've got Sally,' he said reassuringly. 'And your sister. She's a strong woman. She'll help you through it all. She knows what it's like to want a career without all the hassle of nappies and sick. She'll understand that you don't want it. She's never wanted kids, has she?'

'She has Hallam's children. They're over most weekends.'

'But they're not hers, are they?' He leaned forward intimately and put his hand over hers. 'By the time she got together with Hallam, his kids were past the nappies-and-sick stage. All I'm saying is that she'll help you through it. You're not on your own, Louise. You mustn't think that you are.'

She allowed a silence to fall between them and sat turning her glass round and round.

'Louise?' She looked up. 'Are you all right?'

'Of course I'm all right. Why shouldn't I be?'

'If there's anything you need, you only have to ask.'

'Like what?' She threw the question at him and waited for the answer. He was in control of himself again, she noticed. And now he thought he was being munificent.

'I know you won't want me there for the actual thing. Don't worry, I understand that. You'll probably want your mother there for you. Girls stick together at times like this, don't they?'

'Girls?' She stared at him incredulously.

'You know what I mean. Let's not get stupid about semantics.'

'No, let's not. Here are some very sensible semantics for you. You are a selfish git, Jon, and I wish to God I'd never laid eyes on you.'

'That's not exactly fair, Louise.'

'I could sum you up in a few words. In fact I did, last night. You'll get the letter tomorrow morning. I think you might be surprised by how accurate it is.'

'Look, just calm down, will you? I've said I'll back you up if you want to get rid of it. What more do you want me to say?'

'Nothing,' she said. 'Bye then.' She picked up her coat and carefully pulled it on. She was on her way out, but in her own good time.

'Is that it then? At least you'll tell me when you do it, won't you?'

'No, Jon. No information, no contact. You've just forfeited your right to any of that.'

She pulled her handbag onto her shoulder, picked up her lighter and walked away from Jon without looking back.

'How does music publishing grab you?'

Louise flicked the switch on her radio-cassette player and T. Rex were silenced abruptly. She squashed the phone to her ear.

'Are you there, dear?'

'I'm here, Judy.'

'Thank God for that. You need to get yourself round there quickly, this afternoon to be precise. They've been left in the lurch, and it could be temp to perm. It's a good company, Louise, small but successful, and if you got yourself in the door you could be on to something. You'll have to be reliable. No time off. Definitely no sickies. Be there all day, every day and you've got a real chance. Can you smarten yourself up sharpish and show them what you're made of?'

Louise snapped up the pen she'd been doodling with. A job in music publishing? Right now, when she was still lurking in an emotional bombsite? How on earth was she going to find the time and space to work out what she was going to do next? How could she take time off to deal with it?

'It's, um.'

'Louise? Isn't this exactly what you want?'

'Yes, yes it was.'

'Was?' Judy's voice rose. 'Don't mess me about. Yes or no. I've got at least a dozen good candidates on my books who'll leap at this.'

'Judy, it's just that . . .' Her stomach twisted itself into a double helix. A big chance in the industry she'd love to be a part of. It couldn't happen now. 'It's only that . . . Could I start in a week or so?'

'This afternoon. Yes or no.'

Louise played with the pen until it flipped out of her fingers and landed in the washing-up bowl.

'Look, something's come up, it's only temporary but it means I can't work exactly right now. Another week—' She thought of what Sally had said. Sorting this out wasn't going to happen in a hurry. '—or two and I'll know where I stand.'

'Louise?' Judy barked.

'I'm sorry, Judy, I'm going to have to say no.'

'Right,' Judy said in a thin voice and hung up.

The Jobcentre ascended into the swirling grey and white clouds. Louise peered at it from the cocoon of her scarf. The wind was nipping at her legs, but she'd worn a skirt out of habit despite the onset of an early winter. She'd never been into a Jobcentre before and she wasn't sure what the dress code was. Better to look professional in a way that suggested potential. Potential that could begin in a few weeks when she'd resolved her predicament. That was the idea.

She wasn't quite sure what she was going to do inside, but sitting at home writing pertinent obscenities on the backs of her bills wasn't achieving much. She needed time to sort things out, but for the moment she had no job, and no money coming in. Instinct told her that if Party Animals was in dire straits, paying her what she was owed wasn't going to be a priority. She had to find something that would start in a month, perhaps, but in the meantime, she had to sign on.

She'd never signed on before. She'd never had to. She'd always managed to sweet-talk her way into a new opportunity the minute the door slammed on the previous one.

There was one other tenuous option, but something inside her still rebelled against it. Her sister. Rachel had offered more than once to put her name forward for temping options that came up in the record company she worked for. Music was Rachel's thing. She did it brilliantly. She'd blazed her own trail in the company and was doing exactly what she loved now—talent spotting and signing.

But working in Rachel's shadow would be just like being at school in Rachel's shadow. Louise had been called 'Rachel's little sister' by staff until she wanted to prise their eyes out with the corner of her protractor. No, she'd find her own way to where she was going, wherever that was.

'Wing it,' she whispered into her scarf.

It was like walking into an airport lounge. Long, thick, overhead lights ran along the ceiling, and the warm-air vents sent a hum of background noise reverberating through the building. Somebody was saying something over an intercom. It was like being at the supermarket. Clients were being told that there was a special offer on aisle six. She wasn't sure whether it was the clients or the jobs which were on special offer. Rows of stands littered with white cards confronted her. The faces she could see were grey, drawn and lacking in humour. And they were the staff. She wondered what she was going to tell them.

Should she say she was pregnant? Would she be allowed to sign on if she told them the truth? What if she got a job and threw up everywhere? She squashed her fingers into her palms, and realised that they were cold with sweat. What if she wasn't entitled to anything at all? What if Andrew changed his mind and pretended she'd been fired for misbehaviour when he was asked?

There was nobody to tell her what to do. Even the woman at the reception desk was too busy sorting through papers to look up. Louise wanted to blurt it all out, but then she might end up saying the wrong thing. The woman would look up, brush her short bob away from her chin, and tell her that she was on her own.

She walked carefully to the side of the room and took a moment to lean on the stand labelled 'Catering'. Her weight seemed to increase as she hung on to the stand. She grew colder and colder. It was several seconds before she realised that she was in the process of fainting.

'Oh blimey . . .'

The world became a mass of purple and blue blotches. For a

moment, it was blissfully peaceful. If she was dying then everyone else would have to sort everything out on her behalf. Perhaps her father had felt like this? The blotches turned completely black.

'Hey, you all right in there?'

Louise opened her eyes and stared up. It must be a dream. One minute she'd been standing in the Jobcentre contemplating the meaninglessness of everything she'd ever known, the next she was cradled in Ewan McGregor's lap.

If she had died, she knew for sure that this was heaven. If this wasn't death, she sure as hell didn't want it to be a dream either. The wide-apart green eyes looking down into hers stayed right where they were.

'It's OK,' his voice said. 'She's come round now. I'll sit her up. Can somebody get a glass of water or something?'

'I'm not really sure. We only have a staff room. We don't supply beverages to clients.'

'Get a fucking glass of water, will you? Or do I have to do it myself? Jesus Christ, forget it, I'll take her to a café.' The pale eyes looked at her, gentle again. Louise examined them in minute detail. They were mint green, and very calm considering the force of the outburst. 'Can you stand up? I'll get you a cup of tea somewhere.'

'I think I should stay here for a minute,' she murmured. She was going to make lying in Ewan McGregor's lap last as long as possible.

'OK, you just take your time.'

A sigh escaped her lips. He brushed a strand of hair out of her eyes and looked at her intently again. Was it possible to faint lying down after you'd only just fainted standing up?

'Do you think you could sit up now?'

'I'm not sure.'

'It's just that I'm getting cramp in my leg.'

'Oh.' She pulled a noble face. 'I'll see what I can do.'

She reluctantly dragged herself into a sitting position and looked down. Her legs were askew, her skirt ridden up to her thighs, her emerald-green opaque tights right up to the gusset. The woman from reception seemed to have developed a nervous tic, several older men were bending over, apparently fascinated by the emerald gusset, and Ewan McGregor was on his haunches, rubbing vigorously at one of his thighs through torn jeans.

She watched him rub away, bewitched, and stopped herself just before she offered to do it for him. She should stand up now. She heaved her skirt over her thighs and tipped herself onto her knees. She gave her

33

audience a reassuring smile and made it to her feet. She opened her mouth to apologise, and sneezed instead.

'Oh hell. Hang on a sec.' She fumbled around in her pockets for a stringy tissue and gazed through it at her assortment of older men.

'It was kind of you to help. I'm fine, really. No breakfast. I should really eat breakfast, shouldn't I?'

'I'll take it from here,' Ewan McGregor said. The other men smiled sympathetically at Louise and dispersed slowly. Louise groped in her pocket again.

'Need another tissue? I've got one in here somewhere.' He began a search in the pockets of his denim jacket. He came up with a folded piece of lined paper with something scribbled in biro on the back. 'Will this do for now?'

She took it thankfully and wrapped it round her nose.

'Look, why don't I get you into a café and you can blow your nose on some loo paper. It's no wonder you felt groggy. You've got a bastard of a cold, haven't you?'

'That's right.' Louise allowed herself to be led quietly from the building. She hoped the café wasn't far. She didn't want Ewan McGregor to glance at her again and find she had mucus dribbling from her chin.

He stopped at a small café which she hadn't noticed before. It looked wonderful inside. It was bright, cheerful and very relaxed.

'You don't mind a greasy spoon, do you?'

She shook her head and followed him inside. The threat of winter vanished as she was hit by the smell of hot coffee, toast and bacon. The warmth enveloped her face. At the back was a doorway signposting the toilets. She wandered off in that direction, forgetting to mention that she really fancied a plate of toast.

In the toilet she removed the piece of paper from her nose. She could hardly give it back to him, whatever it was. She shoved it in her coat pocket instead, and blew her nose on a banner of soft pink loo paper until it felt safe to stop. Then she glided back into the café and looked around for her saviour, the strange man in the torn jeans with the wide-apart green eyes. He was taking a tray over to a table near a window. No, she hadn't been deluding herself. He was really terrific. After he'd made himself comfortable, she sat down opposite him and slid her coat from her shoulders.

'Hi!'

'I got you some toast and a pot of tea. I'll grab a cup with you, if you don't mind. It's fucking freezing today, isn't it?'

Not backward in coming forward with the expletives, she noted. But he hadn't struck her as one to stand on ceremony. And he'd ordered toast. He was gaining Brownie points by the minute.

'Yep, sure is. It's brilliant in here though.' She sighed contentedly and loosened the collar of her sweater to let in more warm air. 'It's really kind of you to order this, but you must let me pay.'

'I assumed you would pay.'

'Oh. Yes, I would. Obviously.'

'Fine. You're in work, aren't you?'

'Sorry?'

He nodded at her clothes. 'Smart coat, skirt. I noticed that.'

'I've been fired,' she said, cramming the toast into her mouth, and only realising once she saw the surprised look on his face that she was eating it like a pig. 'God, I'm sorry. You should have a bit too.'

'No, I'm fine. I never eat until the evening. Why were you fired?'

'Because my ex-boss is a fat prat,' she said, helping herself to tea. 'No, I'm wrong actually. He's a tart with a heart, or something like that.'

'A fart with a heart, perhaps?'

'So you know him, then?'

He smiled. He had a lovely smile. She stopped chewing, her mug poised in the air, and stared at him.

'I used to have one like that. Not any more. I'm a free agent, now.'

'Oh.' A free agent. That was one way of putting it. It was better than being a statistic. She blinked and looked again. Each time she looked at him he became more gorgeous. Of course, her luck being what it was, he would turn up and rescue her when she was three and a half weeks pregnant and wearing a comedy red nose. She let out an involuntary giggle.

'What's up? It's not exactly the Ritz, but it's dead cheap. Which is just as well, if you've lost your job. I usually pop in here for a cuppa after signing. It's a pain in the arse, but you'll have to get used to that. You just have to know what to say. The pressure's right on, you know.'

'This is all new to me. How are you supposed to know what to say?'

'You are looking for another job, aren't you?'

'Sort of. Soon. Yes.' She twiddled her teaspoon. 'Not this week or next, at least.'

'You do know you've got to prove that you're actively seeking work to sign on, I suppose?'

'I have?'

'Bugger me, you are a novice, aren't you?'

She suddenly wished that he would go away. Just at this moment she didn't want to be reminded by the most gorgeous man in London of what an all-round twit she was.

'I can give you a few tips, if you like. I've been signing over six months now. Hopefully not for much longer.'

She had an ill-defined instinct that he was moonlighting as something, but she wasn't sure what. He seemed too lively, too awake, to be somebody who had spent six months watching *Countdown*. She tried to form questions in her head that wouldn't seem silly. She didn't even know his name. But then, he didn't know hers. He drained his mug.

'I've got to go now, I'm afraid.' He stood up. She gripped her mug tightly and watched him in dismay. 'Thanks for the tea. I'll repay you one day. You sure you'll get home all right?'

'Er, yes. I live locally. Thank you for looking after me, back there.'

'Well, you take care of yourself.' He nodded down at her. 'And make sure you don't miss out on breakfast. Next time, you might not have me to pick you up.'

He sauntered out of the café. And once he'd left it was almost as if he'd never been there. She sat on her own, suffused with her own thoughts, the world outside becoming more distant. She was pregnant, and that was everything.

She'd turned down the career break of a lifetime and fainted in the Jobcentre. Then a gorgeous-looking man with less-than-gorgeous manners had dragged her into a café and been beamed away. As she stared at the mutant toast crumb that was floating around in her mug she vowed that she would make it back to the Jobcentre. She'd pick up some forms, and she'd find a way through it, all without displaying her gusset to anyone.

Chapter Three

'I'M FIFTY-FIVE,' Olivia announced to Sarah, the temp, who was crouching over the computer desk. Sarah looked up.

'Is that all?'

Olivia wasn't sure why she'd announced that fact as she'd arrived at the office. She hadn't been sure where such an opening gambit might lead a conversation either, but that certainly wasn't the response she'd wanted. It was all down to hearing from Katherine Muff again.

It was years since she'd thought about the old school, but one phone call had brought it all flooding back. Louise and Rachel had followed her path through the same school, but they didn't ramble on about it. Olivia had tried to put it all behind her. She had been trying so hard to move on after Bob had gone. But Katherine Muff wanted her to go to a class reunion at a restaurant in the town, in only a few weeks' time. She couldn't face all those girls again, now satisfied women in their fifties. What would she say to them? What had she done with her life?

'You do my 'ead in, you do,' Sarah said, Olivia swung round as her reverie was broken. It was nine in the morning, and she was at work. Carol would be here soon and she wanted to get the mail opened before she arrived. But there were other things on her mind as well.

Sarah's face brightened as if she suddenly understood something.

'God, I'm a plank! I get it. You're fifty-five *today*. You should have said it was your birthday. We can go for a drink at lunchtime. Apart from Cow-bag. Don't tell her.'

Olivia opened her mouth and shut it again. Of course it wasn't her birthday, but since Katherine had rung, being fifty-five seemed important. Why shouldn't they all go to the pub? When it had been her birthday three months ago, she hadn't told anybody at work, and besides, she hadn't been inside a pub for years.

'Yes, let's do that.'

Smiling unsteadily, Olivia attacked a pile of brown envelopes, listening to the beeps and boops coming from the computer Sarah was attempting to use. Carol, whom Sarah had neatly christened Cow-bag after her very first day, had told them to treat it with respect, but she'd showed no sign of planning any training time for them. The only one with any idea was Shaun, one of the social workers. He was trying to do what he could for them, but he soon tiptoed out of the office whenever Carol appeared.

'Aw, fuck. I think I've done something to it.'

'What did you touch?' Olivia asked in a horrified whisper.

'Nothing. I was miles away, and when I looked back at the screen there were these psychedelic boxes coming at me. I'm too scared to touch anything now just in case I mess it up. It could be a virus, or anything. We'll have to ask Cow-bag when she gets in.'

'Somebody's in my parking place again.' Carol entered the room like an avalanche.

They jumped to attention, Sarah physically levitating from her seat and all but clicking her heels together behind her. Carol was so pleasant to look at, with scraped-back black hair, a petite ballerina's face and full, sweet lips. But within this innocuous body was the personality of a T-Rex with chronic PMT.

'What is the current problem?' Carol ranged her ice blue eyes over the two women.

'Good morning, Carol,' Olivia said. Carol ignored the attempt at civility, leaned over the keyboard, pressed a button, and the psychedelic boxes disappeared. Sarah's half-finished memo reappeared.

'The screen saver,' Carol explained tartly. 'I set it on Friday. It will come into action every two minutes. Now I shall know when anybody's daydreaming. I can hear it from my desk, and I can see it. Although why you should have problems understanding a concept as simple as the screen saver, I do not know. Especially you, Sarah. You're supposed to be IT literate.'

Olivia bit her lip and turned back to her desk. When she unclenched her palm, she found that she'd screwed an envelope into a ball. All she needed to do now was to set fire to it and lob it at Carol's head. Her hairspray would feed the flames and they could sit back and have a cup of coffee while they watched.

'I'll look at the post now, Olivia.'

Carol slipped off her chic overcoat and made her way over to her desk, the king-sized one at the back of the room. Olivia watched as she slid into her rotating chair and disappeared from view. She got up quickly, tutting impatiently, and played with the plastic controls until the seat was high enough.

'I think I need a cup of coffee.' Carol turned her attention to her diary and ran a Mont Blanc pen down her notes. 'Not as strong as you usually make it.'

Olivia rested her hot head against the door of the kitchen. If she closed her eyes now, she could fall asleep standing up and stay there until it was time to go home. But she had the day to fight through first. Nobody cared that she had private worries.

'Hi there, Mumsie. How are you doing? I wanted to know if you'd thrown up yet.'

Louise smiled and tutted. It was all about clichés to Sally. She paused to glance over at the kitchen table strewn with paperwork. She had advice on everything now. How to claim jobseeker's allowance, how to jobseek, and how to have a termination. The doctor had told her that she shouldn't make a decision too quickly, but at the same time reminded her that time was of the essence. In other words, she had to rush into making a sensible decision. And all the time she just couldn't believe that any of it was actually happening.

'Hey, Sal, something occurred to me.'

'What's that then?'

'It's four weeks now and I can't feel a thing. Can I sue them for making me believe I was pregnant when I wasn't?'

'What are you on about?'

'I can't be expecting a baby. The only overwhelming instinct I've got is to stay in bed until people stop telling me I'm pregnant.'

'Oh, you're in denial.'

'Of course I am!' Louise grabbed at her packet of Ultra-Lows and lit one in agitation. 'And I'll stay in denial until I have one shred of evidence that it's not a big joke.'

'Face it. You've got a bun in the oven. You're in the club.'

'OK, I get the picture.'

'I just want to help you come to terms with it all.' Sally's voice softened. 'Lou? There's only going to be one way out of it. You know I'll come with you, don't you? You won't be on your own.'

Louise closed her eyes and pressed the receiver to her ear. The words of comfort washed over her. Right over her.

'Thanks, Sal.'

'Tell you what,' Sally concluded. 'I'll take you for a curry on Saturday. How does that sound?'

Louise's stomach gave a sudden, violent rumble.

'Right, you're on.'

'So are you doing something nice tonight?' Sarah asked as she dived into a gin and tonic.

Olivia had opted for an orange juice. She winced as a chink of ice caught in her molar and wedged itself there.

'Sorry?'

'Not going out then?' Sarah said slowly. 'Are you all right? You look cream crackered.'

Olivia smiled. Acknowledgment, at last. Even if it did come from Sarah. And as she looked at Sarah, she decided that she was sweet really. It was just that she was so different, so young, so strange to Olivia. And her confidence was awesome. When they'd walked into the pub, Olivia had instantly felt too old to be there. There was nobody in the building who looked over forty. Sarah had stormed up to the bar, as if she felt at home. Like her girls, Olivia mused. They were at home in the world too.

'I am knackered,' she said.

'Ah, well, never mind. You have to spoil yourself on your birthday, don't you? I always get rat-arsed and tell Neal to surprise me. Does your husband surprise you then?'

Olivia sipped at her orange juice while she considered the question.

'He did surprise me, once.'

'That's nice. What did he do?'

'He died. But that was the only time he ever did anything surprising.'

Olivia fixed her eyes on a palm set on a window-ledge which was wilting through lack of care. It worried her.

'Don't they water their plants in here?' she asked Sarah. It was then she noticed that Sarah's mouth was hanging open. 'What's the matter?'

Sarah's hand flew to her mouth. 'I'm so sorry. I'm really sorry, Olivia. I had no idea your husband was . . . had . . . you know.'

'Died?'

'Yes. That's it. God, the last thing you want to do on your birthday is to think about that. Look, why don't I get us both another drink and something to eat. What do you fancy? A sandwich? A nice lasagne?'

'Er, lasagne sounds lovely.'

Sarah fled.

It was funny that whenever Olivia did want to think about her husband, everybody stopped her from doing it. She couldn't bring the subject up with Rachel or Louise, the only people in the world now who had known Bob almost as well as she had herself. There were other things she wanted to say to her daughters, but she couldn't mention them either.

'Room for a small one?' The sound of Shaun's voice had her smiling before she'd looked up. His impish grin tightened as he gazed vaguely around the bar. 'Not on your own, are you?'

'No, no. Sarah's here too. She's gone to get some lasagne.'

'Great!' Olivia liked Shaun. He was kind. The younger women in the office paid him no attention at all. He had a hook nose, eyebrows that met in the middle, and hair that was trying to escape out of a skylight. He was somewhere in his forties and single. Olivia often thought that it was a pity that the younger women she saw around her didn't seem to appreciate kindness.

'It's very nice of you to come,' she said, shifting along the cushions on the bench to allow him to sit down.

'I'll just perch for a bit. Then I must be on my way. I have to visit the Sheldons again.'

'Oh, you poor thing. It's a difficult one, isn't it?'

'Hmmn.' Shaun fell into thought. 'Still.' He beamed at her. 'You're the birthday girl, so let's be happy about that.'

'Yes.' Olivia dutifully pecked at her orange juice again. She had a bizarre urge to giggle.

'So, you're a scorpion.'

She gazed at him.

'I am?'

'Yes. Tempestuous and strong-willed, but brave and passionate.'

'Really?'

'You know. Smacks life right between the eyes. Mind you, it's more effective that way, I think. I'm not like that myself. I'm a sideways-on type. I'm a Cancer, you see.'

'Oh.' She laughed loudly. 'You sound as if you know a lot about it.'

'Just a bit. I do birth charts as a hobby. I could do yours for you.' He considered her for a moment. 'Yes, of course, why don't I do that? I never got you a card, did I? And I've got to go in a minute, so I could do your chart, as a present.'

'Oh no, really.'

'Yes, I insist.' His eyes sparkled. 'The computer does the chart and I interpret it. But it's amazing how accurate it is. I need to know your time and place of birth.'

Olivia shifted on the bench. She wasn't only an impostor at her own birthday celebration, she was also about to have a fictitious life presented to her on an astrology chart.

But she had to answer Shaun. It wasn't *her* birth chart, and if it made Shaun happy there might not be any harm in it.

She gave him the time and year of her birth, then added, 'And I was born in London.'

For a fleeting moment she felt important. It made the birthday charade worthwhile. Perhaps she should do it more often. Bob never used to take her to the pub, and going without him was unthinkable. But it was nice to be here now.

'Here y'are. Lasagne. And another orange juice. But I've slipped a vodka in there to cheer you up.'

'Thank you, Sarah.'

'And I must be going, I'm afraid.' Shaun leaped up. 'Sarah, Olivia, see you soon. And happy birthday again.'

He looked for a moment as if he might peck her cheek. Olivia leaned away from him. Her cheeks were too dry to be kissed.

'Eat up then. We don't want Cow-bag tanning our arses for being late back, do we?'

Olivia obediently tackled her lasagne. She'd never got used to eating out in public. She hadn't done it often enough. Not like Sarah. And not like her girls. She stopped to wonder for a moment what they were both doing. They were in control of their own lives now, she told herself sternly. And they certainly didn't need her any more. She shouldn't worry about them so much.

Louise threw open the piano lid, heaved the stool into place and launched herself at the keys.

She banged out Handel's 'Largo' with as much bad temper as she could, and trilled along with gritted teeth.

Why couldn't anyone say anything right? Why was it that at the most crucial times in your life, when you most needed somebody to talk to, there was nobody who was just the right person to talk to about it? Then she realised that someone was knocking at her door.

She flung the door wide and growled into the hall. A pair of blue eyes smouldered into hers.

'I'm sorry, Harris, I'm in a bad mood this evening. Can't you get ear-plugs or something?'

She squinted at him as he raised his eyebrows, lowered them and raised them again. The penny finally dropped.

'Oh God, I'm sorry. I've ruined your seduction scene. It must be pretty awful trying to get somebody in the sack while a mad woman's caterwauling in the flat below you.' She gave him a sympathetic smile. 'Sorry. You go back to whoever it is, and I'll just—just hide under the sofa or something until it's all over.'

She closed the door on him. She caught a waft of aftershave as the latch clicked. He had good taste. What a shame he was a love-rat. And if she hadn't been pregnant, she might just have allowed him to be a love-rat on her time.

She decided to ring Rachel. There was just a small chance they'd launch into a warm and sisterly conversation which would end in Rachel offering wonderful advice.

She picked up the phone and after three rings, she got the answering machine.

'Rachel Twigg and Hallam Merton can't take your call right now. Please leave us a message and one of us will get right back to you.'

'Bloody liars,' Louise mumbled.

She could always call her mother. Louise pictured her, at home, in front of the nine o'clock news, with a cup of tea, her eyes gazing mistily over her father's photographs on the mantelpiece, and the one of herself and Rachel looking like a couple of aliens with gapped teeth and bunches. She dialled her mother's number.

'Mum? It's me. Just ringing to say hello.'

'Is everything all right, dear?'

'Of course. I just wondered how you are.'

'I was just going to watch the news with a cup of tea. Did you need to talk to me right now?'

'No, no. Just thought I'd let you know I've had a bit of a cold. Just in case it occurred to you that I might not be well.' She finished with a resounding snap.

'You sound prickly. Are you premenstrual?'

Louise laughed, and stopped herself just before it turned into a shriek. 'No.'

'I could send you a vest. I've bought one for you, but I didn't like to send it without asking you.'

'Please send it if you feel you must.'

'I think I'll go and watch the news. I can't really talk to you when you're in this sort of mood. Shall we try again another time?'

Half an hour later, Louise was stirring up a vat of spaghetti to have with cheese sauce when her doorbell rang.

Jon. The thought of him turned her hot and cold.

She trotted out into the hall as the ringing came again. She stopped in the darkness to take a deep breath, then flicked on the hall light and opened the door. A pair of brown eyes twinkled at her from a sea of black dreadlocks.

'Hi there, darlin'. I was passin', an' I thought I'd drop in. You know, havin' got your letter, an' all.'

'Lenny!' she squeaked. 'How the—how nice to see you again.'

'So what the hell did you do with Lenny?'

Sally waited while Louise chewed and swallowed another mouthful of sag aloo and prawn biriani.

'I didn't do anything.' Louise took a swig of water. 'Lenny likes his women with a bit of zing. I don't think I could have been more lacking in zing that evening if I'd been on display in a coffin. He was really nice, and stayed for about five seconds to catch up on old news.'

Sally watched Louise shovel another hillock of biriani into her mouth. 'You're not too sick to eat?'

'That's the weird thing. I thought eating would make me feel sick, but it's the other way round. I think that might have put Lenny off as well. I took him through to the kitchen, and while I was talking to him I was picking bits of soggy spaghetti out of the saucepan and chewing on them. I didn't even realise I was doing it.'

Sally sat back in her chair and picked up her wineglass. 'So that's Lenny sorted. Now what about Giles? You wrote to him suggesting oral sex, didn't you?'

'Haven't heard a word from him.' Louise dabbed at her mouth with a napkin. 'With any luck, he's emigrated. Or married. Or both.'

'Oh, Louise.' Sally sighed and shook her head. 'Sometimes I feel that we haven't moved on from the fifth form. I still remember coming in all excited that Monday morning and telling you about Guy. He was lovely. I don't know why we ever finished.' Sally's face crumpled into a frown of concentration.

'What about Fergus?' Louise played with the idea of eating the last of the sag aloo, and went for it. Sally looked pensive.

'Fergus is . . . nice. He's attractive, sincere, sensitive, cultured, ambitious, good in bed, rich.'

Louise dropped her spoon as she attempted to deliver half a serving dish of sag aloo to her plate in one go.

'Charming, witty, thoughtful, titled. Did I mention that? His father's the earl of something. Just found out last week.'

'You're lying.'

'OK, maybe not an earl. Sir someone or other. And he's attractive—'

'You've done attractive.'

'OK, he thinks the world of me. He thinks we have a future together,' Sally finished, looking blank.

'And?' Louise was agog.

'It's not so much "and", as "but".'

'OK, but?'

'But . . .' Sally pursed her lips and focused on the flock wallpaper.

'But . . . don't tell me. He doesn't know the words to "Hotel California".'

'No, no. Nothing so trivial. It's just—'

'His fresh pesto just isn't the same as the stuff out of the jar?'

'Stop it.'

'Well, what do you expect?' Louise stared at Sally in horror. 'You've got a man who has absolutely everything that a girl could ever want, and you still say a word like "but". What is it you want, for God's sake?'

'I was hoping you'd understand. I mean, you haven't settled, have you? Even when you were with Jon, you weren't just with Jon, were you?'

Louise licked her finger and stabbed it round the poppadom basket.

'What exactly do you mean?'

'Look, I don't want to say anything dreadful. Especially not now. It's just that you did tell me about , . . things.'

'Jon was behaving like such a git then. I think I was entitled to give some thought to other people.'

'I know that.'

'So . . .'

'So,' Sally continued. She was being careful now, Louise thought. Tiptoeing over a minefield. 'So, nothing really. Shall I get the bill, or do you want a bucket of kulfi to finish things off?'

Louise paused guiltily with the last shred of spinach wrapped round her fork. Sally was smiling again. Louise relaxed and smiled back.

'It's really nice of you to treat me to a meal, Sal. You know I can't afford to do this now.'

'I can't remember a time when you ever could,' Sally said, gazing over her shoulder to attract the waiter's attention. 'If you're ever going to have a decent standard of living, you've got to do something about it now. Before it's too late.'

'Too late for—what?' Louise was troubled as Sally flicked open her leather wallet and pulled out a credit card.

'Everything.' Sally leaned forward sombrely. 'You can't even think about keeping it, Louise. You haven't talked about it all evening, you know. You haven't made any plans, have you?'

Louise shook her head.

'The longer it goes on, the harder it's going to be for you. Believe me, you've got to act quickly. You have to get two opinions, then wait for an appointment. And allow time afterwards in case of complications.'

'How do you know so much about it?'

'It happened to a girl at work who told me all about it. She said I was the only one she felt she could confide in.'

'Oh God.'

'Deal with it, Louise,' Sally said. 'Just let me know where to be, and when. I'll come and sleep on your sofa.'

'Thanks, Sal.' Louise put her hand over Sally's as she turned her attention to signing the slip. Sally looked up in surprise. 'I want you to know that whatever happens, I'll never forget this.'

Olivia jumped as a hand clutching a flat brown envelope appeared in front of her eyes.

It was well after six, and the last person she expected to see in the office was Shaun. She had actually been enjoying herself, without Carol hanging from her heels like a vengeful hamster and Sarah musing about the funny rash on Neal's left testicle. A cold, heavy rain was battering at the window, and it had been calming. It had been nice to lose herself in her own thoughts while she could still occasionally hear footsteps from the office above. It wasn't like being alone at home.

She took the envelope. Shaun perched on the edge of her desk and waited for her to open it. She glanced at his face.

'What is this, Shaun?'

'Something for you,' he said. 'Go on, open it. I promised I'd do it for you, remember?'

She frowned at him as her brain ticked quietly into action, then she remembered. A warm flush spread up her neck.

'Oh, good grief! You don't mean my horoscope?'

'I do. It's fascinating. All your life there for you to see.'

'Oh, no. I couldn't accept it.' She tried to squash the envelope back into his hand. He pushed it back towards her.

'Yes, you can. It didn't cost me anything. Just a bit of time, which is nothing really.'

As she tried to refuse again, her conscience teetered. It was mean of her to disappoint him.

She buried her confusion under a silly laugh. 'It's just that I'm feeling old, Shaun, and you doing this reminds me that I'll be sixty soon.'

'You don't really think about it like that, do you?' he said. 'It's what you feel inside that really counts. Who you are. What you're all about. The things you long to do. The hopes, fears, passions, ambitions, all those things that you never breathe a word of to anyone else, in case . . .'

He had been speaking to the corner of the room, but he suddenly dropped his eyes as if he'd remembered Olivia was there.

'In case?'

'In case they think you're stupid.'

'Yes.' She clutched the envelope between her fingers. 'Yes, I think I know what you mean.'

'I know you do,' Shaun nodded. 'That's why I wanted to do your chart. I don't offer my services to just anyone, you know.'

'I'm very grateful,' she said.

There was a pause. He was waiting for her to open the envelope but she had no intention of looking at the chart with him leaning over her.

'The rain's getting heavier,' Shaun said, standing up and wandering towards the window. 'And it's pretty cold. Christmas coming. I suppose your daughters will be down again this year?'

'Er, I'm not sure yet. They're both very busy.' Olivia stood up and started to clear the papers on her desk into a plastic tray.

'And no grandchildren?' Shaun raised his eyebrows at her again.

'I try not to think about it. The girls have their own lives to lead.'

'But is it what you'd like?' Shaun took a step forward, his eyes questioning. 'It's just that my mother goes on and on about it. Do all women of a certain age go on about grandchildren?'

'I suppose it's to do with feeling that there isn't anybody to make a fuss over. When your own children grow up, they don't need you any more. There's something about small children that makes you feel wanted.'

She frowned as she gazed over the empty office. She'd forgotten something, she was sure of it. Shaun hesitated beside her.

Of course. She made her way round the desks to the king-sized one at the back and dropped the seat of Carol's swivel chair as far as it would go. She patted the seat and stood up again, smiling at her companion.

'What was that for?'

'Oh, just in case the cleaner forgets. One of us tries to remember.'

'I could give you a lift home if you wanted,' Shaun said.

'It's very kind of you.' She patted his arm. 'But I've stood at that bus-stop through rain, wind, sleet, hail, you name it. I shall be there tonight, as usual. We women of a certain age like our little routines, you know.'

She parted company with Shaun outside the building, wondering if she'd been too stubborn in refusing a lift. It was very cold. In the past, Bob would have picked her up if the weather had been so unforgiving. Now their old Ford Escort sat in the garage like a monument.

No, it was better to be getting the bus. It meant that she could sit with other passengers, gazing through the rain-spattered window at the images of the town as they drifted past. She liked the quiet companionship of the journey.

Before she reached the bus-stop, she stopped to stare at the bright window display that always caught her eye, and read the notice that had been intriguing her for the past two months. Somebody in there had a sense of humour.

Why don't you go away?

It was written with red marker pen on fluorescent-green paper. Below it were white cards showing cheap fares to destinations all around the world. She read them all again, then glanced at her watch. If she was quick, she might just make the half past.

Louise waited in the doctor's surgery idling through *Hello!* magazine.

The surgery was turning out to be a fascinating place. She knew that it was run by a husband-and-wife team. They were both Sri Lankan, the receptionist had told her on her first visit, and *he* always had more free slots. Louise had been added to the list of names waiting to see Dr Balasingam, female. She had waited two hours for the privilege, and it had been worth it. While Louise had been waiting she had been curious to see every patient who arrived being offered an immediate slot with Dr Balasingam, male. All had hedged and opted for his wife.

On her second visit, Louise had felt sorry for Dr Balasingam, male. She'd almost wished she had something gender unspecific to deal with. The measles or a bad ear infection. Surely, she'd thought, gazing round the surgery at the stacked bodies who all looked like malingerers, one of them might have had the decency to boost Dr Balasingam, male's, confidence, and opt for a slot with him. But it was not to be.

She had been sitting next to an elderly woman and whispered to her. 'What's wrong with Dr Balasingam?'

The old lady had contorted her face meaningfully.

'He's a bit eccentric. Nobody's quite sure about him.'

'Ah, I see.'

'He doesn't give prescriptions.'

'Ah.'

'Nor them antibiotics.' The old woman lowered her voice and added vehemently, 'Never.'

But today Louise had turned up to see Dr Balasingam, female, and had been told that she wasn't taking a surgery that afternoon. There was only *him*. Louise had thought about putting off her appointment, but had decided that Sally was right. This needed to be dealt with as soon as possible. All she needed to do was follow on from her past conversations, and tell him that she'd made a decision.

A male voice came drifting over the intercom. It was pale, with lilting tones. Louise perked up, intrigued.

'Miss Twigg, kindly be so good as to transport yourself in the direction of room number two where your consultant awaits.'

The receptionist peeped over her appointments book. 'Good luck!' Louise heard her whisper as she walked past.

Louise pushed open the door and walked in. A tiny man was crouched over a wide desk, evidently reading through her medical notes. He seemed much older than Dr Balasingam, female. His bald head gleamed like a dimpled Malteser under the yellow arc of light cast by his desk lamp. He didn't seem to notice that she'd arrived. She cleared her throat.

'Yes, yes. I know that you're here. I have to know all about you, don't I, before you can tell me what ails you today? Please, do seat yourself and be comfortable. I shall be with you in two beats of an eyelash.'

Louise slipped into the leather chair opposite his desk and watched him read. He seemed completely engrossed, as if he was reading a great work of literature. Every so often he stopped to sigh, or to nod, or to raise his eyebrows, and when he did look up, Louise was taken aback. This terrifying character had none of his wife's efficiency or abject professionalism. His deep brown eyes were spiritual. She found herself smiling at him.

'Ah, my dear, you have little to smile about, I think. You are contemplating the great question of life.' He put his hands together in front of his compact body. 'It is such a difficult thing, to face oneself in this way.'

Louise stopped as she was about to open her mouth. She was confused. Her conversations with Dr Balasingam, female, had been nothing like this. She had been given leaflets, told of her options, and it had all been done with enormous sympathy. But this wasn't the same.

'You see . . .' Dr Balasingam got up from his chair and walked across the room. 'This is an important moment for you. You have no support from the man involved, but still you must decide what your feelings are towards your infant.'

'Infant?' The word was odd.

'I only say this because I have seen such sadness. You must think for yourself at this time. People will try to tell you what to do. They feel more relaxed, you see, if the people they love take the same decisions as they would do themselves. But there is only one thing that you must consider here, and that is yourself. How do you feel?'

'I feel . . .' Louise searched her mental thesaurus. The word she came up with was disappointingly ordinary: 'Sick.'

'Oh dear. There is a basin here, and I will not watch if you are embarrassed.'

'No, I mean sick as in tired, if you know what I mean. It's as if this has been going on for ever and I'm trapped in limbo.'

'Ah! Limbo. Yes, I can see why you might feel that.' He wandered over to the window and played with the folds in the net curtain until he had knotted it tightly round his finger. It took him some minutes to extricate himself. Then he turned round with more purpose. 'So, Miss Twigg. You have made a decision.'

'Yes, I'm going to go ahead with it.'

'With . . .?' He opened up his brown eyes and waited.

'With a termination. I have to. It's what I've got to do.'

He nodded, showing neither relief nor dismay, and popped into his chair again. He picked up his pen.

'So, Miss Twigg, perhaps you will tell me why you feel that you must do this. I have to make notes, you see.'

'The thing is, I'm thirty-two, and I haven't got a job. I haven't got a boyfriend either. My—er—immediate prospects are somewhat limited. And I can't do this on my own. Besides, I'm not even sure . . .'

'Yes?'

'. . . if I can afford to support myself, let alone another human being.' Louise let out a long breath. 'The more I see children around me, with fathers and mothers, with a ready-made family to support them, the more I know I can't do this. It's just not fair. And I haven't done anything with my own life yet. I can't impart any advice, or wisdom, or anything to a child.'

'I see.' He turned his attention to her medical card, scrawling notes in a wild hand which seemed to take up half a page per word. 'And is there anything else?'

'Isn't that enough?' Louise pulled herself up in her chair. 'Please don't make me feel guilty. You have no idea how painful this is. You have no right to make it worse. I've never felt so confused in my life.'

His brown eyes studied her as he listened. Louise felt her emotions rising to the surface. She had underestimated herself. She had been suppressing any violent reactions she might be having, but that didn't mean they weren't there.

'Can you imagine how incredible it is to be pregnant? That after years of being autonomous, you're no longer a single being, acting selfishly, only for yourself and your own interests? And to know at the same time that it's impossible to carry it through?' She swallowed hard. 'I'm condemned if I have an abortion, and condemned if I become a single mother. Which would you prefer to be castigated for?'

'This is how you feel?' He looked at her sorrowfully.

'Of course. I'm a statistic whatever I do. That's what nobody realises.'

She reached into her pocket for a tissue, her eyes brimming. She pulled out a crumpled piece of paper and stared at it for a moment. The man with the wide-apart green eyes flashed across her memory. She'd forgotten that it was still there. She pushed it back and accepted a tissue from the box that the doctor passed her.

'I'm sorry.' She blew her nose and took a shaky breath. 'I've been bottling that up. It's just the most unbelievable thing that has ever happened. I've never wanted to cry so much in my whole life.'

'In which case,' the lilting voice came back, 'you must cry until you have drained yourself entirely of tears. And while you are doing that, I will make us both a cup of coffee.'

'Oh.' Louise watched him as he searched through a series of cupboards and finally produced a kettle, waving it at her in triumph.

'One thing I do have, Miss Twigg,' he said, grinning at her, 'is time.'

Chapter Four

THE FOLLOWING MORNING, Louise woke up and found that the sun slanting across her bedroom highlighted a million particles of dust on its way over to a heap of ancient newspapers teetering on the edge of her chest of drawers. She lay very still. Gradually, her conversation with the doctor came back to her. A sense of well-being came over her. It was all going to be all right. All she had to do was get ready for her interview at the Jobcentre, with all her forms correctly filled in. She only had to take things a step at a time, and stay calm. What mattered was that she'd made a decision and that her life had changed. She gave a satisfied sigh and glimpsed her radio alarm to check the time.

'Oh my God!' She sat bolt upright. 'Oh no, oh no, oh no!'

She threw herself out of bed and yanked open the curtains. The sun streamed in, dazzling her. She ran to the bathroom, ripping off her T-shirt and twisting the shower handle as she jumped into the bath. The water was cold. She screamed and twisted the knob the other way until boiling water pounded at her shoulders in a cloud of steam.

She sprinted back to the bedroom, and pulled on a thick green jumper and a pair of button-up red jeans. She grabbed her jacket, collected her forms together and put them in a carrier bag. Then she zipped on her knee-length boots and tramped out of the house.

It was clear and bright outside. And it was December. She paced up the South Ealing road admiring the whiteness of the buildings in the winter sun. Christmas was coming soon.

Christmas. The second one to be faced at home without her father. She could see his photographs now, perched on the mantelpiece, delicately arranged on her mother's dressing table. Her father with his arms round her, squeezing the breath out of her in a bear hug. What would he think of her now?

'Granddad,' she murmured into the air.

She'd found a way round it after all, thanks to Dr Balasingam. He made a lousy cup of coffee, but he was a fantastic listener. He had let her talk and talk until she had found her own way to a conclusion. He'd asked questions that hadn't occurred to anybody else.

She reached the Jobcentre and danced through the door. It seemed much less daunting now. All she had to do was to be sure of her story, and she would get through to the next stage. After that, she would make other plans.

'Short-term goals,' she chanted under her breath. 'One step at a time. Be confident. It's going to be all right.'

She flashed a happy smile at the woman who seemed to suffer a dim bout of recognition.

'Louise Twigg. I'm here to talk about being destitute. I've got an appointment.'

'One moment, please.' The receptionist dropped her head to search through an appointment book. 'Yes, you can wait in the waiting area. Your name will be called. If you can give me your forms, I'll hand them to the officer.'

Louise presented her forms, she found a row of chairs and sat, trying to look poor and downtrodden, yet at the same time keen. She had a sudden empathy with actors going for auditions. 'I can do happy, I can do sad, I can do active jobsearch!' It struck her that a good start would be to wander around and look at the cards. She headed for Office and Secretarial, adopting an expression of fascination.

There was a gentle tap on her shoulder.

She stiffened, remembering to put her active-jobsearch face on before she turned round to impress the benefits officer. A pair of wide-apart green eyes stared into hers. A hot flush covered her entire body.

'Hi!' she said. It came out a little operatically. She swallowed hard. 'What are you doing here?'

'Sightseeing. I usually bring a packed lunch and a Thermos. What about you?'

'Oh, I'm here for an interview.' She cringed. Why hadn't she said something witty? She'd have to try harder. He looked casually unimpressed. But then, he was the one who'd tapped her on the shoulder.

'Listen,' he said. 'I don't want you to think I'm stalking you or anything, but I have been hanging around hoping to see you again.'

'Yes?' Oh joy. Oh thank you, God. Louise decided to forget about being pregnant for the next thirty seconds. A girl had to be allowed to dream.

'The thing is, you know that piece of paper I gave you?'

Louise's hand shot guiltily into her jacket pocket. She fingered the crumpled paper, firmly stuck together with dried mucus.

'The piece of paper I gave you to hold over your nose? You had a cold, and no tissues. You must remember.'

'Oh, *that* piece of paper.' She nodded, feigning enlightenment.

'Well, the thing is, I need it back. There isn't any chance at all that you hung on to it, is there?'

Her fingers tightened on the paper like steel pincers. She was not about to stand in front of the most gorgeous man in London and present him with a piece of screwed-up A4 paper covered in her own snot.

'God, no, I'm so sorry . . .'

'Shit.' He looked thoroughly crestfallen. He pushed his hands up through his pale brown hair, leaving it sticking out in spikes. It made him look even more sexy.

'Do you know where you put it? I mean, it couldn't still be in a bin at your house, could it?'

What was on this piece of paper that was so crucial? Judging by the anguished look on his face it was a matter of life and death.

'When I go home, I'll check through all my wastepaper baskets and see if it's there.'

He gave her a short smile.

'I did ask at the café, once I realised what I'd given you, and they checked the loo at the back. No luck. So trying to find you again was my only hope.'

'What was it? Just in case I find it and don't realise.'

'Oh, it was just something I scribbled. It won't mean anything to you, but it's important to Ginger and the rest of the guys.'

'Yes,' she breathed quietly. This was starting to sound dodgy.

'Louise Twigg.' A voice hailed her from across the building.

'Oh, that's me!'

'I'll give you my number,' he said, casting a glance over his shoulder at the man who was waiting with scarcely concealed impatience for Louise to follow him. He fished around in his denim pockets and found a cigarette packet and ripped off the top of the packet, flattening it out against the Office and Secretarial board while he wrote a number down. He handed it to Louise. She glanced at it.

'I don't know your name,' she said.

'Ash.' He gave a short laugh. 'It's what the guys call me.'

He sauntered out of the building, then he was gone.

Ash, she mused as she trotted over to the benefits officer who led her to a desk, invited her to sit down, and paused to crack his knuckles and scratch his nose with his Biro before sitting down opposite her.

'Good God, what are you doing here?'

'That's a fine way to greet your little sister,' Louise replied as she shivered on Rachel's doorstep. 'You might at least ask me in.'

'Of course you can come in. You're lucky I'm here. Hallam's in Brussels and I've got the place to myself.'

Louise stepped into Rachel's hall, stopping to close her eyes briefly and savour the merits of central heating. She began to sway gently.

'Louise? Are you drunk?'

'No. Wish I was.'

'Great. I'll open another bottle then. Come through to the kitchen. You could have called me, you know.'

Louise plodded after Rachel, watching her tall body gyrating into the bright kitchen. She'd had her dark hair cut very short again. It suited her. She'd always had more than her fair share of eyes and cheekbones. Her eyes were a deep brown, her hair thick and black, and she'd turned heads since she was about fourteen. But she hadn't come here to be churlish about Rachel's looks. She'd come to be churlish about the fact that she never answered her phone.

'How could I have called you? You never answer the sodding phone. There might be an emergency or something, and you'd never know.'

Rachel turned round with a bottle of wine rescued from the fridge.

'I won't have wine, actually. Can I have something soft? Just a glass of water will be great.'

Rachel's fine eyebrows levitated in the air. 'Shit, you're not on the wagon, are you? I was hoping we could get pissed.'

'You can get pissed if you want.' Louise smiled, but Rachel was still staring at her in horror. 'Er, I've got a pig of a hangover, if you must know,' she lied. 'I can still taste the gin today.'

'Ah.' Rachel nodded with understanding. She poured wine into a glass the size of the FA Cup, took a deep sip of it, sloshed tap water into a glass for Louise and motioned her to follow.

They went through into Rachel's sitting room. Louise instantly started to relax. Sometimes she'd wished Rachel and Hallam would adopt her. Whatever her flat was lacking seemed to be present in Rachel's house. She had artful lighting, tasteful throws over the two sofas and the arm-chairs, a spattering of ethnic rugs, and real paintings round the walls.

Rachel collapsed into an armchair and continued to consider Louise. 'You've lost your job again, haven't you?'

'Oh, leave it out, Rachel.'

'You have. You're bloody hopeless. How long at that last place? A couple of months?'

'Well over a year. Anyway, they're downsizing.' Louise emphasised her point with a widening of her eyes. 'It happens to the best of us, you know. They don't need me any more.'

'Oh, Lou.' Rachel shook her head. Louise stared down at the ethnic stick figures on the rug, wishing that Rachel would never have cause to say 'Oh, Lou' to her again. She hadn't been sure whether she would tell Rachel about the baby or not, but her rational head stepped in and warned her away. She knew what she was doing now. She wasn't going to let anyone else muddy the waters for her.

'So that's why you came here.' Rachel pulled a face. 'No wonder you've got a hangover. So are you going to let me help you at last?'

'I'll sort it out. Just don't tell Mum, please. I don't want her to worry about it.'

'OK. Deal. I won't tell Mum. Does that mean no, you don't want me to help you?'

'Rachel!' Louise frowned at her severely. 'Just let me work this one through for myself. Please.'

Rachel shrugged. 'Be a hero then. I've got other things on my mind.'

There was a silence. Rachel lolled back on the sofa.

'Actually, I'm really glad you came,' Rachel announced, curling her black-stockinged legs under her tight skirt. 'I had a weird message from Mum the other day asking me if I wanted a vest. I think she's cracking up. And Hallam's being a git at the moment. His company are downsizing. He thinks he might be on the hit list. The only time we spend together we're being mobbed by those two little bastards.

'I'm surrounded by no-hopers. I'm pissed off with everyone looking to me for an answer. I'm drinking too much, smoking too much, and I haven't had sex for three days.'

Louise took a sip of her water and loosened her coat. This could be a long night.

'Do you know what? Sometimes I just want to throw it all in. Everything I've built up. I just want to give it all two fingers and do something really relaxing. I do get tired, you know. I mean, physically tired. Everybody's so used to me staying up all night at gigs, working all day for those ungrateful, smelly little objects.'

'Hallam's children?'

'The bands.' Rachel sounded irritated. 'They're so bloody keen to show that they can do it on their own. They cling round your neck like drowning men before they make the big time, and afterwards they lie around in mirror shades with a week's worth of stubble and complain about the deal they've got. I just want to be a zoo keeper.'

Louise shifted uncomfortably. Rachel was so good at what she did, and so powerful. She was usually so big-hearted, if mercurial. She seemed more agitated than usual tonight.

'You'll be fine,' Louise reassured her, after a suitable pause. 'Don't worry about it. Hallam loves you, doesn't he? And you love him.'

'To tell you the truth, Louise, I think Hallam and I have reached the end of the road.'

Louise pulled herself up in her chair, her attention grabbed.

'Oh no, Rachel. You can't mean that.'

'I do. I'm sick of it all. His ex-wife, maintenance claims, what's good for the boys. I mean I never said that I was maternal. I've tried, I really have. But I tell you what really pisses me off.' She waved a long, slim finger. 'Just as I get used to them on a Sunday night, they bugger off again. It happens every time. It takes me all weekend to get in the mood to have them here, and then they're gone. Whisked away again. Sometimes I think the only reason I've put up with it for so long is for Mum.'

'What?'

'You know, so that she's got some surrogate grandchildren. I'd feel so sorry for her otherwise, with Dad gone, and nothing else to live for.'

Louise paused to absorb the series of opinions that Rachel had produced, most of which were new to her.

'But—but she hardly sees the boys!'

Rachel sighed, her head flopping against the loose cushions. She spoke again, slowly. 'The thing is, Louise, I've met someone else.'

Louise swallowed. This was seriously dismal news. Rachel and Hallam were good together. Hallam brought out the best in Rachel. Rachel gave Louise a secretive smile.

'You'd better tell me about it.' Louise's voice came out as a sigh.

'I was at a gig keeping an eye on a new band we've signed, and there was a man in the crowd. A doctor. Twenty-seven, blond hair, amazing orange eyes, six foot three. He bought me a drink, and we talked about me, my life, my job. He was really interested. He asked me why I put up with it all.'

'Original,' Louise muttered into her water.

'He's specialising in psychiatry,' Rachel said, her eyes glowing, her face intense. 'I gave him my card.'

'And?'

'I just don't know what to do, Lou.'

'What are the options? You cheat on Hallam, feel awful, and get back together, or you cheat on Hallam, feel awful, and leave him.'

There was another long pause.

'I thought you might understand. I mean, you hop from one relationship to another, don't you? You're not settled?'

56

Louise was glad she was sitting down. To be told by her best friend and her big sister in the space of a few days that she was some sort of role model because all of her relationships had been abject failures was difficult to grasp.

'You've got to decide, Rachel.'

'You could tell me to go for it.'

'Why?'

'Because life's too bloody short, that's what you could tell me.'

'Sounds like you've already made your mind up.'

'God, you sound just like Mum!'

'Have you told her about this?'

'Of course not. I can't talk to Mum about anything. She can't even talk about Dad. All she wants to do is send me vests.'

Louise sat quietly while Rachel catapulted herself from the sofa, stalked out to the kitchen and retrieved the bottle of wine.

'Mum, by the way, has got to get her act together,' Rachel continued. 'I'm damned if I'm spending another morose Christmas down there. All those bloody photographs of Dad all over the place.'

'I like them.' A shard of defensiveness shot through Louise.

'It's like a shrine,' Rachel steamed. 'I can't stand it. It's not as if he was so bloody wonderful.'

Louise stood up and saw Rachel's eyes widen in alarm.

'Calm down, Louise. I wasn't being disrespectful. Just honest. Dad was nice, but he wasn't ever going to set the world on fire, was he? I just think Mum could do something with herself. She could meet someone else. She could get a decent job. She could bare her bum to the whole bloody lot of them. I'm just being honest. I loved Dad, but he was . . . a bit uninspiring, wasn't he?'

'Rachel, how can you say that?' Louise breathed. 'I had nothing but admiration for him. He built that business up from nothing. He could have stayed a brickie, but he set up on his own instead. You get your business head from him.'

'Don't get hysterical. I know you and he were bosom buddies, but I don't think there's any need to get schmaltzy about somebody just because they've died.'

'Schmaltzy?' Louise heard her own voice rising.

'I just think that before we canonise him we might look at the facts. He was great fun, yes, but he'd have loved it if we were just like Mum. You know that's true.'

'He was a family man. It's not a crime. And Mum was happy. If Dad was still around, she'd still be happy. It was what she wanted too.'

'Are you sure Mum was happy?' Rachel gave Louise an even look.

'Of course she was.' Louise was thrown by the question. 'I don't know what to say. He was kind. He cared about other people. He didn't go on and on about himself for hour after hour like you do.'

'Hooray.' Rachel stood up unsteadily, her glass in her hand. 'So I'm selfish. Fine. The truth is that I've had to learn the meaning of the word "ambition" out of a book. Neither of our parents ever had it. If I'd been as willing to jog along as you have, I'd never have had any of this. They never inspired me to do anything different, to go against the grain. I'm not like you, Louise. I can't put up with normality like you can.'

'Fine,' Louise said. 'If this is normality, then I'm Luther Vandross. The real reason I came round tonight was to give you this.'

Louise tossed the piece of paper that Ash had given her at the coffee table. It skimmed across the tiles and landed on the floor. 'It's a song. I wanted you to have a look at it and tell me what you thought. It was because I wanted to do something for someone else. It had nothing to do with me losing my job. The truth is that if I ever had a problem, ever, you'd be the last person I'd turn to, Rachel, and that's why you're so different from Dad.'

'Where are you going?'

Rachel walked unsteadily after Louise as she headed down the hall.

'Away.'

'You can think of this as home, Louise, you're always welcome here.'

'Sod off.'

'Why don't you stay? We can talk this through.'

'No.' Louise stomped towards the door. 'I'm going home.'

'If you need money, I can lend you money.'

Louise knew Rachel would lend her money. She knew she'd help her in a real career. Her sister had always been generous. But what she needed her to say right now was that she wanted to be an auntie.

'I don't want money, Rachel.'

'What's this? Somebody who doesn't want money? It must be Louise. Ah, it is!' It was Hallam, his key outstretched, his bushy eyebrows, half chestnut, half grey, raised in evident delighted surprise to see Louise. She wanted to throw her arms round him and tell him that everything was going to be all right. They were distracted by Rachel losing her balance behind them and falling into a nest of tables. Hallam pulled a comical face at Louise.

'Pissed again, is she? Well, I won't be away so much in the future. If I can just get in and warm up, I'll tell you both what's happening.'

'I've got to go,' Louise said. If she stayed in Hallam's presence too long she just might blurt it all out, and then Rachel would have another chance to tell her how hopeless she was. 'Bye, Hallam.' She pushed a kiss against his icy cheek. 'See you, Rachel.'

Your life is at a crossroads. It is for you to decide which road you wish to travel down. Others will try to influence you, but you must follow your instincts. You are an adventurer, and may find that opportunities to travel overseas present themselves. The stars show distress in the recent past due to the death of a loved one, and confusion. This may soon be replaced by a time of great opportunity. You must listen to your heart.

'What a load of cobblers,' Olivia muttered, leaning back on the sofa and sipping her glass of wine. She finished the page.

Both anguish and joy are promised as the year draws to a close. There may soon be a happy announcement from someone close to you. Above all, your chart shows that your independence is increasing and you will find you have the confidence in yourself to take on tasks which you have been putting off.

It was all there, as she'd expected. Travel, romance, death and a happy event. Of course she travelled. She got the bus to work every day. There was no romance, but she often thought of Bob and their early years together. Death was obvious. Everybody died at some point.

She lay back against the sofa. A happy event was whatever you wanted it to be. Rachel and Hallam were clearly never going to marry. Somehow she couldn't picture Louise announcing her betrothal with shining eyes. She hadn't even mentioned the boyfriend the last few times they'd spoken.

Perhaps the happy event referred to her reunion dinner. She had to ring Katherine Muff. She was putting it off. She took another sip of wine. Words from the chart played around her head.

Increased independence. Being left on your own after your partner of nearly forty years had died could be looked at as increased independence. And what tasks was she putting off, for heaven's sake?

Olivia's skin tingled. There was the garage, and more importantly the Ford Escort that was sitting in it, untouched since Bob had died. She kept meaning to sell it, but she couldn't face that. She'd passed her test, years ago, but Bob always drove.

Annoyed to have discovered the task that she'd been putting off, and even more annoyed that she had allowed herself to be seduced into the idea that anything on Shaun's chart could be pertinent to her life, Olivia tipped another small measure of wine into her glass. She'd deal with the car eventually, but she wouldn't do it now. There was too much to think about first. Including the bloody reunion dinner.

She went through to the kitchen to ring Louise. She was going to screw up the courage, somehow, to mention the dinner to her. If she brought the subject up it might jolt her out of this inertia.

As she dialled Louise's number, Olivia had visions of the other women arriving at the restaurant. There would be Geraldine Fletcher in an off-the-shoulder satin number, with her flowing chestnut hair and big bosoms; Jane Kerr, diminutive in glasses and a velvet suit, snapping at her chauffeur as she climbed out of the limo; Audrey Hamilton, blushing furiously and mumbling under her breath while flicking back a long plait; and of course, Katherine bloody Muff, surrounded by photographers, stopping to sign autographs, waving away her driver and taking the arm of her glamorous escort. Somewhere up the road, Olivia would be stumbling off the bus, brushing the dust from her one nice dress, shivering under the quilted mac she wore to work, and grappling with her umbrella. Olivia held the receiver in a stranglehold as she waited for Louise to answer.

'Yes?' Louise sounded bright. That made a nice change.

'It's Mum. How are you, dear?'

'Oh. Hello.'

'I've caught you off your guard. Are you just going out?'

'No, no.'

'Is Jon there?'

There was a pause. Olivia thought she heard a snort.

'No.'

'Are you in the middle of your dinner?'

'No!' Louise yelled, starting to laugh. 'Nothing was happening, and then the phone rang. How are you, Mum?'

Olivia took another sip from her wineglass. 'I'm a bit—bit worried about something. That's all.'

'Oh?' Louise sounded very alert now.

'It's silly, really. It's just that Katherine Muff rang and wants me to go to a dinner, and I can't go.'

'Muff?' Louise gave an explosive laugh. 'So why can't you go?'

'It's just . . .' Olivia thought of all the reasons that she didn't want to go. She opened her mouth and tried to formulate a concise summary. She didn't want to blackmail Louise into offering to come with her. She didn't want to use words like 'alone' and 'insecure'. She was starting to wish that the girls respected her, just a little bit, for the person she was. 'I—I haven't got anything to wear.'

Louise collapsed into giggles again. Olivia smiled to hear it.

'Blimey, Mum. There's not going to be anybody from the press there, is there? Just a load of women with bubble perms complaining about their corns. Just wear what you're comfortable in.'

'I haven't got a bubble perm.' Olivia tried to joke, but she was wounded. 'Or corns. If I went, I'd like to look nice.'

'Why bother dressing up? It's just going to be a mothers' meeting, everyone going on about how much their kids earn. You'll probably be bored senseless. In fact, why go? You've never kept in touch with anyone from school, have you?'

Olivia's mouth wobbled. Why go? That wasn't what she expected to hear. Olivia stood up straight and frowned at the cupboard door.

'I want to go! And I want you to help me decide what to wear, not to talk me out of it. I never go anywhere. Nobody ever asks me. I want to go to a restaurant!' Olivia realised with a shock that she was almost shouting. 'And what's more, I want you to come with me!'

There was a silence. Louise wasn't used to her mother issuing orders.

'Louise? Are you still there?'

'When is it?'

'Less than two weeks' time. On the Saturday night. You could come down on the train, and we could go together. You could even go back the same night if you wanted to, or sleep in your old room.'

She heard Louise blow out as if she was thinking hard.

'OK, Mum. I'll come with you.'

Olivia put down her wineglass with a clatter, her voice rising an octave. 'You'll come with me?'

'Yes, yes. I haven't seen you for a while, have I? It might be a good thing. And it'll give us a chance to talk properly. Yes, why not?' Louise's voice gained life. 'Why the hell not? I'll come with you, and we'll take the piss out of the bubble perms together. How about that?'

'Oh, good grief!' Olivia put her hand to her mouth. She could feel tears.

'OK, Mum, I'm going to crash out now, but why don't you ring me nearer the time and we'll sort out the details.'

'That's, that's fine.' Olivia cleared her throat. 'Thank you, darling. I think we'll have fun.'

'Oh, and Mum? I've some good news for you. I won't tell you now. I'll tell you when I come down.'

'You're not getting married?'

Louise laughed. 'I thought all mothers wanted their children to settle down, start families, and all that stuff.'

'Not to Jon?'

'Don't panic, Mum. I need Jon like a haemophiliac needs a leech. No more clues. I'll speak to you next week.'

After she'd put the phone down, Olivia finished her glass of wine, pondering over Louise's statement. Was she getting married? Who could she possibly have met in the few weeks since she'd last mentioned Jon? It was far too quick. She couldn't know what she was doing.

She took herself up to bed. For now she wouldn't worry about Louise getting married. She was going to dinner, and she would show off her beautiful blonde daughter who lived in a flat in London. That would show them. And it struck her finally that Shaun's chart had been bizarrely accurate. She *could* feel a surge of increased independence. She had made a stand and got what she wanted. And she had a warm feeling inside telling her that things weren't going to stop there.

Louise headed straight for the vegetables at the supermarket. They looked so good. How could she never have noticed before? Especially the broccoli. She chose a large floret. She tried to move on, but the broccoli called her back. She loaded more into her basket and went for Brussels sprouts and cabbage. And potatoes too. Mashed. With a pork chop. And very thick gravy. Her basket sagged on her arm as she staggered around, piling in her ingredients. It felt so good. The new Louise. Healthy, clean, organised, and full of broccoli.

Chocolate. She didn't normally eat much chocolate. Why not? It was fantastic. She grabbed a handful of Mars bars and sprinkled them on top of her load. So this was what being pregnant was all about. Eating whatever you felt like, with no reason to feel guilty. And as the regular assistant recognised her and reached for a packet of Ultra-Lows, she shook her head, trying not to look as smug as she felt.

'No?' The colour drained from his face.

'No,' she said decisively. 'But if you can hang on a second, I think I need a Black Forest gateau.'

She found a note wedged under her door when she got home.

It looked as though somebody had been trying to get a pen to work, but there were words there if you looked closely. It was from Harris.

'Louise,' she read, puzzled that he had bothered to write to her when he only lived upstairs, 'I am on fire. Harris.'

Her hand dropped to her side clutching the note. She stared up at the ceiling. 'On fire?' She sniffed the air.

She wandered out into the hall and peered up the stairs. There was no smoke, no sign of panic. She looked at the note again. Something did actually smell a bit strange. She put it to her nose and drew in a deep breath. It was aftershave.

There was nothing else for it. She'd have to ask him if he was all right. She walked upstairs and hammered at his door.

'Harris?' she yelled through the wood. 'Are you all right in there?'

Silence. She put her ear to the door. He must be out.

'Oh, Big Boy!' she called coquettishly, making herself giggle. The door flew open. She jumped, clutching her chest. 'Good God, Harris, don't ever do that again!'

Then she realised that he was naked. Completely. It was simply impossible not to stare at his body. He was tanned all over and sprinkled with black hair, and he had a fantastic set of equipment.

He gave her a long, slow smile, his eyes glowing like coals.

'At last, Louise. Now I've got you.' She thought he was going to lunge for her, but he didn't move.

'But I thought . . .' She swallowed nervously. 'I mean, where's the fire, Harris?'

'Here, Louise.'

Her eyes could not have grown any wider as he indicated very graphically exactly where the fire was.

'And you want me too. That's why you came to me.'

'I, um.' She took several small steps towards the top of the stairs. 'Actually, I came to you because I thought you were burning to death.'

'I *am* burning. Burning with desire for you.'

'Look, I'm really flattered,' Louise gulped, backing her way down the stairs. 'But now's not a good time.'

'Now is a *very* good time,' he countered.

It was logical, she supposed, as he pointed down at himself. But she was already halfway down the stairs.

'So you're going to leave me burning?' he called after her.

'Yes.' It came out very lamely. 'Sorry.'

She reached the bottom of the stairs.

'Perhaps I should have given you dinner first,' he said.

'Maybe,' she nodded up at him. 'It was a little direct.'

'OK. I'll give it some thought.'

He turned, allowing her a prime view of his firm, tanned buttocks, and walked back into his flat.

Mother Nature was an odd creature. She was pregnant, for heaven's sake. There was no biological imperative for her to think about men just at the moment. But she was. And amid the jumble of disconcerting images in her mind were Ash's pale green eyes. She had a wild urge to speak to him again. And, being practical about it, she needed advice.

It was a new and strange thing to be applying for the dole. She still didn't have a clue what she was supposed to be doing in order to qualify. She wanted to work, but for the last few days she'd been assaulted by violent attacks of sickness. And she needed to work out a longer-term solution. Ash had been signing on for six months. He could help.

What if she rang him, told him the truth, that she'd opened his piece of paper and read it, realised that it was a song, and given it to her sister to look at in return for his kindness in picking her up when she fainted?

She sorted through her jacket pockets until she found the piece of cigarette packet with Ash's number on it.

She picked up the receiver. She took a deep breath. He was gorgeous. She put the phone down again.

Then she tried again.

He answered the phone himself, but she had to pretend that she didn't know it was him.

'Could I speak to Ash, please?'

'Yeah, speaking. Is that Louise?'

She almost threw the phone across the room. How did he know?

'Yes. I'm the Louise from the Jobcentre.'

'I know which one you are. I only know one Louise, anyway. So, did you find the bit of paper I gave you?'

'There's good news and bad news.' How could she have known that her mind would go blank the moment she heard his voice again? Now she had to think on her feet. 'I've found it, but—'

'You have! I can't fucking believe it. You've saved my life. Oh, Louise, you're a star. You brilliant woman. Have my babies.' She could hear him laughing into the air.

'But—'

'So, can I meet you? Or you can send it to me, if you'd rather.'

'Oh no, I can meet you,' she said. 'I'd like to talk to you anyway. About something completely different.'

He was still laughing. He had a fascinating laugh.

'Great. I could see you in the café again, tomorrow. We can talk about anything you want.'

'It's just about—' She yanked up the verbal handbrake. It made an ugly squeal of rubber on fresh air. She couldn't stall this moment when he was so exuberant. She would find a suitable moment tomorrow to be boring.

'See you there tomorrow.' She could hear him grinning through his voice. 'About eleven do you?'

'Do me?' Oh, yes please, a little voice cried. 'Eleven's fine.'

He hung up.

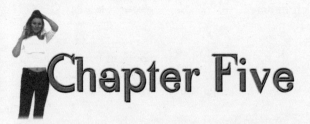

Chapter Five

'So, I WAS WONDERING if you could help me with my jobsearch,' Louise finished. Ash looked at her while he stirred his tea. He'd been very quiet while she'd related the tale of yesterday's interview. Too quiet.

'Do you see what my problem is? I need to know how *not* to get a job just at the moment. It won't be for long. I thought you might give me some tips. You seem to know what you're doing.'

'Why don't you want to get a job?' he asked. She kicked herself. She'd just assumed that it was part of the unemployed thing, to try to outwit the Jobcentre. There was a logical answer, of course, which involved morning sickness for three hours every afternoon and a need to work out a long-term solution, but she could hardly tell him that.

'It's just—you know. Timing.'

'Ah. Timing.'

'Yes.'

He pulled a squashed packet of tobacco out of the pocket of his denim jacket, arranged a Rizla on the table, and began to roll a cigarette. She leaned away from him, towards the door which was constantly swinging open, and prayed that she wasn't going to gag when he lit it. In the last couple of days the smell of cigarette smoke had suddenly made her stomach lurch.

'Timing of what?' he asked, watching her again as he fumbled around in an attempt to find his lighter. He patted all of his pockets in turn, fingered his jeans and swore under his breath.

'Oh, I've got one. Hang on.' Louise found her lighter in her handbag. She flicked the flame for him and he leaned forward, putting up his hands to cup hers and hold them steady.

She jumped as his skin touched hers, knocking the end of his thin cigarette upwards so that it bent in the middle. Slowly, he pulled the crooked cigarette out of his mouth. He assessed it silently.

'I'm so sorry. You can have one of mine instead. Here.' Fumbling pathetically, Louise found her packet of Ultra-Lows. 'In fact, have them all. I've given up.' She tossed the packet over the table. 'There you are.'

He paused again, picking up the packet and peering inside.

'There are fifteen left in here.'

'I don't care. Have them.'

'Impulsive, aren't you?'

'Think of them as a thank-you present for scooping me up when I passed out.'

'Thanks. I'll keep them for emergencies. I tend to stick to rollies. Cheaper.'

She watched him straighten out the cigarette she had bent, then attempted to hold out the lighter for him again. He put out his hand and gently prised the lighter from between her fingers.

'I'll do it, shall I?'

'Yes,' she breathed. 'Why don't you?'

'So,' he asked again as he blew a thin jet of smoke away from her, 'what did you mean about timing? Are you doing something else that you don't want them to know about?'

'I just need a bit of thinking time, to sort myself out. You know how it is.' She tried to look conspiratorial. She had the feeling it wasn't very convincing. The look on his face said that he was either bored witless or deeply unimpressed with everything about her.

It shouldn't have mattered, but he was wearing a chunky black jumper under his denim jacket which stopped just above the waistline of his jeans and left a small expanse of his stomach visible. She could see a layer of soft brown hairs there, and it was doing strange things to her. She'd realised he had nice eyes when she'd woken up from her faint and stared up into them, but until now she hadn't taken in just how appealing the complete package was. That was all Harris's fault. She'd probably never be able to hold a conversation with a man again without expecting him to drop his trousers and point his equipment at her.

'Why don't you tell me how it is.' He gave her a brief smile.

'It's—it's difficult, at the moment. I need to work out what I really want to do. I'm a bit like you, I suppose.' He raised his eyebrows at her. 'You know, with your band. You obviously need time to get your—song-writing off the ground. I assume that's why you're not working.'

'My song-writing,' he murmured. 'So you've brought the song, then? I was starting to wonder.'

'Well, that's what I wanted to talk to you about,' she said, trying to get the upper hand again. 'I'll do you a favour if you do me one.'

He raised his eyebrows again. 'What sort of favour?'

'I need to buy some time. I need somebody to show me how to deal with all these jobseeking requirements so that I don't balls it up.'

'And if I do that, you'll give me my song back?'

'I'll do even more than that. I'll show it to someone who knows about bands. My sister, Rachel, works for a record company. They're always on the lookout for new talent. If she saw your song, I thought she might be able to help you.'

'Right. Have you got it on you now?'

'I—I've already given it to her, actually. I hope you don't mind.'

He lay back in his chair and crossed one knee lazily over the other. She had an odd feeling that she'd done something wrong.

'You're a strange one, Louise. I can't work you out at all.'

'Really?' She blinked. Enigmatic was good. Probably.

'Yeah, you've got everything going for you. Smart, lively, articulate. You could be making a decent living. You could probably walk into another job tomorrow if you really wanted to.'

The finger of guilt returned to jab her in the eye. She tried not to think about her father, her mother, her sister, all of whom would raise their eyebrows disapprovingly. They didn't know she was pregnant. Neither did he.

And on top of that, she'd just offered him an exclusive introduction to someone in the music business, and he didn't seem to have heard her.

'Er, my sister works for this record company,' she repeated limply, 'and I've given her your song. I hope you don't mind.'

He responded this time with a philosophical wave of his hand.

'We've been through record companies. We've sent demos all over the place. We've forced ourselves into people's offices. Of course I don't mind if you've given your sister our song, but you're obviously not in music yourself.'

'Why do you say that?'

'Because a song scribbled out on a scrap of paper, however much detail there is, won't give her a bloody clue what we're like live. I'm sorry, Louise, but she'll probably bin it.'

'But I thought—'

'Don't worry about it. It was nice of you to try. It'd be helpful if you could get the song back, though.'

'You want it back? But what if—?'

'It's the only version of the lyrics Ginger worked out. I can remember the music, but he's going mental about it. Please get it back for me.'

She sat quietly, feeling silly. He shifted and gave her a direct look.

'So why don't you want a job when you're quite capable of getting one?'

'And what about you?' she retaliated. What's stopping you walking into a job tomorrow, if you really wanted to?'

'Can you see me in an office?' he asked, still looking relaxed.

'Yes, if you can see me in one.'

'I am trying to do what I'm actually good at.' He leaned forward, speaking slowly. His eyes had become intense. 'And what I want to do doesn't come with a safety net. You go for broke, or you never do it.'

'You're talking about your band.'

'I don't just mean the band. Nothing I do pays. It doesn't mean it's not a contribution to society, if that's what you're angling for.'

'There's no need to take a moral tone,' she said. 'I only put the question back to you. I've got my reasons for not getting a job just yet. You don't know anything about my circumstances, so don't lecture me.'

'I wasn't lecturing you.'

'Yes, you were. You said I should go and get a job tomorrow. But I can't.'

'Why not?'

'I'm not telling you.'

'Hey, I was only asking you what the dole office is going to ask next time you go in.' He smiled at her and she almost slid off her chair with delight. 'You're going to need a lot of coaching. You haven't got a clue how to handle it, have you? Off like a firework at the first question. That's the one thing that's guaranteed to get you into trouble.'

He seemed genuinely amused by her. It was confusing. Everything about him was confusing.

'Have you been testing me?'

'Something like that. You even turned up to see me in a skirt.' He leaned round the side of the table to gaze at her legs. 'And a very nice pair of shoes. And tights. Pink ones. Interesting.'

She pulled her legs away. He sat up again, his lips twitching.

'I was just checking. If you go to sign on looking as smart as this, they're going to punt you straight off for an interview for a job you'll probably get. If you really do need some time to work things out, you're going to have to be a bit more—downbeat.'

'So what do you advise? Taking a pair of gardening shears to all my clothes?'

'You'll have to be a bit more subtle.' He took another swig of his tea. 'So you're not going to tell me what all this is about, then?'

'No,' she answered.

'So, what is it, I wonder? You want to finish *Lord of the Rings*? The kitchen needs redecorating? You've always wanted to teach yourself Chinese, and now seems like an ideal time to do it?'

He was lolling on his chair, his rolled-up cigarette resting between his fingers, quite at ease with himself. He wasn't the one who was bloody pregnant, was he? Her temper flared.

'Let's see if I can remember. Your band, Ealing's answer to Oasis, has spent a year writing a song that starts "Rolling on the bed with Viola"? Even if I did want to teach myself Chinese, can you tell me why that would be any more pointless than what you're doing?'

'Would you give a fuck if I explained it to you?'

He still looked calm. She was mortified.

'I'm sorry,' she said, not meeting his eyes. 'I didn't mean to be so rude about your song. It obviously means a lot to you.'

He laughed at her, swinging in his chair.

'So, you showed my song to your sister as a trade for me helping you out. But she's already got it, hasn't she, and I haven't agreed to help you polish your job-dodging skills? That was very trusting of you.'

'No,' she said, 'that was to say thank you for picking me up when I fainted under the Catering stand. So we're quits now. I've got your number. If my sister's interested in seeing you live, she'll let me know.' She buttoned up her coat and drained her mug. Pride, she urged herself. Baby first, lust later. Probably much later, when everything had healed up again and there wasn't an attractive man in sight, but she wouldn't dwell on that now. 'Good luck with your song-writing. I might bang into you over the giros some time.'

Louise stood up and turned to go.

'Hey, hang on there.' She glanced back at Ash. Annoyingly, he was still smiling at her. 'I said I'd give you a few tips if you needed them, and I will. Your place or mine?'

'It's not a date,' she said through tight lips.

'I wasn't asking for one.' He looked at her earnestly. 'I don't know what your problem is, Louise, but I'll help. Why don't you give me your address, and I'll drop round some time? In fact, if you're not doing anything now, I could go through things with you. I have something I've got to do this afternoon, but I'm free for a couple of hours if you want to put together a CV that makes you unemployable. Temporarily, of course.'

Louise hesitated.

'Do you want help with this or not? C'mon, Louise, this is all a bit coy, isn't it? Would it help if I answer that question you're mulling over?'

'What question?' The colour rose in her cheeks again.

'You're wondering whether this is all innocent.'

'Well, of course it's innocent. I don't know what you mean?'

'I'm seeing someone. OK? So my offer to help is humanitarian, not some perverse way of trying to get you into a compromising situation.'

'I can assure you that I wasn't angling for a seduction,' she fibbed.

'Good. So we know where we stand. Do you want help or not?'

'I'll ring you,' she blurted out, and fled.

'You're completely bloody mad,' Sally blurted down the phone. 'I don't know what you're thinking of, Louise. You just can't do this. You can't.'

'Why not?' Louise was perched on the edge of her bed eating her way through a plate of salad sandwiches. 'Just because you wouldn't do it, doesn't mean I can't.'

'You're just not thinking straight. I know it's difficult at the moment, but you just can't do what you're suggesting. You'll be in such a state. You'll be tied down with no money, no prospects, no social life. You'll be lonely, sad and desperate. And what will you have to offer your baby, for God's sake?'

'I have lots to offer a baby. I'm going to find a decent job once I've worked out what I want to do, I'm going to have money. I might even have a social life. I want to do this, Sally. I'm really happy about it.'

'And what's Jon going to think about this? Christ, Louise, you're just not thinking.'

'He doesn't want to know about it. He's going to be really relieved if I tell him to stay out of it.'

'He might feel like that now, but how will he feel when he knows there's a baby out there carrying his genes? Every week for ever you'll have Jon turning up on your doorstep and claiming his rights as a father. You'll be tied to him for the rest of your life.' Sally paused for breath. 'No, Louise. You can't.'

'But, Sally . . .' Louise blinked into the air, choosing her words carefully. Friendships teetered at moments like this. 'I wasn't asking for your permission. I was telling you what I was going to do.'

Sally was silent. Louise could hear her shuffling papers on her desk.

'I thought you wanted my advice,' she said huffily.

'I have wanted your advice, and I've valued it, really. But I've made my own decision now.'

'You haven't done anything with your own life yet. And you'll be on your own, with nobody to support you. Who's going to be there for you through all the false alarms? Who's going to drive you to the hospital and go through the experience with you?'

Louise thought hard. 'The midwife?'

'God, Louise. Stop joking.'

'The taxi driver, perhaps? I might get one like John Travolta in *Look Who's Talking*. That would be fortuitous, wouldn't it?'

'Louise, be serious.'

'I am being bloody serious. Look, I didn't ask for this to happen. I didn't even think for one minute that I wanted to keep it at first, and I'm sure that in my position you wouldn't want to, but that's irrelevant. I can't say what's changed, but I'm happy, Sal. Don't you understand?'

'I suppose you'll go all pro-life now, and judge everybody who isn't as dewy-eyed as you. I remember you ranting and raving about choice. You've certainly changed your tune.'

'This *is* about choice. That's what nobody seems to understand.' Louise glowered at the phone. 'I'd be the first one to chain myself to the railings if they changed the laws, but that doesn't mean that I can't make my own sodding mind up, does it?'

'You're shouting.'

'I'm not!' Louise shouted at the receiver.

'Yes, you are. Don't shout at me. I'm only trying to help.'

'I didn't shout. I just have stronger feelings about my own life than I thought. I'm not asking for your approval any more, Sal. I'm sorry, but if you can't say anything more positive, I'm going to have to ring off.'

'Fine,' Sally snapped.

'Fine,' Louise snapped back. Sally crashed the phone down first.

Louise smiled to herself, rubbing her hand on her stomach. A little person. She would do all she could to make life happy for them both. And that meant staying on top of her plans.

If she could just fight through this period of nausea, sign on for a short time to make sure she didn't lose the flat, and work her way into a promising career, the stage would be set. And that brought her back to Ash. He had offered to help her tackle the Jobcentre. She could just pop round, take some newspapers and her forms, and have a cup of tea with him. That might be friendly.

It hadn't taken long to persuade herself. She was back in the bedroom before she knew it, picking up the phone, dialling his number, and breathing erratically into the plastic.

'Ash?' she said quickly.

'Er, I'll just go and get him. Hang on.'

It was a woman's voice. A *woman's voice*. Louise stared at the brick view beyond her window. She heard scuffling from a distance, and he was there on the end of the phone.

'Hi.'

'It's Louise,' she said. She stopped, waiting for him to explain that now wasn't a good time. She suddenly felt like a gooseberry.

'Great. I'm really glad you called. Did you change your mind?'

He sounded almost genuine. His girlfriend must have left the room.

'If you think you can help me, I could meet you tomorrow.'

'Yeah, brilliant. Can you make it early afternoon?'

'That's fine.'

'Why don't you come round here?' he said.

'Is that all right?'

'Course. I'll give you the address.'

Louise scribbled down the details. As she did, her doorbell rang.

'Is that your bell?' he asked.

'Er, yes.' She frowned across the room.

'Right. Well, I'll see you tomorrow.'

'Yes, probably,' she answered, and hung up quickly before she could make more of a fool of herself.

The bell rang again. She flung open the front door.

A bunch of flowers appeared with a pair of grey legs beneath them.

'Flat two?' a nasal voice asked.

'Yes.'

The bunch of flowers was flicked to one side. A man grinned at her.

'Who's a lucky lady then?'

'I don't know.'

He consulted a form in his hand. 'Louise Twigg?'

'Er, yes, but—'

'For you, madam.' He grinned again.

Louise took the flowers and the man trotted off. She closed the front door and searched for a label. She found a small white envelope and pulled out the card. She leaned against the wall as she read it.

To my sweet Louise. Thinking of you. With all my love, Jon.

'Bastard!' Louise issued through her teeth as she ploughed her way through the backstreets of Ealing the following day. 'Git. Sod. Bastard.'

She'd taken the flowers into her flat and sat and stared at them. Jon hadn't rung to ask if she'd got them. There was no letter this morning from him. Just that one, cute little message and enough tiger lilies to buckle the top table at a wedding reception. Finally, out of simple pity for the flowers, she'd stuffed them in a bucket and left them in the kitchen.

She'd read the message over and over again. What exactly did he mean? Without any clarification, she could only think the worst. He would think it was all over by now. It was his way of saying 'Get well soon', but from a safe distance.

Louise began to walk down Ash's street. Judging by the number of bells clustered around most of the doors, she was in bedsit land. She sniffed in a noseful of freezing air and got a whiff of something dreadful. Tarmac? Oil? Whatever it was, quite suddenly her stomach turned over and she knew she was going to be sick.

She dived into the nearest garden, yanked the plastic lid off the dustbin sitting at the bottom of a row of clean white steps, and bent over it.

The front door opened at the top of the white steps.

'Get away from my dustbin!' a woman in a caftan screeched at her. 'Go and do that in the gutter. Druggies. You're disgusting.'

She staggered away as she heard the door slam above her. She reached a low wall at the front of the next house and sank onto it. The branches of a fir pricked at the back of her head. She would just sit here enveloped by an overgrown Christmas tree and think what to do next.

'Louise?'

Ash was standing right in front of her, shivering. Not surprisingly, seeing as he was wearing only his aerated jeans and a T-shirt.

'Blimey. How long have you been standing there?'

'Just a few seconds. I thought you'd fallen asleep.' He grinned at her. 'I, er, saw you from the house. It's just opposite.'

'Oh.' She tried to regain her dignity by sitting up straight. 'Oh, I see. I'm sorry. I just had to sit down for a moment. It's a long walk from my flat and I suddenly felt tired.' She dazzled him with a smile.

'Right. Do you want to come in then? I've put the kettle on.'

She nodded and followed him back across the road. She stopped inside as he closed the door behind her and wandered away to a kitchen at the back of the house.

'This house is bigger than it looks on the outside. It's really nice.'

'Not so big when everyone's home,' he called from the kitchen. 'We share the first two floors here between five of us. Come through. It's only me and Karen here at the moment. She's upstairs, but I think she's asleep. We can just sit in here if you like.'

She went into the kitchen and gazed around. For the moment, she didn't want to think about Karen being asleep upstairs.

'So are you all friends, then? It must be difficult sharing with so many.'

He laughed at her and grabbed two mugs from a heap of washing-up. 'I'm used to it. It's the price you pay for following your dream. I knew Ginger and Karen before we moved here. She's his sister, and he's been my best mate for years. The other two just turned up and refused to leave, which suited us. We needed the rent money.'

'And, er, is Karen . . .' Louise paused to phrase her question inoffensively. 'Is Karen jobless too?'

He stopped for a moment, a frown flitting across his brow.

'Karen's got her own income. So has Ginger. The rest of us here have to scrape by how we can.'

There was something in Ash's tone as he talked about Karen that intrigued her. It wasn't entirely respectful.

'So your parents don't have money?'

'My parents divorced me.'

'They did what?'

'I don't see them. It's a really boring story. What about you?'

'Oh, er, my father died. My mum's in Tonbridge. She works for a branch of the Health Service.'

'Really?' He stopped to look at her as he poured boiling water into the mugs. 'Was that recently?'

'My dad? Over a year ago. I try not to think about it if I can help it. He was a nice man. Fun, friendly, everybody liked him. He was always there, just being him.' She slipped off her coat and arranged it on the back of the chair. 'I couldn't have a glass of water as well, could I?'

'Oh sure. Of course. You still feeling unwell?'

'Just a bit tired. So Karen's your girlfriend then, is she?' she asked. He shot her a cool glance.

'She's Ginger's sister. She sings for us. And we've been seeing each other for a long time.'

'Oh.' Louise opened the first newspaper and flicked through the pages quickly. That was not good news. She found the classified ads and tried to concentrate on them.

'She's got a great voice. Smoky, really sexy.' He flicked tea bags into a bin and brought the mugs over.

'That's nice.' So, Karen was talented. That was even worse news. She focused on an advert for a town planner. He set the mug and glass of water in front of her and sat down. She took a sip of water, read the details of the ad several times, and frowned with concentration.

'I met her through Ginger. We've got a good friendship. I value that.'

'Really.' Friendship. Even worse than lust. Friendships went on for ever. She opened her shoulder bag, picked out a pen, and ringed the advertisement with great care.

'So,' he continued, nodding down at the newspaper, 'you've got a degree in town planning, have you?'

'No,' she said incredulously.

'I just wondered why you've ringed the ad.'

'I thought that was the whole point. If I apply for jobs I'm not qualified for I won't get them, will I?'

He smiled at her, lolling back in his chair.

'You've got to be cleverer than that. You've got to go for something
appropriate but mess it up. The guys at the Jobcentre aren't stupid.'

'Mess it up? What do you mean?'

'I mean you've got to apply for the jobs, go for the interviews, but
make damned sure you don't get offered anything. Just while you need
to sign on, of course.'

'How do I do that?' She looked at him in alarm. 'I've always temped
before. I don't know what you mean.'

'Basically, you have to tell them what they don't want to hear. If that's
not enough, behave as if you're on the edge of a breakdown. And if that
fails, fart loudly when it's all gone quiet.'

Then he smiled at her again.

It was so nice, so warm in this friendly, chaotic kitchen. She wanted
to be like Karen upstairs, cuddled up in bed, with Ash downstairs
making tea for her. She didn't want to have to go home after all this and
be on her own again. Burning tears of self-pity suddenly appeared in her
eyes. She tried to blink them away before he could see them.

'Hey.' He reached out to take her hand. His fingers were warm.

'I'm sorry. It's just that everything's a bit difficult at the moment.'

'I know,' he said softly, standing up to walk round the table and put
his hands gently on her shoulders.

'No, you don't know,' she mumbled.

'Yes,' he said with quiet confidence. 'I do.'

'No.' She turned to look up at him. His eyes were amazing. She gathered herself together.

'Ash, it's kind of you to think you know what's going on, but you
don't. You don't need to know anyway. It's got sod all to do with you.
And I don't know why you're being so kind, but it's very . . . helpful.'

'Louise?'

'Yes?' she whispered.

'Shut up.'

Her mouth opened to argue with him, but words failed her.

'I'm here. I'll help you,' he said.

He dropped his head and brushed her cheek with a kiss. It was such a
gentle action, a mere caress of his lips on her skin, and then he'd walked
away again and seated himself back in the chair out of her reach.

'You didn't have to do that,' she babbled in panic.

'I kissed you because I wanted to. Not because you're pregnant.'

'Oh.' She was relieved. 'All right then.'

She smiled at him. But then it hit her. She couldn't lie, not when he was fixing her with his eyes in that way, but she had to say something.

'What do you mean?'

'Come on,' he said gently. 'It's the only answer that makes any sense. Relax. You've got to have someone to talk to about it, haven't you? You might as well be honest with me. What have you got to lose?'

'Ash . . .'

He was being so—so reasonable. So sensible. So friendly. And so perceptive. There had to be something wrong with him.

'Yes?' he said.

'I should make things clear. I'm having this baby because I want to, not because I have to. I don't need pity.'

'I know,' he said.

'And I don't need anybody to step in and be a substitute for anybody else. This—this has happened, and although I didn't expect it, I've come to realise it's what I want.'

'I guessed that.' He nodded at her.

'And I'm only signing on until I don't feel sick,' she asserted.

'I'd worked that out for myself too.'

'The thing is, I think I've finally grown up. I don't quite know why I'm telling you that. It's just that it's become so important. I've never signed on before, I've never had to think about my security before. Profound things are happening to me.'

His lips twitched, but his eyes remained steady.

'I've never eaten so much broccoli in my life.'

'I can only imagine.'

'I've never given up smoking before.'

'I believe you.'

'And I've never shared such private thoughts with a complete stranger before.'

'I bet you've never thrown up in somebody else's dustbin before either.'

She was horrified. The man had seen her throw up in the dustbin. She looked away from him and back to the newspaper. He seemed to decide to stop teasing her and turn his attention back to why she was at his house in the first place.

'Got your CV?' he asked.

'Er, yes.' She crashed around in her plastic bag and found a handful of papers. She presented it to him. He shuffled through her CV quietly.

'What do you think?'

'There's plenty of potential here,' he said. 'I'll hang on to this and see if I can fiddle with it. OK with you?'

'Yes.' She took a sip of tea while she studied him. 'Listen, I haven't heard from my sister yet. We had a bit of a row the last time I saw her. For all I know, she might have thrown your song away. I just thought I should tell you that. I did what I could.'

Any answer he might have given was interrupted by the thundering of footsteps down the stairs. Louise straightened. The footsteps careered through the hallway and arrived in the kitchen. They stopped behind her. She heard a lazy yawn.

'Hi,' a smoky, sexy voice drawled over her head.

'Hi there. Kettle's just boiled. This is Louise.'

Louise swivelled round in her seat. She saw a woman with impossibly glossy swathes of golden hair, dressed only in a loose denim shirt. Karen pushed her hair out of her face to reveal kittenish brown eyes, a clear creamy skin and a wide, sensual mouth. Louise hated her instantly.

'Ahh. So this is Louise.' Karen nodded at Ash and arched a delicate eyebrow. 'Great, great. I'll just get myself some tea and leave you both to chat.' She flashed a smile at Louise, proving that she could do happy-sexy and sultry-sexy equally well, and swayed over to the kettle, revealing her shirt to be rumpled at the back, half tucked into a pair of maroon satin knickers which were very high cut over the buttock.

Louise remained transfixed as Karen flicked the switch on the kettle, leaned back on the draining board and performed a full stretch, her arms high, the few buttons fastened on the shirt straining to reveal an alarmingly full chest. Louise stuck out her swelling lumps competitively. Ash remained engrossed in her CV, making notes with a Biro.

'So, are you musical too, Louise?' Karen asked huskily.

'Not so's you'd notice.'

Karen nodded, flicking a tidal wave of hair out of one eye so that it fell endearingly over the other instead.

'Ash's really talented,' Karen said, grinning at Ash's back.

'Fuck off, Karen. Haven't you got something to do upstairs?'

'But you are, darling, and you're just so coy about it, which makes it all the more charming.'

'Hasn't the kettle boiled yet?'

'He was brilliant at Guildhall. Blew everyone away. He could be professional now, but he's so single-minded it's scary. If only he wasn't so obsessed with the class war, he'd be up there with the best of them.'

'Hang on.' Louise sat back and fiddled with her pen. 'Guildhall as in the music school?'

'Of course, what's he been telling you? That he was dragged up in the East End and made his own guitar out of orange crates and elastic bands? Don't believe a word of it.'

'Karen!' Ash swung round and eyed her severely. She shrugged at him, flicked her hair backwards and forwards again.

'OK, I'm out of here. Nice to meet you, Louise. See you upstairs when you've finished, working-class hero. Don't be long.'

Ash watched Karen's exit from the kitchen. Louise studied his expression with fascination. There was irritation in his eyes.

'So? What was that all about?' Louise asked him.

'Oh, she's just being a prat. Ignore her.'

'Guildhall School of Music? Not to learn how to play guitar with your teeth, I suspect. What did you do there?'

'Violin and cello,' he said, looking up at her again.

'But you're ashamed of that now, or what? I don't understand.'

'It's not what I do now. Not classical, anyway. I play electric violin. That's the sort of band it is. A bit unusual.'

'So why the allergic reaction to what Karen said?'

He rubbed at his nose with his forefinger. He looked uncomfortable.

'I just can't be doing with the formality of it all. Regular stints in an orchestra, dressing up like a penguin, playing other people's music, toadying to some histrionic conductor, all that ceremony. Treating music as if it's the property of the chattering classes. It's just not me.'

'So—'

'So can we get on with sorting you out? It's just that I don't want to explain it all. As I said, it's really boring.'

'But you did play in an orchestra?' Louise attempted one final push. At last she was getting a tiny glimpse of who Ash might really be.

'Yep. I was thrown out.'

'For . . . What did you do?'

He raised his eyes to her. There was a glint of humour there.

'I mooned at the conductor halfway through the "Sinfonia Antartica".'

'And people saw you?' Louise's mouth dropped open.

'Couldn't miss me really. I was first violin.'

'And your parents didn't approve? Is that why they divorced you?'

'My father was the conductor,' he said flatly. 'So shall we get on with your job applications now?'

'Why do you always do that?' Shaun asked. Olivia looked up guiltily from Carol's chair.

'Do what?'

78

'That thing with the chair. You always lower it before you leave.'

'It's to bring old Cow-bag down to size,' Sarah quipped, reaching up to ruffle Shaun's hair. He blushed violently, and opened his mouth as if trying to think of a suitable retort. 'OK, I'm off now.' Sarah grabbed her leather jacket and winked at Olivia. 'Neal's picking me up.' They heard her crash away down the corridor.

'That girl!' Olivia shook her head at Shaun. 'I remember my first job. I was so terrified of putting a foot wrong I hardly dared speak to anybody. But jobs used to last longer then. Everybody chops and changes now.'

'You can't blame people for that,' Shaun said. 'It's in our nature to change. We only become unhappy if we fight against it.'

'Ah, you're getting philosophical again.' Olivia made sure Carol's seat had dropped as far as it would go, patted it for reassurance, and wandered across to the coat stand.

'Look, Olivia, it really is freezing outside. Please will you let me give you a lift? I hate to think of you at that horrible, cold bus-stop.'

'All right.' She smiled at him. 'Thank you very much. And I can ask you something I've been meaning to ask you for the last couple of days.'

'Really?'

'Don't look so worried. You can always say no.'

They walked out into the street and Olivia waited patiently on the pavement while Shaun played with the lock on the passenger door, which refused to budge from the inside. Eventually, he forced it up and grinned at her through the glass. She slipped into the seat beside him, and after three attempts managed to pull the door properly shut.

'People have love affairs with their cars, you know,' he told her as he repeatedly tried to start the engine. 'I've had Flossie for fourteen years. I wouldn't part with her if I inherited a million. I'm loyal like that.'

'I can believe it.'

'People don't value loyalty any more, do they?' He glanced at Olivia triumphantly as the engine fired into action. They lurched away steering an uncertain course through a network of residential streets. 'It's a rare quality, that's what I say. You can spot it in people.'

'You think so?'

'Oh, yes. People have auras. Some are almost visible, they're so strong. You're a very loyal person, for example. I can sense that.'

Olivia mused. Had her recent thoughts been loyal?

'Sarah's a loyal one,' Shaun continued happily. 'But I'm not sure that Neal's the one for her.'

'Good grief!' Olivia laughed. 'Is this what you spend all your spare time doing? Thinking about people at work and their relationships?'

Shaun didn't answer immediately, and Olivia's laugh trailed away.

'Er, I do the charts, of course.'

'Of course.'

'And I read a lot. Especially poetry.'

'You do?'

'I do.'

'"Courage!" he said, and pointed toward the land. "This mounting wave will roll us shoreward soon." In the afternoon they came unto a land in which it seemed always afternoon.'

Olivia looked at Shaun in shock. He had suddenly turned into John Gielgud. He grinned. 'Tennyson. Great, isn't he?' He drove on quietly for a moment. 'You see, just because I don't spend every night clubbing, it doesn't mean I don't enjoy life. In my own way.'

'I understand, Shaun. I didn't mean to sound rude.'

'No, no. It wasn't rude at all. The truth is, I don't really make the effort. I'm saving up for a holiday.'

'Oh.' Olivia stared out of the windows. How long was it since she'd had a proper holiday, not just for the sake of saying she'd taken time off, but somewhere she really wanted to go? She'd never been where she really wanted to go. And now it felt as if she'd missed her chance.

'Just tell me where to turn,' Shaun said, building up speed as they approached the estate.

'Yes, you need to pull off at this wide road here. Turn left into that small road and I'm the fourth house up.'

'Fine. These are nice houses, Olivia. Have you lived here long?'

'Since I got married.' Olivia released her seat belt as the car stopped.

'Pretty much all your life, then?' Shaun smiled at her pleasantly.

'No!' Olivia said harshly. 'Not all of my life. I had a life before I got married, and I shall have a life now. I was a person, once. With dreams, and ambitions, and visions of what I might do.'

'You sound like me.' Shaun nodded cheerfully, unfazed by the anger. 'I've got lots of things I want to do. And you know what?'

'What?' she said, pulling back her head to look at him properly.

'I'm going to do them. Life's too short, that's what I say. So, Olivia, you were going to ask me something, weren't you?'

'Shaun, I'd like you to do something for me, but I will insist on paying you. The thing is, I wondered if you'd like to teach me to drive?'

'Louise? It's Rachel. About your friend's song—find out when the band's playing and I'll try to be there. Give me a ring, leave a message if I'm not here and I'll see what I can do for you. I can't promise anything, but I'll see them, just for you, OK? I'm sorry you're not there to take the call. Hope you're well. Love you. Bye . . . And, er, sorry about the other night. Of course I loved Dad. Let's not fall out over it.'

Louise rolled over on the bed, stared at the phone, then picked it up and dialled Ash's number. She only realised once she'd pressed out the number that she'd remembered it by heart.

'Ash?'

'No, it's Ginger. Who's that?'

'It's Louise. I met him at the Jobcentre.'

'Oh, Louise. Yeah, right. Hi there.'

'Hi,' she said, trying to picture this orange friend of Ash's, wondering what on earth she should say to him. 'Er, is Ash in, please?'

'Nope. He's got a darts match. Won't be back till pretty late.'

'Darts?'

'Yeah. Local pub. He's usually down there playing or practising. You could always catch him there if you wanted.'

Louise laughed. She could picture Ash in the spartan bar in his tattered jeans, rolling a cigarette, cursing under his breath.

'No, I won't bother him tonight, but I've got something to tell him. Perhaps I could pop round tomorrow?'

'Just call by any time.'

'Oh, yes. Thanks, Ginger.'

She rang off, feeling warm inside. Ginger sounded nice. He sounded rich too, but friendlier than his sister. Part of her wished she could just dash out now to the pub but she was so, so tired. Tomorrow she would deliver the news that Rachel was interested in seeing the band. That would repay the favour he'd done her. The rest was up to him.

Chapter Six

LOUISE TAPPED TENTATIVELY on the green door at eleven the next morning.

She waited, her hands jammed into her coat pockets. She looked smart today, for no other reason than that it made her feel better.

The door opened and she forced a smile just in case Karen was about to appear in a lake of expensively conditioned hair. It was Ginger. She could tell that straight away, not just on account of his hair, but because he also had Karen's striking looks. He immediately grinned at her.

'You must be Louise.'

'Yes, I am. I hope you don't mind me just turning up.'

'No problem. He's fiddling upstairs.'

'Oh look, I won't disturb you all if you're practising or something. Perhaps I can just leave a message?'

'We're not practising. Karen's gone to High Street Ken and the rest are at work. I'm off myself in a minute. He won't be long, then you can talk to him yourself.'

He stood back for her and she entered the dark hall again, wondering what Karen would be shopping for, and musing on the merits of having wealthy parents.

'She's a spoilt brat, isn't she?'

'Sorry?'

'Karen. It's what you were thinking. Ash told me you were signing on at the moment.'

'Oh.' She gave him a cautious look. 'Perhaps I'd be shopping too if I had a bit more money.'

'Don't judge her too harshly. Ash gets intense about it, but it's not going to change the way she is. They're good for each other. They've got a chemistry and it makes the band something special. Ten years is a long time.' He'd maintained a bright smile but beneath it she had the feeling that she was being warned away.

'Why don't you go up and let him know you're here? You can come back down and wait if you want.'

'Won't it disturb him?'

'Yes, but one of us tries to piss him off at least once a day.' Ginger winked at her. 'He's on the first floor. His room's at the front.'

She mounted the stairs. The first floor revealed a short corridor with several off-white doors. She hovered like an indecisive burglar. A muted sound came from one of the rooms. She crept closer and studied the door. She raised her hand but froze.

On her own in her flat, left to her fantasies, she had thought about Ash playing his violin. She had conjured up a romantic image of the lone, brilliant musician, seeking solace in the glory of his music. Karen had said he was really talented.

Slowly, surely, the sound of a violin drifted out to her. It started as a long, low, reverberating note, then it stopped. She shuffled closer to the door. There was a short silence, then the sound came again, a squawk of a sound, abruptly halting. She frowned.

She was unprepared for the blast of noise that suddenly assailed her. Screech after undignified screech. She'd never realised that a violin could produce such bizarre and appallingly tuneless sounds.

He'd said he'd played first violin in a prominent orchestra, if only briefly. But he couldn't have! This horrible noise couldn't be put down to improvisation. It was simple evidence that he couldn't play, and that he'd lied to her.

Bewildered, she crushed her ear right against the wood. The sawing became unbearable. It veered off flatly, then suddenly stopped as abruptly as it had begun.

'Hell's bells!' she exclaimed, and snapped her mouth shut again. That had come out a bit loudly.

The door opened. With nothing to lean against, she staggered and toppled over. With burning cheeks she struggled to her feet and turned to apologise. Ash was standing with his hands on his hips.

'Come in,' he said flatly.

'God, I'm sorry, I was . . .' She stopped. They weren't alone. A boy was perched on an old wooden chair opposite a music stand, a violin lowered onto his lap, his face a blank sheet of astonishment.

'Louise, this is Deepak.'

'H-hi, Deepak.' Louise waved at him. It was ridiculous to wave. He was only a few feet away. But she didn't know what else to do. Deepak stared at her for a long, crushing moment, then looked up at Ash for clarification.

'She mad, or what?' he said in a thick London accent.

'I wish I knew,' Ash said. 'Deepak's my student, Louise. We've got another ten minutes to go before we finish, but you're more than welcome to wait downstairs.'

'I—er.' Louise knew her face was glowing. 'I didn't know you taught music. I thought it was you playing.'

'Ah. That explains everything then,' Ash said with merciless sarcasm.

'We gonna finish this lesson then, or what?'

Ash walked towards the door and opened it wide for Louise.

'He's keen,' Ash whispered to her. 'I like that. Why don't you put the kettle on for us and I'll join you when I can?'

He ushered her out and the door closed gently behind her.

'You two shagging then, or what?' she heard Deepak ask.

'Mind your own fucking business,' Ash's voice came back.

'She's a babe,' Deepak was going on. 'Nice arse. Shame she's mental.'

She couldn't wait to hear any more. She headed for the stairs, downed them two at a time, wrenched open the front door and fled.

'**B**alls,' Sarah said loudly. Olivia looked up.

'What is it?'

'I saved this file,' Sarah hissed. 'And now I've lost the blimmin' thing.'

Olivia left her desk and crossed the office to where Sarah was sitting.

'Problem?' Carol's voice hit them from the other side of the room like a well-aimed snowball.

'Not at all,' Olivia said casually. 'We've got it under control. All right, Sarah, let's try this.' Olivia moved the white arrow over an icon she hadn't seen before and double clicked on it.

The previous screen disappeared and the image of a man who seemed rather attractive imposed itself. She bent right over Sarah's shoulder for a closer look.

'He's a footballer, isn't he?'

'Who's a footballer?'

Carol had left her desk, crossed the office in a series of elegant bounds, and was now examining the image with care.

'Michael Owen?' she said, at first, it seemed, in wonder. Then her voice hardened. 'What is Michael Owen doing on this machine?'

'It was Shaun,' Sarah said, her head dropping.

'He showed me how to download things from the Internet,' Sarah said. 'He said I wouldn't be so scared if I did something on my own.'

Carol stood up stiffly. 'Let me get this straight. You and Shaun have been surfing the net on office time for the purpose of setting miscellaneous men as wallpaper?'

'It was meant to be educational,' Sarah said.

'Delete this please, Sarah,' Carol instructed. Her voice had taken on a deadly quality that Olivia had heard before. 'I shall be looking into the issue of staff using the computers for social purposes. I shall also be speaking to the agency this afternoon and asking for a replacement.'

There was a stunned silence. Sarah's mouth had dropped open, a dark blob within the pallor of her skin. Carol waited while Sarah fumbled with the mouse. Everything disappeared. The computer made a low, reverberating sound and the screen went black.

'Now what have you done?' Carol's voice was deathly quiet.

'I don't know!' Sarah wailed.

To Olivia's horror, Sarah's face crumpled and she started to cry. Instinctively, Olivia leaned down and put her arms round her.

'Come on, dear.'

Sarah buried her face in Olivia's blouse. Olivia stroked her head soothingly. The tears didn't stop. Carol stalked away to her desk.

'Come on, Sarah.' She ruffled her hair. 'I'm taking you to lunch.'

'You'll have to take staggered lunch breaks. I need somebody to man the phones.'

Carol hadn't looked up as she'd issued her order. Her eyes were burning into her paperwork, but Olivia could tell she wasn't reading it.

'Wait for me down in the hall, Sarah.' There was a firmness in Olivia's voice that surprised her. 'I'll be down in a minute.'

Sarah grabbed her leather jacket and fled. The door in the corridor swung shut with a loud bang. Silence fell again in the office. Olivia approached Carol's desk.

'Not now.' Carol waved a hand airily, her eyes down. 'I'm busy.'

'Now,' Olivia stated.

Carol looked up. Her pupils were wide.

'What is it?'

'It's your job to make sure your staff are properly trained. If they aren't, and they make mistakes, it's your fault.'

Where she had found the courage to make that statement, she would never know. In five years she had never raised her voice. She had accepted, pacified, reasoned and put up with hypocrisy, but all without complaining. Something had changed.

'Is that it?'

Olivia smiled.

'I could put my thoughts down in writing if you'd like the complaint formalised.'

Carol drew in her cheeks as if she was sucking a powerful peppermint. Her eyelashes fluttered.

'However,' Olivia continued calmly, 'when I come back from lunch with Sarah, I expect you'll have thought again about replacing her. You might even have thought of arranging for a trainer to show us around the new computer system. That way there'd be no reason to make a formal complaint.'

'Go to lunch, Olivia,' Carol said under her breath. Olivia picked up her mac, checking the contents of her bag and rearranging her desk before she made her way to the door.

'Olivia?'

She turned back. Carol was pretending to write something.

'I had no intention of replacing Sarah. She needed to be given a warning, that was all.'

Without a word, Olivia left the room and broke into a broad grin.

Sarah was shivering on the doorstep, her eye make-up streaked around her face where she had tried to wipe it away. Olivia held out an arm to her.

'Come on, you. I'm going to treat you to wherever you want.'

Sarah looked at the extended arm in surprise, but then linked hers through it.

'Better had as it's my last day. I didn't think things could get any worse. My mum, she relies on my housekeeping money. This was supposed to be temp to perm.'

'You're not going to be replaced.' Olivia patted her arm as they headed towards the town. 'She was only trying to scare you.'

Sarah squeezed Olivia's arm. 'Thanks. I don't think I could have coped with any more disasters at the moment.'

'Why? What else is going on?'

'It's that rash on Neal's testicle.'

Olivia stopped in her tracks. Sarah's eyes were welling with tears again. She found a clean tissue in the pocket of her mac and offered it.

'I've got crabs,' Sarah said in a low voice.

Olivia brushed her fingers over the girl's hot cheek.

'Oh, Sarah. You poor girl.'

'So I rowed with Neal about it, 'cos I knew bloody well it wasn't me. Turns out he's been putting himself about all over the place.'

'I hope you told him what you thought of him.'

'Too bloody right. I told him I hoped his nuts dropped off.'

Olivia buried a smile as they slowly began to walk again. The mating game. Perhaps in some ways she'd been lucky as a young woman. Fate had excluded her from such anxieties.

'Then you definitely need to do something to cheer yourself up,' Olivia said. 'How about a little present to yourself? That's what I do sometimes.'

'There's something I've wanted to do for ages but Neal talked me out of it. It wouldn't take long. We could do it in the lunch hour, and I need someone to come with me, or I'll never have the courage to do it.'

'What the devil is it you want to do?'

'I want to get tattooed.'

Olivia stared at Sarah aghast. 'A bluebell on my shoulder. What do you say?'

Then suddenly she wanted to laugh aloud. It was Sarah's life, her body and her decision. And she'd never been inside a tattoo parlour, although she'd seen one in a side street leading off the main road. This was a time in her life when she had made the decision to explore new ideas, not shut them out. Why shouldn't she go with Sarah?

'I say we go to the tattoo parlour,' Olivia declared, astonishing herself for the second time in less than an hour.

It was Ash.

But what was confusing Louise was that he was on her doorstep. She stared at him in bewilderment for a full minute before she was able to speak.

'Er, how did you know where I lived?' she asked.

'Your CV, remember?'

'Oh, of course.' He didn't seem to want to rush away. 'Would you like to come in?'

'Only if it doesn't put you out. I thought I'd ask you why you ran off.'

'I'll put the kettle on.'

'And I just wanted to make sure you were all right,' Ash added as he wandered into the flat behind her. He stopped to stare at her wrought-iron candelabra, then followed her through to the kitchen. He found himself a chair and settled into it.

'I'm sorry I burst into your lesson,' she said, arranging the mugs.

'Don't worry about that,' he said.

'Is Deepak your only student?'

'Nope, I've got about half a dozen at the moment. Two on cello, the rest violin.'

'Really? And none of them pay you?'

He glanced up at her. 'The money isn't the issue.'

'I didn't think it was. It's just a bit unusual.'

'I advertise locally for kids who can't afford to pay the full whack for private lessons. Word gets around, too. It's just to give them a start. They don't know what they can do because nobody gives them a chance.'

'But you do.'

'I try to. It's helpful, I think, but most of them are beginners. It pays off, but not financially.'

She made tea for them both, slid a mug onto the table beside him and dropped into a chair on the other side.

'It was nice of you to call round.'

'No prob. It was you who called round to see me, remember? I just assumed you had something you wanted to say.'

'Oh.' She sat up straight. Once she was in his company it was easy to forget what the point had been. Of course she'd gone round to see him. She cleared her throat quickly.

'I did have something to say. My sister who works for the record company? Well, she rang and she's interested in seeing you play live. That's if you've got any gigs coming up.'

'Really?' He chuckled. 'Hey, Louise, that's great. You never know what might come of that.'

He stood up and paced around her floor, grinning to himself. Then he sat down again.

'D'you know, I wasn't sure about your sister,' he said. 'It struck me that you'd lost the song and didn't know what the hell to say to me.'

'You mean you thought I'd made it up?'

'Yep. You strike me as someone with a good imagination. I thought it was really funny.'

He thought she was a congenital liar? She should be insulted.

'Still,' he continued, 'you thought it was me hacking away at the violin when you were listening outside my bedroom door, didn't you? So you must have thought I'd been lying to you, too. Call it quits. Wow, this is great news for us,' he went on. 'There's been so much bickering in the band lately, I wondered if it was going to drive us apart. We'll have to get our acts together for this now.'

'Well, don't split up before your next gig then,' she told him firmly. 'Rachel might like you, and then God knows what could happen. I know for a fact she's set a couple of really good bands on their way.'

'We're playing at the Eye of Newt in Battersea this Friday. I expect that's too short notice for you, isn't it?'

'The Eye of Newt?' Louise perked up. She'd been there before with Rachel. It was considered a cult venue for upcoming bands. Were they really talented? Would she be credited personally with discovering a rock legend? 'You must be quite good then.'

'Don't sound so surprised. Some people think we are good.'

'But you'll need the song.' The thought suddenly occurred to her. 'Rachel's still got it.'

'Don't worry about it. We had a row over the fact that I'd given it to someone to blow her nose on but we've got over it. Ginger rewrote it and the music's in my head anyway. It's better now.'

There was a sharp rap at her door. Who? Why? And why didn't they bugger off? Ash waited quietly for her to do something. What she wanted to do was yell 'Hide!' and dive with him under the kitchen table until the intruder had gone away. But she couldn't really.

'I'll get that,' she said, walking to the front door.

It was Harris. She shifted uncomfortably. It was about time that he dropped his amorous intentions and got back to telling her off. A man's unrequited lust could only last so many hours, after all.

'I'm really sorry, Harris. I'll play more quietly.'

'Actually, Louise, I haven't come about your playing. Although,' he added thoughtfully. 'I'm a bit tired of "Paint Your Wagon". Is there any reason it's your favourite this week?'

'OK, point taken,' She frowned at him fiercely.

'I am here to ask you—' he paused again and fixed her with a stare that forbade her to move '—if you'd like to have dinner with me.'

'Dinner?' she echoed.

'I'd like to cook for you. In my flat. I've got a particularly fine bottle of red, and I'd like you to share it with me.'

'Oh, I see.'

'What d'you say?' His eyes sparkled with hope. She crept an inch closer to him. Whispering at this juncture was futile. Even though Ash had started to sing 'I Talk to the Trees' very loudly. It was a gentlemanly gesture on his part, but she was sure he was still listening to everything that was going on.

'The thing is, Harris—'

But Harris was peering over her shoulder.

'Have you got company?' he asked.

'It's just that a friend's dropped round to see me. Now's not a good time. We can talk about this another time, can't we?' She inched the door closed on him.

She took a split second to recover herself, then danced back into the kitchen trying to look as if nothing had happened.

'That's just Harris,' she said brightly, laughing disparagingly. 'Don't mind him. He's an actor.'

'"Paint Your Wagon"?' Ash stood up, the corners of his lips twitching.

'Not that you were listening,' she taunted him. It was better to be casual than petulant about him leaving.

'So you're musical enough to have a piano in your flat?'

'Bloody-minded enough, anyway.'

'I'd like to hear you play some time.' He was definitely aiming for the door.

'I'd like to hear *you* play. I'm sure that's much more fun,' she said, shuffling after him.

'You will. On Friday,' he stated.

'Sally!' Louise grimaced at the figure standing in the dark on her doorstep. 'What the hell are you doing here? I'm just about to go out to a gig. Rachel's going to be there.'

'You're going out? Tonight? To a pub?'

'Yes.'

'But you're pregnant.'

Louise pulled Sally across the threshold and slammed the door.

'Do you mind not proclaiming that fact to the whole of London?'

'I'm sorry. Can I come in, just for a second?'

'Of course, but I'd better not be late.' Automatically, she went back to her bedroom to continue with her superhuman effort to look casually glamorous.

Sally seemed very quiet. Louise waited for the apology that was inevitably forthcoming.

'Not seeing Fergus tonight, then?'

'Oh, Fergus, Fergus, Fergus.' Sally spread-eagled herself on the bed, staring up at a paper lampshade. The slim auburn eyebrows met in a frown. She let out a long sigh.

Louise turned round from the mirror and stared at her. 'What *is* the matter with you?'

'I just don't want to be on my own tonight. Can I come with you?'

'I assumed Fergus would be grilling rainbow trout for you. It is Friday after all.'

'I can't talk about Fergus. I need to think. Think, think, think,' Sally chanted with her eyes shut.

'I take it things have taken a dive then.'

'Hmmn.'

'Otherwise, I guess you wouldn't have come round like this.'

'Yep.'

'Not even, perhaps, to apologise for being such a cow on the phone,' Louise finished a little more firmly. Sally's eyes flew open.

'Louise, I was only saying what I thought. You wouldn't want me to lie to you, would you?'

'Yes.'

'Then I'm sorry. It's just that I saw what the girl I told you about went through. Although it was awful at the time, she said it was the best thing she ever did.'

Louise turned back to the mirror. She wasn't going to let Sally annoy her. She wanted to go to the gig. She was curious to hear Ash's band. She wanted to look at him again, perhaps for the last time.

'Listen, Sal, if you do want to come to this gig, you can, but I don't want you to keep going on about terminations, OK?'

'OK.' Sally heaved herself up. 'So you're going to tell Rachel tonight about being an auntie, are you?'

'No chance.' Louise squinted at her face in the mirror. 'I'm going to introduce her to an electric violin player I met at the Jobcentre.'

'You're kidding?' Sally let out a loud laugh. 'Don't tell me, you're going to freelance as a talent spotter? I would have thought there might be more promising places to find talent than at the Jobcentre.'

'That's an ignorant comment, Sally. And anyway, it depends what you mean by talent.'

Sally gaped and pulled her shoulders straight.

'You've met someone!'

'Er, sort of.'

'God, Louise. I thought you were going to have a baby!' Sally stood up and stared at Louise's reflection. 'You're serious, aren't you?'

'He's a friend, Sally, nothing more than that. Probably not even that after tonight.'

'A friend?' Sally looked sceptical.

'Think about it, Sal. I'm pregnant, he's got a girlfriend. Doesn't augur very well romantically, does it?'

'But you fancy him?'

'I'd have to be cremated not to.' Sally was still looking stunned. 'Well, I'm allowed to window-shop, aren't I? He's sexy, good company, and he's been very kind to me. He has no idea I lust after him.'

'But—but you're going to have a *baby*!' Sally sat down again. 'Unless you've changed your mind. Is that it?'

'No, I haven't changed my mind.'

'So . . . what's going on? I don't understand.'

'So relax, Sally. By the time my bump starts showing he'll be out of my life. He's been thoughtful and I've done him a favour in return. That's all.'

'It's just that I thought that everything stopped when this happened. You know, men, flirting, life. Everything.'

'It's all going to change, Sal, but I'm not digging myself a hole. I'm still a woman, you know, baby or no baby.'

'Louise, Fergus has asked me to marry him,' Sally blurted out, her face very white.

'Oh, why didn't you say so.' Louise was overcome with emotion.

'The thing is,' Sally said, 'I told him to sod off.'

The buzz was exciting as they pushed their way into the pub. A heavy-metal band was playing energetically in the far corner. Nearer the raised stage people were head-banging out of time to the music.

'Nightmare!' Sally yelled into Louise's ear.

'Bar!' Louise mouthed.

'Just tell me this isn't your band,' Sally said as they squeezed together and became mutually audible.

'They must be up next. They always do a couple of bands a night in this place, I think my lot are all classically trained.'

'They'll go down a storm in here, then,' Sally said flatly.

Louise frowned as she called her order at the barmaid. She hoped they knew what they were doing. Rachel wouldn't take kindly to having her hectic schedule interrupted for a bunch of no-hopers.

The wall of sound coming from the direction of the stage stopped suddenly. There were boisterous cheers.

'Fuck you too!' yelled the lead singer.

The four men stumbled from the stage to more cheers. Sally pulled Louise over to stand near a wall where a gap had cleared in the bodies.

'I must be getting old,' she said, giving the band members distasteful looks as they grinned their way through the crowd to the bar. 'Those guys don't look old enough to swear.'

Sally shook back her hair and leaned against the wall. In Louise's jeans, a loose, rollneck jumper and a beaten-up suede jacket she'd borrowed, she didn't look like a terrifyingly good solicitor any more.

'Do you want to know what went through my mind when Fergus asked me to marry him?'

'Er—"when", perhaps?'

'No, no. I thought, "Is Guy still living in Paddock Wood?" I swear to you, Lou, that was it. I was standing there with the tea towel in one hand and the garlic crusher in the other, and there was Fergus, down on one knee, and I was looking down on him, at that lock of hair that always falls over his eyes, while he was presenting me with this tiny velvet box, and everything seemed to stand still while I thought of Guy and Paddock Wood. And then I thought of Nick. And Mark too . . .'

Louise shook her head at her. 'So what happened?'

'Well, then I looked back at Fergus, at his big brown eyes, that floppy bit of hair, that straight nose, those lips of his . . .' Sally trailed away.

'And you wondered why on earth he fancied you?'

'He's too perfect,' Sally announced, snapping herself up straight. 'Something's wrong.'

'Apart from you telling him to sod off, you mean?'

'With him. There's got to be something I don't know. He must be hiding something.'

'I just don't understand you, Sally. One day you're going to think back to this time, realise what you could have done when you had the chance, and shoot yourself between the eyes.'

'I could say the same to you,' she said.

Louise was still searching for an answer when her shoulder was tapped from behind. She swung round, and brightened to see Rachel, in full gig mode. Louise instantly felt frumpy and stupid again.

'I've only just got here. Where's your bloke, then?'

'I don't know. One band's just finished, so I hope they'll be on next.'

'Topping the bill. That's a good sign. They don't take any old shit in here. They make them audition first. Good crowd, too. Very promising. I'll get us a drink in, then. Sally! Lovely to see you!' Rachel and Sally exchanged air kisses and Rachel headed to the bar.

'Louise!' She was engulfed in a hug. 'You came! You're a fucking hero-ine, that's what you are. I need all the smiling faces I can muster. I can't see any of our regulars here. We're going to get killed, I'm sure of it.'

'Ash!' Her heart jumped. He was bristling with nervous energy, his hair all over the place, his eyes black with adrenalin.

'I'm so pleased you're here.' He drew unsteadily on a Marlboro, his fingers trembling. She'd thought he would just saunter into it, as he sauntered into everything else, but he looked terrified. 'I just get jittery before we play. I've always been this way, you know, for live things.'

'It's going to be all right.' Louise squeezed his arm. 'Karen said you were really talented. Just remember that.'

'Yeah, well, Karen's off her face. I just hope she can remember the fucking words. Is this your sister?'

He stuck a hand out to Sally, who was stuck against the wall as if she'd just been nailed into place. Her eyes were like flying saucers.

'Pleased to meet you,' she breathed, shaking his hand limply.

'No, this is Sally, my best friend,' Louise explained quickly. 'Rachel's just getting us a drink. There she is! Oh.'

All three turned to follow Louise's pointing finger. A few feet away, Rachel was locked into a deep-throated snog with a very tall, very blond man. His hands were roaming over her hips and buttocks.

'Well, she'll be with us in a minute, I'm sure,' Louise mumbled.

'Right. I'd better go and set up. We're on in a minute. Clap if you can bear it, and don't heckle me, for God's sake. I can't cope with hecklers.'

'If anyone heckles, just moon at them.' Louise grinned at him with a confidence she didn't feel.

'Thanks.' He smiled. 'I really appreciate you making the effort to be here. I know it can't have been easy for you.'

Louise watched him as he pushed back towards the stage. It was nice of him to say that. It made her feel warm.

'God, Louise. He's incredible!' Louise swung back to Sally. For a moment, she'd almost forgotten she was there.

'He's nice, isn't he?'

Sally was staring at Louise with admiration. 'How did you do it?'

'Do what?' Louise asked coyly.

'Get his attention. I mean, I was flicking my hair around, rolling my eyes at him, and he didn't even know I existed.'

'Listen, I never flirted with Fergus, so hands off.'

'Oh, you can have Fergus if you think he's so marvellous. It's sex appeal that I go for, and that guy's got it in lorry-loads.'

'Sally, for God's sake, you're spoken for.'

'Right. Like Rachel, I suppose.' Sally nodded as Rachel detached herself from the tall blond man, whispered something in his ear, handed him a couple of glasses, and dragged him towards them.

'Hi, everyone. This is Benji. He's a doctor. This is my little sister, Louise, and her friend Sally.'

He was nice, Louise had to admit. He smiled at everyone, made suitably flattering comments, nodded understandingly at the answers they gave. Rachel's dark eyes were luminous with lust.

A series of high-pitched squeaks flooded the room. The crowd jeered at the stage.

Louise turned round. Please, please be good, she entreated.

Karen appeared, being helped by several people up onto the stage. A blast of shouts and wolf whistles filled the air.

'Oh God,' Louise said, closing her eyes. 'She's totally wrecked.'

Karen began a fumbling introduction, but the microphone squealed back through the speakers. There were more jeers. Then a click.

'Hi there, everyone. Same old ugly faces, I see.' Louise opened her eyes as Karen's sultry tones filled the room. Somebody laughed. Louise took a deep breath.

'We're Almanac. I'm Karen, and behind me we have Kerry on lead, Ginger on bass, Ned on drums, and Ash on violin.'

Louise saw her hiccup violently, but her hand covered the microphone. There were more shouts. Louise's eyes smarted. She just couldn't turn round to see the expression on Rachel's face.

'Now if you're not going to shut up,' Karen said, smiling seductively over the sea of faces, 'we're just going to have to shut you up, aren't we?'

Louise backed against the wall as the sound hit them. She had been so afraid that it might be out of tune, out of time, the notes being played in the wrong order.

And it was.

'Stop, stop!' Karen clapped her hands. The instruments died away. Louise's cheeks glowed. Karen seemed unfazed. She chuckled over the microphone, shrugging her shoulders.

'Ooops, that was my fault. I was supposed to count them in. Let's have another go. One, two, three, hit it!'

This time, the sound was incredible. A shiver crawled over Louise's skin. Karen began to hop around the stage. Louise gaped at her. She had no inhibitions, and she was electrifying. And then she began to sing.

'Fucking hell,' Louise heard Rachel behind her. She'd pulled away from Benji, who was too engrossed to notice, and was squinting sharply at the stage. She bent forwards.

'Who is that girl?'

'Her name's Karen,' Louise shouted back. Rachel nodded, and pulled back again to watch with keen interest. After several verses of the song, Karen allowed Ash to take centre stage, his violin clasped under his chin. He drew up his bow and began to play.

The sound he produced was a compelling mix of hard-hitting rock and folk. The drums pounded behind him imposingly. As he finished his solo the pub exploded into cheers. Louise guessed that the loyal bunch of supporters had turned up after all. Sally shook her arm.

'Are you all right?' she called into her ear.

Of course she was all right. The most gorgeous man in London was not only sexy, kind, and great fun to be around. He was also obscenely good at playing the violin. It didn't matter that he happened to be going out with the most gorgeous woman in London. He had come up to *her* when she'd arrived, given *her* a hug, and said that he was really happy that *she* was there.

She hadn't felt more all right for as long as she could remember.

Chapter Seven

ALMANAC PLAYED FIVE more songs before Karen passed out on the stage. Louise realised it wasn't a stunt when the drummer sprang from behind his drum kit and tried to revive her. Ash stared down at the glamorous pile of strawberry-blonde hair at his feet, before putting his instrument to one side and squatting to pick her up.

Ginger took charge of the microphone. 'Small problem, I'm afraid. We'll have to cut the set short. Thanks for all your support.'

It was clear that Karen was conscious again as she threw her arms in the air and grabbed hold of Ash's neck. They managed to get her to her feet, and she immediately fell forwards against him. Pushing the drummer out of the way, he slowly carried her off the stage. Louise watched with increasing dismay. Karen's fingers were linked behind Ash's neck, her head flopped against his chest as if it was a pillow. He manfully kicked open a door leading to a private corridor. They both disappeared, the rest of the band following. God only knew what Rachel would be thinking now.

Rachel was locked in eye contact with Benji while pulling on her jacket. She looked over at Louise and managed a brief smile.

'We're off now, Lou. Thanks for asking me here. I'll give you a call.'

'Aren't you at least going to speak to them?'

'I've told you, I've got to go. I would have had to leave early anyway, I just didn't get a chance to tell you.' Rachel's brown eyes were wide with appeal, and Louise gave up. Rachel always did what she wanted to, and what she obviously wanted to do now was to go somewhere with Benji and bonk him to the last inch of his life.

Just a tiny word of support, Louise implored as she gazed back at Rachel. You're my sister. You're the only one I've got and you're going to be an auntie, like it or not. In a parallel universe, you would stay with Hallam, adore his children, and fall about with happiness at the thought of having a little niece or nephew. But this was reality.

'Go on, then,' Louise said, trying to smile. 'Have a nice night.'

She watched them both as they headed away from the bar, out of the door and into the cold night. She became aware that Sally was standing beside her, a fresh glass of wine in her hand.

'Has Rachel gone, then?'

'Yep.'

'With Benji?'

'Yep. I don't know why she didn't tell me outright that she had no interest in seeing the band, but that it was a brilliant excuse to meet up with Benji.'

'That's that, then.'

'Yep. And the band was crap anyway, so it was a pretty failed mission, all in all.'

'How can you say that?' Sally turned round aghast. 'They were brilliant. I haven't seen such a good band for years.'

But Louise felt totally miserable, and to make things worse, she was overcome with tiredness. The chaotic noise of the pub was crashing in on her. All she wanted now was to be at home, in bed, with a cup of hot chocolate, but first she had to fight her way back across London and Sally would leave her halfway down the District Line and she would have to rumble on down the Piccadilly Line to the unfashionable part of Ealing and dash home through the dark streets on her own. That would underline the fact that it was all over. No excuse to see Ash any more. Just herself, her flat and her pregnancy.

'I want to go home, Sally,' Louise said.

'C'mon then.' Sally took Louise's arm and shunted her forwards. 'And I'll come home and stay over with you.'

'You will?' A silly smile spread over Louise's face.

'Of course,' Sally said in a practical voice. 'I've left all my clothes in your flat.'

'OK, so let's run through it again. Accelerator, brake, clutch. ABC.'

Olivia nodded, pointing her toes at the pedals in turn. One, two, three. It was easy.

'No, you have to do them with different feet. Watch mine again.'

Shaun had offered to take her out to the industrial estate for their first lesson. She had thought it was a bit odd to do it in the dark, but he'd pointed out that if she wanted lessons in the daylight they would only have the weekends. They'd been here over an hour now and Olivia was itching to get on with some driving. When they'd arrived he'd motioned her into the driver's seat, and she'd felt a deep thrill of power sitting behind the steering wheel. He'd run through the controls, some of which, she refrained from saying, were bleeding obvious, then he'd shown her all the gears and she'd changed them with the engine off.

Then, he'd decided to run through the Highway Code.

'Look, Shaun, I know the theory is very important, but since we're here do you think I could actually drive the car?'

Shaun sat back in his seat and looked at her. 'Do you feel ready for that? I thought you might like to gain a bit of confidence first.'

She smiled at him indulgently. 'May I start the engine?'

'You go ahead. Let's do something positive.'

He sat back, placing his hands firmly on his knees, and waited, staring straight ahead.

'I'll just . . .' Olivia swallowed. She reached out her fingers and touched the car keys in the ignition.

Her fingertips tingled. Bob had handled these keys over and over again. It had felt strange to hand them over to Shaun, but not nearly as strange as touching them herself, when they were in position, to fire the engine into life.

As soon as she heard the engine moan into life, instinct took over. She thrust her right foot at the accelerator, and pushed it to keep the revs going. The engine screamed back. She pulled her foot away quickly and the engine stalled.

Shaun cleared his throat. His hands were still clamped purposefully over his knees.

'I—I'll just do that again,' Olivia decided aloud.

When the engine screamed the next time, she touched the pedal gently, pulled away and put pressure on it again. She began to smile.

'I'm going to put the clutch down, and put the car into first gear.'

She lifted her left foot, and elaborately brought it down onto the clutch pedal. Right to the floor. She reached out with her left hand, took hold of the gearlever and pushed the car into first gear.

Shaun whispered something to her that she didn't catch.

'What?' she whispered back.

'Handbrake,' he repeated in a hoarse voice.

She released it and returned to her crouching position over the wheel. The car didn't move. The engine hummed, her left foot was glued down to the floor, her two hands gripped the wheel. Her right foot hovered in the air over the accelerator.

'We're not going to move unless you take your foot off the clutch.'

'I know.'

'Do you want to do it, then?'

'I'm not sure.'

To his credit Shaun neither sighed nor tutted. He just sat quietly as if he was thinking about something else.

'Driving a car's a bit like life,' he said finally. 'You have to decide what sort of car you want, and where you want it to take you. Whether you want to be a passenger or the one with your hands on the wheel.'

Olivia lifted her left foot, stage by stage, from the clutch. Suddenly, she felt the car engage. She pushed down on the accelerator.

'Oh my God. I've done it. Look, we're moving!'

She gripped the wheel as they chugged across the smooth tarmac.

'OK, I think we could turn the wheel now.'

The kerb rimming the car park appeared in the headlamps.

'We need to turn the wheel,' Shaun said, glancing at Olivia as she embraced the steering wheel.

'The wheel. I'll turn the wheel.' She yanked it round as far as it would go. The car swung sideways and careered off towards a concrete stump.

'Brake, Olivia! Take your foot off the accelerator and push the brake!'

The concrete stump was suddenly directly in front of them. Her hands were stuck on the steering wheel, her feet paralysed into position.

'For God's sake, Olivia!' Shaun's voice lost all its gentle persuasion and became a bellow. 'Will you stop being such a bloody wimp and take control? Is it what you want, or isn't it?'

The car rolled into the centre of the tarmac again, Olivia's mind sharpened by Shaun's loss of temper. Instead of letting the car stall, she remembered to put her foot on the clutch as it slowed down. And she put her right foot on the brake. They came to an abrupt halt, and lurched forward in their seats. The engine remained humming as Olivia reached for the gearlever and pulled it back into neutral. She wrenched the handbrake up.

'How dare you call me a wimp? You hardly know me.'

She heard Shaun expel a long breath. Then, when he turned to look at her, she saw that he was smiling.

'You're laughing at me,' she said, ruffled.

'Not in the slightest,' he laughed.

'I drove, didn't I?' Olivia began to smile.

'Yes. You drove the car.'

Now she couldn't stop laughing. She slapped her hands on the steering wheel in triumph. 'Can you see me, Bob? I drove the car!'

Louise and Sally crashed through the front door.

Sally had insisted on stopping off for a few drinks on the way back, saying that if it wasn't closing time she didn't feel normal being at home. Louise had been surprised at how much Sally had thrown back. Tonight she'd seemed determined to get steaming drunk.

'Where did the flowers come from?' Sally frowned across the kitchen at the bucket. 'I didn't see those before.'

'They came from Jon.'

Sally pulled a dramatic face.

'Jon? Do you think he wants a reconciliation?'

Louise laughed loudly.

'He wanted to make himself feel better, that's all.' She filled the kettle and plugged it in.

'Oh.' Sally sniffed and sat down at the kitchen table. 'Fergus sent me flowers. All the time. It really got on my nerves.'

Louise glanced at Sally.

'Sal? Why are you talking about Fergus in the past tense?'

'It's obvious, isn't it?'

'Not to me. I like Fergus. He's a decent, good-looking, friendly, intelligent bloke. I don't understand what's wrong with him.'

'Hmmn.' Sally stuck her head in her hands and stared at Louise. '*You* don't like it, do you?'

'What don't I like?' Louise wished whole-heartedly that she was as drunk as Sally. Then she might be able to follow her trajectories.

'Being told what to do. When people suggest something to you that they think's good for you, you just go off and do the opposite.'

'You can't honestly be suggesting that I'd have a baby just to go against popular opinion?'

'Well, no, not exactly,' Sally reasoned. 'But in a way, yes. It's as if you've always got to make up your own rules.'

'What rules?'

'The rules. You know. The things I abide by. I've done it all in the right order. I should be feeling totally smug. And look at us! You're the one who's up the spout with no job, no money and no man, and you're the one who's happy!'

Louise stopped to think. Sally was being frivolous. It was fine, as long as she didn't push it too far. 'I've got a lot on my plate, Sal. Don't envy me, whatever you do.'

They looked at each other. Then Sally smiled and leaned over the table.

'Is that your phone ringing, or have I got Almanac still buzzing in my ears?'

Louise concentrated. The phone was ringing. She looked at her watch quickly. It was far too late for anybody to call her. Unless it was Ash. She sprinted out of the kitchen, through the hall and into the bedroom, then dived onto the bed and hoiked up the receiver.

'Yes?' It came out as a pant, but she wasn't that bothered. She just had to hear his voice again.

'Louise? How are you?'

Something wasn't right.

'Ash?'

'Er, no. It's Jon.'

She was silenced. Sally had decided to come into the room and lie down next to her on the bed, her face a picture of drunken repose. Louise shuffled over to make room. Sally groaned and snuggled up to the pillows.

'Have you got someone with you?' Jon asked.

'Er, not really.'

'So, did you get the flowers? I thought I might hear from you.'

'Yes. Tiger lilies.'

'I know you like them.'

'Right.'

Sally began to snore.

'You have got someone there, haven't you?'

100

Louise sniffed back her indifference to the question.

'OK, can you just hear me out?' Jon continued. He was on a sales roll. She was too tired to fend him off. 'I rang to ask you how it went, and to see if you needed anything.'

'It's all fine.'

'Right. And I wanted to apologise to you as well.'

'Hmmn.'

'Louise? Did you get that? I was a shit, and I know it. It was something that happened between us, and I should have been there for you. I realise that now. I've talked to a few people about it, and not one of them has stood by me.' He gave a self-deprecating laugh.

'That's good.' Sally's snoring was getting louder.

'Louise, I wanted you to know that I'm really, really sorry. I treated you abominably, and it'll live with me for ever.'

'Right.' Louise felt her eyes closing. It had been such a long day.

'And I wondered if I could make it up to you in any way. Perhaps I could take you out to dinner.'

Louise opened her eyes again. Her stomach started to rumble.

'What, anywhere?'

'Yes, Louise, anywhere. The thing is . . . I've been thinking. Perhaps it was a mistake for us to split up in the first place. Perhaps we had a good thing going, but I just didn't realise it.'

Louise smiled at the ceiling, then held the receiver towards Sally as she snorted, turned over and farted.

'Jon? I'll call you. Bye now.'

She put the receiver down, rolled over and fell asleep next to Sally.

'**W**hat's wrong with your mouth, Rachel?'

Rachel felt her shoulders being shaken. She groaned, swore and buried her face in the pillow.

'Rachel? Are you going to play on the computer with us now?'

'Shhh, Ricky. She'll play with us when her mouth gets better.'

'Rachel, if you're not awake, just say so, and we'll go away.'

Ricky. He couldn't help being seven. He couldn't help coming out with the sort of comments that cut through her veneer and cracked her face into a smile.

'I'm not awake,' she rumbled through the pillow.

'OK, we'll go away,' the whisper responded earnestly. 'We'll come back with a cup of tea later to make your mouth better.'

Glen erupted into a shriek of laughter.

'You're stupid. She's awake. How can she talk if she's not awake?'

Rachel sat up and shook her hair around her head.

'Don't be a smart-arse, Glen. Ricky's trying to be thoughtful.' Her voice emerged as a croak.

She surveyed the two faces. Ricky's, small and delicate, broke into a delighted smile as if he wasn't sure what she'd said, but knew she was on his side. Glen looked cautiously at her, then sprang away, shouting as he headed for the stairs.

'I don't care. I'm going to tell Dad you've got a bad mouth.'

She pressed her lips together. They felt swollen and numb. She put a tentative finger up to her face, and opened her eyes in alarm. Her mouth felt huge, as if she'd got mumps from her chin up to her nostrils.

'Ricky, go and help Daddy with the breakfast. I promise I'll come and play on the computer with you if you give me a chance to get up.'

He cast a final, fascinated glance at her face, then fled.

She lay back against the pillows. Her thighs were sore. Her breasts were sore. Her mouth was sore. What had happened with Benji last night had been totally anticipated in some ways, and a shock in others. She'd planned it, even to the point of arranging to see Louise's friend's band. She hadn't meant to be so calculating, but fate had offered her the first opportunity since she'd been living with Hallam to start an affair.

And now that she'd started one, how did she feel? She felt exhilarated with sexual pleasure. Benji had been harshly passionate, and it had been amazing. She waited for guilt to consume her. She thought about Hallam. She wondered how Benji felt waking up to the memory of their lovemaking. He had said it was unique. She believed him. Was it any more than that? Did it matter if it wasn't?

She got up and walked slowly through to the bathroom and looked at herself in the mirror.

What had Benji done to her face? She'd realised he had stubble but the only time she'd ever looked as disfigured as this was when she'd had her four back molars out to make room for her wisdom teeth.

'Oh my God!'

She started to laugh. What would Louise say now?

Louise didn't understand what was going on in her own sister's head. Nobody was ever going to take her side in this situation. Everybody loved Hallam. Everybody thought he was the right sort of man for her to be with. Nobody stopped to consider what she herself could see.

She doused her face in cold water and mopped it with a soft towel. It was Hallam who was splitting her down the middle. Men. They always had to impose themselves, to imprint their personalities.

She threw on a silk wrap, ruffled her hair and wandered down the stairs. Hallam looked up at her. She stopped, her throat tight. He was an elegant man, even in jeans and a jumper. Her heart stuttered as his eyes roamed her face. He blinked, then smiled before going into the kitchen.

'I'm just going to make a phone call, Hal.'

'Fine. Breakfast's ready when you want it,' he called back.

She flicked through the Filofax on the table until she found the number she needed. She took a breath and dialled.

'Is that the Eye of Newt? Oh hi, Keith, it's Rachel Twigg. Sorry I didn't get to speak to you last night, but that last band you had on, Almanac . . . Yes, I thought so too. Have you got a contact number for them?'

She picked up a pen and waited. A squeal of laughter came from the kitchen. Ricky. Hallam was pretending to be the electric fence in *Jurassic Park* again.

'Hi, Keith, yep.' She scribbled down a number. 'Gotcha. Cheers.'

She wandered through to the kitchen in time to see Hallam helping the boys into their coats.

'We're going for a quick stroll,' he said, glancing up at her. 'There's a bacon sarnie there for you.'

'Well . . .' Rachel rubbed at her hair. 'Just give me a sec to throw some clothes on and I'll come with you.'

'Listen, we'll only be half an hour or so. It'll give you time to sort yourself out, won't it?' Hallam said.

'It's no problem. I can just bung my jeans on.'

'But we're going now, Rachel. And you look like you need a shower.'

Rachel hesitated. Once again she was being treated as the outsider. If she could have sat Louise in the kitchen right now and shown her what was happening perhaps then she'd understand. But although her heart was sinking, she wouldn't let the boys know.

'Oh. All right, then.' Rachel grinned at Ricky quickly. He was looking from Rachel to Hallam, his round eyes worried. 'I'll set the computer up, shall I, Ricky? You can thrash me when you get back.'

'Actually, I was going to take them to the pictures later,' Hallam said, not looking at Rachel. 'There's something they really want to see.'

'Great!' Rachel forced herself to sound bright. 'That gives me time to get on with some work, then.'

'Won't you come to the film?' Ricky said, his bottom lip dropping.

'Can't, love. Sorry.' Rachel pulled a hideous face, and he giggled. 'You lot buzz off then and leave me in peace.'

The front door slammed shut. They were too excited to shout a good-bye. She sank her chin into her hands. There was still tomorrow. She'd got a surprise for them. A game they'd been talking about for weeks.

Even Hallam didn't know that she'd bought it for them. He'd be pleased. Tomorrow they could have a day playing games together. She was looking forward to it.

The house was uncomfortably quiet without the boys. She wandered through to the living room, clicking on the stereo and twisting the volume so that the CD blasted out. Benji had wanted to know when he could see her again. She wouldn't ring him yet. She'd think about it.

Louise wasn't imagining it. *Madame Butterfly* was blasting through her door. The music was so loud it had to be coming from the hall, but that wouldn't make any sense. She leaned against the door and listened hard. There was definitely a radio or cassette player at full volume out there. She fumbled with the catch and yanked open the door.

Harris was lying on the floor outside her door. Next to him was a portable cassette recorder. He was wearing Ray-Bans and had his arms comfortably tucked behind his head.

'Hello, gorgeous!' he said.

'What the hell are you doing?'

'Serenading you.'

'Harris,' she sighed, leaning against the door. 'I think it's time you and I had a little talk.'

'No, I don't think so. I don't think we should talk. I think we should make love.'

'Harris,' she sought for words. 'What have I done to deserve this?'

'You want me!' He grinned at her. 'You can't pretend you don't. You came up to my flat and practically threw yourself at me.'

'Look, why don't you come in?'

He sprang up, grabbed the cassette recorder and readied himself to enter her flat.

'To talk,' she clarified.

'If you say so.' He bounced past her and headed for the bedroom.

'In the kitchen!' she instructed loudly.

She'd have to find a way to explain things to him that was tasteful. He had put a lot of effort into seducing her. A man had to maintain his pride. And Harris was an actor. His ego was a significant consideration.

'Harris?'

It had all gone very quiet.

'Harris! Get your pert butt into this kitchen right now, or I'll throw you out!'

She jumped as he emerged from her bedroom just as she reached the open door. He was holding out her book of babies' names.

With his other hand he proffered a pair of diminutive knitting needles gummed together by a wedge of yellow wool. The pair of booties that she'd attempted to create. She could tell that it was a deeply painful discovery for him.

'Look, Harris, none of this is really your business but I feel I should tell you that—'

She stopped. She couldn't really do anything else. He had whipped away his Ray-Bans and he was crying.

'It's so beautiful,' he said in a choked voice, holding out her knitting.

'No, it isn't,' she said factually. She knitted in the way that bricks float.

'You!' he said, thrusting out an arm and pointing at her. 'Mother!'

Harris captured her in an embrace that winded her. She struck a rigid pose, but after several minutes had passed and he seemed in no immediate danger of releasing her she decided it was easier to relax and be cuddled instead. And his arms were warm, and it felt very nice to be hugged so strongly.

'Thanks,' she muttered throatily into his shoulder. He set her away from him and looked at her.

'God, it's overwhelming, Louise. I'm so happy for you. I'll look after you!' His announcement was so triumphant, she didn't have the heart to explain that she was intending to look after herself.

'It's nice of you to think so, Harris.'

'I can give you anything you need,' he said without apparent fear of contradiction. 'All you have to do is ask. What a woman!'

He engulfed her again and she allowed herself to sink against his chest and experience what it felt like to be pregnant and embraced by a man at the same time.

Chapter Eight

'IT'S SO GOOD to see you, Louise!'

Louise gave Jon a short smile that turned into a long smile. It was difficult not to be generous. She'd rung him and asked him if he'd like to meet at very short notice. He hadn't even pretended that he'd got something else planned, which was odd. He'd sounded pleased that she'd phoned him. So she'd dressed herself up, and she'd even produced a co-ordinated outfit, a striking royal blue velvet shirt with a figure-hugging skirt to match. The whole process had been quite fluid, and she'd hummed her way through it, squirting a puff of Opium on each wrist and smiling at her own radiant image before leaving the flat.

She'd chosen a bistro in Kensington that was light, airy and buzzing with activity. Jon had already been at the table when she'd arrived. Usually he made a point of being at least half an hour late. Tonight it almost felt as if she was at the top of his agenda.

He picked up the menu and ran his eyes over it. He was still a gorgeous-looking man, and she could see why she'd fallen for him. She dwelt on the gleaming chestnut highlights in his hair. Would the baby have them? Would his brown genes and her blonde ones be wrestling it out down there? Or perhaps the baby would be more like her father—bald and rugged. Or even like Jon's parents? That was a thought. What the hell did they look like? She hadn't got a clue. If she'd planned this she might have demanded to see the family photo album in advance. What if they all had Prince Charles's ears and Jon had spent his child-hood having corrective surgery? She'd never thought to ask.

'Lou? You're not listening, are you?'

'Sorry?'

'I said, Chardonnay all right with you?'

'You don't usually check with me first,' she smiled pleasantly. 'But I'll just have a weak spritzer, please.'

He gave her a teasing look and ordered the wine from the waiter.

'I'm on a new regime. I've given up smoking, and I'm down on drink-ing. I feel a thousand times better for it. You should try it.'

Jon tried to ease the unlit cigarette in his hand surreptitiously back into the packet.

'But you do what you want,' she continued airily.

'Perhaps it's about time I thought about giving up. Hell, why not? I'm going to start a new regime, right now.'

'Really?'

He surprised her by winking at her. 'You'll see what I mean as the evening goes on, Louise. I've changed. I'm not the same person you used to know.' Jon leaned across the table intimately. 'So how did it go, Louise? Don't talk about it if it's too painful.'

She realised that the clawing of his fingers in her direction was an attempt to take her hand. She squashed them firmly into her lap.

'I'm not sure why you want to know. It's all over, as far as you're concerned.'

He sighed deeply. That wasn't one of his usual sales pitches. Sighing just wasn't his style.

'I wish I'd handled it better,' he said. 'There were times when I wished I'd persuaded you to keep it. Perhaps we could have made a go of it. That baby was half mine, you know.'

She was speechless.

'Oh, I know what you're thinking. It's bloody arrogant of me to think I could have persuaded you one way or the other. But sometimes these things just jump up and bite you. You don't plan them, you don't mean them to happen, but just like that,' he clicked his fingers, 'your life changes for ever.'

'I'm with you so far.'

'Well, my life has changed through this, even though it's been dealt with. It made me think about where I am, what I'm doing, what it's all about.'

'So, what are you saying?' she asked casually.

'I'm saying that if I could do it all over again, you meeting me in the pub, dropping your bombshell, me saying what I did . . .' He took a gulp of his wine and swallowed thoughtfully. 'I'd do it differently.'

'How, exactly?'

He looked at her squarely. She felt a shiver of guilt. Should she be telling him about the baby right now? But she was intrigued. Not yet.

'I'd be more understanding,' he said. 'I'd ask you what you felt. And I think I'd have talked to you about marriage.'

Louise's glass thudded back onto the table. Her voice emerged as a whisper. 'You're not serious, Jon. Tell me you're not serious.'

'I don't know. It did make me think about it. Neither of us is getting any younger. I mean, why do any two people get married anyway? What reason is there, other than starting a family?'

'I did think there might be something about love squeezed in there somewhere.'

'Of course, of course. This is all coming out wrong.'

The waiter reappeared as Jon was settling into another long sigh. He sat up straight, rearranged his jacket and regarded the menu seriously. He put on a formal voice that was as new to her as everything else he was producing.

'Louise? Are you ready to order, or shall we tell him to go away for a few minutes?'

'You can *ask* 'im to go away, but you'll be bloody lucky if 'e comes back.' The waiter smiled down at Jon without humour. 'It is Saturday night, sir.'

'I'm ready.' Louise settled on a first course and a hefty main dish, and placed her own order. Jon was staring blankly at Louise.

'You never have a starter!' he said.

'How do you know?' she asked pleasantly. 'Are you ready?'

Jon looked flustered. He ordered a main course for himself and flapped the menu closed.

'This is so unlike you, Louise. Can you really get through all that?'

'You'd be surprised,' Louise said, picking at the edge of her bread roll and popping it into her mouth. 'I've been eating like a horse recently.'

'There's something about you, Louise. You've changed. No, it goes right back to the pub, when you told me about all this. You were—I don't know—odd.'

'Odd?'

'Calm. In control. Just different from how you usually are. I just thought you'd be more upset. You don't seem flustered at all.'

She tried to concentrate on what Jon was saying but her mind was trying to work out how many of the women around her were pregnant.

'Sorry?'

'I think it's because you've got someone else.' Jon put his glass down. She stared back at him.

'And if I had someone, why would you have a problem with that?'

'There was someone there in your bedroom when I phoned you. I need to know if it's important to you. Please tell me, Louise. Have you got someone else? Yes or no.'

'Yes, Jon. Yes, if you must know, I'm in love with somebody, and it's not you. All right?'

Jon blanched.

'Jesus,' he said finally. He lit a cigarette without looking at her.

Her attention was gripped now. There was something badly wrong with him. He was behaving out of character in every possible way. Now he had dropped any semblance of cool and was muttering to himself as he smoked and drank heavily in front of her very eyes.

'Calm down,' Louise said.

'Why should I be calm?' Jon's voice was intense. 'I've realised I'm in love with you, and you don't give a toss.'

'In love?' she gulped.

'Yes. With you! And your Dad's a brickie, for Christ's sake.'

'*Was* a brickie,' Louise corrected, stunned.

'My parents wouldn't even let me play with the council estate kids. God knows what they'd make of me falling in love with one.'

Louise sat very still. She wasn't surprised by what he was saying.

She'd heard him say similar things before, but not aimed at her.

He'd made comments about her family and her background that she wasn't prepared to hear. Not from anybody.

'Jon, I think I'm going to go.' She took her napkin from her lap, folded it and placed it on the table.

'You can't go,' he said flatly. 'We haven't finished our meal.'

'Jon, if I want to go I'll just walk out of here.'

'I don't want you to. Please don't. Not yet. I haven't explained anything properly. I want to say this.' He reached out for her hand. Reluctantly, she extended it for him. 'Louise, I'm sorry. I'm so bloody sorry for everything. I've been a total bastard.'

She swallowed. He had tears welling in his eyes. He seemed to have lost all ability to control himself.

'Louise, I love you. I *love* you, don't you see? And so,' Jon continued with determination. 'I'm going to give you this. Throw it in my face if you must, but I came here intending to give it to you, and I am going to give it to you. No, don't pull away.'

She watched, mesmerised, as he fumbled with one hand in his jacket pocket, while maintaining a secure hold on her with the other. Finally, he produced a small velvet box and placed it in front of her.

He flipped open the lid to reveal a ring. It was a solitaire. Tasteful, discreet, probably expensive. Her hand became limp in his.

'Louise, I know I've been a sod, but I've realised that I love you. And,' his voice broke, 'I came here intending to ask you to marry me. So I'm going to do it. Will you marry me?'

Louise sat motionless while the world kaleidoscoped around her.

He'd asked her to marry him, even though he thought she was no longer having his baby. He thought that he loved her. There was no other reason. He sat opposite her, his soul bared in his eyes, the father of the baby she was having.

'Louise?' he mouthed at her across the table.

The whole restaurant was hushed, waiting for her response. She dropped her head so that she didn't have to look at the desperation in Jon's face. The tense silence around them was shattered. She looked up sharply and realised that her action had been taken as a nod. Saturday night exuberance crashed in on them as people laughed with relief and glasses chinked. Someone clapped.

Jon slipped the ring onto her finger. He gave a disbelieving laugh. He stood up, reached over the table, pulled her up into his arms and smacked a kiss on her lips.

Should she patronise him? Reason with him? Hit him? By now their audience was too enthusiastic to be disappointed. She tried to smile at him. This was no time to talk anything through. The momentum had overtaken them. 'She said yes!' Jon turned round and threw his arms out to his audience. Louise watched him. Something profound had happened, but she wasn't sure what it was. She could feel tears on her cheeks.

'Congratulations, madam,' said the waiter. 'Would you like a glass of champagne, or a valium? Either way, it's on the 'ouse.'

Olivia stood at the back door, peering out at the garden. It was black outside, and when she readjusted her eyes she saw only her own reflection in the smooth sheet of glass. She took a step back. Was that really what she looked like?

She smiled at herself as an experiment. Her own indistinct image was ten years younger, the rebounding light unable to capture every worryline on her face. It was very satisfying. She'd been thought of as very pretty when she was much younger. Like Louise. She had more in common with her youngest daughter than Louise could imagine. They had both gone adrift, come off the rails, at some point in their young adult lives. The thought made her turn away from her reflection, almost as if to stare at it any longer while thinking such thoughts would will upon Louise the same destiny that she had found herself.

She poured herself a glass of wine and sat pondering Shaun's present. It was silly to have put off opening it for so long, but she liked to have something to look forward to at the end of the evening.

She pulled the bag towards her, peered inside and removed the dusty-looking book. It was blue, a lighter, faded blue around the edges as if it had been exposed to the sun. She turned it over to read the spine. The gold print read *Tennyson's Poems*.

She stared at the book, confused. It was only today, that she'd told Shaun she liked him quoting Tennyson. But he'd come to meet her with the book ready to give to her. How could he have known?

She opened the cover and a note slipped out. She unfolded it and tried to read his looped scrawl. *Dear Olivia, I hope you enyoy these. I have put a blip of paa-per in a couple of palaces—places for you. But it's op to yov to see what you hike. No, like. With Shergar? Regards. Shaun.*

She laid his note on the table. It was well creased as if he'd pondered over it for some time. Something stirred inside her.

She got up, walked into the living room, and aimed for the stereo. She squatted down and thumbed through the edges of the album sleeves and slid out the Mamas and the Papas. She laid the record flat and guided the needle over to the track she wanted to hear. The speakers crackled as they were awakened from sleep.

Olivia wandered over to the back door. She twisted the key in the door as the track began to play its stirring introduction. It had been their song, if it was ever possible for them to have a song seeing as they never courted in the way that other couples did. But later, once they were married, and once they had realised that there was love between them, it had become their song.

Olivia opened the back door and stepped out onto the even paving stones of the patio. The haunting melody of 'Dedicated to the One I Love' floated out to her. She gazed round the garden trying to adjust to the darkness while she stood in the arc of light cast by the kitchen, then wandered to the edge of the patio and dipped a toe onto the damp grass.

She threw her head back and gazed right up into the night. The clouds had cleared. It sent a cold rush of excitement over her. She could see the stars! And there was a moon, a crescent moon.

Her exhalations coming in white streams, she rolled her head back as far as it would go. And this sky, these stars, this moon, were being seen all over the world. All she had to do was become like one of the stars, then she could shine down wherever she wanted.

She began to spin round, her arms outstretched, very slowly, with the crescent moon as her focus. The song dug like a trowel into her chest. She had to endure it. She saw a light go on in next door's bathroom. Olivia stopped spinning. It was no use trying to pretend she was a star when her neighbour was gargling so loudly.

She walked back up the garden and into the house. She closed the door firmly behind her. She went back to the table, sat down and pulled Shaun's note and the book towards her. She opened it at one of the pages he had marked. He had put a pencil scribble in the margin to show that he wanted her to read a verse of a poem. She glanced at the title of the poem. 'In Memoriam'. Her pulse slowed. She read.

> I sometimes hold it half a sin
> To put in words the grief I feel;
> For words, like Nature, half reveal
> And half conceal the Soul within.

'My God,' she uttered, throwing the book down on the table. What did Shaun think he was doing, for God's sake? Did he think that she thought it would be sinful to talk about her grief? Did he think she *should* talk about it? What did he mean, and what did it have to do with him?

So, she thought, it was still impossible for her to cry for Bob. She'd played the song that would have made it happen if anything could, and still nothing. But it was a blessing that she couldn't cry, because if she did, all her plans would probably come crashing down around her ears.

It had been the obvious thing to do, to invite Jon back to her flat. They weren't going to be able to talk in the restaurant after he had swallowed his second bottle of wine. Outside, he'd hailed them a cab and insisted on paying. All the way home he'd clutched her hand and exchanged mother-in-law jokes with the cab driver.

'Jon, we need to talk.'

'Certainly, my dear. Once I've found your brandy.'

Louise leaned back against the kitchen table and turned her hand over slowly. The solitaire glinted under the harsh strip light. She twisted it round until the stone had disappeared and all she could see was a thin gold band round her finger. Her wedding-ring finger. She pulled at the ring until it was halfway off her finger.

'Where is that bottle?' Jon reappeared and leaned against the door frame. He grinned at her lopsidedly. 'You can't have guzzled the lot.'

She slid the ring back into place. They must talk, first.

'It was Sally. She was on a bit of a bender when she came round. She pretty much cleaned me out of booze.'

'Sally?' He straightened his face and raised his eyebrows. 'What was she doing here?'

'She's my friend. She needed to talk about something.'

'Really? Bitching about me, were you?'

Louise decided not to answer. He ambled back into the kitchen and yanked open her fridge door.

'Don't answer that if you don't want to. Blimey, no beer and only half an inch of wine. And food everywhere. You really are serious about changing your lifestyle, aren't you?' He pulled out the wine bottle and tipped the contents into a glass. His eyes roamed her kitchen and rested on the drooping heads of the tiger lilies hanging out of the plastic bucket. He frowned. 'Not a very prominent place to display them, Lou.'

'Jon, I need to tell you something.'

He pulled out a chair and draped himself over it, loosening the collar of his shirt. It made him look rakish. She felt a reluctant stir of attraction.

'OK.' He smiled. 'In which case, you'd better tell me about the guy you thought you were in love with. That way we can wipe the slate clean and start afresh.'

Louise slowly sat down on a chair and faced him across the table.

'It's not about anybody else. It's about me. There's something I didn't have a chance to tell you in the restaurant.'

'Blimey, you're not pregnant, are you?'

He stretched his eyes in fake horror, then collapsed into giggles, his glass to his lips.

'Sorry, Louise. I couldn't help it. It's just the look on your face.' She stared back at him solemnly and he buried his smile quickly. He sat up more elegantly and crossed one leg over the other. 'I'm really sorry. That wasn't funny. Not after what you've been through.'

He pulled her onto his lap and reached out for her hand. She looked down too. Her hand in his, the engagement ring binding them together. Except that the ring was a trinket. The thing that bound them together was growing inside her, and was going to last a lifetime.

'Jon, I'm still pregnant,' she said.

There was a long silence. She tried to get up, only to find that his arm was still clamped round her waist.

'Say that again,' he said quietly.

'I—' She swallowed. She was not going to apologise. 'I'm still pregnant. I haven't had a termination.'

He cleared his throat. He still seemed unwilling to release her.

'And—you're saying that it hasn't happened *yet*, or what?'

'It's not going to happen. I'm going to have the baby.'

His arm dropped from her waist. She glanced at him quickly. He seemed deluged with his own thoughts. She got up and busied herself with making a mug of coffee. She couldn't turn round and look at him.

'I, um . . .' She stirred the coffee frantically. 'I was going to tell you, at the right time. But there hasn't been a right time yet.'

'When did you decide on this?' he asked.

'Er, a little while ago. Not immediately. I wasn't sure what I was going to do at first.'

'And you're sure about this? Or are you going to change your mind again in another couple of days?' She swung round on him. 'I only ask that, Louise, because you're turning my head inside out.'

She watched him, her pulse thumping. His head. His life. His feelings. What about hers?

'I'm going to have the baby, Jon. It's my decision, and I'm happy about it. I'm not asking you to be happy. I'm just telling you what's going to happen. You can have as much access as you like after the baby's born.' She paused and added, 'If you want it, that is.'

'You were planning to do this on your own, then?'

'Of course. There's no need for you to be involved. You're still a free agent.'

He stared at her open-mouthed.

'I expect you'll want this back.' She twisted the ring from her finger and laid it on the table top. 'I didn't actually say yes, you know. I think you misinterpreted me.' She felt she should say something else. 'I'm sorry this is a shock for you. I wasn't expecting you to propose.'

He chewed on his lip. She was starting to feel very uncomfortable. It was completely unlike him to be silent for so long.

'The baby's going to need a father around, Louise,' he said slowly, breaking his silence. 'You know how important that is. Look at the relationship you had with your own father.'

It wasn't what she expected him to say. He looked remarkably sober all of a sudden.

'This isn't an ideal world,' she said.

'No, but we can do our best for the child, can't we?'

'I always intended to do that, from the moment I made my decision. It's my priority now. Anything else is going to come second.'

'Like a man?'

She gave him a sharp look.

'If necessary, yes. That depends on the man.'

'I think I'm saying that I still want to be with you,' he said. He carefully picked up the delicate gold ring. He turned it over. 'This is so typical of me, isn't it?' He gave a disparaging laugh. 'I go charging in with fanfares and banners, and all the time I could have been talking to you, putting things right. It didn't need this, did it?'

She felt oddly moved by his behaviour. He took the ring and slid it back into the small velvet box. 'Maybe another time.'

'Yes. Maybe,' she said.

'Lou?' he began hesitantly. 'Do you think I could stay here tonight? It's just—I don't want to go.'

She watched him shifting awkwardly as he waited for her response. It was a different Jon she was seeing now. One he had hidden from her in all the time they had been together. If only this was the real Jon. There was only one way to find out.

'Stay tonight, Jon,' she said. 'If we're going to get to know each other, we might as well start now.'

Rachel smiled as she heard the front door banging.

'In here!' she called.

Ricky came racing into the study. Rachel hopped away from the computer. 'Tum-tum-TARA!' She flung her hand out to indicate the boxed game which she had wrapped and placed next to the screen. Ricky's eyes opened wider.

'Another one!' he breathed.

Glen piled into the room, pulling Hallam after him.

'Now!' Glen was begging. 'Please, can I put it on NOW!'

Rachel absorbed the scene around her. Glen was swinging a plastic bag, Ricky was still gawping at the wrapped present Rachel had left on the desk. Hallam smiled at her briefly.

'Hi, Rach. Get much done?'

'I'm not working this afternoon,' she said, failing to keep the irritation from her voice. 'I thought we could all play a computer game. In fact, I thought that's what we'd planned.'

'We *are* going to play a computer game.' Glen glanced at her as he edged his way onto the chair and pulled a box from the red plastic bag. 'A brilliant one. Dad's bought it for us.'

Rachel stared at the game that Hallam had bought.

Bitterness swelled inside her, a strange mixture of unreleased sorrow and anger. Hallam was leaning over Glen's shoulder. His eyes fell on Rachel's present.

'Hello, what's this?'

'It's nothing,' Rachel snapped, thrusting herself forward and yanking the box out of sight.

'Rachel?' Hallam stood up and gave her a quizzical look.

Rachel fought with her angry tears. She had to maintain control, for Ricky's sake, if nobody else's. Ricky slipped his hand into hers.

'It's all right, Rachel,' he said, his eyes luminous. 'We can play your game too.'

Something inside her broke down. She gave a wrenching sob and fled from the room, raced up the stairs, not daring to stop or look round. She hurled herself onto the bed, the present gripped in her hand. She hammered it against the duvet, wishing it was a mallet and the duvet was Hallam's skull.

'You bastard. You bastard. You bastard!'

The door to the bedroom clicked shut. Hallam was standing there behind her, watching.

'Am I the bastard?' he asked quietly.

She took several ragged breaths before flinging the box across the room at him. It bounced off his head and into the laundry basket. He looked confused for a moment, then rubbed at his forehead.

'I'll take that as a yes, shall I?' he asked.

'I bought that same bloody game for them. It was meant to be a surprise. I wanted to show them that I'd listened to them, that I knew what they liked. And you *ruined* it!'

'Why didn't you tell me?' he asked.

'Because then it wouldn't have been a bloody surprise, would it?'

'I see,' he said, leaning against the door. 'Now I know the problem.'

'Don't . . .' She shook her head. 'Don't make me feel stupid.'

'I'm not trying to. I thought you might be tired, that's all.'

'I'm not sodding tired!' She began to cry again.

'No?' He inclined his head. 'You got so little sleep on Friday night.'

He turned and let himself out of the bedroom, pulling the door closed behind him. She heard his footsteps on the stairs, and his voice from the study as he joined the boys again.

She hauled herself off the bed, walked across the room and thumped her fist against the white gloss of the closed door.

'So why don't you bloody well ask me about Friday night then?'

'Ash!' Louise was unable to stop her delighted grin from spreading to her ears. 'What are you doing here?'

It was a fair question, seeing as she was in Totz baby shop.

But it was just so wonderful to see him that she couldn't disguise it. He was in his denim jacket, his jeans and his thick black jumper. His hair was in more disarray than usual. It looked as if he'd been teasing the strands mercilessly with his fingers.

'I, um . . .' A flush touched his cheeks. He lowered his eyes and fingered a small teddy bear he was clutching. 'You've caught me out, haven't you?'

'Buying teddy bears? Certainly looks like it. What is it, band mascot or something?'

'Oh, no, not really.' He fiddled with the bear. 'What do you think of this one? Is it cute, or does it look like a psychopath? I can't decide.'

'Psychopath.'

'Good. That's what I thought. I prefer the bunnies really, but they're more expensive.' He pointed over to a counter of soft toys.

She folded her arms and gave him a firm look. 'Just how long have you been in here?'

He glanced at his watch. 'Blimey, nearly an hour now. Time flies when you're in your local supplier of baby goods, doesn't it?' He smiled at her, and she felt as if summer had arrived. 'So, how are you? Did you get back from the gig OK? I came to look for you, but you'd gone.'

'I'm sorry about that. I had a sudden attack of tiredness. Has Rachel been in touch with you?'

'No, well, you can't expect her to be seriously interested in us, can you? It was a fiasco.'

'Oh.' She was disappointed, but it was as she'd feared. She clenched her fingers inside her gloves, trying to think of something to say that would stop him from running away. Dwelling on his blown opportunity wasn't the best tactic. And what was he doing in Totz anyway? She was itching to ask. She could even dare to hope that the reply might have something to do with her. But then again, if she and Jon were going to try to forge a relationship, she shouldn't be hoping anything of the sort. She should be telling him right now about Jon, but when she opened her mouth what she said had nothing to do with Jon.

'I came to look at prams.'

'I'm not rushing off if you want a second opinion.'

'Would you mind? I know it's early days, but I just thought I'd check them out.'

They wandered over to the selection of prams.

'Hey, this one's cool.' Ash pulled out a light buggy and fiddled with a series of levers. 'Folds down into a sofa bed. You can put all your friends up too. Plenty of room for your shopping.' He squatted down and patted the tray beneath. 'You can fill this up and use it as a paddling pool when the baby gets older. All you need is go-fast stripes and alloy wheels.'

'No way!' she laughed at him. 'And no furry dice.'

Louise nearly fainted as she turned over the price tag. She linked her arm through Ash's and carted him out of the shop. His legs were almost dragging with reluctance.

'But I was having fun.' The stiff wind assaulted them. 'And at least it was warm in there,' he said ruefully.

'Warm, and poignant. I can't afford any of it. Not now, and certainly not when the baby's born. Not unless I get my act together pretty damn quickly and do something about it.'

He nodded at her. His eyes were serious now. 'Do you need to talk it over with someone?' he asked. 'I've got just enough for a cuppa if you can face the greasy spoon.'

She was about to protest, but she stopped herself. He was being friendly. There was no harm in that. And with Ash she really could think. It was as if her head cleared when he was around.

'Well, all right,' she said. 'If you really don't mind. I won't keep you for long, though. The last thing you want to spend a Wednesday afternoon doing is listening to a pregnant woman trying to plan her—'

'Louise?'

'Yes?'

'Shut up.'

'OK,' she squeaked, and took the arm that he extended to her.

Chapter Nine

'HERE Y'ARE, LOVE. Late delivery. It came apart, this one did. And there's a letter for you too.'

The postman handed Louise a heavily Sellotaped brown package and a flat envelope that looked like a bill. She tucked the envelope under her arm and concentrated on the parcel. It was ripped at one end and the pointed toe of a garish slipper was sticking out.

As the postman whistled away down the path she leaned on the door frame, pulling the offending slippers from the paper. She dropped them on the ground and slipped her feet into them. Together with her yellow socks they looked amazing. She laughed quietly. A pair of pointy, circus clown slippers. They really were hideous. She felt inside the remains of the paper and pulled out a folded Marks & Spencer's bag. Inside was a thermal vest edged with frills. She shook it out. It was huge. Her mother had a habit of buying everything for her at least four sizes too big, as if she couldn't get over the idea that Louise would grow into things. She didn't know how right she was at the moment. She pulled the vest over her head to test it. It stretched easily over the polo-neck sweater she was wearing. Louise left it there. She took a deep breath of cold air. It wasn't exactly fresh, but it was invigorating. She gazed down her path at the main road. The afternoon rush-hour traffic was mounting, but it didn't annoy her. Life was extremely bearable at the moment. She was only going to take things one day at a time, and since the weekend she had tentatively been feeling more settled. Jon was surprising her more and more. He'd rung her from work each afternoon to ask if she'd mind if he came back for the night. It was the end of the week and he'd spent all his free time with her since Saturday night. He was still protesting his feelings for her, and she allowed him to say what he wanted without gushing back at him. There was a chance that love would grow between them. She owed it to them all to try.

She turned her attention to the envelope and ripped it open. Her eyes widened with surprise. It was a cheque from Party Animals. It was much, much more than she might have expected.

'Please find enclosed the salary we owe you, plus a bonus to help you through Christmas,' she read in a murmur. 'Good luck with your job hunt. Sorry about everything, Andrew.'

She looked at the cheque again. It was only money and money didn't usually have the power to stir her into euphoria, but this was security. It would cover the phone bill and next month's rent, and it would keep her head above water while she moved on with her plans. It was another step towards independence.

She nudged the door to close it, but caught sight of a figure turning into her path. Damn it. It was Jon, and she still looked like a wreck. But the cheque had lifted her spirits, and in a burst of spontaneity she threw open the door, rushed down the path at him and waved the cheque in front of his eyes.

'Look, Jon, it's money. From Andrew. Money they owed me!'

'Fine.' He held her away from him with a frown. He glanced around, as if to be sure they weren't being watched, and edged past her quickly towards the door. She stood on the path and watched him try to distance himself from her.

She looked like a wreck. Jon wouldn't want to be associated with her in public until she'd done her hair and slapped a bit of make-up on. She looked down at herself in horror. She had a frilly vest on over her jumper, and was sporting a pair of long, thin slippers on her feet. It was no wonder Jon was so embarrassed.

'Jesus!' She turned to get herself inside as quickly as possible.

'Louise! Hey!'

She swivelled round. Excitement and shock stampeded over her.

'Ash!'

She shot a fearful glance over her shoulder. Jon was now standing in the hall casually, watching.

'Um . . .' She looked back to Ash, who was striding towards her, his eyes bright, his hair a tangle of brown knots. He enveloped her in a hug which knocked the remaining breath out of her lungs. It struck her that he couldn't have seen Jon languishing in the shadows of the hall. She squirmed within the forceful embrace.

'Ash, what—what—why are you here?'

'Your CV, remember? I said I'd bring it round for you. And I have to talk to you. Is now a good time?'

'For—for what?'

'For this.' He winked at her, then, to her shock, planted a kiss directly on to her lips. His mouth was so warm, so insistent, that it was difficult to pull away, but she had to.

'God, Ash.' She pushed him away, flustered. 'What did you do that for?'

'You're brilliant. It's all sorted, and I've never been so happy.'

'What—' She looked quickly over her shoulder to see if Jon was still in the hall. She had a feeling that he was hiding round the back of the door. Ash was still holding her tightly. He laid his cheek against hers and waltzed her up and down her path. She laughed nervously.

'You've sorted my life out for me, Louise, and you don't even know it.'

'What's going on?'

'Rachel, your sister.'

'She called you?'

'Yes, but it's not what you think. She called Karen. They're not interested in the band, just her. It looks like Karen's going to make it.'

'What?' Louise stepped back, horrified. Ash was nodding cheerfully.

'It's just great. We had a totally destructive house row and she went off to live with a mate of hers instead. The band's split up, Ginger's not talking to me. I've never been happier.' He grinned to prove the point. He glanced down at her body, allowed his eyes to roam right down to the yellow socks and slippers and back up again to the frilly vest over her jumper, then grinned even more broadly. 'You're totally fucking mad, do you know that?'

'Er—'

'And I want to ask you out. I'm free. I'm going to start all over again, doing things I really want to do from now on. And that includes asking you out to dinner. What do you say?'

Louise's mouth dropped open. She delved deep inside for some sort of word, anything would do just to tide things over, but nothing came. She just stood in her vest and slippers and gaped at the most gorgeous man in London who had just asked her out on a date.

'Um, you see, the thing is . . .' She swam in his pale green eyes, wishing that the world would vanish and leave the two of them alone.

'The thing is, she's pregnant.' Jon's harsh voice cut across them from her doorstep. Louise knew without turning round what his expression would be like. 'And it's mine,' Jon finished firmly.

Slowly Ash took his hand from Louise's shoulder.

'So you're back,' Ash said bluntly. Louise's eyebrows shot up to her hairline. That wasn't what she expected him to say at all. Ash glanced at Jon again, then dropped his eyes on Louise. His expression softened.

'If you need me, you know where I am.'

She nodded dumbly.

'She won't,' Jon stated. Louise could sense that he had left the doorstep and was walking slowly towards them. Surely not a fist fight over her? A pregnant woman with flyaway hair in a vest and slippers?

'Relax,' Ash said calmly. 'I realise this is a private matter. I'm going now. I said what I came to say.'

He turned and walked away, very slowly. Louise stared after him. He disappeared from sight. That, without doubt, was the last she would ever see of him.

'Come on, Lou,' Jon said, gripping her arm and hauling her inside the main hallway. Once inside, she shook his hand away, pushed the front door shut and leaned back against it. Jon stalked ahead of her into the shadows of the hall and waited for her at the door to her flat. 'Whatever that was all about, it's over now, Louise. You can explain it to me.'

'And you'll tell me all about Kelly then, I assume?'

'Who?' He blinked innocent eyes at her.

She jumped as the doorbell blasted suddenly over her head.

'If that's him again—' Jon took a purposeful step back down the hall. 'Just let me get the door, then for heaven's sake let's get into the flat.'

She pulled the door open roughly, her emotions churning.

'Yes?' she bellowed at the figure standing on her path. Recognition dawned.

'Louise!' The eager smile on Giles the accountant's bearded face was failing rapidly. 'I—I got your letter and I was driving home from work this way. I—I thought we could . . . perhaps . . .' His voice tailed away.

'Oh, just go away!' She slammed the door violently in his face. She blew out sharply, her nerves in tatters, and swung round to face Jon. He was frozen into position, his key pointed at her door. His expression had flattened out into total astonishment.

'Right then,' she said, striding across the hall. 'I think that's my past dealt with. Let's go and talk about the future, shall we?'

The conversation had not exactly resolved anything, Louise thought on Saturday as she sorted through her wardrobe and tried to find something that might be appropriate to wear down to Kent. Something suitable for her mother's reunion dinner which would also do for her announcement. What would her mother like to see her daughter in at the moment she found out that she was going to be a grandmother?

She had told Jon exactly what had happened between herself and Ash. The fact that he had been there to give her advice about signing on, that they'd met several times and that she'd asked Rachel to go and see his band to return the favour. What she hadn't told Jon was how she felt about Ash. She wasn't even sure herself what she felt. All she knew was that when she thought about him she felt uplifted. In another life, she and Ash might have started something.

'At least let me drive you down.' Jon was standing in the doorway. 'You're going to miss the train at this rate, Lou. I don't like the idea of you cavorting across London and down to Kent in your state.'

She frowned at him. 'I'm not in a state. I'll be fine.'

'I'd like to see your mum again anyway. We got on like a house on fire the last time we met. I'd like to be there when you tell her about us and the baby. I'd love to see the expression on her face.'

'No, Jon. I really need to see her on my own first. Maybe you can come down another time?'

Louise forced a smile. She was also wondering what the expression on her mother's face would be when she told her. There was the baby, and there was Jon. She had a feeling that her mother's reactions to the two developments were going to be different. The two of them had met when Olivia had come up to visit Louise in London. Louise had cooked a meal and Jon had joined them. Jon had talked about his career prospects for three hours without taking a breath. When Olivia hugged Louise goodbye, she suggested it was a little odd that Jon hadn't talked about their relationship at all. Her mother, annoyingly, had been right about Jon, not so much in what she said, but what she didn't say.

'Great. And, er, you won't mind if I stay here for the weekend then?'

She looked up at him. 'Do you want to?'

He shrugged. 'I might as well now I'm here. It'll make me feel closer to you, Lou. If you don't mind.'

'No, I don't mind.'

'Now you'd better get a move on. Isn't your mother supposed to be meeting you from the train?'

'Yes, I'm nearly ready.'

'And when shall I expect you back?'

'Probably late on Sunday. We're going to have a lot to talk about.'

'You just take as much time as you need.'

Louise glanced at her watch as the phone rang. 'Shit, who's that?'

She listened to the odd sound that was coming through her answering machine. It sounded like a child whining down the phone. No, it was somebody crying. Louise realised it was Rachel.

'Louise, are you there?' Rachel's voice tailed away into tears again.

Louise grabbed at the phone.

'Rachel, I'm here. What's wrong?'

'Oh, Louise.' Rachel started to sob uncontrollably. 'It's Hallam.'

'What's happened, Rachel?' Louise asked firmly. 'Take a deep breath and tell me.'

'I've told him about Benji. He said we should split up. He offered to leave but I couldn't let him, so I've left instead.'

'What about Benji, Rachel? Have you told him you've left Hallam?'

'No,' Rachel gulped. 'No, he doesn't know. He wouldn't want to know. It's only sex, nothing more. I can't tell him.' Rachel's voice broke into tears again. 'I just grabbed a few things and left.'

'Rachel, everything's going to be fine. Just tell me where you are.'

'I'm in my car.'

'Fine. Where is the car?'

'In your road,' Rachel said, her voice cracking. 'Outside your house.'

'Oh.' Louise stood up.

'And there's a traffic warden walking towards me!' Rachel finished, her voice becoming a sob again.

'OK. Now you're going to start the car, take it round to a side road and park it. Then you're going to come to my house, and the door's going to be open. We'll take it from there,' Louise said.

'OK,' Rachel sniffed.

'I'm putting the phone down now. I'm going to the door and I'll be there when you get to the gate. Will you be OK without me?'

'Yes,' Rachel said. 'And Lou?'

'Yes?'

'I love you.'

Louise nodded, a lump rising in her throat.

'I love you too, Rach.'

'Everything all right?' Jon asked.

'Slight change of plan.'

Just don't tell Mum I was crying. I don't want her to worry,' Rachel said as they climbed out of the BMW and stood on the driveway next to their bags. 'Let me just finish this fag, then we'll go in.'

Louise took several deep gulps of air. It was a miracle that she hadn't thrown up in the car. She turned slowly in a circle and allowed the familiarity of the estate to envelop her. The evenly spaced houses and neat gardens were orange in the street lamps. There was no jarring thunder of lorries and buses. She was home and somewhere in the house her mother was waiting. It was a lovely, familiar, comforting feeling. Rachel was looking up at the pebbledashed façade of their old house as she ground her cigarette under her heel.

'Weird coming back, isn't it?'

'I expect Mum heard us arrive,' Louise urged. 'We'd best knock.'

'Let's go for it. And remember, not a mention of me and Hallam. Poor Mum's got enough on her plate and I'll only get a lecture.'

'Mum'll just be happy to see you,' Louise said, taking Rachel's arm as they marched up to the front door together. 'She sounded thrilled that you were coming too.'

'But worried about table placements, I know.'

'It's just habit. You know what Mum's like.' Louise lowered her voice just in case their mother could hear them through the door. 'You've got to be nice to Mum. She's got her own way of doing things. She's set in her ways, but I think that's something we should be grateful for.'

'Grateful? When she's so depressed?'

Louise sighed. 'She's going through a grieving process which is totally natural. We've just got to give her time.'

Louise pressed the bell and moved closer to Rachel. She gave her arm an impulsive squeeze. 'Great to be home though, isn't it? Thank God there are still some things that you can rely on.'

Louise felt her lips spread into a smile as she saw their mother fumbling with the catch on the door. The door swung open.

'Surprise!' their mother called at them, spreading her arms wide and curtseying in the hall. She giggled, and did a turn for them.

Rachel and Louise had both opened their mouths ready with an affectionate greeting. They shut them again. Neither of them moved. Olivia giggled again.

'Well, aren't you going to say anything?'

'You've changed your hair,' Rachel said vacantly.

Louise ranged her eyes over the elegant figure who was now striking model poses. She had changed her hair. That was probably the easiest fact to get a grip of. Instead of the loose, soft wings that had framed her head, her hair was now cropped into a chic cut, high around the ears, with a light fringe that emphasised her eyes. But her eyes were different too. She'd changed her make-up. And she was wearing trousers, fashionable ones, of a soft suede material, with a pair of ankle boots brushing the hems. A silk top of a muted gold was tucked into a thick leather belt, and a casual jacket which matched the trousers swung jauntily round her waist. The complete ensemble knocked ten years off her.

'Hello, Mum,' Rachel said, recovering herself as they stepped inside. 'You look absolutely fantastic.'

'Have you been drinking?' Louise asked. It wasn't just how her mother looked, it was how she was acting. She seemed light-hearted, flippant, dizzy.

'Oh, hark at you!' Olivia slapped her daughter's arm playfully, and danced through to the living room. 'Just dump your coats and bags and come on through. We're going to have a glass of something together, then you two can get changed. The water's hot if you want showers.'

Louise glided into their old living room and gazed around. Thankfully it was the same as ever.

'Now, Rachel can only have a tiny sip of this seeing as she's driving,' Olivia breezed on. 'But Louise can have as much as she likes. She can keep me company, then she can't make rude comments about me drinking on my own.'

Olivia struggled to open a bottle of champagne. She had set three fluted glasses out on the table. Louise couldn't remember the last time they had been used.

'Here, let me.' Rachel took the bottle gently while Olivia flushed and waved her hands.

'I'm sure I could have done it.'

'Yes, but I've got it down to a fine art,' Rachel smiled at her mother. 'Real champagne! What's got into you, Mum?'

'What hasn't? I've got so much to tell you both.' She sighed in happiness. 'It's so, so good to have you both here.'

The champagne cork flew out of the bottle, hit the ceiling and skidded across the floor. Olivia hummed to herself as she held out the glasses one by one, ignoring the fact that a spume of champagne had erupted from the bottle and was now dripping off the edge of the table. Louise was becoming more confused by the second.

'Right!' Olivia declared. 'What shall I tell you first? Shall we sit down?'

Her cheeks were pink and her eyes were sparkling. They gaped back at her in silence as they sat in the armchairs.

'Well,' Olivia laced her fingers together on the table. 'I've done a lot of thinking recently. It was after Katherine bloody Muff's phone call. I thought of all those women, and what they'd all done with their lives. I thought of myself, and what I'd done. A wife and mother. That was it.'

'But—being a mother's so important,' Louise asserted. 'You should be proud of it.'

'I am proud.' Olivia held up a hand to Louise. 'But I had Rachel very young. There were things I always wanted to do, but I never did them. So—so I thought I could do some of those things now.' She stopped to sip her champagne. 'In fact, I thought I'd do all of those things now.'

Rachel leaned forward, her face full of anticipation.

'So what are the things, Mum?'

'Well . . . Shaun's teaching me to drive the Escort, I've told Carol to get stuffed, I'm going to resign from work and take a trip abroad. Round the world, in fact. Via India. I've always wanted to go there.'

Olivia looked startled now as both her daughters sat bolt upright.

'And I've joined the Liberal Democrats,' she finished breathlessly. She picked up her glass of champagne and finished it in one gulp.

There was a long, long silence. Louise was unable to move, even to twitch her fingers towards her glass, much as she needed to drink it now. Rachel stared in amazement.

'Bloody hell!'

'Can't you just vote for them?' Louise asked weakly.

'Bugger the Liberal Democrats, what's this about going round the world?' Rachel had started to laugh. 'I thought you were afraid of flying.'

'It was Bob, don't you see? He never wanted to go abroad. How can I know if I'm afraid of flying? I've never been inside an aeroplane.'

'When?' Louise voiced. She could feel the blood draining from her cheeks. 'When are you going away?'

'I'm not sure yet, but soon. There's a nice little travel agent in Tonbridge, and they're going to help me sort it out.'

'But—Mum—what will you do for a job when you come back? What about security? I thought that was important to you.'

'I've been secure for nearly forty years, Louise,' Olivia said abruptly. 'And Bob's insurance policy left me well looked after. I'll do something else when I come back. I'm not going to plan that far ahead. For once, I'm going to try to—to wing it.'

'Wing it,' Louise echoed.

'God, Mum!' Rachel rested her chin in her hands and gazed at her mother in admiration. 'I didn't think you had it in you.'

'You mean that you thought I was a wimp!' Olivia blushed.

'No, never.' Rachel took her mother's hand and squeezed it. 'But I knew you were unhappy.'

'Well, I'm not unhappy any more,' Olivia said with quiet certainty. 'I've never been more sure of what I'm doing. It doesn't mean I don't have fears. But I'm going to carry on in this direction now.'

'Bully for you, Mum. It's brilliant.'

'Oh!' Olivia glanced at her watch. 'Look at the time. And I've got one last thing to show you.'

She stood up, her face reddening again, then suddenly slipped her jacket down over her shoulders. Louise squinted at a small, red patch on her mother's upper arm. It looked like a scab.

'You fell over?' she offered.

'It looks disgusting at the moment, I know,' Olivia said. 'But when it all clears up it's going to be a little crescent moon.'

'You've got a tattoo?' Louise emitted faintly. She was prepared to believe anything now. If her mother had suddenly announced that she'd been the sixth Beatle but had never thought to tell them, she would have just nodded.

'Do you think it's tacky?' Olivia gave Rachel a worried look. 'I wanted to know what it felt like. It's—it's sort of symbolic really.'

Louise stood up. She wandered away through the living room, listening to her sister and mother exchanging jokes.

'We'd better hurry up,' Olivia said. 'I'm just dying for Katherine Muff to ask me what I'm doing now. We don't want to be late for my grand entrance, do we?'

Louise sat in the back of the car as they drove into the town. It suited her to sit sulking while her mother and sister chatted at high volume over the gearlever in the front.

'Not just one, but two glamorous escorts!' Olivia exclaimed after she had directed Rachel into the restaurant car park. 'And I'm arriving in a silver BMW. Really, Rachel, you should have dropped us off at the front just in case.'

'I tell you what, I'll drop you two off at the steps, then come back and park the car. Then if Katherine Muff's watching she'll be blown away.'

Rachel swung the car round and veered back to the front of the restaurant. She drew up with a screech of tyres that sent them all flying towards the windscreen.

Louise wrenched open the car door and crawled out into the night. She inhaled cold air into her lungs. Olivia snapped the passenger door closed and tapped spiritedly on the roof. Rachel squealed away, waving a hand at them, and rounded the corner into the car park. Louise heard her mother give a deep sigh. She was patting at her hair and blinking widely into the gloom as if she'd dislodged a contact lens.

'I think my eyes have stuck together. It's this non-stick mascara Sarah made me buy. Let me just sort it out. I don't want them all to think I've got a nervous tic.' She straightened herself. 'Louise, you said you had something to tell me when you came down. Some good news.'

'Oh, it's not important right now, Mum. Maybe later.'

Louise looked at her mother illuminated under the multicoloured bulbs around the door of the restaurant. She watched her fiddle with her handbag, her scarf, the lapels of her coat. Her heart softened. Olivia was extremely nervous, that much was obvious. And she was doing courageous things, wonderful things. She couldn't know that her timing was particularly bad for her youngest daughter.

'Here, Mum,' Louise held out her arm. 'If you want to make an entrance, why don't you grab hold of this.'

Olivia hesitated, then stalked forward in her ankle boots to take Louise's arm. She beamed at her.

Louise kissed her cheek. 'I'm proud of you, Mum. I'm sorry I've been so quiet.'

'It's all right, dear. I know what the problem is,' Olivia said, reorganising her scarf once more.

'You do?'

'That boyfriend of yours.' Olivia nodded. 'Good riddance to bad rubbish, that's what I say. Good Lord, I sound just like Shaun!'

'Who's Shaun, Mum? You mentioned him before.'

'He's a very nice man. I have a feeling he understands me very well. Come on then, shall we trip the light fantastic?'

'Yes, let's.'

Louise stopped as they heard footsteps hurrying towards them in the darkness.

Olivia glanced over her shoulder. 'Is that you, Rachel?'

'Who's that, then?' came an answering, breathless voice. Louise let go of her mother's arm and they turned to examine a woman who was trotting across the road, grabbing at an umbrella.

'It's, er, I'm Olivia. Who's that?'

'Olivia!' The woman reached them, panting uncomfortably. 'Just let me get my breath back. I expect the others are all inside by now. It doesn't do to be late, does it? Public transport's just getting worse, isn't it?'

'We wouldn't know,' Louise entered smoothly on her mother's behalf. 'We were whisked here in a BMW.'

'A BMW?' Louise regretted her boast when she registered the wiry greyness of the woman's hair, blown into chaos by the wind, and the tired look round her eyes. 'Oh, that's nice. This must be your daughter, Olivia. I'm so thrilled to meet you. What a beautiful girl. You must be so proud. And you look wonderful!' the woman said. 'But you always were a beauty, Olivia. I used to be so jealous of you.'

Olivia surprised Louise by suddenly enveloping the woman in a hug. 'Katherine!' Olivia gulped aloud. 'It's so—so wonderful to see you!'

'And you too, but we'd better go in, hadn't we?'

'Katherine Muff?' Louise voiced her surprise aloud.

'Stacey, actually.' Katherine coughed again. 'Well, we mustn't stand out here in the cold.'

'Oh, and here's my other daughter!' Olivia exclaimed, standing back to welcome Rachel as she arrived, jangling her car keys. 'I hope you don't mind me bringing one extra. Rachel, this is Katherine.'

'Katherine Muff?' Rachel raised her eyebrows expressively.

'Stacey,' Katherine corrected.

'Let's go in,' Olivia said quickly, allowing Katherine to plod up the steps ahead of them, and giving both of her daughters long, warning looks before following.

'This is driving me mad,' Rachel whispered to Louise as she dug an elongated spoon into her Strawberry Heaven. Louise bit back a sympathetic smile.

'Never mind. Nearly over.'

But Olivia was enjoying herself. Louise cast her a sideways glance. The sixteen women were seated along a row of narrow mahogany tables that had been pushed together for the occasion.

Katherine Muff was at the far end of the table, engrossed in conversation with a pale woman who was pecking at her bread, despite the fact that they were on dessert. Olivia was opposite a woman called Geraldine, whose eyebrows spread from her eyelids to her hairline, and whose breasts were comfortably resting on the table. Louise sipped her Coke and smiled at her mother's animated profile. She looked fantastic. By far the most vibrant of the women at the table. Louise felt a surge of pride. Her mother had so much to talk about, because so much was happening for her. And it was about time, too. Rachel had been right.

It had been comforting to think that her mother would be there for her. Even while Jon was battling to prove to her that they could make it work as a couple, she had always felt that there was a safety net. If it all went wrong, she could dive back into her old bedroom, baby in tow, and sort herself out. She'd even wondered if her mother might be keen to babysit while she forged her way in a new career. When she made her situation clear, later, when they were alone together, would Olivia abandon her plans and offer to stay? Would it ruin the new life she was charting out for herself?

But if she explained that she and Jon were going to stay together then Olivia would still be free to explore her new ideas. Perhaps that was it, Louise decided, brightening. She should explain that she wasn't relying on her mother for anything, and then they could all be happy about it. Apart from Rachel, of course. Rachel had talked incessantly about Hallam's children on the journey down, and how ill-equipped she felt to be a stepmother. No, there would be no joy on Rachel's behalf.

'We're going to give Katherine a lift home,' Olivia announced to Louise in the lobby. Rachel had gone to get the car.

'We are?' Louise glanced around her. At the door, people were saying goodbye in a much more tactile fashion than they had said hello. She wondered whether the wine had anything to do with that, or whether all of the women had turned up to the reunion gripped by the same fears as her mother.

'Yes,' Olivia said distractedly, grabbing one of her rediscovered friends in a farewell hug and stepping back to look around. 'Ah. Here she is!'

'I can get the train,' Katherine was saying as she crossed the lobby. 'It's very kind of you to offer, Olivia, but it's right out of your way.'

'Nonsense!' Olivia said firmly. 'It's a small detour, and besides, I've hardly had a chance to talk to you all evening. I don't know what you've been doing.'

'Let's get outside,' Louise said, nudging her mother's elbow. 'Rachel won't want to be kept waiting.'

Louise sighed as her mother stopped in her tracks to wait for Katherine. For a moment she'd thought she could get all three of them through the door and down the steps in one fluid motion.

As they made it out onto the porch, Louise hissed into her mother's ear, 'If it takes you this long to get out of a restaurant, how many years is it going to take you to go round the world?'

They jogged through the rain to where Rachel had stopped the car. Louise dived into the back and shuffled her way along the seat. There was a long wait while the rain hammered at the car roof and Louise and Rachel waited for Katherine to stop protesting and get in the front. Finally Olivia pushed her into the seat, closed the door on her, and slipped into the back. Rachel paused with the keys in the ignition.

'Where are we going?'

'Hildenborough,' Olivia said assertively.

Rachel pulled away from the restaurant and out into the traffic in the main road.

'You need to take this fork, Rachel,' Olivia said.

'She knows, Mum,' Louise said quietly. 'You're forgetting, we used to live here too.'

'Oh, you!' Olivia muttered with a hint of annoyance. 'When are you going to stop telling me off, Louise?'

'It's like that, isn't it?' Katherine contributed, settling into her seat. 'It all changes when you get older. My sons tell me off all the time.'

'Oh yes, tell me about your family!' Olivia squeezed her head between the two front seats. 'I'm dying to hear all about them. And about you. What did you do after school? Somebody told me you trained to be a journalist. That must have been exciting.'

'Well, I did some training. I had it all worked out then. I wanted to be a foreign correspondent. Can you imagine that now?' Katherine peered down at herself bleakly. 'But then I got married and the boys came along, and it never really happened how I'd planned it.'

'You were always good at languages,' Olivia said supportively. 'You were always good at everything. I used to think you might be a translator or something.'

'You were good, too,' Katherine said. 'If you hadn't left—'

'Here, Rachel!' Olivia banged Rachel's shoulder. 'The back way's quicker.'

'I speak four languages,' Katherine confirmed. 'But I've never really used them. The boys have travelled. Greg's in Australia now, and Mark went to California. We used to go to France a lot as a family, but that was when Graham was alive. I don't go there any more.'

Rachel drove on into the rain. The roads became narrower.

'Are you sure this is the right way, Mum?'

'Yes, dear, just keep driving. So Graham isn't—isn't with us any more?' Olivia's expression showed that the words hadn't come out quite as she'd intended. Katherine swallowed noisily and gave a small cough.

'He—um. I lost him four years ago. I—'

Katherine startled them by choking back a violent sob. Rachel was so shocked she swerved, mounted a low bank and scraped the car along a hedgerow before bringing them back onto the road again. Olivia sat forward, putting a hand on Katherine's shoulder.

'Slow down, Rachel,' she urged in a low voice.

'Right,' Rachel said. 'Are you all right Mrs Muff?'

'Stacey,' Katherine corrected in a wobbly voice. 'Just call me Katherine, please. I'm all right. I really am sorry.'

She delved into the pocket of her coat and pulled out a handkerchief. Silently, she mopped at her cheeks. Rachel slowed the car to a crawl.

'Rachel?' Their mother's voice was uneven. 'Pull over, please, in the next safe spot.'

'We're in the middle of nowhere, Mum.'

'Find a lay-by or something, and pull the car right off the road.'

The car purred on until they reached the entrance to a field with a five-bar gate set back from the lane. Rachel edged the car off the road.

'Mum?' Rachel whispered.

'Shhh!' Olivia shot her a severe look.

In the warmth and peace of the car, Louise felt as if she was picking up the vibrations coming from Katherine's heaving chest. For several moments, the four women sat, alone with their thoughts. Olivia broke the hush.

'Katherine?' Louise turned to look at Olivia in surprise. Her own mother's voice was trembling, as if she was close to tears. But she hadn't seen her cry since her father had died. 'Do you want to talk about Graham?'

Katherine nodded, pulling her handkerchief away from her face. Louise could see a stream of tears cascading down her chin.

'Nobody lets you talk about it, do they?' Olivia said, struggling with her words. 'Since I lost Bob I haven't been allowed to talk about him to anybody. I can think about him, but I can't let it out.'

'I know!' Katherine turned in her seat and looked back at Olivia. Louise watched her mother's face crumple. Olivia was going to cry, and it wasn't just going to be a dribble of tears.

'Graham was such a lovely man. I loved him so much!' Katherine said in a high voice. 'We used to do everything together. After he retired, we had so many rows. He became so difficult, but I never stopped loving him. He was my companion. And now he's gone and life's so empty.'

Louise clamped her teeth together. If she wasn't careful she was going to cry too. Olivia drew in a deep breath beside her, tried to speak, then let out a long wail. Louise stuffed her hands into her pockets and fumbled for a tissue. Olivia cried into it as if her heart was breaking. Louise glanced quickly at Rachel in the driving mirror. To her shock, Rachel's eyes were brimming.

'I loved Bob,' Olivia gulped, 'and he loved me, too. He was so kind. And I felt so guilty when he died. I still feel so gu-guilty.' She rammed Louise's tissue into her eyes. The two older women cried and cried. Louise closed her eyes and swallowed the hard lump in her throat. From the driver's seat, she could hear Rachel sniffing loudly. She opened one eye in time to see her sister bend her head over the steering wheel and release a long sob.

'I—I'm so s-sorry,' Katherine emitted.

'It's not you,' Olivia wept forcefully. 'It's me.'

'It's me.' Rachel brushed jerkily at her face with her hand. 'I've left Hallam. But I love him. I love him so much. I wish I'd never left him!'

Olivia gripped her daughter's shoulder.

'And—and I'm pregnant!' Louise contributed. Without warning, she too burst into tears.

Olivia moved her hand swiftly from Rachel's shoulder to Louise's knee. She squeezed it until it hurt. Then, as if Louise's words had sunk in, she gathered her youngest daughter into her arms in the back seat and they hugged as if they couldn't let each other go.

The inside of the car suddenly seemed to get brighter. Louise stiffly pulled away from her mother and squinted. Somebody was shining a torch at them from the outside.

'Rachel?' Louise whispered in alarm. Rachel blinked into the torch-light as somebody tapped on the driver's window. She pressed a button and the window dropped with an electronic whine.

'Oh hello, officer,' Rachel swallowed. 'How can we help you?'

'I wondered if everything was all right in here.' Louise could see a uniformed policeman peering into the car. Now she could see the squad car that was parked a few yards up the lane ahead of them. They hadn't heard it drive past or pull over.

The four women nodded at him mutely, stifling sobs. He regarded them for a moment longer in fascination, then flicked off the torch.

'It's not a very safe place to stop, madam. I'd suggest you move on from here.' He paused as they all seemed to choose the same moment to wipe their eyes. 'There's a large lay-by about a mile ahead.'

Rachel nodded and gave him a weak smile.

'Thank you.' She stabbed the button again and the policeman wandered away to his car, which moved off and rounded the corner.

'Well,' Olivia said at last. Katherine made a noise of agreement. Rachel and Louise nodded. Rachel readjusted her seat belt and put the car into gear, dropping the handbrake. She glanced around her.

'Are you really pregnant, Lou?'

'Yes,' Louise admitted.

'Fuck me,' she breathed.

'Language!' Olivia and Katherine interjected as one. Rachel turned back to the wheel.

'Right then. Are we all ready to move on now?'

Chapter Ten

'IT'S JUST SO INCREDIBLE!' Rachel grinned. 'I still can't believe it. Me, an auntie! A real live auntie!'

'It's still incredible to me too, Rach.'

Louise was becoming confused. She was sitting at the kitchen table sipping on a cold glass of water, Rachel was pouring wine into her glass, and Olivia was standing at the kitchen door.

She'd expected to get two contrasting reactions to her announcement. On that count, she'd been dead right. But what was confusing her was that it was her mother who had started to look as if she was sucking lemons while Rachel was bubbling over with excitement.

'But what does it actually *feel* like? I can't imagine it.'

'Well, it's weird. It's not like anything else you've felt before. It's like being a chauffeur. You just drive around wherever you're told to go.'

'I can imagine that.' Rachel looked vague and took Louise's fingers. 'I'm just so sorry I was a cow to you before. I wish you'd told me.'

'I needed time to work it out on my own.' She smiled back at her sister.

Olivia drew an audible breath. 'You surely don't mean you're going to keep it?' she exclaimed.

'Oh yes!' Louise nodded at her forcefully. 'Yes, I am.'

'Louise,' Olivia sat down with them and laid her hands flat on the table. 'I don't think you've thought this through.'

'I have.' Louise folded her arms across her chest.

'It's not as easy as you think,' Olivia said with emphasis. 'Having a child on your own's a terrible thing.'

'Terrible?'

'You'll have no life. You won't be able to go out. Your life will come to a standstill.'

'Mum,' Louise said, biting back her disappointment, 'I've thought about it very carefully. I've got plans and ideas. I don't need you to bail me out. I need your moral support, that's all.'

'I can't give you that!' Olivia looked as if she was going to burst into tears for the second time that night. 'You don't know what you're doing. Goodness, Louise, what's the matter with you? It's not difficult to sort it out these days. Not like it was when I was young. It was illegal then. If you got pregnant you were stuck with it. Single mothers were stigmatised.'

'I—' Louise sought in her confused brain for answers. 'I'm not going to be a single mother. I'm going to stay with Jon.'

'I thought you two had split up?' Olivia looked distressed.

'We did, but we got back together again.' Louise stumbled over her reply. She'd never seen her mother look so overwrought. 'We're going to try to be a family. If that doesn't work out, I'll—'

'You're going to marry him?' Olivia's voice soared. 'Because of the baby?'

'I'm not sure. He wants to marry me anyway, I think.'

Olivia stood up. She paced across the floor, wrenched at the key in the back door and threw it open. A blast of December air assaulted them. She took several short, sharp breaths and closed the door again.

'What are you doing, Mum?' Rachel asked.

'Savouring the big wide world. It's all out there, you know.' She turned round. 'Louise, I can't let you do this.'

'You really can't stop me.'

'I'm telling you that I won't be there for you. You can't rely on me for financial support, or to help you bring up the baby. You can't expect me to play the role of the doting grandmother. I've got my own life to lead now. You just can't be this—this selfish.'

Louise was aware that Rachel was gripping her hand tightly. She squeezed it back. She had an ally, if an unlikely one.

'I don't expect you to do anything, Mum. Nothing's going to change.'

'How can you say that?' Olivia pleaded. 'Everything will change. You'll need me. Jon won't stick by you. I can't leave you all alone with your baby. You'll need somewhere to stay, and a babysitter while you sort your life out. Who else is going to do that for you?'

'You've only met Jon once,' Louise asserted. 'He's changed. He's really happy about this. I owe it to the baby to try.'

'You're talking about marrying a man you don't love!' Olivia protested, waving her hands in agitation. 'You'll spend the rest of your life regretting it. That's if you stay together. And if you don't, you'll be alone with your child anyway. I—I had such hopes for you. For both of you. And look at you. All you seem to want to do is destroy yourselves!'

'That's enough, Mum,' Rachel said in a low voice.

'No, it isn't enough!' Olivia thumped her fist down onto the table. 'You don't understand! I married a man I wasn't in love with. I wasn't in love with him! I stayed with him for years because of you two girls.'

Louise stared. Their mother? Not in love with their father? How could this be?

'What do you mean? Of course you loved him. You've just had too many glasses of hock. You're getting maudlin.'

'I mean I *had* to marry him. Don't you understand?'

'What do you mean, you *had* to?' This was ludicrous.

Rachel sipped her wine without comment.

'Because of her!' Olivia pointed at Rachel. 'Because I was pregnant, and because in those days you had the choice of dying on the table of a backstreet abortionist, or getting married. But it's not the same now. You've got a choice. Why can't you see that? Why can't you take advantage of the way things have changed?'

'You OK, Lou?' It was Rachel's soft voice in her ear. She nodded.

'I just don't understand what's going on.'

'Do you want to go to bed? You look tired.'

Olivia stood up abruptly, marched over to the kettle and waved it in the air.

'Coffee, anyone?' She filled the kettle from the tap and plugged it in. Rachel shook her head woefully at her mother's back.

'Poor Mum,' she said under her breath. 'All these years. It's no wonder you've been so unhappy.'

Olivia collected crockery from the cupboard and crashed the cups onto the saucers. She pulled a handful of teaspoons from a drawer and banged them down on the unit.

'I'm fine,' she sniffed. 'I'm sorry that I had to tell you like that, Rachel. I didn't mean to throw it in your face. I've never regretted having you.' She grabbed at a jar of coffee and yanked off the lid. Louise and Rachel followed the resulting explosion of granules down to the kitchen tiles.

'Mum?' Rachel said softly. 'I knew it all anyway.'

The teaspoons clattered.

'You can't have done,' Olivia said, patting at the side of the kettle to see if it was warm.

'I did. Dad told me.'

'He did?' Olivia played with a teaspoon that catapulted through the air and landed in the sink. She replaced it with another one.

'Yes, he did.'

'When?' Louise's voice was a squeak.

'A long time ago. He made me promise not to tell Mum I knew.'

'Then—then why didn't he tell me? We talked about everything.'

'I know you and Dad were bosom buddies, but this was something that didn't involve you. It was because Mum was depressed at the time, and seeing the doctor. I wanted to know why, and he told me.'

'Depressed?' Louise looked back to her mother for confirmation. 'I don't remember you ever being depressed!'

'That's the advantage of being the youngest,' Rachel explained. 'At the time you were busy drooling over *Starsky and Hutch*. You were too young to notice.'

'Mum?' Louise wanted to run round the room with her hands over her ears, shouting. Olivia didn't answer. She banged open the cupboard and pulled out a packet of biscuits.

'Jammy Dodger, anyone?'

'Mum? Are you going to explain?' Rachel pressed.

'Explain what, dear?'

'You want Lou to do the things you didn't do,' Rachel began. 'When you were in the sixth form at the grammar school you had your life ahead of you. Bright prospects, good qualifications, and supportive parents. But then it went horribly wrong. You left early without a word of explanation to anyone. Suddenly, it was all over.'

'No. I—'

'Your supportive parents threw you out on the street.'

Olivia's face was like chalk.

'My mother didn't understand. Things were different then.'

'You had no choice. You were on your own. You had to marry a brickie.'

'I—'

'She threw you out?' Louise looked at her mother in horror. 'Granny?'

'She was a prize bitch, Lou.' Rachel's black eyes flashed. 'She abandoned Mum when she needed her the most.'

'Oh God.' Olivia put her hands over her face.

'So it's not Mum's fault that she sees the same things happening to you.' Rachel's grip on Louise's hand was so tight it had started to hurt. 'In fact, she's manufacturing the same situation. It's all she knows.'

Louise wanted to rush to her mother and put her arms round her.

'Mum—' She stood up.

'Not now, dear,' Olivia said, taking her hands from her face. 'I—I'll talk to you tomorrow. I'm going to bed now. I need to be on my own.'

'But—'

'You go to bed,' Rachel inserted. 'It's all right, Mum. We're all too tired tonight to think anything through. We'll see you in the morning.'

Olivia nodded. Her eyes were glassy. They watched her drift away as if she was walking through water. The door to the hall clicked and they heard her footsteps as she mounted the stairs.

Rachel emptied the bottle of wine into her glass. Louise had the feeling that she was going to say something meaningful.

'Shall we scoff all the Jammie Dodgers now Mum's gone?'

'Oh, Rach.' Louise lunged towards her and engulfed her in a hug. 'You've been so amazing. I'd never have thought you'd be my champion. What would I have done without you?'

'I just think it's about time we were all honest with each other.' Rachel returned the hug. 'Hey, it's a profound moment, finding out you're going to be an auntie. Probably much, much more profound than knowing you're going to be a mother.'

Louise sank back into her chair and gazed at her sister fondly. She put her hands under her clothes and felt for her stomach. It was an unconscious gesture, but she felt better with the warmth of her fingers over her skin.

'You've been so strong. You're always strong. I don't know how you do it.'

'It happens when you're the eldest. You grow up fast. I'm so happy for you.' Rachel's eyes had dropped to Louise's stomach too. 'And if you get bored, you can off-load it on me.'

'I thought you hated children.'

'I don't hate children at all.' Rachel gave a wobbly smile. 'I love the boys, you know. Hallam kept shutting me out. It's difficult trying to be a good stepmother when nobody will let you in. I've got maternal instincts, too, you know, if only somebody will give me a chance to show them. I should have explained it to him, but I didn't.'

'You're going back to Hallam, then?'

'If he'll have me.'

'You really do love him, don't you?'

Rachel nodded. 'I never realised how much until I left. He's everything I want. I—I think it's really important to be with the man you love, Lou, whatever packaging he comes in.'

'How do you know, though?' Louise frowned. 'You have to weigh it all up, don't you?'

'Nope. You know in the pit of your stomach. I think Mum's right about that. You shouldn't tie yourself to Jon unless you're very sure about him. You might meet someone in the future who you can really love. What would you do if he walked into your life and you were already married, for all the wrong reasons? It'd be a mess. You've got to think about that.'

'Rachel, there was just one thing I was going to ask you.'

'Shoot,' Rachel said.

'It's just about work.' Louise stopped. 'It's, um—'

'There's going to be a temping slot coming up in January in promotions. One of the assistants is leaving, and we usually try out a temp first to see what happens. It'd be up to you to prove yourself, of course, but if you're interested, it'll get your foot in the door. If you can impress the right people you could have a break waiting for you after the baby's born.'

Louise felt a warm rush of pleasure. She hadn't even had to beg, and Rachel wasn't going to make her feel stupid for turning down opportunities in the past.

'But I'd have to be interviewed.'

'Of course.'

'I—I'm not dynamic in the way you are. I wouldn't want them to think they'd got another Rachel Twigg turning up.'

'You'd be treated on your merits along with the rest, Lou. I reckon you'll be fine, though. All you've lacked is motivation. This department would be perfect for you. You've got a good eclectic interest, imagination, and you're a charmer. I think the company will snatch you up.'

'God, it almost sounds as if you like me.'

'Don't push it.'

Louise beamed at her.

'Aren't you going to be smug and unbearable?'

'Nope,' Rachel smiled. 'But I will say it's about bloody time. Music's always been your thing. It's the right career for you.'

'Thanks. This means so much to me.'

'Go to bed now. You look bushed. We can talk about it again when you've had a good night's sleep.'

Louise made her way through the hall and up the stairs. Her mother's door was ajar. She nudged open the door. A shaft of light fell across the flat bedspread. Olivia was sitting at the window, holding open the curtain and looking out at the sky. She seemed to sense somebody was in the room and turned round.

'Oh, Louise. I was just watching the clouds. They fascinate me.'

Louise padded across the carpet and stood behind her mother.

'You never really see the sky in London.'

'That's a shame. I like to see the sky. It's always changing, always moving on to somewhere else.'

Louise kissed the top of her mother's head.

'You'll see a different sky when you travel. It will be wonderful. You'll have to write and tell us all about it.'

'I will.'

'I'm really excited for you, Mum.'

'And I'm excited for you, too, dear. You know when something's right. You can feel it.'

'Yes, you can.'

'I can feel it now, and I think you can too. It was wrong of me to try to tell you what to do.' Olivia's face was concerned. 'I hope you forgive me.'

'Hey, let's say no more about it. Tomorrow we'll start all over again.'

'Louise?'

'Yes, Mum?' She turned at the door.

'I was thinking.' Olivia looked ghostly in the gloom. Like a spirit freeing itself from an earthly body. 'You could stay in the house while I'm away. It—it's a family house really. You and the baby could come here.'

Louise leaned against the door. 'Thanks, Mum. It's nice of you to offer, but it won't be necessary. Good night.'

'Go back in, Mum, you'll freeze out here. It looks as if it's going to snow.'

'I wish you didn't have to leave so early. I was hoping to have you both all day.'

'I know, but if it does snow the traffic's going to be a pig.'

'I understand,' Olivia said regretfully. 'And you're sure you don't want to ring Jon to tell him you're on your way, Louise?'

'God, no!' Louise laughed. 'He's probably sleeping off a hangover.'

'I want to wave you off. I'm not going to see you both until Christmas.'

'Oh, yeah, and that's years away.'

'And you will come down with Hallam and the children if he has them this year, Rachel?'

'If it works out, we'll come down together. I'll ring you and let you know.'

'I thought I might invite a few friends too,' Olivia said hesitantly. 'Just perhaps, you know, from work maybe. And I thought Katherine might like to join us for Christmas dinner. What do you think?'

'You wouldn't be talking about Shaun, would you?' Louise teased as she leaned on the car. Olivia's cheeks went pink.

'Heavens, I don't know what he'll be doing, do I? It's just that he's been so helpful and I feel I should repay him somehow. Come here, sweetheart.' Olivia impulsively cantered forward to hold Louise tightly. 'I'll ring you all the time, and if you need anything you just have to ask.'

'Thanks, Mum, but don't worry. I'll be fine.'

'And you'll be back for Christmas?'

'Of course.'

'And remember the house is yours if you want to stay. You only have to let me know. And use that cheque I've given you for heating. You mustn't be cold, you know.'

'How could I be cold in a brand new pair of slippers and a thermal vest?' Louise widened her eyes.

'They arrived!' Olivia said happily.

'And it took you this long to ask!' Louise laughed. 'You've really surprised me this weekend, Mum. I'm so proud of you.'

'And I'm proud of you, too.' Olivia's eyes misted over. She clutched her younger daughter to her chest.

'Time to go.' Rachel jangled the car keys.

Louise and Rachel chatted sporadically on the journey home. Rachel declared that she was determined to beat the weather, and before Louise could blink they'd sped round the M25 and were near home. Now she had plans, and even bright prospects. Her family understood. And Jon would be waiting for her in her flat.

'Will Hallam be at home when you get there?' Louise asked. Rachel looked for a place to pull over.

'I bloody hope so. I'll be stuck if he isn't. I threw my door keys at him in a fit of self-destruction.'

'If not, I'll put you up.'

'I know. Thanks.'

Louise gathered her bags, kissed Rachel, and waved as the BMW shot out of sight.

She trudged down her front path. She paused with her keys in the air. Should she ring? It was an absurd thought, but she wasn't used to arriving unannounced. With any luck he would still be in bed and she could slip in beside him. A warm cuddle was just what she needed.

She heard a giggle as she was inserting the key and twisting it. It hadn't taken Harris long to find himself another distraction. She pushed the door open. As she did, the giggle came again, very loudly, followed by a male chuckle. The noise had come from inside her own flat.

She came face to face with Jon, as she'd expected, dishevelled in jeans and a half tucked-in shirt. He was sitting astride a woman on the floor, and he was tickling her. It was some moments before Louise had the presence of mind to focus on whoever it was squirming under him. She did so when the woman sat up abruptly, pushing Jon off, and shook back her auburn hair.

It was Sally.

Louise took a moment to absorb the scene completely. She leaned back against the door and gazed at them both. Sally's face was redder than Jon's but the flush over his chin was spreading up to his cheeks.

Louise opened her mouth and closed it again. Sally squatted down quickly to retrieve her hair clasp from the floor and gathering her hair behind her head, snapped it into place. Louise watched her put a finger up to the corner of her lip and wipe the skin there. But Louise hadn't needed to see that small gesture to know that Jon had been kissing her. He had a tiny but visible smear of lipstick just under his mouth.

'Sally came round to see you,' Jon stated, standing up straight now. 'She hasn't been here long. I was going to make her a cup of tea and tell her about our plans. It seems you hadn't got round to telling her about us yet, Lou.'

His expression was an attempt at a playful reprimand, but his eyes were startled. She ignored him and looked back at Sally instead.

'It's true, Louise. You must believe him. I brought the Sunday papers round for you. I wanted to see how you were, and I thought if I rang you might try to put me off. I had no idea you were away. I didn't think Jon would be here, did I?'

Louise felt her pulse rising. It was as if the reaction had been delayed by shock. Now her heart was thumping painfully inside her rib cage, but still the words wouldn't come.

'C'mon, Lou,' said Jon, brushing back his hair in a swift gesture and resuming his appealing stare. 'Don't make more out of this than there is.'

'I'm sorry, Louise,' Sally gushed. She was picking at her clothes, fingering her hair. Her hands were trembling. 'I'm really, really sorry.'

Jon put out a hand and touched Louise's arm.

'Let's not ruin things. Not now.'

'Please remove your hand from my arm,' Louise said breathlessly, her chest starting to heave. She took several short breaths, then found the strength in her legs to move away from the door.

'Which one of you would like to leave first?'

'I will,' Sally mumbled. She turned to Louise as if she wanted to say something else.

'One question, Sal,' Louise managed. 'Is this the first time?'

There was a long pause.

'Yes,' she replied.

'Now go,' Louise said in a whisper.

Sally let herself out. They heard the front door close after her. There was a brief silence in the room. Then Jon erupted.

'For God's sake!' He began to pace round the room. 'This is so like you!'

'And this is so like you,' she replied. Now that Sally had gone she felt calmer. Now at least she only had to deal with one of them.

'Listen—'

'No, *you* listen!' she instructed with such force that he stopped dead in the middle of the room and stared back at her. 'I'm going to go into the kitchen and I'm going to make myself a cup of tea. I want you to gather anything of yours that you can see and leave. I don't expect you to interrupt me, I don't expect you to come into the kitchen for any reason at all.'

'But—'

'No, Jon. That's it. The next sound I expect to hear is the front door closing on your way out. Leave the keys where I can find them.'

She gritted her teeth, determined not to say more. She held his gaze with absolute determination.

She made her way to the kitchen door and pushed her way inside, then stopped. Jon was watching her, his face dejected. His shirt was still loose round his chest, and it occurred to her that he looked puny.

'You're a shit,' she said.

'I know,' he replied.

She closed the door.

'Hallam?' Rachel shivered inside her long coat on the doorstep. 'Can I come in?'

He stood for a moment on the threshold, but then he stepped back and leaned against the wall, kicking open the door. Rachel was shocked at his appearance. His shirt was unbuttoned halfway to his waist, his hair looked as if he hadn't bothered to comb it and there was a distant look in his eyes. For the moment at least, he had abandoned the elegant, poised bearing that had seemed so much a part of him.

She caught the aroma of whisky on his breath as she walked into the hall. He straightened himself and walked away, turning into the living room and leaving Rachel standing in the hall with the front door wide open. She closed it.

At least the boys weren't here this weekend. It was just the two of them. Rachel chewed on her lip. She'd clarified her feelings in her own mind now, but there was a long way to go before she would be able to make him understand. That was if there was a chance that he would forgive her. She took off her coat, draped it over the peg, and walked straight through to the living room. Hallam was crouched on the sofa, a bottle of whisky in one hand. He glanced at her and held out the bottle.

'Want one?'

She shook her head.

'Course not. You're driving, aren't you?' He tossed back the contents of his glass. 'Or are you? Has he given you a lift here?'

'No, I'm on my own.'

'Well, go right ahead.' He cast out an arm. 'Help yourself to what you want. I haven't packed for you. I couldn't bear to do that, but you won't mind doing it yourself, will you? I can't remember exactly who bought what. We should have kept receipts, Rachel. That way there'd be no argument. Oh, what the hell!' He tipped another measure of whisky into his glass. 'Take what you like. I don't give a toss.'

She walked slowly round the coffee table and sat down on the armchair opposite him.

'Hal, I want to talk to you.'

'Fine!' He smiled at her unevenly. 'Tell me all the reasons you're leaving me. I'm waiting.'

Rachel stood up. She clenched her fists. 'Hallam, you're being pathetic.'
He sat back, shocked, and focused on her.

'I am?'

'I said I want to talk to you, and I am going to talk to you.'

'Talk away.' He flung a hand out. 'I can't wait to hear what you've got to say.'

Rachel sat down again. She had never seen him like this. It was daunting. But she had to be honest with herself, and honest with him. For the moment, at least, his attention was on her.

'You've been an insensitive, inconsiderate bastard. You've made assumptions that you never should have made. You never stopped to ask me what I thought, or what I felt.'

'But you,' he said, pointing an unsteady finger at her, 'went off and slept with somebody else. I never did that.'

'I know,' Rachel said, her colour rising. 'And I wish I hadn't. I wish I'd had the courage to be honest with you and tell you why I was so unhappy, but I ran into someone else's arms instead. I can't undo it. At least I told you about it. I wanted to be honest with you.'

He sat back in the cushions, gazing at her. 'Go on.'

'I—' She stood up and clasped her hands together. 'It was because you already had a family. A ready-made one. And you always assumed that I was happy with that. You never stopped to ask what I wanted. You thought the kids got in my way, but they never did. I became fond of them, but you always put yourself between us, as if I had no right to love them too. And it made me doubt everything I'd built up for myself. You thought you knew what I felt, but you never asked.'

He cleared his throat and pushed away the bottle.

'I thought the boys were an irritation to you. I just assumed—'

'That's exactly it!' Rachel cried at him. 'You just assumed, and assumed, and assumed.'

'But you love your job, don't you? I always thought it came above everything else.'

'I do love my job! But I'm a woman too, Hal, don't you see?' She turned to implore him with her eyes.

He stood up. He self-consciously did up a button on his shirt and tucked the tails into his jeans. It was as if he was suddenly aware of how he looked.

'Rachel, I—' His brows were drawn together in concentration. 'The thing is, I was trying to protect you. I thought they got in the way of your work.' He sounded completely sober now. 'I tried to do what I thought you wanted. I thought you disliked children, and that my children from my former marriage would be an intrusion into your life. It's the impression you gave me.'

Rachel tutted with impatience.

'I thought you wanted them all to yourself. I wasn't going to get in your way. I tried to be all the things I thought you liked about me. Independent, free, interesting.'

'And I was trying to be all the things I thought you liked about me. I thought you wanted me to give you space.'

'Well, it looks as if we both got it wrong then, doesn't it?' Rachel snapped at him.

There was a silence. Hallam rubbed his fingers round his chin.

'Does this mean you're not about to walk out? I just need you to warn me so that I know how to feel about this.' He pushed his hand through his hair. 'I've missed you so much and I couldn't believe that it was you at the door. I was so happy to see you.'

'That was you doing happy?' Rachel smirked at him.

'I can—' He cleared his throat noisily. 'I can do a better happy if you like. But first you have to tell me that you're not going to go.'

'I'm not going to go. I'm going to stay here and work this through with you.'

He looked away from her as she spoke. 'And what about the doctor?'

'He's nothing, Hal. He was never the issue. Forget him if you possibly can. I have.' She waited as Hallam walked across the room to the stereo and gazed at their pile of CDs.

'What are you doing?'

He held a finger up to her as he found what he was looking for and slipped it into the machine.

'I know I'm not very good at expressing myself,' he said over his shoulder, his eyes still not meeting hers. 'But I love you, Rachel. I love you very much. I think you should know that.' He pressed a button and walked towards her as the introduction played. She felt her heart melt as she saw the intense look of longing in his eyes. He had played this song for her when they had first fallen in love. If anything, she loved him more now. And he was mouthing the words to her.

'Anything you want, you got it.' He touched her face cautiously.

She drew him into her arms.

'If you ever go silent on me again, I'll nail your testicles to a turntable.'

'Promises, promises!' He lowered his mouth to hers.

Louise saw Sally as soon as she entered the restaurant. She was sitting at a table in the corner with her head in her hands. Louise sat down opposite her. Slowly, Sally raised her head. Her mouth was pale and devoid of lipstick, her cheeks white.

'Louise—'

'Shut up. It's good of you to meet me for lunch, but I haven't come here to listen to you. I've got some things to say. First of all, I've been thinking about this. I know it wasn't the first time, so don't lie to me any more. I've had all day yesterday to think about it, and I've put it together. Your reactions when I talked about Jon, his when I talked about you. There was an undercurrent, something I was too stupid to put my finger on. Even your reactions about the baby were to do with Jon. When you said Jon and I would be tied together for the rest of our lives you were horrified, but not on my behalf. On your own.'

She stopped to take a breath. An Italian waiter offered them menus. Sally didn't move. Louise took them both and gave him a curt smile.

'Can you give us a few minutes alone, please? I'll call you over when we're ready.'

'Certainly.' He departed silently.

'It explains why you didn't want to marry Fergus, and why you seemed to envy me. It explains everything. So can we start from that basis, please? I'm going to leave if you feed me a load of bullshit.'

Sally ran her tongue over her top lip.

'Nothing had ever happened before this weekend,' she said.

Louise smiled sardonically. 'There's not much reason for me to hang around then, is there? I'm not going to have my intelligence insulted any more.'

She stood up. Sally shot out a hand and hung on to her arm.

'I haven't finished, Louise,' she said. 'Sit down.'

She sat down again and laced her fingers together.

'Go on then, Sal. You'd better speak fast.'

'He made a pass at me. Some time ago.' Sally swallowed, her face twitching. 'It was that night we all went out together, a few months ago. We were all drunk. I—I suppose I was quite flattered at the time. But I was shocked too. I've never had a fling, not with anyone who's involved with someone else.'

'It must have been exciting.' Louise gritted her teeth.

'I—you two seemed to be drifting apart. I thought you were better off without him, and I didn't want to hurt you by telling you, although I think he thought I would. Especially after you split up.'

'It would explain why he was so twitchy about you,' Louise said, her heart thumping.

'I haven't been like you, Louise, you see.'

Louise studied Sally's face. She was wearing no make-up at all today. Her eyes were small and pink within her pale skin, her lashes light brown without mascara. She looked like the girl she'd known at school.

'I've always done the sensible thing.' Sally's lips wobbled. She bit them between her teeth. 'You see, I've had problems to deal with too, but I buried them under the surface. I got on with what had to be done. I always did that. Just took the straight line to wherever I was going.'

'And it got a bit boring, did it?' Louise suggested.

'I—the girl at work. The one who had the termination.'

'Yes?' Louise said with feigned interest.

'That was me,' Sally said in a small voice.

'When?'

'About a year ago.'

'Who was the father?'

'Fergus.' Louise raised her eyebrows but said nothing. 'It made sense. I'd just been offered the partnership. He had opportunities in his career. It wasn't the right time.'

Louise didn't want her feelings to soften towards Sally. She hated her for what she'd done. She wanted to throw a punch across the table and knock her flat. But she sat still, turning her words over in her mind.

'I know it was the right thing to do,' Sally went on in a low voice. 'I don't regret it. But it's killed any feelings I had for Fergus. Perhaps if he'd been less sure of what we should do I might have thought about it differently, but it's too late now. I just feel this dreadful sadness. It won't go away. You—you can't know how this feels. I hope you'll never know.'

'And then he asked you to marry him?'

Sally nodded.

'I'm not making excuses, Lou. I don't expect you're ever going to want to see me again after this, and I don't blame you.' It wasn't a question, Louise realised. Sally's voice was devoid of hope. 'On Sunday I think I had a moment of total madness. It was the first time I'd ever done something that broke the rules. I don't know what I was thinking. It was only flirtation. And you have to know that there was a kiss. Just one. Even if you hadn't walked in, I'm sure I wouldn't have let it go further than that. But I know it was still a shitty thing to do to you. I suppose as it was happening I was trying to justify it to myself. I thought of you and Andrew—'

'Hold it right there.' Louise put up a hand. 'Me and Andrew?'

Sally raised her eyes.

'You slept with Andrew. You told me. I'm not even sure now that the baby's Jon's. Are you?'

Louise froze, shocked. She tried to understand what had been going through Sally's mind.

'Two months ago, Sally, when Jon was treating me like a doormat, I went for a drink with Andrew. We went back to my flat, fumbled a bit, then he left.'

Sally sat up straight.

'But you implied—'

'No, that was your imagination working overtime. I felt guilty because I was still theoretically going out with Jon and I'd played with the idea of sleeping with someone else. It never happened.'

'God, Lou. Sorry.'

'So you thought that I could be lying to Jon about all this, presumably because he was my best option.'

'Hell, I just didn't know. I said I'm sorry. I—I understood your confusion better than you think, you see. I've been there. I know how bewildered you become when you're pregnant. You turn into a different person. You can think desperate things.'

'Oh, Sal.' Louise could not keep the sadness from her eyes. 'I thought we knew each other, but we don't at all, do we?'

Sally didn't answer.

'And you didn't tell me when you were in trouble,' Louise went on. 'I wonder why not.'

'I didn't tell anyone apart from Fergus. I just swept it under the carpet. If—if I'd talked to anyone else, they might have influenced me, and I knew what I had to do. I couldn't bear to be distracted.'

Louise considered Sally. She was a wreck. She surprised herself by reaching a hand out across the table.

'C'mon, give me your hand.' Sally cautiously put her hand in Louise's. 'You're a complete bitch, Sally.' Sally looked away. 'I hate you for what you've done.'

'You—you don't love Jon,' Sally said quietly. 'I don't expect you to believe me, but if you'd loved him, it—it never could have happened. I would never come between you and . . .' Her voice tailed away.

'And?'

'And someone you really loved. Or who loved you.'

Louise released Sally's hand. She pushed back her hair and tried to think clearly. 'Will you see Jon again?' she asked directly.

'No. Never. Will—will you?'

Louise gave a humourless laugh. 'That depends on how good a lawyer he gets himself. I don't mean that really. The baby's still his. He'll have rights.'

'But you won't—I mean, you're not going to try to . . .' Sally left her sentence unfinished.

'Have a meaningful relationship with him?' Louise suddenly wanted to laugh. She had felt so relieved when the front door had banged for the last time. She was angry, yes. Furious. But with Sally. Jon seemed unable to stir her emotions any longer.

'I'll take that look as a no,' Sally said, twisting her lips ruefully.

'Absolutely. From now on, I'm on my own. And it feels bloody good, I can tell you.'

Sally looked exhausted, but the corners of her lips twitched into a dry smile. 'That makes two of us, then.'

'You won't be on your own for long, Sal. You'll meet someone. It won't matter about Fergus, and Jon, and all that history then. You'll put it behind you.'

Louise was amazing herself. Where had this munificence come from? She was sitting down to lunch with her best friend, who that weekend had been discovered frolicking on the floor with the man who was supposed to be fathering her family. It was so odd. It wasn't that it didn't matter, because it did, and it would have consequences. No doubt in the future she'd flash back to the shock, the pain and the anger she'd felt. Maybe she'd even think twice about trusting Sally with a boyfriend again. But that could be dealt with. Sally had been trying to prove something to herself. Jon hadn't been relevant to what happened. Louise herself hadn't even been relevant. It had been a way of breaking free of the bonds Sally had created for herself. In one destructive act she had exploded the shroud of pretence they were all hiding under. Louise didn't love Jon. Jon didn't love Louise. The truth of it had always been there, but now it was exposed.

And Sally was still her best friend.

'I'm going to make you suffer for this, Sal.'

A muted light appeared in her friend's eyes.

'You mean you're not going to disown me?'

'I'll let you sweat about that for a bit, but probably not. I need you. And you need me. Men come and go but friendships don't. You're a bloody idiot for trying to throw what we've got away.'

Colour flashed into Sally's cheeks.

'Tell—tell me about your weekend. How was your mother? Is she keeping well?'

Louise tried to keep a straight face, but failed. Sally's voice had been peculiarly polite, as if she was trying to impress Louise with her best behaviour.

149

'Well, let's just say you're not the only one showing signs of lunacy at the moment.' She dropped the façade and grabbed Sally's hand again. 'I've got so much to tell you, and you're just not going to believe any of it.' She glanced at her watch with a sudden thought. 'But how much time have you got? Won't you have to be back at work soon?'

'I'm going to play truant. That'll shock them all, won't it? They'll just have to manage without me this afternoon. I'm going to spend the day trying to win my best friend back instead.'

'Can you do that?'

'Just watch me. You've lasted longer than any job I've had, and I'm not about to let you go now.'

Chapter Eleven

'I LOVE IT UP HERE,' Shaun said, coming to a halt next to a bench. The castle grounds were Olivia's favourite lunchtime venue, especially in the summer, and sometimes in the winter too. Today she had felt the need to get right away from work, away from the town, and climb the twisting pathways which spiralled up the old castle mound. Shaun had been hovering in the office as she was putting on her coat so she'd asked him if he wanted to walk with her.

'So, shall we sit here then?'

'Plenty of benches to choose from,' Shaun noted, pulling his thick jacket round his body. 'We seem to be the only ones braving the weather today.'

'Oh, are you cold?' Olivia looked at him in concern. The tip of his nose was red but he shook his head bravely.

'No. It's nice to be out. With you,' he added in a quiet voice.

Olivia sat down, feeling warmer for his comment.

'Not hungry?' Shaun glanced sideways at her.

'Oh, yes. But first I've got some things to say, Shaun. I wanted to tell you first, before anyone else at work knew.'

'Nothing you do ever surprises me, Olivia.'

She laughed, flattered and pleased by his comment. But she was going to surprise him, she was sure of that.

'No, Shaun. Even with all your insight, I don't think you can antici-
pate this.'

'Ah!' He put up a gloved finger. 'But I've done your chart, remember.
You've got no secrets from me any more.'

'Oh, the chart.' But perhaps that was a good place to start. 'I've got a
confession to make about that. The day that we went to the pub, when I
said it was my birthday?'

'Yes?'

'It wasn't my birthday. I don't know why I let you believe that it was. I
was just in need of some attention, I suppose. But I'm sorry, Shaun. The
chart you did was all wrong. You had the wrong date of birth, you see.'

He took a bite out of his sandwich, and noticing the thickening group
of grey birds around them, crumbled up a large portion of crust and
tossed it out.

'I knew that,' he said.

'You did?'

'Yes. I did the chart for your real date of birth, not the one you gave me.'
She turned to him in astonishment.

'I should have owned up, but I thought you might be offended. You
know, see it as an intrusion of privacy, or something.'

'Good Lord.' She laughed at him. 'I thought I was the one who was
going to surprise you. I underestimated you, obviously.'

'Yes,' he said. 'I think you have, but never mind. The thing is, I notice
everything about you. I have done ever since I joined the team. Your
husband was still alive then but it didn't mean I didn't notice you. I
knew enough to know exactly when your birthday is. I know every
mood you have, every expression your face is capable of.' His voice died
away.

'I—I don't know what to say,' Olivia said, when she could speak
again.

'Don't say anything. I didn't tell you that to embarrass you or to make
you say something back. I know how things are.'

'Thank you, Shaun.' Olivia patted his hand. 'I like you very much too.
You always make me happy. When I think back over my time at work it
has always been you who cheered me up. When Carol was at her worst,
when I thought I couldn't deal with it any more, you'd come into the
office, and before I knew it, it would all be bearable again.'

'But that's not so important any more, is it? You're not going to be
around for much longer anyway, are you? So you won't need me to
cheer you up.'

'How do you know that?'

'You're talking about work in the past tense. My guess is you've got another job.'

'Another job?'

'Well, you've got different clothes and you've changed your hair. You know what they say. When a woman changes her hair, it's not all she's changing.' He nodded at her meaningfully. 'So tell me what's happening.'

'It's not a job, Shaun. I'm going away.'

'Away?'

'I'm going to go abroad for a few months.'

'Really?' His face was a mixture of delight and disbelief.

'Yes. I'm going to stop off at a few places, but by the time I come back I'll have flown around the entire world. Can you imagine that?'

'Gosh. I've been saving all this money to go away myself but you're the one who's gone ahead and done it first.'

'We must be kindred spirits.' She nudged him. He smiled.

'You know—' He jammed his hands in his pockets. 'You don't have to go alone, Olivia. Not if you don't want to.'

'Don't I?'

'No. It's just that—if you wanted a companion. Someone to travel with. You know.'

She let him struggle for a moment longer, but her heart softened towards him.

'I know, Shaun. And it's very kind of you to offer. But I'm not going to be travelling alone.'

'You're not?' His eyes were disturbed as he turned to look properly at her newly cut hair, her animated face. 'Oh I see. I've been dense, then. I'm sorry.'

'I met up with her again recently. It turns out we have a great deal more in common than we thought, so we've decided to go together. I'm going to go away with my old schoolfriend, Katherine.'

'Oh!' Shaun looked entirely relieved. 'Oh. That's nice for you both. Yes, very nice.'

'We'll probably end up murdering each other, but you never know. We might have a lovely time. And then I'll come home, Shaun. When I've been away and visited the places I want to see, I'll come home.'

'Oh, yes. I suppose you will.'

'And when you've travelled, and you've visited the places you want to see, you'll come home again too, won't you?'

'Well, yes. I will.'

'Yes.' Olivia beamed at him. 'And then when we're both at home together again . . .'

He looked at her with hope in his eyes.

'Then you might want to ask me out to dinner. And I might say yes.'

'Oh. Oh, I see.' His cheeks dimpled into a secret smile.

'But that's a while off,' Olivia continued. 'And if you don't mind, I'd still like you to teach me to drive, and I'd love you to come to Christmas dinner with me and my family if you'd like to.'

A squall of wind blasted them both into a shudder, but he turned with confidence and smiled at her. A glow spread from her stomach to warm her whole body. As she looked at him, at the unashamed love in his eyes, the straightness of his lips, his upright demeanour on the low park bench, she wondered why she had never seen him as attractive before. There was nothing to be laughed at in the look he was giving her now. One of discovery, elation and understanding. The sort of look a man gave a woman at the moment when he realised that his feelings were shared. It was rare, and it was to be treasured. She would carry the memory of it with her while she was away and hold it to her heart like a talisman. It would bring her home safely. Back to him.

'Louise?'

Louise turned, but she didn't need to see Ash to know it was him. He hadn't tapped her on the shoulder this time, but had spoken her name softly next to her ear as if to avoid making her jump. She had been loitering next to the Office and Secretarial board, examining the cards with solemn intent and wondering if it was possible that he might appear. She'd been in the Jobcentre nearly all day every day since Jon had left.

'Oh, hello.' She smiled at him.

'Hi. I just saw you there. So I thought I'd say hello.'

Her smile widened. They looked into each other's eyes. Somebody had to say something.

'And what brings you down to the Jobcentre?' she asked. 'Got your Thermos flask, have you?'

'Not today. It's my signing day today. But I shouldn't be signing for much longer, thank God.'

'Really? What's happening then?'

'I—have you got time to talk?' He glanced around as if to confirm that Jon wasn't with her.

'Yes, all the time in the world.'

'Do you want to get a cup of tea?'

'Why not?'

They walked out of the Jobcentre together.

'Shall we go in here?' Ash stopped as they reached the glass front of the greasy spoon. 'We're almost regulars now.'

'It'll do fine.'

They pushed open the door. Louise approached the counter.

'Oh no, I'll get this,' Ash said, patting at the pockets of his jeans as if to work out how much change he had on him.

'No, this is on me,' Louise said.

'No, I'll pay for it.'

'Listen. Why don't we each buy our own? It's simpler that way, isn't it? Neither of us can afford it really.'

She ordered two teas and some toast for them both, and followed Ash over to the table he'd chosen. It was the one next to the window with the ripped plastic seats. She sat down opposite him.

'So!' he said, running his eyes over her. 'You look good. Really good.'

'I do?'

'Yes.' He scrutinised her more closely. 'You've changed something about you. It's not just in your face.'

Louise raised an eyebrow but kept silent. Finally Ash chuckled under his breath.

'It's your hair. You've had a different cut.' He laid his hand on his chest in relief. 'Thank God I worked it out. It's a capital offence not to realise when a woman's had a haircut, isn't it?'

'I think I'd commute your sentence to life imprisonment,' she said. 'But it's nice of you to notice. I did have something done. Not that I paid, of course.'

'Oh, right. Of course. It was a present.' Ash nodded. He gave her a tight smile.

'My friend paid. Sally. You met her, didn't you?'

'The ginger one.'

Louise liked the fact that Ash had referred to Sally as 'the ginger one'.

'I shouldn't have let her pay really, but she insisted. She's being particularly nice to me at the moment.'

'Is she? Why's that then?'

'She snogged my ex-boyfriend.'

Ash put his mug down carefully.

'Your ex-boyfriend?'

'The thing is, I knew what Jon was like but I thought he'd turned over a new leaf. But he hadn't, so now he's gone, and Sally's spending lots of money on me. I don't really need her to do it but I'm emotionally blackmailing her to make sure she never does it again. I'm starting a new job after Christmas, you see. A proper job.'

'Are you?' Ash seemed to be increasingly surprised by Louise's announcements.

'So.' She swallowed her toast. 'What are you doing now?'

'Hang on, Louise. I can't keep up with you.' He laughed and held out a hand. 'It's like this every time I see you. There's always something new. I don't know how you do it. You make me dizzy, you know.'

'It's not as complicated as it sounds.'

'You make me feel boring. It's quite a revelation. I know how my friends have been feeling for years now.'

'Look. I'll explain. I'm staying in my flat. It's big enough, it just needs tarting up. I've talked to the landlord and he says I can give it a lick of paint. I've had a cheque from my old employer and at last some money's come through from signing on which is going to tide me over until I start a new job. See? All sorted. When it's time for the baby to be born I'm going to stay with either Sally, Rachel or my mother until I'm over the birth, then I'm going back to work. Mum will be back from going round the world then.'

'I envy your child, Louise,' Ash said sincerely. 'For what it's worth, I think you'll be a great mother.'

'You really do?' Louise swelled with pride at the thought.

'I really do.'

'Thank you.' Louise beamed at him in gratitude. 'That's the best thing anyone's ever said to me.'

'No problem.' He picked up his mug and drained his tea. 'Well, I'd best be off.'

'But you haven't told me what you're doing.' Louise shot out a hand. She pulled it back again self-consciously. 'I mean, you said you probably wouldn't be signing on for much longer.'

'It's nothing really.'

'Go on.'

'Well, it's just that I've been thinking about things. And I've had to be frank with myself. It was after that last gig.' If Louise hadn't known him better she'd have thought he was blushing. 'It's about stage fright, really.'

'Stage fright.'

'Yes. Pretty prosaic next to what you've been doing, I know. But that's what it boils down to. I'm not a performer.' He played with the handle of his mug. 'If I'm honest, it's probably why I struggled with the band. It's why I've struggled all along with music. I'm not a front man.'

'Oh, I see.' She remembered his pupils, dilated with fear when he'd been about to play at the pub. He'd been terrified, but then he'd gone on to deliver a fantastic performance.

'I know what you're thinking.' He gave a small smile. 'I was all right once I was on stage.'

'I thought you were amazing.'

'But it was miserable. I hated it. Just like I used to hate it when I played in the orchestra.'

'But, Ash, you can't give up music. You're so talented.'

'I'm not going to,' he said. 'I'm thinking of taking a professional qualification so that I can teach in schools. The sort of schools where I can really do some good. Where I can enlighten kids who've never heard the sound of a violin. Where I can bring something good into their lives.'

She rested her chin in her hands, moved by his words. He glanced away from her dismissively.

'I'm being nauseous, I know.'

'I'm not Karen,' she stated boldly. She even held his eyes when he looked at her.

'I know you're not Karen.' He lowered his voice. 'I didn't mean that.'

'But you don't have many people around you who understand how you feel, so you assume I'm going to take the piss out of you.'

'No. I thought you'd be the one person who'd understand.'

'I—well, I wish you luck, Ash. I envy your children.'

He looked up at her, startled.

'What children?'

'The children you're going to teach.' She patted his hand reassuringly. 'Unless you know about any others out there?'

He laughed in an unrestrained way that made her feel happy.

'So!' She buttoned up her coat ready to face the cold. 'We'd better pay for this delectable experience, hadn't we? It looks as if we both have a lot to get on with.'

'Yes, I'd better get back. I've got a student coming later.'

They paid at the counter and wandered outside. The door swung shut behind them. Louise stamped her feet on the pavement to prepare herself for the walk home and glanced up at the sky. She'd told her mother that they never saw the sky in London, but she could see it clearly now, a strip of silver far above the reaches of the leaden buildings lining the road. A soft, cold snowflake landed on her nose. She brushed at it with her finger.

'Odds on for a white Christmas?'

'Well, we can dream, can't we?'

She fumbled in her pockets for her gloves and pulled them on.

'So,' she said.

'So,' Ash echoed. He suddenly enveloped her in his arms. She held her breath as her body was pressed against his. Then he released her. He stood back, rubbing his hands together. 'Well, good luck, Louise. I'm really glad I bumped into you.'

'Yes, and me you. I wanted to thank you for everything you did. You were so kind.'

'It was nothing. It really was . . .' He squinted along the road, as if he had already left her and was several paces away. 'Nothing. See you.'

She watched him walk away. She hadn't meant to, because she'd thought she'd be the one to walk away first, but she'd been wrong. She turned quickly on her heel and walked away too.

She began at a brisk pace, but there were too many people in her way. She slowed down and calmed herself. Then she stopped completely. It was no good, striding around Ealing like this. She had the baby to think of, and she had her own frame of mind to think of, too.

Ash was a lovely man. He would always be a lovely man. She had his phone number, and he had hers. There was no point in them both being strangers to each other. Why should they be? Before too long she would ring him.

She walked on, a smile touching her lips. It would have been unusual to start a relationship with such total honesty. There was nothing they could pretend to each other now. And if there could be no relationship, there was a friendship, one that she would value. It had shown her how things could be, and for that she would always be grateful to him whether he knew it or not.

She turned the corner. Her body was grabbed from behind. She was swivelled round by a pair of strong arms and her lips were crushed with a kiss. It was a kiss that seemed to go on for ever. She opened her eyes in shock. She recognised Ash. She put her arms round his neck to keep her balance. Eventually he released her.

'Jesus!' The minute she was free she slapped his arm in agitation. 'Don't you ever, ever do that to me again, do you hear me? I nearly had a heart attack!'

Ash was grinning at her, a dusting of snow on his head.

'I just wondered if I could walk you home.'

'You said you had a lesson!'

'I lied,' he said without shame.

'Well,' she puffed at him. 'If you're going this way anyway, I suppose you can walk with me.'

'I'm not, but I will.' He offered his elbow to her. She considered it with due care, then threaded her arm through his.

'I wouldn't mind the company. But you shouldn't read anything into it.'

157

'Oh, I won't,' he said. 'I'll just walk back with you, drop you at the door, and be on my merry way.'

'That's right,' she said firmly. They began to walk together. 'Unless,' she added after a few paces, 'you just want a cup of tea to warm up once we get there. And you promise that you're not going to startle me with any more surprise kisses?'

'Sort of promise.'

'That's not good enough.'

'I promise I'll offer to leave after a cup of tea and stay only if you want me to stay, but I can't promise not to kiss you again. How about that?'

'I'll think about it,' Louise said. 'But I'll let you know as we go along. That suit you?'

'I think I can work with that.'

'The thing is, the flat's a bit of a mess and last night I cooked up a huge pan of broccoli. I'm sure the smell's everywhere now, and I haven't had a chance to open the windows so you might think—'

'Louise?'

'Yes?'

'Shut up.'

LINDA TAYLOR

I had arranged to meet Linda Taylor in *Brown's* restaurant, Oxford, not too far from where she lives, and arrived a little early. As I sat waiting for her, I looked closely at every woman who came in—students, mothers of students, businesswomen, tourists. But the moment Linda Taylor entered, I just knew it was her—tall, striking, with an air of fun and frivolity, she couldn't be anyone but the author of *Going Against the Grain*.

As we sat chatting over lunch, Linda told me about how she left school with just O levels, worked for the Foreign Office in Angola and Sri Lanka and then left to head for Japan with the man of her dreams. 'It was a bit daft, really,' she says with a wry smile. 'I gave up everything, and once I had left the Foreign Office I soon realised that I did not have any actual skills. It was a crisis of confidence time and I decided to come back to England and start again.' She studied for A levels and then got a place as a mature student at Harris Manchester College, Oxford, reading Anglo-Saxon English, and received her degree when she was twenty-nine.

'I always wanted to be a writer, though,' she admits. 'For me, it is not so much the use of words but the way the imagination works. I am always

play-acting little scenes in my head and working them into the pages of my novels. It's like when you have an argument with someone and you go away and replay the scene over and over again in your mind and think "I wish I had said that". The next step for me is to write it all down.' Her first novel, *Reading Between the Lines*, published in 1998, was an immediate success, winning the Romantic Novelist Association's New Writer's Award, the WH Smith Fresh Talent Award and making the *Sunday Times* top ten. 'Not bad for a first novel,' she recalls with relish. 'It was all very exciting, but a publishing deal also means more pressure. The plot for my first novel was written on the back of a bank statement, but now I was a fully fledged novelist, I had to be more professional. I was determined not to be predictable and get writer's block with the second novel, but that is exactly what happened. I guess the reason is that you write the first book for yourself, but by the second one you are trying to understand what people liked about the first and trying to repeat it. Once I had realised that was the wrong way to go about it, *Going Against the Grain* emerged.'

So what's next for Linda Taylor? 'Writing more novels and I hope that I will get better and better at them. Writing can be a very solitary occupation, but it is not at all lonely, especially with my cat Fred about! For someone like me, with very diverse interests, being a novelist is just brilliant because is allows me to dip into lots of things and live the fantasy. What more could a girl ask?'

Jane Eastgate

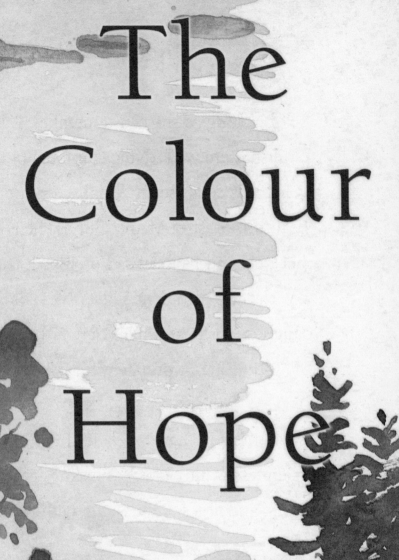

The Colour of Hope

of

Hope

Susan
Madison

For as long as she can remember, Ruth Carter has enjoyed idyllic summers in her family's cedar-scented house on the beautiful coast of Maine. But as she and her husband Paul set sail on a boat trip with their turbulent sixteen-year-old daughter, Josie, and her younger brother Will, they are unprepared for the shock waves of tragedy that will shatter their lives, threaten their love and drag them, relentlessly, into a heart-rending search for life and a desperate battle with death.

One

ALL HER LIFE, Ruth Connelly had feared death by water.

Once, standing as a child at the sea's edge, foam covering her feet, she had been filled with the sudden knowledge of terror, clear and sharp as the knife her parents sliced bread with.

She held their hands, as water heaved away from her and lunged back again, heavy with intent. Wrinkles of water, glinting where the sun caught them. Diamond fingers, beckoning.

Terrified, she tried to move away, out of its reach, but they urged her forward. Go on, don't be frightened, it won't hurt you. Unconvinced, she pulled at their hands but they stepped nearer. It's the sea, the sea, they said in high bright voices, come on, honey, the sea.

Pebbles shifted under her toes. Slippery. Cold. She stumbled and fell. Mommy! Daddy! She heard them, miles above her, laughing. She tried to stand but an unexpected wave slammed into her, green and glassy, determined. Daddy! She screamed again and the sea poured through her, swamped, deluged her. The gasp, the choke, clutching at green, at water which slid through her fingers: she remembered it still, salt stinging in her eyes, burning the back of her throat. She would never forget the purity of her panic, the premature step into adulthood as she sensed something of which she should not yet have been aware.

Death. Oblivion. Nothingness.

You were only under the water for a second, her father soothed, big, jovial, as he swung her up against his chest, it's all right, baby.

It was a second that would last a lifetime.

All her life, she had feared death by water. All her life, she had imagined that the death would be her own.

Standing on Caleb's Point, the low bluff which marked the ocean-most edge of their property, she looked down at the scene of that unforgotten moment. Beyond the fallen boulders was a tiny strip of sand, not even sand, small pebbles really, ground over the centuries to the size of peas. A beach, that was all. Nothing to be frightened of. But all these years later, she still feared the sea. At some instinctual level, she knew that it would destroy her if it could. And yet she loved this place. Up here, with the murmur of the waves, the waving grass, brilliant with devil's paintbrush and field daisies, she found solace. She had come here so often during the years of her growing up. She did the same now, as an adult, a mother, a wife.

The Point pushed out into water dotted with lobster-pot buoys. Arms of green woodland curved round the horizon on either side, trees falling down to narrow shorelines of rocks crushed and scarred by the fierce winter tides. The woods were broken here and there by the shingled roofs of summer cottages. Further out, in the open channel, lay the grey hump of Bertlemy's Isle, a barren piece of granite that rose from the water like a turtle shell, crowned with a stand of spruces. Tomorrow, the four of them would be sailing out there to celebrate Will's fourteenth birthday.

Wind flattened the dry grass of the bluff. Behind her, a granite boulder reared out of the earth. Ruth leaned against it and sighed. It was so peaceful up here. No arguments. No bickering. No tension. Maybe she should get one of the local carpenters to make a bench.

Every time they came up to Maine from the city, she toyed with the idea of suggesting that they move here permanently. Paul already held a part-time visiting professorship down at Bowdoin; he would surely find it easier up here to finish the book he was writing than in the Boston apartment, spacious though that was. The children, it went without saying, would be ecstatic. What held her back were her own needs. She would probably find work with one of the legal firms in Portland or Bar Harbor, but she had worked too hard, for too long, to want to start again at the bottom.

She stared at the distant whale-shapes of Mount Desert Island on the horizon. Triangles of white sail were scattered across the water, heading out to sea from the little yacht club down at Hartsfield. One of them belonged to the children. At her back, higher up the slope, were the pinewoods. Spruce, red and white pine, balsam, hemlock. The hot resin-scented air recalled the simplicity of summer days when she was still just a mother and not a lawyer as well. Picnics under the trees. Hide-and-seek. Swimming in the pond. All the innocent things which, as a child, she had done in this dear and familiar place with her own parents.

Where had it all gone, that security, that sweetness? Time had rushed by, leaving her to wonder what had happened to the chirping voices of her children, to their unconditional love, their trust. The slipperiness of pine needles under her feet, the taste of crab cakes, freshly made whole-meal bread and chocolate brownies. She had been happy then. Glad to subsume ambition in the treasure of her children. Will, with his freckled face and cowlick; Josie, hair tied back in bunches on either side of her head, smiling, adorable in tiny raggedy shorts and a stripy top. They had filled her world. Had *been* her world. Often, overcome by a rush of love, she would squeeze the little creatures close and murmur, 'I love you, I *love* you,' pressing the words into the nutty fragrance of their hair, while they squealed and wriggled and said they loved her too, they would always love her, she was their mommy, she was squeezing too tight, she was *hurting*.

Will had not changed much since then, but Josie had grown so secretive, so distanced from them. She knew this was only to be expected, part of her daughter's reach towards adulthood, something to be endured. But even so, Josie's hostility was hard to live with.

Her spirit sagged. Time to go back into the real world. She took the trail which led down through the woods, past the boulder from which Josie had fallen and torn open a gash above her eyebrow which had required six stitches, across the tree trunk that spanned a shallow ditch. Halfway down the hill the trail forked, one path leading on further into the woods, the other descending sharply towards the house, passing the wild cranberry bog, and the bend towards the freshwater pond, before ending at the rear porch at the back of the house.

The boundaries of their property were wide—though, strictly speaking, it was not *their* property but hers alone, deeded to her on her marriage by her parents, who had retired thankfully to Florida after a lifetime of New England winters. There was hardly a square yard which did not hold special memories of her own childhood and that of her children.

As she came out of the trees, Carter's House stood before her. Foursquare, white clapboard, wrap-around porches, shingled roofs and turrets. It had been built more than 150 years earlier by Ruth's seafaring great-great-grandfather, Josiah Carter, who spent thirty years on the China run before making his final landfall. He had worked his way up from ship's boy to owning his own clipper, probably indulging in more than a little piracy on his way to amassing a considerable fortune. Over the years he had purchased a number of fields and a large acreage of wooded hillside above the little cluster of stores and houses that comprised the village of Sweetharbor; there he built his cedar-lined house and filled it with the spoils of his many voyages. Succeeding generations had cared lovingly for the place. There had been some modernisation, but essentially the house had remained unchanged. Were old Josiah to rise again from beneath the white marble cross that marked his final resting place, he would find his home very much as he had left it, still smelling of cedar, still full of the curiosities he had brought back from distant shores.

 # Two

'I'M NOT COMING tomorrow,' Josie said. 'I have better things to do than go off on some kid's picnic.'

'I'm not a kid,' said Will.

'What kind of better things?' Ruth asked.

Josie looked belligerent. 'I said I'd drop by the Coombs'.'

'Who're they?'

'You wouldn't know them, Mom: they're only year-rounders, not worth your while cosying up to.'

Josie's contemptuous tone was infuriating. 'You're coming with us,' Ruth said shortly.

'Why should I?' Josie had been working on one of her canvasses; there was a smudge of blue oil paint on her face, and more on her fingers. 'Anyway, I've had it with sailing.'

'What do you mean by that? You've been sailing since you were a little girl.'

'Yeah, and now I'm all grown-up, Mom, in case you hadn't noticed.'

'I want you to come with us,' Ruth said. 'It won't be the same without you. Besides, it's your brother's birthday.'

'So what?'

'So he'd like us to take the boat out one last time before we go back to the city.' Ruth began spreading chocolate butter frosting on the cake that Will, with a little help, had made earlier in the afternoon. 'We all would.'

'Not me. I don't care if I never set foot on a boat again.'

'That's nonsense, Josie. You were out sailing yesterday. If you don't come, you'll ruin Will's day.'

Will, the peacemaker, flashed a smile at the two women. 'I'd really like it if you'd come, Josie, but you don't have to.'

Will was always so equable, so reasonable. Like his father used to be, Ruth thought.

'Count me out,' Josie said.

Ruth felt her temper rise. 'That's enough out of you, young lady,' she snapped. 'You're going to come to Will's picnic—and you're going to behave yourself.'

'I'm nearly seventeen: why do you still treat me like a kid?'

'Why do you still behave like one?'

'How come we have to go to the Trotmans' first?'

'Because it's important. Because Ted Trotman has put a lot of business my way. Besides, he's asked someone specially to meet me and he and his wife are driving up from Brunswick. I can't just not show up.'

'Jesus Christ, don't you ever stop sucking up to people like this guy, in the hope of getting business from them? Why do we always have to do *your* stuff, but you never do ours? Like, *we're* supposed to show up at some nerdy party, but *you* couldn't be bothered to come to the school art exhibition last semester, which had no less than *three* of my paintings.'

'I explained why I couldn't come, Josephine. I have a responsible job, I can't just take time off whenever I feel like it.'

'Dad seems to be able to manage it.'

'Dad doesn't have the demands on him that I do.'

'You mean he's not as interested in making money.'

Ruth put down the frosting knife. 'You know as well as I do why I work so hard. It's because I want you two to have—'

'The truth is, we'd rather have you around so we could fuckin' *talk* to you just *sometimes*, just every now and *then*, instead of having all this money piling up in some bank.'

'Mom,' Will said, changing the subject. 'Why can't we live up here all the time?'

'Because we live in the city.'

'But we're year-rounders, really. I mean, Granddad was the local

167

doctor for years. You and Dad are the first Carters—'

'Dad's not a Carter, thank *God*,' said Josie nastily.

'—the first ones not to live up here all the time.'

'First off, although your granddad was the doctor here, we moved down to Boston when I was little. After that, we only summered here, so I don't think we count as year-rounders, especially since your dad's from California. Secondly, your father and I had to go where the work was.'

'You could have found something if you'd really wanted,' said Josie. 'Anyway, I thought the point of coming up here in the summer was to get *away* from work. So you can spend *quality* time with your kids.'

Nobody did contempt like Josie. 'I thought that's what we were doing,' Ruth said, as mildly as she could.

'Except you *so* can't bear to be cut off from your office for even a single day that you have to bring *zillions* of computers and modems with you. And now we've got to hang around while you schmooze with some fat guy because he'll be good for business. I'd have thought you could forget the job just for one day. Will's birthday.'

'To which you've just announced you won't come,' said Ruth.

'I expect I will in the end.' Josie made a face at her brother.

'Which is why, as soon as we decently can, we're going to leave the Trotmans', come back home, pick up the picnic hamper and take the boat out to Bertlemy's.'

Josie stuck out her chin. 'If we go to the Trotmans', you know Dad'll just drink too much. And if he does, we shouldn't be going out sailing, it wouldn't be safe.'

'If we're going out on the boat, obviously your father's not going to drink too much,' Ruth said. 'Anyway, I don't know why you're making such a fuss about going to the Trotmans'. All your friends'll be there.' She scraped the knife against the edge of the bowl. 'You used to enjoy those parties, Josie.'

'That was before I discovered what a *murderer* Ted Trotman is.'

'How do you work that out?'

'All those companies he's on the board of? I bet you don't even *care* that they're all releasing dangerous toxins into the environment.'

Looking at her daughter, Ruth felt a kind of anguish. Under the tan, Josie's face was pinched and there were shadows beneath her eyes. Was her truculence due to something more than her age? Was she, God forbid, experimenting with drugs? With boys? It was hard being adolescent these days. Let me help you, Ruth wanted to say. Tell me about it. I'm your mother.

'Is anything upsetting you?' she said.

'Apart from the mess this country's in, do you mean? Not to mention the rest of the globe.'

'You always seem so uptight.'

'Well, I'm not.' Josie moved restlessly round the kitchen. Her arms were sunburnt, the faded T-shirt she wore clung to rounded breasts. Does she know how heartbreakingly pretty she is? Ruth wondered. And with a pang, thought, Where was I, what meeting was I chairing, when she turned from a girl into this almost-woman?

Josie pulled open a drawer and examined the contents before slamming it shut. Then she tugged it open again.

'Are you looking for something specific?' Ruth asked.

'No.'

'If you want something to do, you could go down in the basement, take the clothes out of the machine and put them into the dryer for me.'

It seemed to be the cue Josie had been waiting for. She turned, leaning against the cooking surface. 'God, I *hate* the way we are,' she said. She pressed her long hair back behind her ears, exposing lobes pierced by a pair of turquoise studs which set off the grey of her eyes.

'What way's that?'

'The way we live.'

Ruth's heart sank. Please, not another argument about the rain forests and tuna fish, both of which Josie seemed to think was personally down to her mother. 'Which particular aspect of it do you have in mind?'

'*All* of it. Do you know how much damage people like you are doing to the environment?'

'People like me, huh?'

'Yeah. Like all that yucky foam in the rivers and on the edge of the ponds? That's because people like you use so much laundry detergent.'

'Josie, if you want to take your clothes down to the creek and beat the hell out of them between two flat stones, feel free. I'm going to go on using modern conveniences because I haven't time not to.'

'You've never got time for *anything*. Why can't we at least hang our clothes out to dry outside, like the year-round people do? The Hechsts, for instance. Or the Cottons.'

Ruth made a face.

'God, you are so *mean*!' screamed Josie. 'Just because Marietta Cotton's a bit slow doesn't mean she isn't just as good a human being as anyone else. And *way* better than some.' She glared at Ruth.

'Did I say that? Did I say anything like that? Feel free to use the clothes line. You'll find some clothes pins in the basement. Or perhaps,' Ruth added, 'you'd rather protect the environment and carve your own.'

SUSAN MADISON

'Yeah, great,' said Will, trying to ease the tension. 'You could sell them, door to door. Like those guys who come round with onions and stuff. Gypsy Josie.'

'Shut up!' Josie yelled, as though she were back in kindergarten, instead of pushing seventeen. Her face went red.

'Shut up yourself.'

'Be *quiet*, both of you.'

Josie folded her arms across her chest. 'The way we live's so artificial. I mean, the people here live *real* lives, close to the land and the water. They're part of it all. Not like *us*, only interested in *money*.'

Ruth had a sudden flash of foreknowledge. Josie at college, rallying her peers round the flag of some unlikely cause. The way Paul used to be. The way she herself used to be. Engaged with life, idealistic. 'Did you say real lives?' she said.

'Yes.'

'I hope you realise that there's more than one reality.'

'As you'll appreciate when you grow up,' put in Will, quoting his grandmother.

'Shut up,' Josie said. She frowned at her mother. 'And there's another thing,' she began.

'I don't want to hear it,' said Ruth.

'See what I mean?' Josie said. 'You never talk to me. Never. Not about anything *real*.'

'Oh Josie . . .' Ruth shook her head. 'That's not true. So why don't you just tell me whatever it is you want to say.'

'You know what it is.' Josie touched her ear studs with long paint-stained fingers. 'I want to leave school.'

'Don't we all?' said Will.

Ruth sighed heavily. 'Not this again, Josie. I've already told you what a ridiculous idea that is. I really can't be bothered to discuss it any further.' Ruth looked at her watch. 'Come along, kids, we've got—'

'I mean it, Mom. *Really*.' Josie's voice rose. 'I want to leave school right now and go to art school instead. I want to paint.'

'She's really good,' Will put in.

Ruth drew a deep, exasperated breath. 'And for the hundredth time, I'm telling you that you don't have the slightest idea how difficult it is to make a living as a painter.'

'Money isn't everything. What about job fulfilment?' Josie straightened. 'Besides, if you took the slightest interest in what I do, if you ever bothered to *look* at my work, you'd know I could make it.'

'There's no way I'm allowing you to leave high school without

170

graduating.' Ruth could feel her own voice rising. 'What you do with your life once you've left home is your business. But while you're in my care, Josephine, the answer's no.'

'Fuck you!' Josie shouted. Kicking one of the chairs as she passed, she slammed out of the kitchen.

Ruth was exhausted by being kept constantly on the defensive. In the office, nobody questioned her, nobody disputed what she said. Who gave this furious feisty adolescent the right to argue all the time?

'Dad'll be back soon,' Will said. He had a smear of frosting on his chin which he was trying to reach with his chocolatey tongue. 'We're going out in the *Lucky Duck*—want to come along?'

'I've got some papers to look at,' said Ruth. 'And some reading to do before we meet this man tomorrow.'

'Sure.'

Ruth said defensively, 'I need to be prepared. Otherwise I would.'

'That's OK. Just thought I'd ask.'

That evening, after another bad-tempered discussion about the sterling qualities shown by the year-rounders, as opposed to the decadent lifestyles of the summer people like her parents, Josie bounced off the couch in the living room. 'You two are so *smug*,' she declared. 'You think you know it all, don't you? You and your rich materialistic friends. None of you ever talk about anything interesting. It's always yak, yak, yak about stupid things like movies and vacations and recipes and stuff. Not about *important* things.'

'Give it a rest, Josie,' Paul said, not looking up from the *New York Times* book pages. 'How would you like it if your mom and I nagged you the way you feel free to nag us?'

'At least the people up here don't just sit about marking student essays. They're making a living from their *hands*. Using their *skills*.'

'And when you finally run away from home to live with the *real* people, as you've threatened to do ever since you could walk, what skill would *you* use, Josephine, if you had to?' Paul asked in a softly reasonable voice intended, Ruth knew, to infuriate.

'I could sell my paintings.'

'Oh yes?' Paul raised his eyebrows.

'And if that didn't work, I could—I could help on the lobster boats.'

'Like they're *really* looking for extra crew,' said Will sarcastically.

Josie flushed. 'At least I wouldn't be working in a fucking bank or selling stocks and shares, for God's sake. Or poisoning the environment. Or tearing up the rain forests with a fucking bulldozer.'

'Moderate your language, Josephine.'

'Dad used to make those neat wooden bowls and boxes and stuff, didn't you, Dad? That's pretty real,' put in Will.

'He gave that up years ago. Anyway, he wasn't trying to live off it. It was just a stupid *hobby*.'

'Not that stupid,' said Ruth. 'He was really good at it.'

'And *I'm* really good at painting.'

'Not that again,' Ruth said sharply.

'Not what?' Paul asked.

'Your daughter has decided she wants to leave school right this minute and set up as an artist.'

'I could do it, too,' said Josie, 'if you'd let me.'

'Uh-uh.' Paul shook his head.

'You two make me *sick*.' Josie turned round and flounced out of the room, managing to catch with her bare foot the base of one of the two Chinese porcelain vases that stood on either side of the door. It toppled against the wall and then rolled down onto the broad pine planking; although it did not smash, a large triangular chip broke from the rim.

'Josie!' Ruth was furious. She picked up the chip and ran her finger across the ragged edge. '*Damn* it. Can't you be more careful?'

Josie walked away without responding. Ruth ran out into the hall to find her halfway up the stairs. 'Josephine!' she shouted.

The girl stopped, one hand on the banister. Her shoulder blades were defiant. She did not look round. 'What?'

'Get back here this minute,' Ruth said.

'Why?'

'You know why. The very least you could do is apologise.'

'Sorr-ee, Moth-er,' Josie said, with singsong insolence.

Ruth bounded up the stairs faster than she would have thought possible, and grabbed hold of her. 'How dare you speak to me like that? Especially after damaging my property through your own sheer bloody-minded carelessness.' A bubble of her spit landed on the girl's cheek.

Josie rubbed at it, smiling contemptuously. 'That's the trouble with this family,' she said. 'Objects matter more than people.'

'As so often, you're talking crap.'

'Am I?'

Ruth stared at her. Josie's eyes were blank with hostility. Ruth opened her mouth to argue, then closed it. The wall between them seemed all of a sudden too high for her to climb.

She let go of her daughter and turned on the stair. 'It's not because it's an *object* that I'm upset,' she said wearily. 'What bothers me is that it's that particular object. Great-Great-Grandfather Carter brought it back in his boat all the way from China. It's been here as long as the house.'

'I said I was fucking sorry, didn't I?'

Paul came into the hall with the newspaper in his hand. He stared up at the two of them over his reading glasses. 'Don't use language like that to your mother, Josephine,' he said. 'Can't you see it's not the vase she regrets? It's the way you've violated the spirit of the house.'

'The *spirit of the house*?' sneered Josie.

'That's what I said. Now, apologise to your mother.'

Both her parents could see Josie contemplating further belligerence before she eventually decided to mutter an ungracious apology. Then she marched on up to her room.

'Jeez,' Paul said, staring after her. 'What did we do to deserve this?'

Ruth was grateful for his support. These days she felt she seldom had it. A rush of affection swelled inside her. She put her hand on his arm. 'Thank you, darling,' she said.

He patted her hand absently.

'Do you think I should give up my job?' she said suddenly.

'Get real, Ruth. You'd hate that.'

Ruth was reluctant to admit it. 'I don't know . . .'

'The time when they really needed you is long gone.'

'I suppose so, but—'

'And let's face it,' Paul said dispassionately, 'the money you make keeps us in the style we've grown accustomed to. God knows, my salary doesn't come anywhere near yours. Besides, don't you think it's a bit late now for you to go back to being a mommy?'

It was one of those rare Maine days when the temperature hits the nineties, and everyone in the Trotmans' garden was bathed in a light sheen of sweat. This was the last party of the season: tomorrow the vacationers and summer visitors would begin heading back to New York City, Boston and Philadelphia. School would be starting, university semesters getting under way. Most of the people with cottages up here had already begun packing them up for the winter.

Although the weather would not deteriorate for a while longer, and there were families who would continue to spend weekends up here before winter gripped the state, the party had a nostalgic air. People, all of them from away—Ruth was not sure the Trotmans knew any of the year-rounders—drifted languidly across the well-watered lawns.

'Ruth! I've been looking for you.'

She fixed a smile to her face and turned. Ted Trotman, dapper in madras shorts and a polo shirt, was coming towards her, accompanied by an older man. 'Ted,' she said warmly. 'Wonderful party.'

'I want you to meet Phil Lavelle, who's driven up from Brunswick specially to meet you.'

'Hi.' Ruth put out her hand and shook the beefy paw which Lavelle extended.

'Ted's been talking you up a storm,' he said.

'With good reason.' Ruth eased back her shoulders, knowing she looked good in her beige linen shorts and navy halter top.

'I'll leave you two together.' Trotman patted Lavelle on the shoulder. 'Watch out for her, Phil: she's as sharp as an ice pick.'

'So.' Lavelle hoisted a plump buttock onto the deck rail. 'Ted's obviously hooked.'

'He gives us a lot of business.'

'Persuade me that I should, too. For a start, what do you think your firm can do for me that the others can't?'

'You probably have a pretty good idea already, or we wouldn't be talking,' Ruth said. 'There's a lot of companies out there, but our particular strength lies in helping corporate clients at a turning point in their development, assisting them to identify market position and to form strategic alliances.'

The heat was getting to Lavelle. Sweat rolled down his face and gathered in the folds of his neck. 'Any firm touting for new accounts would say the same. But what can Landers Keech Millsom do for *me*?'

'For a start, we aren't generalists,' Ruth said. She loved moments like this, playing the mark, reeling him in. 'We specialise in mergers and acquisitions, debt refinancing, contract negotiations, real estate development.' She looked at him shrewdly, persuasive and in control. For another ten minutes, she outlined a strategy. By the time their glasses were empty, Lavelle was sold. When they shook hands he told her that he would phone to make a lunch date.

Ruth stood looking at the crowd of guests. Conversational snatches from the grass below reached her in bursts, like the sound of a warning buoy, now close by, now far away. Her mission accomplished, they were now free to go. Automatically, she checked on her family. Will was playing Frisbee with Ed Stein and one of the Trotmans' golden retrievers. Josie was standing with her friends Chris and Shauna. When she moved her head, responding to something Chris had said, the sun caught the shining highlights of her hair, somewhere between clear honey and maple syrup.

In spite of herself, Ruth smiled, remembering a rare moment of empathy with her daughter. Last fall, Josie had dyed her hair a raw bright orange. Running out of the bathroom, she had collapsed dramatically against the kitchen table. 'I can't go to school like this,' she said, her voice throbbing with self-pity. 'I'd rather *die*.'

Ruth, knowing that she must treat this as the tragedy it was, had soothed and comforted, and, eventually, had gone down to the nearest drugstore to buy another shade of hair dye nearer Josie's natural colour.

The next day Josie had come back from school carrying a sheaf of white freesias. 'Thanks, Mom,' she had said.

'They're beautiful, Josie.' Ruth had admired the delicate white blooms on their thin green stems.

'They're my absolute favourite flower.' Josie had stroked one, sniffed the overwhelming fragrance. 'Don't they smell fantastic?'

'Just wonderful.' Ruth had hugged her. 'Thank you, sweetheart.'

As Ruth recalled the moment, Josie looked up and caught her mother's eye. She scowled and turned away. Don't do that, Ruth wanted to call. You cannot imagine how much that hurts. She longed to bridge the gap that lay between them, but the task seemed beyond her.

Standing in the shade of a juniper tree, Paul watched his wife. A classy lady. He'd always thought so, from the first time he saw her walking across College Green, her books clutched to her chest, laughing with a friend, glancing sideways at him, catching his eye. Catching his heart.

He wiped his forehead. Jeez, it was hot. He wondered if Ruth had impressed the fat little man from Boston. Lavelle, was that his name? She was good, no question about it. No wonder Bob Landers kept promoting her, telling her how much the firm valued her.

Chris Kauffman strolled into sight. He looked up at Ruth and the side of his mouth lifted briefly as she caught his eye. They'd become lovers for a brief few weeks last summer, both of them left temporarily spouseless in the city. Several people had made sure Paul knew about it. He had never let on that he knew about Ruth's affair. He guessed it would mortify her, perhaps even precipitate some action on her part which he was not prepared to accept. Besides, there'd been a couple of episodes on his side, too. He was not going to stand in judgment on her. They got along at least as well as most of their friends, and considerably better than many.

A pleasant alcoholic blur sat inside his head. Lovely day. Reasonable job. Pretty wife. Beautiful children, even if Josie was sometimes a pain in the butt. On the whole, a good life. He pushed himself away from the tree. Time to get another drink.

Three

RUTH STOWED thick sweaters in a duffle bag. In the cooler she packed the birthday food she had prepared for Will, who had fairly sophisticated tastes: cocktail sausages, chicken legs baked in satay sauce, cold cooked lobsters, a ginger-and-lime dressing for the avocado. She added local raspberries, a bottle of chilled wine, cans of Diet Pepsi and Tango. Finally she slipped the chocolate cake into a container.

Josie came in and flung herself around the kitchen. 'You don't like me much, do you?' she said suddenly.

The words pierced Ruth. 'What a terrible thing to say.'

'I saw the way you looked at me, when we were at the Trotmans'.'

'And I saw the way you looked at *me*,' said Ruth. 'As if you hated me.'

'Maybe I do.'

Ruth gripped the cooler tightly, suddenly close to tears. 'Why, Josie? Why would you hate me? What have I done?'

'It's more what you haven't done,' muttered Josie.

Ruth shook her head. 'Well, I don't hate you.' She held out her arms. If only Josie would run into them, the way she used to. 'I *love* you.'

'Yeah. Sure.'

Ignored, Ruth let her arms drop. Yet Josie was right, she did not *like* Josie much. Not the alienated Josie she had been this summer. It makes no difference, she wanted to say, love is the important thing, and the love was still there. The liking was only in abeyance until the former Josie came back from wherever she had been. But she did not say it.

'Would you love me whatever I did?' Josie asked. 'Would you love me no matter *what*?'

'Of course I would. You don't turn love on and off.' What on earth was Josie about to come out with? Could she be—oh Lord, no—pregnant? Was she trying to explain why she was so much at odds with her family this summer? In her ears glinted the earrings Ruth had bought for her last Christmas, small silver rectangles with a copper heart set in the middle. Was it a signal of some kind, that she should have chosen to wear those particular earrings? And if so, what was the message?

'If you didn't love me, I wouldn't blame you,' Josie said. 'Parents get stuck with their kids, don't they? The same way children don't get to choose their parents. Just because they live in the same house doesn't mean they have to like or love each other, does it?'

'I can't speak for how you feel about me.' Ruth tried not to show her hurt. 'I can only assure you that I—and your father—love you and Will more than we can possibly say.'

'You'd give your life for Will, wouldn't you?'

'Of course.'

'Would you give your life for me?'

'Of *course* I would.' Ruth stared at Josie. Trying to lighten the conversation, she added, 'Why do you ask?'

'Oh.' Josie shrugged. 'No reason.'

The angle of light slanting over the trees already spoke of autumn. Although it was still warm on land, it would be chilly out on the water. The motionless heat had given way to sudden gusts of wind that were catching the cedars and hemlocks up on the hill. Rain was on the way.

The sea was her enemy; it would destroy her if it could. Knowing that unless fear was conquered, it would consume, at college Ruth had made herself learn to swim, and found that the containment of a swimming pool somehow eased her terrors. Nonetheless, as they walked in single file along the catwalk, Ruth felt the old anxieties surge. It was safe enough here, close to shore, but once they left the confines of the land-encircled water, the sea would have her at its mercy.

The children's Beetle Cat bobbed restlessly on the water as they climbed aboard the *Lucky Duck*, the thirty-five-foot, wooden-hulled sloop Paul had bought ten years earlier.

Ruth shaded her eyes against the sun and looked apprehensively up at the sky. 'You don't think the wind's going to get any stronger, do you?'

'Don't worry, darling.' Paul put his arm round her shoulders. 'The worst we'll get is a bit of a blow.'

'Which is fun, right?' Will said, reaching for the cooler and the picnic basket. 'It's a perfect day for sailing, isn't it, Dad?'

'You bet.' Paul tripped over a rough plank in the pontoon. 'Absolutely.'

'OK.' Once she and Paul had become engaged, Ruth had forced herself to crew for him, but she was always going to be a fair-weather sailor.

As they cast off, Josie produced her Walkman and slipped the earphones over her head, blotting her family out in a manner which proclaimed she was only here because she had been forced to come. Ruth wanted to tear them off. Tell her to stop behaving like a spoilt child. To grow up. What held her back was the wry knowledge that growing up was exactly what Josie was, in her own awkward way, trying to do.

They got up a fair speed once they reached open water. Sunshine glittered along the ridged surface of the sea, blue-grey under the bow. Ruth sat back in the cockpit with her eyes closed, listening as Paul and Will discussed tactics for tomorrow morning's race. 'If we come in the first three,' Paul said, 'I'll be happy.'

'I want to do better than that,' said Will. 'Last race of the summer, Dad. You and me, we gotta really go for it.'

Ruth smiled sleepily, warmed by the fine salt-flavoured air. Below her, the water chuckled and splashed against the hull. The sun was hot on her shoulders. This was how it should always be. Just like this.

'**W**e'd better get going,' Paul said. The weather had taken a sharp downturn, and out to sea the water was unpleasantly choppy. Thunderheads were piling up along the horizon; the sky had turned the dark purplish colour which announced an approaching storm. Nothing very unusual for this time of the year, but nonetheless it would be best if they reached land before it broke.

'OK.' Will started packing away the remains of the food. 'Great picnic, Mom,' he said. 'Thanks.' He and Josie stowed the stuff in the flat-bottomed dinghy which they had used to row ashore. Small waves slapped ill-temperedly at the sides of the craft and set it rocking. Already water was breaking high up the shallow beach.

Getting into the dingy, Ruth felt vulnerable. The sea was so much closer, it had only to reach out and grab hold of her.

Paul waded in waist-deep and shoved them off and then scrambled in over the stern. The two children rowed the dinghy to the sloop, anchored a hundred yards offshore. On the highest part of the coast, the lighthouse above Sweetharbor stood like a white finger against the swollen clouds.

Even as they prepared to cast off, the gusting wind changed again. Standing at the wheel, Paul cursed as it blew straight off the land towards them. The squall was closer now, and the spruces which crowned Bertlemy's Isle were whipping frantically to and fro.

Paul spoke, his voice calm. 'OK, crew. First thing we're gonna do is shorten the sail.'

'Right.' Will grinned, peering down at the water racing past the hull.

'Put your safety harness on first. You too, Josie. We'll set the small jib and put two reefs in the mainsail. After that, I want you to check the halyards and sheets, make sure they're free to run.'

'Aye, aye, sir.'

Paul spoke to Ruth without taking his eyes off the weather. 'Ruth, go below and make sure everything's secured.'

'Fine.' It was a struggle for Ruth to match his calmness. Having checked that there was nothing loose in the cabin, she stood on the bottom step and looked forward across the deck to where Josie and Will were struggling to control the huge folds of sail whipping about them. It began to rain, blinding sheets of water flying horizontal to the sea.

With the sails set, the children clambered back into the cockpit, sliding their safety harnesses along the jackstay. Josie took the wheel while Paul went up on the foredeck and got the anchor up. The chain rattled; at the same time, a clap of thunder seemed to split the heavens in two.

'Watch out!' Paul yelled suddenly and the boat heeled over, the lee rail almost submerged. Ruth ducked down again into the cabin, only to hear, over the buffeting wind, Paul yelling for her to come up. 'Bring the life jackets, too, while you're down there,' he commanded.

'Life jackets?' Her eyes widened with panic. 'Oh, my God, Paul, what does—'

'We should have put them on before we left Bertlemy's,' he interrupted. 'Always best to wear them. It doesn't mean anything.'

Ruth fastened her own life jacket and brought the other three up into the cockpit. In the short time she had been below, the afternoon had undergone a transformation. Overhead, the clouds were now the colour of a wet coalface, and visibility was down to no more than a few yards. Whitecaps rolled relentlessly across the sea, each one slamming against the hull, tossing the boat around as if it were made of paper. Soaked through, Paul and the children fought their way into their life jackets against the rolling pitch of the boat.

'OK, the anchor's up,' Paul said. 'Let's do it.'

Wind filled the sail as he sheeted it in. As they moved off, Ruth took the wheel, feeling the deck buck beneath her feet. Spray from an oncoming wave slapped across her face and sloshed into the cockpit, covering her, but she forced herself to stay calm, told herself that this was nothing to worry about. Below her feet, the sea sucked greedily at the boat.

'The wind's still straight off the shore,' said Paul, after a while. 'Even if we try tacking, we're not going to go anywhere. I'll put the engine on. We'll have to motor-sail home.'

He turned the key in the ignition. The engine coughed, sputtered, died. He tried again. Again it died. He muttered something about the line being blocked. Ruth fought rising panic: she knew that there was always a lot of crud in the bottom of the fuel tank and in this sea it had probably been shaken around. He tried once more and this time the engine caught.

Ruth could see he was relieved. Moving closer to him, she caught the smell of wine on his breath. The hysteria she had been trying to batten down took over. 'Jesus, Paul,' she said angrily, keeping her voice low. 'How much have you had to drink?'

'Only some of the wine you packed, to drink to Will's health.' He kept his eyes on the horizon as the rain flattened his hair.

'Some? Most of the bottle, if we're being honest here. How much at the Trotmans'?'

'Not a lot.' He grinned, face roughened by the fierce wind. 'But they do make awful strong martinis.'

The boat heeled violently to port, and all four of them grabbed on to anything solid they could find. 'Clip on, kids!' Paul shouted at the children, and added brusquely to Ruth, 'You too. And watch out for the boom. The last thing we want is you getting knocked overboard.'

They motored for a while, parallel with the coast. Through the drumming rain, Ruth could see the green wooded shoreline and the white stub of the lighthouse, so close she could almost have reached out and touched it. Behind them, the distant trees on Bertlemy's had disappeared from sight. The sky was night-time dark. Over to starboard, Ruth saw the lights of a lobster boat. 'Look,' she said excitedly. 'Couldn't we attract their attention?'

'What the hell for?'

'They could give us a tow in or something.'

'For God's sake, woman. We don't need a tow,' Paul said. 'And will you, for Pete's sake, let go of my fucking arm.' He shook her off violently.

Ruth was cold and wet and frightened. 'Don't talk to me like that!' she yelled. 'You bring us out here when you're completely smashed and—'

'Shut up! Shut up!' Josie screamed at them. 'Can't you two stop quarrelling for even five minutes?' Her face, screwed up against the rain, was full of animosity.

Exasperated, Ruth turned on her. 'Shut up yourself!' she shouted. 'You self-righteous little prig.'

'You make me sick,' Josie said. The hostility in her gaze was chilling.

Ruth knew from experience that the seamanlike thing to do would be to head further out to sea and ride the storm out there. She knew too that without her, that was unquestionably what Paul would have done. But she could not stop her mouth going slack with fear when he suggested it. 'No!' she said. 'For God's sake, let's get home.'

'We'll have a hard time, with the wind dead on the nose like this. The best thing we can do is either ride out the weather or head round the coast a bit to Ellsport.'

Ruth kept her eyes on the wheel. If she looked at the sea, she would be paralysed by the sight of those angry, hungry waves. 'Why Ellsport?'

'The harbour there faces northeast, which means we could make some use of the wind.'

As he spoke, the boat smacked heavily into the space on the far side of a wave and Ruth screamed, clapping her hands to her mouth.

Will took her hand. 'It's OK, Mom,' he said. 'We're gonna be OK. It's not nearly as bad as you think, is it, Dad?'

'It's just a bit of a blow, that's all,' Paul said. 'Happens all the time in these waters.'

'Why don't we put out to sea?' the boy asked. He had been sailing since he was a baby and was not frightened by anything. 'Wait it out.'

'I already said we should. But your mom apparently knows best and thinks we should head for shore . . .'

'You're the skipper, Dad,' Josie said. 'We should do what *you* think's best—which everyone except Mom knows is putting out to sea.'

Ruth longed to give in to her terror. She wanted to scream at them to get her home, get her off this quivering, heaving, vessel. 'I'd . . .' Her lips were trembling. 'I'd rather get back, if we can.'

'Then Ellsport it'll have to be,' Paul said. Shouldering Ruth aside, he took the wheel, bore away to starboard and began heading parallel to the shore up the coast towards the next harbour. For a while, with the wind on the beam, they motored in comparative quiet.

There was a sudden clunking sound from somewhere under the boat. The engine stopped dead. Without power, the boat veered round and the fierce weather caught it again, throwing it from side to side. Each crashing wave seemed higher than the previous one.

'What the hell was that?' Paul said.

'There's some netting floating about,' Josie called out, hanging out over the stern.

'Shit.' Ruth watched Paul steady himself with a hand on Josie's shoulder. The boat wallowed heavily, clumsy as a walrus, and he clenched his fists with frustration. 'Damn it all to hell! We've got something wrapped round the propeller. Which means the engine's fucked.'

'Can it be fixed?'

'Only by going over the side. Not something I fancy doing in these conditions.'

'So what now?'

Paul glanced up at the sail. 'I don't know.'

'You don't *know*? Jesus, Paul, you're supposed to be the expert.'

'Shut the hell up, Ruth.' Paul turned away from his wife and spoke to the children. 'What do you think, kids? More sail?'

'Wind's awful strong,' Josie said.

'Unless we head out to sea,' said Will.

They all stared at Ruth. Tears gathered in her eyes and mingled with the rain. She felt excluded by the other three. The sky overhead was the colour of night. Clouds hung above the trees on shore, only a few hundred yards away. Lights twinkled on the low bluffs. It looked so comforting. So safe. She wanted to be there. Fighting for self-control, she wiped surreptitiously at her eyes.

'Dad,' Will said suddenly. 'We're getting kind of close in to shore.'

They had been drifting with the current. Paul glanced overboard. 'Christ! You're right. *Much* too close. Jesus!'

Under these relatively shallow waters was a whole slew of hidden rocks and shoals. As though to prove it, there was a second thunk beneath them, much more severe than the last. All four were thrown heavily forward against the cabin bulkhead.

Josie screamed, clutching at her left arm. 'My wrist!' Her face screwed up with pain. 'Mom! I think it's broken.'

'Hang on,' Paul said. There was a split second of uneasy quiet and then, somewhere beneath the boat, a noise like a giant chewing glass began down in the bilges. The boat groaned.

'Paul!' Ruth felt numb. As she moved towards Josie, the cold rain drove against her face, forced itself down her throat. 'What's that noise?'

'Sounds like we've been holed,' Paul said, his voice unnaturally calm.

Josie was sobbing. 'My wrist, it really hurts.'

'Don't worry, Josie,' Ruth said shakily to the chalky smudge of her daughter's face. 'It'll be OK.' She did not believe it. What were they going to do if the boat capsized?

With every wave, the boat reared several feet out of the water and smashed down again with a splintering sound. Water was pouring into the cabin with each shuddering crash of wave against keel. There was a mighty crack as the mast suddenly snapped off and disappeared over the side, dragging the sails with it.

'We're sinking!' Ruth screamed. Her knees faded under her. She tasted salt at the back of her throat. This was the end, then. They were going to drown. My children, she thought. My darlings. The sense of anticipated loss was unbearable.

'Oh God,' Paul moaned. 'My beautiful boat.'

'Guess that's us out of the race tomorrow,' said Will. 'What now, Dad?'

'Best get into the dinghy, son. We need to get away from these rocks.'
Paul pushed Ruth roughly towards the rear of the cockpit. He ordered Will to climb down the ladder into the little boat and motioned Josie after him.

'I can't, Dad,' Josie said. She was holding her injured wrist at an odd angle against her chest. It took much longer to lower her down than seemed reasonable. All the time, the sea hammered at the hull, demanding entrance, demanding sacrifice.

'I'll give you a hand,' Paul told Ruth. His eyes were cold and condemning. This is your fault, they seemed to be saying.

Ruth tried to follow Paul's orders. Standing with one leg over the stern-rail, she saw her children below, their white faces upturned in the near-dark. Will was reaching up for her. Below, the tiny craft pitched about on the black water which foamed and crashed around it. Fear locked Ruth's legs to the rail. 'I can't,' she said.

Paul was behind her. 'Take my hand,' he said.

The sea reached up towards her. 'I can't.' Terror had trapped the breath in her throat. 'I *can't*, Paul.'

'Ruth, get a grip, will you? We don't have much time.' He reached into his back pocket and brought out his mobile phone. '*Do* it, Ruth.'

The boat lurched. Paul pushed her and screaming, Ruth fell towards the sea before landing awkwardly in the bottom of the dinghy, banging her head against the side. Will put his arms round her. She felt his cheek against hers and his breath warming her neck.

Ruth saw Paul drop towards them and scramble to untie the painter. The dinghy swirled away into the gloom. A mighty wave suddenly swelled out of the black sea and caught the underside of the dinghy, lifting it so that it stood almost perpendicular, tipping them out in a tangle, thrusting them down under the surface. Ruth heard Josie's shriek of agony as the force of the water caught her damaged wrist.

Ruth's head was full of blinding pain. As she broke the surface and snatched in some air, the sea rushed into her mouth, choking her. She closed her throat against it, forced it out again. She could see neither of her children. Where were they? 'Will!' she shrieked. 'Will! Will!' Frantically she reached out, felt something under her fingertips. The webbing of Will's safety harness. She pulled it close. 'Will. Thank God.'

Paul was beside her, his hand strong over hers. 'The Coast Guard . . . I managed to get through . . .' he shouted above the noise of the water. 'They're on their way.'

They heard another scream. 'Dad! Mom! Help me! I can't hold on . . .'
In the near-dark, Ruth could see her daughter's terrified face, white

against the thrashing sea. Her mouth was open, a dark circle against her pale skin. In the curious half-light, her silver earrings glinted.

And then she disappeared.

'Josie!' Ruth screamed. 'Oh, God, *no*!' Desperately she lunged towards the space where only a moment ago Josie had been. 'Josie! Where are you?' The sea crashed down on her again, forcing her below the churning water. For a second, there was something solid under her feet before she was fighting her way upwards once more, gasping for breath. She yelled again but the only answer was the whack and groan as the boat crashed down again onto the reef. As she and Paul and Will clung to the safety ropes round the dinghy, they all three shouted Josie's name, but there was no answer.

Ruth felt consciousness fading. The bone-chilling cold had removed all feeling, was creeping towards her brain. Will already seemed to be unconscious. Fingers clumsy with cold, she wound the strap of his harness round her wrist. 'Josie,' she screamed desperately. 'Josie!'

'Josie!' Paul yelled. 'Can you hear us? I'll come and help you.'

Anguish was building under Ruth's ribs. None of this was happening. How could they be so close to safety and yet be in such danger? Where was her daughter? Above her, the boat was half lifted by the incoming waves, and smashed down again. Once more they heard the crunch of the keel as it connected with solid rock.

Ruth began to shiver, huge tremors running through her body. My girl, she thought, my beloved daughter. Images fluttered about in her head like tattered rags: it can't be, the unthinkable, the ultimate horror, she can't be dead, not Josie, not my Josie, it isn't true, it isn't . . .

Afterwards, none of them knew how long had passed before they heard the throb of a helicopter overhead. For all of them, the only reality was that Josie had vanished. Paul kept repeating like a mantra that she had her life jacket on, she couldn't drown, the crew of the helicopter would find her, there was every chance that she would be picked up.

Overhead, a powerful beam arced across the sky before moving over the water to focus on them. With an effort, Ruth forced her frozen body to function and looked up at it. A figure in a survival suit was swinging down towards them.

'We're going to be all right,' Paul said, but Ruth knew that if they had lost Josie, then nothing, ever, was going to be all right again.

News of the accident spread quickly through the little community. The Connellys' friends telephoned, or called round, urged them to say if there was anything they could do to help.

Though less vocal in their sympathy, the year-round people were more practical. There were bunches of summer blooms from their gardens, lilac branches tied with a ribbon. But for the most part, they brought food. Every day Gertrud Hechst came up to the house, carrying a dish of dumplings or a sauerbraten, or a blueberry pie, and stayed to brush down the porches and scrub the kitchen floor. Their nearest neighbours, Ben and Marietta Cotton, dealt with other practicalities.

Ruth was aware of their presence, of their compassion. Nonetheless, they seemed inhabitants of another world to which she no longer belonged. Each day her whole being was concentrated on two things. First, on keeping hold of her sanity. Secondly, on the certainty that Josie was still alive. She spent hours up on Caleb's Point, a pair of field glasses round her neck, scanning the blank face of the ocean. Sometimes she screamed Josie's name to the heavens. She went down to the shoreline and clambered over the rocks and boulders, searching, searching, wild-eyed, hands bleeding where she cut them on the stones, emotions wound tight with desperate expectation. She took the car along the coast and doggedly searched the beaches and coves.

She refused to accept that her search was futile. The Coast Guard cutters had swept up and down the coastal waters a dozen times, to no avail. All along the coastline, from Portland up to the Canadian border, the locals had been alerted, fishing boats had been asked to keep a lookout, pleasure craft warned. But she would not give up.

After several days, when there was still no news, Paul rang Will's school principal. Mr Fogarty, expressing his deep sympathy, suggested that since the semester was about to start, it might be a good idea if Will came back to the city; he was sure that Will would be welcome to stay with the family of his best buddy, Ed Stein.

'I agree with him,' Paul said. 'I've called Carmel Stein and it's OK with her.'

'It's not OK with me,' said Will. He stared at his mother, who sat hunched with misery in the kitchen. 'Don't make me go, Mom.'

'I think your dad's right,' Ruth said expressionlessly.

'He's *not*.'

'You shouldn't miss school,' said Paul.

'Who cares about school? She's my sister. I want to be here when they . . . It's not *fair* to send me away.'

'I know how you feel, Will,' said Paul gently. He put a hand on his son's shoulder. 'But it'd be best, son, if you went back.'

'I want to be with *you*.' Will was trying not to cry, his freckled face flushed red with the effort of holding back the tears. 'Please. If it hadn't been for my birthday—' He began to sob.

With a terrible anguish, Ruth realised that he was blaming himself for Josie's loss. 'Will, it's not your fault,' she said. 'It's absolutely not.'

'It's nobody's fault,' said Paul. He pulled Will close against him. 'I promise we'll call you, son, the very minute there's any news.'

'But I want to—'

'You can come right back here as soon as . . . as she's home.'

As if recognising that arguing with his father was futile, Will gave in. 'OK,' he said quietly.

The Steins were leaving for the city that afternoon. Paul drove a silent Will over to their cottage, set deep in the woods a mile away.

'I hope we've done the right thing,' he said, when he returned.

Ruth scarcely heard him. Buried deep in their grief, the two of them exchanged no more than half a dozen sentences a day.

Early one morning someone pounded at the front door. In the kitchen, Ruth felt her body swell with anticipation. 'They've found her!' she said. 'Paul, she's come home!' She pushed back her chair, stumbled down the passage, across the hall and opened the door.

'Ms Connelly?' The young man on the porch tipped his cap.

'Yes.' Ruth looked beyond him. 'Where's my—'

She heard Paul's footsteps behind her on the pine planking, and his voice, desperate. 'What've you found?'

'Coast Guard, sir, ma'am.' The young man looked awkward. 'Lieutenant Edwards. Mind if I come in?' As he stepped past her into the hall, he pulled something from a holdall. 'Do you recognise this?'

Paul looked down. His hand sought for Ruth's. 'It's her life jacket,' he said. 'Josie's. See? It's got her name printed on it.'

'It was found washed up among the rocks miles further up the coast.' The lieutenant's weather-beaten face was solemn.

Ruth took it from him. Looking down at the ripped, red canvas life jacket, something broke inside her. She held the jacket to her chest, pressing it against her breastbone as though she might squeeze one last precious drop of Josie from it. This was the final connection she would ever have with her daughter. She remembered Josie struggling into it as the waves crashed about them.

Paul wept, pressing his fingers against his eyes. Ruth knew she ought to hold her husband, comfort him, but she was too immersed in her own pain. When Paul put his arm round her, she moved away. They could not speak, numbed by the realisation that there was no longer any way to avoid the fact that Josie was dead.

From the porch, Ruth watched the dark blue Coast Guard vehicle drive away. She looked at the field grass which spread down towards the sea, the bright flowers dotting it, the lichen-yellowed rocks emerging from ancient earth. 'I will never come here again,' she said. 'Never, ever.'

She stepped off the porch and walked away from her husband, towards the freshwater pond behind the house. Hands tucked under her arms in an attempt to ease the pain which constricted her chest, she paced slowly round its perimeter. Every summer Paul towed the wooden raft out of the centre of the pond and tethered it there; from it, both of the children had learned to swim, as Ruth herself had done years before. As she walked the reedy borders, the mental snapshot of her daughter as she dived from the raft into the water was so clear that she almost expected to hear the splash and the sound of Josie's laughter as she pushed upwards again into the summer afternoon.

She picked up the trail and followed it through the woods up to Caleb's Point. She wanted views, wide horizons, to prove that there still remained something more than the stifling imprisonment of grief. Needed, too, the confirmation that in these woods, on this bluff, Josie had been happy. She remembered being pregnant, the wonder and the fear she experienced at knowing that something had begun which could not be reversed. She had dreamed of the baby swimming in her womb. She remembered how it had felt as, new-formed and naked, the child had dived from her body into the new world.

How long had Josie struggled, choking as the sea rushed in, desperate for breath? Had she known which was her last gasp? Or had it been the cold that killed her, and not the water? Under the warm blue sky, Ruth shivered. Was there any pain worse than this loss? Not able to forget the hostility between them over the recent summer weeks, her mouth loosened and twisted.

If she were to kill herself, this tearing grief would be over. She moved to the very edge of the bluff and looked down at the rocky beach. For a minute, the earth wheeled in front of her and she thought—hoped—that she was falling. One more step would end it all.

But there was Will. She did not have a choice. She had to live, and suffer this endless loss. It would be her punishment.

She lay on her side in bed, staring at the round shadow of the lampshade on the wall. Her heart felt as though it was made of lead, heavy as a coffin. Misery pressed down on her, weighting her to the bed.

Paul came out of the bathroom and she listened to him moving about the room. He would be naked except for the towel round his waist. She heard the soft thud as he dropped the towel on the floor. The bed dipped as he climbed under the covers. She felt the long weight of him as he stretched out beside her. He tried to put his arms round her, as he had done a thousand times before. 'I'm here,' he whispered. 'We'll get through this, Ruth. Somehow we'll—'

She whipped round. 'Don't,' she said, her teeth clamped together. 'Don't touch me.'

He raised himself up on his elbow. His eyes were red from crying. She ought to have been moved, but the sight only inflamed her anger. After what he had done, he had no right to tears.

'What are you talking about?' he said, bewildered.

'It's your fault.' She dropped her voice. 'It's your fault that Josie's dead.'

'Ruth,' he said sadly, 'come on, honey. I understand how you feel—'

'You don't understand anything,' she interrupted.

'We have to support each other, we have to. No one else can.'

'If you hadn't been drinking . . .'

His body stiffened. 'Yes,' he said. 'If I hadn't, what then?'

'You'd have been more careful.'

'You mean I wouldn't have allowed a freak storm to catch us like that, is that what you mean?'

'You'd have left Bertlemy's before it started. You'd have taken more notice of the weather.'

'So it's all down to me?'

'Yes.' Her throat tightened. '*Yes*.' It had to be, didn't it? Someone had to be responsible. Otherwise, there was no justice in the world, no reason for anything. Only chaos.

'You're telling me that if I hadn't drunk three martinis, we'd still have Josie?'

'And most of the wine.'

He sighed, the sound almost a sob in his throat. 'If you hadn't forced her to come,' he said, ticking the points off on his fingers. 'If you had let us ride out the storm at sea, instead of insisting that we make a run for home. If you hadn't been knocked down by a wave when you were a kid. If you . . . what the hell good are "ifs", Ruth? Where are they going to lead us? It happened, and now we have to find a way to live with it.'

His face softened and he tried to pull her closer to him.

Again she twisted savagely away. 'This is our daughter we're talking about, our *daughter*, goddammit, and you act like it doesn't matter.' She pulled herself to her knees, her body trembling. 'Don't touch me. Just *don't*.' She began pummelling his chest, trying to hurt him. Screaming abuse. Yelling at him. 'Murderer, murderer!'

# Four

THE MEDICAL EXAMINER came up from Bangor to hold an inquest in the little wood-lined room behind the Cabot Lodge Inn. Fingers peaked in front of his mouth, he listened impassively to the evidence presented by the Coast Guard, a meteorologist and a marine expert.

Finally the ME nodded at Ruth. 'Mrs Connelly, I know how difficult this is for you, but could you tell us in your own words what happened in the moments leading up to your daughter's disappearance?'

Seated at a scarred wooden table, Ruth opened her mouth. Her hands clutched at the table's edge as she tried to force out the words. 'I—I . . .' she began. 'She . . .' She shook her head.

The ME turned to Paul. 'Professor Connelly?'

Voice husky with grief, Paul explained about the storm, the netting which had fouled the propeller, the drift towards the rocks.

'And once you were all in the dinghy?' prompted the ME.

Paul cleared his throat. 'We were overturned,' he said. 'We were s-swept overboard. My wife and son were able to hang on but . . . m-my daughter Josie was . . .' His voice cracked as he tried to explain.

Will was absent. Having already given a written deposition, he was spared the ordeal of describing once again how his sister had vanished.

While the sound of Paul's tears filled the room, the ME shuffled the reports in front of him. Finally he spoke. 'The circumstances are unusual,' he said. His voice was grave and fitting. 'We are holding an inquest without a body. We have heard the witnesses describe the condition of the boat and the weather conditions prevailing on the afternoon in question. All proper safeguards appear to have been taken. Life jackets and safety harnesses were worn. We know that this is a treacherous coast.' He paused. 'In my opinion, there is little to be gained in waiting, in the hope that the missing girl's body will appear. I therefore propose a verdict of death by cause or causes unknown.'

The locals who had crowded into the makeshift courtroom nodded in agreement. They had all lived too close to the sea for too long not to know that sometimes it refused to yield up what it had snatched.

'I offer my deepest condolences to the bereaved family,' continued the

ME. 'It should always be remembered that even with the utmost dili-
gence, accidents can happen. Nobody could have foreseen the violence
of the storm which caused this present disaster.' Smiling gravely in the
direction of the Connellys, he stood up.

Someone led them away. Paul leaned against a stranger's shoulder and
cried but Ruth could not weep. So swiftly was Josie's death disposed of.

A few days later, they held a short service in the little Episcopalian
church in Hartsfield. 'It's not a funeral,' Paul explained to Will, who had
travelled up from Boston with Ed Stein and his parents, Franklin and
Carmel. 'Because there's no . . . no body.'

'Does that mean she could still be alive?' Will's voice shook.

'No.' Paul held his son close. 'I'm afraid not.'

'You can't be sure, Dad. Suppose someone picked her up and took
her somewhere,' persisted Will.

'They'd have contacted the Coast Guard.'

'Maybe she can't tell them who she is. Maybe she's lost her memory.'

Paul squeezed Will's shoulders. 'I don't think so,' he said quietly.

A plaque was placed on the Carter tomb in the graveyard alongside
the church. Josie's friends stood in a red-eyed group, holding each
other's hands. Ruth's parents and Paul's mother came too, along with
almost the entire population of Sweetharbor.

Ruth stood between her husband and her son, pinched and silent.
Beside her, Paul wept. Will carried a sheaf of white freesias. He rested
his head against his mother's sleeve, his face wet with tears. Ruth's heart
continued to beat, to pump blood round her body, but she felt detached
from it all, as though her capacity for emotion had been destroyed. Josie
had been so full of life, and now she was dead. Since her body had not
yet been recovered, this was not even her last resting place.

'In the midst of life, we are in death,' intoned the pastor. 'This young
life . . . fulfilment of potential . . . so tragically taken from us . . . we
must have faith . . . put on this earth for a purpose . . .'

For what purpose? Ruth wondered. Why should we have faith? And
in what? The words meant nothing. 'Josie,' she said once, aloud, cutting
through the pastor's prayers. It was the only sound she made.

After Paul had gone back to Boston with Will, Ruth made an appointment with Dee's Realty in Sweetharbor. Belle Dee, the proprietor, was a
tiny, energetic woman. She shook hands with Ruth and poured coffee
for both of them.

'How can I help you, Mrs Connelly?'

'I'm planning to close my house—Carter's House—for some time. I'd like your firm to take over the maintenance of it.'

'Maintenance?'

'That *is* what you do, isn't it? One of the services you offer?'

'Yes, but—'

'Then please give me the papers and I'll fill them out,' Ruth said.

Mrs Dee put down her cup and foraged for the paperwork in the drawers of her desk. 'You said you plan to close the house for some time,' she said carefully, passing the forms to Ruth.

'That's right.'

'Will you be back next summer?'

'No.'

Mrs Dee was not put off by her prospective client's brusqueness. 'Then have you considered letting? Our books are full of people anxious to rent for the summer.'

'I don't want strangers in my house,' Ruth said.

'I hate to sound fanciful, Mrs Connelly, but to my way of thinking, houses have personalities just as much as people do, and if you neglect them, they suffer.'

'You're used to managing properties for the out-of-towners, aren't you?'

'Yes, but—'

'Then please add Carter's House to your list.'

Ruth pushed completed papers back across the desk and stood up. 'It was good to talk with you,' she said, then turned on her heel and went out.

Later that day, driving away down the track, she did not look back. Behind her, Carter's House stood mellow in the sloping autumnal sunlight, the black shutters fastened across the windows, incarcerating her memories. An era was ended. That part of her life was over.

In late September, Paul told Ruth that while he was up in Brunswick one afternoon, he had run into Dieter and Gertrud Hechst's nephew, Sam.

'And?'

'We talked. I told him we wanted something to remember Josie by. A kind of memorial. He said, why not make a bench?'

'He's a carpenter, isn't he?'

'Yes, Ruth.' Paul sighed. 'He replaced the dining-room floor at Carter's House five years ago.'

'I remember now.' Ruth did not want to think about graveyards and memorials to a dead girl.

'I asked him if he'd do it and he asked why I didn't make it myself. What do you think?'

'A bench.'

'My tools are all up there in the barn. I could do it. Get Will to come along, maybe.'

'She loved Caleb's Point,' Ruth said.

'I know. Will and me—we could make a good strong bench, put it somewhere where we can sit and remember her.'

'She loved it up there,' said Ruth. She felt like someone walking across a frozen pond, not really sure if the ice would hold.

Most weekends that fall, Paul and Will drove up to Sweetharbor and worked on the bench. Ruth insisted that they were not to go into the house so they stayed overnight at the Cabot Lodge Inn. Although Paul tried to get her to come with them, she always refused.

'It's a great bench, Mom,' Will told her, just returned from Maine. 'Dad's carved the middle bit in the back into the shape of a heart. He's really good.'

'You're not bad yourself,' Paul said. He turned to Ruth. 'Will's a killer with the sanding machine. Smoothest wood I ever did see.'

'You should see the way Dad shapes the slats,' countered Will. 'I gotta admit I'm impressed.'

'Never knew the old man had it in him, did you, son?'

'You made that box for Mom's earrings one summer. Remember that?'

'So I did. I'd forgotten all about it.'

Ruth looked away, hating them for being so contented with each other. Hating them, too, for being able to return to Carter's House when she knew she never would. Going to bed that evening, she took the small, heart-shaped wooden box from the back of a drawer and put it on her dressing table. Paul had made it for her when Josie was born.

When the bench was finished, Paul had a small brass plate set into the top rail engraved with Josie's name and the dates of her birth and death. He tried to show it to Ruth, but she would not look at it.

She still refused to go to Maine, so Paul and Will drove up without her. At Carter's House, they heaved the bench into the back of the car and took it up to Caleb's Point, where they poured concrete and set the bench fair and square, facing out to sea. They bolted it down and rubbed linseed oil into the wood until it gleamed.

Paul gazed bleakly at the grey, wintry water of the Sound. Was it his fault that Josie had died? Could he have done more, done something else which could have saved her life? The wind blew in off the sea, cold and salty, and tears ran down his face.

'It's OK, Dad,' Will said. He slipped his hand into his father's, his own eyes full of tears. 'We'll be OK.'

'I hope so.'

'I kinda wish Mom would talk about it, though.'

'Not talking is her way of handling it,' Paul said.

The next morning, before returning to the city, Paul and Will went up to Caleb's Point to give the bench a final coat.

'Smells good,' Will said, when they were done.

'It does that.' Paul reached over and touched his son's shoulder. 'You miss her?'

'Of course I do. She was my . . . she was my friend, as well as my sister.' Will bit his lip. 'Yeah. I miss her lots.'

'Me too. All the time.'

'Dad . . . do you think she could be . . . might she still be . . . I mean, sometimes I really wonder if she's out there somewhere, still alive.'

'Oh, Will.' Tears came into Paul's eyes. 'I wish I thought she was. But she's not, son. We just have to accept it. She's not.'

'I guess you're right.'

They drove back to the city without mentioning Josie's name again.

Ruth had found a way to manage. She worked late nearly every evening and came home too tired to talk, with a legitimate excuse for going early to bed. At weekends, she brought papers home with her, crowding out the spaces in her life where Josie might otherwise have lurked.

She was very conscious of the fact that Will needed her more now than formerly. Every day she made time in her schedule to talk with him, be there for him. She tried to factor in weekend treats for him: movies, ball games, trips to New York. He was now an only child; because of this she told herself she must make allowances when he argued with her or refused to go along with some plan she had made.

'I'm going to eat vegetarian from now on,' he told her one morning.

'No, you're not.'

'Why not?' He was truculent.

'You're still growing, Will. Vegetarianism doesn't provide all the nutrients you need.'

'I can take vitamins and stuff.'

'Why not just eat meat occasionally, instead?'

'I don't want to.'

'But, Will, you know how much you enjoy cooking.'

193

'I'll cook vegetarian.'

'But you always used to make fun of . . .'

It was a sentence impossible to conclude. Josie had decided she was a vegetarian at the beginning of the summer, becoming adept at producing combination salads and meatless dishes. Ruth had grown increasingly irked by the way she wrinkled her nose at the food the rest of her family were eating, and exclaimed 'Gross!' at least three times during every meal, gazing at her parents and brother with disgust.

'I know.' Will turned awkwardly away, hunching one shoulder. 'Now I wish I hadn't.'

'You do realise, don't you, how much longer it takes to shop and cook for a vegetarian diet? I'm stretched as it is.'

'I'll do it myself,' Will said.

She was wrung by the expression on his face, a mixture of need and dread, but at that moment she did not feel able to deal with either. She was needy enough herself.

Five

TOWARDS THE END of October, Bob Landers came into Ruth's office. 'Do you know what the time is?' he asked.

'No.' She glanced at her watch. 'God, is it really eight?'

'Ten after. You're working too hard, Ruth.'

'Probably.' She glanced down at the papers spread over her desk. 'But there's a lot to do.'

'Haven't you got a family to go home to?'

'Actually, no. Paul's taken Will to visit his mother.'

'So you're all on your own.'

'That's right.'

He leaned over and swept her documents into a heap. 'Time to call it a day,' he said. 'Come and have dinner with me.'

'Um . . . I'm not sure I can.'

'If the family's out of town, of course you can. And I warn you, it's not just for fun. I've got a proposal to put to you.'

She flushed. 'A proposal?'

'We'll discuss it over dinner.'

They took a cab down to a harbour-front seafood restaurant. Bob ordered a Californian chardonnay. The waitress poured it, greenly golden, into tall glasses, and they sipped it quietly, looking out at the reflections from the other side of the harbour rocking on the water. Ruth ordered the crab cakes; Bob had lobster. When they were halfway through their food, Bob said, 'How's it going, Ruth?'

She knew that he did not mean her work. 'Fine.' She put down her fork and sipped her wine. 'Just fine.'

'Is that the truth? I know you have good cause, but recently you've been looking extra stressed. I'm not the only one who's noticed it. It's none of my business, but is everything OK between you and Paul?'

'Of course. Why do you ask?'

'You've lost a lot of weight and the Lord knows you didn't have much spare in the first place.'

'I don't seem to have time to eat these days,' she said. 'Which is why I'm grateful to you for suggesting we go out. Hey, these crab cakes are—'

'Don't try to change the subject,' he said. He put a hand out towards her, strong and square. She looked down at it, fighting inexplicable tears. She and Bob went back a long way, to college days, to before she began dating Paul. 'It's natural that you should be under strain. Losing a child must be the worst thing that can happen. I can't begin to imagine how I'd cope if it were one of mine.'

'I'm coping,' she said. 'You didn't bring me here to complain about anything I've done, did you?'

'Quite the opposite. I should have said before now that you did a fine job of bringing Phil Lavelle on board. A very fine job indeed.'

'Thanks.' That day at the Trotmans' party came back to her. When Josie, belligerent, feisty, had been so much alive. Her throat closed.

'You're doing me a lot of good in the firm,' continued Bob. He looked at her affectionately. 'You're more than justifying my choice. Frankly, at the time, some of the other partners thought you were too young to be promoted.' Bob loaded a fork with lobster meat and held it halfway to his mouth. 'Now listen, Ruth. I'm going to say what I brought you here to say. Then you go home and think about it. No obligations attached, no strings. It's entirely up to you, and accepting or refusing will make no difference to your career prospects with us.'

'Intriguing.'

'As you already know, some time in the new year the McLennan Corporation is scheduled to be fighting an anti-trust infringement case through the British courts. The hearing's supposed to last about three weeks but might take as long as six, and during that time LKM are going to need someone on the ground over there. You've worked on McLennan's affairs for nearly five years now. Nobody knows the ins and outs as well as you do, which is why I think that you'd be the ideal person to have there in an advisory capacity.'

'It's tempting,' Ruth said slowly. A breathing space: it was exactly what she needed. There was only Will to worry about. 'I'd have to talk to Paul, obviously.'

'Do that. Take a while, consider the angles.'

'How long a while can I take?'

'Like, till the end of the week?'

When she told Paul about Bob's offer, he seemed almost relieved. 'You should go,' he said.

'I don't want to upset Will. What I mean is, am I being unfair, leaving him? Will he feel neglected if I go?'

'You could always take him with you. Put him in school in London for a month. It'd be a real experience.'

When she suggested that he come to England with her, Will was adamant that he did not want to. He looked down at the ground. 'I want to be with my friends.'

'You might make some new ones.'

'I've got enough already,' he said. 'Besides, I just want to go on the way I am now.' He looked at her with a carefully neutral expression on his face. 'Do you have to go, Mom?'

'I don't *have* to. But it's quite an honour to be asked. It'd certainly be a good career move to go.'

'Right.'

'Would you rather I stayed here, Will? Because if so, I'll tell Bob Landers I can't do it.'

'Hey, good career moves don't happen that often, do they?' The effort he was making wrenched Ruth's heart. How could she leave him? Will had to come first. She opened her mouth to say this, but before she could do so, Paul spoke.

'I think us two guys could manage for a while, don't you, son?'

'I guess.' Will spoke halfheartedly.

'Look,' Ruth said, 'I'll tell Bob I can't go.'

'If you do that, you won't be able to bring us back some of that nice warm British beer,' Paul said.

'Nor a deerstalker hat,' said Will. 'With the earflaps? So you gotta go, Mom. I really want one of those.'

Hugging him, Ruth asked, 'Will you miss me?' and realised as she said it that the moment to turn down Bob's offer had passed.

'What do *you* think?' Will managed a grin. 'I'll have a ball while you're gone. Dad lets me get away with a lot more stuff than you do.'

'Hey, you little fink,' said Paul.

'And what will you do while I'm gone, Paul?'

'What I usually do. Work, write, deal with my students, visit friends from time to time.'

He sounded as if her absence would be an ideal opportunity for him to have some fun. Once, just being together had been fun enough. Since when had being apart become better than being with each other?

The next day, Ruth told Bob that she would accept the offer and go to England.

Will came into the kitchen where Ruth sat at the table staring into a cup of coffee. 'Are we going up to Carter's House for Christmas?' he said.

'I don't think that'll be possible.' Ruth kept her expression steady.

'Why not?'

'Because . . . because I'm not up to it.'

'I want to, Mom.' His voice twanged with emotion. 'I *need* to go back.'

'You've *been* back. You and Dad. Making that bench.'

'Not into the house.'

'It might be more than you can handle, Will.'

'Jesus, Mom. I'm not a kid any more.'

You are, she wanted to tell him. Just a kid. My precious kid. 'I know that. You'll just have to trust me.'

He sounded mutinous. 'I *like* it up there. We always go up there.'

Used to, she wanted to say. *Used* to. But that is all over now. 'Discuss it with your father when he gets in,' she said.

'Aw, Mom. What a cop-out.'

When Paul came in, Will tried again. 'Dad, are we going up to Maine for Christmas?'

Ruth could see that the thought had never crossed Paul's mind. 'To Carter's House?' He looked at his wife. 'I don't think so.'

'Why not?'

'I think you can imagine why, pal.'

'I can't.' Will's freckles stood out sharply against his face.

'Then try,' Paul said shortly.

'Please, Mom?' Will stared at Ruth. 'I don't understand why we can't go,' he repeated. Recently, he had begun to avoid her attempts to embrace him, just as Josie had once done, otherwise she might have been tempted to stroke his cheek, put an arm round him. What would he say if she told him that he was the only thing that made her life worth living at the moment? That she existed only because of him?

'If you really can't,' Paul said, 'that would tell me you were not very sensitive to other people, Will. And I don't want to believe that.'

'I want to go with you two. Like a family.'

A family? Ruth almost laughed. That was far beyond them now. 'No,' she said. She was undoubtedly blocking something that was important to Will. Nonetheless, the thought of opening the doors upon the ghosts in Maine was more than she was able to face.

'Why can't we go and live up there permanently, anyway?'

'We've already had this discussion,' Ruth said. 'We live in the city because that's where we work. I do not want to discuss this any further.'

'You never want to discuss *anything*,' Will said. 'Never. You just shut me out. And Dad.' His eyes were stormy as he slammed off to his room.

'It's the only way I can cope,' Ruth said helplessly.

'He needs to talk, Ruth,' Paul said. 'Both of us do. All three of us. Maybe we should see a professional, a grief counsellor or something.'

'No.' The thought was too alarming. A professional would require her to dredge up her grief, to remove her armour. 'I'm not ready for that.'

'I don't think we can go on like this for much longer.'

'Like what?'

'Living this kind of lie. Not talking about what all of us are thinking about.' Paul came over to stand behind her. 'It's not healing us, Ruth.'

She picked up her coffee cup. Because Josie's body had never been found, the reality of her death would always remain clouded. 'Do you ever think she might still be alive?' she asked suddenly.

'Will's asked me that.' Paul came round the table and took the chair opposite Ruth. 'Of course she's not alive. What kind of damned stupid speculation is that?'

'I only wonder sometimes if by any chance she could have—'

'Stop it, Ruth. Stop deluding yourself.'

'I only said I sometimes *thought* about it.'

'She's *dead*. To think anything else is madness.'

Later, Paul came and sat down next to Ruth on the sofa in the living room. 'I'm sorry,' he said. 'I shouldn't have reacted like that.'

'That's OK.'

'Don't you think we should find some room in our schedules for ourselves?' He put his arm round her. Squeezed her shoulder.

She remembered the first occasion they had made love. She had never slept with anyone before. She smiled at him, vaguely. 'We're together all the time, except for work.'

'*Proper* time,' he said. 'Quality time.'

She had been so nervous. His hand on her breast. Not really sure what she was supposed to feel. He had kissed her nipples. It had been pretty much of a non-event for her, though she had never said so.

'We've been through an unbearably stressful time,' he said. 'It's been nearly six months.'

'Six months is nothing.' Ruth could think only of her daughter, lost at sea, rolling with the tides. 'It'll be with us for ever.'

'I think we—you and me—need to find each other again.'

'We still have each other. The way we always have.' It was not true, but Ruth did not want to discuss it. She looked over at the table where her papers were spread, and started to get up. 'I've got work to do.'

Paul held her back. 'Leave the damn work, Ruth.' He tried to kiss her, but she turned her face away.

'Don't,' she said.

'Why not? We haven't made love since—'

'Sex, is that all you can think about?'

'Life doesn't stop. Life goes on. It has to. I need you, Ruth. I need your love. I need the intimacy of sharing. There's nothing wrong with that.'

'I don't want to,' she said, her voice sharp. 'I can't bear to, not after what happened.'

She looked down at her hands, and noted how thin they looked. She spread them on her lap and moved the wedding ring up and down her finger. She had thought he was such a good person, in their college days. So committed, so inspiring. He had ideas about the world which she had never heard articulated before; he moved with a crowd who marched in protest for their principles, who believed in things. And it had all ended up like this.

He took her chin in his hand and forced her face round to his. 'Ruth,' he murmured. 'I'm your husband and I want to make love with you. I need to feel that life is going on, that it hasn't come to a stop.'

Once this man could move her. Once, the words he spoke would have made her soft and damp. She would have fitted herself to him, moved under him in the expert way of a loved and happy wife, waiting to ease him into herself and enjoy him. Now she shifted away from him, keeping her body tight. Making love would seem like a betrayal.

'What are you doing to us, Ruth?' he asked, his face set. 'Don't you feel anything for me any more?'

'Of course I do.'

'For the past months you've been so . . . closed. It's not just me who needs you, it's Will, too.'

'You know I try to make time for Will.'

'Oh yes. I bet it's even on your schedule: one hour with Will, in between the appointments and the papers.'

His words pierced her. She stared at him, her mouth trembling. 'That's bullshit.'

'I can't imagine having to . . .' his voice was heavy with sarcasm, '*make time* for my son.'

'You know what I mean. No one can say I'm a neglectful mother.'

'How about a neglectful wife? Ever think about making time for your husband?' He took her hands and forced her to face him. 'We're married, Ruth. We're supposed to be a team. Don't you think I have needs?'

'I also have needs,' she said sadly. 'And for the moment, this is the only way I can handle them.'

Despite Will's continued pleas that they spend Christmas in Maine, the three of them flew down to Florida to visit Ruth's parents. Though they all pretended to be enjoying themselves, there was something manic behind the silences which frequently fell.

Eventually Ruth's mother could hold it in no longer. As she and Ruth prepared food in the kitchen, while Will walked on the beach with his grandfather and Paul was shopping at the supermarket, Betty Carter said, 'Why?'

'Why what, Mom?'

'Why Josie? Why did it have to happen? I can't understand why it . . . Was there anything either of you could have done to—'

'Nothing.' Ruth shook her head, trying to banish the resurrected image of Josie's face in the curious purple-black stormlight, the earrings underwater, the dark space of her mouth, her terror, her . . . '*Nothing*, Mom, OK? I really don't want to talk about it.'

'But I do. I need to, Ruthie. She was my granddaughter. Don't you realise your father and I have suffered, too? And still are?'

'I know that. But talking about it doesn't do any good. It just revives the memories.'

'That's what I'm afraid of, dear. That I'll lose the memories and then she'll be gone. You both seem to take it . . . what happened . . . so well but your father and I, well, it's devastated us.'

Ruth was seized with a swell of rage. 'How did you *want* us to take it?' she demanded. 'Our lives will never be the same. But what good does it do to scream and howl and bang our heads against the wall?'

'It's a natural thing to do,' her mother said mildly.

'Well, it's not the way Paul and I are dealing with it.'

Suddenly, her mother began to sob. 'It was so terrible, Ruth.'

'I know.'

'We were so . . . I remember the night she was born . . . funny little moppet . . . that hair . . . like you when you were . . . so *lovely* . . .'

'Mom—'

'She was so talented . . . her painting . . . your father thought she could . . .' Betty blew her nose, tried to pull herself back into coherence.

'Don't, Mom. Please.' Ruth's eyes were wet.

'You were so hard on her, though.'

'*Hard* on her?'

'Whatever she did . . . nothing seemed to please you . . .'

'*What?* That's a terrible thing to say.'

'But it's true. Your dad and I used to think . . .' Betty quailed before the look Ruth gave her. 'I know you wanted her to be the very best she could be, Ruth, but sometimes—'

'Sometimes what?' Ruth demanded fiercely.

'You could have praised her a bit more, criticised her a bit less.'

'I can't believe I'm hearing this.'

'You were always so much more relaxed with Will, that's all I'm saying.' Betty broke open the head of a lettuce and tore it into pieces.

Ruth was amazed at how much the accusations hurt. Was her mother right? *Had* she been harder on Josie than on Will? The way she saw it, Will was just easier to handle, always had been. And yes, she had wanted Josie to fulfil her potential, and if that meant pushing a bit, was that so wrong? She was pierced by her own last words to her daughter, and by the way she had refused to take Josie's concerns seriously.

'What about Will?' her mother asked, breaking into Ruth's mood of self-condemnation.

'What about him?'

'Is he really as adjusted to it all as he seems?'

'What can I say? I just hope so.'

Back in Boston, Will went down with a chest infection that kept him off school. Frantically, Ruth juggled with her schedules so as to be at home earlier and leave later, all the while fearful that she might be damaging her career prospects. She was leading a team handling a complicated bank merger, and in addition she was trying to find time to submerge herself in the complex details of the McLennan merger plans, preparing for the case scheduled in the British courts in the next few weeks.

Though worried about Will, she was conscious of a feeling of irritation. Why did he have to get sick now, of all times?

'The antibiotics don't seem to be doing him much good,' she told Paul.

'I guess that's because they're only masking the symptoms.'

'You think this infection is a psychosomatic reaction to what . . . what happened?'

'Don't you? He's hardly had a sick day in his life until now.'

Ruth massaged her temples wearily. 'I know it sounds really unsympathetic, but this couldn't have happened at a worse time.'

Paul looked at her with disgust. 'Right now he needs support, not more guilt.'

'I know, I know.' She felt panicky. 'But I'm in a severe time crunch. I've piles of paperwork to get through and frankly, if Will doesn't get better soon, my position at LKM's going to be up for grabs. There're thousands of hopefuls out there, just dying for a chance to score.'

'Is that all you care about these days? Your career? What about me and Will?'

'After the . . . after what happened, I have this constant feeling that nothing's going to last. I know there's still the three of us, but deep down I kind of expect it all to crumble.' She looked at her husband wistfully, longing for him to understand. 'Do you know what I mean?'

'No. You're being totally irrational.'

She cringed inwardly at the indifference in his voice.

The night before she left for England, she said, 'You're sure about this, aren't you? Me leaving you and Will?'

'Absolutely,' said Paul. Avoiding her eyes, he said, 'Actually, it couldn't have come at a better time.'

'What's that supposed to mean?'

'I've been thinking for a while that we need some space.'

The word filled her with dread. 'Space?'

'The time away from each other will do us both good. With you gone, at least we'll both have a chance to think things through.'

'What things?'

'Us.'

'You mean our marriage?'

'That too.'

She was silent. Tears gathered at the back of her throat. If she gave in to them she might drown. Instead, she stiffened her shoulders. 'What are you saying exactly? That you want a trial separation?'

'Sounds good to me,' he said.

'Thank you, Paul. That is so exactly what I needed right now.'

'I'm sorry.' He did not sound it. 'It seemed better to get it out in the open, before you left.'

She did not answer him. There was nothing she could say.

Six

THE MCLENNAN CORPORATION had provided Ruth with a luxurious two-bedroomed company apartment in Chelsea. A woman came in a couple of times a week to housekeep and buy the groceries that Ruth required.

There was a small balcony overlooking the Thames, and she sat here sometimes, wrapped up against the January cold, watching the play of light on the water, drinking her coffee before setting off for the office. The river was always busy. Big barges drifted past on the tide, tourist boats chugged down towards Greenwich, smaller craft hurried by.

Ruth had been afraid she would be lonely in England. Instead she found it liberating. She began to see that Paul was right, this intermission was exactly what they had needed. The McLennan case had already generated a ton of paperwork. Despite that, Ruth made one rule. The case could have her for the rest of the week, but Sundays were hers. Although the weather was wet and cold, she took buses from London out to Cambridge, to Oxford, to Canterbury. She stood beneath Gothic roofs, walked through ancient cloisters, and marvelled. It was a world away from the life she was used to.

Ruth's absence had panned out conveniently for Paul. Even before Bob Landers's offer, he had arranged a sabbatical semester in order to make a final push on his book. He could spend most of his time in Boston, in order to be around for Will and, with any luck, he would be able to deliver the book to his publishers by the end of the month.

On the way back from seeing Ruth off at the airport, he had a serious discussion with Will about mealtimes. 'I'm warning you,' Paul said. 'I'm not intending to live off vegetarian glop for the next few weeks.'

'Who said anything about glop?' said Will. 'Some vegetarian food is real gourmet stuff.'

'Prove it.'

'OK, I will. But hey, I'm not gonna end up on kitchen duty every night. That wouldn't be fair. I mean, I've got stuff to do.'

'OK. Turn about's fair play. I'll be chef one night, you the next. But you ought to eat meat every other night, if I've got to eat veggie.'

'Dad, trust me. After tasting my stuff, you'll never touch meat again.'

The two spent a lot of time shopping for food together, dreaming up elaborate menus for each other, cooking, eating together, enjoying each other's company.

One night, as Paul watched the late movie, he heard Will moaning in his bedroom. Quietly opening his door, Paul saw that the boy was asleep but tossing restlessly. As he watched, Will moaned again, flinging out an arm as though pushing something away.

'Will.' Paul put a hand on the boy's shoulder. 'Wake up, son.'

Will groaned a few indistinguishable words.

'It's OK,' Paul said reassuringly. 'I'm here. You're all right.'

Slowly, Will opened his eyes, stared up at his father, the shreds of the nightmare still clinging to his expression.

'What was it?' Paul demanded. 'What were you dreaming about?'

'It was awful. I dreamed I was—' He broke off. 'That we were all . . . all drowning.' Will grabbed Paul's hand so tightly that the bones cracked. 'We were out in the boat and the sea came . . . and—'

'Sssh.' Paul sat down and put his arm round Will's shoulders. 'It was just a dream.'

'She swam away,' Will said painfully. 'She said if it wasn't for me, my birthday, none of this would have happened. And then she vanished under the water. I could see her, Dad, her face disappearing under the sea, all white, and she was saying it was my fault she was drowning.'

'That's nonsense, Will,' Paul said, shaking the boy's shoulders. 'How could it possibly be your fault? You weren't responsible for the storm. Or for anything else that happened that day. Look, it's nearly two in the morning. Want to come and keep me company in bed, the way you used to when you were little?'

'I'll be OK, Dad.'

Paul bent to shake up his son's pillow and as he did so, something fell onto the floor. He picked it up and put it beside Will's head. A cuddly bear with a spotted bow tie and big brown eyes of glass. He frowned. 'Isn't that—wasn't that Josie's?'

'Hardy, yeah.'

'Where did you get it?'

'From Carter's House. After the accident.'

'Will . . . It's not going to be easy, to get over losing Josie. It'll take time, you know that, don't you?'

'That's what the school shrink said. I—I went to see him the other day.'

'Did you?' Paul hoped his voice sounded sufficiently casual, though he could feel the thump of his heart. 'Did someone suggest it?'

'No. It's just, he told me a while back that if I ever needed to talk to him, to go right on in. So I did.'

A bubble of guilt and sorrow filled Paul's chest. Oh, Will, he thought. What can we do to help you?

When Ruth next called from London and asked how Will was, Paul said forthrightly, 'Not good.'

'What is it?' she demanded. 'What's wrong?'

'He's not sleeping well. Having nightmares.'

'What about?'

'Would you believe death? By drowning?'

'Oh, no. Maybe he needs to talk things through with someone more objective than his parents, like the school psychiatrist?'

'He already has. I spoke to the guy myself, and he said that it would take a very long time for Will to get over the trauma of bereavement. Told me that these chest infections Will gets could be down to that. Frankly, I'm worried. He's not eating well. And he's doing such a lot at school at the moment that some days he gets really tired. But that's adolescence for you. He's got an iron supplement to take: they thought he might be anaemic. I've arranged for him to take a blood test. Did you know that he sleeps with . . . with her teddy bear?'

'Hardy? I thought he'd been left at Carter's House.' There was a pause. 'Paul, should I come back? I can, if you think it would be best. I mean, it would be really difficult but—'

'I can't see the point.' Frankly, Paul was happier to be alone in the apartment with Will.

'So we just go on showing that we love him.'

'I do that,' Paul said sharply. 'All the time.'

Want to go up to Maine for the weekend?' Paul said.

'Cool.'

'We could take off in the afternoon, be there by supper.'

'Don't suppose we get to stay at Carter's House, do we?'

'Not this time. I'll book us in at the Cabot Lodge. I thought we might go for a hike, get some air in our lungs, check up on our bench.'

It was almost dark by the time they reached Sweetharbor. They took their bags up to the room they were sharing then walked down Old Port

Street to stand on the harbour quay. Snow was falling. Yellow dusklight was reflected in the ice which hemmed the harbour waters. The stony shores were bleak, the trees and rocks powdered with snow. The wind rammed across the grey water, tugging at the boats at their moorings.

'Aren't you glad you're not a fisherman?' Paul said, his breath pluming into the freezing air. Even through layers of winter-proof clothing he could feel the bite of the cold.

'One winter, Josie went out fishing with Ben Cotton,' Will said. 'She told me it was the coldest she'd ever been in her life. Took them thirty minutes just to get through the ice to the mooring.'

Paul shivered. 'No wonder your granddad moved to Florida.'

That evening they took in a movie playing at the little local cinema before turning in. The next day, after a big breakfast, they drove up to Carter's House and parked in front of the barn, then struck up through the trees towards Caleb's Point. The going was tough. Snow obscured the trail, making it easy to trip over concealed roots and creepers.

'Still want to move up here permanently?' Paul asked, taking a breather. He leaned against a tree trunk and clapped his arms several times round himself. 'Jeez, it's cold.'

'You got to admit, Dad, it's kinda gutsy living up here.'

'Guess I'm happier being a coward down in the city.'

'Think about the Cottons and Hechsts,' said Will. 'And all the other year-rounders.'

'I do think about them,' Paul said. 'Which is exactly why I don't want to be up here in winter, thanks very much. There's only so much the human spirit can endure.'

'We've endured, haven't we?' Will looked very small under his layers of wool and flannel.

Paul was moved by his son's expression. And by his words. There was so much left unsaid. 'Yes,' he said quietly. 'We have.'

When they finally reached the bluff, they sat for a moment or two on the bench they had made together. The wind roared at them, burning their cheeks with minute slivers of ice.

Will stood up and stroked the carved heart on the back of the bench with his gloved hand. 'Josie,' he said softly.

'Josie,' echoed Paul. He took his son's hand.

'We had some good times here, didn't we, Dad?'

'We sure did. And will do again.'

'Except Mom doesn't want to come back.'

'One of these days . . .' Paul said vaguely, able to promise nothing.

As they came down the trail, Ben Cotton's pick-up eased round to the back of the house. The back of it was piled high with frost-covered logs. He waited until they reached him, then got out and shook Paul's hand, enveloped Will in a bear hug. 'How ya doin'?' he said.

'Fine. And you, Ben?' Paul asked.

'Good. Good. Things is kinda slow, though.'

'Always the same, this time of year.'

'Don't know that it's been this bad before.' The old man let out a long breath. 'Heard you was back, so I brung you some wood.'

'That's good of you, Ben.' Paul moved his shoulders around, searching for warmth, then unzipped his jacket and reached a hand inside.

Ben stepped back, holding up mittened hands. 'No,' he said. 'Don't want payin'. Old Doc Carter was good to us. Looked after Marietta real kindly. Never asked for one red cent. Besides, what's a load of wood?'

'It's money, Ben. You could sell it elsewhere. Besides, we're not staying.'

'No?'

'Not this time.'

After talking a while longer, the old man turned away. 'See you some time.' Raising a hand in farewell, he climbed back into his pick-up.

'Will and I went up to Carter's House,' Paul said, telephoning Ruth from Boston one evening.

'Oh?' Ruth closed her mind. She did not want to hear about it.

'Didn't go in. Just looked around outside. We went up to the Point, too. Checked out the bench Will and I made.'

'Did you?' Ruth was seized by a sudden sense of loss and rejection. Her husband and her son had formed a unit of two, while she was here on her own. She changed the subject. 'How's the book coming?'

'Fine. The publishers had a few queries and one chapter's going to have to be rewritten, but otherwise they're pleased with it.'

'I'm so proud of you, Paul. I'll be able to tell people I'm the wife of a published author.'

'That'll be almost as good as having a wife who's a partner in a prestigious law firm.'

His tone was cool and Ruth felt a sudden need to break through his distance to the warm reservoir of his love.

'Paul, I—'

'Here's Will.'

'Hi, Mom.'

'Hi, honey.' Hearing her son's voice, Ruth was overwhelmed with regret. 'How're you doing?'

'Fine.'

'I'll be back very soon, hon,' she told him. 'Promise. I really miss you.' Her voice skipped a beat, broke.

'Hey,' said Will, awkward. 'Don't go all weepy on me.'

She tried to laugh but could not. 'Weepy? *Moi?*'

'I'm being a good boy and drinking up my milk.' As always, he tried to lighten the atmosphere. 'And I promise to quit smoking, cut down on the booze and stop gambling, OK?'

This time she managed to laugh. 'OK.'

Putting down the receiver, she thought she had never been lonelier.

Two days later, Ruth sat at the apartment's dining table, her papers spread across it. She was going over them one last time before sitting in on a meeting the next day between Nick Pargeter, McLennan's English lawyer, and the Commission people. Suddenly she heard a squawk from the intercom. When she went to the speaker by the door, she was astonished to hear Chris Kauffman's voice asking if he could come up.

'Second floor,' she said. She pressed the buzzer and opened the door. 'Chris!' she exclaimed as he appeared on her landing. 'What are you doing here?'

'I'm in town for a couple of days,' he said, giving her his almost-smile. 'I ran into Bob Landers a couple of weeks ago, and he said you were in London. I thought I'd look you up.' He handed her a sheaf of freesias. The faint sweet fragrance pierced Ruth's heart.

She poured Chris a drink. They chatted inconsequentially, and all the while she wondered why he had come, what he wanted. Eventually he put his glass down.

'Ruth,' he said, leaning towards her. 'I haven't seen you since the memorial service for Josie. I guess you know how I—how I felt about that.'

'Yes, Chris. I do.'

'It was just a terrible thing to happen. Terrible.' He shook his head. 'So young. And she was such a pretty girl.'

Stop, she wanted to shout. Don't. But it was too late. Her defences had been breached. Grief, long dammed, poured through her. 'We loved her so much,' she whispered. 'So very much.' Helplessly, she began to cry.

Chris took her hand.

'You can't—you cannot imagine the pain I feel.' Tears streamed from her eyes. 'It haunts me. And she was so . . . so hostile that last summer.'

Chris was holding her. 'Kids her age are like that.'

His shirt was wet under her cheek. 'I never—I never told her how much I loved her, Chris.'

'I think all our kids know we love them,' Chris said.

'She was full of some kind of pain, that summer, and I was too busy to find out what was causing it,' said Ruth. Her tears seemed to well up from some inexhaustible spring, as though they had waited all this time for release. She pressed her fists against her wet face. 'She asked me if I would give up my life for her and she didn't believe me when I said yes. I would have done, Chris. Gladly.'

'Don't, Ruth. Don't.' Chris put his arms round her.

'It can never be put right,' Ruth said. 'That's the very worst thing of all. She's gone and I'll never ever see her again.'

'Ruth, Ruth.' Chris leaned forward to kiss her lightly on the cheek but Ruth turned her head so that his lips met her mouth.

'Make love to me,' she whispered urgently. 'Please, Chris.' Suddenly she understood what Paul had meant when he said that making love was an affirmation that life continued after even the darkest tragedy. 'Please.'

'Honey, I don't think this is what you really want.'

'It is. Oh, Chris. It's exactly what I want.'

He pulled her roughly against him. She began to undo his shirt, pulled at his tie. He put his hand inside her blouse and down into her bra. As he held her breast, brushed her nipple with his finger, excitement flowed through her body like electricity. She tore at her clothes. Then Chris was pushing into her and the old familiar fire raced through her, blotting out her pain, blotting out her loss.

Seven

PAUL GREETED THE NEWS that Ruth was coming home with mixed feelings. 'That's wonderful,' he managed to say. He wished he meant it.

When Will came in from school, Paul told him the news.

'Oh no!' Will said.

'What's up? Don't you want to see your mom again?'

'It's not that.' Will looked round the apartment. 'We better do something about this place.'

'Looks OK to me.'

'To me, too. But it won't to Mom. Especially with Bess being away sick the last two weeks.'

Paul ran his finger across the coffee table and held it up for Will's inspection. 'Something must be done.'

'And you, Dad, are just the guy to do it. I've got a history project to get on with.'

'Oh, *right*. When the going gets tough, huh?'

'You got it.'

Ruth's absence had crystallised one thing for Paul: he could no longer live with the barriers she had built between them. He had talked about needing space; space was all there was now. The only thing they shared was Will. Even their grief over Josie was separate and individual. When Ruth got back, he would move out. Not for ever, maybe, but for a while. He had already looked for an apartment near the Boston campus, a one-bedroom bachelor apartment he could lease for six months.

But what would Will think of him? Could he just walk out on his son? He had longed to be able to talk to someone about it.

A couple of evenings later, as he walked across the campus parking lot, he ran into Carole Barwick from the Philosophy Department.

'Hi, Paul,' she said, holding an armful of files, trying to fit her key into the lock of her car. 'Good to see you again.'

'Welcome back,' he said. 'Enjoy your sabbatical?'

'Very much. I got a lot of work done.' A couple of files slid from the pile in her arm and he bent to pick them up, thinking he had not realised how attractive she was. 'You're on one now, aren't you?'

'That's right.'

She surveyed him critically. 'You're looking pretty down. Anything in particular that's wrong?' Her voice was soft and sympathetic, reminding Paul of how much he longed for a bit of kindness. He tried to remember if there was a husband, a family.

'Do you have time for a coffee?' he asked, hoping he did not sound desperate. 'A beer? A bottle of wine?'

'Make it a glass and I'll say yes.'

They ended up in a nearby wine cellar, squeezed together on a padded bench under a low whitewashed ceiling. Carole was persuaded after all to share a bottle of wine; talking together, Paul found her quiet voice as soothing as warm oil. Three glasses of wine in and Paul found himself pouring out his problems. 'And now Ruth's coming home after working on a case in England, and somehow I just can't face it. I'm thinking of moving out,' he concluded.

Carole had listened attentively, her kind face concerned. 'Do you want a divorce?'

He shook his head. 'I still love my wife. At least, I love the Ruth she used to be. Some of it's down to me, I know that. But I feel as if I've been trying against all the odds to hold things together, whereas she's simply opted out.'

'What's it going to do to her if you leave?'

Paul laughed bitterly. 'On recent form, she probably won't even notice.'

'More importantly then,' Carole said, 'what will it do to your son?'

'He's the one I worry about. He's already pretty screwed up by the accident. For a while there, he seemed OK, but it's all coming out now. Nightmares, infections, withdrawal.'

'Is he seeing anyone about it?'

'The school psychiatrist. If there was anything I could do to help him out of it, I'd do it. But I don't see that there is.'

'So you're going to walk out on him.'

'Put like that, it sounds irresponsible of me.'

'Isn't that what it is?'

Crammed against her in the vaulted space, he could smell her perfume. 'Don't think I don't know that I'm acting like a shit. But what else is there to do?'

'Stay. Tough it out.'

'I've tried that, and it didn't work. I keep telling myself I'll be a better father to him if I'm happier myself.'

'Sounds like the usual hypocritical bullshit men your age come up with when they're trying to justify their decision to abandon their responsibilities.' Carole lowered her eyes. 'It's what my husband said before he left me for somebody else. "Think of it as creating two happy homes for the children," he told me, "rather than one unhappy one."'

'But I can't just go back to the situation we were in before Ruth went to England. The coldness. The distance.'

'She's lost a child, Paul. How do you expect her to be?'

'I feel like I can't talk to her about anything. Maybe one of these days we can start over, but for now, I've just got to get out.'

'That's the coward's way,' she said crisply.

'Is it?'

'Yes.'

Walking her back to her car, Paul found himself wanting to ask if they could do this again. And might have done so if he had believed there was the slightest chance she would say yes.

Paul met Ruth off the plane. Despite the heavy workload of the past weeks, she looked younger and more carefree and he knew that she had made a great success of the job in London. He recalled other meetings after separation, when he would sweep her into his arms, call her name, feel his heart soar with the sheer joy of seeing her once more. He put his arms round her.

'Where's Will?' she said.

'He had to stay after school. Basketball practice.'

'I can't wait to see him again.'

'He's shaken off that cold at last. Eating everything in sight.'

'I'm glad he's got his appetite back. From what you told me, I was seriously worried about him.'

'Not *that* worried,' Paul said. 'Or you'd have come home earlier.'

Ruth felt her gut clench with anger. 'That's unfair. And you know it.'

'If you want to know what I think—'

'I don't. And I'm far too tired to argue about it now.'

They walked together to the parking lot, the silence thick between them as Paul backed the car out and made his way onto the freeway. Ruth closed her eyes and leaned her head against the back of the seat.

He felt sick. What would she say when he told her that he was leaving her? He glanced at her and noted the familiar little chocolate mole just below her left ear. She had once been so dear to him. And now there was a void where love used to be. Although he had gone over the arguments a hundred times during her absence, he still found himself debating his decision. Was he doing the right thing? What about Will?

They travelled up in the elevator without speaking, avoiding each other's gaze. When he let her into the apartment, she looked around appreciatively. The furniture was polished, the rugs vacuumed, there was a vase of white freesias on the coffee table. 'Wow! You must have paid Bess extra, to get it looking like this,' she said.

'Bess is off sick.'

'Are you telling me *you* did this?'

'I would—if I thought you'd believe me,' Paul said. 'No, I found someone in the Yellow Pages.'

'It looks great. Wonderful.'

Paul went into the kitchen. 'Coffee?' he called. His hands were damp with sweat.

'I have to take a shower before I do anything else.'

In the shower, she closed her eyes as the water fell over her shoulders. Despite the spat at the airport, there was still so much between them. It had been a long time since they made love, far too long. It was her fault, she knew that. She was ready to acknowledge how wrong she had been. Above all, she wanted to tell him that it was not his fault that Josie had died.

She came out of the shower with a towel wrapped round her and said, without preamble, 'Let's go to bed.'

'What?'

'I want to make love with my husband again, Paul. It's so good to be back with you. Let's do it, before Will comes home.'

'Ruth, I . . .'

She stood on tiptoe and kissed him, pressed closer to him. 'Paul,' she murmured. She undid his shirt and let the towel slip. His tweed jacket was rough against her body. She ran a finger along the hard line of his ribs, touched the jutting bones of his hips. When she moved down his stomach to his crotch, she expected to feel his erection, hot and strong, ready to take her quickly and fiercely. But . . .

'Paul,' she whispered. 'What's wrong?'

'I don't know,' he said.

'Don't you want to?' She stepped back.

'Not now.'

'Then when?'

He looked at her hard and she could see the shine of tears in his eyes. 'I don't know.'

She turned away. 'I feel such a fool,' she said. In silence, she bent to pick up the towel, covered her nakedness, went into the bedroom. When she came back, fully dressed, he was sitting at the kitchen table drinking coffee. 'OK,' Ruth said. 'Let's talk.'

He drew a deep breath into his lungs. 'I'm . . . I'm moving out, Ruth.'

'You mean, leaving us?'

'Not Will. Just you. You, the way you are. I told you before you went to London, we just don't seem to have anything in common any more.'

'Is this all because of the . . . what happened?'

'Let's face it, Ruth. Things weren't going right before that. When you joined LKM, you became a different person. Your work always seems to be more important than we are.'

'That's so unfair,' Ruth said furiously. 'I *have* to work. But you've always resented the fact that I earn more than you do.'

Paul sighed. 'Most men would. I do my best. But whatever I do, I am never going to match your salary. I can't take your disapproval any more.'

'I *don't* disapprove of you.'

'That's not how it looks from where I'm standing. You've put such a distance between us that I don't see how we can ever cross it.'

'Don't say that, Paul,' she begged. 'Please don't.'

'We've been apart for weeks, and I'm afraid I've enjoyed being on my own with Will. It's been such a relief not to be shut out by the person

I'm supposed to be closest to.' He shook his head. 'Every time I think about us, all I can remember is you keeping me at arm's length.'

'You're right. I know that. But I realise it now and I didn't before. Oh, Paul . . .' She was crying. 'Don't go. Please don't.'

'We want different things,' he said quietly.

'No, it's not true.'

'I just don't seem to figure in your life any more.'

Ruth wiped the tears from her face with the back of her hand. Anger had begun to build where only minutes ago there had been anguish. He was going to walk out on them. He had been planning it all the time she was away. 'You've made up your mind, haven't you?'

'That's right.'

'Does Will know?' she asked.

'It seemed only fair to wait until you got back.'

'Fair? Did you say *fair*?' She looked down at her wedding band. 'I suppose there's another woman, is there?'

He tried to speak but she rushed on. 'What is she, one of your students who props up your ego and makes you feel like a stud? Stares up at you with big adoring eyes every time you speak? Well, believe me, Paul, that won't last. Ten years down the road, you'll be in the same situation with her as you think you are with me, except you'll be supporting two families, not just one, and you'll be ten years older.' Ruth pushed back from the table. 'You're crazy if you think—'

'Ruth.' He reached over and put a hand over hers. 'There isn't anyone else.'

'Then—why?'

He spoke very deliberately. 'I need to talk about Josie. You don't know how many times, since she died, I reached out in the night for you, and you pushed me away. The truth is . . .' He hesitated. 'I'm more comfortable when you're not here. I can cope better on my own.'

She gazed at him in disbelief. 'That is such a hurtful thing to say.'

'If you'd just allow yourself to show some emotion. If you would only talk to me . . .'

'How many times do I have to tell you I've changed? The time in England was just what you said: it gave me space to think. But since you've made your mind up, what is there to say?' Tears began to roll down her cheeks again.

'If you'd just tell me you still loved me, then I'd stay.' He stared at her challengingly. 'Tell me, Ruth.'

For a long moment, she hesitated, then she looked away. 'If you're leaving, better do it before Will gets back,' she said.

He left before Will came home from school. His bags had been packed and stowed in the back of his car. Sitting in the driver's seat, he leaned over and popped open the glove compartment where he kept a photograph of Ruth. She gazed at the camera, laughing. Clear grey eyes, just like Josie's. God, they were so alike.

Suddenly, he was weeping. A grown man sitting in his car, sobbing. He smudged the tears away and stared into the bleak concrete space of the underground parking lot. If she came down now and asked him to stay, he knew he would.

He turned the key in the ignition, floored the accelerator, gunned out of the parking space and up to street level, just missed hitting a messenger on a bike. He slammed on the brakes, his hands trembling. At the lights, he flipped the indicator, ready to turn, ready to go back. But if he changed his mind, the situation would simply revert to what it had been. She had said things were different now, but he did not really believe her. 'Tell me, Ruth,' he'd said. Meaning, tell me you love me. But she hadn't. As the lights blinked from red to green, he pulled straight ahead, hearing the indignant horn-blasts of the drivers behind him.

After so many weeks in the anonymity of Chelsea, Ruth had looked forward to being among her own things again. Instead, she moved about the big apartment in a daze. Jet lag made her brain feel sluggish; she could scarcely keep her eyes open.

Paul. The thought of him quivered in her heart. There had never been anyone else but Paul, not really. Chris Kauffman, briefly. Nobody else. She sat on one of the two broad window seats and stared down unseeing at the traffic. All she could think of was that Paul was gone.

Much later, she heard Will's key in the lock. 'Mom!' he said, his face alight. 'You're back!'

She hugged him, held him tight. When she finally let him go and looked at him properly, she was suddenly alarmed. In the weeks she had been away, he had changed. He looked ill. Exhausted.

Sitting with a coffee in the kitchen, while he drank most of a half-litre of milk, she said carefully, 'Your father has moved out.'

He wiped his mouth with the back of his hand. 'Where to?'

'I don't know.' Before Paul had left, he had said something about writing down his new address and leaving it on the pinboard in the kitchen, but she had not yet looked at it.

Will's eyes widened. 'You mean, like, moved *out*?'

'Yes.'

'I don't get it. Has he gone to live with somebody else?'

She could not comprehend it, so why should he? 'He says not.'

'Are you upset?'

'We've been married for nearly twenty years.' She got up and hugged him again, trying to hide her tears. 'Honey, I'm sorry. I'm really sorry.'

'It's not your fault.'

'I sort of think it is. Or *he* does, which comes to the same thing.'

Will bit his lip. She watched him trying to be brave, trying to pretend it did not matter. 'I don't see why he's all of a sudden got to go,' he said.

'I think he's realised he's happier living on his own.'

'What about me?' His chin trembled. 'I'm his *son*.'

She started to weep. 'Ah, Will. Sweetheart.'

'We had some good times together while you were in England,' he said. 'I thought he loved me.'

'He does. He does. His leaving has nothing to do with you. You must believe that, Will.'

'First Josie, now Dad,' he said unsteadily. 'Why does shit like this happen? What did we do?' He began to sob. 'What else is going to happen to us, Mom?'

'Nothing, Will. This is as bad as it gets. From here on in, it'll start getting better.' She put her arms round him. 'And maybe, after a while, Dad'll realise it's more fun living with us than on his own.'

'He said we'd rebuild the *Lucky Duck*,' Will said. His body shook with repressed sobs. 'Him and me. He said it'd be our spring project.'

'It still will be. Just because he's—he's living somewhere else doesn't mean he's stopped being your dad.'

The two of them swayed together, mother and son, until Will jerked himself upright. 'Don't cry, Mom.' He put his hand up and curved it round the line of her jaw in an oddly adult gesture. 'We'll be OK.'

'Will we?'

'Paul's gone, Dad.'

'How do you mean, he's gone?' Ruth's father sounded as if she had just woken him up.

'He's left us. Moved out.'

There was a silence, then Jonathan Carter said, 'Oh, dear God. Oh, honey, I'm so sorry.'

'Dad, I . . .' She could hear her father telling his wife, and her mother's sudden alarmed response as she snatched the phone away from him.

'Ruthie. Darling. What's happened? What's wrong? These days Dad's hearing's not all it—'

'He heard OK.'

'Paul's *left* you?'

'Yes.'

'Why? Why?' Betty Carter's voice rose. 'Was it because you went to England? I always wondered if it was wise, leaving him on his own. Men are kind of—'

'There isn't anyone else, no other woman,' Ruth said. 'Or so he says.'

'Ruthie. Oh, Ruthie. Are you all right?' Her mother began to weep. 'Of course you're not, how could you be? I can't believe it.'

'Nor me, Mom.'

'What about Will?'

'Poor kid. He's being so brave about it. Oh, Mom . . .'

'Want us to fly up and be with you?'

'Not just yet. Not till I've . . .' Pulled myself together, Ruth wanted to say, then wondered how long that would take.

'We love you, hon.' Her father came back on the line. 'Remember that, Ruth. You'll always be our darling girl.' His voice fogged with emotion. 'Ruth, I'm so sorry . . .'

'Dad, Dad. I don't know what to do.' Ruth broke down. She rested her head against the wall beside the telephone and let herself cry. Dimly she could hear her father's tears, and behind him, her mother's inarticulate cries of distress. They were there for her now, as they had always been. The way she had not been for Josie.

Suddenly there was such a rush of work that Ruth barely had time to scramble through the days. At the office she was treated with a respect which helped to fill some of the hollows in her heart. The successful outcome of the McLennan Corporation's case was seen as a triumph for her. Bob Landers hinted at further promotion.

Her initial concern about Will's health abated somewhat. She put his paleness down to the fact that he was growing too fast; his clothes appeared to have shrunk, sleeves halfway up his arms, trousers way above his ankles. The nightmares Paul had spoken of seemed to have stopped. But almost overnight, he had become difficult and uncooperative. His response to her grew increasingly hostile.

'How did it work when I was away?' she asked him. 'You guys had some kind of routine for running the place, didn't you?'

'What's your point?' he said rudely.

'Dad told me on the phone that you were taking turns to cook. Want to go on with that?'

'You're back now.' He gazed at her resentfully. 'Cooking's what moms are supposed to do, isn't it?'

He was punishing her. For going to England. For Paul's departure. She tried to be patient. 'Fine. But listen, with Bess still off sick, you're going to have to help more around the place.'

'Ever heard of the Yellow Pages?'

'Thanks for the advice,' she said, determined not to let him rile her. 'But you could start by not leaving wet towels all over the bathroom.'

'Anyone would think this was a friggin' showhouse or something.'

'If it was, you certainly wouldn't be allowed to leave your room looking like a nuclear disaster zone.'

'It may look like a mess to you—'

'It most definitely does.'

'—but I know where everything is.'

She clenched her teeth, not wanting to shout at him.

Later, she came home after work to find him watching *Star Trek* instead of getting on with his homework. Buttered popcorn was spilt all over the scatter rugs.

'Will,' she snapped. 'What the hell's all this mess? Clean it up.' She picked up the remote control and switched off the set. 'You know the house rules: no TV until your homework's done.'

'Don't do that!' he shouted. He grabbed the remote and flicked on the TV again.

'Will,' she said. 'Turn it off.'

'I want to watch it.'

'You heard me. I said no.' She dropped her bags on the table. 'Besides, I've got a terrible headache.'

'You don't care about anything except yourself, do you?'

'Don't talk to me like that.' Frustration made her peremptory.

'No wonder Dad left,' he muttered.

'That's enough,' she said, her voice rising.

He stood up and strode menacingly towards her. 'Well, it's true.'

She stepped back, her heart beating in doublequick time. 'I'm not going to argue with you,' she said, trying to stay calm.

'That's because you know I'm fucking right.'

'Don't use that kind of language,' Ruth said curtly. She bent and pulled the plug for the TV out of the socket. 'And get on with your homework.'

She went into the kitchen to start preparing supper. Chopping vegetables, she took several deep breaths, trying to calm herself. For a moment, she had almost thought he was going to attack her.

Later, Will emerged grumpily from his room when she knocked at the door to say supper was ready. Slumped in his chair, he stared at the roasted vegetable lasagne she had prepared and pushed his plate away.

'Aren't you hungry?' she asked, concerned.

'Starving. But that looks disgusting. I'll throw up.'

'Eat it,' she shouted. 'Eat it, Will, or I'll feed you myself.'

He stared at her. 'What did you say?'

'I said I'd feed you, Will, just like I did when you were a baby. And I mean it. I'm sick and tired of your behaviour. Have some consideration for me, will you? I know you miss your father. But you're not the only one suffering. Whatever you're feeling, I'm feeling the same.'

'It's not *my* fault he went.'

She had been here before. She had seen that same look of hostility in Josie. She was not going to let it happen again. She shut her eyes and counted to ten, then said as calmly as she could, 'I can't go on like this, Will. I just can't cope with your rudeness and surliness and the way you act as though you can hardly bear to be in the same room as me.'

'Maybe I can't.'

'Then perhaps you'd better go live with your dad.'

'Everything fuckin' *sucks!*' Will shouted. '*Everything.*'

'Tell me about it. I've got feelings too, dammit.' Her hands shook as she tried to lift her water glass and drink from it. 'I'm hurting inside, just like you are. I understand how you feel, Will. I honestly do.' She drew in a ragged breath and covered her face with her hands. She began to weep. 'I d-don't think I can c-carry on like this for much longer.'

Will seemed bewildered by her outburst. 'Hey, calm down, will you?'

'Please, please stop taking everything out on me. *Please.*'

'Look, I'm sorry . . .'

'I'm doing my best. You may not like it, but I'm really trying to do my best,' she said, sniffing.

'OK. I'm sorry.' He reached for the dish on the table and took a large helping. 'All right?' He dug his fork into the pasta and began to eat it.

After a while, she peeked through her fingers. 'You're right,' she said.

'What about?'

'It does look disgusting, doesn't it?' She tried to laugh.

'Kinda. See, what you did, Mom, was you didn't make a cheese sauce and pour it between the layers.'

'Didn't I?'

'No. That's why none of it's sticking together.'

'I'm sorry, darling.'

'Tastes OK, though,' Will conceded. He drank half a Diet Pepsi, then said, not looking at her, 'Maybe I could do some cooking at the weekend or something. Show you a few things.'

'I'd really like that,' she said humbly.

'I asked you to take the laundry out of the machine and fold it,' Ruth said one evening, about a week later. The two of them were living in an uneasy partnership. Explosion was never far from the surface, but Will was obviously trying to be less surly and Ruth made an effort to hide her irritation at the listless way he dragged himself about the apartment.

'I know you did.' He was lying on the couch in the sitting room. 'I was too tired when I came back from school.'

'And you were too tired last night to put the dishes in the dish-washer,' she said. 'But you weren't too tired to go up to Sweetharbor with your father last weekend.'

'We didn't go in the end. We stayed in his apartment instead, took it kind of easy. Went to the movies. Watched football on TV.'

'At your age you shouldn't be tired. Is it just that you're trying to do too much? Or is there something else wrong that you're not telling me?'

He did not answer for a while. Then he said reluctantly, 'I haven't been feeling real good lately. I keep throwing up. And I get these pains in my joints.'

Frowning, Ruth got up and stood over him. 'What's this?' There were a couple of angry boils on his neck and another halfway up his arm.

He ducked away from her. 'Nothing.'

'Are there any more of these on you?'

'One or two.'

Her heart began to beat faster with anxiety. 'Are you sleeping prop-erly? You've got terrible shadows under your eyes.' Was he doing drugs?

'Don't fuss. I'm just tired, that's all.'

'You still hanging out with Ed and Dan?'

'Course I am. They're my friends. The guys in the band. Dan's father thinks he might get us a gig.'

'I heard that Dan had a problem.'

'Dan Baxter is a problem,' Will said. He grinned at her. There was a group of red pus-filled spots near one corner of his mouth.

'I meant a drug problem,' Ruth said.

'So what if he has?'

'Are you involved with anything like that? I promise I won't be angry if you tell me you've been trying stuff out.'

'I haven't.'

She shook her head at him. 'I have no way of knowing whether you're telling me the truth. But if you're in trouble, let me help you.'

'Read my lips, Mom.' He closed his eyes wearily. 'I do not have a drug problem, OK? Dad says I'm growing too fast, that's all.'

It would have to do for the moment. She was overloading. No longer in control. Exhausted, Ruth went back to the papers she was preparing for the next day's work.

The following morning, she went into Will's room to hurry him along for school, and found him still under the covers. That was all she needed. She looked impatiently at her watch.

'Come on, Will,' she said briskly. 'Up, up, up. We're running late.'

'I don't think I can get out of bed,' he said, his voice rasping. It sounded like he was coming down with yet another cold.

'We all feel like that sometimes,' she said. Ruth felt his forehead. 'You don't have a fever.' She made some quick calculations. The only really urgent thing was her ten o'clock meeting. If she could rearrange the rest of her schedule, maybe she could get Will up and running. She tried not to sound impatient. 'Look, I'll tell the office I won't be in until later.'

'Sorry, Mom. I . . . I don't know what it is.' His eyes were suddenly frightened.

Ruth looked at him, biting her lip. She headed for the phone. This was exactly why her firm was so leery of promoting women: when there was a family emergency, they always put the family before the job.

Ruth called her assistant. 'I'm going to be late, Marcy.'

'Nothing serious, I hope,' Marcy said.

'My son's not well. Will you reschedule my ten o'clock appointment for eleven? Better still, eleven thirty.'

'What about your lunch date with Baker Industrial?'

'I can't imagine I won't be in the office by eleven.'

She called the Health Maintenance Organisation clinic and explained that Will had no fever, but seemed weak. The receptionist put her through to a nurse-practitioner. She was asked when Will had last had a blood test and said that as far as she remembered, it had been just after Christmas, when he had been tested for anaemia.

'You say he's too weak to get out of bed?'

'Yes.'

'Mmm.' A pause. 'Can you get him down here so we can take a look?'

When she went back into Will's room, Ruth was fighting panic. Seeing him lying there, trying to smile, his face almost as white as the pillow, it was hard to disguise her fear.

'Anything you want, darling? The bathroom?'

He looked embarrassed. 'I do sort of need to go,' he said.

'Here. Let me help you up.' She slid an arm round his shoulders and tugged him into a sitting position. She had not realised how thin he was. She swung his legs sideways so that by pulling him forward he was standing on the floor. He stood, knees trembling like a newborn foal's.

'Come on, now. Put your arm round my waist.' She grabbed hold of his other hand and together they tottered towards the bathroom.

'I can manage now, Mom,' he said. 'Thanks.'

'Are you sure?'

'Really. Perhaps I just kind of got locked into position or something.'

'Call me if you need help.'

She heard the flushing of the toilet, then Will called from the bathroom door. He sounded stronger. 'Maybe I'll take a shower.'

She went into the passage and looked at him leaning against the bathroom doorpost. 'Do you feel like eating something?'

'Not really.'

A wave of fear swept through her, leaving her weak. Hot tears stung her eyes. There could not be anything seriously wrong with him. 'I think you ought to try to get something down you. And then . . .'

'Then what?'

'I'm going to run you to the clinic. We need to get this dealt with,' she said firmly. 'Whatever it is.'

While he showered, she called Paul's office. Melda, the department secretary, answered. 'Ms Connelly,' she said. 'It's good to hear your voice.'

'Hi, Melda.' Did she know Paul had moved out? 'Is my husband there?'

'Professor Connelly has classes right now. But I can get him to call you, soon as he comes back. Should be here midmorning.'

'Please do, Melda. Tell him it's important.'

'Not something serious, I hope, Ms Connelly?'

Oh, God, so do I, Ruth thought. 'Just say it's about Will. He's . . .' Ruth tried not to burst into tears. 'I'm taking him down to the HMO clinic.'

Water was still running in the bathroom. She went into Will's room and began pulling his sheets off the bed. By the time she had finished making it up with fresh ones, Will was shuffling back into the room, a towel round his waist. So like his father, she thought. The shoulder blades were the same, and so was the way his back muscles lengthened into his waist. The man he would become was plain to see. She wanted to kiss him, tell him how much she loved him. When had she last done that? There were bruises on his body, by the elbows, at his shoulder. More of the boils flared on his back, red and angry.

'Are you OK to get dressed by yourself?'

'Think so. I feel a bit better.' He sat down on the edge of the bed and closed his eyes. 'Sort of, anyway.'

'Sure about breakfast? There's cereal? Eggs? Waffles? Or blueberry pancakes? I could easily do some for you.'

'I'm not real hungry, Mom.' He reached for the shirt she had put out and began to pull it on. The bones of his arms pushed against the transparent skin, almost fleshless.

My God, Ruth thought, can he be anorexic? It was supposed to be a disease which mainly afflicted girls, but she had read that boys suffered from it too.

'Put your down jacket on,' she said. 'It's subzero outside.' She hoped she sounded calm, businesslike.

'OK.'

Searching for her keys in the kitchen, she held on to the edge of the counter and bowed her head for a second or two. Anorexia would explain the weakness, the loss of appetite, the tiredness. Maybe even the pains in his joints he had complained of recently.

Driving across town to the clinic, it seemed as if every light turned red as she approached it. Will was collapsed in the back seat. His breath crackled in his chest. Her own breath was coming quick and short. Her thoughts churned, panicky, terrified. Anaemia. Anorexia. Anaemia. Anorexia. They were not life-threatening diseases. Hang on to that. Will was ill, but he was going to be all right. He was. He would be all right.

She pulled up untidily in front of the building. The air glittered with frost particles as she ran in and told the receptionist who she was. Someone followed her out and helped transfer Will from the car to a wheelchair, then took him inside and waited while she parked the car. Once inside, she pushed him down the polished corridors.

Greg Turner, the paediatrician, was waiting for them. She watched his expression change as his eyes fell on Will. He checked the boy's mouth, pushed up a sleeve and examined the skin of his arm. Asked if he had any pain. When Will mentioned his stomach, the doctor's fingers probed gently, withdrawing when Will winced. He picked up the phone on his desk and spoke discreetly into it.

Then he looked at Ruth. 'I want him to go down to the hospital,' he said. 'Right now. I want him to have some tests done.' He made no attempt to soothe, or to play down the gravity in his voice.

'What is it?' Her heart was revving up like the engine of a racing car. She stepped closer to the paediatrician and spoke quietly so that Will would not hear. 'Is it something serious?'

Greg took her hands in his. 'I wouldn't presume to make any kind of diagnosis without proper tests. Now, I've called an ambulance to take him in. You can ride along with them.'

Ruth looked at Will. He gave her a ghostly grin. 'Mom, chill out.'

More than anything else, she wanted Paul.

Eight

MELDA PASSED PAUL a note. 'She's taking your boy to the HMO clinic. Wanted you to call her.'

'When was this?'

'About an hour ago.'

Paul picked up the handset and dialled the number of the apartment. All he got was the efficient voice of Ruth's answering service. He called her office number, but Marcy could only tell him that Ruth had not yet shown up. Taking out his wallet, he searched through it for the small plastic card with the HMO's phone number. When the switchboard answered, he asked for the paediatrician. 'Which one?' he was asked.

'Greg,' he said, desperately trying to remember the doctor's surname. 'Uh . . . Greg Turner.' What was this all about?

'Hello?'

'Dr Turner,' Paul said. 'It's Professor Connelly. Will Connelly's father? I got a message to call my wife but she's not—'

'I sent her down to the hospital, along with William.'

'But why? What the hell is wrong?'

'I can't be sure, Professor.' Turner's voice was remote, impersonal. 'As I said to your wife, I'm not going to make any kind of diagnosis just off the top of my head. I suggest you join her down there.'

Paul replaced the handset. He stared at Melda, at the familiar office, without really seeing either.

'Cancel my classes for the rest of the day,' he said.

He got to the hospital just before noon. He was directed to the Haematology Department, where he found Ruth alone in a waiting area. She was sitting with a magazine on her lap and her eyes closed. He took a moment to watch her. She was much too thin, the cheekbones aggressive, her body angular. She looked so frail. Was all this the result of a summer storm eight months ago? Before then, surely things had been good, when they were still that dull and unusual thing, a happy family. A fairly happy family, at any rate.

How could he have walked out on her? On Will? He called her name and she opened her eyes with a jerk of the head, rising to her feet. When he spread his arms, she stepped inside them and leaned against his chest. Just for a moment, he allowed himself to think that this was the way it was, instead of the way it used to be.

'I'm scared,' she said.

'What the hell is going on, Ruth?'

'I can't . . . I can't really t-take it all in. They're running all s-sorts of tests, Paul. It's something . . . something bad.'

'What kind of bad?'

For answer, she began to sob. 'They're talking about . . . they've done some blood tests and I overheard one of the technicians saying it could be—' She seemed to be too frightened to pronounce the word.

'What, Ruth?' He shook her impatiently.

'Cancer. Leukaemia.' The word barely made it through her lips.

'Oh, my God.' He drew her down to sit beside him. 'Leukaemia? Oh God.' He took her hand, squeezed it, hoping to tap into her strength. The word spelt a horror he felt too drained to contemplate. Leukaemia meant pain and the ravaging of a body. And little kids dying. How could any of that have relevance for Will?

Ruth shivered as though she were in the winter chill of outdoors instead of an overheated hospital wing. 'I should have seen it, Paul. I knew he didn't look right, he was so tired all the time, but I was too wrapped up with my work. I was too fucking involved with my stupid shitty *job!*' Ruth screamed out the last word. She tore her hand from Paul's. Picking up the magazine from the floor where it had fallen, she threw it violently against the wall. 'Because I'm a lousy, godawful mother who never deserved to have children in the first place.'

He shook her, then slapped her face. 'Stop it, Ruth. We don't even know for sure what's wrong with him. Maybe Greg Turner was just play-ing safe, sending you down here.' He was talking for his own sake as much as for hers. 'Besides, if . . . *if*, God forbid, it *is* . . . leukaemia, it's nothing you or I've done that's caused it, nothing we could have done to prevent it. Blaming yourself isn't going to achieve anything.' He pressed shaky fingers against his forehead.

Someone joined them. They both looked up at him. A doctor. *The* doctor? He nodded at Paul. 'Hi. You must be Professor Connelly. I'm Mike Gearin. Staff haematologist. Sorry to keep you waiting.'

'What's . . .' Ruth swallowed. 'What's wrong with our son?'

The doctor tried to smile. 'Well.' He looked down at the notes in his hand. 'At this stage it does look as though your son has a serious blood disorder.'

'Oh God,' whispered Ruth.

'What blood disorder?' Paul said.

'He's currently being checked out by a team of experts.' The doctor ticked them off. 'A haematologist. An oncologist. A urologist. A neurologist. Not much is going to get past those guys, believe me. We've done the blood work, but now we have to wait for the results of the other tests. If there's something there to find, we'll find it.' But his eyes said more than his mouth. Paul felt cold. Those eyes said he knew already that something had been found.

When he had gone, they sat in silence, the minutes dragging as they might have done before an execution.

It was almost six o'clock when Gearin reappeared. This time he asked them to follow him to a small side room that held a low couch and two chrome upright chairs. One of them was occupied by an older doctor.

He stood up and held out a hand. 'Good to meet you both,' he said. 'I'm Dr Caldbeck, Chief of Haematology.'

Gearin took the other upright chair. 'Right,' he said. He had a very direct gaze. 'William.' He looked sideways at his colleague. Laced his fingers together. 'Yes,' he said. 'Well, there's no point trying to soften the blow for you. As we suspected, William is seriously ill.'

'What is it?' Paul was the one who asked. Ruth's hands trembled in her lap. She could not have put the question.

'Looks like acute lymphoblastic leukaemia,' Gearin said.

'But leukaemia's almost incurable, isn't it?' Ruth began to shiver.

'By no means. ALL is extremely responsive to therapy. We—researchers in the field, that is—are constantly expanding our understanding of the disease, which means that the chances of recovery keep on improving as we discover more effective treatments. These days, we look for cures in as high as eighty per cent of the cases presenting.'

'Are you absolutely certain of the diagnosis?' Paul asked.

'As sure as we can be, I'm afraid. The blood work we've done seems fairly conclusive, though we'll have to perform a bone marrow aspiration to come up with a precise diagnosis. After we've seen the results of that, and have determined the extent of the disease, we can begin the treatment. Now, how much do you know about leukaemia?'

'It's cancer of the blood cells, isn't it?' Again it was Paul who spoke. Ruth had shrunk inside herself, not wanting to hear any of this.

'That's right. What happens with leukaemia is that the body begins to produce large numbers of abnormal white blood cells that don't function properly. The disease starts in the bone marrow, which is essentially a mechanism for producing blood cells. If one of these cells mutates, it multiplies at a rapid rate, overwhelming the other healthy tissues. Looking at Will's medical history over the past few weeks, he's been subject to chest infections, poor appetite, fatigue, joint pain. All of them are classic symptoms of the disease.'

'He had a blood test only a few weeks ago,' Paul said. 'Why wasn't this picked up sooner?'

'He wasn't given a broad spectrum blood count,' Gearin said. 'According to his file, they were looking for anaemia, not leukaemia. Because some of the symptoms are similar, it's possible that the one masked the other. On the other hand, he might not even have developed the disease at that stage. It can occur very suddenly.'

Caldbeck nodded in agreement. 'We could give tests on one day which showed there was nothing wrong, and twenty-four hours later, do the same tests and find he's got the disease.'

'What are his chances?' Paul asked.

'We can't really say at this point,' Dr Caldbeck said. 'So much depends on the patient himself and his response to treatment. I can only repeat what Dr Gearin told you that ALL is very sensitive to chemotherapy treatment, and these days we look to an eighty per cent cure rate.'

Gearin began to outline the treatment choices available. 'There's chemotherapy, which uses drugs to kill the rogue cancer cells. Or radiation therapy, where high-energy rays are employed to zap the cancer cells and inhibit their growth. Sometimes we choose a combination treatment, depending on which looks right for the patient.'

The patient. Will. It sounded so cold, so distant from the boy who waited for them somewhere in a hospital room.

'There's a downside to all this, isn't there?' Paul said.

'The use of high-dose chemotherapy to kill the cells destroys the bone marrow,' Gearin said quietly. 'If the loss of bone marrow becomes critical, we have to find a healthy donor and infuse bone marrow from him or her into the patient. In other words, replace Will's own bone marrow with that taken from the donor.'

Ruth heard what he was saying, but could not take it in. 'I'm so cold,' she said. Shock and stress had set up a reaction in her own body.

Gearin lifted a phone and pressed in some numbers. 'Could we have some coffee in here?' he said. 'As soon as possible.' He gazed at Ruth with concern.

'Take my coat.' Paul removed his jacket and draped it round her.

'Thank you.' The jacket carried the heat of his body and Ruth's shivers subsided. She leaned against him and felt his hands strong on her shoulders. She reached up and grasped them.

'Will's going to be all right,' Paul said. 'You heard what the man said. Eighty per cent of cases are cured.'

'Which means twenty per cent aren't.'

'Don't talk like that,' said Paul angrily. 'Don't even think it.'

'I should have noticed. I should have brought him in sooner.'

'Don't blame yourselves,' Caldbeck said. 'That's always the first reaction parents have when they hear a diagnosis like this—that somehow it's their fault.'

She did not believe him. It *was* her fault. Her boy. Her son. She had been so blind. If she hadn't gone to England, maybe this would not have happened. She started to sob, covering her face with her hands.

Gearin gave them papers to sign, to allow the surgery involved in taking bone marrow samples from Will to be performed. 'He won't be able to leave for a while,' he told them.

'Can we stay with him?' Ruth asked.

'If you wish.'

A call for Dr Caldbeck came over the intercom, and he got up. 'I'm sorry,' he said. 'I'm truly sorry. There is no news worse for a parent than to learn that their child has cancer. But we have every hope that between us we can beat it.' He held out his hand. 'Unfortunately, I'll be seeing you again. Meantime, just stay strong, for your son's sake.'

When he had gone, Dr Gearin led them through the benefits and disadvantages of chemotherapy. There would be unpleasant side effects, but most of them would be transitory, and meanwhile, healthy new cells would be developing.

'What sort of side effects?' Paul asked.

'Hair loss, ulcerated inflammation of the mouth and throat, nausea and vomiting, a change in food preferences. Uncomfortable while they last, but like I said, they're usually temporary.'

'Usually?'

'Nearly always. And not all patients in chemotherapy will experience all the adverse side effects.'

Gearin's mouth opened and shut. Words. Pouring out of him. Telling her things she did not want to hear. Nausea. Hair loss. Ulcers. My poor Will, Ruth thought. My poor boy. She wanted to be anywhere else but here, with her child nearby lying on a bed, deathly sick, among other sick children. The thought of the clean air of Caleb's Point came back to her. Brightness of sun on sea. Clearness of wind. Sound of the pine trees murmuring at her back. Where had it all gone, the treasures that she once had owned: children, husband, home? What fool's gold had she traded them for?

As soon as Ruth could get to a phone, she called Bob Landers at home.

'Ruth!' he said. 'I heard you didn't come in this morning. Don't worry—'

'I'm resigning, Bob.'

'You're what?'

'From the job, from the partnership.'

'Resigning? For God's sake, why?'

'I'm phoning from the hospital.'

'Hospital? Which hospital?'

'Will has just been diagnosed with leukaemia.'

'Oh, my God. Ruth, how appalling. Oh, I'm so very sorry.' Landers expelled a deep breath. 'But I'd urge you not to do anything drastic at this initial stage. Especially not to resign.'

'I have no choice.'

'We'll grant you an extended leave of absence instead.' She could almost hear the whirr of his brain as he calculated the pros and cons of letting her go. The temporary loss of one expensive partner versus the difficulty of finding and then training someone to take her place. 'Quite apart from anything else, there's the health insurance benefits. You may find you need them.'

'I hadn't thought of that.' The future stretched ahead, bleak and cold.

'Don't resign, Ruth. Not yet. That way, if and when—'

'There may not be any ifs or whens, Bob. Will is seriously ill.' Her voice trembled. 'Believe me, I'm grateful for your thoughts, Bob.' She put down the phone.

She called her parents. 'Mom, it's me. I'm calling—'

Her mother cut in, instantly aware that something dreadful had happened. 'What's wrong? What is it, Ruth?'

Ruth explained and listened to her mother's harsh sobs on the other end of the line. Her father took the phone and she explained again. She could feel his bewilderment.

'Why?' he said. 'So many cruel blows . . . Why?'

'If I knew that, Dad . . .' Ruth felt stronger and calmer than she had for months. If Will was to survive, then she must be strong.

'We'll come up at once,' her father said heavily. 'Take an apartment nearby, stay as long as we can be useful.'

'It's good of you to offer,' Ruth said gently. 'But for the moment, there's no need. You stay and take care of Mom.'

'But, Ruthie, we want to help.' Her mother came back on the line, her voice distorted by her tears. 'We want to be with you. And poor little Will. Cancer . . . oh, my *God*. And Florida's so far away.'

'There's nothing you can do for now.'

'Will you tell us when there is?' Jonathan Carter had taken the phone from his wife.

'I promise, Dad.'

'Just remember, girl, that we want to help. That we *need* to help. Will is our only grandchild. And you're our daughter. We've always been so proud of you, so . . .' His voice wavered, bringing Ruth to the edge of breaking down.

'I know that, Dad. And I'm so grateful to both of you,' she said. 'Not just for now but for . . .' Her throat jammed. '. . . for everything.'

Her father seemed to understand what she wanted them to know. 'We love you, hon.'

Tears slid down her cheeks. She had never been good at saying it, but now she did. 'I love you too, both of you, more than you can imagine.'

At last they were allowed in to see Will. He was in a glass-fronted room off the corridor leading from the nurses' station. He was lying on a bed, wearing a loose green hospital gown. An IV drip led from a plastic bag of clear liquid attached to a pole beside his bed into the vein inside his elbow. Behind him was a tall table holding a tangle of transparent tubing and a box which looked like part of a stereo system. A monitor stood on top of it, lines of electronic green marching erratically across its screen.

Seeing them, Will smiled, trying, as always, to break the tension with a joke. 'Hey, what kept you? I was beginning to think you folks had gone on vacation.'

'Oh, honey . . .' Ruth took his hand and Will winced.

'Careful, Mom. I've had so many needles stuck in me I don't dare have a drink in case it all leaks out onto the floor. Bet I look like a pincushion.'

'You look fine,' Ruth said. 'Just fine.'

Paul cleared his throat. 'Like the outfit.' His voice shook slightly.

'Hope none of the guys from school come by. Anyone sees me dressed like this, that's my rep gone.' He looked from Paul to Ruth. 'Are we going home soon?'

'Not just yet,' Ruth said. 'They still have some tests to do.'

'I'd really really like to go home,' Will said, his eyes sliding away from them. 'I don't want any more needles.' His mouth began to quiver.

'Hey,' Paul said gently. 'Hey, there.' He held his son's hand tight.

'They've pushed the darn things in everywhere,' Will said. His eyes filled. 'It hurts.'

'It's not for much longer. Just till they—till they find out what's wrong and how they're going to cure it.'

Will stared at them both. 'I'm real sick, aren't I?'

Paul knew they had a choice. They could either fudge, pretend, distance themselves from Will by dishonesty. Or they could tell the truth.

He bit his lip, then said, 'Kind of looks like it.'

'Am I gonna die?'

'Not if we have anything to do with it.' Like Paul, Ruth forced strength into her voice.

Paul wanted to get out of this room. He wanted a drink. Instead of having to be strong for Ruth and Will, he wanted someone who would listen and understand, someone who would be strong for him.

'Have I got cancer?' Will's matter-of-fact voice broke into Paul's thoughts. He glanced across at Ruth. Her face white and drawn, she nodded fractionally at him.

Paul took his son's hand. 'Yes.'

'Can I be cured?'

'They told us most cases are cured,' Ruth said.

'How long do I have to stay in here?'

'A little while longer,' said Paul. 'But one of us will stay with you.'

'I wish I had my Walkman.'

'I'll drive back home a bit later,' Ruth said. 'Anything else you want?'

'Books, maybe.' He sighed. 'Guess you'd better bring in my school tapes, too. I'm supposed to be studying *The Crucible*.'

'One of those plays whose sum is greater than its parts.' Paul adopted his solemn professorial face. 'A comment, if you will, on our contemporary culture which adds a whole new perspective to—'

'Knock it off, Dad. Gimme a break, just for once, will you?'

The chemo treatments left Will too weak and disorientated to do much for himself. When he came home after each treatment, in order to give his blood time to recover, Ruth found herself having to care for him in the same intimate fashion as she had when he was still a baby. He who had grown into self-reliance was forced to revert to dependency. She could only guess how much he hated the physical weakness which resulted from the drugs. He found it acutely embarrassing to have his personal privacy invaded.

As well as the drugs needed to fight the disease, Will was taking medication designed to combat infection, which often made him nauseous. His skin broke out into rashes and boils. He developed serious ulcers in his mouth and throat, making swallowing extremely painful. Ruth knew that along with all this was the fear he must be feeling.

Her grief at seeing him so weak and incapacitated was profound. His heavy eyes, his lethargy, his wounded skin, wrenched her. She had to clap her hands over her ears to hide the sound of his retching. She, so desperate to help, was powerless.

Going back to the hospital for each new treatment was traumatic for both Ruth and Will. There was no way to avoid seeing the ghostly army of hairless children, whose treatments were further advanced.

'They look like aliens,' Will said once.

'I know.' The deep-shadowed eyes, the gaunt faces, haunted Ruth.

'Am I going to lose *my* hair?'

'If by any chance you do, it'll grow back.'

What made the return visits even worse was Will's dislike, bordering on phobia, of needles. The pain made him scream aloud. Sometimes his arm swelled up like a balloon. Yet there was no way to avoid them. After one particularly harrowing session, he wept.

'I don't want any more treatment.'

'Hold on, honey. It's not for much longer,' Ruth said. She pressed a hand to her leaping heart. Even worse than the sight of his pain was her inability to stop it. It should be *me*, she wanted to shriek at the nurses. Let *me* suffer, not him. Not him.

'I'd rather die now than have to go through that again.' Tears rolled slowly down his white face. His bloodless lips quivered.

'Well, I'm not going to let you,' Ruth said. 'Who'd I have to nag at, if you weren't around?'

He was usually quick to respond to even the feeblest joke, as though he felt that laughter was the only way they would survive all this. Now, the effort to move his lips into a smile seemed too much for him.

When he had fallen into a frowning doze, Ruth went into the hospital washroom and stared at herself in the mirror over the handbasins.

One of the other mothers came in. Ruth had noticed her before, a too-thin bubbly blonde who always looked as if she was dressed up for a night out on the town. She smiled at Ruth's reflection. 'You're Mrs Donnelly, aren't you?'

'Connelly, yes. Ruth. And you're Michelle's mom.' It was known on the ward that eight-year-old Michelle was not likely to survive for very much longer.

'Lynda Petievich.' For a moment the woman's face crumpled. 'I wish I could be as brave as you are.'

'Brave? Me?' Was she putting on such a good front that someone actually believed that she, Ruth Connelly, was being *brave*?

'You seem so *strong*.' Lynda gulped, and her eyes filled with tears. 'Will is a lovely kid. He spends hours playing games with my Michelle, even though she's so much younger. Most boys his age wouldn't be bothered with a little girl.'

'She's such a pretty child.'

'Shoulda seen her when she still had her hair,' Lynda said. 'Your boy's OK that way.'

'So far.'

'And touch wood. It would be real hard for you if he . . .'

'He won't.' Her doubts vanished. 'He *won't*.'

'I wish I could say that.' The other woman's face melted like wax and anguish darkened her eyes.

Ruth reached out and took her hand. 'I'm not brave,' she said. 'Not in the least. I'm terrified. Every minute of every day. I see you and Michelle and all the moms and dads, and I feel truly humbled.' She glanced down at her creased jeans. 'And you always look so glamorous, too.'

'That's for Michelle's sake,' Lynda said. 'Before she got sick, I used to slob around like we all do, but I want her to know what a special person she is to me, that she's worth taking some trouble over. So now I always dress good. I don't know if it helps her, but it sure helps me.'

'Of course it helps her. We've all seen the way she lights up when you appear—it's like having a movie star visit. I should take more trouble myself. I always assumed Will would know I think he's special.'

'He is, he really is.' Lynda's eyes were again full of tears and she laughed shakily. 'Look at me. It's kind of strange, isn't it, that I can get emotional over your boy but I just don't dare over Michelle.'

'Perhaps I should cry for Michelle, and let you cry for my boy,' Ruth said. Her own eyes filled. 'Then we needn't bother about being brave because we're each crying for someone else's kid.'

'That's *such* a great idea.' For a moment, Lynda almost shone.

'It is, isn't it?' Ruth smiled too.

'**R**uth . . . it's Paul.' He hated talking to the machine but ploughed ahead. 'I'd like to come round tonight, see Will, if—'

She picked up. 'Hi, it's me.'

'Can I come round later?'

'I'll tell Will, he'll be glad to see you.'

'It'd be nice to see you too,' he said awkwardly. 'Maybe we could have a drink or something. I'll bring a bottle with me, if that's OK with you.'

He felt absurd, being so hesitant about it. She was still his wife, after all. There was nothing strange about the two of them sharing a glass of wine.

At the door, he gave her a hug and handed her the bottle and a package.

'What's this?' She fingered the pretty gift-wrap.

'Well,' he said. 'You have two choices: either you stand there all night feeling it and guessing. Or you open it and see.'

Inside was a necklet. Four little wooden hearts strung on a leather lace. Her face lit up. 'How lovely, Paul. Where did you find them?'

'Would you believe I made them?'

'As a matter of fact . . .' She smiled at him. 'Yes, I would. They're lovely,' Ruth said. 'Unusual.' She laid the hearts in a line on the coffee table. Ran a finger over the delicate carving. 'Thank you so much.'

Paul drew the cork and poured them each a glass of wine. 'May I say, Mrs Connelly, you're looking particularly good tonight.'

'Thank you.'

'Where's Will?'

'In bed. It hasn't been a good day for him.'

'I'll go and visit with him a while.'

Carrying his wineglass, he went down the passage to his son's room, thinking: she didn't pick up the necklace again. Didn't put it round her neck. Four hearts. One for each member of the family they used to be.

He knocked at Will's door. 'Can I come in?'

'Hi, Dad.'

Paul pushed open the door and went in. 'How're ya doin', son?'

Will lay back against his pillows, his face pale. 'OK, I guess.'

'Anything I can do for you?'

'Actually, Dad . . .'

'What?'

'I'm feeling kinda tired. I'd like it if you—if you'd read to me?'

'Be my pleasure.'

'Great.' Will lay back against his pillows, closed his eyes.

'What shall I read? Grown-up stuff? Kids' stuff?'

Will pointed to the nightstand. 'Actually, I'm halfway through this vampire book.'

'Vampires? Give me a break.'

'It's neat, Dad. All about this handsome young vampire who's fallen in love with this beautiful girl whose brother was murdered by a—'

Paul groaned. 'I just remembered there's something else I'm supposed to be doing.'

Will laughed, a quiet, weary sound so unlike his normal laugh that Paul almost burst into tears. 'I'm on page fifty-seven,' Will said. 'You'll love it, when you get into it.'

Will was back in the hospital for the next in his series of treatments. Arriving to spend time with him, Ruth heard voices through the open door of his room. Peeking through the half-drawn blinds which covered the window, she saw Michelle sitting on the edge of the bed. The little girl had Will's hand on her knee and was painting his nails with different coloured varnishes. Her face was very serious as she surveyed the most recent nail. 'It's gonna look so pretty, like a rainbow,' she said.

'Hey, Michelle.'

'What?'

'You know guys don't usually wear nail varnish, don't you?' Will said.

'Course I do, silly.' Michelle screwed the cap back onto a bottle of varnish and picked up another. 'This one's called Inca Gold. My mom wears this one for special, like when she and my dad go out dancing.'

'Do they do that a lot?'

'Every Friday. My mom's got these gowns she wears, all covered in sparkly stuff. She made them herself. She made me one, and Kelly, too.'

'I'll bet you both look really good.'

'My dad says we're the prettiest girls in the world.'

'What colour is Kelly's gown?' Will asked.

'Kind of shiny blue, to match her eyes. And mine's pink.'

'To match *your* eyes?'

'Nobody has pink eyes,' said Michelle sternly. 'It's pink 'cause that's my favourite colour. My mom mostly wears green 'cause that's what she was wearing when my dad fell in love with her. Where did your mom and dad fall in love?'

We were walking across College Green, Ruth thought. Buds just breaking, blue sky, the hint of spring in the air, the promise of hope. That's where we fell in love.

'I don't know,' Will said. 'Maybe at our house in Maine. It's called Carter's House.'

'Why?'

'Because it was built by somebody called Carter. My great-great-grandfather, I think.'

'What's it like?'

'It's painted white and it's got black shutters, and there's trees all round and the sea in front,' Will said. 'It's perfect.'

Ruth felt a knife twist in her heart. They should have spent last Christmas up there, as he had begged to do. But even as she thought this, she could feel her own fear at the possibility of pain. Josie was up there. What was left of her. The Boston apartment had been rendered bearable by clearing out her room, having it repainted, the furniture shifted around. But Carter's House was just as it had always been.

'The sun always shines up there, and the birds sing,' Will said.

'Even at night?'

'Specially at night.'

Michelle put her head on one side and regarded with satisfaction the golden nail she had just painted. Her tiny fingers clasped Will's hand. 'I bet you never had a manicure in your whole life, did you?'

'Boys don't have manicures.'

'My brothers do. But that's 'cause Kelly's practising on them.'

'You tell Kelly she can practise on me any time she likes. She's kinda pretty, isn't she?'

'She's *real* pretty,' corrected Michelle. 'She's going to work in a beauty parlour when she grows up.' She picked up a brilliant green varnish and took off the cap. 'Go on about the birds singing at night. Don't they keep you awake?'

'There's this special cap I wear,' Will said. 'I pull it down over my ears if I want to sleep.'

Michelle touched the pink gingham mobcap she was wearing to hide her naked skull. 'My sister made this for me.'

'It's real cute,' said Will. 'Think she'd make one for me?'

'No, 'cause you'd look *stoopid*,' Michelle said. 'Now, what shall we do for the last nail?'

'How about purple?'

'OK. Pink's my favourite, but purple's good too. What else do you do up there in your house by the sea?'

'I go out in my boat. Catch lobsters and crabs.' Ruth could hear the longing in his voice. 'Just look at the rocks and the trees. Smell the air.'

'Can I come and see your house when I'm better?'

'Sure. I'll take you out in my boat.'

Will looked up and saw his mother on the other side of the glass. He smiled at her and she raised her hand, not wanting to interrupt, but he called out, 'Mom! Come in.'

Ruth walked into the room. 'Looks like somebody's been getting the beauty treatment.'

Will splayed his hands girlishly across his T-shirt. 'Hey, whaddya think?'

'Truly gorgeous,' Ruth said.

'Hi, Mrs Connelly,' said Michelle.

'How are you today, honey?'

'Very well, thank you.'

The little girl's cheeks were unnaturally swollen, puffed out with the drugs she was taking. Her face was chalky white, except for around her eyes, which were set deep into their sockets. She looked very frail. 'I love your hat,' Ruth said. God, how difficult it was to behave normally, faced with such sadness.

'My sister made it. Will wants her to make him one, too, but I think he'd look *stoopid*.'

'I don't know . . .' Ruth smiled as the little girl began to pack her nail varnishes into a pretty bag. 'Are you going to stay for a bit?'

'I gotta go see Billy,' Michelle said. 'He's feeling bad today.'

Ruth stood at the door of Will's room and watched the child walk away down the corridor. From behind, she looked like any other little girl, skipping occasionally to catch up with herself.

Nine

RUTH'S FATHER TELEPHONED one evening. 'I was talking to Rick Henderson the other day—remember him?'

'Vaguely.' Rick had been a colleague of her father's in Maine.

'He tells me that Rick Junior is going on vacation for a couple of weeks, and his apartment will be empty. It's right around the corner from you. So your mom and I thought it would be a good idea if we came up. Get a chance to see you, see Will.' There was a pause while her father audibly swallowed. 'Give us a chance to do something.' Jonathan Carter's tone was full of entreaty. 'Lord, you don't have any idea how useless we feel down here. Your mother just sits and cries.'

He was asking for something she could not refuse him. 'That would be wonderful, Dad. I'd really appreciate it.'

'We'll be up at the end of the week. Don't worry about meeting us, we'll take a cab from the airport.'

'Will will be so happy to see you. Me too.'

Having her parents near at hand made it both harder for Ruth, and easier. Harder, because the pain they were so visibly experiencing only exacerbated her own, and meant that she had to be brave for their sakes as well as for Will's; easier, because she was able to break down and admit that she despaired.

'Will's looking better than I expected,' Jonathan Carter said.

'But not good.'

'He's going to get better. I promise you, darling,' her mother said.

'Yeah.' Ruth dared not allow hope to creep into the tight hold she forced herself to maintain over her feelings.

When Ruth took her parents to the hospital to have a blood sample taken, Dr Gearin was reassuring. 'We hope this procedure will be unnecessary,' he said. 'Will's doing well. We're very hopeful of beating the cancer.'

'Right. But since we're in town . . .' Jonathan Carter said, rolling up his shirtsleeve.

Gearing swabbed the inside of the older man's elbow with alcohol. 'As you know, we took blood from Professor and Mrs Connelly some months back. Unfortunately without any success.'

'I thought the immediate family provided the best hope of coming up with a match for Will?' Ruth's mother said.

'Even so, there's still less than a one in three chance.' Gearin picked up a disposable syringe and tore off the wrapping. Carefully sliding the needle into the vein on Dr Carter's arm, he added, 'With any luck, a bone marrow aspiration won't be necessary, but if it is, then at least we'll know where to look.'

'Or where not to look,' said Betty Carter.

Will was not in his hospital room. Frowning, Paul went in search of him. Anxiety thumped inside his rib cage but he tried to ignore it.

At the nurses' station he asked where Will was, trying to sound unconcerned but knowing he did not. The stress of the past weeks was getting to him in a big way. 'He's just fine, Professor Connelly,' one of the nurses said. 'He's with Michelle.'

'Michelle?'

'He's in her room, been reading her a story. You've got a real nice boy there, Professor. Takes a lot of trouble with the younger kids in here. Just go down the corridor. Michelle's room's on the right-hand side.'

'Thanks.'

Paul hurried along the passage, his head spinning with relief. He heard a weak burst of laughter, then a wheelchair containing a little girl turned into the passage towards him. Paul stopped. Will was pushing the child, talking to her. She lay back with her eyes closed. She wore a pink gingham mobcap. Unselfconsciously, Will wore a similar one.

Paul gulped. 'Hello, son,' he said softly.

'Hi, Dad.'

'I guess this must be Michelle.'

'That's right.' Will bent over the chair. 'Can you say hi to my dad, Michelle?' he asked tenderly.

With enormous effort, the child opened her eyes. 'Hi,' she said, and closed them again.

'I'm taking her for a walk,' Will said.

'Can I come?' Paul said, his voice unsteady.

'Sure.'

Side by side, Paul and his son walked along the corridor. 'The hat suits you, Will,' he said.

'Kelly made it for me. That's Michelle's sister.'

'Looks good.'

'Looks *stoopi* . . .' Michelle said, scarcely audible. ''S like mine . . .'

'I can see that. You look real pretty in pink.'

''S my favourite co . . .' The sentence drifted away, unfinished.

'You ever see that movie, Michelle?' Will said. '*Pretty in Pink*? Ever see it?' There was something desperate in his voice.

The little girl nodded infinitesimally.

'It was a good one,' said Will. 'I enjoyed that. Not as good as *Home Alone*, though.' Wearing a funny hat to please a little girl, he pushed the wheelchair along, talking, talking, while Michelle leaned her head back, her eyes shut. Her mouth drooped open a little, the lips bloodless, the eyelids as delicate as silk.

Ruth telephoned Paul. 'Now Will's between treatments again and back home, it would be good if you'd plan to sleep over every now and then,' she told him. 'I think he'd find it easier if you were around more.'

The thought of returning to their apartment made Paul's heart sink. He was often lonely in his one-bedroom place, but at least it was of his own choosing. Could anything be worse than sitting in the same room as your wife and being lonely? Doubt made him sound hostile. 'Why?'

'I don't think you're behaving well over this,' she said, her tone unfriendly. 'I've got a hell of a job to do, with Will so sick. Not that I grudge him a minute, a second, of my time or my love. But you should be helping too. For his sake, as much as for mine.'

'OK.' Paul sighed inwardly. If Will needed him, then he must do whatever was best. 'I'll work out some kind of a schedule so I spend more time with you.'

'Not with me, Paul, with Will. If you prefer, I can make arrangements to be out of the apartment while you're there.'

'That won't be necessary, for God's sake. Just tell me what you want me to do.'

'I'd like you to spend three nights a week here in the apartment, until this course of chemotherapy's been completed and evaluated.'

He wished she did not sound so impersonal. 'When would you like me to start?'

'Let's say after the weekend. How about next Tuesday?'

He turned the pages of his diary. 'That looks fine.'

'We're talking maybe months of this, Paul,' Ruth warned.

'I know that.'

Ruth was in the kitchen when Will got up on Monday morning and went along to the bathroom. Listening from the kitchen to his slow, old-man's step along the passage, she closed her eyes. She heard the swish of the shower curtain along the chrome rail, the sound of water splashing against Will's body. Ordinary noises. Soothing sounds. Suddenly, Will screamed. Terrified, Ruth ran to the bathroom and rapped at the door.

'Will! Honey! What's the matter?'

'Mom,' he moaned. 'Oh, Mom.' His voice was muffled, anguished.

'Can I come in?'

He did not answer and she pushed open the door. The water in the shower was still running, but Will stood naked in front of the full-length mirror on one wall, gazing at his reflection.

'My God.' Ruth stepped into the bathroom, aghast. Apart from a few wisps of hair, Will's skull gleamed white, startlingly naked above his bony face. Much of his body hair had also gone, she saw most of it lying in the shower tray, clogged round the plughole.

'I was soaping myself,' he said, 'the shampoo . . .' He choked, inarticulate, and turned towards her, face screwed up in despair, eyes full of self-disgust. 'Mom, *look* at me.'

Anticipating this moment, dreading it, she had rehearsed what she would say when it came. Now the words stuck in her throat.

'Dr Gearin told us this might happen. It's normal. You've seen the kids down at the hospital,' she told him.

'I didn't think . . .' Will swallowed hard, tears standing in his eyes. 'I just hoped it wouldn't happen to me.'

'Honey, I promise you it'll all come back. It's just temporary.'

'It's fucking shitty, that's what it is. This whole thing is shitty.' He began to cry again, his expression utterly miserable. 'Look at me, Mom,' he gulped. 'I look like some weird space monster. And . . . I feel lousy.' He clutched at his stomach suddenly and heaved. 'I'm gonna throw up.'

'You don't look *that* bad,' Ruth said, and he tried to laugh before he vomited into the bath.

Later, when she had cleaned him up and the bathroom, she went into his bedroom.

'Oh, *Mom*.' He swallowed hard. There was a hand-mirror on his desk into which he kept staring, tears rolling down his cheeks.

She wanted to tell him he did not look nearly as bad as he thought he did. She wanted to say how the lack of hair made his face stronger, more adult. She wanted to kiss him and tell him she loved him, but was afraid that if she did so, he would think she was only saying it because she thought he looked so terrible.

After school, Ed Stein came round. Before Ruth could warn him to be tactful, he was knocking on the door of Will's room at the same time as he pushed it open. There was a moment's stupefied silence. Then Ruth heard him say, 'Hey, *dude*. You look really cool.'

'Fuck off,' Will said.

'No, man, I mean it. You look—jeez, I've been trying to get my mom to let me shave my head for months now.'

'I didn't fucking shave it,' Will said.

'You mean, your mom did?'

'It fell out, asshole.'

'Fell—you mean your medication and stuff? Man. You look wicked.'

'Think so?'

Ruth guessed Will was looking into his hand-mirror again, reviewing his image in the light of Ed's envious tone.

'You bet I do. Wait till I tell the others. You could oil it, make it really shine. Hey, you know what you need?'

'What's that?'

'One of those ear studs. Diamond. That'd be *sooo* cool.'

Later, when Ed was leaving, she called him into the kitchen. 'I'm so grateful to you,' she said.

'What for?'

'Telling Will he looked OK. He wouldn't believe me.'

'Hey, I meant it,' Ed said. He was broader than Will was ever likely to be. 'Uh, Mrs Connelly, could I ask you something?'

'Go right ahead.'

'Will is pretty sick, isn't he?'

'About as sick as he can be.'

'Is he going to—you know. Is he going to die?'

She ought to deny it, but she could not. Tears filled her eyes. 'I don't know, Ed. And that's the truth. I just don't know.'

Paul was staying the following night for the first time since his departure. Ruth found herself taking extra trouble with her appearance, opening a bottle of expensive wine, getting the ingredients together for a green pepper steak, which she knew he liked.

'Will went to bed early,' Ruth said, kissing his cheek when he arrived. She led the way into the sitting room. 'You look like you caught the sun.'

'One of my colleagues has a son with a boat,' Paul said. 'We went sailing last weekend.'

'I see.' What had she hoped from his presence here overnight? It was over between them. When Will had first been diagnosed with cancer, there had been a certain rapprochement between them. Since then, Paul seemed to be growing more distant. Looking at his tanned face, his blue eyes, she remembered how they had talked over beers in the student bars, held hands at the movies. From the moment she had seen Paul she had been drawn to him. He had been the first man she slept with and, apart from Chris Kauffman, the last.

'I've got steaks,' she said. 'Salad. A baked potato.'

He looked stricken. 'Oh, no. Sorry, I didn't realise you—I already ate. I was round at a friend's and we made salmon steaks.'

'A female friend's?' Ruth asked, before she could stop herself.

'As it happens, yes.'

Well, isn't that just peachy, thought Ruth, determined not to let him see how disappointed she was. 'That's OK. It'll keep.'

'A drink would be good,' Paul said.

She handed him a glass of wine and put the bottle on the table.

They sat together on the sofa without speaking until Ruth, for something to say, said, 'Are you going up to Sweetharbor soon?'

'Maybe next weekend. Why do you ask?'

'The agent rang. She thinks someone's been in the house.'

'I don't know what I could do about it that she can't.'

'I think she wanted to check that nothing's been stolen.'

'She's got the inventory, she probably knows more about it than I do.' He leaned over and refilled his glass, offered her the bottle.

She shook her head. That she should be trying to make conversation with her own husband cast a shadow on her heart. 'I think I'll go to bed,' she said. 'You're all clear on Will, right? What to do if he wakes?'

'I think so.'

She stood up awkwardly, wondering if she ought to kiss him, thinking how absurd it was, the two of them in the home they had shared for most of twenty years, and she did not know whether she should kiss him good night. In the end, she smiled briefly and went.

Had he detected a hint of jealousy in Ruth's voice when he mentioned eating with a friend? It had not occurred to him that Ruth might want to cook for him. Eat with him.

He wished she had at least put her arms round him before she went to bed. He switched on the TV, surfed the channels, settled down to watch an *Inspector Morse*. He was dozing to the staccato theme music at the end of the programme when he heard Will's voice. 'Dad . . .'

Paul jumped up, disorientated, wondering for a moment where he was. Will was standing at the door of the sitting room.

'Will. Hi, son.' It was the first time he'd seen Will since the hair loss and he did his best not to look surprised.

Will came in and sat down on the sofa beside his father. 'What're you watching?'

'Some British thing. *Inspector Morse*. Ever seen it?'

'A couple of times.'

Paul faked a double take. 'Hey, love the haircut.'

'Thanks for pretending you didn't notice.'

'And did you know you've got a diamond stuck in your ear?'

'It's fake,' Will said. 'Mom and I went out the other day and had it done. We bought a hat, too. But you can still tell I'm bald.'

'Have to say it's kind of startling, first glance. For a moment there, thought I was watching *Kojak*, not *Inspector Morse* at all.'

The two of them burst out laughing. Paul spread his arm across the top of the sofa, and Will snuggled in close. He picked up the remote and pressed it. 'Hey, look. Clint Eastwood in *Unforgiven*.'

They sat together in companionable silence, Will held close by his father's arm.

From the bedroom, Ruth, sleepless, heard them talking, laughing. She wished she was in there with them, sharing, a family again, not out here in the dark. She wished she was not so alone.

Ten

IN EARLY MAY, Will returned to the hospital for his final dose of chemotherapy. As Ruth pushed him down the corridor, they had both glanced into Michelle's room, only to see that there was another child lying on the bed.

'Gone home for a couple of days, probably.' Ruth kept her voice light though a weight of anxiety was tying a knot in her chest. Michelle was far too ill to go home.

'Let's ask.' Will grabbed her hand. 'Oh, Mom, I hope she hasn't . . .'

'So do I, darling.'

Ruth found one of the nurses and asked where the little girl was. There was no need for an answer, the expression on the woman's face was enough. Will began sobbing, his thin shoulders heaving. 'No, oh no,' he said. 'No. Please no.'

'Will . . .' Ruth put her hand on her son's shoulder. There was nothing she could say. 'When?' she said softly to the nurse.

'Two days ago.'

'Michelle,' Will said. 'Oh no.'

Ruth covered her face with her hands. Poor Lynda. Poor, poor Will. No fourteen-year-old should know what death meant.

'It was very quiet,' said the nurse. 'We all knew it was coming. Her mom and dad were there, and grandparents. And her big sister. She just kind of smiled at them all and closed her eyes.'

'It's not fair,' Will said, his voice breaking. 'She was only a little kid.'

As they walked down the passage to the room waiting for him, Ruth said, 'Michelle loved being with you, Will. You helped her such a lot.'

'She helped *me*.' Will dug into the bag resting on his knees and fetched out the pink gingham mobcap Kelly had made for him. He sat in the chair, clutching it, trembling.

When he had been settled in his room and Dr Gearin had arrived to examine him, Ruth walked to the phones and called Lynda. 'It's Ruth Connelly,' she said to the answering machine. 'Will's mom. I'm so very, very sorry. Please, Lynda, get in touch.' She left her home number.

That evening, Lynda called back. Michelle's funeral was the following afternoon and she hoped Ruth would join them afterwards.

'Does Will know?' she asked.

'Yes,' Ruth said. 'He's so upset. He's due for treatment. Means he won't be able to come to the funeral.'

'Perhaps that's a good thing,' Lynda said.

'Maybe. His blood counts are up again. The doctors are very hopeful.'

'I'm so glad.'

The next day, Ruth spent some time deciding what to wear to say good-bye to Michelle. Sombre colours seemed wrong to mark the death of a child; in the end, she chose a daffodil-yellow suit in a fine wool, with a green silk scarf tucked into the neckline, the colours of spring, the colours of hope. She drove to the address Lynda had given her. It was a hall attached to the back of a restaurant called The Old Warsaw. The place was packed with people and noise and laughter. One long table was covered in platters of food, and another was stacked with bottles of wine. Someone handed her a glass and she pushed her way through the crowd towards Lynda, who stood at the end of the room, flanked by her husband and three children. A large portrait of Michelle stood on a table, draped in long strands of pink and white ribbon and surrounded by soft toys and dolls. Rainbow-coloured balloons hung from the walls and ceiling and vases of pink rosebuds stood all round the room.

'We're having a party to celebrate her,' Lynda said, hugging Ruth. She wore a dress the colour of strawberry ice cream. She dabbed at her eyes. 'I'm not crying for her, I'm really not.'

'She would have loved it,' said Ruth, looking around. 'Such beautiful roses.'

Lynda introduced her husband Mike, a big man in a bright blue suit, who seized Ruth's hand and pressed it against his chest. 'Thank you for coming,' he said. 'Lynda has told me about your boy.'

'I'm so sorry,' whispered Ruth. 'Michelle was such a lovely child.'

'An angel,' her father said simply. 'A little angel.'

A man in baggy black trousers and a grey felt jacket fastened with silver buckles stepped forward. An accordion hung on an embroidered strap round his neck. He squeezed off a few chords and the crowd fell silent. Lynda took her husband's hand and addressed them all. 'You know why we're here,' she said. 'To say goodbye to Michelle. We said our own private farewells to her at the church this morning. But Michelle always planned to have a party when she was better— and this is the party she would have had. If you want to cry, go right ahead, but remember that she was just a little girl, the bravest in the world, and she didn't cry much in her short life, so we shouldn't either. She was a real special little girl and we're so glad that we had her for eight years. Kelly—Michelle's big sister—is going to read you something now.'

Kelly stood very straight. She was wearing a pink top over a black microskirt and had tied her blonde hair back with a pink ribbon. 'This was Michelle's favourite poem,' she announced. 'I read it to her lots when she was sick. I loved her so much and I'm—I'm going to miss her all the rest of my life.' She opened the book she held.

Listening as Kelly read a poem for her dead sister, grief and guilt overwhelmed Ruth. Josie had been allowed to go from their lives without any of this celebration. And it was *her* fault. She was the one who had refused to allow her family to mourn.

When Kelly had finished, Michelle's father shouted, 'To little Michelle.' Everyone lifted their glasses.

The mood changed again. People were talking now, eating, drinking. Dancing began. The temperature rose, the food disappeared, the bottles emptied. Ruth was pulled into the throng, dancing with pale-haired youths, with old men, with Lynda herself. 'You're wonderful,' Ruth managed to gasp. 'Michelle would have loved this.'

'Wouldn't she, though?' Clasping each other, the two women whirled round the room.

'Please let's keep in touch.'

Red-faced, Lynda shook her head. 'If Will gets better, I don't reckon you'll want to be reminded of these sad times.'

Where did a woman like this learn to look with such clarity into the human heart? Driving back to the apartment, Ruth was ashamed of her own inadequacies.

Though classes were over, there was still a lot of college paperwork to deal with. That evening, Paul was hoping to be done in time to watch the game on TV. He made himself a gin and tonic and had just taken the first sip when the telephone bleeped. He picked it up. 'Yes?'

'Paul?' The voice was so faint he hardly recognised it.

'Ruth? Is that you? What's wrong?'

'I don't know. I came home to find a message from Dr Gearin. He wants me to call him as soon as I can and—and the thing is . . . Paul . . . I—I don't think I can face any more bad news on my own.'

'I'm on my way,' Paul said.

Was Ruth worrying unnecessarily? Paul switched on the car radio. Will had to be all right. He was going to be all right. Definitely.

He parked and ran into their apartment building, taking the stairs two at a time. Ruth was waiting for him. He put his arms tightly about her and they stood locked together in silence. After a while, he stepped away from her. 'Come on,' he said. 'There's two of us now.'

He dialled the number Gearin had left. 'It's Professor Connelly,' Paul said. 'You asked us to call you.'

'Yes.' Gearin's voice shifted a notch or two, from exhaustion to elation. 'Yes, I wanted you to know the good news as soon as possible.'

Paul hardly dared hope. He kept his voice unemotional. 'Does that mean what I think it means?'

'The leukaemia's in remission. The last tests we did showed no traces of the disease. For the present, Will is cancer-free.'

'Oh God.'

'We hope the disease won't recur, but of course we'll be keeping a close eye on him over the months to come. We can never be completely sure that the cancer will stay in remission. We just have to keep praying that it will.'

In other words, it's gone away, Paul thought, but maybe only for the moment. We shall never be able to sleep easily again. He did not say this aloud. Ruth had carried a heavy burden over the past months and he was not about to add to it by being less than enthusiastic. 'I can't tell you how grateful we are for everything you've done,' he said. 'Thank you, Mike. Thank you so very, very much.' Paul slammed down the phone and turned to Ruth.

'It's OK,' he said. 'It's OK!'

Ruth held a hand to her mouth, scarcely able to believe him.

'He's beaten it, Ruth! The cancer's gone.'

'He's going to be OK.' She collapsed onto the sofa and began to cry. 'I can't believe it,' she said numbly. 'I just can't.'

'Nor me.' He leaned over her, seized her face between his two hands and kissed her wet cheeks, her closed eyes, her mouth. 'Is there any champagne in the fridge?'

'Sure is. I'll get some glasses.'

They sat on the sofa together. She leaned against him, her head on his shoulder. 'I tried to believe that he would be cured, but I was still terrified he wouldn't be. All these months—looking at him, wondering how much more suffering he had to go through. And now . . . he's cured.'

'Cured . . .' Paul pressed her against his side, refusing to remember Gearin's qualified approval of the term. 'It's a strong word.'

'It's a good word,' Ruth said. 'The *best* word.'

Paul leaned towards her, took the glass from her hand and set it down on the table. 'The very best,' he said softly.

'Oh, Paul . . .' Joy made her hair seem almost incandescent and lent a golden glow to her skin. She kissed the corner of his mouth. 'Will is waiting. Let's go and tell him.'

Driving to the hospital with her beside him, he was consumed with the sense of something infinitely precious which had been wantonly discarded. Gently, he put his hand over hers.

As Will picked up his life again, gradually going back full-time to school for the last days of the semester, Ruth was able to return to the office. Surveying the crowded city streets, noticing as though for the first time the clothes in the store windows, the flowers in the public gardens, she realised how narrow her existence had become.

As long as Will stayed well, they could look forward to the future, though she knew that she would watch him, listen out for him, worry about him every second of every day. One cough and she would flinch. One bruise and she would know the cancer had come back.

A couple of weeks after the summer vacation had begun, she came home to find Ed Stein in the kitchen. 'Hi, Mrs Connelly,' he said.

'Hello, Ed. How're your mom and dad?'

'Just fine.' He glanced across at Will. 'By the way, we're leaving tomorrow for Maine and they wanted to know whether Will could come up, spend some time with us.'

'I wonder what on earth could have put that notion into their heads.' Ruth glanced sharply at Will.

'I did, Mrs Connelly.' Ed's gaze was one of limpid innocence. 'It'd be really great for me if Will could join us this summer.'

'I don't think so,' Ruth said brusquely.

'Why *not*?' demanded Will.

'I'll think about it,' Ruth said.

'Well, I'm *going*.' Will shouldered out of the kitchen, followed by Ed, who turned at the door and smiled. 'Don't worry about it, Mrs Connelly. The only thing Will needs to worry about in Maine is my sister Mamie. She's a real pain.'

'Is that right?'

'Honest, I think he'd be OK.'

That evening, Carmel Stein rang.

'Let me guess why you're calling,' Ruth said. 'You want Will to join you in Maine for a few weeks.'

'How did you—'

'Ed already asked,' Ruth said, 'and I told him I didn't think so. The truth is, I don't like the thought of Will being so far away from the hospital. His whole system is vulnerable. I'm still worried sick about him. Maybe I'm overprotective, but you can understand why.'

'I can understand. I'm not sure I can go along with it. You've got him virtually imprisoned in that apartment. The only time you let him out is to go to school, or when you can go with him.'

'But he's been so ill.'

'All the more reason to give him some freedom now that he's in remission. You've got to let him go. He's an intelligent boy. He knows that he has to take care. Just think how much better it'll be for him to be breathing that clean sea air down east than the Boston traffic fumes. And Ed's a good kid,' said Carmel. 'He'll keep an eye on him. And it goes without saying that Franklin and I will.'

248

'I don't know . . . Will'd enjoy it,' Ruth said thoughtfully. 'And he does love it there.'

'So you'll let him come?'

Ruth took a deep breath. 'Yes,' she said.

'Good. That's great. What about you, Ruth? Why don't you come up and visit too?'

'I . . . I can't. Because of what . . . happened.'

Carmel hesitated. 'Honey, maybe I never put it into words, but you don't know how we've felt for you over the past twelve months.'

'At least Will has come through. I hardly dared hope that he would, but the doctors say he's OK now. If I let him come up to Maine, you'd call me instantly if there was the slightest thing wrong, wouldn't you?'

'Trust me.' There was a sudden exclamation. 'Hey, Ruth! Will's birthday.'

'What about it?'

'Why don't you celebrate it up here? You can stay with us. It would do you good after these past months.'

'I'll think about it, Carmel. I'm not just saying that, I really will.'

'Let's fix it right now.'

'I'm not sure I—'

'Get your schedule, Ruth Connelly. If not before, I definitely want to see you up in Maine for Will's fifteenth birthday.'

Will had telephoned his father from the Steins' house, suggesting he come up and visit. 'We could get in some sailing,' he said.

'Sounds good,' Paul said. 'Sounds *wonderful*.'

'Mr Stein'll let us use one of his boats. Ed can come along too, can't he, Dad?'

'Listen—' Paul wanted to say that Will could bring the entire State Assembly along if he wished. To hear his son's voice bubbling and eager again was like being given back his own life. 'Yes, Ed can come. Hey, Will . . .'

'What?'

'Did you check this with the Steins?'

'Course I did. You don't think it was *my* idea to have you come busting in on my vacation, do you?'

'So young, and yet so cruel,' Paul said.

He took the I-95 up as far as Brunswick, then turned off onto the back roads. With each breath of pine and kelp, each sighting of the flat-calm sea, his exhilaration grew. Summer in Maine. And Will well again.

He remembered how he and Josie used to be out on the water together all through the summer. He'd taught her the rudiments of

SUSAN MADISON

sailing when she was only five or six, first in the Beetle Cat and later in the *Lucky Duck*. And then Will started to come along with them, and that was good too, a father and his children, handling a boat, being a family. Except that last summer she didn't sail with him and Will once. He hadn't thought about it before but now it bothered him. She'd sail with Will, but not with him. Was she jealous of the closeness between her father and her brother? Had she felt excluded?

His mood dampened a little, he arrived at the Steins' house, where Franklin and Carmel were sitting out under sun-umbrellas.

'You two look really busy,' he said.

'We are.' Carmel waved a languid hand at him. 'Busy doing nothing.'

Franklin made a half-hearted attempt to get out of his chair and abandoned it. 'Paul. Good to see you.'

'And you.' He bent down to kiss Carmel.

Paul cocked his head. 'I don't hear the merry sound of boys at play.'

'They're down at the yacht club. Sailing, I think, but maybe playing tennis with the girls.'

'I'll see if I can find them before I settle into sluggard mode,' said Paul.

'Lunch at one,' Carmel called after him.

The yacht club looked much as it had done since his first visits there. There were rockers on the porch, half of them occupied by ancient ladies knitting, chatting, dozing.

A few boats still lay tied up to the dock built out into the little deepwater harbour; the rest were out on the water. From the courts next door came the thud of tennis balls on rackets and the calls of the players. Laughter floated on the air.

Inside the club, the shaded rooms were empty. He walked across the sanded pine floor and stood looking out at the water, remembering the countless times he'd come here over the years. So much had changed.

'Professor Connelly?'

He turned. Two teenaged girls in Sweetharbor Yacht Club T-shirts were standing side by side under the slowly whirring electric fan. 'Hi,' the older of the two said. 'I'm Amy Prescott. This is my sister Lizzie.'

'Prescott? You must be Sue Prescott's girls.'

'Yes, sir. That's right.' Amy smiled politely. 'I guess you're looking for Will. But he and Ed are off racing this morning. He's looking real good, Professor Connelly.'

Beside her, Lizzie nodded. She glanced sideways at her sister. 'He's a real hunk, isn't he, Amy?'

Colour burned its way up Amy's face. 'He's OK,' she said, glaring at her sister.

'Thank you, girls.' Paul smiled at them and went out again, trying not to laugh. He liked that. The girls beginning to sit up and take notice of Will. That was good. As a matter of fact, it was more than good. It was fantastic. At the bar he bought a beer and sipped it, wondered if Will was taking notice back.

A month after Will had left for Maine, Carmel Stein rang Ruth at her office. 'Now, you're not to panic, Ruth.'

'Cue for instant hysteria,' Ruth said lightly, striving to remain calm.

'It's Will. He's been running a fever.'

'No.'

'Not a very high one, Ruth.'

'No,' moaned Ruth. Blackness filled her.

'We took him straight down to the hospital in Hartsfield, but they didn't seem too worried. Paul said—'

'Paul?'

'He's come up a couple of times to visit Will, yes.'

Ruth was silent.

'Don't be like that,' Carmel said. 'We love you both. You're both our friends. We don't want to lose either of you.'

'I understand,' Ruth said. 'Of course I do.'

'Will's back with us now,' Carmel said. 'Everything's fine and Paul said I shouldn't worry you about it but I thought you should know.'

'Thank you,' Ruth said. Guilt consumed her. Paul had already been up to visit Will twice while she had not yet been up once. 'Shall I come up and get him?'

'There's no reason why you should. Like I said, they seemed to think he was fine. I wouldn't even have bothered to call you if it wasn't for his medical history. And because I promised you I would.'

Despite her friend's reassurances, Ruth felt nauseous. 'Thanks, Carmel. I'll get back to you.'

Not again. Please, not again.

The waves grabbed at her. She tried to get out of their reach, but found she could not move. The water glittered cruelly, sharp as razor blades, receding as though to reassure her then lunging back again when she least expected it. Terrified, she watched it lap at her knees, her waist, her breasts, her throat, icier than the frozen Arctic waters. It's the sea, the sea, someone said above her head as one roaring green wave detached itself from the rest and slammed against her, devouring her.

She woke sweaty, buried under a tangle of sheets. Gasping, she pushed herself up against the headboard, tried to force herself awake. The nightmare clung to her brain, the panic refusing to let go even when she flicked on the light, went into the kitchen for a glass of water.

It was futile to try to reinvent the past. Nothing would bring Josie back, nothing would return any of them to where they had once been. Sitting at the kitchen table, she shivered, although the trapped heat of the day still hung heavily in the air. Of all the abundance she had once possessed, Will was the only thing left.

She dressed quickly, flung some things into a bag, found her car keys. Out in the street, the night air was almost cool. She drove with the windows open, relishing the damp air which flowed past her.

Carmel Stein was surprised to see her. 'You should have telephoned.'

'It was a sudden decision,' Ruth said. 'I woke in the night and started worrying.'

'Will's fine. I told you. He's down at the yacht club, sailing with Ed.'

'OK. Then maybe I'll drive down to Sweetharbor and have a coffee there. And then . . . I thought I'd take Will back to the city with me.'

'What about his birthday?' Carmel frowned. 'I already invited people. Ordered a cake and everything.'

'I need to have him where I can keep an eye on him.'

'He's OK, Ruth.' Carmel put her arm round her friend's shoulders. 'You have to believe that he's fine. You should let him have these precious summer days up here. This is where he's happiest.'

Parking the car behind the little convenience store in Sweetharbor, Ruth sat for a moment, eyes unseeing, as the past came flooding in on her. Only two days before the accident, she had hiked down from the house with Josie. They had sat on high stools at the counter of the donut shop, she with a coffee, Josie with an apple-cinnamon donut. She remembered the powdered sugar on Josie's upper lip, and how she had laughed, reached out a finger to wipe it off, saying Josie looked like an old man who had forgotten to shave. It was one of the few moments that summer when Josie had behaved like an untroubled teenager.

She got out of the car and walked down Main Street to the quayside, where the water lapped against wooden pilings and the lobster boats bobbed on the swell. She moved on to look in the window of the little craft shop. The window display featured driftwood draped with swatches of batiked silk. Set against the fabric were carved wooden bowls, dishes, salad servers, photograph frames.

'Mrs Connelly?' The voice was deep and warming.

She looked up to see a tall, bearded man, vaguely familiar.

'Sam Hechst,' he said. He held out a hand and she took it. Warm fingers, rough at the tips. A wide smile showing strong square teeth. Eyes dark enough to be almost black.

'You're Dieter's nephew,' she said.

'That's right.' He wore jeans and a denim shirt with the sleeves rolled up. 'Are you all up here?'

There was no reason why he should know that Paul had left them and she was not well enough acquainted with him to explain. 'I'm just visiting my son—he's vacationing with friends up here.'

'You're not staying at Carter's House?'

'No.' Ruth swallowed, knowing that words had to be spoken. 'Josie—my daughter—I'm sure you heard that she was drowned last summer. Our cottage is too . . . I can't bear to be there, knowing that she'll never be there again herself.'

He glanced at her, indicated the Cabot Lodge Inn across the way. 'Would you—do you have time for coffee?'

'That would be nice,' she said.

In the dining room of the inn, they found a table by the window which gave on to Old Port Street. When the waitress came over, Sam asked for coffee while Ruth ordered breakfast, the full works: hash browns, two eggs, bacon, a stack of pancakes, coffee. She was suddenly ravenous, having left Boston without eating.

'You said you were visiting your son.'

She looked down at her plate then back at the man sitting opposite her. 'He's—he's been very sick with leukaemia.'

She braced herself for some knee-jerk expression of sympathy but instead, he said, 'I'm so sorry. I didn't know. But you're not opening up Carter's House?'

'No, I . . . I'm not here for long. And as I said, I haven't felt like staying there. Too many memories.'

'Of Josephine?'

'Of . . . happiness.'

'Mrs Connelly. Ruth. If memories are all you have, then you should glory in them.' His dark eyes moved over her. 'You should go back to your house. I'm sure that the memories you have of your daughter are good ones. She was a remarkably talented painter. Some of her insights into what artists were trying to achieve in their work—' He broke off. Smiled. 'She also had a very strong personality.'

'Yes, indeed.'

'But she had a sorrowful soul.'

A new Josie was forming in Ruth's mind. Not a daughter, but a person. 'Sometimes I think I never really knew her,' she said simply. She glanced out at the street. 'What do you do, Sam?'

'I work in wood. But I can turn my hand to anything, from house painting to carpentry. Up here, you have to. Lobstering isn't enough.'

She looked surprised and he laughed. 'I've had a string of lobster traps since I was a child.'

Josie had talked about going lobstering, had it been with this man? She glanced at her watch, then turned her gaze on him. 'I must get on.'

As they stepped into the street, he turned to her. 'Your son is cured?'

'Yes.'

He laid his hand over hers. 'That is so good to hear.'

Driving back to the Steins' cottage, she passed the turnoff which led to Carter's House. Slowing down, she peered between the tree trunks. Wild flowers nodded along the sandy track which ran towards the meadow in front of the house. Butter-yellow sunshine glowed where the trees broadened out.

A gift from a true love . . . Paul had read the words to her one summer afternoon, as the two of them sat under a shady tree in a rare moment of shared peace. The children were swimming in the pond with friends. Paul looked up from his reading. 'Listen to what E. B. White wrote about returning to Maine after being away from it ". . . I do not ordinarily spy a partridge in a pear tree, or three French hens, but I do have the sensation of having received a gift from a true love."'

She had laughed. 'I like that. I know just what he means: it's how I feel when we see the house for the first time each summer.'

He had smiled at her. Reached for her hand. 'We're lucky, Ruth.'

Back then, she had thought it was true. Would she ever drive down the track again?

Carmel, Will and Ed were sitting on the porch of the Steins' house, waiting for her. The dogs lay at their side, panting in the heat.

She got out of her car and ran towards Will.

'Mom!' He jumped up. 'Good to see you.'

'Darling, you look marvellous!' In the weeks he had been up here, his pale face had acquired a light sea-tan. He had put on some weight.

Now he looked apologetic. 'Sorry, Mom, but we gotta get back down to the yacht club. We'll see you later, OK?'

'Guess you're going to meet up with some nice girls,' Carmel said.

'*Some* girls?' Ed punched Will's shoulder. '*A* girl, don't you mean? *A* girl beginning with *A*? Am I right?'

'Get outta here,' said Will.

As the boys charged off, Ruth turned to her friend. 'Thank you,' she said quietly. 'Will looks absolutely great.'

I think you should come home with me, Will,' Ruth said when the boys returned from the yacht club. 'After all, the summer's nearly ended.' She was trying it out, knowing he would not agree.

'There's my *birthday*. You promised I could have it up here. And you have to admit I look really well, don't I? It's *good* for me to be here.'

'Really, Mrs Connelly,' Ed said gravely. 'I think he ought to stay.'

Ruth held up both hands in mock surrender. 'OK, OK. You convinced me.'

'Yo!' The boys gave each other a high five and jigged round the room.

Ruth laughed. 'So I'll see you again soon, Will.' She smiled at her son. 'I can't tell you how much it means to see you looking so good.'

'Right, Mom.' Will looked embarrassed. 'Come on, I'll walk you out to the car.'

Saying goodbye, she held him close, not wanting to let go of him. He let her for a moment then broke free. 'Mom,' he said. 'Don't worry about me. I'm OK. We licked it, between us, didn't we?'

'We did,' she said, elated. 'Yes. We really did.'

 # Eleven

'I'M GOING UP to Sweetharbor for Will's birthday,' she told him on the telephone.

'Oh.' Paul's heart dropped. Even though they seldom met, now that Will was better, he nonetheless gained a measure of satisfaction from knowing that she lived in the same city as he did.

Can I come too? The phrase screamed inside his skull. He was silent, remembering Will's last birthday. 'How long will you be gone?'

'Only a couple of days.'

He cleared his throat. 'If you want some moral support for the celebrations, I'm willing to volunteer.'

He could hear her smile. 'That's good of you, Paul.'

Thanks a lot, but no thanks, in other words. 'Ruth,' he said. 'I've been thinking about things.'

'So have I.'

He wanted her to reassure him but she wasn't going to. 'Maybe . . . maybe we could have dinner when you get back?'

'I'd like that.'

The children had long since gone about their own affairs, and the three adults were able to linger over dinner. A warm breeze blew in off the sea. 'Last time I was up here, I ran into Sam Hechst,' Ruth said idly.

'Hechst? The carpenter? He put in a new parquet floor in the living room for us last winter,' said Carmel.

Franklin nodded. 'What a craftsman. He did the whole thing by eye.' He drank vigorously from his wineglass. 'Interesting guy. Used to teach art history at a private girls' school down in Connecticut. Gave it all up to come back here. Told us he'd try doing what his forefathers had always done, working with wood. Not just carpentry, but sculpture as well.'

Carmel passed round a platter of local lobster, set out bowls of home-made mayonnaise and melted butter. 'I bought a piece of his only the other day. Absolutely exquisite.' Candles stood on the wooden table, smoking in the wind from the invisible sea.

Ruth picked up her wineglass. 'He told me Josie was a remarkably talented painter. He said she had a sorrowful soul. She was certainly upset about something last summer. I wish I knew what it was. I guess although kids today seem so much more in control than we were at the same age, they aren't really.'

'That's right,' agreed Carmel. 'They still find themselves in situations where they're way out of their depth.'

'A sorrowful soul,' repeated Ruth.

Later, in her bedroom, she leaned out of the window and stared into the night. There was no moon, no sea to cast back the silver reflection of the sky. She breathed in the rich fragrance of the junipers surrounding the Steins' house.

What had been troubling Josie so much last summer? Had she found herself trying to cope with a situation too complex for her? I do not even know if she was a virgin, Ruth thought. I did not know my own daughter. Those summer vacations they ran free, the two kids, they could have gone anywhere, done anything, and I would not have been aware.

She thought of Paul. Where was he tonight? Did he stare into the darkness, as she did, and wish they were still together?

In honour of Will's fifteenth birthday, the Steins threw a lunch party. Most of the guests were old friends, people Ruth had not seen since the previous summer.

Finding herself next to Chris Kauffman, she said quietly, 'Forgive me, Chris.'

'What the hell for?' He put a big arm round her shoulder.

'London—that evening you came round. I put you in a difficult position and I'm—'

'London?' he said. He smiled his lopsided smile. 'I don't know what you're talking about.'

'Thanks, Chris.'

Ted Trotman came towards her. 'Ruth, it's good to see you. You're looking great.'

'You too, Ted.'

'Hey, listen, Ruth. I'd like to set up a lunch date. I'm thinking of transferring a big percentage of my business away from the guys currently handling my affairs. Think LKM could take us on?'

'I'm absolutely sure they could,' Ruth said. Bob Landers would be ecstatic if she could bring Ted Trotman on board.

'What I hear, you're doing well.' He put a hand on her shoulder. 'Wanted to say, Ruth, how bad I felt about your kid. Josie. She had guts. Always taking me on.' He chuckled. 'And I'm real glad to know your boy's better. Must have been pretty bad for you, this past year.'

'You could say that.'

Raising a hand, he moved away, leaving her standing alone. Light fell between the branches of the junipers. Her body felt honeyed with contentment. She had thought she would never feel happy again.

That evening they ate dinner at the yacht club. Will sat at the head of the table, laughing, kidding around with Ed.

Franklin offered a toast to the birthday boy and they all raised their glasses. Afterwards, Will leaned towards her. 'Thanks for being here, Mom,' he said quietly.

'You don't think I'd miss your birthday, do you?'

'Except it's not just my birthday, it's also the day that . . . that . . .'

'That Josie died,' she said steadily.

He looked down at his plate. Pushed the cake around with his fork. 'All day long I've been thinking about her. Remembering.'

There were so many things she could have said. In the end, she sighed. 'Me too, Will. Josie's part of us, part of up here. It's taken me far too long to accept that she has a *right* to be remembered.'

Both of them were silent for a moment. Then Will said, 'Sorry I haven't spent more time with you while you've been visiting, Mom.'

'That's OK.'

'It's just it's summer and there's such a lot to do up here, and I—'

'Listen to me, Will.' She picked up his hand and squeezed it. 'You don't have to apologise to me for anything. It's more than I could have asked for just to see you here, where I know you're happy. OK?'

'OK, Mom.' Awkwardly, he put an arm round her shoulders and hugged her, crushing her up against his chest.

The fall semester began. Although Will had to work hard to catch up on his missed schooling, he managed to play hard as well. Most of his spare time was spent with Ed and Dan.

'It's the band, Mom,' he said, when Ruth told him not to overtire himself. 'This gig that Dan's father fixed up for us.' He threw spinach leaves into a bowl and shook the skillet in which he was roasting pine nuts. 'It's the week after Thanksgiving and people are *paying* to hear us, so we gotta be good.' In the skillet, the pine nuts danced and spun.

'Can I come?'

'*You?*' His expression was horrified.

'Yes, Will. Me, your mother.'

Will sighed. 'Why do parents always want to come to things?' He emptied the pine nuts into the salad bowl and began to shave fresh Parmesan cheese.

Watching him, marvelling at him, Ruth savoured her martini. 'I seem to remember you getting annoyed because I *didn't* come to things.'

'This is different.'

'In what way?'

Will scraped at a blackened pan of roasted vegetables which he'd removed from the oven. He lifted a piece on a fork and tasted it. Chewing, he surveyed his mother. 'They're putting this dance on for disabled kids, not adults. You'd hate it. We don't play your kind of music.'

'How do you know what my kind of music is?'

Will rolled his eyes heavenwards. He crushed garlic cloves with the flat of his knife.

'OK. I guess you can come if you really want to. Just don't do anything that'll destroy my rep, OK?'

'Like what? Dance naked on a table?'

'Like . . . *kiss* me or something like that.' Deftly, Will used a fork to mix oil, mustard and vinegar with the garlic.

Ruth laughed. 'I promise.'

'**S**he's pretty smashed up,' Paul said. Hands tucked inside their jackets and caps pulled down over their ears, he and Will walked one last time round the *Lucky Duck*. Fog hung over the boatyard, burrowing into their throats, thickening their lungs. The autumn storms had begun and the winds were beating down the coast, whistling round the masts of the boats tied up to the boatyard's dock. 'What do you think?'

'I reckon it could be repaired.' Will's nose was red and his eyes were tearing up with cold. He ran a hand over the boat's wooden hull. Smashed timbers surrounded the gaping hole in her side. Where the mast had snapped, there was a splintered stump. 'Lotta work, though.'

'The inside's not so bad, it's the hull which really took a beating. Maybe we should ask Sam Hechst to give us a hand. He knows a lot more about this sort of work than I do.'

'Sounds good to me.'

'What I'd like,' Paul said wistfully, 'is if we could get her ready for next season. So we can get some racing in.'

'Can't see why not.'

'It'd mean coming up here most weekends before the winter sets in.'

'Don't know about that,' Will said. He was almost as tall as his father now. 'There's the band. I gotta be ready for our gig.'

'When's that?'

'Week after Thanksgiving. Can't do anything at weekends until after that.' Will looked round the boatyard, at the boats shrouded for winter. 'How about we get them to move the *Duck* up to Carter's House?'

'What for?'

'If we, you and me, cleared out the barn a bit, the *Duck* could go in there. At least until her mast's replaced. That way, once Thanksgiving's over, we could work on her right through the winter.'

'Hey, good idea.' Paul clapped his son on the shoulder. *You and me*: he loved it when Will said that. They began to walk towards the iron gates of the yard. Paul said, 'Want something to eat?'

'You bet. I'm starving.'

They drove towards the nearest eatery, fog thick against the windscreen. With the first frosts, the grass that lined the rutted sandy lanes round Sweetharbor had turned yellow and brittle. Barberry and rowan gleamed crimson under the trees, each berry dripping with moisture.

Biting into an overfilled crab roll, Will said, 'I *love* it up here.'

'Me too.'

'I wish we could live here for ever.'

'Yeah.' Unlikely, Paul thought. Ruth would never agree to them leaving the city. Then he remembered that he and Ruth led separate lives.

259

As though following his thoughts, Will asked casually, 'You coming by the apartment for Thanksgiving?'

'Your mom hasn't asked me.'

'Would you if she did?'

'I guess I would,' Paul said, 'if she did.' Now that Will was recovered, Ruth and he appeared to be drifting further apart. He could scarcely remember when they had last spoken.

'Can Dad come for Thanksgiving?' Will said.

'Dad? What makes you think he'd want to?'

'I asked him, that's what. He said he'd come if he was invited.'

'It'll be sort of . . . awkward.'

'Thanksgiving is a time for everyone to be sweet to everyone else,' Will said. 'For families to get together. And even if you and Dad don't live together, you're still my family.'

'Well . . .'

'You don't hate him or anything, do you?' Will's eyes were wide with the need for her to say no.

'Of course not,' Ruth said.

'So will you ask him?'

'All right. I'll ring him this evening.'

Much later that night, Ruth was woken by some sound. She lay under the covers, still half-asleep, and heard Will retching in the bathroom. Instantly she was wide awake, swinging her legs out of bed, reaching for her robe. She stumbled out into the passage. Will had left the door open and she could see him hunched over the pedestal.

'What's wrong?' she said, when he had rinsed out his mouth and washed his face. Her face felt stiff, sodden with sleep. Inside her rib cage, her heart thumped with rediscovered fear.

'Nothing, Mom.' He grinned shamefacedly. 'I went out with the guys after school, pigged out on fries and a toasted cheese sandwich. Plus a couple of Cokes. Guess they didn't mix too well.'

In the morning he seemed fine, though Ruth examined his face minutely, looking for—for what, exactly? Boils, shadows under his eyes, unexplained bruises? There were none: he looked well, the last of the summer's tan still on his face. She tried not to worry, kids threw up all the time, especially if they ate too much junk food. It was nothing.

A couple of weeks later, she came back from the office to find Will asleep on the sofa in the living room. Ed was sitting next to him, watching TV with the sound turned right down.

'What's going on, Ed?' she said quietly, dumping her bag and papers on the table. With her head, she motioned him into the kitchen, where they could talk without disturbing Will.

'I came back with him, Mrs Connelly. He was throwing up.'

'Oh, Ed . . .'

'Don't worry, Mrs Connelly. We had to eat this really gross fish thing at lunch: I should think it was that. But they said I was to come home with Will in a cab and wait for you, because of Will's being sick earlier.'

'Thanks, Ed. You're a star.'

When Ed had gone, Ruth went back into the living room and looked down at her son's sleeping face. Devoured it. Try as she might, she could see no sign at all that he was sick. She clasped her hands together and raised them to her mouth, pressing back dread.

Her parents arrived at the beginning of Thanksgiving week. Ruth's father held his grandson by the upper arms, appraised him, let him go. 'Hey, boy. You're looking wonderful,' he said. 'Really good.'

'Hope you brought some warm clothes, Granddad,' Will said.

'Listen, I lived up here for most of my life. I know to bring warm clothes,' Jonathan Carter said.

'Oh, sweetheart.' Betty Carter hugged Will. 'You look great.'

'Still vegetarian?' Jonathan asked.

'Only way to go, Granddad.'

'Do we get to eat turkey on Thursday?' Will's grandfather wondered plaintively. 'That veggie stuff does my digestive system no good at all.'

On Thanksgiving Day, Will complained of earache. His summer tan had faded, and he was looking very pale. Fiercely questioned by Ruth, he admitted that he had been feeling tired lately, that he'd thrown up a couple more times recently.

'Why didn't you *say*?' Ruth tried to cram the panic back inside her but it refused to stay put.

'I'm OK. Just this earache.'

'I'll give you a painkiller for the moment,' Ruth said.

She walked down the passage to her parents' room. 'Will's got earache,' she told them flatly.

She saw her own anxieties reflected in her father's eyes. 'Anything else?' he asked.

'He's been feeling tired. He's thrown up again.'

'But when we arrived, he looked great,' her mother said.

'Oh God,' her father said heavily. He sat down on the side of the bed and leaned forward, staring at his shoes.

'Do you think I should take him down to the hospital right now?'

'Better carry on as planned,' her father said. 'Another twenty-four hours won't make much difference either way.' He moved his head slowly from side to side, his expression despairing.

When Paul arrived, Ruth did not tell him about Will's earache. He had made a cherrywood bowl for her mother, and as he showed it to Will, as he poured wine for her parents, Ruth thought how easy it would be for a stranger to conclude that this was a normal happy family. But watching her son picking at the elaborate vegetables she had prepared for him, Ruth realised she would have to face the truth.

While Paul and her parents stacked the dishwasher in worried silence, she went into Will's room. He was lying on his bed, looking exhausted. 'Show me your arms,' she commanded. 'Your legs.'

There were bruises around his elbows, purple blotches behind his knees. Watching her face, he said defeatedly, 'It's come back, hasn't it?'

'Don't be ridiculous, Will,' she said, more confidently than she felt. 'We won't know anything until we've had you checked out. It's probably nothing more than a minor infection.'

'It's back.' He turned his face to the wall. 'I've been feeling bad for a while now.'

'Why didn't you tell me?'

'Don't know.'

But she knew that he had kept silent from fear. 'It could be anything,' she said, keeping her voice calm. 'The treatment you had—this could just be some delayed reaction.'

'Yeah. Right,' Will said bleakly.

'We'll have the doctors look at you.' She sat down on the bed and cradled his head against her chest.

'I can't stand it, Mom,' Will said. 'I'm not going through all that again. The needles. Aching all over. Wanting to throw up all the time.'

'You're giving up before we even know.'

'*I* know.'

'You don't.'

'And even if I do have more treatment, it'll all be for nothing.'

Ruth put her arm round his shoulders. 'You're wrong. Life is good, Will. You have to go on believing that.'

'Not for me. Not if I'm sick again. I'd rather die.'

'Don't.' Savagely she pulled his face towards her, ignoring his cry of pain. 'Don't *say* that, Will. Not ever.'

'Why not? It's the truth.'

'You're going to live. You *will* live.' She produced a shaky laugh. 'Listen to us! We don't even know for sure that there's anything wrong.'

He stared into her face and the territory behind his eyes was the bleakest of landscapes. 'Don't we?'

As soon as she came back into the room, Paul knew. He'd been aware of tensions from the moment he'd arrived. Now Ruth's face said it all. He got up and put his arms round her. She rested her head against his shoulder and he held her tight, neither of them speaking. Behind him, he heard Betty Carter begin to cry.

'We'll take him to the hospital tomorrow,' Paul whispered into Ruth's hair. 'I'll be there for you.' And yet, even as he spoke, he wondered how true that was. Could he go through the horror of it all again? Could Will? If the cancer had come back—and he felt sure it had—this time it would be even worse. It would mean—wouldn't it?—that Will's chances were much slimmer than before.

He squeezed his eyes shut, pushing the images of Will to the back of his mind. My son . . . my son. Wind in our hair. The *Lucky Duck* . . . The future receded, contracted.

They waited in a small room with a low ceiling. There were two armchairs upholstered in brown corduroy, separated by a square wooden coffee table. To one side was a love seat upholstered in contrasting beige. There was a picture on the wall of mountains covered in snow. This was not the room that had become so familiar during Will's previous illness; Ruth wondered if it had been chosen in order to avoid dredging up memories.

Doctors Caldbeck and Gearin came in, looking subdued. 'Professor Connelly. Mrs Connelly.' They shook hands before sitting down together on the love seat and opening the files they carried.

'We're very disappointed,' Dr Caldbeck said, after a few moments. 'After such a prompt remission, we had hoped for better results.'

'Did you stop the treatment too soon?' Ruth asked bluntly.

'I don't think so. His blood was clear, the disease had gone.'

'What are his chances?' Paul asked. 'Last time you told us eighty per cent of cases like Will's end in a cure. What's the percentage now?'

Gearin answered. 'Somewhat lower than eighty. I can't pretend otherwise. But we have every hope that we'll be able to combat the disease.'

'You told us before that you were confident Will would be cured,' said Ruth. 'And now he's ill again. How can I believe anything you say?'

'You can't,' Caldbeck said. 'You just have to do what *we* do, which is to go on hoping that we'll find the successful combination of treatments.'

Gearin glanced down at his folder. 'Since Will's form of the disease is proving resistant to the standard drugs, we think we should move to the next level of therapy and this time combine chemo with radiotherapy. It isn't as painful as chemo, in terms of actual treatment. But the side effects are much the same: nausea, vomiting, joints aching. Luckily, as with chemo, they're mostly temporary.'

Ruth held the sides of her chair. If it was like this for her, what must it be like for Will?

'In the last few days, Will's just sunk deeper and deeper into depression,' Paul said. 'How psychologically prepared is he for another course of treatment?'

'We'll arrange for him to see the family psychologist. And you should talk to her, too, both of you. This is equally hard on the parents.'

'Worse, Mike. Much much worse.' Ruth had intended to be strong, to fight, but suddenly she was weeping. She buried her head in her hands and felt the tears flow.

Gearin got up and came and stood beside Ruth. He put a hand on her shoulder. 'Let it out, Ruth. It's better that way.'

'Have you told Will what you've found?' asked Paul.

'Not yet.'

'He knows,' said Ruth harshly. 'He's known for days. He didn't want to admit it, that's all.'

Five days later, Will was given his first dose of radiotherapy. Despite the determined cheerfulness of the technicians, Ruth knew there was little to be cheerful about. She held Will's hand as he was lifted onto a vinyl-covered table and then stepped back as they began to wrap him in sheeting. Even his face was covered. Just before the cloth was placed over his head, his eyes met hers, and she saw in them the same look she had seen, months before, in the eyes of other children.

The table slid slowly into the dark cavern of the machine. A sob rose in her throat and she backed into a corner, pressing her hands to her mouth, trying to hold it in.

One of the technicians approached her, brushing at her green scrubs. 'It looks worse than it really is,' she said. 'Honestly it does. They don't feel anything, and it doesn't last too long.' She glanced across at the sinister glow inside the machine, and added, 'Poor kid.'

Because his immune system was still low after the previous series of treatments, Will had to spend more than two weeks in hospital. His needle phobia made each jab an ordeal. Standing by and watching while the nursing staff dug needles into his flesh became almost as painful for Ruth as it was for him. That is my son's body, she wanted to shout. Don't let him be hurt any more. Hurt me instead.

'Nearly Christmas,' Ruth said to Will. 'Got any ideas about it?'

'Plenty. Or . . . just one, really. But you won't go along with it.'

'Try me.'

'I want to go up to Carter's House.' Small spots of colour stood out on Will's cheekbones, emphasising the bony contours of his face. 'We always used to spend Christmas up there.'

'I know we did, but . . .' Her whole being rebelled at the thought of entering the house, especially at Christmas. 'I'll think about it,' she said.

She found Mike Gearin in his office. 'What do you think?' she said. 'Will wants to go up to Maine for Christmas.'

'Sounds like fun.' Dr Gearin took off his glasses and rubbed the top of his nose. He looked exhausted.

'But is he going to be OK to travel?'

'I can't see why not.'

'Even though he'll be away from the hospital . . .?'

'Ruth, I'm sure you're aware that one of the best treatments of all for any kind of cancer is a positive attitude. If Will's going to be happy spending Christmas in Maine, then let him do so. If you decide to go, what I can do is call the hospital in Hartsfield—it is Hartsfield, isn't it?—to check that if an emergency arose, they could care for him there.'

'All right,' she said doubtfully.

In spite of Will's pleas, the more she considered it, the more Ruth knew she could not go back to Carter's House. She circled round the problem, seeking a compromise.

And then it came to her. The next day she said to Will, 'Shall we have Christmas up in Sweetharbor . . .'

'Oh great! That's really—'

'But not,' Ruth said, 'at the house. Suppose we stay at the Cabot Lodge?'

Will looked at the wall behind her. 'It wouldn't be the same.'

Ruth stepped towards him and gently stroked his thinning hair. 'I want to make you happy, truly I do. I know how you want to go back to Carter's House, but I'm simply not ready yet.'

His eyes were huge, luminous with suffering. He gave an immense shrugging sigh and stared at her, flexing his mouth. 'I suppose if we went to the Cabot Lodge, it'd be better for Granddad and Grandma.'

Ruth wanted to say that her parents would gladly spend Christmas in an igloo if it would make their grandson happy. She recognised that Will too was compromising. 'That's true,' she said. 'So what do you think?'

'Guess it wouldn't be too bad.'

'Shall we call them, ask what they think?'

'If you like.'

Ruth phoned her parents. 'Mom! Hi, it's me.'

'What's wrong?' her mother instantly demanded. 'What's happened?'

'Nothing, except—Will and I decided that it'd be kind of nice to spend Christmas up in Maine. Thought we'd book some rooms at the Cabot Lodge Inn. We hoped you might join us.'

'You know we'd go anywhere for the chance to be with you two.'

Ruth telephoned the inn and spoke to Tyler Reed, the manager.

'Mrs Connelly.' His voice was warm. 'How nice to hear from you.'

'It's been a long time, Mr Reed. I'm coming up with my parents—'

'Dr and Mrs Carter—it'll be good to see them again.'

'—and my son. He's . . . I don't know if you've heard but he's been very sick and he'd really like to spend Christmas in Sweetharbor. Will you have rooms for us all? And if so, could we bring some decorations, a tree? I want to make it as much like home for my son as possible.'

'How about if you took a couple of our two-room suites? You could do what you liked then.'

'That sounds perfect.'

'I'll book you in. We look forward to seeing you then, Mrs Connelly.'

When she put down the phone, Will said, 'What about Dad?'

'*What* about Dad?'

'Is he coming too?'

'If he wants to,' she said lightly.

He hardly ever saw her now. They passed each other in the hospital corridor, bumped into each other briefly in the parking lot. That was it. Nothing deliberate about it, just the way things were. They were both suffering and it seemed easier to suffer alone than together. Last time he'd seen her, she had looked dreadful, too thin, eyes over-bright, skin stretched across her cheekbones. Always with a frown. When she looked at him, he wasn't even sure she saw him.

Will was finally allowed home. He was much weaker than he had been previously. Ruth had persuaded him that this time it would be easier, but it was not. His reaction to each stage of treatment was more intense: darker bruises from the insertion of needles, deeper depression from the drugs given to combat infection, greater pain from the ulcers which inevitably accompanied the treatment. His emotional withdrawal, too, was greater than before: daily she watched him growing further away from her.

Paul knew this was wearing her down. Destroying her. He nerved himself to pick up the phone and call her. 'Want me to come round, give you a break?' he asked.

'It would help Will, I guess. At this stage, that's more important than either of us.'

'You're important too, Ruth,' he said quietly.

Her tone softened. 'Thank you, Paul.'

'What are your Christmas plans?'

'My parents are coming up from Florida.'

'Will mentioned you were going up to Maine.'

'Yes.'

'Staying at the Cabot Lodge.'

'That's right.' She waited a fraction too long then said, 'What about you? What will you be doing?'

'Nothing in particular,' he said.

There was another pause then Ruth said unwillingly, 'I'm not sure about this, but Will would like it, so why don't you join us?'

'Gee, you really know how to make a guy welcome.'

'A guy who walked out on us, Paul.'

'A guy who made a mistake he bitterly regrets,' he said. He bit his lip. 'We chose each other years ago and you're still the one I want to be with,' he said doggedly, almost sure it was still the truth. 'You and Will.'

'Too bad you didn't think of that before you left.'

I wish we were working things out together, he wanted to say. I wish we could share our pain. But he was the one who had walked out and he had to accept her hostility. Will was what mattered, not her, not him. 'You haven't let me help with Will this time round.'

'You haven't asked to.'

'I'm asking now.'

Ruth sighed. 'Why don't you join us for Christmas, Paul?'

 Twelve

RUTH FOUND HERSELF becoming obsessed with the determination to ensure that this Christmas was as good as it could possibly be. Instead of just one, she bought several Christmas trees—one for the hall, one for the living room, a smaller one for the kitchen—and, with Will's help, loaded the branches down with golden stars and silver bells, iridescent ornaments, trails of silver tinsel. She purchased armfuls of greenery from the flower shop, covering mantelpieces and furniture surfaces with pine and holly and eucalyptus leaves until the apartment smelt like a forest. She sat up at night stringing cranberries and popcorn, she purchased seasonal tablecloths and table napkins, played CDs of massed choirs singing carols.

This was going to be a good Christmas. The *best* Christmas. The very best she could make it. Because always, at the back of her mind, was a possibility she could scarcely bear to contemplate.

'What're you doing now?' Will asked one evening, as she busily assembled sultanas and glacé cherries, pecans, almonds, candied orange peel, brandy.

'I'm making mince pies,' she said. 'Remember how you kids used to chop the goodies for me?'

'Remember how we needed a chisel to break through your pastry when they were done?'

'You're so mean.'

'Just teasing, Mom. But you have to admit you're not the world's best pastry maker.'

'And you are, I suppose?'

'Better than you. Grandma showed me how. Look, how about I make the pastry and you chop the stuff, OK?'

He came round the table. A medicinal smell emanated from his clothes, from his skin, his hair. His fingertips were white, his chalky nails edged in blue. She almost asked if he could manage but was able to bite the words back. 'OK,' she said and turned away so he would not see the anguish in her face.

Paul picked Ruth and Will up from the apartment. Though the invitation to join them had originally been prompted by Will, she had felt a rush of compassion at the thought of Paul alone and unhappy, throwing a TV dinner into the microwave, opening a bottle of wine and getting maudlin drunk. Now he seemed to find the situation as awkward to handle as she did. Stopping in Portland to buy coffee, they drank it quickly, standing by the car, stamping their feet, shoulders hunched against the cold, avoiding each other's gaze.

As they headed north, the harsh reality of a Maine winter drew them in and enclosed them. On either side of the road the land lay leaden under thick, steel-grey clouds. Trees crowded the edge of the road, bent under the weight of the last snowfall.

For this part of the drive, Paul sat in the back with Will. Every time

Ruth glanced in the rearview mirror they both seemed to be asleep. But as they approached Sweetharbor, Will sat up. Ruth turned off the highway and began to negotiate the narrow lanes. As they passed the turn down to the Hechsts' house, he said, 'Can we stop at Carter's House, Mom?'

'Will, I don't think I—'

'Let's at least go look at it. Please?'

'Good idea,' Paul said, awake now. 'Check the place out.'

She felt his finger lightly brush her cheek. Did he understand how she felt? 'Just a look, no more than that,' Ruth said, and was surprised at how unsteady her voice was. To come here at this special time of year, with her estranged husband and her sick son, was an experience she shrank from. 'Just a look.'

'That's all,' Will promised.

She reached the turnoff to the house. The track was covered in snow, but the overhanging trees had provided some protection so that they were able to bump along until they came out of the pine woods.

'Oh,' breathed Will. 'Look at that, will you?'

The house and barn glowed in the last of the winter daylight. The sun hung low in the misty sky, indistinct and hazy as though submerged in dry ice. The flat pasture was a thick pale blue, and beyond it the spired spruces stood black and cold.

Will sighed with pleasure. He squeezed Ruth's hand. 'It looks great.'

'Just the way I remember it,' said Paul. He leaned forward and Ruth felt his breath against her neck. 'It's so good to be back.'

We're *not* back, Ruth thought. We're here, but we're not *back*. We can never be back.

'Can I get out?' Will asked.

'If you want,' she said. 'Just make sure you've got your—' but he had already opened the door and jumped into the snow. They watched him struggle towards the house, whooping faintly with joy, tumbling into the snow and dragging himself up again. His breath hung in the icy air.

'Will he be OK?' asked Paul.

'Tomorrow he'll be bruised and his joints'll ache, but the hell with that. It's so good to see him happy again.'

'He looks like one of Santa's little helpers in that red ski-suit.'

'Not so little any more.'

'And that ridiculous woollen hat: where'd he get that?'

'Amy Prescott knitted it for him.' Ruth put a hand to her face. Her throat was thick.

As though he understood what she was feeling, Paul said, 'We can't worry about the future.'

269

'Easier to say than to do.'

'I know that.'

Ruth said softly, 'I'm so afraid he's not going to make it.'

'I can't possible reassure you.' Paul took her hand. 'Let's at least try to enjoy the next few days. Give Will the best Christmas we can.'

Dr and Mrs Carter arrived the following morning. While they were settling into their room, Will announced that they—*all* of them—had to go up to Carter's House and find a tree to decorate. 'And not just any old tree,' he said, 'but the *perfect* tree.'

'I think Granddad and I'll stay behind and unpack,' said Betty, glancing out at the sombre sky. A few snowflakes whirled and danced on the other side of the glass. 'You don't mind, do you, dear?'

'You two can't skulk in here for the rest of the holiday,' Ruth said.

'OK, but we don't have to look for it this afternoon, do we?' Betty shuddered elaborately. 'Snow: I hate the stuff.'

'Me too,' said Jonathan. 'Don't forget I'm an old man, and shaky on my pins.'

'You're not that old,' said Will firmly, 'and not that shaky. You've *got* to come. You always used to.'

Dr Carter allowed his gaze to wander over his grandson's face. He tutted theatrically. 'OK,' he said. 'We'll come. But we get to eat lunch first, right?'

'Right.'

After lunch, while Paul and the Carters lingered over coffee, Will and Ruth went out into Old Port Street. They walked along the waterfront, bent against the wind. Overnight the temperature had plummeted. In the harbour, the water slapped hard at the wooden pilings of the dock, grey and troubled; further out, it dashed itself repeatedly against the tumbled rocks of the little bay, sending up clouds of spray. The lowering sky bleached everything of colour except the lobster floats.

Ruth shivered. 'Doesn't it look chilly?'

'The water's always cold up here,' said Will. He had his hands plunged into his pockets. A thick lumberman's cap was pulled down over his head. 'Even in summer.'

'Want to go to Don's Donuts?' Ruth asked.

'OK.'

Ruth brought two coffees and a donut over to the narrow table by the window where Will was looking out at the street. 'There you are.' She watched him lick a finger and touch the sugary coating, the way his sister used to do. 'Apple-cinnamon. Josie's favourite,' she said.

He shook his head. 'No, Mom,' he said patiently. 'It wasn't. She liked the chocolate ones much better.'

'Did she?' She frowned. 'Are you sure?'

He nodded, lifting the donut to his mouth and taking a bite which left his lips covered in fine white sugar. Looking at his illness-ravaged face in the unforgiving light off the sea, Ruth was struck by a despair so profound that she could scarcely find strength to lift her mug. 'There's sugar on your—' she began, but could not finish the sentence.

When they had finished their coffees, they went out into the street. Lights were strung across it, and round the eaves of the buildings. Snow lay piled up at the edge of the sidewalks; red-ribboned garlands of evergreen decorated the shopfronts. On the other side of the road, the Cabot Lodge had several small spruces set upon the roof of its front porch, trimmed with tiny white lights which blinked on and off. Will walked back to the hotel while Ruth went into the drugstore.

As she was choosing gift-wrap, someone said, 'It's good to see you.'

'Mrs Hechst . . . Trudi,' Ruth exclaimed. 'How are you?'

'Just fine.' Gertrud Hechst examined her from large pale eyes. 'And you, Ruth?'

'I'm doing OK.'

'I'm glad you have come back here for Christmas. Carter's House full again, this is good.'

'We're not actually staying up at the house. We're at the Cabot Lodge.'

'But why?'

'Will wanted to come, and I couldn't face opening up the house. So we compromised.'

'Such a compromise.' The broad round face was creased with concern. 'This is not right, to be in a hotel at Christmas time . . .' The older woman suddenly took Ruth's arm. 'I have an idea. Ruth, why do you not bring your family to my house for dinner on Christmas Day?'

'What a kind thought,' said Ruth, somewhat taken aback.

Gertrud Hechst smiled delightedly. 'A good idea, yes?'

Ruth shook her head. 'Thank you, but we couldn't possibly intrude on you. There are far too many of us. My parents are with us. And—' And besides, we hardly know you, she wanted to add. Although we have been acquainted all our lives, we do not know you.

'The more the merrier—isn't that what they say? Especially on Christmas Day.'

'I'm very touched,' Ruth said. 'It's so kind of you. I think that would be a wonderful idea. But only if you let us make some contribution.'

'It isn't necessary. We always have way too much.'

'We'll see.' Ruth smiled. 'Thank you, Trudi.'

Crossing the road, she went back into the hotel and up to her room. Will was sitting on the couch, earphones on, reading an Asterix book. She tapped him on the shoulder. When he looked up, taking off his ear-phones, she asked, 'Gertrud Hechst invited us over for Christmas dinner and I said yes. Is that OK?'

'Cool!' he said. 'I really like the Hechsts.'

With the temperature falling even further, Paul drove them all up to Carter's House and parked in front of the barn.

'OK, people, out you get.' Paul glanced at Ruth. She looked pinched and pale. Had coming up here been a good idea?

'Lord,' grumbled Dr Carter, climbing down into the snow, then help-ing his wife out of the vehicle. 'What did we ever do to deserve this?' He put his arm round her shoulder. 'Want to move back up here, hon, or shall we stay in Florida?'

Paul looked at the wide doors of the barn. Will was right, they could easily get the mastless *Lucky Duck* in there. The day after Christmas, he might go down to the boatyard, ask about getting the boat moved. Paul glanced across at his son: the initial euphoria of their arrival had given way to exhaustion and there were grey hollows under his eyes.

Whatever he had said to Ruth, Paul knew it wasn't enough to live for the day. For Will's sake they had to act as though there was a future as well as a present. 'Right.' He clapped his mittened hands together, issu-ing instructions, taking charge the way he used to do. 'Just so we don't all get exhausted, as well as soaking wet, I suggest we confine our search for the perfect tree to the area round the house. How about we meet back here in what, ten, fifteen minutes?'

'How about we just jump in the car and go back to our nice warm hotel suite?' Jonathan said.

'Silence in the ranks,' Paul said.

'Granddad, what a wimp you are.'

'My feet have turned to blocks of solid ice just standing here,' the doctor complained.

Paul knew the moans were exaggerated, part of a show put on for Will's benefit. 'OK, Dad, quit bellyaching,' he said. 'You can manage ten minutes rummaging round in the snow, can't you?'

'Do I have a choice?'

'No,' Will said, laughing.

'Remember we're not looking for some giant tree, we want something about three or four feet high, that's all,' said Paul. He moved to stand beside Ruth who was hugging herself against the cold, a fur hat pulled down low over her fair hair. 'Are you all right?' he asked, reaching for her hand.

'Just fine.' She pulled away. 'Let's get moving, shall we, before we all freeze to the spot?' She began trudging towards the edge of the pasture where the trees began.

Paul followed, snow crunching under his boots. Fog was drifting in from the ocean, damp and wet. He pulled at her sleeve. 'Stop, Ruth. Look at the light on the house. It's beautiful, isn't it?'

She turned. 'Yes.'

'We had some good times here.'

'Yes, we did.'

'And could do so again.'

'I don't think so.'

'Different good times, Ruth.' His heart felt heavy. She looked so beaten down. If only he could have taken her in his arms as he used to do. Soothe her, tell her things would work out somehow. 'I'm glad we're going to have dinner with the Hechsts tomorrow.'

'You know what's strange,' Ruth said. 'I've lived here all my life, and I've never once been inside their house. That's part of what—what Josie used to object to, wasn't it? The way the summer folk act as though the year-round people hardly exist.'

'Josie exaggerated things, but yes, she was right.'

Will's voice travelled across the snow towards them. 'Here it is! I found it. The perfect tree!'

'OK,' Paul shouted back. 'We're coming.' He took Ruth's arm again and this time she did not shrug him away as they tramped across the frozen pasture towards their son.

After dinner in the hotel restaurant, they went back to their suite. An artificial log fire burned in the open hearth. Dr Carter poured whisky for the adults, gave Will a Pepsi from the icebox by the television. 'It's almost like home here,' he said.

'And it's so beautifully warm,' said Betty.

Ruth sat on the floor, wrapping presents for the Hechsts. The room was filled with the spicy scent of fresh pine from the tree they had cut. Before dinner, Paul and Will had decorated it; now it sparkled and shimmered, its delicate ornaments and tinsel streamers lifting with every tiny current of air.

'You could have gone skating today, Grandma,' Will said. 'We've got skates in the barn at Carter's House.'

'Yes, dear.'

Ruth had a mental image of her daughter, dressed in something blue, leaving tracks across the icy pond as she spun and twirled, golden in the light reflected from Carter's House. She suddenly felt the need, in this family gathering, to talk about the daughter she had enclosed inside herself for so long. She opened her mouth. 'Remember how good a skater Josie used to be?'

'Until she got scared off, because of that girl at her school,' Will said.

'Went skating one winter and drowned, didn't she?' Paul got up and began refilling their glasses.

Will nodded his head. 'The ice broke up under her. That's why Josie wouldn't skate any more.'

'I'd tell her over and over she couldn't possibly fall through,' Paul agreed. 'She never believed me. Stuff'd be inches thick but she wouldn't put so much as a toe on it.'

We're talking like a normal family, Ruth thought. A sudden rush of optimism filled her. Things would turn out all right. All would be well.

Will peered between the heavy curtains which covered the window. 'It's snowing again, Granddad,' he announced happily.

'Lordy. *Please* can I go back to Florida?'

'No way. You gotta tough it out.'

The others laughed.

This is good, Ruth thought. We're making the best of things. She thought of Carter's House, alone in the snow, empty except for its ghosts. She wished she had felt able to open up the place for Christmas. She saw Will watching her and forced herself to smile.

On Christmas morning they drove along the snow-thick lanes to the Hechsts' big weathered house. The day was dull again, trees beaded with fog, sky shrouded, almost as dark as at sundown. As they pulled up by the wicket gate, the dogs began to bark, the sound echoing, thrown back to them by the mist. Lemon light spilled out onto the snow as the genial figure of Dieter Hechst stood in the doorway. 'Happy Christmas,' he called. 'And welcome.'

'Hi, Mr Hechst.' Running up the icy steps of the porch, Will slipped and ended up at Dieter's feet in a shower of snow.

'How're you, son?' Laughing, Dieter gave the boy an arm to help him back onto his feet. 'Take your things off and go inside, where it's warm.'

As she reached the top of the steps, Dieter took Ruth's hand in both of his and pressed it against his chest. 'Welcome to our house.'

'It's so kind of you to have us.'

'It's good of you to join us.' Dieter was a handsome, placid man with a direct gaze. 'Trudi is some pleased.'

Ruth heard him greeting the others as she passed into a small cloakroom area full of snowshoes and boots and heavy winter outerwear. She removed her coat and hung it up, changed her shoes and went in to where Gertrud stood waiting for her, dressed in a thick woollen skirt with a flowered shawl pinned across her shoulders.

The wood-lined living room was a single large space stretching the entire length of the house. The ceiling was wooden too, the crossbeams carved and painted in red and green. Bookshelves covered half of one wall, beautiful objects were set about the room: pieces of silver and glass which caught the firelight, hand-painted plates, carved angels with golden wings and shining faces. And everywhere there were candles, dozens of them, on the floor, on the polished surfaces, on the elaborately laid table and on the piano at the far end of the room. A Christmas tree stood between the windows, unornamented except for small creamy candles set into holders attached to its dark green branches.

There were other people already seated on the deep sofas on either side of a wood-burning stove: an elderly lady, a man in a Scandinavian sweater, a woman with the same round face as Trudi, another man in a forest-green jacket with silver buttons, a fair-haired young girl. The long room was full of fragrances: woodsmoke, roasting meat, aniseed and oranges, wine and spices, candle wax.

Ruth opened her mouth in surprise and delight. 'How beautiful,' she exclaimed. 'How lovely.'

As though in a dream, she saw Will's face, its angularity softened by the light from the candles, saw Paul greeting the other people, saw her parents come in, shaking snow off their jackets, changing into indoor shoes. Paul was carrying a supermarket box which he took into the kitchen. Her father embraced Gertrud, saying it had been a long time, far too long, and rubbed his hands together as he advanced towards the open doors of the wood-burning stove and held them to the flames.

'This is wonderful,' he said. 'Happy Christmas to all of you.'

They were introduced to each other: Dieter's mother; Trudi's sister and her husband, and their daughter; Dieter's brother. Mugs of mulled wine were passed round, hot and spicy, each one topped with a clove-studded sliver of orange peel.

Ruth followed Trudi into the kitchen. It was large and warm. A big table stood in the centre of the room, laden with plates and glasses, dishes ready to be filled with food, baskets of nuts and rosy apples, a platter of cheeses, mince pies, stollen, chocolate-covered stars.

Gertrud began lifting the lids of pans and sniffing their contents.

'This is so kind of you, Trudi. Inviting us to join you.'

'It is nothing.'

'Five extra people is nothing?'

'We are glad to have you.'

How generous she was. How warm. Ruth recalled the way she had come into Carter's House and helped in the sad days after Josie's death.

Trudi said, 'What exactly is wrong with Will?'

Ruth clasped her arms protectively across her chest. 'He has leukaemia.' The word sounded sharp and jagged in this warm room.

'Oh, my dear, that is terrible.'

'During the summer we thought he'd recovered, but it's come back.'

'The poor boy. From the way he behaves, you would hardly know he was sick. You must be a very special person, Ruth.'

'Me?' Ruth laughed a little sadly. 'I don't think so.' She began to unpack the box Paul had brought.

'Yes,' insisted Trudi, opening the oven to look at the turkey. 'To have such wonderful children is an achievement. Josie too was very special.'

'She was—but it was not because of anything I did.'

'Children do not grow in isolation. So much depends on what they are given by their parents.'

Ruth bent her head over the box, not wanting Gertrud to see the tears in her eyes. 'We argued all the time. Especially that last summer, before she . . . before the accident.'

'This is so normal, Ruth. We have not had children of our own, Dieter and I, but we have seen it often in the families of our friends.'

Was she right? From the box, Ruth pulled out the bottles of wine she had brought, a bottle of Scotch whisky, Swiss chocolate candies, a honey-roasted ham, a whole Camembert and the wrapped gifts.

'Such gifts,' said Trudi, turning from the stove and catching sight of the wrapped presents Ruth had placed on the table. 'So much . . .' She smiled at Ruth. 'Thank you.' She bent down to look in the oven again. 'I think it is time to eat. This bird is telling me he is ready for the table.'

It took them more than two hours to do justice to the Dickensian feast Gertrud had prepared. The turkey was moist, the vegetables delicious, the cranberry and orange sauce outstanding. There were piles of moistly golden corn-bread, a dish of sweet potato puréed with butternut squash, red cabbage cooked with onion and apple, wild rice, roast potatoes, homemade sausages.

There was a lull in the conversation as they drank their coffee. Outside, the dark day was disappearing into night. Wind rattled the windows.

'Why don't you play us something?' Dieter said to his wife.

Gertrud smiled at the company, swallowed the last of her coffee and wiped her mouth on her linen napkin. 'Now I will play, but only for a little.'

She went over to the grand piano and sat down. For a moment she stared at the keys. Then she began to play, her work-roughened fingers moving effortlessly from Debussy to Mozart and on to Chopin.

Ruth was amazed. It had never occurred to her that such talent was to be found up here. Catching the deep calm gaze of Dieter Hechst, she blushed, hoping he had not been able to read her thoughts. He smiled a little, and she knew that he had.

'That is it,' Trudi said eventually. 'I have played enough.'

Though the others begged her to continue she shook her head. 'In a minute, we shall sing together,' she said. 'But first we must all make a toast. Here's to family.' They raised their glasses. 'How lucky we are to be together yet another year.'

Will lifted his glass. 'To Josie,' he said. 'To my sister.' He looked round at them with sparkling eyes. 'I just wish she was here.'

As the others raised their glasses to Josie, Ruth got up and went over to the window to stare out into the darkness, blinking away the tears that had filled her eyes. After a while, she felt Trudi's hand on her shoulder.

'Now, we must sing,' Trudi said. 'Come, Ruth.' She returned to the piano. 'Dieter. Please . . .' Dieter rose to his feet and then, when his wife had played the introduction, sang Schubert's *Elf King* in a rolling tenor. As the last German phrases faded away, they all applauded.

'Goodness,' Betty Carter said. 'You sound like a professional.'

He nodded. 'For a while I hoped I might be. But there were too many other young men with good voices. And my family needed what I could earn, so I became a carpenter instead.' He looked at his mother. 'Now who is next? How about you, *Mutti*?'

'I have no longer the voice,' the old lady said, 'but I will sing a song from the old country, which was so lovely, even though it became a song of the last war.'

Gertrud nodded. Softly, she began to play 'Lili Marlene' and gradually everyone joined in except Will and Gertrud's niece, both too young to know the song.

One by one, others round the table performed. Trudi's sister produced a violin and the two women played a piece of Bach together. Jonathan and Betty Carter sang 'Drink To Me Only With Thine Eyes', Will half sang, half spoke a rap number while Paul accompanied him by rhythmically slapping the edge of the table.

They finished by standing round the piano singing carols, while the candles flickered on the Christmas tree.

Later, as they began their goodbyes and thanks, struggling into coats and boots, preparing for a dash to the car through the deepening snow, Dieter Hechst took Ruth's hand and raised it to his lips. 'You must not worry,' he murmured. 'Things will work out.'

She looked up at him. 'I don't think so,' she said sadly.

'Be strong, Ruth.'

Paul appeared, put his arm round her shoulders, kissed the side of her neck. 'Come on, Ruthie, you look tired,' he said. 'Better get you home.'

Back at the hotel, they sat round the fire, opening their gifts. Will's cheeks were flushed. 'That was great,' he said.

'Wasn't it fun?' Betty said. 'I don't know when I've enjoyed myself so much.'

'Remember when we used to sing together at parties?' Jonathan responded. 'We should do it again.'

'I wish *we* could be year-rounders.' Will said. He lay back tiredly against the pillows on the sofa. 'I'd *really* like that.'

'No real reason why not,' said Paul.

'Well, then. Let's do it.'

'The winters!' Ruth's mother shuddered.

'It'd need some planning,' Paul said. 'I'd have to give up my Boston job if we came up here permanently. I guess I could still manage to teach at Bowdoin twice a week, but getting down to Boston would be a killer, especially in the winter.'

It was as if he had forgotten that he had made other choices, chosen to follow different paths.

 # Thirteen

JUST BEFORE THE EASTER weekend, Dr Gearin called Ruth into his office. She knew already what she would hear. It was impossible to ignore the fact that Will was not thriving. 'Will's last blood count was discouraging,' he began. His brown eyes were dulled by the difficulty of what he had to say. 'There's been no improvement in his blood count for some

THE COLOUR OF HOPE

weeks. Quite the opposite, in fact.' He gazed mournfully at Ruth. 'Things are looking less good than we might have wished.'

Ruth had tried to pretend away her doubts and fears. Now hopelessness ran along the narrow byways of her body, saturating her with grief. Rocking forward, she put her hand over her mouth.

Gearin half rose from behind his desk. 'Are you all right, Ruth?'

'No, Mike. I'm not all right. I'm about as far from all right as I could be.' Harsh gasps of pain were torn from her throat. 'How can I stand by and watch him die?'

He came to stand beside her. 'It hasn't come to that yet. Not anywhere near it. As you know, your parents were not a match for Will so our best hope now is to find a bone marrow donor.'

'Even if you did, it's not going to make any difference in the long run,' Ruth said dejectedly. 'I might as well face the fact that Will is going to die.'

'Do that if you want to, Ruth.' Gearin's voice was deliberately contemptuous. 'If that's how you choose to deal with it, then you must go that route. If you want Will to pick up the vibes from you, then you just go right ahead and make it even worse for him.' He tidied his case notes. 'Maybe you should change to another specialist—'

'What?'

'—because I don't think I can go on working with someone who gives up so easily. Someone who's only concerned with her own thoughts and feelings.'

There was a silence. Ruth twisted the wedding ring on her finger. 'You're right, of course,' she said quietly.

'Good.' His smile was sad. 'We're now going to undertake a serious search for a non-related bone marrow donor, since we haven't found a match in the immediate family. So we consult the worldwide register.'

'How does that work?'

'It's a register of non-related bone marrow donors. Their blood samples have already been analysed and registered. There are three million names on it, so there's a good chance we might get lucky. Basically, a technician will sit down at a computer and feed the details of Will's tissue type into the database, hoping to come up with a match.'

Unspoken inside Ruth lay the knowledge of how much higher Will's chances would be if Josie was still alive. The likelihood of sibling bone marrows being a match for each other was infinitely greater than anyone else's. Numbness filled her.

A couple of weeks later, Dr Gearin waylaid Ruth in the corridor outside Will's hospital room. His voice was high with excitement, the words tumbling over one another. 'I spoke to our technician today. I think we've got it!' he exclaimed.

'A match for Will?'

'That's right. I think at last we're there.'

'If you're right, what next?' Ruth bundled the relief and delight she felt behind a screen of brisk efficiency. There was no point celebrating until they were absolutely sure.

'He's only got one more dose of chemo. Let him take that, then have a period of convalescence at home. We'll build his strength up, then he can come back in and we'll go for it.'

'Please God,' Ruth whispered, the way she used to as a child, desperately wanting something to come right.

'My sentiments precisely,' Gearin said.

'When will we know?'

'Soon. A couple of days at most.'

'What's the result?' Paul asked the question, even though it was unnecessary. Ruth's body language as she came towards him across the restaurant was all the answer he needed.

She shook her head, crushed, unable to speak.

'Oh, Ruth.' Paul poured wine into a glass and held it towards her. 'I'm so sorry.' The stress is killing her, he thought. Is killing *us*. At Christmas, he had felt her unbend towards him, he had been hopeful. But since then, with Will's condition deteriorating, she had been as distant as ever. He felt an anger towards his son which he recognised as inappropriate, but nonetheless could not help. 'Where do we go from here?'

'There's still a chance that another bone marrow match will come up.'

He refilled his own glass. 'Shall we order?'

She set down her wine. 'What?'

'I said, shall we order?'

Under the surface of her face, emotions struggled for precedence. Anger won. 'How can you be so indifferent?' she demanded. 'Shall we order? Shall we order? As if I give a damn whether I ever eat again.' She flung down the menu he had handed to her. 'Our son is dying and all you can think about is food.'

'Calm down, Ruth.'

'No, I damn well won't calm down. I never realised before how . . . how *uncaring* you are,' she said fiercely. Her body was shaking.

'Oh, Ruth,' he said, wearily. 'I'm just so tired of all this.'

'There you go again. It's Will we should be worrying about and not ourselves.'

'I worry about Will all the fucking time. Taking an occasional break, eating a halfway decent meal with you isn't going to change anything for him, but it could help us.'

Ruth lifted her glass and tried to sip her wine, but her hand trembled too much and she put it unsteadily back on the table.

Paul pressed his hand over hers. 'Listen to me, Ruth. We can't keep watch at the hospital round the clock. We should recognise our own needs occasionally, as well as Will's.'

'I daren't,' she said miserably. She picked up her bag and pushed back her chair. 'It's hopeless, Paul.'

'Ruth, for God's sake. This is . . .'

'Hopeless,' she said again, and marched out, back straight.

He watched her go then poured more wine into his glass. He missed her. Her presence. *Her*. Scent on the pillow. Papers strewn across the dining-room table. He had come to realise how much he used to resent her job, the energy she put into it, but in these months away from her, he had begun to see that her desire to succeed was as integral to her as her laugh, her walk. And that new understanding made him miss her even more.

His mind drifted back to that last afternoon, coming home from the Trotmans' party, following her into their bedroom, pushing her down on the bed under him. He had slipped his hand inside her navy-blue halter top, felt her nipple harden.

'No, Paul,' she had said, pulling his shoulders against her warm breasts, saying, 'No, we mustn't, the children . . . the picnic,' but meaning yes, yes, lifting her hips so he could pull down her shorts and panties. Smelling the excitement between her thighs, pushing into her, their mouths hard against each other. Then he had come, emptying into Ruth while she moaned in his ear, not wanting the children to hear, writhing under him as she came too, saying God, that's wonderful, Paul, wonderful, while her body clenched and relaxed around him.

Looking back, he could see that that had been the final moment of their lives together.

He finished the bottle of wine, watching the pale wet light outside. He could not go on like this. He was afraid that Ruth's grief would swallow him up. Unless his own did first.

'We have to face it, Ruth. Unless a miracle happens and a bone marrow donor suddenly appears from left field, there's almost nothing further we can do for Will. The entire register's been checked and there simply isn't another match anywhere.'

Ruth listened, heard what Dr Caldbeck, the Chief of Haematology, was saying, felt nothing but a vast emptiness.

She managed to move her lips. 'How long do we have?'

Gearin glanced at his superior before speaking. His face drooped. 'I can't say. The will to live—or die, of course—is always a determining factor in these cases. I'd say—God, I'm sorry, Ruth—six months maybe. Perhaps more. The human spirit so often confounds us.'

'What about another course of chemo?'

'I don't think Will's body will stand it, Ruth. Even if he himself would go for it.'

'You're telling me we've reached the end of the road?'

Gearin was silent for a while. Then, very slowly, he bent his head.

Now Ruth stood by Will's hospital bed. He lay asleep, flat on his back under the covers. So thin, she thought. So pitifully thin, except for his face, unnaturally swollen by the drugs. He has almost left us, almost slipped away. What right do I have to try to tug him back? Sunlight slanted through the window and lay across his chest. She had scarcely had time to notice that summer had come once more.

Will opened his eyes and, seeing her, tried to smile. 'Hi, Mom.'

'Hi, darling.'

'They didn't find a match, did they?'

'Not yet, darling.'

'Not ever, Mom. Get real.'

'You can't be—'

'Even if they find a match, I don't want any more treatment. I've had it, Mom. I'm tired. Let me go. Don't make me feel bad about it.'

'Letting go is not on the agenda, William.'

'Give me one good reason why.'

Because, she thought, if you die as well, my whole life will have been worth nothing. 'Because I'm not going to allow it. Just try to be brave a little while longer.'

'I'm sick of being brave. I want to be done with all this crap. The only thing I want to do is to go back to Carter's House. With you and Dad.'

'Look, Will. We have to stay close to this hospital.'

'I don't care. I want to go up there,' Will said stubbornly. 'It'll be the last time.'

'Don't fucking say that!' Ruth yelled. 'Just don't *say* it.'

'OK.' Wearily he turned away from her. 'I just hope you'll remember that you refused my last request.'

'Shut *up!*'

Ruth ran from the room. She stood in the washroom, staring at herself.

His last request . . . No! She pulled a brush out of her bag and tugged at her tangled hair with it. Despair weighted her down, hung from her limbs so that each movement required all her strength to complete it. A world without Will. Images paraded through her head, so clear she could almost see them in her reflected eyes. His coffin. Lowered into the earth. Covered. Gone.

'*No!*' she howled. She pounded the heavy porcelain of the washbasin until her fists hurt. '*No!*' Anguish pushed against the confines of her skin. Everything was breaking down. There would be nothing left. She pressed her forehead against the cool mirror glass and closed her eyes.

Don't die, Will . . .

Ruth took a deep breath. Will was right. How would she feel if she refused him something he so desperately wanted?

That evening, she called Paul. Since leaving him at the restaurant they had not run into each other at the hospital.

Hearing her voice, his own grew wary. 'What's up?'

'Will wants to go back to Carter's House. He wants to spend the summer up in Maine . . . with us.'

'How do you feel about opening the house up again? I thought you couldn't bear to go back?'

'It's what Will wants. So I'm going along with it, because—because . . . oh, Paul, he's going to die. Unless there's a miracle. I'll go up a week before you drive up with Will, open the house up, get it ready.'

'Ruth, let's be sensible about this. He's too sick to travel. In the hospital they can at least make him comfortable.'

'He wants to be up there,' Ruth said stubbornly. 'I've already called Mrs Dee and told her we're coming up.'

'I don't think he should go.'

'So you won't help me by bringing him up? You want me to go up there, open up the house, get things organised and then come back down to pick him up?'

'I didn't say that. I just don't think it's wise.'

'Will wants to be there. That's enough for me. He wants to be there with us. When he's dead, I just hope you remember that you refused the last wishes of your son.'

'Ruth, I didn't—I can't handle this,' Paul said. He put down the phone.

He was wrong, he knew it. He walked the streets, not too steady, too much whisky, not quite sure where he was heading. Had to get out, walls crowding in on him, crushing him. Warm evening, navy sky turning velvet black, air heavy with the smell of exhaust and rubber, someone screaming abuse from an apartment window across the way. Will needed him. Ruth needed him. If only she would tell him. If only she could bring herself to say it: Paul, I *need* you.

Derelicts were setting up for the night in dark doorways, gathering their bags and newspaper round them. Eyes watched him, furtive, collars turned up round matted hair. Coffee shop across the road, Irish pub down the street. Had he been here before? He tripped over something, someone's feet and heard curses.

The last wishes of my son. It sounded so damn final. My dying son. Ruth was right. How would he feel if he didn't help? There was little else he could do for his son . . . didn't even have the right blood.

Tears clogged his throat and he found himself choking, the whisky he'd drunk earlier raw on the back of his tongue. If that's what Will wanted, to travel up to Carter's House, then of course he would drive him up. Whatever she wanted. Dying. He began to weep. Kid of fifteen. 'So needlessly, fucking senselessly cruel,' he shouted. He knuckled away his tears, tried to get control.

He stumbled again, put out his hands to save himself, hit the sidewalk, felt his palm scrape raw. Pain pulled his lips back from his teeth. He got to his feet, let his head swing, tidal wave of whisky drowning his brain. He groaned, feeling nausea loose in the pit of his belly. Where did it go? The Connellys? Ordinary family, doing the best they could by each other. He staggered towards an intersection, saw lights, traffic, cab. Cab home. Take a shower.

On either side of the road out of Sweetharbor, new bracken had sprung up, hooks of green uncurling from the layers of winter gold. Blossom was ripe along fresh-leafed branches and the fields were brilliant with harebells and daisies. At the turnoff to Carter's House, she bumped down the sandy track under the trees and wound down her windows, letting in the smell of the ocean. Coming slowly out of the pine stand to the pasture, she saw the sunlit house waiting for her, patient and unchanging.

For a while she sat, hearing the sea-sigh from below the meadows and the lonesome shriek of the gulls. Eventually she got out of the car and walked slowly towards the porch. Resolutely, forcing herself, she took the steps two at a time, put the key in the door and let herself in.

She had expected stuffiness, perhaps a sense of grievance emanating from the neglected rooms. She had certainly expected pain. What she felt instead was a deep sense of peace. Belle Dee had done a good job of maintaining a semblance of current domesticity. The house felt lived in.

The living room was more or less as it had been when they left. Furniture was polished, surfaces shone, there were even flowers—ironically enough, a vase of freesias—on the oriental chest which did service as a coffee table. The piano was open, as though someone was just about to play or had just been playing. On the stand attached to the upright lid was a song sheet—'Mr Tambourine Man', a Bob Dylan song she remembered from college days. Where had it come from? *In the jingle-jangle morning I'll come followin' you . . .*

As she had feared, everything was a reminder of Josie: the chipped Chinese vase, the piano which she had loved to play, one of her paintings given pride of place on the dining-room wall. Ruth had thought the memories would be impossible to cope with but, to her surprise, they were not. Time had gentled them.

Ruth picked up her sunglasses and went out of the front door and round to the back where the trail began. It was overgrown, almost invisible in parts. The familiar scents of woodland terrain filled her nostrils: leaf and wet earth and rotting wood, a gentle scent of blossom.

She climbed up to where the trees opened out and stood on the edge of the bluff, looking at the rocky beach below. The sea spread before her, blue-grey, falsely unthreatening.

She sat down on the bench—Josie's bench—lifted her face to the skies, closed her eyes. Silence, broken only by the gently deceptive murmur of the sea, the mewl of a bird dipping above her head, the whisper of the pines behind her. She was filled with a sense of Josie's presence. Her spirit is here, she thought. Somewhere, close by.

Eventually, wearily, she got to her feet. As she turned to leave, she saw something glinting in the grass at her feet. She bent to pick it up. It glittered in the sunlight. Metallic. An earring.

'Oh God!' She spoke aloud, wildly staring round her. She began to hyperventilate, her heart hammering. 'Josie!'

The earring lay in her palm like a precious insect, long legged, steel shelled. She turned it over. Silver. Rectangular, inset with a tiny copper heart. Exactly like the ones Josie had been wearing on the afternoon she drowned. Pressing her fists against her chest, she breathed deeply, in and out, in and out.

Rationalise this, she told herself. Be logical. The earring was not, could not be, Josie's. Someone had sat on Josie's bench, gazing out at the Sound, and then gone away, leaving the earring behind. It was simply a coincidence.

Walking unsteadily back along the trail, she turned off at the Hechst house. The watching dogs scrambled on the porch, checking her out. She murmured soothing words, pulling open the screen to rap at the door. Before she could do so, Gertrud Hechst appeared.

'Ruth! What a pleasure this is.'

'Trudi,' Ruth said warmly. 'How are you?'

'I am good.' Gertrud examined her with her head on one side. 'And you, Ruth?'

'I'm good too. We're bringing Will up to Carter's House for the summer at the end of the week.'

'How is he?'

'He's bad, Trudi. The hospital has sent him home. They—they don't know what else to do for him at the moment.'

For answer, Gertrud came down the steps and held out her arms. 'I am so sorry. So very sorry. But you must not despair.'

'I can't do anything else. We seem to have run out of options.'

'You never know what is waiting round the corner.'

'No.' For a moment, Ruth drooped, then she stepped back. 'Trudi, I came to ask if your husband or nephew, maybe, would be kind enough to help me move some furniture about. I'd like to have things ready for when Will gets here. He's been longing to come up here again.'

'I will ask one of them to come by one morning.'

As she stepped into the hall of Carter's House, the scent of freesias was strong, almost overwhelming. She had just closed the door behind her when the telephone rang.

'Mrs Connelly? It's Belle Dee, checking that everything's all right.'

'Very much so, thank you. The house looks very well cared for.'

'If you need someone to help in any way, you only have to call.'

'A friend is going to come by and help me set up a room on the ground floor for my son. Other than that, it's all under control.' Ruth remembered something. 'And thank you very much for the flowers.'

'Flowers?'

'So welcoming. The freesias in the living room. They have such a lovely scent.'

'I'd like to take credit, Mrs Connelly, but I can't. We have to be careful, as I'm sure you appreciate. We never leave flowers or even groceries. Our clients may have allergies or special needs, and we've found it best only to do so if specifically required.'

'How strange. I wonder where the freesias came from.'

'I'm sure there's a simple explanation,' Mrs Dee said. 'Now, don't forget: if there's anything I can do for you, let me know.'

In the living room, she touched one of the trumpet-shaped blooms and heard Josie's voice again: *My absolute favourite flower.*

The words seemed to hang in the air . . . *favourite flower.* The effect startled her. For a long moment she stood without moving. Had she really heard the voice, or only fantasised it? Had the phrase been spoken aloud or was she imagining things? Silent, she listened for a footfall, a breath, anything that might indicate the presence of someone else. *My absolute favourite flower* . . . her daughter's voice sounded again and this time she knew it was only inside her head.

In the evening cool, she sat out on the porch with a glass of wine and a paperknife. Better late than never, she thought, slitting open envelopes posted two years ago, reading the notes of condolences. *Deepest sympathy . . . such a lovely girl . . . you must be so bereft . . . we knew her well.* Josie opened in front of her like a blossom unfurling in sunshine, *much missed . . . lighted up our home . . . so much talent . . . her concern for others.* Reading the letters moved Ruth unbearably.

One of the envelopes was stiffened with board and had DO NOT BEND printed on the outside. Opening it, she drew out a charcoal sketch of a young girl, head bent, holding something in her hand—a flower, a paintbrush, hard to say which. Ruth drew in a sharp breath. The model was undoubtedly Josie. She turned the sketch over and saw a pencilled note scrawled on the back: *I thought you would like this.* The signature was one she did not recognise: *Annie Lefeau.* It meant nothing to her.

She went into the house and propped the sketch up in the kitchen. Annie Lefeau—who was she? Was she the person who had made the drawing? When had Josie posed for it?

That evening she lay half dozing in the bedroom she used to share with Paul, lulled by the sea-murmur. Will would be here in a few days, and there was a lot to organise. She began making lists in her head. As she did so, gently, almost inaudibly, she heard the tune, Josie's tune . . . *In the jingle jangle morning* . . .

She sat up, straining to listen. Had she really heard it, or was the sound simply an extension of her thoughts? It sounded again, faint music, the notes from the piano, words.

She got out of bed. At the top of the stairs she listened once more, but this time the old house was still.

'Is anyone there?' she called. Then, feeling idiotic, added, 'Josie?' But, of course, there was no answer.

Had she disturbed something more than just memories? Was the strength of her longing conjuring up illusions?

Back in bed, she lay under the covers knowing she would not sleep. She picked up the phone and telephoned Paul.

He was asleep when the telephone cheeped beside his bed. He groaned, his head thick with last night's whisky. He groped for the receiver, found it, held it to his ear.

'Ruth!' He tried to clear the alcohol fog in his brain. 'What's wrong?'

'Nothing.'

'What then?' He squinted at the clock beside his bed. Jesus, it was two o'clock in the morning.

'Don't laugh but . . . do you believe in ghosts?'

'Sorry?'

'Ghosts. I think Carter's House is haunted.'

'Haunted. What the hell are you—'

'By Josie.'

He sat up against his pillows, blinking away sleep, feeling the throb of a hangover at the back of his skull. He said quietly, 'Maybe you need to talk to someone, Ruth.' Ridiculously, he wanted to tell her he loved her.

'I'm not crazy, if that's what you think.'

'I know that, but . . .'

She began to talk, her voice growing stronger. He could not understand everything she was saying. The piano. 'Bob Dylan,' he said. 'What's he got to do with anything?'

She swept on, her voice rising. 'Her earring, Paul, the one she was wearing that . . . and flowers, freesias, the scent of them in the house, and the singing. I thought I was mistaken, but she's here, Paul. Or something of her is.'

He sighed. 'Look, darling.' The endearment slipped out before he could stop it. 'I'll be up at the end of the week. Just hang in there until then, OK?'

'You think I'm mad, don't you?'

'Of course I don't.' He tried to make her smile, put on a pleading voice. 'Can I go back to sleep now?'

'Sorry,' she said. 'Sorry if I woke you up.'

'Any time,' he said. And realised he meant it.

Wrapped in a throw against the cool night air, she went out of the house and sat on the porch in her grandmother's rocker. From beyond the meadow came the sea-whisper of the ocean. She adjusted the old herb-stuffed cushion in the small of her back, thinking: She is out there somewhere, I know she is. Not her ghost, not some spirit being, but the living person. She is out there. And she knows I am here. Hunched in the creaky old chair, the possibility of Josie's existence burned inside her. She stood up, walked to the edge of the porch and leaned on the railings, shivering with excitement.

Was she being given a second chance? The opportunity to put right whatever had been so wrong between her and her daughter that last summer?

All around her, the night hummed with expectation and longing. Ruth lifted her head and stared into the dark, transmitting a wordless message. *Josie, come back. I'm here. I love you.*

There was another thought which she could not repress. *I need you, Josie. Will needs you. Only you can help him now.*

Fourteen

RUTH OPENED the Yellow Pages and looked for *Investigators*. Of the three listed names, one appeared to be mainly concerned with business security, and one offered a list of services, including fraud enquiry and video surveillance. The third was a firm based in Hartsfield.

A gruff male voice answered her call. 'Fielding's Enquiries. Derrick Pearson speaking.'

'I'd like to make an appointment,' Ruth said.

'What's it in connection with?'

'A missing person,' Ruth said. 'My daughter. I want to find her.'

'How long's she been gone?'

'Maybe for almost two years.'

'Maybe? Aren't you sure?'

'Uh . . .' She cleared her throat. 'It's complicated.'

Pearson began extracting further details from her and eventually offered her an appointment at four o'clock that afternoon. Putting down the telephone, she felt breathless, unnerved. A private eye. She would not tell Paul about it. Not yet.

Mr Pearson had told her to bring anything she could that might be helpful in tracing Josie. 'Her bag,' he had said. 'Driver's licence. Date of birth. Social Security number. Anything that might be relevant.'

She went into the kitchen and took a key from one of the cabinets.

Then she took a deep breath, braced herself and went up to the first floor. The broad-planked passage which ran from one end of the house to the other had been kept burnished; the long Turkey runners brought home by Josiah Carter stretched towards the pine door at the end. Ruth walked slowly down the hall towards it.

In front of the door, she put the key into the lock and turned it. Josie's room. Opening the door, the smells came at her: oil paint, sun cream, old polish from the sanded boards. Mrs Dee had been given instructions that no one was to go into this room, so nothing had been touched in here for two years. Jeans still lay crumpled on the floor, a pair of white cotton panties hung from a half-open drawer, a hairbrush had been flung down on the bed. There was a spill of cassette tapes on a bureau top, open magazines, crumpled tissues.

The table under the window was covered in a dusty mess of papers; she picked up and examined each one, searching for significance, but found none. Most were reminders to call someone or meet someone. There were several scribbled phone numbers, but no diaries, no revealing snaps, no address book. She could not see Josie's painting equipment, which she thought had been carried up from the enclosed side porch after the accident, but she could have been mistaken.

She had a sudden picture of her daughter coming down the trail from the woods, taking the key from its hiding place under the side porch, letting herself into the house after the rest of the family had gone grieving back to Boston. She saw her sitting at the piano, singing to herself. *Hey! Mr Tambourine Man, play a song for me* . . . The image was disconcerting and painful. Had she felt that her family would be better off without her, or that she would be better off without them?

Canvasses were stacked against one wall. She turned them round and examined them. Local scenes. A portrait of Will. A portrait of Dieter and Trudi Hechst. An abandoned boat. A view of the sea, with Bertlemy's Isle in the distance. A forest, thin trunks gilded with sunshine, and a man somewhere in among them, half person, half tree. Josie had been sixteen when she painted these, but there was already a maturity of execution, a clarity of vision which was quite startling. Ruth wondered why she had not encouraged Josie more. Why she had not truly believed in her.

On the shelf above the bed were books, a mug holding a silk rose, a carved decoy duck, not painted in the usual bright colours but left so that the whorls of the wood melted naturally into the curves of wing and breast, the grain itself suggesting the feathers. It was beautiful. She turned it over and saw the initials SH burnt into the wood, and a date from two years earlier. SH—that must mean Sam Hechst.

Returning it to the shelf, she wondered where Josie's bag was. It should have been on the table, slung over the back of a chair, tossed on the bed. It would have held money and personal items which might be of help to Derrick Pearson.

Money. The thought triggered another. Ruth hurried down the passage to the walk-in linen closet and felt around behind the thick plastic storage bags in which the winter bed covers were stored. A contingency fund had been hidden there for as long as she could remember. Last time she looked, the box had contained $500. Now, when she drew it out and opened the lid, it was empty.

Empty!

It was all the confirmation she needed. Only Josie would have known where the box was kept, only Josie would have been able to go straight to it and then tidily replace it without disturbing the blankets and quilts.

Ruth shut the closet door. Looking up and down the passage, she smiled. 'I know you're out there,' she said aloud. 'I *know* you are.'

'You're not giving me a whole lot to go with.' Derrick Pearson raised his eyebrows. He was a large untidy man, with a weather-beaten face. Occasionally making notes, he had not reacted to Ruth's reasons for believing that Josie might not after all have drowned. 'I can make some calls, access some of our databases, but even if she is still alive, she could be going under another name—most likely is. I mean, she's old enough to be married, isn't she?'

'I can't believe she would have—'

'It seems the most likely explanation. How else would she have managed to exist for two years without contacting her family? Unless she had friends—or more likely *a* friend—to help her. Apart from a few hundred bucks, which anyway you think she didn't get hold of until some time after the accident, she'd have been entirely on her own, poor physical condition, soaked to the skin, penniless. The more you look at it, the more it make sense that she found someone to help her, at least at the beginning.'

'You mean some man?'

'You'd have to think so, wouldn't you? Some guy she's got involved with, there she is, missing presumed drowned, ideal opportunity to run off with him, wouldn't you say?'

'I find it hard to believe she knew anyone irresponsible enough to go along with such a plan.' It was harder still to imagine Josie married, living a life somewhere, maybe with a child of her own. What sort of man would she have chosen? Was it this unknown man who had been behind Josie's distress that summer, the cause of her hostility? Was he the man who stood motionless among the trees in Josie's painting?

'She probably pitched some kind of story,' Pearson said. 'Her family's been wiped out in a car crash, or she's an orphan trying to make it on her own.' He leaned back in his chair, stared up at the ceiling. 'Or mentions these abusive parents. Any one of the above. Story like that, someone would be bound to lend a hand.'

Ruth felt helpless. Although Pearson seemed entirely familiar with it, this was a world she did not know.

He picked up a pen. 'Meanwhile, better give me the names of any known associates and their phone numbers. People she might have turned to for help. Teachers, particular friends, places she liked to hang out.' When he had made notes of the information, he stared hard at Ruth. 'Is there anything else at all that might be helpful? Identifying features such as scars or birthmarks? A missing limb—' He saw Ruth's expression and added hastily, 'or something?'

'There's a possibility she might have broken her wrist in the accident,' Ruth said. Her certainty was beginning to wither. 'Is there any chance at all of you finding her?'

'If she's still going by her given name, we could turn her up by tomorrow, no problem. If she's not, then . . .' He shrugged.

'I can't tell you how important this is.'

'Do my best,' he said. 'That's all I can promise you. If I come up with anything, I'll let you know right away.'

'Why would she have gone to such lengths to avoid coming back to her family?'

'You tell me.'

'We're not—we weren't a dysfunctional family,' Ruth said.

'Sorry, but I don't buy that,' Pearson said bluntly. 'There had to be something wrong. Seems to me like she's saying loud and clear that she doesn't want any of you in her life.'

'I don't believe that,' Ruth said. 'Whatever happened back then, I think now she wants to be found. The clues she's left—like the earring and so on . . .'

'If that's what they are.'

'I'm sure that she's trying to tell me she wants to come home.'

'Maybe. But if you want my honest opinion . . .'

'Yes?'

'I'd say that the poor kid was drowned two years ago. End of story. Which is not to say that I won't do my damnedest to find her.'

'I appreciate your frankness.'

'I'll be in touch as soon as I have anything to tell you.'

Back at Carter's House, Ruth dialled Belle Dee's number. 'It's Ruth Connelly. I forgot to ask how long ago you opened up the house?'

'Three or four days before you arrived.' Hostility hardened the realtor's voice. 'Are you suggesting that our service is substandard? It's a busy time of year for us and we can't always arrange our schedules to match the—'

'I already said everything was fine. Just fine.'

Reassured, Mrs Dee grew friendlier. 'It was a real pleasure to be able to tell people that the house would be occupied this summer.'

'Which people?'

'Well, I say people but only two, really. One was a gentleman from Montreal.'

'How would he know about the house in the first place? It's not as if it's advertised.'

'Word of mouth, maybe? Most of the locals here know the house has been empty.'

'What about the other enquiry?'

'That was from a young woman. She called only two days ago.'

'So . . . after you'd opened the place up?'

'That's right. She said she was interested in renting the house for the summer and when I said the owner would be in residence, she just hung up.'

Was it far-fetched to wonder if this had been Josie? But if so, why was she staying hidden? What was holding her back?

Ruth was drinking coffee in the kitchen when Sam Hechst rapped lightly on the open door and came in. 'My aunt tells me you need some help moving furniture,' he said.

'That's right. Want some coffee first?'

'Good.'

They sat on either side of the table, taking stock of each other. Ruth started to speak but he cut across her. 'What's happened? Do you want to talk about it?'

Ruth's hands shook; she pushed them into the pockets of her shorts. Through the open door she could smell the wind off the pines, blowing seawards. The kitchen suddenly seemed too small for both of them. 'Let's go outside. The thing is, there are . . .' She stopped. 'I don't really know where to start.'

Standing in the sunshine, she watched the play of light on the pond. The reeds quivered as a breeze caught them and ruffled the water. 'First of all, I know it sounds crazy, especially after all this time, but . . . I think that Josie's still alive.' He drew in a sharp breath and she held up her hand. 'Don't say anything until I've finished.' Carefully she enumerated her reasons.

When she had finished, he asked, 'If Josephine survived the storm, why do you think she didn't come home?'

'Maybe she didn't want to.'

'Why not?'

'I'm not sure. Over these past months, I've realised how little I knew about her. What she thought about, what her hopes were, what she did with herself. Not even who she spent time with.'

'Isn't that perfectly natural? How *could* you know? When you were that age, did you tell your parents everything you did or thought or felt?'

'No, but—'

'Secrecy is an essential part of growing up.'

'I tried to be a good mother,' Ruth said anxiously. 'I thought I was. But now I can see how neglectful I was, how much more concerned with my own career than with my children. I should have put myself on hold. I should have concentrated on being a mother.'

'Would that have been enough for you?'

'Maybe not.'

'Then don't blame yourself for not doing it. Stop trying to take on the guilt of the world. It's pointless to try to be something you aren't.'

'There's something else,' she said. 'If she *is* around here, then it becomes all the more important that I find her. You see, my son is . . . he's . . . dying.'

'You told me he was cured.'

'We thought he was. Late last year the disease came back. He's been through all the treatments available now. Our last hope is a bone marrow aspiration, but we can't find a match for his tissue. Josie might be one.' She stared at the trees climbing up the hill away from the house.

Hechst took her hand and held it lightly. 'This is terrible. I had no idea, Ruth.'

'Time's running out for him. If she's alive then she could . . . she might . . . Josie is Will's last chance.' Ruth began to weep, clinging to Hechst's hand. 'Oh God . . .'

He gripped her arms, not moving towards her, just holding her. 'Can I do anything at all to help?'

'Do you have any idea of where she could have gone when she . . . if she . . . after the accident? Or even who she might have gone to? She seems to have talked to you more freely than she did to me.'

'We did talk a lot. And yes, she did fantasise about running away from home. She always had this romantic notion about living with "real" people. By which I think she meant people concerned about the environment, people who helped others, who made a living using their hands. She had this romantic idea of joining a commune.' He tightened his grip on Ruth's hand. 'If—*if*—she survived the accident, maybe she saw it as an opportunity to—to test her theories. To see if she could earn a living from her painting. Prove herself to you.'

'By allowing us to believe she was dead?' Ruth was horrified. 'I can't believe it.'

'If you're determined to look for her, I can tell you several places in the area she might have headed for. Communes. That's kind of a sixties concept these days, but they do still exist. I guess artists' colony might be a better phrase.'

'I'd be grateful for any information at all. I've hired a private investigator, but he's not very hopeful of finding her.' She looked up at him. 'I haven't told Paul that yet. He thinks it's completely irrational to jump to the conclusion that Josie's alive just because of an earring. I don't see that, I don't agree. There were the flowers, too. And the piano . . .' She was talking wildly now, shoulders shaking.

Hechst gathered her against his chest. His big hand gently stroked her hair. He smelt of wood and of turpentine. Of strength. She was grateful to him for not trying to argue her out of her conviction that Josie was alive. Even if he considered her search hopeless, at least he was not deriding her for wanting to undertake it.

Away from the coast Maine changed, no longer the guidebook fantasy but a place undeveloped, almost primitive, where living was pared right down to the basics of water, shelter, food. Along the endless, deserted roads, Ruth passed mobile homes, fields of daisies, unexpected graveyards full of granite headstones. Abandoned wooden buildings stood beside the road; once barns or homes, they now leaned like drunks towards the ground.

Ruth was heading for the tiny hamlet of Colbridge. 'It's a sort of collective,' Sam Hechst had told her. 'Artists and crafts people, getting together to market their work. Given the short season, it makes sense for them to pool their resources. Up here you have to catch the tourists while the summer lasts.'

'How would Josie know about them?'

'She came with me once when I was dropping some of my carved pieces off. She liked the set-up they had.'

Colbridge was off the highway, a small hamlet set round a triangular village green with an episcopal church at one apex, a post office at another and a tiny general store on the third. Ruth parked in front of the store and went in. She took a bottle of juice from the glass-fronted refrigerator case. Paying for it, she said she had heard that there was an artists' commune somewhere nearby.

'Ayuh,' the woman behind the counter said. She came out onto the wooden steps which led up from the road and pointed. 'See that kinda ramshackle place, the grey one? That's where they're at.'

Ruth took out a photograph of Josie which she had brought with her. 'Have you ever seen this girl?' she said. 'She may have been living with them, might have come in here.'

The woman stared at it for so long that Ruth's hopes began to rise. But finally she shook her head. 'I don't believe so,' she said. 'Mind you, they all look the same to me. After a while, you can't tell one from the other.'

Ruth left her car and walked down the road. This far from the coast, the air was windless and dusty. The heat leaned on her, inescapable. By the time she had reached the grey house, her legs and face were sheened with sweat. She climbed the shallow wooden steps and pressed the bell. After a while, the front door opened and a man looked out at her through the screen mesh.

'Yes?' He had very short hair dyed an improbable yellow, with the black roots showing, and several silver rings in his ear.

'My name's Ruth Connelly,' she said. 'I'm looking for my daughter, Josephine. She's a painter.'

He had a quiet, educated voice. 'What makes you think she could be here?'

'She came visiting, a couple of years ago, and liked it. I thought she might have come back.'

'Ah. Let me guess,' he said. 'She left home, right? Hasn't been in touch since?'

'Something like that.'

He scrutinised Ruth in silence. Then, as though some conclusion had been reached, he said, 'OK. Got a picture?'

Ruth showed him the photograph of Josie, holding it up against the screen door. He looked at it briefly before shaking his head. 'Sorry. The coast might be your best best. Bar Harbor, or Northeast Harbor—that's where people buy paintings.'

'I'll try them.'

As she turned to go, the man said, 'Ever thought that she might not want to be found?'

'I'd like her to tell me that herself,' said Ruth steadily. She had thought about almost nothing else since first deciding to look for her daughter.

As soon as the telephone chirped, Paul knew it was Ruth. 'Hi!' he said. 'How's things?'

'Fine. How's Will?'

'OK, I guess. Anxious to be out of hospital. Looking forward to seeing you again. Where are you? I tried ringing the house a couple of times.'

'I've stopped for a coffee in a place called Sawton.'

'Abandoned sawmill, polluted river, stench of urban decay . . . what are you doing up there?'

'I'm looking for something.'

'Looking for what?' He eased the phone against his jaw, imagining her in some grubby phone booth, leaning against the Perspex sides.

'I don't want to talk about it.'

'OK. Ruth . . .'

'Yes?'

'What are you wearing?' It was what he always used to ask, when they were courting: did she remember, too?

'Green linen slacks, a white T-shirt, sandals. And this rather nice carved necklace somebody made for me. Four hearts strung on a leather lace.'

'Are you really?' he whispered.

'Yes. Really,' she said, and he heard the smile in her voice.

He picked up the phone once more and called the flower shop. Asked them to arrange for a dozen red roses to be sent to Carter's House, in Sweetharbor, Maine. Told them to write *Love, Paul* on the card.

Ruth had spent the night at a fine old Victorian house which had been converted into a b. & b. She was tired; it had been a long and disappointing day. She had stopped at more galleries and craft centres than she could remember, but nobody knew Josie's name, nobody recognised the girl in the photograph she showed them.

Towards the end of the afternoon, she found herself driving into Millport, a small town set far up one of the many inlets off the coast. The sun had broken through the heavy cloud cover and sunlight slanted off the wet roofs of the main street. Between the buildings was water, boats, buoys. Squeezed in between a small bank and a garage was a medicinal herbs store. Further on, outside the Docksider Diner, a hand-lettered sign pointed down a short dirt track to Annie's Gallery.

Annie. Could that be Annie Lefeau? The woman who had sent her that sketch of Josie, nearly two years ago?

Ruth drove down the track and parked. The gallery's windows held none of the usual cute tourist-tempting artefacts. In the one on the left of the door, there were paintings, a wooden bowl of bird's-eye maple, several pieces of hand-thrown pottery with subtle glazes. The window on the right held a spread of hand-loomed textiles, some beautiful glass jars and a painted wooden chest.

Inside, the floors were wooden and bare, the glass shelves carefully lit to show to best advantage the objects displayed.

The woman who was sitting behind a table laden with glossy art books was in her mid-thirties, wearing a low-cut black top and a floor-length skirt of Indian cotton. A long braid of red hair hung over one shoulder.

'Can I help you?' she said.

'Are you Annie Lefeau?'

'That's right.'

'I'll just look round.' Ruth was reluctant to plunge in and ask directly about Josie. She walked slowly between the carved wooden boxes, the pottery plates and bowls, the wooden dishes, and baskets of various sizes. At the end of the gallery, one of the walls was covered in mirrors and textile hangings. The other two held paintings.

They were mostly local scenes: seascapes, rocks, boats pulled up out of the water, weathered houses with the wide grey sky of a Maine winter behind them. The fishing boats were not pleasure craft, designed for sunny days and holidays, but year-round working boats, oil-stained and dirty. The houses were not the brightly painted gingerbread cottages expensively restored by people from away, but shabby places, their shingles peeling, their lines plain and workmanlike. A graveyard, a boat turned upside-down, an abandoned anchor on an empty shore: the paintings were powerful and bleak.

One in particular caught Ruth's eye: a marble headstone leaning as though against the sea wind, its white surface pitted with salt. Carved in elegant italic script were the words: *Death is Swallowed Up in Victory*. As though to emphasise the point, withered leaves lay piled at the foot of the stone and among them, a single white flower.

Ruth stared at it for some time then made her way back to the front of the gallery. 'I'm interested in the paintings you have in the back,' she said.

The woman put her finger into the book she was reading and looked up. 'Any one in particular?'

'There's one of a gravestone. And another of a boat pulled up onto a beach. Some others which seem to be by the same person. I can't see a signature, though. Are they signed on the back? I didn't like to take them off the wall to look.'

Annie smiled. Her whole body seemed to light up. 'They're great, aren't they?' Getting up, she led the way to the end of the big room. Over her shoulder she said, 'I admire all the work but I think I like the tombstone best. I love that juxtaposition of life and death, the promise of springs to come. I wish I could paint like that, but . . .' she spread her hands in a gesture of resigned defeat.

'Is it a woman painter?'

Annie turned. Her gaze was suddenly wary. 'Why do you ask?'

'Partly because of the detailed observation, and partly because the sentiment the painting conveys seems to have a woman's perspective about it.'

Annie remained silent.

'Perhaps I'm reading too much into it,' Ruth said, unnerved.

Unexpectedly, the other woman laughed. 'I think you're right, and yes, the painter is a woman.'

'What's her name?'

Distrust closed down Annie's face again. 'All the paintings are signed.' She stroked the auburn braid on her shoulder and narrowed her eyes like a cat.

'If they are, I can't read the signature from here.' This Annie was behaving more like someone anticipating attack than like a gallery owner eager to make a sale. She said boldly, 'I'd like to buy that one, the gravestone one, please.'

Silently, Annie lifted it off the wall and began carrying it back to her table.

Ruth followed her. 'Where's the signature?'

'There.' Annie pointed to a dead leaf curled at the bottom left-hand corner of the picture. Ruth squinted at it and could just make out the letters JO.

JO. Excitement swelled inside her. 'What do the initials stand for?' she asked.

Annie stared at Ruth. 'Janie O'Donnell,' she said. She folded her arms across her chest. 'You seem to be a lot more interested in the painter than in the picture. Before I give any more information away, I'd like to know why.'

The two women faced each other belligerently. Finally Ruth said, 'Because I think they may have been painted by my daughter. My estranged daughter.'

'Oh God.' Annie paled. 'You're Mrs Connelly.'

'How do you know that?'

'I'm . . . I was a friend of Josephine's.'

'You sent me a drawing of her when she . . . after the accident.'

'That was before . . . yes, I did.'

'Then you'll know I haven't seen her for two years.'

'She drowned. That's why I sent you the drawing.'

'Maybe she didn't.'

Annie Lefeau's eyes widened. 'Why do you think she's alive?'

'Instinct.' Ruth took a step closer. 'Have you seen her, Ms Lefeau? I've been searching all over. Asking everybody.'

'No.' Annie shook her head violently from side to side.

'I don't believe you.'

'That's your problem, not mine.'

Ruth clenched her jaw to prevent the angry words escaping. Writing out a cheque, she said curtly, 'Perhaps you'd wrap this up for me.' As she opened the door, she turned. 'I know my daughter painted this,' Ruth said quietly. 'And I know she did it recently.'

Sitting in her car, Ruth looked at her watch. She drove up the track from the gallery and over the main road to park in the lot behind the Docksider Diner. Inside, she ordered an iced tea, then sat in the window, watching, waiting. At five fifteen, Annie Lefeau appeared, driving a dirty green Camaro. She drove cautiously to the edge of the main road, looked in both directions, then turned left. Hurriedly, Ruth stood up.

At the door of the restaurant, she turned to the waitress. 'The person who runs that place across from here. Annie Lefeau. Does she live far from here?'

'A couple of miles the other side of town,' the waitress said. 'Little place called Troy Ponds.'

'Right. Thanks.'

She drove fast along the road Annie Lefeau had taken. Before long, she saw the green Camaro, three cars ahead of her. Shortly after that, a sign indicated a right turn towards Troy Ponds, and Annie swung off the road, followed by one of the cars behind. Keeping back now, Ruth trailed the other cars into Troy Ponds, a tiny ribbon development along a rural road. After a while, the other car peeled off.

Two or three hundred yards further on, Annie turned off into a rough area of gravel and grass in front of a one-storey house. Ruth continued up the road then found a place to pull off. She turned off the engine and waited for fifteen minutes by the dashboard clock before driving back again to the Lefeau house. Pulling in past the entrance, she parked on the grass at the side of the road, out of sight of Annie's windows.

Hoping she was not observed, she ran across the gravel to the front door. Before pressing the bell, she pulled the screen door open. Ms Lefeau came to the door almost immediately. She had released her rich hair from its braid and it hung below her shoulders like a fall of water. Her face paled when she saw Ruth. 'What the hell are you doing here?' she demanded.

'I have to talk to you,' Ruth said. As the woman opened her mouth to speak, Ruth rushed on. 'Ms Lefeau, I *must* find her—'

'I suppose you want her to come home with you?'

'If she's willing, yes, I most certainly do.'

Annie made a sound of disgust. 'So her stepfather can go on abusing her?'

'*What?*'

'Please . . .' Annie held up her hand. 'Don't pretend you didn't know.'

'So she *is* alive?' Ruth put a hand against the doorpost for support, afraid she might otherwise fall.

The other woman moved back. 'Don't think I have any intention of helping you find her.' She tried to push the door shut, but Ruth crowded after her.

'I don't know what Josephine's told you,' she said, 'but there is no stepfather. Nor was she ever abused by Paul, my husband, her father.'

'How do you know that?'

'Because . . .' Ruth stopped. 'Because I know my husband,' she said simply.

'I wonder how many other wives have said that.'

'Ms Lefeau—Annie. I want Josephine back. I love her more than I can say—we both do. If there's anything I can do to make up to her for what she perceives I've done to hurt her, I would willingly do it. But that's not the only reason I'm here. My son Will—' She broke off. 'Ms Lefeau, please let me come in.'

'Why should I?'

'Because I don't think you're in possession of all the facts. And if you would listen to me for a few minutes, you might view the situation somewhat differently.'

Seeing Annie's hesitation, Ruth hurried on. 'Perhaps if you'd let me explain why I'm here, you would feel less hostile. So may I please come in?'

'I suppose so,' Annie said reluctantly. She motioned Ruth to go ahead of her into a pleasant sitting room where antique furniture had been skilfully combined with modern glass and wood. She faced Ruth nervously. 'Go ahead,' she said. 'Let's hear what you have to say.'

In her head Ruth assembled the salient facts. 'For a start, whatever she may have told you, Josephine was a much-loved child. If she was abused, it was not by anyone in her family. However, I don't believe she was abused by anyone at all, not in the way you think.'

'Go on.' Annie Lefeau narrowed her eyes.

'As you're obviously aware, there was an accident, and Josephine was lost. We all believed she was dead. We've all mourned her ever since, and missed her desperately. It's only in the past few days that I've begun to believe that perhaps she survived and, for reasons I can only guess at, didn't want to come home. What you've said so far confirms it. I'm sure you don't need me to tell you how painful it is to know that.'

Annie reached a hand towards Ruth and then withdrew it. She stared wildly around her. 'Oh God,' she said. 'I don't know what to do.'

'My son is desperately ill with leukaemia.' Ruth was pleading now. 'His only hope lies in a bone marrow transplant, and so far we've been unable to find a match for him. His sister might be able to provide that match. You can see how important it is for me to locate her.'

'This is terrible.' Annie Lefeau bit her lip, nervously twisting her ring-less fingers. 'I don't know what to do,' she repeated.

Aware of the other woman's mounting distress, Ruth pushed on relentlessly. 'If you know where she is, Ms Lefeau, for God's sake think of my boy.'

'What have I done?' Annie said suddenly. She took a hank of her bright hair and thrust it against her mouth. 'Dear Lord, I shouldn't . . . I can't . . .'

'You should. You can.' Ruth seized the other woman's wrist and held it tightly. 'You know where she is, don't you? You know she's alive.'

Annie drew in a deep breath and then exhaled it. 'Yes. Yes, I do. I told her. I said it was wrong, she shouldn't leave you in ignorance, it wasn't fair, whatever she felt about her parents, it wasn't right—'

'Where is she?' Ruth said, scarcely able to breathe. 'Where is she, Ms Lefeau?'

'She's . . .' Annie's eyes filled with tears. 'I—uh—oh God, I wish I'd met you long ago, before all this came up. I'm so sorry, Mrs Connelly. Truly I am. I never did think she was telling the whole—'

'*Where is she?*'

'She's been—she's been living here, right here with me.'

Blindly Ruth reached for the armchair and sank into it. The room began to waver and dim.

'She'd been into the gallery a couple of times before, you see, we'd got on well, talked about a lot of things. We had a lot in common, even though she was so young. She was very passionate, very . . . strong. When I read about her disappearance in the papers, I was devastated. That's why I sent you that sketch. And then, later, I—I . . .' Ms Lefeau took the top off a crystal decanter and poured whisky into two glasses, handing one to Ruth. Her hands were shaking.

'You what?'

'I went down to—' Again she broke off.

'*What?*' Ruth wanted to shake the woman, shake the information out of her trembling mouth.

Annie squared her shoulders, took a deep breath. 'One afternoon, about a year ago, someone came in and when I looked up—it was her. I could hardly believe it . . . While we were talking, she told me that she'd been sleeping in her car, some old rustbucket she'd picked up some-where, so I offered her a room. She's used this house as a base ever since.'

'Why didn't she . . .' Ruth shook her head in bewilderment. 'One phone call would have . . . she can't have hated us that much.'

'I thought so too—until she told me about her stepfather molesting—'

'But she doesn't have a stepfather!' cried Ruth. 'And her father's a good man. A good father.'

'Oh God!' Annie cried despairingly. 'If only I'd known . . . I have no family of my own. She's been like a—like my daughter. She trusts me. I just can't betray her. I can't even be sure that you're telling the truth. She told me that if anyone ever came looking for her, I wasn't to give her away. She actually made me raise my hand and swear it.'

It was precisely the kind of melodramatic gesture Josie would have gone in for. 'If she doesn't want to see us or be with us, that's her choice and however hard it is for us, we'll respect it. But for Will's sake . . .'

'She doesn't know about him being ill,' Annie said softly.

'If she did, wouldn't she want to help?'

'I'm sure she would.'

'Then tell her that Will needs her.'

Annie lifted the weight of her hair in both hands and let it fall against her neck. 'I can't do that.'

'Why not?'

'Because I don't know where she is. She's taken off again. She does that. She'll ring me eventually, but I have no way of knowing when.'

A choking despair swept over Ruth. To have come so close to her daughter, only to lose her again . . . she buried her face in her hands.

Annie put a hand on her shoulder. 'Don't give up now,' she said.

Fifteen

WHEN THE TELEPHONE RANG, he was watching some crap on the TV, not really watching, just thankful to have the bright images to focus on rather than the thought of his son's white face. Still staring at the screen, he reached over and lifted the receiver. When he heard her voice, he hit the mute button on the remote. 'Ruth . . . Did you find what you were looking for?'

'Almost,' she said.

'Want to tell me about it?'

'Maybe.'

'What do I have to do?'

'Listen, Paul. Just listen, OK?. It's about Josie.'

'But—'

'She's alive, Paul. She's really alive.'

He had not the slightest doubt that Ruth was making a terrible mistake. But he understood the pressures she was under. He wished he was with her, could hold her in his arms and gently explain how life didn't work like that. Drowned daughters didn't just show up after two years, however hard you might desire them to.

'Where is she now?'

'You don't believe me, do you?'

'I do.'

'I think,' Ruth said, and he could tell she was choosing her words with extreme care, 'I think she needs me to find her.'

There was silence. 'Ruth, we'll be with you by six tomorrow night,' Paul said quietly.

'Good. Everything's ready. How's Will?'

'Glad to be coming up to Maine.' Paul sounded bleak.

'What's wrong?'

'He seems to be getting worse by the day. It's almost more than I can bear.'

'At least we'll be able to support each other when you get here.'

'True.' He sighed heavily. 'Will, his illness, it's going to take every ounce of strength we have to get through the next few months. Or weeks.'

'At least we'll be together.'

'I worry about you, Ruth.'

'Thank you for thinking of me.'

'You wouldn't believe how often I do.'

'And thank you for the roses you sent. They're beautiful.'

'You know what red roses mean?'

'Yes,' she said quietly. 'Yes, I do.'

Putting down the phone he thought, I'm falling in love with her all over again.

Will seemed in much worse physical shape than when Ruth had last seen him. The pallor of his drug-swollen face and the grey shadows under his eyes belied the temporary animation he displayed as he moved heavily from room to room, checking the place out, making sure that everything was as he had remembered. Trying to hide the grief she felt, Ruth followed him, not wanting to let him out of her sight.

'It's great,' he kept saying. 'It's just so great to be back here.'

'I've put you downstairs.'

'But I wanted to be in my own room.'

'I thought you'd like to be able to step directly onto the porch. Sam Hechst helped me bring all your things down from upstairs.'

'But I . . .' He was about to protest some more, then saw her face and stopped. With an effort, he said, 'Thanks, Mom.'

'Come and talk to me. I'm going to make supper.'

They walked together down the passage to the kitchen. 'Where did that come from?' Will asked, nodding at the sketch of Josie.

'Someone gave it to me.'

'It's good.'

'I know.'

'You've changed, Mom. A year ago you wouldn't have allowed yourself to mention Josie's name, let alone had her picture up.'

'I chose the wrong way to come to terms with what happened,' Ruth said. 'I realise that now.' Should she tell him what she had found out, or should she wait until he was rested from the journey?

'Ed and his family'll be up on Monday.' Will sat on the edge of the table. 'Mind if I go down to the shore?'

'Just don't overtire yourself.'

He stood up again. 'I'm not a kid, Mom.'

'I know you're not.'

From the front porch, she watched him walk slowly and with obvious effort across the meadow towards the stony strip of beach below it.

When Will had gone to bed, Paul sat opposite Ruth, watching the fire-light play on her hair. She was wearing some musky perfume which, enhanced by the heat of the flames, filled the air around her.

'What's wrong?' Ruth smiled at him.

'You look so pretty,' he said.

'Me?'

'Like you did when I first met you.'

'Oh, sure.'

He got up and went to sit beside her. He lifted her hand. 'You're still wearing your wedding ring.'

'That's because I'm still married.'

'Tell me about Josie.' He slipped an arm round her shoulders and felt her yield, melt into the curve of his body, lift her face towards him and open her mouth to speak.

Then the telephone rang, and she pulled away, suddenly frantic, scrambling for the receiver, her face tight with anticipation.

Annie Lefeau was on the other end of the line.

'Janie—Josephine—called me this morning,' Annie said. 'I told her about her brother being sick. She was terribly upset.'

'Did she say where she was?'

'No. We didn't get a chance to talk for long. I told her about the bone marrow thing, that she might be a match, and it was Will's last chance. She was distraught, Ruth, sobbing on the phone.'

'Did you tell her I'd been looking for her?'

'She knows.'

'Did you tell her how much I need to see her?'

'Yes.'

'Did you tell her I love her?'

'She knows that too, Ruth. She said she'd be in touch.'

'Did she say when?'

'No. I told her over and over she should call you right away.'

'Thanks for trying.'

'Ruth, I'm going to be in Sweetharbor tomorrow,' Annie said slowly. 'After what's happened, I'll understand if you say no, but—but would it be OK for me to come by? I'd like to meet Will. And your husband.'

'Good idea,' said Ruth. 'I haven't told Will yet about his sister. If you're here, you can at least confirm to both of them that I haven't totally lost it.'

'There's something else. Something I need to talk to you about.'

'What sort of thing?'

'I'll—I'll explain when I see you. I'll be with you early afternoon.'

'OK.' Hanging up, Ruth closed her eyes, exhausted.

'Tell me about Josie.' Paul tried to pick up their conversation where it had been broken off.

For the length of a heartbeat, she gazed into his eyes, wondering if the lost mood could be recaptured and deciding it could not.

'Maybe tomorrow,' she said.

Was Josie really alive?

Staring into the not-quite-darkness, Paul didn't dare allow himself to hope. He lay in bed, listening to Ruth getting ready for the night. She had prepared a bed for him next to the room they used to share. There was a big old-fashioned bathroom between the two, which gave them a vestige of the old shared intimacy while at the same time keeping them apart. He hadn't slept in this bed before, nor in this room. It smelt of herbs and lavender water. Wavy shadows played across the ceiling, as though reflected off the sea, though he didn't know how that could be since it was dark outside.

Ruth and he had started their married life here at Carter's House— maybe ended it. Coming up here with Will, he'd hoped—he didn't quite know what he had hoped, but he knew it involved holding Ruth in his arms. He could hear her moving about in the bathroom, the spurt and hiss of water from an air-locked tap as she ran a bath, the clink of a bottle against the glass shelf above the basin. He could imagine her in the bath, lying in scented bubbles, her eyes closed. He was aware of a desperate longing, fierce as a flame, an absolute desire for her.

'I'm starving,' Ruth said, when Will appeared in the kitchen the next morning. 'Are you up for breakfast at the Cabot Lodge?'

'You betcha.'

'Let's go.'

'What about Dad?'

'He's gone down to the boatyard. Wants to take another look at the *Duck*.'

'We were going to try to rebuild it,' Will said. 'Before . . . all this.'

'You still could.'

Tyler Reed, the hotel manager, was standing by the reception desk when they came in, and at Will's request he seated them at a table overlooking Old Port Street. Will stared avidly out of the window. 'It's so good to be back,' he said. 'I really wish we lived here all the time.'

'I'm thinking,' Ruth said slowly, 'that maybe we should.' She smiled at him. 'I should have thought of it long before now.'

'If we did move up here, what would happen with your job?'

'These days it's much easier to work from home.'

'Really? Honestly?'

'Why not?'

'Everything'll be great again.' He sighed with pleasure as the waitress placed a stack of pancakes and a jug of blueberry syrup in front of him.

'Will . . .' Ruth leaned across her coffee cup, closer to her son. 'I don't know if this is the right place or time to do it, but there's something desperately important I have to tell you.'

The joy ebbed from his face. 'Is it about my cancer? Cause if so, don't worry. It doesn't bother me any more. It did at first, dying and stuff, but I'm OK about it now, I really am.' He cut into the pancakes and lifted a forkful to his mouth.

'You break my heart when you talk like that.'

He looked directly at her. There was a smear of blueberry syrup by his mouth, and the spectre of death in his eyes. 'I'm not frightened, Mom. I've had plenty long enough to get used to the idea.'

'Don't, Will. I can't bear it.'

'OK. What's so important? You can tell me. I promise not to faint.'

'Will, it's . . .' she began, then shook her head.

'Tell me, Mom.'

'It's about Josie.'

'What about her?'

'She's alive,' Ruth said.

Eyes wide, he stared at her. She saw his hand tremble as he put down his fork. He looked down at his plate. 'Don't, Mom. Please. Don't drop this on me. I can't take any more, I'm just a kid.'

'Yesterday you said you weren't,' she said, smiling. She reached across for his hand. 'Will, believe me. I'm not dreaming this up. It's true.'

'How do you know?'

Ruth described what she had learned from Annie Lefeau.

Will listened without comment, then said, 'Where did she go at the beginning? How did she handle it all?'

'I don't know. Not yet. She'll tell us.'

'It'd better be good,' said Will. He sounded angry. 'I thought—I kind of kept hoping that she'd made it after the accident. But when she didn't get in touch with us, I realised she must have died. Otherwise she'd have called us. She'd have let us know she was OK. Oh, Mom . . .' There was a break in Will's voice. 'Are you *sure*?'

'I'm sure. Annie Lefeau is coming to visit this afternoon. She can tell you herself.'

'Do you think Josie knows we're back in Carter's House?' Will pushed at the tears in his eyes.

'Yes, I do. Oh, darling Will, if only she'd get in touch with us.'

There was a flush lying along Will's over-prominent cheekbones. 'Josie alive after all! That's my last wish come true.' His eyes filled again. 'Maybe Josie and I can take the boat out when she comes home. I really want to go sailing, and I know you're not up for it.'

When she comes home . . . How ordinary it sounded. 'I could try if you like. Crew for you, I mean.' Ruth's stomach began to churn. 'If that's what you want.'

'That's OK. I don't want you getting worried. Dad and I can go. Or I'll wait until Josie can take me.'

Mother and son smiled at each other. Unspoken between them lay the treasure of a Josie refound and all it might mean.

Annie Lefeau arrived at four o'clock. She shook hands with Paul, greeted Will with delight. 'I'm *so* happy to meet you,' she told him. 'Your sister talked about you such a lot.'

Ruth led the way out to the porch and they sat down. Reaching into the leather pouch slung over her shoulder, Annie took out a package. 'I brought you this.'

'Thanks,' Will said. He undid the wrapping to reveal a small picture of a boy leaning against an upturned boat. He stared down at it. 'Hey, it's me.' Blindly Will passed the little painting to his mother.

'It's beautiful.' Ruth showed it to Paul.

He looked at it with a mixture of surprise and pride on his face. 'I'm impressed.'

'You have a very talented daughter, Professor Connelly.'

'*Have?* Are you really sure you mean what you're saying?'

She drew in a deep breath and clasped her hands together in her lap. 'This is so hard . . . I guess . . . I better just get on and say what I've come to say.'

'Which is what, exactly?' Paul said.

'I own a cabin in the woods, along the shore. Unless you knew it was there, you'd never find it. If I'm working on a painting I sometimes stay there overnight. It's kind of primitive but there's packaged food and cans, an oil lamp, candles, a sleeping-bag. Even water, rainwater, collected from an old cistern.' She leaned towards Paul and Ruth. 'After the sailing accident, three or four days after Josephine's disappearance, I went down there to work on a canvas and—' She broke off.

'And what?'

SUSAN MADISON

'She . . . Josie was there.'

Ruth looked at Paul and then back at Annie. '*What?* I can't—she was in your cabin?'

'I couldn't believe what I was seeing. She was dead, I knew that—I'd read the papers, I sent you that drawing of her—and yet there she was, alive, in my cabin. She was feverish, rambling. She told me that when she was swept away, the current was much too strong to swim against, all she could do was let it carry her. The sea was crashing over her, she was choking, semiconscious, certain she was going to die. And then she found herself flung forward by a wave and she managed to grab on to a spar of rock and eventually to crawl higher up onto dry ground. It took her nearly two days to make her way to my cabin.'

'But . . . I don't understand.' Ruth pressed her hands against her temples. 'Why didn't you let us *know*?'

'Ever since you showed up on my doorstep, I've asked myself that a thousand times. There are no excuses, Ruth. None. But at that stage I didn't know you and I did know Josie. So I believed her when she told me that her stepfather . . . that she had been molested . . .'

'Josie said that?' Paul's eyes had grown smoky with suppressed anger.

'I can see now that she was lying, but at the time she was hardly rational, raving and hysterical. She kept pleading with me not to let anyone know. In the end, I agreed.'

'A phone call,' Ruth said helplessly. 'That's all it would have taken. One call to say she was all right.'

'I told her that. She said . . . she said foolish things, hysterical things. That you wouldn't miss her. That you didn't care about her.'

'That wasn't true,' Will burst out. There was colour in his pale face. 'We loved her. All of us.'

Ruth stood up. Anger rushed through her. 'All this time you knew she wasn't drowned, after all.' Raging, she turned away from Annie. 'How could you have behaved like that? How *could* you?'

Annie drew in a shuddering breath. 'I *couldn't* make the call. I moved her in with me, so I could take care of her while I decided what to do. We had so many rows about it over those first few days. In the end, she said she'd call you. When I came back one evening, she'd gone.'

'Where to?'

'Ruth, I swear I thought she'd gone back to Boston, taken up her life with you again. I sometimes thought how happy you all must be.'

'And when you saw her again, what did you think then?' Paul asked coldly.

'I . . . I don't really know. I was so happy to see her well again.' Annie

310

fiddled with the combs which held her russet hair back from her face. 'I've behaved so . . . terribly badly.'

'Yes, you have,' Ruth said.

'So has Josie,' said Will.

'If what you've said is true,' Paul agreed, 'then you've caused more pain than you can possibly imagine. If this really is our Josie you're talking about.'

'You still don't believe she's alive, do you?' Ruth said.

'I'm exercising my right to feel sceptical. For instance, if she was who she said, why did she run away from Annie's house?'

'She was always taking off,' said Annie. 'When she had enough paintings, she'd load up that old car of hers and go out on the road to sell them.'

'Making her living from her work, like she always said she would,' Will said softly.

'She deliberately kept away from Sweetharbor and Hartsfield,' said Annie. 'From anywhere she might be recognised.'

'This is all extremely painful for us.' Paul reached across and took Ruth's hand.

Annie stood. 'I can only say that I'm desperately sorry.'

'I should damn well think you are!' shouted Paul.

'I don't suppose we shall meet again,' Annie said humbly.

'If I have anything to do with it, no, we shan't,' said Paul. He was breathing heavily, his nostrils white and pinched with rage.

When Annie had left, they sat silently on the porch. None of them wanted to discuss what they had just been told. They waited. Hoped. Now that Josie knew of Will's illness, she would surely come as soon as she could.

One phone call, Ruth thought, over and over again. How different our lives might have been.

That evening, they lit a fire and played cribbage for a while. Will found it difficult to concentrate.

Ruth put her hand on his. 'She'll come,' she said softly.

'I wish she'd hurry up,' he said fretfully. The firelight threw long shadows across his face as he put down his cards. 'I'm tired. I'll go to bed, guys, if you don't mind.'

Later, having kissed him good night, Ruth was about to close his door behind her when Will called out. 'Mom!'

'What, sweetheart?'

The smudged shadows beneath Will's eyes lay like puddles in the pallor of his face. The picture Josie had painted was propped against the wall at the end of his bed, where he could see it from his pillow. 'When she comes, you'll wake me up, won't you? Even if I'm dead asleep?'

She shuddered inwardly at his choice of words. 'Whatever time it is, I swear I will wake you up,' she said. 'OK?'

'OK.' He smiled the gaunt, pale-gummed smile she had grown used to over the past months. 'Please don't think I'm frightened, Mom. About dying. Because I'm really not.' He lifted his arms. 'Mom.'

'Yes?'

'Give me a hug.'

'As many as you like.' Tears pooled behind Ruth's eyes as she walked back and put her arms round her son. His bones felt as fragile as breadsticks, as though they would snap under the slightest pressure. She screwed her face up to prevent herself from weeping.

Will pushed his naked head into her shoulder, snuggling like a puppy. 'I love you, Mom.'

'And I love you, Will, oh, with all my heart.'

Before getting into her bed, Ruth stood at the balcony rail. A bright sliver of moon hung against the intense lavender of the summer sky, its fragile reflection floating on the black glass of the deeper water beyond the bay.

Josie would come. For Will's sake, she had to.

 Sixteen

FOG HAD CREPT in during the night and now lay heaped across the pasture. The house felt damp, as though the sea-mist had seeped in through the screens and under the door; a thick white light filled the rooms.

Will spent the morning walking slowly from room to room, as though, if he tried hard enough, he could force his sister to materialise at the kitchen table, on the living-room couch, in his bedroom. 'When do you think she'll get here?' he asked, standing at the windows, gazing into the fog.

Ruth put an arm round him. 'Soon.' Carefully, she hugged him.

'But *when*?' He put a hand against the wall, as though he needed support to remain standing. '*How* soon?'

'The minute she can, sweetheart.'

The hours went by, and Josie did not appear. 'But she will, darling,' Ruth said to Will, now lying on the sofa in the living room. 'She will.'

Will lifted his head. 'I just wish she'd hurry up, that's all.'

Around noon, Ruth made sandwiches but Will barely touched his. It was difficult to keep up any pretence of normality. The seconds, the minutes, sluggishly changed into hours.

As the afternoon began to fade, she found Will lying on his bed. 'I thought I'd drop by the Cottons',' she said. 'Come with me, Will?'

'Suppose Josie telephones?'

'We won't be long.'

'Is Dad coming too?'

'Let's go ask him.'

Paul was at the edge of the woods, chopping logs from a sapling birch that had fallen during the winter storms. His face was flushed. Seeing them coming, he stopped and wiped his forehead with his arm.

'Getting ready for winter already, Dad?' Will asked, giving his ghostly grin.

'Can't start too soon,' Paul said.

'We're going to visit the Cottons,' Ruth said.

'On second thoughts, Mom, maybe I'll stay here. Give Dad a hand.'

'Are you sure?'

'In case there's a phone call.'

Tucked up against the edge of the woods, the Cottons' house was painted red, its woodwork picked out in white. Ruth banged at the door but it seemed they were not home. She sat on the porch of their weathered little house and waited for a while, enjoying the solitude, the peace. On the rough grass behind the house, laundry was pegged to a clothes line, billowing and filling with the fresh breeze off the water. She remembered Josie demanding to know why she too didn't hang the laundry out to dry in the fresh air and could not recall what her response had been. Something to do with not having enough time, probably.

Eventually, she set off to climb up through the woods towards Carter's House. The fog had finally begun to roll back. Wisps of it clung to the trees like cotton candy and then were suddenly gone. Although the sun was not yet visible, the thinning mist took on a golden glow, promising late-afternoon heat. Where the trail forked, Ruth hesitated. I'll only stay a couple of minutes, she promised herself. Just a few minutes.

Up on the bluff, a breeze blew fitfully off the sea, not quite cold. She stood behind the bench, tracing the letters of her daughter's name on the brass plate set into its back. Josephine Carter Connelly. A steady certainty possessed her. Today, Josie would come home. She knew it as surely as she knew that tomorrow the sun would rise.

The garnered images of Will's and Josie's childhood crowded into her mind and suddenly, despite herself, despite her defiant optimism, she was overtaken by a tide of grief.

'Don't cry . . .'

The voice behind her was so low she thought she must have dreamed words into the sound of the wind.

'Mom . . .'

Slowly she turned. For a moment, she wondered whether she was seeing real flesh and blood or merely a mirage conjured up by desperations. 'Josie . . .' she whispered.

'Mom . . .'

'Josie!' Ruth held out her arms and her daughter came running and the two women wrapped themselves round each other, clinging together tightly, tightly, for moments that seemed to last for ever.

At last, Ruth thought. My daughter, at last. Lost and found. The miracle of this reunion was almost overwhelming. The swell of love inside her threatened to break through the frail barriers of body as she drew into herself the youthful scent of skin, fragility of bones under flesh, smooth slide of hair. 'I love you,' she murmured, her lips fierce against her daughter's cheek. She remembered how she used to crush the little girl Josie had once been against her, lost in a welter of passion. 'I *love* you.'

'Mom,' breathed Josie. 'Oh, Mom.'

'We've missed you. *Missed* you, Josie, more than . . .' Ruth stopped. What she wanted to say was beyond words. She held her daughter away from her. 'How did you know I'd be here?'

'This has always been our special place.'

'You look so . . .' Josie was taller than she had been at sixteen. The long-legged slimness of girlhood had given way to feminine curves. She had cut her hair short. Her eyes were older, wiser. 'Josie . . .' Ruth said softly. 'It's so good to be able to say your name. To see you. To . . . have you here.'

Josie did not move. 'Mom, please forgive me.'

'You're back now,' Ruth said. 'That's all that matters.'

'Please, Mom. We have to talk about this,' insisted Josie.

'Will's desperate to see you. And your father . . .'

'I don't want to see them until we've discussed this, Mom. You and me. It's so important. Why didn't I call? That's what you want to know, isn't it?'

'Now isn't really the—'

Josie's gaze was direct, anxious. 'How could I have let you go on believing I was dead? You can't push the question away, Mom. It lies at the heart of everything. You don't know how many times I wanted to call you.' Her voice failed briefly and she cleared her throat. 'Not at first. But then, after a while, it got so difficult. The longer I left it . . . what would I say? After what I'd done, how could I expect to come back into your lives?' She lifted her shoulders. 'I don't know . . . I guess I was afraid.'

Josie walked to the edge of the bluff and looked down at the rocks. 'I've thought about it so often. At first, I was just mad. At you, mostly. Then I was hurt. When I fetched up on the beach, coughing up seawater, aching all over, I felt such hurt . . .'

'But why?'

'Because—' On the edge of the bluff, she turned. 'It sounds so petty—because you'd called out for Will, but not for me.'

'He was younger, smaller . . .'

'I know.' Josie caught her lip between her teeth. 'I guess the truth is, I wanted to punish you.'

'It's enough that you're back,' Ruth said gently. 'I don't need to know anything else.'

'You *have* to know. Because I want to tell you that I realise there was nothing to punish you *for*. It was just . . . I didn't appreciate how lucky I was to have you for a mother. I keep asking myself how I could have been so—so unfeeling. How I could have let you suffer.'

'Josie, it's not necessary.'

'Listen to me, Mom . . . I need to say this. Now. Before we go back to the house.' Josie shook her head. 'You're so strong, you see. And I wanted to be like you. I admired you so much for being made a partner, for doing so well. And yet, at the same time, I wanted you to be home in an apron, baking cookies and apple pies.' Josie gave a laugh that was almost a sob. 'It's only recently I've begun to see that nobody can do everything. And then I remembered that you *did* do all that when we were little kids, and it was only when we got older that you picked up your own life again.'

'Josie, you don't have to—'

'I want to. I *need* to. I was so unfair. So hard on you.'

'Your grandmother thinks *I* was hard on *you*.'

'But that's *good*, Mom. Don't you see? You set standards for me—for

315

all of us. I just couldn't see it then. Any of it.' Josie walked slowly towards her mother and then stood with her hands hanging at her sides. She began to cry. 'Mom, I'm so ashamed of myself.'

'Sweetheart, it's all right. Everything I know about you, Josie, everything I've come to realise, hearing what people think of you, has made me so proud . . .' Ruth tilted Josie's face towards her and with her finger wiped the tears from her cheek. 'I only wish I could be as proud of myself.' They were both silent for a moment. The wind off the sea blew through Ruth's hair. 'Losing you . . . I didn't handle it well.' She hesitated. 'Dad and I split up. It just seemed less difficult for us to cope alone than together.'

'It's all my fault,' sobbed Josie. 'You guys were so close.'

'We still are,' Ruth said quietly. 'We've kind of got back together for the moment.'

'Mom . . .'

'Hush,' said Ruth. 'I love you more than I can say, Josephine. I always have. I always will, whatever you do. You're my child. It's a bond which can't ever be broken.'

'I realise that now.'

'If you hadn't left the earring,' Ruth said, 'even now, I'd never have thought for a minute that you were still alive. I'd never have gone looking for you.'

'Which earring?'

'The one you put right here for me to find. One of the pair I gave you, silver, with a copper heart in the middle. You remember—you were wearing them when you . . . on the day of the accident.'

'I've still got them. Both of them.'

'But it's because of the earring that I first started to—'

Josie shook her head. 'It wasn't mine.' Out on the water the bell buoy clanged once. She clutched at her mother's hand. 'I used to go into the house from time to time. I took my painting gear away. And some money. The contingency fund. Sometimes I'd play the piano, sit, be there where we used to be happy, and just wish we . . .'

'Oh, Josie . . .'

'And I used to ring Mrs Dee, pretending I wanted to rent the house, to find out if you were coming back at Christmas or in the summer. Thought I might sneak round, you see, try to catch a glimpse of you, check out how you were all doing.'

'We were here at Christmas.'

'But not at Carter's House.'

'No. I—I wasn't ready for that.'

'Oh, Mom . . . what have I done to you?'

'I bought a picture of yours. "Death is Swallowed Up in Victory".'

'Annie told me.'

'I think it's amazing.'

'Mom, I never said this enough, if I ever did at all, but . . . I love you so much.'

'As I love you.' Ruth squeezed her daughter's hand. 'Come on, darling, let's go find the others.' Everything is going to be all right now, she thought. We can go back to being a family again.

They began to walk down through the woods. In single file, they crossed the tree trunk. 'When I found out you were opening up the cottage for the summer, I put some flowers there for you,' Josie said over her shoulder.

'Freesias. Your absolute favourite flower . . .'

'That's right.'

Skirting the cranberry bog, Josie stopped. 'Mom. How sick is Will?'

'He's going to die,' Ruth said bluntly. 'Unless we're able to find a tissue match, so he can have a bone marrow transplant. There's a worldwide register, but nothing's come up. His best chance is from within the family, but none of us is a match.' Ruth expelled a deep breath. 'He'll be *so* happy to see you, Josie.'

When they emerged from the woods, Will was standing at the edge of the pond, staring towards the trees, as though he already knew that his sister had returned. When he saw them, he began an awkward limping run towards them, arms outspread. 'Josie!' His face seemed to be one enormous grin. 'Josie, Josie! You're back.'

Watching her, Ruth saw Josie's shock at the first sight of her brother and how fear drew the colour from her face as she hugged him, kissed his pale cheek, carefully reached up to pat the top of his head. 'You've grown,' she said.

'It happens,' Will said.

'Where'd you get the ear stud?'

'Mom bought it.'

'C'mon,' Josie said, glancing over at her mother, digging into herself for the strength not to exclaim over Will's appearance. 'Get real. Ruth Carter Connelly bought her son an *ear* stud?'

'It's true.'

'Things must've changed round here.'

'You can say that again.'

Josie touched her brother's arm. 'You aren't going to believe this, but I've really missed you.'

317

Will sighed. 'It's been so great not having a big sister to boss me around. But I guess I could get used to it again.'

'Did you get the picture of you I painted?'

'Yes. And I hate to admit it, but you're *some* good.'

'Think so?'

'Know so.' Will put out his hand and Josie took it tenderly in hers.

'Anybody want anything?' Ruth asked, her eyes misting over. 'Because I'm going into the house to pour myself some lemonade, take some to your father who's chopping up logs.'

'I'll come and . . . and see Dad in just a minute,' said Josie. To Will, she said, 'How about a walk down to the shore?'

'Great.' Clumsily, Will turned. Every movement he made seemed to hurt him. 'You'll have to go slowly, though.'

'As slowly as you like, Will.'

As they disappeared round the side of the house, Ruth went into the kitchen and poured a glass of lemonade which she took out to Paul.

'Do you think she's going to show up today?' he said as soon as he saw her.

'Paul . . . she's already here.'

'Josie is?'

'She's just gone down to the shore. With Will.'

'Why didn't she come and—'

'She's ashamed, Paul. And a bit afraid.'

He slammed his axe into the tree stump so that it stuck there. 'I'll go and—'

Ruth held him back. 'Give her a few moments alone with Will first.'

'But I want to—' He broke off. 'I suppose you're right.'

'Paul?'

'Yes?'

'I can hardly believe it that we're all together. A family again.'

Paul nodded. 'I guess.'

'Tomorrow, Josie can go to the hospital and have a blood test and if we're lucky, we'll find a match. Then maybe everything will be all right again.'

'Maybe it will,' he agreed. He wiped his hands on the front of his shirt. 'Sorry, I can't wait. I'm going to find them.'

He ran across the rough grass of the pasture towards the little slope leading to the shore. He could see them standing facing each other down by the water's edge. Coming closer, the breeze carried towards him a sound so unusual he barely recognised it. Will, angry? Will, yelling at his sister? Paul wanted to rush forward, stop him, put a hand across his mouth, warn him to take care, in case she vanished again.

'. . . not fuckin' fair!' Will was shouting.

'I know that—'

'Do you have the faintest idea what you've done to us? Mom and Dad, *me*? We thought you were fucking *dead*.'

'I'm sorry.'

'Sorry's not good enough.' Will was weeping now, picking up pebbles from the beach and lobbing them into the water. 'You even told that Lefeau woman that Dad was—was feeling you up. That's disgusting. Horrible.'

'I know, I know. But it was the only thing I could think of that would stop her contacting them. And don't call her "that Lefeau woman"— she's been a good friend to me.'

'I just don't get it, Josie. Why did you let us go on believing you were *dead*, for fuck's sake?'

'I—it sounds so stupid now—I guess I wanted to punish them. Especially Mom. I can't really explain it. I wanted to leave school, go to art college, and I knew Mom wouldn't let me in a million years, even if I could persuade Dad. And neither of them seemed to have the faintest idea of what it meant to me. Nor . . . nor how *good* I was.'

'So you were going to make them pay, is that it?'

'Sort of, I guess.'

'That's so horrible, Josie.'

'I know. I hate myself. It was like I'd dug myself into a hole. It just got harder and harder to get out of it.'

'And me, what about me, what did I ever do to you?' Will's thin body twisted as the sobs were wrenched from his chest. 'I've had this fucking awful time, being sick and all, and the whole time I'm worrying about you not being around and what it'd do to Mom and Dad if I wasn't either.'

Josie too was crying. 'Will, you're not going to—'

'I hate you, right? I hate you for what you did.' Will stopped and knuckled the tears from his eyes. He bent down and picked up a drift-wood branch and threw it into the water. As it floated away, he said quietly, 'Which doesn't mean I don't—I don't love you, too.'

'Oh, Will . . .' Josie put her arms round her brother and rocked him against her chest.

After a moment, Paul cleared his throat.

Josie broke away from Will and looked up at him. 'Dad.'

He stared at her. It really was her, standing below him, hair riffled by the wind lifting off the water, his daughter, his Josie, his little girl. Restored to life.

'Dad,' she said again. 'I'm home.'

He held his arms wide. A pulsing rush of joy filled him as she ran towards him and flung herself into them. 'Josie,' he said. He felt her heart leaping against his and knew, with unstoppable certainty, that here, now, everything at last was put right. Tears sprang from his eyes and he suddenly began to sob. 'Oh God. Josie . . .'

'Dad, I'm sorry, I'm sorry.' Josie wept too.

He wanted to tell her it was OK, but his voice would not function.

'I'm *sorry*,' Josie said again.

He held her tighter, never wanting to let her go again. Tears ran down his face, dropping into her hair—so clean, so well remembered—while the pain of the last two years vanished as though it had never been.

'I *love* you,' he whispered, but could not have said whether he spoke the words aloud or simply felt them. Then Will walked slowly across the beach to join them and they stood together, clinging to each other.

That evening, he couldn't take his eyes off his daughter as they sat round the table. Celebrating, Ruth had laid a formal table in the dining room, taken the heavy silver-gilt candlesticks from their hiding place in the linen cupboard. The return of the prodigal daughter. She that was lost is found again.

She'd changed so much. Her hair was cut close to her head and coloured a darker brown, her face was too thin, far too thin, the bones much more clearly defined than they had been two years ago. How slight she looked. How beautiful.

Josie was talking to Will. 'So this total *prick* asks me to paint a mural all round his indoor swimming pool. Offers to pay me a small fortune.'

'How much is that?' asked Ruth.

'Enough to live on for a month or two. Anyway, he says he wants something to remind him of his mother, who's originally from Greece, right? So I spend hours and hours painting this scene with olive groves and grapevines and, like, the Acropolis in the background. And then, when I'm finished, know what he does?' She picked up her glass and drank from it, keeping her eyes on Will.

He shook his head. 'What?'

'He finked out. Refused to pay me. Said I hadn't carried out the commission. Then I discovered he does that all the time. Gets people to do things for him and then refuses to pay. Wanna know what I did?'

'What?' said Will.

'The guy spends half the year at his house in Pacific Palisades, right? So next time he was out in California, I got into his house one night—'

'Broke in, you mean?' Will's eyes were round.

'Sort of. And then I painted over the entire mural. Painted it white. Two coats.'

'Wow!'

'Takes guts to obliterate a piece of work like that,' Paul said.

Where had Josie learned how to force her way into someone else's house? What other dubious skills had she picked up in the time she had been away from them? Where had she been? Was there a man in her life? How had she survived? There was so much Paul wanted to know. Smiling at her through the candle flames, he found that he wanted—*needed*—the answers. Why? *Why?*

Josie caught his eye. Her expression changed. 'I can't explain, Dad,' she said quietly. 'I just can't.'

He poured more wine, guessing that in the future it might simply have to be enough that Josie was back. He tilted his glass to her in a toast. 'To you, darling heart. You don't know how happy we are to have you home.'

Sam Hechst telephoned. 'I promised to take Will out in my boat,' he began, but Ruth cut in.

'Josie's home,' she said.

'Thank God. Oh, that is truly wonderful news.' His voice was warm with pleasure. 'You must be so happy. How is she?'

'About how you'd expect.'

'How are *you*, Ruth?'

'I think you can imagine how we feel.'

'No doubt you'll find it a little strange to have her back, as well as joyful.'

'Well . . .' She did not want to lie. 'Maybe a little. But it's all going to work out just fine.'

'Let's hope so. Now, I wondered if I could pick Will up tomorrow morning?'

'He'd love that, Sam. Especially since . . .' Ruth lowered her voice. 'Josie's going down to the hospital in Hartsfield to have blood taken, see if it matches her brother's. I know he won't want to be there.'

'I'll be at the house by nine thirty, OK?'

Paul lay listening to Ruth in the bathroom. It had become a nightly routine for him, to lie there imagining her undressing, recalling the line of her leg as she stepped into the scented water, her full breasts. It was a kind of self-inflicted torture, as though he were pressed against the locked gates of a lost Eden. He knew precisely how she would look lying in the bath, the way she would reach for the towel when she was through, the smell of her warm skin.

He switched off the lamp and lay on his back under the thin summer quilt. The uncurtained window was a rectangle of silvery blue against the larger darkness of the room. He could hear the faint swish of the waves down on the shore.

He was half asleep when he heard quiet footsteps across the wooden floorboards. Before he could sit up, the quilt was gently pulled back and Ruth slid in beside him.

'Ruth . . .' He opened his arms and she came into them, naked, still damp from the bath. She placed a hand on his chest, above his heart and he drew in a long deep breath. The feel of her fingers against his skin was like a valuable gift which he had thought lost for ever.

'Ruth . . .' With a hand low on her buttocks, he pulled her even closer. 'Oh, Ruth, I want you so much . . .'

Her breasts were pressed against him. He moved his hand slowly about her body, feeling each separate and particular change of her skin, the soft curve of her breast, her nipples, the delicate jut of her hip, the thick pelt at the base of her stomach. He wanted to possess her, to taste her. 'This is what I want.' He moved down the bed and lowered his head to the dark sweet space between her legs, tasting it, breathing it deep into his lungs. Outside, the sea beat against the shore, in time with the blood which coursed through his body. Behind his eyes, a thousand other lovemakings shared with this woman fused into this single one. He lifted his head. 'Or this.' He touched her delicately with the tip of his tongue, hearing her gasp. 'And this.' Slowly he slid his fingers inside her, feeling the damp red lusciousness of her.

'Come into me, Paul. Now. Quickly.'

He moved over her, positioning himself, giddy with the prospect of being inside her again.

'Be there, love me, fuck me, quickly, quickly.' She spread herself to his strong urgency, throwing back her head, moaning. 'Just love me, Paul.'

'I do, my darling, I do,' he said, entering her in a swift sure surge, knowing it would be over quickly this time, because the ecstasy of the long drive towards the centre, towards the very heart of her, was already causing him to expand, to erupt, to explode into a million white-hot shattering stars.

Outside the window, the sea crashed and roared, the wind raged in the trees, thunder cracked and lightning fizzed across the sky as she grabbed his hips, kept him tight inside her, moved against him, swelled and bloomed around him. He heard her soft cries as she arched beneath him, cresting towards her climax until she fell back, while the core of her leapt and shuddered and he felt the convulsive gush of her at last.

'I love you, Paul,' she said.

'And I love you, Ruth. More than you'll ever know.'

 # Seventeen

'SURE YOU DON'T want to come along, Will?' Josie asked.

'I've had enough of hospitals to last me for a lifetime.' Will's spectral grin lengthened across his pale face. 'Besides, I've got better things to do.' He seemed very frail this morning, as though drained by the excitement of yesterday.

'What time did Sam say he'd come for you?' Josie was nervous, picking at a thread in her jeans, tapping her foot, constantly trying to push her hair behind her ears although it was far too short.

'About nine thirty,' said Ruth.

'Here he comes!' Will said. For a moment excitement glowed in his eyes, then dimmed, as though it was an emotion too strong for him to sustain for very long.

Sam's pick-up bumped its way along the track and up through the meadow to park in front of them. He swung down from the cabin, adjusting a deep-crowned baseball cap on his head. He had another in his hand.

'This is for you, Will,' he said, his brown eyes sweeping over Ruth's face, lingering for a moment on Josie's. 'Nobody steps on my boat without one of these.' The cap had a multi-clawed lobster embroidered on it and underneath, the word LOBSTERMAN.

'Hey, *cool*.' Will settled it over his skull. 'Whadda ya think, Mom?'

'You look like a real professional,' Ruth said. She wanted to fuss over him, ask if he had brought a sweater, tell him not to get overtired, beseech Sam to take proper care of him. Instead, she came down the shallow steps of the porch and put her arms round the big man. 'Thank you, Sam. You will remember that Will's very frail, won't you?'

He nodded. 'Don't worry, Ruth. He'll be safe with me.' He sketched a

323

little bow to Josie. 'Good morning, Miss Connelly. I heard you were . . . back with us. I'm so glad you're home.'

'So am I.'

Sam helped Will into the pick-up and drove away while Josie stood with her hands in the back pockets of her jeans watching them go.

Paul and Josie sat holding hands, huddled together on a leatherette couch in a side room at Hartsfield Hospital. Under the harsh light from the neon strip hanging from the ceiling, their faces looked grey and haggard. A pile of children's building blocks stood in one corner, the bright colours crudely garish.

Neither of them was able to talk about what really occupied their thoughts. Every time someone passed the door they tensed. 'God, I wish they'd hurry up,' Josie said. 'I can't stand much more of this.'

'I'm sure they're rushing the tests through. They know how urgent it is.'

Josie glanced up as a white-coated doctor paused at the door, looked at them, then continued on down the passage. She leaned towards Paul. 'Can you understand how desperately I want this to work? If it did, it'd be like making up for all the harm I've caused.'

'Josephine, I want you to understand something very clearly.'

'What?'

'If you can provide a bone marrow match for Will, that'd be fantastic. That would be more than . . . than . . . But that's not why we're so terribly happy you're home. We love you because you're Josie. Our daughter. Remember, whatever you've done, whatever you do, we love you.' Paul looked down at her hand, softly ran a finger across the knuckles. 'You do realise that the chances of this working are pretty slim, don't you?'

Josie's face crumpled. She took a sharp breath and squeezed her eyes shut. 'I don't want to think about that.'

'If it doesn't work, it's not your fault, OK?'

She nodded.

'At least you tried.'

'Dad, whatever the result, let me be the one to tell Will.'

'OK.'

Down the hall, a baby began to cry. A little red-headed boy ran into the room and, after a cursory glance at them, began to throw the plastic bricks about.

'Will used to look like that,' Paul said softly.

A young woman came through the door. She stopped when she saw them. 'Hi,' she said. Her gaze lingered on their faces for a moment. She turned to the child. 'Now listen, Max. You just better stop that. You're disturbing these people, can't you see?'

Max threw a blue brick at her and laughed.

'Ooh, you're such a bad little boy,' said the woman, smiling. She bent to pick up her son and swing him into her arms. 'Such a bad, bad little boy.'

Max laughed again, beating at her with his fists. 'Bad boy,' he said delightedly.

'Good thing I love you,' his mother said. At the door, she smiled apologetically at Paul and Josie. 'Sorry about my son.'

And I'm sorry about mine, Paul thought. 'Did Will tell you that we were going to try to do up the *Lucky Duck*?' he asked Josie a little later, breaking into the silence.

'Can I help?'

'Of course you can.'

'It'd be good to do some sailing again. I kind of . . . went off it.'

There was another pause. 'Wonder if Will'll bring some lobsters home for supper tonight,' Paul said.

After a while, Josie leaned her head against Paul's shoulder. He rested his cheek on her hair. They sat again in silence.

Another white-coated doctor stood at the door. 'Josephine Connelly?' he said, looking down at the clipboard in his hand.

'That's me.'

'If you'd like to come with me, Ms Connelly . . .' He stepped back and stood waiting in the passage outside.

Josie stood up. She turned to look down at her father, her expression anguished. 'Dad . . .'

'You'll be fine,' Paul said.

'Suppose it doesn't work?'

'Suppose it does.'

She hesitated as though about to say something more, then joined the doctor. Paul heard the sound of their footsteps receding down the corridor. Even though he knew she was an adult now, he wanted to be with her when she heard whatever news the doctors had to give her. After a while, he got up and walked slowly along the passage, looking in at the windows of the side rooms as he went. Halfway down, he saw Josie. She was listening with head bent, hands clasped tightly in her lap, as the doctor pointed to a sheet of print-out, tapping it here and there with a pen. His lips moved though Paul could not hear what he was saying.

But he knew anyway.

Ruth left Paul sleeping and went downstairs. There was a lingering smell of coffee in the empty kitchen. Early-morning sun slanted through the windows, golden and hopeful. It was going to be another glorious day. There were two mugs on the table and a milky cereal bowl.

'Will?' Ruth called. 'Where are you? Josie?'

No answer.

'Are you OK?' There was still no reply. She stepped out onto the side porch. 'Will? Josie?' Her voice floated up into the astringent sea-sharp air and was lost. Maybe they had both gone for a walk.

Slowly she went up to her bedroom. She had been surprised at her reaction to the news of Josie's tests. Having pinned all her hopes on there being a match between Josie's blood and Will's, she had expected to be crushed if the results proved negative. Instead, her mind was already spinning ahead, turning over the possibilities that might still remain. More chemo, a sudden match discovered on the register, another remission, a miracle.

On the balcony, she lifted the binoculars she kept there, swept them round, across pink rock and pale water and blue spruce. Out on the water a lobster boat was pulling up traps. She swept the glasses round once more. There was nothing out there except trees, grass, boulders thrusting up from the ancient earth. And the sea. All along the rocky shore was a dark line left by the receding tide. A couple of sloops lay at anchor, hardly moving on the still surface of the water.

Where would Will have gone?

She slipped the strap of the glasses over her neck. The sun was still low as it danced and dazzled across the water; the scattered pot buoys swayed in the glare. Josie could not possibly appreciate just how weak Will was. And they might not even be together. Perhaps they had had an early coffee then she had driven off somewhere while he decided to go for a walk. Or a sail in the Beetle Cat, as he had done many times before.

A jolt of alarm shook her. Suppose he had collapsed, suppose he was lying somewhere, unable to help himself, waiting for them to find him. She ran into their bedroom. 'Paul!' She shook his shoulder.

'Mmm,' he said sleepily. Eyes still shut, he reached for her. 'I love you, Ruth.'

'Darling, Will's gone. And Josie.'

'They've probably gone down to the shore together,' he murmured, stretching lazily, opening his eyes to look at her, lust kindling in his face as he saw her bending over him, her breasts loose inside her robe. 'God, what a gorgeous sight to wake up to.' He stretched out a hand to fondle her but she pushed him away.

326

'I'm worried, Paul. Suppose Will's in trouble?'

Hearing the anxiety in her voice, he pulled himself up, swung out of bed, walked towards the chair where his clothes had been flung the night before. 'Let's both of us get some clothes on and we'll go look.'

Ten minutes later, standing on the porch, a second pair of binoculars round his neck, he said, 'Where do you think he'd go?'

'Up to the Point. Or sailing.'

'Is he strong enough to take out the dinghy on his own?'

'I don't know.'

'Then let's go up to Caleb's Point.' Paul put his arm round Ruth's shoulder. 'Don't worry, Ruth.'

She kissed his cheek. 'It's so hard not to.'

Hand in hand, they took the trail up into the trees. As they climbed towards Caleb's Point, sunlight slanted between the fog-dampened branches.

It was still too early for the boats from the yacht club to be out, but one little dinghy bobbed on the water, haloed by the brilliant light. Ruth focused on the white sail, gilded by the sun behind it.

'There they are,' she said, relieved. She raised the glasses again. Out on the water, the dinghy skimmed along against the sky, a wake forming a line of white behind it. Small waves glittered. She could see Will leaning back in the cockpit, one arm spread along the gunwales, the other lightly on the tiller. He was smiling at his sister.

'Paul.' She took his hand. 'Seeing them together again, our children . . . it's wonderful.'

'A true miracle, darling.'

In the little boat, Josie was talking, apparently exhorting Will, one hand slapping through the air as she made whatever point she was trying to convey. And Will, still smiling, kept shaking his head.

'She looks well, doesn't she?' Paul said. He raised his own glasses.

'She looks *lovely*.'

'She always did. Takes after her beautiful mother.'

Ruth looked at Paul. 'It's what he wanted most of all, to go sailing with her.'

The little boat veered away across the calm surface towards the open water. It sailed between the wooded arms of the bay before turning and tacking back again, while brother and sister sat, scarcely moving, and talked.

'It's so peaceful up here.' Paul sat down on Josie's bench.

Ruth sat beside him. She lowered the glasses to her lap and closed her eyes, turning her face up to the sun. The breeze brought the fresh tang of salt and kelp off the water below them. Gulls screamed distantly out in the bay.

'Ought we to do something about this bench?' Paul asked.

'Leave it here?' Ruth murmured.

'As a reminder?'

'That's right.'

They sat quietly, hand in hand, the air between them rich with promise. Happiness filled her like water. Every now and then she lifted the glasses to watch her children talking while the dinghy drifted gently between the pot buoys and the water danced. A yellow-gold light shone across the bay, the colour of honey, the colour of hope.

'I wish this day could last for ever,' she said lazily. 'Just this bit of it, with them out there and . . . us here.'

She lifted her glasses again. Josie had now moved to sit beside her brother. She put her arms round him for a long moment, hugging him tightly. She rubbed her face against his, touched his cheek with her hand. Will took her hand and held it. He talked earnestly for several minutes, while Josie heard him out, her head bent.

The little boat came in right below the bluff, so close to shore that Ruth could hear the *clunk* as the boom swung over. Neither Josie nor Will looked up, however, too engrossed in their conversation. She saw Will lean forward and kiss his sister. As they headed out into the bay again, Ruth's contentment began to dissipate. What were the two of them discussing so earnestly? Although the scene seemed idyllic, something was dragging it awry.

Through her glasses, she saw Josie speak and then turn away, her face grim. At the same time, Will let go of the tiller and stood up. He had the anchor clasped against his chest, the chain wrapped round his wrist. He rested one hand on the edge of the cockpit, sat down and swung his legs over the side.

'What's he doing?' Ruth asked. A wave of fear engulfed her. Something was wrong.

'What's he doing?' she demanded. 'Paul . . . Why's he holding the anchor like that?' Alarm drummed, louder now.

'Ruth,' said Paul suddenly. 'Ruth.' He closed his hand tightly round her arm as Will slowly, slowly, slipped over the side of the boat into the sea. As he hit the water, a silent splash of spray rose, sparking a brief rainbow as it caught the sun, and then he was gone. Disbelieving, Ruth watched him disappear beneath the surface of the sea, remembering the bitter chill of the water, the numbing cold that burned like fire.

'What's he doing?' Ruth cried, while fear clutched at her heart and threatened to freeze her lungs. Will had not yet surfaced. 'Paul, what is he . . . Why hasn't he . . .'

Paul stood up, holding the glasses to his eyes. 'Oh God,' he whispered.

Below them, Josie resolutely sailed away from the spot where Will had disappeared.

'Where is he?' Ruth said loudly. She too rose to her feet. 'Why has she left him alone? He hasn't come up, Paul. Why isn't she helping him?'

Paul said nothing.

Ruth stared at the spot where she had last seen her son. Will did not reappear. Josie, her head bent, steered across the water towards the open sea.

Understanding finally came. And horror.

'No!' Ruth screamed. 'Will . . . Oh my God. Oh, Will, my darling, no!' The words flew across the water and mingled with the cries of the seagulls. 'Will! Will! I love you. I love . . .'

She turned and began to run downhill to where the bluff grew less steep and it was possible to gain access to the beach. Paul ran too, pounding along behind her, calling her name, but she paid no heed. If she could swim out to the spot where he had disappeared, she could find him, she could save him, she could breathe life back into him, resurrect him. *Will!* . . . But even as she scrambled across the rocks, slipping on the seaweed, she knew it was useless.

One part of her mind insisted that this was not happening, that somewhere another Ruth still stood at the edge of the bluff and looked across the water to where a little boat bobbed and her children laughed together. As she plunged into the waiting sea, straight into the oncoming waves, and began to swim out into the bay, the only message her distraught brain could process was this: he had chosen his own path and there was nothing now that she could do.

As she swam further and further out, she screamed Will's name and the sea poured through her, swamped, deluged her. The gasp, the choke, clutching at water which slid through her fingers: she remembered it still, the purity of her panic in that long-ago moment as a child when salt had stung her eyes, burned the back of her throat, and she had been aware of death, oblivion, nothingness.

Would you die for me? Josie had asked. *Would you give your life for me?*

Encumbered by her clothes, heart bursting with terror, salt water heavy in her mouth, the answer was so blindingly clear that Ruth wondered why Josie had needed to put the question. Oh *yes*, without any doubt whatsoever. If it was necessary, I would gladly give my life for you. For both of you. But neither of you ever asked.

Shivering, she stood passive while Paul silently removed her wet clothes and guided her into the shower. She felt his hands on her body, washing away the salt, washing away the sea. A cold numbness filled her, blotting out all feeling except grief. Will . . . She would never see him again, never joke with him, never hold his hand again or kiss his rough hair.

Paul towelled her dry, found her robe on the back of the door and wrapped her in it. He began to weep and she took his head in her hands and held it against her breast, as though he were her child, not her husband. The two of them stood there together, stunned with grief, each seeking comfort from the other, each giving comfort, too.

'Paul,' she said, tears sliding ceaselessly down her face. She gripped him tightly. 'This time we must treasure each other.'

'Yes.'

'Not be careless of the richness we have together.' She bent her head over his, the seaweed smell of salt still on her skin, and began to weep, her shoulders bowed over the sobs which came ripping up her body in an explosion of grief and pain.

He could not speak. Tears flowed across his face, pulsing out of his eyes. He nodded slowly. Together they went downstairs to the kitchen where Josie was sitting at the table, staring at her clasped hands.

Seeing them, she hesitated for a moment then got up and stood between them, touching them lightly on the shoulders, like a bridge. 'He was going to die anyway,' she said.

'But not like that. Not drowning.' While Paul walked towards the back door and stood looking out, Ruth sank down on a chair and buried her face in her hands. Despair ate into her body. 'Will,' she moaned. 'Oh, Will.'

Josie put her arm round her mother. 'He said he had hoped he'd have the whole summer. But he was getting weaker and weaker. This morning he could hardly stand. He didn't want you to know, but he was afraid he soon wouldn't be able to get up. Said he was damned if he was going to spend a perfect summer lying in bed, looking out the window.'

'Oh, Will. My poor boy.'

'I told him the results of the tests this morning. He said he'd already guessed. He asked me to take him out in the boat and I knew he was planning something. He didn't say so, but I could see it in his eyes. He didn't want to live. He told me this morning. He was tired of being ill. He didn't want any more treatments. Just a few last days up here and then, finished, over, ended. The way he wanted to go.' Tears gathered in Josie's eyes but did not fall. 'We talked for hours this morning. I'm so glad about that. My poor little brother. He was just waiting for me to come back so he could go himself.'

'You didn't try to stop him?'

'Not once I realised it was what he wanted. What he'd planned.'

'He's like you, isn't he? Both of you are so . . . strong.'

'We got that from you.' Josie put a piece of folded paper on the table beside Ruth. 'Mum, Will asked me to make sure you got this.'

Mom, Dad, don't be sad. I couldn't take any more. I wanted to be in control, not like the kids in the hospital, like poor little Michelle. Thank you for all the things you gave me. I love you all. Please don't cry.
From your loving son William

Ruth thought of his swollen-knuckled fingers struggling to hold the pen to write the words. Grief welled up again. But now, as well as anguish, she felt a sudden kind of peace. She turned to Josie and rested her head on her daughter's shoulder and felt her daughter's hand on her hair. Heard her husband's footsteps across the kitchen, and felt the comfort of his arms round them both.

They sat on the bench at Caleb's Point, looking out to sea. Bertlemy's Isle lay on the water, the tips of the spruces at its centre gilded by the setting sun. Out of sight, on the strip of stony beach below them, the sea whispered, sucking at the pebbles and falling away with a sigh. A single star was already out, low on the horizon.

Ruth stared at the place where she had last seen Will. I gave birth to him, she thought, I gave him life and raised him, my sunny, funny Will, and now there is nothing left of him. In her mind she saw Will's face when they took him from the water, and the way his pale lips were curved into a little smile.

'Mom,' Josie said. Heartbroken, she began to sob.

'It's all right.' Ruth forced herself away from thoughts of her dead son to the business of comforting her living daughter. Of being a mother. 'It's OK. It's . . . OK.'

Thank you for all the things you gave me, Will had written. He had endured so much and yet he still thanked them . . . Ruth too wept, quietly, hopelessly. This death could not be reversed.

'He said he thought you'd be happier here than in the city,' Josie said.

'I think he's right,' said Paul. His arm tightened round Ruth's shoulders. 'We'll have to think about it.'

For so long Ruth had not had time to consider the simple matter of happiness. Now she realised that somewhere a kind of contentment waited for them. Along the way, she would find it. And Paul, too. Josie. The three of them.

'One of the awful things, when we thought you were dead,' Ruth said, 'was that I couldn't talk about it. The grief, the sorrow . . . I tried to pretend it had never happened. I refused to let anyone mention your name.'

'We mustn't do that with Will.' Paul tightened his hold on his family.

'There was this little girl called Michelle,' said Ruth. 'Such a cute child. Will was kind of taken with her sister. Kelly. She made him a pink gingham hat to cover his bald head.' She smiled at the remembrance, looking across the water. One child had been exchanged for another. For the rest of her life, whenever she came up here, she would see, in slow motion, tiny and foreshortened, the figures of her children in the little boat out on the water. Her resurrected daughter. And her doomed son, bending, slipping, falling slowly into the welcoming sea.

All her life she had feared death by water, but until that moment, she had always imagined that the death would be her own.

SUSAN MADISON

I met Susan Madison at the historic Randolph Hotel in Oxford, on a cold, crisp, sunny day in February. Over a delicious lunch, with exceptionally attentive waiters, the author told me that she has been writing novels for over eighteen years. She explained that she had adopted a new pen name when writing *The Colour of Hope* as it marked a new departure in her writing career, which to date has consisted mainly of crime and suspense novels. '*The Colour of Hope* started out as a suspense novel, but as I got closer and closer to my characters it changed. I became more and more engrossed in the family drama and all the emotion. It was quite unlike anything I had written before and I had to keep stopping to cry. By the time it was finished I was emotionally drained.'

Susan Madison was born and brought up in Oxford, where her father was a Don at the University. She then went to Paris to work when she was quite young and met her American husband and moved to Tennessee, where they lived for ten years. 'Tennessee was a wonderful place to bring up my two sons. Lots of space and lots of air and lots of lakes. I did not appreciate it as much as I should have done at the time because I was terribly homesick.' She returned to England when her marriage broke up and eventually remarried. It was when her third son started school that she decided to study for an Open University degree

and afterwards began to write. 'The OU was an excellent training ground for the discipline you need to be a writer,' she told me.

Research for *The Colour of Hope* took her to Maine, where she drove around for a week, getting the feel of the place and taking lots of photographs, especially of the different types of houses. She also studied a variety of books on Maine and the people who live there. In addition, she researched the subject of leukaemia extensively. 'Thank God, I had no personal experience of the illness. However, I do think that any parent, of any sensibilities, is terrified for their child. So I was writing in one sense out of ignorance of actual fact, but absolutely from the deepest possible emotion.'

Susan Madison is currently writing her next book which is called *The Hour of Separation* and will be set in Vermont. 'By setting my novels in America it gives me the freedom to create character and vision which will take readers away from their everyday lives. So much better than having a character stand in a shopping queue at Sainsbury's or Waitrose!'

As we ended our meal, I asked Susan Madison what she would have liked to have been if she hadn't become a writer? Without hesitation she replied, with a smile, 'A country-and-western singer. I just adore it and would have loved to have been up on stage in those glittering costumes, belting out songs for all the guys in cowboy hats.' Her many new readers will be very glad she made the choice she did.

Jane Eastgate

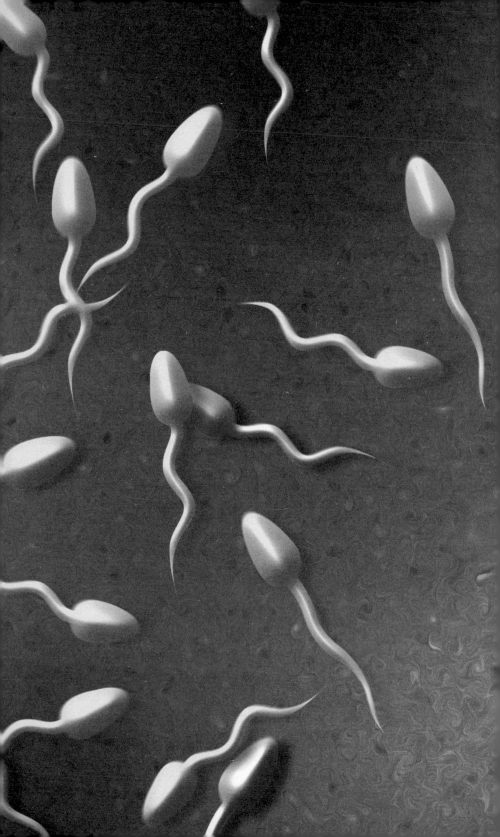

BEN ELTON
INCONCEIVABLE

For over five years Lucy has been trying to get
pregnant. She longs for a baby more than anything
else and can't walk past Mothercare without getting
all teary. Sam loves Lucy and would love to have a
baby with her but he has problems of his own. His
job at the BBC is rapidly going downhill and his
ambition to write a hit movie is a non-starter
because he hasn't had a decent idea in years.
As they embark on IVF treatment it seems just
possible that both their dreams can come true. But
sometimes you can want something too much.
That's when you risk losing what you have.

Dear . . .?

Dear.

Dear Book?

Dear Self? Dear Sam.

Good. Got that sorted out. What next?

Lucy is making me write this diary. Except it's not a diary. It's a 'book of thoughts'. 'Letters to myself' is how she put it, hence the 'Dear Sam' business, which of course is me. Lucy says that her friend, whose name escapes me, has a theory that conducting this internal correspondence will help Lucy and me to relax about things. The idea is that if Lucy and I periodically privately assemble our thoughts and feelings then we'll feel less like corks bobbing about on the sea of fate. Personally, I find it extraordinary that Lucy can be persuaded that she'll become less obsessed about something if she spends half an hour every day writing about it, but there you go. Lucy thinks that things might be a whole lot better if I stopped trying to be clever and started trying to be supportive.

It's now five minutes later and I find I have no thoughts and feelings to assemble. Lucy has been right all along. I'm a sad, cold, sensitivity-exclusion zone who would rather read the newspaper than have an emotion. I always thought she was exaggerating.

Dear Penny

I'm writing to you, Penny, because in my childhood you were my imaginary friend and I feel that I'll be more open and honest if I personify the part of myself to which I'm addressing these thoughts. Does that make sense? I do hope so because, quite frankly, if ever I needed an imaginary friend I need one now. The truth is that I want to have a baby. You remember how our favourite game when I was a child was looking after babies? Well, things haven't changed at all, right down to the fact that I still haven't actually got a baby to look after. This thing, so simple to many women, is proving very difficult for me. Sam and I have been trying for five years and so far not a hint. You could set your watch by my periods.

Sometimes I feel quite desperate about it and really have to struggle not to be jealous of women who have babies, which I loathe myself for. However, and let me say this very firmly, Penny, I'm determined that I am not, I repeat NOT, going to become obsessed about all this. If, God forbid, it turns out that I cannot have children, then so be it. I shall accept my fate. I shall not acquire eight dogs, two cats, a rabbit and a potbellied pig. I shall not be mean about people who have children, calling them smug and insular and obsessed by their kids. Nor will I go on about my wonderful job (which it isn't anyway) to harassed mums who've not spoken adult English for two and a half years and have sick all over their shoulders and down their backs.

Whatever the fates decide for me, I intend to remain an emotionally functional woman and I absolutely SWEAR that I will not get all teary when I walk past Mothercare on my way to the off-licence like I did last week.

What does she find to write about? I've been sitting watching her for ten minutes and she hasn't paused once. What can she possibly be saying?

The most important thing to remember, Penny, is that there are many ways of being a whole and fulfilled woman and that Motherhood is only one of them. It just happens to be the most beautiful, enriching, instinctive and necessary thing that a woman can do and is entirely the reason that I feel I was put upon this earth. That's all.

However, as I say, despite remaining resolutely unobsessed, I do not intend to give up without a fight. Five years is too long and I have decided that after two more periods I'll seek medical help. Sam doesn't like this idea much. He says that it's a matter of psychology, claiming that while at the moment we can still see ourselves as simply unlucky, if we go to a doctor we'll be admitting that we are actually infertile and from that point on we'll be forever sad. Of course the real reason that Sam doesn't want to go to a doctor is because it's the first step on a road that will almost certainly lead to him having to masturbate in National Health Service semen collection rooms.

This really is very depressing. And to think that I had dreams of being a writer. If I can't even write a letter to myself, then scintillating screenplays and brilliantly innovative television serials at the very cutting edge of the zeitgeist are likely to be somewhat beyond my grasp.

Oh good, she's finally stopped.

So what I'll do is I'll just carry on writing this sentence I'm writing now for a moment or two longer . . . so that it doesn't look like I stopped just because she did . . . Ho hum, dumdy dum . . . What can I say? Saturday tomorrow, going to see George and Melinda plus offspring.

Brilliant, Sam. Give the boy a Pulitzer Prize. That's it, finito.

Dear Penny

I must admit that going to see Melinda and George with their new baby today was a bit difficult. I hate being envious, but I was. It was so sweet, a little boy and absolutely beautiful. Couldn't get over his little fingers, I never can with brand new babs. Just gorgeous.

Dear Book

I'm very worried about George and Melinda's new sprog. Ugly as a monkey's arse. Couldn't say so, of course, but I could see that poor old George was dubious. He calls it Prune, which I think is fair, although 'old man's scrotum' would probably be closer to the mark.

I had hoped that the sight of young Prune (or Cuthbert, as he is called) might put Lucy off a bit, make her see that there are enormous risks involved with propagation. The thought of having to face those chasmic, gaping, bawling toothless gums five times a night would, I imagine, make any woman reach for the condoms. Quite the opposite, though. She thinks he's utterly adorable. Amazing. It's like we're looking at different babies.

Quite frankly, I began to see King Herod in a wholly different light.

I got home feeling all clucky and sad but I am determined to resist maudlin 'I'm barren' mawkishness. The truth is, though, I fear that I am barren and if that isn't enough to make me mawkish I don't know what is. I mean, some girls are up the duff straight off. My friend Roz from college could get pregnant just by phoning her husband at work and if you believe what you read in the papers half the schoolgirls in the country are teenage mums.

However, as I say, I am determined to approach this period of my life positively. Hence these letters to you, Penny, the point of which, according to my friend Sheila (who saw an Oprah on the subject), is that Sam and I become proactively involved in our emotional journeys. Sheila says that according to several American experts whom Oprah spoke to, the desire to have children is entirely natural and good and we should embrace it whether it turns out that we are fertile (I hate that word, it makes me feel like a failed heifer) or not.

Dear Book

Another evening, another desperate effort to think of something to write about.

God, I'd love a shag. I really really would like a shag. But we can't. We're off sex at the moment and I must say I miss it. Lucy is over there looking saucier than the condiments shelf at Sainsbury's. The very definition of the word shaggable. Sitting on the bed, wearing nothing but a pyjama top, bare legs raised, tongue pointing out of the side of her mouth, nose wrinkled in concentration. She really is so beautiful sometimes. But I'm not allowed to jump on her. We're saving up my sperm, you see. It's this month's theory and it's one of my least favourite.

Dear Penny

Sam's rather grumpy at the moment because he's feeling sexually frustrated. I can't deny I miss it myself a bit. But no. No, no, NO! We can't and there's an end to it. I should explain, Pen, that this is an RBM, a Restricted Bonking Month. What's happening is that I'm making him save up all his sperm. It's this month's theory. Wait for the right time and then have one concentrated, day-long, high-density, sperm-rich assault on my ovulating eggs. But when is the time right? To have it off or not to have it off, that is the question.

The only way I can determine the optimum ovulatory moment is to apply scientific methods of research, which I've never been very good at, not even being able to programme my mobile phone. In theory it should all be quite simple. Just a question of counting days, studying your pee and taking your temperature all the time. But it really is a horrible and soul-destroying business. I count days, I collect urine, I pee on a little traffic light from Boots, I take my temperature, I fill in my chart, I do some more pee, I put some more little red dots on my calendar until it's completely covered in little red dots and crossed-out little red dots so that I don't know which little red dots are which. It's like trying to have it off in an intensive care unit.

And the biggest problem of all in these meticulous calculations is when do you begin them? When do you start the counting? Are you supposed to start counting at the beginning of your period or at the end?

I remember reading in Elle or some such mag that clues can be gleaned from the colour of your menstrual blood. Well, frankly.

I preferred last month's theory. That one was a cracker. I loved it. We were experimenting with the 'bonk all the time' theory. Based on the idea that fertilisation is an unknowable, unplannable lottery. Which of course it is.

Lucy made a list in an effort to marshal her thoughts. I reproduce this list below. If nothing else it will fill up a bit of space.

Lucy's Shag All The Time Theory List.

1. No one can ever be sure exactly when ovulation occurs.

2. No one really seems to know at what point during ovulation fertility is at its most likely.

3. If you did know these things it would not make any difference at all. Because no one knows how long it takes a lazy and reluctant sperm with attitude to swim what, I seem to recall being told at school, is the equivalent of a piranha fish swimming the length of the Amazon. Hence, even if you did know when ovulation was going to occur you would not know how long before that you should do the business.

The conclusion that Lucy drew from this list was that the only way to be sure of hitting the mark was to shag all the time. When I say 'all the time' I mean once a night which is all the time as far as I'm concerned.

It was a good month, except when Lucy scalded herself. Nothing to do with me, I hasten to add. The problem was that after we'd done it she insisted on propping her bum up with a pillow for half an hour so that my sperm would be able to swim downhill. This is not an ideal position in which to enjoy a cup of tea and so, one day, over her and the duvet it went.

I must say I thought she deserved it. I resented the assumption that my crappy, lazy, undermotivated sperm would only be able to reach her eggs if given the unfair advantage of being allowed to swim downhill.

The other thing I find a bit sad about Restricted Bonking Month is it means that Sam and I don't really have much physical contact at all at the moment. Sam's not much of a cuddler, he never has been. He really only tends to cuddle as a sort of pre-sex warm up. Personally I often crave a bit of physical affection that isn't sexual and is, well, just affection. Sheila says that in her experience (which is considerable, she having had it off for the Home Counties in her time), non-sexual physical attention isn't something that men do, and certainly not after about the first year of the relationship.

Dear Book

First entry for four days. I really must do better or Lucy will think I'm not trying. The whole problem with the theory of writing down your feelings of course is that it takes so long to come up with one. I remember trying to write a diary when I was at school. All I could think of to write was what I'd had for dinner.

Lucy is enjoying doing her writing, of course, surprise, surprise. She's sitting there now, across the bedroom, scribbling away. She gets the bed, obviously. I have to do mine on the dressing table, which is of course completely covered in bottles of moisturising stuff.

What the hell is she writing about? I'm not allowed to ask. Apparently, if we read each other's books we'll be writing them for each other, which is not the purpose of the exercise.

I expect Lucy's writing about what an emotionally retarded shit I am. That'll be it. She can never forgive me for being more relaxed than her about whether we have children or not. I know that secretly she thinks this attitude has infected my sperm. She thinks that their refusal to leap like wild salmon straight up the river of her fertility and headbutt great holes in the walls of her eggs is down to a belligerently slack attitude which they've caught off me.

Dear Penny

Sam hates this. I'm looking at him now, hunched over his laptop, resentment radiating from his every pore. I really don't see why he has to be so negative. Perhaps it's because the exercise is making him confront his own shallowness. I don't think he even knows whether he wants children. I'm going to ask him. I don't think I've ever really confronted him with the question.

Lucy just stopped writing and asked me for the millionth time whether I was sure that I even wanted children because she didn't think I did. God, we keep having these conversations. I think we should just tape one and put it on a loop. It's not that I don't want children. I'm not made of stone, for heaven's sake, but children are not the only thing I want. I happen to believe that when God made me he made me for a purpose beyond that of devoting my entire life to reproducing myself. To which Lucy replied that when God made me he made a million other people the same day and probably doesn't even remember my name. I suggested to her that if my presence on the planet is so insignificant I should probably just kill myself right now, relieving our overstretched planet of a pointless waste of resources. She said I was just being pompous and unpleasant and then started to look a bit teary. Actually, sometimes, I think I'd quite like to die young. That way I could avoid failing to fulfil my potential.

What he dresses up as self-doubt and humility is actually frustrated arrogance. He only gets depressed about himself because he doesn't write any more. But it's becoming a self-fulfilling prophecy. He says he can't write, so he doesn't write. It's as simple as that. I told him he'd get a lot further as a writer if he spent less time moaning about it and more time doing it. To which he said he'd like to but that I was taking up all his spare time making him write a stupid book of letters to himself. Actually, I think it might do him good as a writer to get in touch with his feelings occasionally. All he seems to do as a commissioning editor at the BBC is encourage people to write ever ruder jokes. This must surely eventually coarsen his creative soul.

Anyway, he didn't answer that because he knew I was right. He just snorted unpleasantly and now there's an atmosphere.

It's all very well her telling me to write. I can't bloody write. I'm a creativity-free zone. She is wrong about my attitude to kids, though. Of course I want children. Well, I think I do. There's been so much angst surrounding the subject for so long now that I've forgotten what I originally felt. But I'm sure that if I do want children it's because I love Lucy. That's the only way I can think about it. If I try to think of kids in the abstract I very quickly come up against the end of life as I know it, and I like life as I know it. I like to work, I like to drink, I like to sleep in and have clothes and furniture with no dribble and sick on them.

Kids, however, as a part of Lucy, as an extension and expression of our love, I can relate to, and if it happened I'd be delighted. If we have children it will be another part of us, of our love. If we don't, then we'll still have us. Our love will be no less whole.

Dearest Pen Pal

I was talking to Drusilla today at work. Sheila (my boss, the one who told me to write to you) had rushed out of the office (she'd heard there was a bloke on Oxford Street selling dodgy fags at a pound a box), so Joanna and I were being slack. In fact we were playing the Spotlight game, which is great fun. What you do is you get the Actor's Spotlight (which is a book full of photographs of actors) and open it at random. Whoever you pick on, you have to sleep with. Not actually, obviously, but just as a thought.

I'd just been landed with Sir Ian McKellen and was rather thinking that I had my work cut out there when Drusilla popped in. Drusilla is an actress and recently played a mad mystic in an episode of Casualty and I'm here to tell you that she was typecast. Anyway, she has got very interested in my fears about being barren and is convinced that the answer lies in the runes. She's been reading up on some ancient Druid-like fertility rites or other and came in today waving a crystal about. She says that Western society is the only society which has dispensed with its fertility rites and the only society in which the birth rate is falling. 'Hello-o,' she said. 'Obvious connection, I think.' Then she suggested an impromptu fertility ceremony.

Unbelievably, she wanted me to lie on the floor while she and Joanna squatted over me. I swear I'm not making this up. Then she wanted us all to make

some sort of appalling vaginal symbol with our thumbs and forefingers. While
doing this we had to chant the words 'womb' and 'flow' in low rich tones so
that the sounds reverberated deep within us.

Let me tell you I felt a right fool when Sheila came back with her fags and
found us. If Restricted Bonking Month works and I get pregnant, Drusilla will
of course claim victory for her fertility ritual, but I shan't mind. I'm that des-
perate I'd give credit to the fairies at the bottom of the garden.

Dear Book

Lucy decided that the optimum moment of Restricted Bonking
Month had arrived during lunch. My lunch, not hers. She wasn't there,
she was at home surrounded by calendars, thermometers, red felt-tip
pens and urine. I was lunching at One Nine Oh (so called because it's
situated at 190 Ladbroke Park Gate—brilliant, eh)? One Nine Oh is
something of a media haunt and I often lunch there in my capacity as
one of the BBC's most senior and experienced lunch eaters.

My guests were Dog and Fish, a comic double act who seem to be
doing quite well on the circuit at the moment. They are two Oxbridge
graduates who are of the opinion that current comedy is 'completely
crap and useless' and what we need is a new, post-comedy comedy. *Time
Out* says that they are important and mould-breaking (no mention of
funny, but that would be selling out), so the BBC must of course beat a
path to their door. If for no other reason than that if we don't Channel
Four will get them and yet again look more hip than us.

They told me that they wanted to do a postmodern docusoap sitcom.
The idea being that we supply them with cameras and a crew and that
they record their lives. Each week they'll present us with a half-hour of
the best bits. They claim that by this means they'll cut out all that false
crap which TV comedy normally gets bogged down in, like scripts and
jokes and acting in an amusing manner, and get straight to the raw
improvisational bones of their genius.

Anyway. Lucy's call came along with the starters. Finally, it seemed,
after days of intense number crunching, the ovulation result had come
up and we were on. By a curious coincidence I'd ordered Oeufs
Benedict to begin my meal. Her eggs were ready at exactly the same time
as mine.

I hate mobiles but Lucy had made me buy one for just such a circum-
stance as this. I'm going to have to work out the volume control,
though, because unless I'm being paranoid her voice seemed to be being
broadcast through the restaurant PA.

'Sam, I think I'm ovulating. Come home and fuck me now.'

Well, people may have heard and they may not have heard, but either way they could not have helped but hear my reply, which was intended to be in a whisper but emerged as a sort of loud gasp.

'Fuck you? I'm in a meeting.'

Dog and Fish smiled broadly at this and I could tell that in the delicate dance of mutual respect I was losing ground somewhat. Thinking fast, I repeated what I'd said but with a different emphasis.

'Fuck you! I'm in a meeting.'

Dog and Fish laughed out loud at that and Lucy must have heard them because she absolutely made me promise not to tell them what she was phoning about. This was all very well, but she was also demanding that I jack in the lunch immediately and hurry home. It's not an easy situation to think up a decent excuse for. I mean cancelling a meeting is easy. But attending a meeting, a meeting that has been set up for months and then suddenly getting an abrupt phonecall after which you leap up from the table and leave your busy and highly fashionable companions to dine alone, that requires an explanation. What do you say? All I could do was act casual and try to keep it ambiguous.

'Sorry,' I said. 'My wife is ovulating and she wants seeing to.'

'Nice one, geezer,' they said and laughed in a grunty, cynical, fag-ashy kind of a way.

I left a credit card number with the Maître d' to cover Dog and Fish's lunch and grabbed a taxi. All the way home I tried to think erotic thoughts, knowing what would be required of me the moment I walked through the door. Sure enough, when I got home Lucy was already in bed, shouting, 'Come on! Come on!'

I hate myself sometimes. All month I'd been wanting a shag and now I get stagefright. Well, who wouldn't? It isn't easy to get a hard-on when your partner is desperately staring at her watch and bleakly contemplating a lonely and emotionally unfulfilled life of childlessness ahead. Lucy tried her best, of course, but it wasn't much help.

We succeeded in the end. I managed to just about sustain a sort of semi-half-master until achieving a lacklustre orgasm. I felt really unmanned and that I'd let Lucy down. She said it was all right, but without a great deal of conviction. I told her that I didn't think I'd produced enough but she said it didn't need much. 'It's quality, not quantity,' she said, which was nice of her.

Dear Penny

It was Bonk Day today, the culmination of Restricted Bonking Month. This sort of thing is definitely not good for the sex life. I mean sex ought to be spontaneous and erotic, not contrived and mechanical, but what could I do? I needed servicing and there's an end to it. I could see that Sam was a bit upset afterwards. I fear that he feels he's being used like some kind of farmyard animal. Nothing more than a breeding stud, brutally milked for his sperm. Not that he was much of a stud today.

It was the pressure, of course. After all my calculations he knew he had to produce the goods. Difficult for him, I'm sure, but as a woman with feelings I do rather wish it hadn't appeared quite such an ordeal.

When we'd finished he rushed off, of course. I asked him not to because I think it's important to spend a bit of time together after sex or else it's just sex, isn't it? But Sam said he had to go back to work, which, considering he claims his job consists entirely of telling arseholes how clever they are, didn't seem like much of an excuse to me.

When I got back to TV Centre there were three messages to ring Aiden Fumet, Dog and Fish's manager. He's also the manager of sixteen other acts whom *Time Out* and the *Guardian* have sequentially announced as 'quite simply the best in Britain today'. Aiden Fumet seems to see any failure on the part of the BBC to grant a series to any of his acts as evidence of a vicious conspiracy to deny the young people of Britain the comedic nourishment for which their souls are clearly crying out.

'What the fuck was that malarkey all about, then, Sam, dumping my boys at One Nine Oh?' Fumet said when I called him back. 'I'd better warn you now, mate, that Dog and Fish are one phone call away from going to Channel Four. And the BBC can fuck off.'

Well, I was in no mood for this. Normally I have to admit that I'm a bit of a pushover. The worm, however, can turn and show his teeth (if worms have teeth) and a worm who has just been crap in bed with the wife he loves is likely to turn like a U-bend.

'What is going *on*, Aiden, *mate*. . .' and I commenced to give him the most exquisitely phrased bollocking of his entire life. Unfortunately it was all wasted because after he'd told me to fuck off he'd hung up.

Later, I told Lucy about the whole incident over supper, and that led to a slight misunderstanding. She said that she was sorry about today, and I thought she meant she was sorry about me getting shat on by arrogant, no-talent twatheads. So I told her not to worry. I told her that it was my job. Well, it turned out that she was actually talking about our lunchtime sex session. She's been concerned that I might feel used—'milked for my sperm like a farmyard animal' was how she put it. So when I said, 'Don't worry, it's my job,' she thought I meant having sex with her was my job and said, 'I hope you don't see it as a job,' in a very tart voice indeed. But I of course still thought she was talking about my work and therefore took her tart retort as a snide reference to the pathetically unfulfilling way I earn a living and said, 'Yes, it's a job, a bloody boring job. There's certainly no satisfaction to be had in it.'

Misunderstandings all round and quite an atmosphere had developed before we got it sorted out. After that we didn't talk any more and she started clearing the plates in a marked manner.

Dear Penny

I got my period today.

I'm writing this with a hot-water bottle clamped to my tummy because of the cramps. Oh, how I love being a woman.

Drusilla says I have to learn to love my periods, that they're part of the sacred cycle of the earth and the moon. Words failed me at that juncture, which was fortunate really because had I thought about it I would have told her to get on her sacred cycle and ride it off a cliff.

It really is so depressing, Penny. The grim, clockwork inevitability of my body failing to perform the functions for which it was designed. A few months ago I broke down on the M6—my car, that is, not me, although quite frankly I nearly did as well. It was awful, just sitting there waiting for the breakdown people to come. Millions of other cars kept whizzing by and they were all working but I was stuck. I cannot tell you how frustrating it was. Well, my whole life's like that really. Month after month I'm stuck, my car won't work and I have no idea how to make it go. Meanwhile, the rest of the female sex are whizzing past in Renault people-carriers with eight baby seats in the back.

Look, I know I'm whining here, but if I can't whine to my imaginary friend who can I whine to? My periods are absolutely horrible and the crowning nightmare of my apparent infertility is the idea that this abject misery, which I have endured since I was thirteen, might be for nothing.

Dear Book

Failed again. Arse. Lucy says that Sheila says the bloke on *Oprah* said that I'm not supposed to use that word. 'Failed', that is, not 'arse'. Apparently the 'fail' word implies a value judgment. If we say that we've failed then that means in some way it's our fault, which of course it isn't. Lucy has read eight and a half million books on the subject of infertility and while they don't agree on many things they do all seem to feel that a positive outlook is essential.

Well, bollocks to that. We've failed again. Lucy has got her period, Restricted Bonking Month was a complete washout. I'm sure the main reason she wants a kid is to have nine months off having periods.

I always feel at such a loss at these times. So impotent. Whoops, wrong word there, but you know what I mean . . . I mean I know what I mean . . . for heaven's sake, I think I'm going mad. Nobody's going to read this but me and yet I'm beginning to address this pointless exercise to a third person. I must get a grip.

Dear Penny

Felt better today, physically, anyway. Mentally I'm still feeling low. The brutal truth is that it is now sixty-one periods since Sam and I started trying for a baby. That's five years and one month. What's more, when I come to think about it, prior to that we weren't exactly being careful. In fact we had at least a year of relying on withdrawal.

Basically, I have to face facts. I am Sad. I'm Barren. My womb is a prune.

There, I've said it. I don't care, it's how I feel. What's the point of this book if I can't be honest? Excuse me, Penny, got to get a tissue.

I've been crying, Penny, sorry. I tried reminding myself about the homeless and the starving people in Africa, but it didn't work. Anyway, I'm back now. And, yes, I know that a lot of women wait a lot longer than five years and a month (actually six years and one month in my case, if you count the careless year) and then all of a sudden they start spraying sprogs about the place like a fish spawning. I've heard all the stories.

'I know a couple who waited decades!' people say. 'Yet once they'd had one they couldn't stop. Ended up with enough for a football team and a crowd of supporters!'

Mum says that she's sure it's all in the mind. Everybody says that. She says I concentrate too much on my career. Everybody says that too. Besides which, career? Ha! Ha ha HA! One thing I do not have is a career. I am not a theatrical agent, I am a theatrical agent's assistant.

Melinda says I've got to relax. Everybody says that as well! In fact, that is the thing that everybody says most. They say, 'Relax, the thing to do is put it out of your mind and then it will happen.' It is simply not possible to bloody well relax with your body clock ticking away in your ear at five million decibels, and your eggs getting more ancient by the day.

Melinda and George brought Cuthbert round today, which was nice. No, really it was, I'm not so bloody sad that I can't enjoy my friends and their babies. Sam still refers to Cuthbert as Scrotum, which is ridiculous because he's beautiful. I held him for a while and all I could think was, 'Wish I had one.'

Dear Sam

Scrotum may have improved slightly, difficult to say. George has overcome his initial qualms, and given the lad the benefit of the doubt. The prospects of young Cuthbert ending up wrapped in a blanket outside a police station are receding. I mean it's clear that he's not going to be a male model, but George thinks he could probably do something in the City or on the radio. Or a boxer, perhaps? We certainly wouldn't have to worry about his looks getting ruined.

I'm probably being unfair here. I suppose all babies look this way in the very early stages, but I have to admit that they do absolutely nothing for me. I try to get clucky but no go, I don't even want to hold them. I'm an arm's-length man. That funny pulsating bit on their heads completely freaks me out. The first time I saw that I confidently expected the Alien to burst forth from it with Sigourney Weaver close behind. Of course Lucy went potty over the lad and had to hold him and I knew that all she could think was that she wished she had one. I wish that she did too. I wish that we both did. I would love to be the father of Lucy's child.

Dear Penny Pal

I feel a bit sad. I know Sam loves me and I suppose he still fancies me, but he doesn't bother to show it very much and he never says it. He says he does, of course. He claims that I have selective ears. I don't think that's true. I think he only really says nice things when I ask him to say them, but I can't be sure. I think that perhaps his mother didn't cuddle him enough as a child or something. Tonight I made him massage some oil into my lower back and although he did do it I could tell that it was a major inconvenience for him, which made the whole thing pointless. I mean, if aromatherapy is going to have any effect at all I imagine it will be a pretty subtle one, dealing as it does with one's most delicate biorhythms. Let's face it, delicate biorhythms are not exactly going to stand a lot of chance against a great big lump of negativity that just wants to read its newspaper.

Dear Book

I think Lucy is at the end of her tether. She's been a bit quiet these last few days and I know it's because she's thinking about fertility. There's been this documentary running on the Beeb about IVF couples and she seems to have learned it off by heart. Personally I can't watch it. I just cannot bring myself to be interested in the sad and desperate experiences of complete strangers. Lucy, on the other hand, tapes it. She tapes anything about fertility. She cuts articles out of the papers (incredible how many there are) and writes off to all sorts of organisations. It's all a bit heartbreaking, although she's very good about it, determined not to become emotionally dysfunctional, she's quite clear on that one.

But I must say I do find it slightly alarming how attractive she seems to find baby clothes. Mind you, this is something I've noticed in many women. They look at a pair of tiny socks and say, 'Ahh, isn't that just so-o-o sweet and just lovely.' Why is this? I simply cannot fathom it. These are empty socks we're talking about here, socks with no baby in them. How can women go gooey over a pair of socks?

Better stop. Got to read a script tonight, a comic play that has developed out of a new writing workshop we've been running at the Beeb. The author has already had a one-act piece put on at the Royal Court or some other gruesome oversubsidised London centre of theatrical wankdom. The new play is called *Fucking and Fucking*. I told him that we'd have to change the title and he looked at me as if I was some kind of fascist. It's so depressing. It seems only yesterday that I was considered a hip and dangerous young producer because I commissioned sketches about tampons. Now I'm a Nazi for telling young writers they can't use the word 'fuck' in their titles.

I can't believe how quickly I'm turning into a sad, reactionary old git.

Dear Penny

I'm not putting it off any longer. I've made an appointment to go and talk to my doctor. There is obviously something wrong and quite frankly it will be a relief to know the truth. Anyway, it seems to me that the best way to get pregnant is to go and start the process of some sort of fertility treatment. You hear constantly of people who know people who had decided to start IVF only to get pregnant by conventional means on their way to the first appointment! There are also any number of stories of couples who failed at IVF but then immediately got pregnant by conventional means or by sitting on wet grass or something. Add to this the numerous people who have a cousin who signed up to adopt and then immediately fell pregnant. All in all I have come to the conclusion that the only absolutely sure way to get pregnant is to be pronounced infertile.

Sheila took on an important new client today. An actor called Carl Phipps. He came into the office. Very arrogant. Good looking, certainly, but what does that signify?

Dear etc.

Depressed. Very depressed. I met the new BBC1 Controller today. He's younger than me! This is the first time this has happened. I mean me being older than one of my bosses. I don't like it at all. He's a whiz kid from Granada. I think he made some documentary proving that the Conservative Party is funded by a gang of Middle Eastern prostitutes, so obviously that qualifies him to schedule the entertainment of a nation.

I feel very sorry for poor old Lucy at the moment. Not only has she got all this fertility business on her mind, but now it sounds like she's got a real idiot to look after at work. That new actor, Phipps guy, can't remember his first name. He sounds like a right pain. She went on about him a bit over dinner, so I could tell he's got right under her skin. As if she didn't have enough to worry about.

Dear Penny

I'm going to see Dr Cooper today. I feel better now that I'm finally acknowledging that there actually probably is a problem and that I'm beginning the process of dealing with it. All the girls plus my mum and Sam's mum continue to assure me that five years and one month (nearly five years and two months) is not that long to be trying. I continue to be bombarded with the same old drivel about various women who tried continually and energetically for seven years and then—bang!—out popped triplets. It will be so good to get an informed opinion rather than all this anecdotal hearsay.

Just got back from Dr Cooper's. He says that five years or so is not actually that long to be trying and that he knows any number of women who tried for seven years and then had twelve apiece. I feel a huge gin and tonic calling.

Dr Cooper has, however, offered to do a blood test to check my hormone levels and a sperm test for Sam. He took it very well. I thought it might bother him a bit but he was great and said it was simply not a problem and did not bother him in the slightest.

The blood test is set up for next Tuesday. Apparently this will ascertain if I'm ovulating or not. My God, I shall be so annoyed if I'm not. Ten years of condoms, caps, coils and abstinence followed by five years of thermometers, counting days and weeing on traffic lights would all be completely wasted.

Drusilla is horrified at the prospect of me having a blood test. She thinks that modern medicine is totally intrusive (and I suppose wandering about naked at Stonehenge isn't intrusive). She wants me to visualise a baby inside me, in my stomach, in my arms, in my very soul, a complete and perfect part of me. I said, 'Drusilla darling, that's all I ever bloody do,' and she said that was the problem. I'm obsessive, I need to visualise mystically rather than desperately. I need to allow myself the freedom to dream. Sounds like absolute bollocks to me.

I've booked a class for tomorrow night.

Sam seems to be going a bit funny over the prospect of his sperm test.

Dear Self

Heard an interesting fact about sperm today. Not that sperm is on my mind or anything but the subject came up in a taxi, as it will from time to time. Sperm counts, it seems, are generally down in the Western world. It seems that for whatever reason, be it additives in the food, pollution, radiation from our mobile phones, or the gunk at the bottom of Pot Noodles, we modern men are considerably less flush in the sperm department than our grandfathers were. Isn't that strange? I mean modern society's attitude to old people is basically one of contempt. We don't want to look like them and they cost too much to run.

'Poor old Grandad,' we think. 'Look at him, sitting in the corner dribbling and sucking his gums, always wanting to watch a different television channel from the rest of the family.' Now it turns out the man's got bigger bollocks than all of his patronising male descendants put together!

Recently I've been feeling slightly old, which is ridiculous at thirty-eight. I don't like thinking this way. In fact, I don't really like thinking at all. I'm not really an introspective sort of person. It's writing these stupid bloody letters that's making me all self-conscious. Perhaps I should cut down on the booze a bit. I'll have a drink and think about it.

Dear Penny

I'm afraid Drusilla's visualisation class was a complete and utter washout. Why is it that anything interesting and different always has to be championed by the most unprepossessing people?

I arrived at the Community Centre and a large woman with more hair (hennaed) than an old English sheepdog and breasts like Space Hoppers asked me if I wished to purchase some washable hessian sanitary napkins! I mean I ask you, Penny! Ugh, or what?! I'm happy to recycle glass, collect newspapers and rinse out tin cans but I do draw the line at recycling sanitary pads. If that is to be the price of saving the world then I fear that the world must die.

I nearly turned around and ran for it there and then, but I'd made the effort so I decided that I'd better give it a go. Well, first off there was a 'greeting session'. This involved us all sitting in a big circle and chucking a beanbag at each other and whenever you caught it you had to say your name. A simple enough exercise, one might have thought, but it was astonishing how difficult some of them found keeping the rhythm.

Anyway, after that the leading lady (who was American) took us on what is called a 'guided fantasy'. You have to imagine a cool forest and a path by a stream, damp mist, a green canopy above, you know the sort of thing. An infinity of calm. I rather enjoyed this bit and nearly nodded off.

Once she'd got us feeling all sort of 'drifty', the American lady told us to try and visualise an imaginary baby being welcomed into our wombs. Well, I'm afraid that was where I lost it. All the relaxation disappeared and was replaced by anger and frustration. My cool forest suddenly turned into London as of now.

Afterwards I told the American lady that I really didn't think that this was the right approach for me. She said that she understood but that I have to allow myself to want, to dream and if necessary to grieve over my current lack of baby. She said that I was fighting my body, resenting it, seeing it as the enemy of all my hopes and that this self-created tension might in fact be getting in the way of conception. Actually, it did sort of make sense and I ended up rather liking the woman, but I still shan't go again. I just get too frustrated. I keep screaming inside, why the hell should I have to imagine a baby? Why can't I just have one! I know I'd be a much better mum than half the women I see letting their children put sweets in the trolley at Sainsbury's. I'd read my child Beatrix Potter and Winnie the Pooh and the only glue it would ever get involved with would be flour and water for making collages.

Sam's sperm test is looming. I had originally thought that he was taking it well but now he does seem to be dwelling on it rather.

Dear Self

I had lunch with Trevor and George from work today and was determined to touch on the subject of sperm. Pick their brains, so to speak. I mean, George ought to know something. He produced Cuthbert and I wouldn't like to meet the sperm that fathered him. Trevor's gay so he should have some opinions on the subject. All in all I had been looking forward to airing my fears re my upcoming (if that isn't too loaded a phrase) sperm test.

I didn't get the chance, of course. We talked shop. We always do. It's a funny thing about this biz we call show: whenever people involved in it get together they can talk about nothing else. I'm as bad as anyone. Telling people in showbusiness not to talk about showbusiness would be like telling the Pope to lay off the religious stuff.

We were lunching in Soho at a posh place called Quark. All restaurants in Soho are posh these days. Those nice, rough and ready little Italian diners are just a distant memory. I'd already made an arse of myself, of course. I arrived first and the waitress (wearing a skirt that was little more than a big belt, why do these girls torment us so?) immediately put this plate of prawny things down in front of me. I said they must be someone else's because I hadn't ordered anything yet. She laughed and said they were 'for the table', a complimentary pre-appetiser appetiser. 'Don't worry,' she said, 'you won't be charged for them,' like I was some sad tourist way out of his depth and worrying about his budget. Silly mistake. Particularly for a professional eater of the sacred meal called lunch.

Anyway, as I was saying, I'd been hoping to draw the others out on sperm, but before I could even bring the subject up we got into this terrible row about our job titles. It all came up because Trevor was talking about some script he wanted to commission and he said . . .

'I don't want to throw my weight around here, but as the BBC Head of Comedy, Television Group South, I feel that . . .'

Well, he didn't get any further because George and I both protested that we were the BBC Head of Comedy, Television Group South. I knew that George wasn't because I knew for a fact that he was Chief Coordinator, BBC Entertainment Group, Television. I'd seen it on an invitation to a party. I also knew that he was angling for the post of Network Regional Channel Controller because I'd read it in the *Independent* only the previous morning. George insisted that he didn't care what it said on his invites, or what I'd read in the *Independent*, that he was BBC Head of Comedy, Television Group South.

'Well, what are you angling for, then?' Trevor asked, and George said that he was very excited about his current position and had no plans to move, which of course means he's angling for something at Channel Four.

That got us thinking. Because if George did go to Channel Four, and if he is, as he insists, BBC Head of Comedy, Television Group South, then either I or Trevor will be able to take over his job (which we both thought we already had anyway). That would leave whatever job that person currently held vacant for the other.

Trevor insisted that he knew what my job was because he'd been offered it ahead of me (slightly disheartening). Apparently, I'm BBC Controller, Broken Comedy and Variety, which if true is disappointing because only last year I was BBC Entertainment Chief, Comedy Group, London and South East. Which would mean I've taken a step down without realising it and am further away from becoming a Network Channel Controller than ever.

We all agreed that at this year's Christmas drinks we really would pluck up the courage to ask the Deputy Director General what our jobs are.

After that the talk drifted on to other things. Trevor and George had their usual row about booze. Trevor no longer drinks, which George strongly disapproves of, particularly since Trevor has been through 'recovery' (another thing of which George disapproves) and feels the need to mention his 'problem' on a regular basis.

'As an alcoholic in recovery I have no problem with the alcohol on this table,' said Trevor.

'Look, Trevor,' said George, 'you don't drink any more, that's great, not that you ever drank that much in the first place, but now you're cured, isn't it time you moved on?'

'But that's the point, George. You can never be cured. I'm an alcoholic. I'll always be an alcoholic. I could have nothing to drink for fifty years and I'd still be an alcoholic.'

This is the bit George hates most.

'Well you might as well have a fucking drink, then!' he said loudly enough for people at other tables to turn their heads.

At this point I thought I could bring up the subject of sperm to smooth things over a bit but George, having dealt with Trevor's obsession, moved on to his own, producing some photos of little Cuthbert. I had thought that producing pictures of one's baby in all-male company was against the law but, like everything else, that seems to have changed.

As a matter of record, though, I must confess that young Cuthbert is beginning to shape up a bit. He's definitely filling out and losing his scrotal appearance. He looked quite jolly in his togs from Baby Gap. George said that Cuthbert's clothes cost more than his own do, which he thought was obscene. Trevor, on the other hand, wished his boyfriend had half the dress sense of young Cuthbert. To which George replied that it was all very well for him because being gay he would never have to face the appalling cost of bringing up a baby. Trevor said that George was not to be too sure about that; with a Labour government in, who knew what might happen to the adoption laws?

Oh, God. Trevor is going to get kids before I do and he's a homosexual.

Dearest Penny

You know I was telling you that Sam isn't very tactile? Well, I'd been thinking that perhaps it was partly because our sex life has become so clinical. You know, it's got so inextricably wound up in my quest for fertility that I thought perhaps I was turning him off. So I tried to broach the subject. I said to him that I was sorry that things have got a bit dreary for us in the lovemaking department of late and told him that it was only because of the baby thing taking my mind off it. He just pecked me on the nose and said I mustn't worry and that he was fine. Quite frankly, this was not the reaction I was looking for.

This evening I tried to snuggle up when we were watching Channel Four News *but when Sam watches telly he really watches it, no distractions allowed, even during the adverts. It's amazing. There he is, concentrating on the golden crispiness of a packet of fish fingers or the sheer joy of driving a Fiat Uno and nothing must intrude.*

Yesterday I had one more go at the visualisation class. Drusilla made me. She said it was absurd to do it just once and that if I didn't go again then I might as well not have gone at all. So I gave it another chance, but it really isn't for me. We're all supposed to know each other now so the American lady

was a bit bolder and she hopped straight in with some cathartic role-playing.
She made us all cry like babies. Ten grown women sitting in a circle, crying
and wailing. I think the idea was to physicalise and project our need for chil-
dren and hence stop us feeling like it was some kind of guilty secret. That may
have been it. Anyway, it was bloody embarrassing. After that we had to hug
each other and offer comfort, sharing our sadness and recognising that we are
not alone. Well, I tried to be communally supportive but it was pretty grue-
some. I ended up clamped to the bosom of a woman who smelt of dogs. One
strange thing, though. During the meditation bit of the class (which happens
at the end) I found myself thinking about that appalling hoity Carl Phipps.
Can't think why; I don't even like him or find him attractive. Although he does
have a nice smile—that is, when he deigns to bestow it upon one so lowly as I.

Dear Book

Trevor and I played squash today. God, I am so unfit. I coughed up
something that looked like it lived in a pond. I hardly smoke at all any
more but I do like a drink. I think I'll try and switch to Spritzers.

Anyway, I talked to Trev a bit about my impending examination re
sperm and we both agreed that it is not a test of my manhood. He was
actually very sensitive. He asked me whether I'd think him any less a
whole man if it was him who was suspected of having a sad sorry sack
full of bugger-all banging betwixt his legs. I said of course I wouldn't.

But I *would*! I know I would. I'd pretend I wouldn't but I would. 'Poor
old Trevor,' I'd think, 'not much going on in the bollock department,' I'd
think, 'something of a testicular void'.

I told Lucy about my fears and, here's a funny thing, she burst into
tears, which I wasn't expecting at all.

'Hang on,' I said. 'I'm the one with the suspected empty balls, aren't I?'

I thought she was going to hit me. She said that I was already thinking in terms of 'fault', which was pathetic and destructive! She said that
the truth was that the problem was far more likely to rest with her than
with me because a woman's tubes are a lot more complicated than any
stupid horrible little knob and that if my sperm proved acceptable our
infertility would henceforward be her 'fault' and I would blame her!
This was of course followed by more tears.

I hate seeing her cry. It really makes me sad. On the other hand I do
think it's a bit much that I can't worry about my sperm count without
her turning it all back on to herself. I mean, I'm in on this too, aren't I?

But life goes on. There is after all more to it than my bollocks,
although I do tend to forget that fact with a sperm test pending. But
turning to other subjects, I've been thinking about the conversation I

had with Trevor and George at Quark about our job titles. Perhaps I should be moving on from the Beeb? After all, there's so much independent production going on, and what with my Beeb experience I'd probably be in huge demand. Of course I would. And I must say that I quite fancy a bit of that indie cash that's swilling about the place.

Of course, what I'd really like to do is write an original script myself, but since even coming up with an initial idea seems to be beyond my creative powers I might as well do my present job but for a decent salary, which means the indie sector.

Only eight days to go until the big test and I am definitely feeling quite relaxed about it. In fact, it's actually seven days and thirteen hours, so what's the problem?

Dear Penny

I can't believe it! All Sam thinks about is his sperm test. I mean for God's sake! From what I can gather, as a younger man he practically had a degree in masturbation. His horrid hand was never still!

What's more, he's desperate to get a good result! Terrified that he might be found lacking in the tadpole department. This is unbelievably selfish of him, because basically and in reality what this means is that he's desperate for there to be something wrong with my body. I mean, that's what it comes down to, surely? Because, let's face it, it's either him or me. We can't blame Mrs Thatcher for everything like we used to when we were young.

And this is the whole point. There is basically only one thing that can go wrong with a man. N.E.S. Not Enough Sperm. That's it and once you know you know, and you can start to deal with it.

But with a woman! Well, a woman's plumbing is like . . . well, I don't know what it's like. I'm trying to think of something really complex but also very beautiful. The ceiling of the Sistine Chapel, for instance, or Paul Simon's Graceland *album. There's a hundred things to be checked and every single one of those checks involves a gang of doctors placing something up one's doodah not dissimilar to the equipment they used to build the Channel Tunnel! How could he wish that upon me?*

Dear Self

I feel much better about the sperm test now.

I've decided that it's actually politically offensive to get all worked up with fear and shame about something that is simply an accident of nature. So enough of this nonsense. I'll take my sperm result like a man and if it's a poor one then so be it. I'll simply shrug, *c'est la vie* style. In fact I'll take pride in the way God made me.

Nonetheless, despite not caring at all, I'm planning to go into a bit of training. Well, you want to do as well as possible, don't you? I might as well give it my best shot, so to speak. I've resolved therefore to cut out the booze for a few days and eat a lot of fruit. Also George told me that he'd heard that zinc was good, so I've bought a tub of five hundred tablets from Boots. I've also got a crate of Energizer sports drink and an American book entitled *The Testicular Workout*. Having said all this, I wish to stress again that I'm not in the slightest bit concerned about my test result.

Turning once more to other matters, I did something a bit devilish at work today. I instigated a bit of tentative job exploration and on BBC time too. I wrote a letter to Simon 'Tosser' Tomkins, with whom I was at college. Old Tosser's done very well of late, having practically cornered the market in supplying the BBC with programmes fronted by posh smart Alecs. He and his partners have had a quite extraordinary run of success, producing quiz shows (fronted by posh smart Alecs), chat shows (fronted by posh smart Alecs) and endless travelogues (fronted by posh smart Alecs). Anyway, Tosser recently floated his company on the stock market and it turned out that it's worth 7 million quid! I just sent him a friendly note, you know . . .

'*Dear Tosser. The Beeb's a bit crap these days or what? Too many shows full of yobs going on about how much they like football. I was thinking of putting myself about a bit. What do you think?*'

I signed it '*Sam Bell, Executive Chief Commissioning Editor, BBC Worldwide,*' which is actually a post I made up but I didn't want old Tosser thinking I'm not a major player. Of course, being me, as I was putting the note into an envelope I began to worry about it. I suddenly felt all guilty and started to think that I might be burning bridges at the Beeb. Suppose my negative thinking is showing in my attitude? So I also sent a note to the new Channel Controller asking if he'd like to come to dinner. I very much doubt he will, since as I believe I've mentioned he's younger than me and also knows pop stars and people like that, but it's nice to ask him. A bit of smarmy arselick never hurts. I sent the letters through the BBC franking system. Let the licence payers stump up the cash. I've given them the best years of my life.

Dear Pen Pal

I spent yesterday lunchtime at a women's clinic for alternative medicine and therapy. As I've said, all that New Agey stuff is not really for me, but on the other hand it's foolish to dismiss things out of hand. Anyway, while I was there I bumped into Drusilla. She'd just been to an aromatherapy session and she reeked of orange and liquorice oils.

Anyway, Drusilla (who seems to be nearly as fascinated by my infertility as I am myself) asked how long we'd lived in Highgate.

'Five years,' I said, to which she positively shrieked and said that this was our problem! Apparently it's well known that there's an unfriendly and infertile ley line running right through Hampstead and Highgate. I pointed out that other people conceive in Highgate, but apparently ley lines are very personal and can be a fertility drug for some and an absolute vinegar douche for others. Drusilla is convinced that our problem is geographical. She claims that the most powerfully positive ley line within this, our ancient and magical land of Albany, runs right across Primrose Hill! Well, I half guessed what was coming, but it was still a shock. She wants Sam and me to have it off on top of Primrose Hill! At midnight under a full moon!

It's not on, of course. Absolutely out of the question. Under no circumstances would I dream of doing such a thing. Well, it's ridiculous.

Incidentally, I nearly shouted at that arrogant sod Carl Phipps today. He came in to pick up some faxes, from an American producer no less, very grand. I must say he was looking rather nice, wearing a maroon-coloured corduroy suit, so I said, 'Oh you're looking rather nice, Carl,' and he said, 'Well, one tries.' I mean the arrogance! Anyway, then he sat right down on the corner of my desk and said, 'You're looking like something of a sex bitch yourself today, Lucy,' which was simply not true. All I had on was a silly little miniskirt, my kinky boots and that little tight top I quite like. Frankly I looked awful, so it was stupid of him to pretend I didn't. Carl is terribly popular with the public. He's definitely our biggest client. He gets loads of fan mail from that costume thing he did at the Beeb. I can't think what people see in him.

Dear Book

Good news and bad news. Lucy has vetoed my all-round scrotal fitness plan. She says that the test must not be rigged. If we're to get anywhere with discovering why we're infertile I must present an honest picture of myself and my life. i.e. half pissed most nights and occasionally at lunchtime. Lucy suspects, I fear, that my fondness for booze (which though sociable is by no means excessive) may be the problem. She imagines that the inside of my scrotum resembles the Groucho Club at 1.45 on a Saturday night, i.e. nearly empty but with a thin smattering of pissed-up free-loading liggers who have no real skills or purpose and appear to make no positive contribution to anything whatsoever that might justify their comfortable and socially exalted existence.

Anyway, Lucy's decision not to let me prepare for my test has certainly made life easier. I'm particularly pleased to be able to give up the *Testicular Workout*. It promised firm, full and rounded testicles in a wrinkle-free scrotum inside one month, but it required a kind of tensing of the arse and lower gut muscles which made me frown furiously. I'm glad not to be bothering with that any more. I have enough new lines on my face without deliberately grimacing for ten minutes a day.

Anyway, in four days' time it will all be over. Which means from tomorrow onwards I'm not allowed to ejaculate. Apparently a three-day period of being left alone in quiet contemplation will give my sperm time to consider their characters and pull themselves together a bit.

No reply yet from Tosser, or indeed the Channel Controller, but I take this as no slight. They're both very busy men, as, of course, am I.

Dear Pen Pal
I gave blood today. This test is to consider my hormone level to see if I ovulate. I did it at an NHS Female Health Clinic in Camden. I didn't do it at my normal GP's because Dr Cooper is on holiday and I don't really like Dr Mason.

The clinic was depressing, as it would be. All these women having their bits and their boobs checked, or barren like me. One tries to maintain a positive outlook but it's not easy.

There was an old TV Times in the waiting pen (I won't call it a 'room', that would make it sound too cosy; it was just a sort of square of plastic chairs with a couple of broken toys on the floor). Anyway, the TV Times contained quite a good article about Carl Phipps, when he was still in that awful thing Fusilier! on ITV. Quite nice pictures, although I must say I prefer him now he's got longer hair. That crew cut was rather brutal. Still, his eyes haven't changed, still soft and limpid. He knows how nice they are, though, like David Essex used to. I'll bet he uses twinkle drops. The text went on and on about how girls are always getting terrible crushes on him. You can see how they might, but God, some women are stupid.

Dear etc.
Quite astonishing development at work today. I've been to *Downing Street*. I didn't meet the Prime Minister, but it's still amazing. It completely took my mind off my sperm test.

It happened like this. I'd just sat down to another morning of brooding over the lack of direction or passion in my career, leafing through another pile of scripts, wondering why the hell I can't seem to find it in me to write one myself, when Daphne said that the Channel Controller was on the line. Well of course I was thrilled, he could only be phoning personally to accept my dinner invitation. I was mentally leafing through Delia as I grabbed the phone and had already decided on the salmon mousse to start when it turned out Nigel had called about something even more exciting. He was phoning from Barcelona, where he was (of course) attending an international television festival. Perhaps the single greatest perk of being at the Beeb is the international festival circuit. Even I get to go to a few.

Anyway, it turned out that the Prime Minister's office had been on to the BBC about the PM appearing on *Livin' Large*. *Livin' Large* is our current Saturday morning kids' pop and fun show and every week they have a sort of interview spot where the children get to ask questions of a celebrity. Now, unbeknownst to me (surprise, surprise) our PR people had had a brilliant idea. (I must digress here to remark that the fact that our PR people had had a brilliant idea was shocking news in itself and evidence of how much things have changed around the old place. BBC press and public relations used to consist of an office with a large enthusiastic woman in it whom everyone ignored. Now it's a huge and entirely separate company called something like BBC Communications or Beeb COM, whose services I have to *hire*.)

Anyway, BBC Communications' idea had been to ask the Prime Minister if he would like to appear on *Livin' Large* and take some questions from 'the kids', thereby cutting through all that cynical adult bullshit and plugging in to the pure unsullied enthusiasm of youth.

The problem for Nigel (the Controller) was that Downing Street (which is a vigorous, 'can do' sort of a place these days) wanted to meet *today*! and no other later date would do because the PM's diary is chocka-block with summits and Cabinet crises right through till Christmas. Nigel had of course tried to get a flight back from Barcelona but there was a football match, or the French air-traffic controllers weren't letting anybody out of Europe today or something. Anyway, the upshot of it was that I would have to go to the meeting!

So this afternoon there I was, fronting up to the gates of Downing Street and being saluted through by a policeman. I must say it's bloody dowdy inside, or at least the bits I saw are. Amazing. The entrance hall is like a rundown hotel. Nobody could accuse any of the previous fifteen administrations of wasting money on decoration, because I swear that the place hasn't had a lick of paint since Chamberlain was waving his bit of paper about.

Anyway, after about ten minutes one of the PM's 'forward planning team' arrived, a young woman called Jo, who I think I recognised from her having been on *Question Time*. She ushered me into a small room with a chair and an old couch and some dirty coffee cups on a table. Here she 'briefed' me on the background to this particular 'outreach initiative'. She told me that the Prime Minister was Britain's newest, youngest, hippest prime minister since Lord Fol d'Rol in 1753 and that her office had the job of reminding people of this fact and generally demonstrating that the PM was neither fuddy nor duddy.

'We want the kids to know that their PM is not just the youngest, most energetic and most charismatic premier in British history but that he's also their mate, a regular bloke who likes pop music, wearing fashionable trousers, and comedy with proper swearing in it. Which is why we think it's important to place him on *Livin' Large*.'

'God yes, great idea,' I said, pathetically. It's amazing how even the proximity to power seduces a person.

'But in a dignified context,' Jo added firmly. 'No gunk tanks or "gotcha"s. It struck us that some kind of "youth summit" would be appropriate, you know, the boss chats with the future and all that.'

I said it sounded fantastic and that the BBC would be honoured.

'But nice questions, of course, not political. Questions about the issues that matter to kids. Pop music, fashion, computers, the Internet, that sort of thing.'

My mind reeled. This was *fantastic*. A genuine television event! Like Mrs Thatcher getting grilled about the *Belgrano* on *Nationwide* or the *Blue Peter* elephant shitting on John Noakes.

'This means a lot to the PM,' Jo continued. 'Dammit, as far as ordinary people are concerned politics is boring! The kids don't want a lot of old fuddy-duddies telling them what to do. We need to let people know that things have changed. Basically, it's very important to us that the premier gets a chance to point out that he likes pop music and that he actually plays the guitar. Will that be possible?'

Well, as far as I was concerned he could point out that he liked liver and onions and played the didgeridoo if he wanted, but I said that I thought everybody knew that the PM played the guitar; it seemed to have come up in every interview he'd ever done.

'People have short memories,' said Jo, 'besides which we need to make it clear that it's the electric guitar he plays, not some strummy-crummy, clicky-clacky, classical fuddy-duddy stuff.'

Well, I nodded and agreed and pretty soon Jo signalled that the meeting was over.

And so there it is. I, Sam Bell, have successfully brokered a historic live TV encounter between the PM and Generation Next. Trevor and I spent the afternoon trying to think of a good hook for the trailers. Trevor kept coming back to 'The Premier meets the Little People' but I'm sure that'd just make everyone think of leprechauns.

I must say this business has changed my attitude to my job entirely. I mean, if I was in the independent sector I certainly wouldn't be meeting the PM. Besides which, it has occurred to me that I could use my newly acquired inside knowledge of Downing Street to write a political thriller. It could be just the inspiration I need.

Good old Beeb, say I. When Tosser offers me a job I'll turn it down.

Dear Penny

Guess what! Sam nearly met the PM today. I could hardly believe it when he told me. Now that's what I call cool. I'm so proud of him. I'm married to a man who deals with the very highest in the land and from what he tells me he handled it incredibly well. The only thing that made me a bit sad is that if we never have kids then I won't be able to tell them that their dad once nearly met the PM. I really must stop thinking things like that.

Dear Self

Another bit of good news today. They tell me that I can produce my sperm sample at home! Yes, apparently sperm survives for one hour once outside the body (if kept warm) and as long as you can get the stuff back to the clinic within that time it doesn't matter where you pull one off the wrist. Great news.

Anyway, I went in to see Dr Cooper after work to pick up the sterilised pot (you can't just hand it in in a teacup). You can get the pots at Boots, but I'm not asking some sixteen-year-old girl for a sperm pot.

I must say I'm delighted about this 'home-tossing' development, generally much more relaxing I feel. Interesting as well, because this will be the first time in my entire life that I will be able to have a completely legitimate hand shandy. Amazing really, when I think back over all the sly ones I've had over the last twenty-five-odd years, all the lies and stratagems I resorted to, particularly as a child, and here I am positively being encouraged to abuse myself by the National Health Service. Ironic.

Dearest Penny Pen Pal

I think Sam's quite proud of his pot. He's put it on the mantelpiece in the sitting room like it was a darts trophy. I hope he doesn't imagine that's where he's going to fill it.

I adopted a baby gorilla today. She's called Gertrude. She was advertised in the Big Issue. You don't actually get to have Gertrude at home but for £90 they send you a picture of her and a certificate of adoption.

Sam gave me a rather patronising look when I told him about the adoption, which infuriated me because I acted out of ecological concern and for no other reason. I must say Gertrude does look very sweet. £90 well spent.

Dear Idiot

Rather an unfortunate development arose today workwise. And when I say 'rather' what I actually mean is 'unbelievably' and such a bugger coming so soon as it did after my Downing Street triumph.

I was sitting at work trying to read a treatment for a game show that had been sent in by Aiden Fumet on behalf of one of his acts. Something about contestants having to identify their partners by smelling their socks and looking at their bare bottoms pushed through holes in the set. The bit they seemed most proud of was that the game would also feature gay and lesbian couples. This alone, the authors seemed to feel, made the idea important, alternative and at the cutting edge.

Anyway, I was just applying my 'Loved it but seems more Channel Five to me' rubber stamp when the phone rang and Daphne told me it was someone called Tosser. Good, I thought. Tosser has always been a tiny bit patronising with me and I'd been looking forward to telling him that I was no longer in the market for employment so he'd have to head-hunt elsewhere. Sadly I was not to have this chance.

'Sam,' said Tosser, 'love to come to dinner, old boy, except I'm going skiing. But as it happens I'm not sure the invite was intended for me anyway. It said "Dear Nigel" on the note.'

Oh my God. Oh my Goddity God. Wrong envelopes!

A man did not need to be Stephen Hawking to work out the permutations of the plot. If I'd sent the dinner invitation to Tosser Tomkins, then I'd sent my enquiry about leaving the BBC to . . .

Daphne took another call.

'Sam. The Channel Controller on line two.'

I made my excuses to Tosser. 'In shit, Toss, got to go!'

And picked up the phone. Nigel's voice was cold as a penguin's arse.

'Sam, I have a memo here in which you address me as a tosser.'

'It was a mistake.'

'Yes,' said Nigel, 'it certainly was, mate.'

He went on to assure me that he was flattered that I had thought to seek his advice about whether I should leave the BBC and intrigued that I wanted his opinion on whether I should 'put myself about a bit'. He thanked me for my consideration and promised to give the matter his fullest and most immediate possible attention.

Click. Dial tone. Bugger.

Well, I couldn't leave it there, could I? I rushed along the corridor to his office. Television Centre is of course famously circular and I was so flustered that I missed the Controller's office entirely and had to run round the whole building again. I've done that before, of course, many times, but only when pissed and trying to find a Christmas party.

Responding to my urgent pleading (conveyed to him via one of his icy receptionists), Nigel allowed me into his office.

I can remember (just) that office when it was a friendly place. When the BBC really was a family. A family of fat, boozy old time-servers who earned little and drank much. Men and women who went through their entire lives without once wearing a stylish garment or having a fashionable haircut. Well, those faggy, boozy days are long gone and it's probably for the best. None of those jolly old boys would last a second in a climate where there're 500 channels competing for the audience and the money's all going to cable and satellite.

'Look, Nigel,' I said, still dizzy and clutching at a Golden Rose of Montreux for support and nearly cutting myself on its petals. 'This is awful, I wanted to invite you to dinner.'

He answered me with nothing more than a raised eyebrow.

'That note I sent you was meant for someone else. Simon Tomkins, you know, he was on the panel with you at last year's Edinburgh Television Festival. He was the one who said the BBC was an ageing tart trying to flag down a curb crawler on the information superhighway.'

'So what you're telling me, Sam, is that this note dissing the BBC' (he used the word 'dissing' even though he's a thirty-six-year-old white freckly philosophy graduate from Durham University) 'was actually intended as a job application to one of the foremost independent producers in the country?'

'Uhm,' I said.

Not good, but the best I could do at the time.

'Well?' said Nigel.

I was clearly going to have to do better than 'Uhm'.

'Oh, you know, just a punt, Nigel, really more to see what sort of shape the independent sector's in than anything else.'

He did not believe me even slightly.

'Uhm . . . did you see my emails regarding the Prime Minister? Tremendously successful meeting we . . .'

'Yes, I saw them,' said Nigel, and there our meeting ended save for Nigel assuring me that if I was at all unhappy at the BBC I had only to offer my resignation and he would consider it most favourably.

Needless to say, dinner was not discussed.

Dear Penny

Got my picture of Gertrude today and was slightly disappointed to discover that it's the same as the one in the Big Issue. *You'd think they'd have taken more than one shot of her. Still, at least it's a better print.*

I do have to admit, Pen, that I'm just a little bit concerned that those less environmentally aware than myself (my mother, for instance) might consider my adoption of Gertrude as reflective of my hopes for a child. This is definitely not the case. The plight of the mountain gorillas is an international tragedy and my involvement in the issue is entirely political.

Dear Book

Lucy has put a picture of a baby gorilla into a clipframe and placed it on the mantelpiece. She says we've adopted it. I'm now rather worried that her nurturing instincts are getting the better of her.

I went for a quickie in the BBC club bar after work today. The club bar always depresses me these days. It's been franchised out and now has a name, Shakers or Groovers or possibly Gropers, I'm not sure, I'm always pissed when I try to read the beer mats. Anyway, I bumped into George and Trevor at the bar and they had clearly been sniggering about something when I approached, but on seeing me they stopped dead. It could only mean one thing. My arse-up with the Channel Controller is now public knowledge and it will only be a matter of time before the whole incident is recounted in *Private Eye*. Not good, I fear.

Still, it's taken my mind off the sperm test.

Dear Penny

Sam's a bit quiet and rather down at the moment. I know he had a row at work with that appalling Channel Controller. (Who else but an arse could spend £7 million of public money adapting Finnegans Wake*? FINNEGANS WAKE! I ask you. A road map of Birmingham is easier to follow.*

I do feel sorry for Sam. I mean he really does seem a bit depressed, but it's so hard to know how to help. The fact is he doesn't want any help. He'd rather read his newspaper. If it was me I'd want tons of attention, in fact I do want tons of attention. Sam, however, neither craves it nor gives it very much and this leaves me feeling in extreme want of warmth. This evening I knew something was on his mind and I tried to reach out to him but he'd have none of it. He just drank beer and cracked silly jokes about if we do have a kid we'll have to send it out to work at the age of seven because we'll be so poor. Ha ha. So now we're going to be penniless as well as infertile. Hilarious.

Dear Sam

Well, it's done. Conjugal visit to hand completed. Funny to think that my sperm is in some laboratory somewhere waiting to be tested, darting this way and that for the benefit of a total stranger. Hope they're looking after it, keeping it warm. I feel very slightly paternal about the stuff.

Producing it was a close-run thing. Originally we had planned for Lucy to attend possibly even lending a hand, so to speak. This was her idea. She doesn't really like the thought of me having sex without her, even if it's only on my own. She's convinced that I'll not give her a single thought throughout the whole proceedings but offer my entire fantastical erotic being to Winona Ryder, and of course she's right. Well, for God's sake! I get to sleep with Lucy every night, I only get to do it with Winona when required to produce a sperm sample. I tried to explain this, saying that psychologists had established that an uninhibited fantasy life was part of a healthy, monogamous sexual relationship. Well, Lucy wasn't having any of it. In fact she acted quite hurt, which I find truly extraordinary.

Thank goodness I didn't tell her I'd also been planning to invite Tiffany from *EastEnders*, the Corrs and Baby Spice to the party.

Anyway, as I said, Lucy seemed to feel it was important that she be involved in the process, so this morning when we woke up I went and got the pot from the sitting-room mantelpiece. I handed it over to Lucy, got back into bed and took up my limp appendage whilst she held the pot out expectantly, clearly anticipating an immediate outpouring.

Well, I'm here to tell anyone who cares to listen that masturbation with an audience (particularly an impatient one that hasn't yet had a cup of tea) is not easy. I felt a complete prick, both personally and of course literally. There I was kneeling on the bed, portion in palm with Lucy holding out the pot like some kind of beggar, and nothing was happening. Lucy, bless her, had a rather self-conscious go and disported herself about the bed a bit, you know, cupping breasts in hands and pouting, that sort of thing. I really don't know which of us felt more stupid. After about thirty seconds I could see she was getting bored and beginning to think about breakfast. It was as much as she could do to stop herself looking at her watch. Quite obviously it was never going to work. I love her and I fancy her but a fellow can feel self-conscious even with a woman he's shared a bed with for six years. I just could not get things going and in the end I had to decamp into the spare room.

Anyway, left to myself I came up with the goods, so to speak. I say 'goods', if that isn't too grand an expression to describe the sad little sample I produced. I couldn't believe it. It looked pathetic, dribbling down the inside of a plastic pot. Like a sparrow sneezed.

Interesting, really, how vulnerable the whole exercise made me feel. I felt genuinely exposed, like my very manhood was being tested. I'd always presumed I'm a pretty relaxed, modern sort of bloke. I didn't think I'd ever bought into any of that macho bullshit about being a big noise in the trouser department. Yet there I was staring at my sample thinking about trying to eke it out with a bit of flour and water.

I suddenly realised that I'd spent about two minutes worrying about how little I'd produced and of course I only had an hour to hand it in before the stuff died. I had to get to the clinic or I'd have the whole business to do again.

Now the advice that Dr Cooper had given me was to pop the pot down my pants, because at all costs its contents must be kept warm. In fact he had told me that if possible I was to work it into a warm crevice, which I assume is doctor code for shove it up your bum. It's a very strange feeling waddling along the street trying to hail a taxi with a pot of sperm clenched between your buttocks. I was immediately consumed with the irrational conviction that everybody knew what was going on. Policemen seemed to glare, toddlers tugged at their mothers' skirts and pointed, office girls veered across the pavement apparently to keep well out of my way. Perhaps it was my desperate, hurried air that drew people's eye. Let's face it, a man is hardly going to look his most relaxed and urbane when he is charging along the street, agonisingly aware that his sperm has only minutes left to live.

Eventually I spotted an empty cab but inevitably another bloke spotted it too. We both dashed for it (well he dashed, I waddled) and arriving at the same time we wrestled over the handle together.

'Mine, I think,' I said.

'Well, you think wrong,' said the man. 'Bugger off and get your own cab. I'm having this one.'

Normally I would have given up without a fight but I was desperate by this time, having only twenty-eight minutes left.

'Look,' I said, 'I have to have this cab; it's a matter of life and death.'

'Tough,' said the man. 'I've got a very important meeting.'

'Well, I've got some warm sperm up my arse and it's dying.'

I'll have to remember that one. The bloke let go of that door handle like it was a live snake.

It wasn't an easy journey, unable to sit down as I was. I had to curl up on the back seat in a sort of foetal position and I could see that the driver didn't like it. But we got there in the end, with a few minutes to spare even, and I rushed into the clinic and handed in my sample. I was so desperate to get there in time that I just rushed through the front door and went straight up to the reception desk. It was only as I was actually fishing the pot out of the back of my trousers that I realised that it might have been more tactful and polite to have retrieved the thing in private. The nurse stared at it as if to say, 'And you want me to touch that now?' before going off to get some rubber gloves and a bargepole.

My God, I can't believe I've just spent half an hour writing about taking sperm to a clinic! If I could only be half this committed at work I might not be in the shit I'm in. Things are still very edgy at the office. It seems to me only a matter of time before Nigel finds a way to get rid of me, and if I'm honest I'm really not particularly employable. Lunch-eating is not a skill for which there is much demand these days; it's not the eighties.

I sent another note to Tosser (this time I checked the envelope three times) to try asking him again about a job. I didn't bother with any matey-matey, beating-about-the-bush stuff this time. I just basically asked the bastard for a job. Hope I didn't sound desperate. Does 'Give us a job, you bastard,' sound desperate, I wonder?

Looking back over the last few pages I've written, I've come to the surprising conclusion that the American expert Lucy's friend Sheila saw on *Oprah* was right: writing letters to yourself is actually a very good idea. I came home today all fired up with my success at delivering the sample on time and looking forward to telling Lucy the story (particularly the bit about hailing the cab), but she seemed all distant and distracted. She said it had been a difficult day at work and she didn't feel like talking. Fair enough. I almost always feel like that. Still, it's helped to write it down.

Strange, Lucy not wanting to talk. I hope she isn't working too hard. Actors can be such pains.

Dearest Penny

I have to tell you that something very strange happened at work today, which I hardly like to write about. I was on my own again. Sheila is still bronchial (self-prescribed cure: forty cigarettes a day) and Joanna is in LA. There I am on my own and who should turn up but, yes! Carl Phipps, all brooding and Byronic looking in a big coat. Well, before I know it he's telling me that fame is a lonely burden and asking me out to lunch! Extraordinary. I can't imagine why he picked on me. I'm sure I haven't given him the slightest indication that I enjoy his company or find him remotely attractive.

As it happened I couldn't go out with him because I was all alone and who would man the phones? So I told him that I was too busy, and I said it slightly hoitily. I rather resent the assumption that mine is the sort of job that you can just drift in and out of, even though it is. 'Fair enough,' says Lord Phipps and off he goes in a flurry of brooding, wuthering menace, and I thought that was the end of it.

Well! Ten minutes later he's back with a positive hamper from Fortnum's full of fantastic stuff from their food hall. Oysters, olives, foreign nibbles and champagne, no less! He said he was celebrating getting a recall for a very big American film. Usual thing, dastardly Brit to play villain. It seems that the English are the only racial group left on earth whom absolutely nobody minds seeing marmalised. Honestly, ten years ago it was costume drama or nothing for our boys. If nobody was making Robin Hood or Ivanhoe, they didn't work. Now they get to crash helicopters into Bruce Willis!

Anyway, so there we were in the office, just the two of us, and I asked Heathcliff, if he was celebrating, didn't he have someone special to celebrate with? Do you want to know what he said to that, Penny? He said that that was exactly what he was doing!!!! Arggh!

Oh, my God! I could feel myself going beetroot and that rash on my neck coming back (when I was a teenager, if ever a boy asked me out I invariably instantly looked as though my throat had just been cut).

Anyway, of course I told him not to be silly and asked him what he meant by such familiarities. Well, he didn't say anything, he just smiled in a sort of soft way that he knew brought out his dimples, and took my hand.

Yes!

Sorry about the breathless style, Penny, but I am much moved.

Because here, I'm afraid, is the terrible thing (none but you must ever know, Penny). I did not withdraw my hand! I left it there and we just sort of, well, looked at each other and his eyes went all melty (just like his close-ups in The Tenant of Wildfell Hall when he really was very good). He looked like the dispossessed lord of a bleak moorland estate. God knows what I looked like— an electrified rabbit with a rash, no doubt.

Then, and I don't know if I imagined it, but I think, in fact I'm sure, I felt his finger playing in the palm of my hand which, as far as I know, is silent code for 'I would not be averse to rogering you, ma'am.'

If this is true, I just can't BELIEVE the man's cheek. He knows I'm married. Married to a good, solid, honest, ordinary, boring, far better man than he, if not quite so dishy, bloke.

Anyway, after a bit I did take my hand away, thank God. I don't know what would have happened if I hadn't. I think he would have kissed me. And then short of making a scene I don't know what I would have done. He is our biggest client, after all. I probably would have had to kiss him back, which would have been terrible! Instead I thanked him for the lunch in an extremely cold 'not today, thank you' voice and said that I had to get on with my work. To which he shrugged, smiled a knowing little smile, picked up his fan mail and left.

I must say, I feel most peculiar.

But also very angry.

I love my husband, dull, sexless bore though he may be. What is more, I want to have his children, something that is not proving easy, and I can do without arrogant actors trying to interfere with my already unbalanced hormones.

Dear Sam

No news on sperm.

No reply from Tosser re him giving me an important new job.

My life is on tenterhooks, whatever tenterhooks may be.

I saw Nigel the Controller today and he didn't remind me about my appalling *faux pas* over the letters, which I think is a good sign. Mind you, he didn't really have an opportunity because it wasn't just him and me, he'd summoned all the commissioning editors in the Entertainment Group (if indeed that is what we are), plus the finance and marketing people, for a big strategy meeting, so there were about ten of us festooned about his office. The subject of the meeting was the BBC's plans to get into movies, so it should have been an exciting discussion, but with the cloud hanging over me I couldn't get worked up.

'Nobody watches television nowadays,' Nigel began, 'or at least none of my friends do. Television is wallpaper. Television is fast food. Movies are the millennial art form. Where do you think I'm going with this? Come on, come on, anyone!'

'The BBC should be getting into movies,' said a young woman with pink hair and Nigel positively beamed at her.

'Exactly, Yaz,' he said and proceeded with great self-importance to rap out the names of recent British movie hits.

'*Four Weddings, Full Monty, Trainspotting, Lock Stock and Two Smoking Barrels*. British movies have never been healthier. There were at least three last year that the Americans quite liked. We need to be a part of that revolution. We need to be making movies.'

Everyone seemed terribly excited at this idea but I always thought the BBC was a television company and said so.

'Boots is a chemist, Sam. That doesn't stop them selling chicken tikka sandwiches with yogurt and mint dressing. Jesus Christ, Sam! At least try setting your brain for the twenty-first century! As Britain's premier media provider, the BBC is perfectly placed to connect up with the real cutting-edge talent that is out there making New Britain hip. We need to interface with these people. We have the resources to make films, we have the budgets to make films, all we need is the ideas.'

Later, discussing the meeting in the BBC bar, George and Trevor were very excited about it. After all, for people like us who spend our time commissioning new ways of humiliating the public for the early

Saturday evening schedules, the idea of making proper films is pretty seductive. I tried hard to join in with their enthusiasm but I couldn't summon up much jollity. Jealousy really, I suppose. I don't want to commission films; I want to write one.

George and Trevor saw things differently.

'This is your big chance!' they said. 'Commission yourself. Write a script and green-light it. The man's crying out for ideas and he's asking us to find them. You'll never get an opportunity like this again!'

For a moment I was almost seduced, but then I remembered two things. Firstly my current relationship with the Controller does not lead me to imagine that he'd accept a script with my name on it. And even if he did, *what* script? I haven't written a thing in years. I've forgotten *how* to write and even if I hadn't I have nothing to write about.

They say comedy is about conflict and pain. Where's my conflict? Where's my pain? I'm a boring bloke in a boringly happy marriage. Apart from my own monumental lack of talent and an impending sperm result there isn't a cloud on my horizon.

Dear Penny

I simply cannot believe it. Sam handed in his sample three days ago and since then he has been jumpy as a kitten. He pounces on the post in the morning even though he knows the result will take five days. He grabs at any envelope that comes through the door. He tears them open in terror that they might also be concealing a failed sperm test certificate. I swear that's what he thinks he's going to get, a certificate, possibly with a ribbon on it or a red wax seal, saying 'sperm test FAILED'.

Anyway, my blood test result came through with the second post and it seems my body has passed that particular hurdle, insomuch as the indications are that I ovulate. Hooray and whoopidydingdong. There are now only 14 million things that could be wrong with my sad, dysfunctional tubes. Sometimes it really is hard to be a woman.

I had to send off loads of signed pictures of Carl 'Will you fuck me for a sandwich?' Phipps today. I have very mixed emotions about that whole episode. Obviously I'd never do anything about it, I mean obviously. Nonetheless it's quite flattering. At thirty-four and married it's rather nice to discover that one could still get laid if one wanted to which one doesn't and one certainly wouldn't even if one did.

When I told Sam that my blood test indicated healthy ovulation he acted most unpleasantly. Instead of being pleased that at least one part of my body functions as it should, he immediately took it as proof that he's going to fail his sperm test and that he's some kind of sexless eunuch.

Yo, stud!

Yes! Yes! *Yes*!!! All RIGHT! Result, my son! Here we go, here we *go*! Result! Passed! Passed my sperm test. The letter arrived this morning.

At first I didn't want to open it. It was just like my 'A' levels. I was grape-picking in France and I had to ring home and get my mum to open the envelope. I can remember walking round that French phone box for half an hour, too nervous to make the call. Of course I couldn't hang around for half an hour this morning because I had to go to work, but I did make Lucy open the envelope and read the letter for me.

I must say things started pretty grimly. There was no personal element at all, no 'Dear sir,' no 'Brace yourself, mate.' Just a printed form on which they fill in your results with a ballpoint pen. So much for our more caring society. They do not even offer counselling.

Well, Book, at first I thought that all was lost. The very opening line (under the deceptively bland heading 'motility') said '30% sluggish'. Honestly, that was the very word they used. *Sluggish*. A horrible, horrible word, reminiscent of slimy snail-like creatures that can't be bothered moving their arses on garden paths in order to avoid being stamped on. Sluggish! And if they're going to use unscientific language couldn't they have thought of a more friendly expression? Like 'relaxed', perhaps, or 'unhurried'? If they'd told me I had relaxed sperm I could have handled it. Cool, laid-back sperm. That would be fine. But 'sluggish'? It's almost as if they were trying to be unpleasant.

Anyway, the next line was worse! Yes, worse! I nearly cried. It said '41% swimming in the wrong direction'! I mean, what a thing to say about the very stuff of a man's loins! My head was spinning. Then I thought, 'Hang on, this is ridiculous!' This test is rigged. How are they supposed to know what's the right direction, for heaven's sake? They're in a plastic pot! I had this vision of all my sperm desperately groping about hither and thither, banging their heads against the sides of the container, lashing their tails around like fish in a bucket.

By the end of the letter I was ready to slit my wrists.

In conclusion it said, '90% useless'! Bad swimmers, poor motility. A load of rubbish in general. So now the full and terrible truth was upon me. I'm not a man. I've failed my sperm test!

I was already asking myself whether they'd let me take it again. I mean, if it was like your driving test, I had four goes at that. I was on the very point of phoning my MP and demanding a full recount when Lucy pointed out that stamped at the bottom of the form in big letters was the word NORMAL.

Oh, the relief! It turns out that my pathetic percentages are par for the course, that pretty much all sperm is 90 per cent rubbish. Apparently there's only a couple of decent wrigglers in an entire wristful. For all the macho pride and posturing of us men, most sperms just simply aren't up to it. They're sluggish. They're stupid. They're always wandering off in the wrong direction. Lucy said they sound exactly like a pub full of blokes, which was *quite* funny, I suppose.

Anyway, that was it. Passed. Normal. I was so pleased I danced round the kitchen. Then I thought, hang on, normal? Ordinary? A bit disappointing, really. I mean, let's face it, 'Superb' would have been a better result. Probably just an off day. Still, whatever, I'm off the hook.

Dear Penny

Well, I must say I did laugh at Sam's letter and not just because it nearly made him cry either. The bit about 41 per cent swimming in the wrong direction! Well, I ask you. I'm surprised it wasn't 100 per cent.

Anyway, armed with both our test results I took an hour off work and went to see Dr Cooper and he said that having established that nothing obvious is wrong with either of us, the problem might be that we are incompatible. (I felt like saying that this thought had crossed my mind too, but I didn't.) Dr Cooper says that my juices and Sam's sperm may simply not like each other.

I was a bit taken aback at the thought. The idea of all Sam's seed drowning in agony in the hell waters of my poisonous vagina made me quite teary. Like a murderess. Well, it seems that in order to discover whether this horrible possibility is in fact the case we must do a postcoital test. Which basically means Sam and me having it off and then a doctor having a look at the aftermath. Quite frankly, one of the most horrible suggestions anyone has ever put to me.

What has to happen is that Sam and I must get up early on the appointed day and get straight down to business. This is not regular morning practice for us, I hasten to add, both of us preferring a cup of tea and a slice of toast first thing. Once I've been properly serviced, so to speak, I have to go to some ghastly specialist clinic or other and up me the doctors will go. Surprise, surprise. Who would be a woman? Looking back over the years of smear tests, non-specific infections, fertility bizzo and all, my poor old muff has definitely been a well-trodden path for the medical profession.

God, I hate this. Why can't I just get pregnant!?

I rang Drusilla from work and asked her when the next full moon was. I'm not going to do it on Primrose Hill, but I can't afford to discount anything.

Dear Sam

Going to dinner at Trevor and Kit's tonight. Had the usual hoo-hah about what to wear. Not me, of course. I know what to wear. Trousers and a shirt. But Lucy finds these decisions much more perplexing. What's more, she insists on dragging me into her dilemmas and then blaming me for them! She stands there in her underwear and says 'Which do you think, the red or the blue?' Well, I know of course the clever thing would be to refuse to answer, because there's no chance in this world or the next of saying the right thing. Nonetheless, inevitably I have a stab at it.

'Uhm, the red?'

'So you don't like the blue?'

'I didn't say that.'

'I was going to wear the blue.'

'Wear the blue, then.'

'Well, I can't now, can I? Since you obviously think I look horrible in it . . . Now I've got to start thinking all over again. . .'

Madness, absolute madness, particularly since it's only Trevor and Kit, for heaven's sake. George and Melinda were invited too but they couldn't get a baby sitter. I pointed out to Lucy that that sort of thing will happen to us if ever we do score. I don't actually think that she's thought through the whole social side of having babies at all. I said to her, here we are, two highly educated, fully rounded people and yet we are *desperate* to totally subsume our existence in the abstract concept of a being who will suck us dry physically, emotionally and financially and will not even be able to form a decent sentence for at least five years.

Sam's in the bathroom shaving, having just delivered a little monologue on the downside of having children, and I'm trying very hard not to get upset because I've already done my make-up. How could he be so thoughtless and selfish? He doesn't mean to be cruel, I know, but he just doesn't understand. I was born to have children. There's never been a moment in my life when I didn't want, some day, to be a mother. When he talks like that, as if children are some kind of lifestyle option to be taken or left, I feel a million miles away from him. Children are the reason for being alive.

I just reminded Lucy that kids are, in the end, just another lifestyle option and I think I made her feel better.

On the other hand. Sometimes I must admit that I catch a glimpse of Lucy, or look at her while she's asleep, and I think how pretty she is, and how much I love her. And I think how much more I would like to love her and how I would like to find new and more complete ways of expressing that love. That's when I think that perhaps having a baby might be the most wonderful thing in the world.

Dear Penny

Last night's dinner with Trevor and his boyfriend Kit was great fun, despite Sam getting me a bit upset before we left.

Sam and Trevor are of course colleagues in lunch at the Beeb and are terribly funny when they start sneering at the more awful of the artists they have to hand over all our licence fees to. Trevor was telling us about these ghastly Oxbridge-educated yobbos whose job is to make jokes about football on some beery late-night sports chat show. It's called A Game of Two Halves *and it's Trevor's biggest hit. Apparently the idea of the show (I haven't seen it) is that clips of various sporting events are played and then the regular panel members compete with each other to see who can mention their penises most often.*

It was nice to have a really good laugh. We always do with Trevor and Kit. Trevor is good at taking the piss out of himself and it seems he's become a victim of his own success with this alternative sports quiz he's developed. Two of the blokes on it have inevitably been picked up for representation by the bull-like Aiden Fumet. Fumet has been to see Trevor and explained that, on the strength of their current 'ballistic' status, his 'turns' must immediately be given their own sitcoms. When Trevor asked if before committing hundreds of thousands of pounds worth of licence payers' money to an untried project it might be possible to see a script, Aiden Fumet threatened that any suggestion of artistic interference from Trevor or the 'BB-fucking-C' would result in Aiden Fumet's entire 'stable' being no longer available to the Corporation.

Trevor, George and I all agree that artists are a lot more arrogant with the BBC than they used to be. I suppose it's down to the incredible diversity of employment options that anybody half good (or not even) is presented with these days. I mean, there was a time when there was only one channel and anybody, no matter how talented, who wanted to be on telly did so by the grace of the BBC. That was how we used to get those incredible long runs of things. People did what they were told, and if that meant doing sixty episodes of the same sitcom then that was what they did.

Trevor is always good at telling stories about work because you see he doesn't really care about it very much, unlike Sam, who cares desperately and actually thinks that you can 'plan' comedy hits.

Anyway, then Sam (possibly trying to be funnier than Trevor) brought up our impending postcoital business, which I suppose I didn't really mind because Trevor and Kit are very good pals. Although it is slightly disconcerting to discuss one's vaginal juices at the dinner table. Trevor and Sam were both being most amusing, saying things about vaginal genocide and Sam's sperm swimming back from the fray carrying little white flags.

We actually laughed until we cried and then I'm afraid to admit I nearly did cry a bit because the truth is, hilarious though it may be, it isn't very funny wanting kids and not being able to get them.

Kit was so lovely. He's a set designer for the theatre (mainly fringe; he told me that recently he had to do Burnham Wood moving to Dunsinane for about five quid). Anyway, Kit asked what we would do if we failed the test and it turned out that my body really did reject Sam's sperm. Well, before we knew it we were discussing Trevor making a donation! Ha! Apparently, Trevor has already done it for a lesbian couple in Crouch End that he and Kit met on the Internet. He explained that you don't actually have to do it, you know, have sex together ('Not even for you, Lucy love,' said Trevor), you just use a turkey baster! Seems incredible to me, but apparently it's true.

Sam laughed at all this, but I could see he was a bit taken aback at the idea.

Life is becoming rather strange. My wife appears to be plotting to conceive with my gay friends using a turkey baster. That'll be an interesting story to tell my mother over the next Christmas dinner.

It has made me think, though. I mean, what if Sam and I aren't compatible? What are the alternatives? Adoption? Artificial insemination? Oh well, I suppose I'll just have to try not to think about it.

Dear Sam

A sort of half-exciting thing happened at work today. It started off very exciting, but then got slightly less so. I was just completing a particularly difficult level of *Tomb Raider* on my PC when Daphne looked in and said that the Director General's office had been on and would Lucy and I care to go to dinner at Broadcasting House!

Well, *would I*? I mean the DG's dinners at BH are legendary. He has cabinet ministers, captains of industry, footballers, bishops, *everyone*. But *never*, to the best of my knowledge, has a lowly executive producer of broken comedy and sitcom been invited. The DG must have heard of my trip to Downing Street. I doubt he could have missed it: I've talked about it loudly in every single nook and cranny of the Corporation.

Anyway, for whatever reason, we'd been invited. We were 'in'.

'When is it?' I said. 'I'll cancel everything. If my mother dies, she dies alone.'

'Tomorrow night,' she said.

Slightly disheartening. Obviously an invitation at such short notice means we're to be fill-ins for somebody who has jacked. Still, I thought, I'd never have expected to have been asked at all.

Then the phone rang. It was George.

'Guess what?' he said. 'Melinda and I got asked to a DG's dinner for tomorrow night! Obviously we're a fill-in for somebody who jacked but, still, pretty amazing. The appalling bugger of it is we can't go! Melinda just can't get a sitter she trusts. There's only two sitters in the world it seems who aren't mass murderers and they're both busy.'

'When did you get your invitation?' I asked.

'Yesterday, late afternoon,' said George. 'I rang the DG's office first thing this morning to say we couldn't do it. I could scarcely believe I was actually turning down the Director General this morning.'

After George got off the phone I tried not to be miffed. 'Who cares?' I thought. 'So what if I was second choice?'

And then Trevor rang.

'You're not going to believe this,' he said, 'but Kit and I got invited to have dinner at BH with the DG and we can't go! His office rang first thing this morning. It's for tomorrow night so obviously we were to be the replacement for someone who's dropped out, but all the same! Pretty amazing, eh? I had to ring them back half an hour ago to decline. It was like pulling teeth but there's no way Kit can break his rule.'

Kit, sadly, is HIV positive and although he's doing incredibly well he does have to be careful about overexertion. He and Trevor have a strict rule that they have only one social occasion a week.

'And we used it up having *you* to dinner,' Trevor said, and I must say that I didn't much like his tone. We parted slightly coldly.

So there it is. Lucy and I are to be the replacement for a replacement for a replacement. Nonetheless we are going to dinner with the DG, which is not to be sniffed at. I'll have to make sure that Nigel hears about it. He can hardly sack me if I'm friends with the PM *and* the DG.

Tosser also phoned me today. No chance of a job with his company, which was a bit dispiriting, I must admit. I had thought, vainly, that he'd jump at the chance of recruiting me, that I'd be rather a prestige signing for his company. You know, top BBC man and all that, but obviously he doesn't think so. 'The BBC is just another player,' he said to me, which is a bloody ridiculous thing to say considering the BBC is the largest broadcaster in the world and he has a floor and a half in Dean Street.

Dear Pen Pal

I'm writing this having just got back from dinner at Broadcasting House. The Director General was hosting one of his evenings for the great and the good so obviously we'd only been invited to pad out the numbers (Sam did some spying and it turned out that the Editor of the Daily Telegraph had jacked at the last moment. Sam said other people had been asked to fill in before us, but he was very vague about who they were—very important people, he said).

Anyway, when I say we had dinner with the Director General we barely actually spoke to him, of course, being at the other end of the table, but it was still very nice. BH really is a fantastic building, even though some idiot or other ripped most of the Deco out in the fifties and replaced it with the interior of a Soviet prison.

Of course actually having dinner there is particularly magical. It takes you back to another age, like the twenties or something. You start with drinks in a sort of antechamber and then go through into a marvellous dining room, all wood lined and shimmering crystal. I got sat next to a bishop who was very nice, and a junior member of the Shadow Cabinet who was not. He immediately made it quite clear that he was not happy at being seated next to a mere 'wife' and, what's more, a mere nobody's wife to boot.

We attempted smalltalk for about a minute.

Me: 'So you're in the Shadow Cabinet? How fascinating. Although I always imagine that being in opposition must be very frustrating.'

Him: 'Hmm, yes. So your husband works in television comedy, you say? I really don't think that any of that rubbish is funny any more. There hasn't been anything remotely decent since Yes, Minister.'

After that he completely ignored me until the cheese, by which time he was pissed enough to try a bit of bored flirting.

Him: 'I expect with you both being in showbusiness there must be terrible temptations. Do you ever get jealous? Does he?'

I wasn't having any of it. 'What a strange question,' I said, not only hoitily but also fairly toitily and turned back to the bishop, with whom I was getting on like a house on fire. He must have been ninety-three if he was a day and he was telling me about his hobby, which was collecting eighteenth-century Japanese erotic art! Extraordinary! Where does the church get them? What's more, while describing a porcelain figurine of a naked ninja (in rather too much detail), he squeezed my leg under the table! The randy old goat. Sam was scarcely being any better than the bishop. He was sitting next to this tart with extraordinary knockers (not entirely her own, I fancy) and I could see him just ogling them. I mean, at first he'd at least tried to be discreet, although I knew what he was up to, of course, all that reaching for the salt and passing the bread. Sad, really. And after a few glasses of wine he just gave up any pretence at subtlety and started simply staring at them with his tongue hanging out. I've no idea who this overly boobed slapper was, she was only *about twenty-three or four and clearly a second wife to someone, but I didn't find out whose. I looked for a man with a smug smile on his face but there were too many contenders.*

All in all, what with Sam drooling and the shadow minister sneering and the bishop's hand beginning to gather a tiny bit too much confidence, it was a great relief when the DG made us all move round for the pudding. I ended up talking to his wife, who seemed very nice. I found myself telling her all about Carl Phipps. Not the hand-holding lunch, obviously, but about being an agent and representing him. I must admit I suddenly heard myself being altogether more enthusiastic about him than I'd intended to be.

On the way home Sam insisted that he wasn't pissed, but he did his usual pissed thing of worrying about whether he'd put his foot in it to anyone. I said he might as well have put his foot into that woman's cleavage because he'd done everything else but climb into it (which he denied, pathetically). Sam always comes home from parties worrying that he's said something wrong or offended someone. He's so bad he's got me doing it as well. Sometimes we spend the whole cab ride asking each other if we were embarrassing and reassuring each other that we weren't. It's sad.

Anyway, he'd better not have been too pissed. He knows damn well what he's got to do tomorrow morning.

Dear etc.

I *think* it went all right tonight. Bit worried I might have said the wrong thing. As far as I can recall I only spoke to the Director General twice. I said, 'Good evening,' at the beginning and later on I said, 'Yes, I think things are fairly healthy in the arena of entertainment and comedy at the moment.' I don't think either of those comments could be misconstrued.

What's more, I *certainly* didn't spend the evening staring at that woman's tits, as I've been unfairly accused of. I mean they were *there*, for God's sake! I simply couldn't avoid the things. I could hardly sit and look at the ceiling all evening, could I?

Anyway. One thing is for absolutely sure. I am *not pissed*. I was *very* careful about that. Because, as I'm well aware, I have to provide a shag in the morning. What is more I intend to make it a cracker, because I really love Lucy. I really really do and tomorrow, before I go to work, I am going to make love to her so passionately and so beautifully that she will remember it always, because I love her.

Dear Penny

This morning I think I had the worst shag I have had in thirteen and a half years of moderately continuous lovemaking. I doubt that I shall ever forget it.

Sam reeked of stale booze and fags, plus I was still seething about him spending the whole evening staring down that enormous cleavage, which he continued to deny, of course.

Anyway, we both knew we would have to go through with it. The postcoital examination had been booked for ten and you do not mess with a confirmed appointment on the NHS.

I had just decided to ignore the beery, faggy fug that surrounded him when Sam said, 'I'm afraid we're really going to have to be quick, darling, because I've got a meeting.'

Well, I screamed at him! 'Oh, I'm so sorry!' I said. 'Trying to start a family when you've got a meeting! Perhaps if I phoned your secretary we could schedule our sex life into your diary. Just in pencil, of course. Wouldn't want to be inflexible about it or put you under any pressure!' Sarcastic, I know, but I was furious.

Anyway then, of course, the inevitable happened and he couldn't do it. I told him to think about Ms 'look at my gargantuanly fulsome funbags' from the previous night but he got all angry and said that he didn't wish to think about other women, but that bonking to order was not as bloody easy as it might appear.

Well, to cut a short story even shorter he just about managed it. Actually I felt a bit sorry for him. I could see he felt he'd let me down a bit so I said he wasn't to worry because it wasn't his fault that he had a small and unreliable penis.

I really did mean it nicely but it just seemed to put him in an even worse mood.

So, Sam got dressed and went to his meeting, and I went off to the clinic. Obviously worried about all the stuff falling out on the way. Horrible thought. I didn't want to have to go through the whole ghastly palaver of a pre-postcoital examination bonk again.

So there I was, hobbling to the car and trying not to cough. Once in the car it was worse. It is simply not possible to change gear with your legs crossed, and trying to do the whole journey in third makes things very juddery when you pull away at the lights, which of course shakes things down even more.

Then when I got to the clinic the road was blocked by a car with its hazard lights on.

I hate hazard lights.

They should be bloody well banned. People think that if they have them on then everything is all right. They can do exactly as they please.

So of course I had to reverse back up the street (with people reversing behind me, and making V-signs as if it was my fault). By a miracle I managed to park in a space exactly the same size as my car. I don't know how I did it. Extraordinary achievement and it only took seventy-two manoeuvres. Thank God for power steering!

Anyway, out I got and hobbled back along the street to the clinic, still trying to keep my knees together, past the car with its hazards on. I'm afraid to say that I gave way to anger and snarled at the bloke at the wheel, shouting, 'You're blocking the road, you fool!' which was rather stating the obvious.

So, feeling all hot and bothered I announced myself at the reception desk. Most embarrassing.

'Hello. I've come to see if my vagina poisons my husband's sperm.'

I didn't actually say that but the receptionist knew anyway. She smiled wearily and told me to take a seat.

I only had time to get halfway through a fascinating article in Woman's Own *about Prince Andrew's exciting engagement to his new fiancée Sarah Ferguson. I must say medical waiting rooms are incredibly nostalgic places. They are the only places where you can pretend that the Princess of Wales is still alive.*

So anyway, then it was into the torture chamber and all the usual appalling cervical intrusions, legs up in the stirrups, fanny prised apart, invaded and inspected. There was a student there as well, having a good old stare.

I hate that!

I absolutely loathe *it. I mean I know they have to learn and all that but I really can do without spotty teenagers wanting to mess around between my legs. It reminded me of being back at school.*

Anyway, what with one thing and another I was in a foul mood as they slapped on the freezing cold lubrication and the doctor shoved up his horrid contraption, cold again, of course, and began scraping out my cervix. And what did he say? Well, of course, he said what they always say.

'Do try to relax.'

Oh well, of course. A perfect stranger is sticking bits of cold, greasy metal up your vagina, staring deep within, tutting in a worried manner and then asking an adolescent boy what he thinks of it, but do try to relax.

Normally these things take ages to come through but amazingly the doctor whipped his spatula out of me, slapped the smear under the microscope and gave me the result there and then. Satisfactory, he said. Everything had turned out fine. Except, that is, for the fact that when he extracted the metal duck it made a disgusting loud wet raspberry noise, which was excruciatingly embarrassing. It's all that jelly they use and he used far too much. Every time I braked on the way home I slid off the car seat.

Anyway, as I say, the news is good. Sam and I are definitely chemically compatible. I am of course very pleased about this because despite his being a pig I do love him and I had been dreading having to pop round to our gay friends with a turkey baster and asking them to fill it full of sperm.

So there we are. It seems that compatibility is not the problem. Nor is my ovulation and nor is the motility of his sperm.

And yet we are still not preg! Why? WHY? Bloody why?

It is completely baffling and most distressing. What's more, we're running out of options. I fear a laparoscopy looms. Oh, shit. The very thought of a doctor inserting a television camera into my bellybutton makes my knees wobble!

I can scarcely believe I'm going to write this but I'm beginning to seriously think about Drusilla's theory re: ley lines and Primrose Hill. She does seem very certain of her facts. I know that Drusilla is a witch but she's a good witch, which is a very different thing from the wicked variety.

Dear etc.

Well, this morning was a pressure job all right, our postcoital compatibility test. Doctor's orders. Shag and then straight round to the clinic to check the juices. Not much fun for the woman certainly but let me tell you it's a horrible situation for the bloke who is called upon to provide the wherewithal. I mean, it's not ideal, is it? Sex on demand is tricky enough at the best of times, but in the morning, particularly after a big night at the Director General's, it's a very tough call indeed.

Besides which, the whole problem was compounded by the fact that I happened to have a particularly early and rather important meeting.

Lucy says, 'When don't you have a meeting?' But actually that's not true. I am, in fact, often there at her beck and call. The point is when I *am* available to her she's not interested. She's only interested in presuming on my time when she knows I have other things to do.

So, what with the hangover (which I think I managed to disguise from Lucy), the earliness of the hour, and the impending meeting, instant and impressive erections were not massively in evidence. We pulled it off in the end, so to speak, but it was a very close-run thing.

I did, however, manage to make my meeting, which I was pleased about because it was a special one, concerning as it did Nigel's major new film-making initiative, an area in which considering my current standing with the Controller I cannot afford to screw up. Actually, I was rather excited about it. After all, film is film and we humble telly people do not normally get to dabble in so exalted a medium.

It was to be a 'breakfast' meeting at a posh hotel, I'm sorry to say. Whichever American it was who invented such a deeply uncivilised idea should have his eggs boiled, his muffins split and his pop-tarts toasted on an open fire. You can't make sense of a meeting over brekkie! How the hell are you supposed to take anything seriously when you're eating Rice Krispies? Or, worse, Coco Pops, which was what I had.

This was Claridge's, so I could have ordered porridge or salmon or the full English but I've never been big on breakfast, and the smell of kippers and kedgeree before eleven quite frankly makes me nauseous. Fish for breakfast has always struck me as wrong, like having a croissant for supper or coffee in a pub. Apparently, however, fishie brekkie is the last word in traditional, crusty, old English chic. Not for me, though. Let's face it, how often do I get the chance to have a bowl of Coco Pops?

Anyway, to 'cut to the chase', as people in film say, I was meeting some people from Above The Line Films.

I *do* beg your pardon, I was meeting *with* some people from Above The Line Films. One must of course speak American English when moving in film circles these days (sorry, *motion picture* circles).

The people from Above The Line are very hip at the moment, the reason being that they recently made a film that some Americans quite liked. It's an interesting thing about the Brit film industry (such as it is) that for all the gung-ho, Cool Britannia jingoism we spout about our cool new British talent, we judge our product exclusively on whether or not people in America go to see it. You could make a British film that every person in Britain went to see twice, plus half the population of the European Community, but unless at least 5,000 Americans have also been persuaded to go the style fascists will judge it naff and parochial. On the other hand, if we make a movie which flops everywhere and which *only* 5,000 Americans go and see, the director will still be seen as a major burgeoning international talent.

Anyway, there I was sitting at Claridge's 'doing' Coco Pops and kedgeree with three of Britain's brightest motion picture talents. Justin Cocker, an estuary Oxbridge mid-Atlantic drawler who called the toilet the 'bathroom' and asked if they had any bagels and lox. A snarling Scot called Ewan Proclaimer, who took one look at the Claridge's breakfast room and said, 'God, I fuckin' hate the fuckin' English. I mean they are just so fuckin' *English*, aren't they? D'you ken what I'm saying here?'

Also a pencil-thin woman called Petra. On the phone the previous day I had asked Justin Cocker if Petra had a surname and he said that if I needed to ask that question I did not know the British motion picture industry. Which is right, of course. I don't.

Weird meeting. Like a summit between people from different planets. The BBC being vaguely located on earth, and Above The Line Films being located somewhere far beyond the galaxy of Barkingtonto. The extraordinary thing is that they think that *they* are the ones who live in the real world. Amazing how these days it's hip to assume that the money supplied by vast multinational media conglomerates (writing off their tax losses) is somehow more real and proper than that raised by the public for the purposes of their own entertainment.

Anyway, I told them that the BBC was interested in co-producing more films with a view to theatrical release prior to TV screening and that my special area was comedy. They said if I wanted comedy they had comedy. Real comedy. Not crap comedy, they assured me; not all that *fuckin' crap* that the BBC passes off as comedy, but sharp, witty, edgy, in-your-face, on-the-nose and up-your-arse comedy. 'Two words,' they said, 'Zeit' and 'Geist'. In other words, 'Tomorrow's comedy today.'

Well, I can't deny I was excited. This surely was what we wanted. Ewan Proclaimer produced his script, the eagerly awaited follow-up to his film *Sick Junkie*, which had been 'hugely successful', i.e. some American critics liked it, although it was actually seen by fewer people than watch the weather on Grampian. *Sick Junkie* had been a career breaker for Ewan, but now he explained that he wanted to move totally away from all that stuff.

His new script is called *Aids and Heroin*.

'It's a comedy about a group of normal, ordinary kids,' said Ewan Proclaimer, 'all heroin addicts, of course. Probably Scottish, perhaps Welsh or Irish. . .'

'Although we'd shoot it in London,' interjected Pencil Petra.

'Well, of course we'd shoot it in London!' Ewan snapped. He was clearly not a man who liked to be interrupted. 'Morag and I have only just got wee Jamie into a decent school . . . Now these kids survive on the edges of society, right? The movie is a week in their ordinary mundane lives. They inject heroin into their eyeballs, they have babies in toilets, they get Aids, they kill a social worker, they have abortions, they're raped by gangs of English policemen. . .'

'Excuse me,' I risked an interjection. 'I hope I'm following. This is a comedy we're discussing here?'

'Total comedy,' Ewan assured me, 'but *real* comedy, about what's *actually* happening to kids today, not escapist *English* crap.'

It all sounded very post-watershed to me. But broadcastable or not, I wasn't having any of it. This never-ending diet of sex and drugs and urban horror that well-heeled highly educated young film makers seem to feel duty-bound to serve up as stone-cold naturalism. For heaven's sake, I know that life is tough out there but it's not exclusively so. There are more adolescents in the Girl Guides and the Sea Scouts than there are teenage junkies, but nobody ever makes a film about them.

I finished my Coco Pops in a marked manner, resisting the temptation to drink the chocolatey milk out of the bowl, and rose to leave.

'Thanks for explaining your idea to me, Ewan,' I said. 'Unfortunately the BBC is not in the business of funding cynical tales about drugs and prostitution that purport to reflect everyday Britain merely so that the fashion junkies who make them can swank about at Cannes and then bugger off to work in the States the first chance they get.'

Then I took up the bill and left feeling proudly self-assertive.

By the time I got back to Television Centre I had worked myself into a right old self-righteous lather. The first thing I did was to get Daphne to take down a sarky fax telling Above The Line Films where they could shove it. I had no sooner finished doing this and was contemplating a calming game of *Tomb Raider* on my PC when Nigel called and summoned me to his office.

I trudged along the circular corridor convinced that this was it, that the long-awaited shafting was about to be administered. As I entered the hallowed office, however, it seemed that I was wrong. Nigel was positively beaming at me.

'Sam!' he said. 'I just heard you did breakfast with Above The Line and met with Justin, Ewan and Petra. Congratulations, mate! Excellent move. Ewan is a genius and a God-sent antidote to all the crap your department normally commissions.'

Alarm bells began to ring.

'Yes, that's what *he* said,' I replied limply.

'He's just the kind of raw, edgy talent we need for the new film initiative. It would be absolutely sensational if you could bring him and the whole Above The Line ethos into the Beeb. As it happens I'm having dinner with Justin and Petra at Mick and Jerry's tonight so I'll do everything I can to push it along. OK, mate? Well done.'

I arrived back in my office just in time to see the fax I had dictated to Daphne emerge from the machine having been transmitted as instructed.

Dear Penny

I've decided. Since the next medical step for me is a laparoscopy, which is intrusive and not to be entered into lightly (like my bellybutton), it is foolish for me to ignore other possibilities.

Tomorrow is a full moon, my traffic light says I'll be ovulating and Sam will just have to like it or lump it.

Oh my God.

I got home today and Lucy told me that tomorrow night, at midnight, she wants me to take her to the top of Primrose Hill, which is a *public park*, and shag her under the full moon.

I'm still hoping that this is some kind of joke.

INCONCEIVABLE

Dear Penny

Tonight is the night! Full moon! The forecast is for a mild night with gentle breezes. Perfect. Perhaps the fates are finally going to be on my side.

Drusilla and I went to a fairy shop in Covent Garden at lunchtime and got some crystals. Drusilla assures me they'll help. We sat together on a bench in Soho Square and energised them. This involved squeezing the crystals in the palms of our hands and, well, energising them. I had a tofu pitta bread sarnie from Pret A Manger in the other hand so I imagine that I energised that too.

I've bought a nice thick picnic rug from Selfridge's, because you want to be as comfortable as possible on these occasions.

I also went to Kookaï and bought an incredible new frock. It's just a sheath, really, and I'm afraid my tum will bulge, but I'll hold it in. The dress cost an entire week's wages but Drusilla insists that this must be a sensual and erotic event, not just a sly bonk in a park. There's to be wine and candles and I must reek of musk and primrose oil and ancient pagan scents. I really didn't know where I was supposed to get ancient pagan scents in London on a Friday after-noon but Drusilla had it all sorted out. Rather conveniently, Boots do a set of soaps that cover the lot and she'd bought me a box as a present.

I played Celtic music on my Walkman on the tube home to get me into a mood of fertile pagan spirituality. I'm quite excited in a funny sort of way.

I hope Sam cheers up about it, though. I regret to have to report that last night, when I told him what was expected of him, he was most unenthusiastic. In fact he got quite hostile. Obviously I can sort of understand his doubting the effectiveness of the plan. It's a long shot, certainly, relying on the faint echoes and rhythms of the ancient world to jolly his sperm along. I'm highly sceptical myself, but I do wish he'd see that we must try everything.

It's always the way, though, isn't it, Penny? The poor woman gets the short end of the stick. It's like with contraception. The things women have to go through (all pointless in my case, it seems). I remember when Sam and I first started doing it regularly he wanted me to go on the pill or have a coil fitted because he didn't like condoms. He said they were a barrier between us (well of course they are, that surely is the point). Basically what he was saying was that he didn't want to put his dick in a bag. So instead would I mind either fill-ing my body with chemicals or having a small piece of barbed wire inserted into me? In the end, I got a Dutch cap and God was that a palaver! Trying to put one of those in when you've had a bottle and a half of Hirondelle is not easy. The damn thing was always shooting across the bathroom and landing in the basin. Then there was that awful cream you had to put on. The nights that I nearly shoved toothpaste up my fanny and brushed my teeth with spermici-dal lubricant! Makes my eyes water just to think about it.

Anyway, I'm digressing. As I often do when on the subject of the selfishness of men. Let's face it, there's so much scope. But as I was saying re Primrose Hill, I just have to give everything a try, it's a matter of life and . . . Well, life and no life, I suppose, which is a pretty terrible thought. And anyway who knows what strange and powerful forces there are in the world? I mean the moon does definitely affect people, we know that. You only have to look at dogs. They go potty at full moon. As for ley lines, I admit that it sounds pretty unlikely. On the other hand, certain places do have a special energy. I can remember once feeling very strange during a walk in the Devil's Punchbowl in Surrey, and that's supposed to be a mystic place, isn't it? Sam claims it was the macaroni cheese I'd had for lunch in that pub, but I know it wasn't.

And what's more, apart from any spiritual and mystical considerations, I had hoped that Sam might find the whole idea a bit raunchy. After all, we are lovers, aren't we? Besides being boring old marrieds? Surely we can see all this in the light of a naughty, saucy adventure?

No chance, I'm afraid. Sam didn't get home until half an hour ago (last-minute preparations for the PM tomorrow), and he's insisting that he still has some calls to make. I'm writing this while he whinges and whines about comedy in his study. I've had my bath (by candlelight with rose petals floating on the water) and used all the soaps. I was really beginning to feel quite goddess-like and fertile and Sam is acting like it was just any other bloody night.

I bet Carl Phipps wouldn't be in his study making calls about stupid comedy programmes while his lover lay damp and scented and naked upon their bed.

No! I must not think that sort of thing. It's wicked.

T'will be dark in an hour. The moon is on the wax and the witching hour is nigh. Do you know, Penny? I've got this funny feeling that it might just work.

Dear Self

It's four o'clock in the morning and we've just got back from the police station. They were quite nice about it in the end, once they let me put my trousers back on. I thought I handled the whole matter pretty well, actually.

Dear Penny

Sam was ridiculous tonight, quite bloody ridiculous. I mean, you just do not give false names to the police, do you? Particularly 'William Gladstone'. I mean, bonking isn't illegal, is it? But of course when he claimed to be a nineteenth-century prime minister they asked for ID and immediately the game was up.

He looked like one of those men who stand on the end of train platforms. Not much of a turn-on at all. I explained to him as patiently as I could that Drusilla had insisted that a steamy passionate atmosphere was essential. We must both be highly, throbbingly, almost primevally sexually charged. Timeless animals of passion, caught up in the eternal spinning vortex of all creation.

Anyway, I made him go and put on his black tie and dinner suit, which he wears to the BAFTA awards every year. He's always been disappointed when wearing that suit, having never won a single award. I prayed that the ancient and timeless deities of the firmament would change all that tonight and give him the most important prize of all.

Lucy made me put on black tie, which quite frankly made us look like Gomez and Morticia, particularly since she'd really gone to town with the black eyeliner. I must admit, though, she did look fantastic. Like a beautiful model, I thought. I really did and I said so.

Sam suddenly started being rather sweet and I must say he looked very nice in his dinner suit. Most men do look good in black tie. Dinner jackets even make a paunch look sort of stately and dignified. Not that Sam has a paunch. Anyway, I thought he looked lovely, even though he still insisted on wearing his anorak 'just till we got down to it'.

Actually I can scarcely credit it, but it was all beginning to get rather fun. Lucy had prepared some bits of artichoke on biscuits (fertile fruit, apparently) and oysters! We had them in front of the fire with a glass of red wine (just one) before getting in the car. Lucy had also bought a beautiful black crocheted shawl to keep her warm and it just looked fantastic with her white skin showing through the black, like a Russian princess or something. And she'd put on some long droopy silver earrings I'd never seen before.

All in all, she'd really made an effort, which I loved her for. I myself had tried to enter into the spirit of things by putting on the silk boxer shorts I got last Christmas and had so far never worn.

I do wish Sam hadn't put on those Donald Duck pants. I know he was trying to be nice but you don't need Disney characters when you're trying to be all pagan and ritualistic, even if they are silk.

Anyway, we got there and amazingly found a parking place almost immediately. And having got over the usual car palaver (Sam set the alarm off, I don't know how he manages to do that so often), we stood there together at the foot of the ancient hill. It was only eleven thirty, so we had a good half-hour to climb up it and get down to it, so to speak. It was a very quiet night for London and I must say the hill looked fantastic against the moon. We seemed to have it to ourselves apart from the birds and squirrels and, of course, the spirits of the night. *I thought I saw one but it turned out to be an unconscious homeless alcoholic slumbering on a bench near the children's playground.*

If we succeeded, if the gods really did bring us luck, I was going to bring my children to play on those swings every day.

Funny, as we made our way up the path, to my surprise I really did begin to feel all ancient and beautiful. I tried to allow my body to respond to the timeless rhythms and vibrations of the eternal cycles of life on earth that were swirling about me.

It would have been easier if Sam had not kept telling me to watch out for dogshit, but I suppose he meant well.

I trod in this huge turd the moment we entered the park. Huge. No mortal dog could have passed such a turd. Honestly, I went in almost up to my knee. Any deeper and I would have had to call for a rope. London Zoo is situated at the bottom of Primrose Hill and I was forced to conclude that an elephant must have escaped.

At the top of Primrose Hill I was amazed to discover that I was starting to get quite motivated. I mean I had expected to be petrified with embarrassment, but in fact I felt quite sexy. It was such a fine night and Lucy looked so beautiful standing there in the silvery light of the full moon. There's a sort of look-out area at the top of the hill, with benches and a map of the panoramic view of London. We had it all to ourselves and it was suddenly very beautiful, like we were on a flying saucer hovering over London or something. Lucy took off her shawl and put it on a bench. She looked so stunning in her sexy crimson dress and with a gentle night breeze playing in her hair. I'd been worrying that I might get stage fright but no way! I was a tiger! I think I fancied her at that moment as much as I've ever fancied her, and that's quite a lot, as it happens.

London looked like a great starry carpet spread all about us. I thought for a moment about all the thousands of centuries that had gone before, when we could have stood on that very same spot and seen nothing but darkness below us. Suddenly our time on earth and the fact of being human seemed very small indeed. Completely insignificant in the grander scheme of things. Except that what we were hoping to do, what this night was meant to achieve, was as big as the whole universe! New life! A brand new beginning. Should we succeed, this very moment would be the dawn of time for that child.

We chose a place on the grass behind the concrete summit (Sam having first thoroughly checked the area with his torch for dog-do and used hypodermic needles, which was sensible) and laid our blanket on the ground. Then I put out the circle of candles around the blanket (little nightlights in jamjars that would not be spotted from afar) and sprinkled primrose oil about the place.

Then I lay down with the moon on my face and, ahem, raised the hem of my garment. I had decided to be sensual and wear no knickers. Sam lay down on top of me, and, rather incredibly, we had it off. I must say I was proud of him. I'd been half expecting him to fail to deliver, but apart from complaining a bit about it being painful on his knees and elbows he was quite romantic about it.

I won't say that I actually had an orgasm, the situation was rather too fraught for that, I'm afraid, but I nearly did and I definitely enjoyed it and when we'd finished I thought we'd done well. After all, it's not every girl that has it off wearing a new satin frock surrounded by candles on the top of Primrose Hill at midnight under a full moon.

Afterwards we lay there for a little while on the rug gathering our thoughts and listening to the breeze in the trees. Anyway, that was when Sam screamed.

This, I'm afraid, brought an abrupt end to our idyll, as well it might.

What had happened was this. As Sam and I had lain there together in the warm and spiritual afterglow of our lovemaking, a squirrel had found its way into Sam's trousers, which Sam had left nearby along with his silk jocks, having stepped out of the whole lot in one. I don't know what had led the squirrel into this dark territory. Perhaps it was after Sam's nuts. What I do know is that the squirrels of Primrose Hill and Regent's Park are incredibly cheeky on account of the manner in which they are indulged by all and sundry. As Sam stood bent and hovering above his trousers, one foot in and the waistband firmly gripped, the squirrel popped out its head to see what was what. There was of course a confrontation.

They faced each other in the night, Sam staring down at the squirrel, the squirrel staring up at Sam. It was Sam who screamed first.

Lucy says it was a squirrel but if it was a squirrel then someone's been feeding them steroids. I'd just risen to my feet, contentedly contemplating the large and joyful whisky I'd be treating myself to when we got home. I reached down to pull up my trousers and instantly I felt this hot breath upon my bollocks! Looking down between my legs I saw it, eyes blazing, teeth bared, talons poised. Whatever it was, it appeared to me to be getting ready to rip my scrotum off! Of course I screamed. Who wouldn't have? Of course I know that Lucy is convinced it was a squirrel and it's true that Primrose Hill is amply supplied with squirrels. Nonetheless I contend that what I saw fossicking around in my trousers tonight was like no squirrel I have ever seen. It was big and tough and toothy and wicked looking and it will haunt my slumbers for many a night to come.

The police were upon us almost before we knew it. We did not hear them coming because Sam was leaping about beating his hands between his legs and shouting, 'Ahh! Ahh! Get a stick!' I think that the squirrel must have seen the coppers first, actually, because by the time they arrived Sam's trousers appeared to be empty (apart from him, of course). They were nonetheless still very much unhitched, which was all rather embarrassing. I should mention here that Sam's Donald Duck pants were also round his knees so that there was a second full moon shining on Primrose Hill tonight. I think we were very lucky that they didn't do us for indecency.

Anyway, as I say, had Sam not attempted to give the police a false name I think they would have let us off there and then, but instead they took us in.

We sat about a bit at the police station and after a cup of tea and one or two off-colour innuendos from the young constables they let us go. Sam got quite shirty about the jokes the coppers made, which I thought was stupid since they were no worse than the sort of rubbish he commissions every day. They even dropped us off back at our car, which I thought was nice of them.

Anyway, it's all over now, for better or worse, and here I am, lying in bed. Sam's already snoring, sleeping the sleep of the great and powerful lover, but I'm wide awake, clutching my crystals, humming Celtic hymns and praying to Gaia to deliver new life into my body. Let Mother Nature make me a mother too!

In my heart and my soul I truly believe she will.

Well, it's now the evening following our Primrose Hill tryst and today has not gone well.

On the plus side Lucy is very happy about our success last night. She seems to have convinced herself that the power of positive thinking has been the missing factor in us getting pregnant. When I got home this afternoon I found her sitting in front of the fire watching a Saturday afternoon film on Channel Four and looking wistful, sipping camomile tea and gently trying to will her eggs to envelop my sperm. It's a strange thing, but you know she did sort of look pregnant, I can't really say why, but sort of serene and womanly and, well, fertile. Perhaps Lucy is right. Perhaps positive thinking is what we need. Anyway, if there's any balance of fair play in the world we'll be pregnant, because the rest of my life is double buggered squared.

I have not mentioned my inner torment to Lucy, of course. When she asked me how things had gone today I said, 'Fine.' I did not feel that in her present state of self-induced mystical empowerment she would want to be told that her husband was an utter joke. I did not feel it fair to tell that sweet, trusting, potential nestbuilder that the career of her champion and protector now hangs by less than a single thread. That we are shortly to be paupers. I simply could not bring myself to tell her that the Prime Minister's visit to *Livin' Large* was the most right royal cock-up since Henry VIII discovered girls.

Despite my late-night run-in with the law on the previous evening, I was up bright and early this morning. *Livin' Large* goes out live at 9.00am and I had promised to take my niece Kylie along. Kylie is the daughter of my sister Emily and has apparently, of late, taken an interest in politics. My sister, anxious to encourage this new maturity in a girl who up until now has liked only ponies and Barbie, asked me to take her along. To add to the excitement, Grrrl Gang, a kind of post-post-Spice Girls group, are also appearing on the show and Emily says that Kylie worships the ground they walk on.

Kylie was something of a shock. I had last seen her about six months before at a family do and she had been a very sweet and pretty little eleven-year-old who had a picture of a horse in a locket round her neck. I'm afraid to have to report that the butterfly has reverted to a caterpillar and that Kylie or 'K Grrrl', as she now wishes to be known, is a horrid little pre-teen brat. Her nice blonde hair has red streaks inexpertly dyed into it. She has a nose stud and wears enormously baggy army combat trousers. Her tummy is bare save for a tattoo of a rat holding a hypodermic needle (mercifully a transfer). Her crop-top T-shirt has the words 'DROP DEAD' printed on it and her once-pretty face is now contorted into a permanent sulky scowl.

I asked her if she was excited about going to the studio. The look of astonished contempt she gave me would have scrambled an egg.

'Oh *yeah! Right, as if!* Like I'm *really* going to get excited about going to a crap *kids'* show. Yeah, *right*, that's *really* likely.'

I could not have felt more withered if I had been a sultana. I did my best to engage her interest, which was, of course, fatal.

'The Prime Minister will be there.'

'The Prime Minister is a meat-eating fascist.'

'Grrrl Gang will be playing live.'

'Grrrl Gang are crap and sad.'

'I'll introduce you to Tazz.'

'Tazz is a moronic duh brain who wouldn't have got anywhere if all the sad old men at the BBC didn't fancy her.'

I thought this was extremely unfair. Tazz is an excellent presenter and a lovely girl. Yes, it's true that she's fairly gorgeous and does indeed have the factor that in showbiz is traditionally called 'something for the dads'. But being consistently perky for three hours on a Saturday morning is more difficult than a lot of people think. It takes real talent.

We got in the car and Kylie sorted through my tapes, rejecting every one with pained groans of contempt before turning up the radio full to prevent further conversation.

Whatever Kylie might have felt, I personally was very much looking forward to the morning and meeting Tazz. She really is gorgeous and quite simply every heterosexual bloke in the country fancies her. Tazz is also, I'm told, very nice, and a real enthusiast about things like Comic Relief. Besides all this, she wears tiny little crop-tops and microscopic little skirts which for somebody like me who spends his time at TV Centre talking to plump, grumpy, unshaven comedians about whether they can say knob before nine o'clock is a very welcome change.

This morning, rather disappointingly, Tazz was wearing trousers. Probably a directive from Downing Street. I don't think the PM is an ogler, but he's only human, for God's sake. Many a strong man's eyes have twitched downwards to check out the knicker triangle when facing Tazz on the 'Hot Seat' sofas. The last thing Downing Street wants is the PM caught having a perv on a twenty-two-year-old's gusset.

The show started off fine. I got Kylie sat down among the other kids, whom at first she affected to despise, but I soon noticed that she had hooked up with two eleven-year-old sisters whose mother seemed to have dressed them as prostitutes, in so much as their skirts were the merest pelmets and their tops barely covered the fact that there was as yet nothing to barely cover. Having seen Kylie settled in, I went up to the control box. I was surprised to discover that I was clearly the most senior figure present. I recall reflecting how generous it was of Nigel to stay away and let me take my rightful place centre stage as the BBC's official Prime Minister host. Ha! And double ha!

Anyway, after the usual half-hour of cartoons ('We hate showing them but it's what the kids want'), Tazz introduced Grrrl Gang. None of these groups is ever going to do what the Spice Girls did in '96, but Grrrl Gang are pretty hip at present. They were 'In the Dock', which was another of these sections in which the star guest takes questions from the kids in the audience and on the phones. Which in reality means a series of tremulous voices from Milton Keynes and Dumfriesshire asking, 'How do you get to be a pop star?'

'You just got to be yourself, right? Livin' it large. Kickin' it big. That's all it takes,' the grrrls of Grrrl Gang assured the kids of Britain.

'You gotta kick it, girl! Big yourself up!'

'Yeah, and don't let no one disrespect you, right?'

'Yeah, if you want it, grrrl, just grab it. It's a babe revolution.'

The rest of the Grrrls nodded wisely at this.

Then Tazz announced that it was environment week on *Livin' Large* and that the show was committed to biggin' up the environment big time, right. The grrrls from Grrrl Gang all let it be known that they had big respec' for this concept. Tazz had brought on the *Livin' Large* 'Green Professor', a nice, wacky, bearded git called Simon. The idea was that Simon would discuss green issues with Tazz, Grrrl Gang and the kids.

Sometimes these things can be a little sticky, but one of the grrrls from Grrrl Gang had a question right off.

'Talking about the environment, right,' she said, 'do you know about animals and stuff, then?'

Simon positively glowed. 'Well, a little. I'm Chief Zoologist to the Royal Natural Academy.'

'All right, answer me this, then,' said the grrrl. 'How come birds have rude names, then?'

Simon was clearly not following.

'You know,' the grrrl continued. 'Cock, tit, thrush.'

Up in the control box we all froze.

'Warbler.'

The kids giggled and Simon stuttered.

'Well, I. . .'

In control the phone lines were lighting up already as irate parents all over the country began to call in to complain. The producer screamed into Tazz's earpiece telling her to move on.

'My brother used to have a white mouse called Big Balls,' said a second member of Grrrl Gang.

'Yeah, but that's just a personal name, innit?' replied the first. 'Not a breed.'

Looking back, I suppose I should have taken it as a warning. The warm complacent glow I had been feeling (Lucy stonked up; me about to be the sole facilitator of a glorious TV moment with the PM) suddenly chilled a bit. This was live telly and things could go wrong. But the panic in the box subsided and I comforted myself that it was probably good luck to get the gremlins out of the way first. A glance at my watch informed me that the PM was due in twenty minutes so I decided to make my way to the front of TV Centre to be ready to receive him.

Oh, how naive I'd been.

When I got to the reception area I discovered that a welcome committee had already assembled. Nigel was there, of course, standing on the red carpet trying to look both relaxed and important in equal measure. In front of Nigel, all jostling for position, were the Corporation's Chief of Accounting, also the Heads of Marketing, Networking, Global

Outreaching and Corporate Affairs-ing. Also present were the Head of Television and the Head of Radio, also the Head of Television and Radio (Radio and Television Group) and the Chief Programming Coordinator and the Chief Coordinating Programmer and the Deputy Director General, of course the Director General himself, the Chairman of the Board of Governors and the Board of Governors. Basically, the entire senior executive management structure of the Corporation had turned out so that they could say they had met the PM.

I took my place at the back of the crowd quietly determining to find a moment to proclaim loudly that despite being the most junior senior executive present I was in charge on the ground. It was my gig.

There were five or six Downing Street minders buzzing about the place as well, phones and pagers going off like the martians were about to land. I saw Jo Winstón and waved but I'm afraid she either didn't see me or didn't recognise me.

Then they were upon us. Outside the main gates heading south towards Shepherd's Bush was the mini cavalcade, two motorcycle out-riders at each end sandwiching three cars of which the PM's Daimler with its darkened rear windows was the middle one. As the procession drew up opposite the main entrance the front motorbikes pulled across the road into the oncoming traffic to block the northbound traffic. Leaving behind the two secret service cars, the Daimler pulled up to the famous IN barrier of BBC Television Centre.

And then came the first of the day's truly momentous disasters.

Book, my hand shakes as I report that the barrier did not rise.

The entire top brass of the BBC (plus me) stood transfixed with horror as the prime ministerial Daimler drew to a reluctant halt while a little old man in a peaked cap emerged from the security hut that stands beside the barrier.

None of us could speak. We just watched in dumbstruck silence as down at the gate a negotiation began to take place between the BBC guard and the Prime Minister's driver.

The BBC gate men are notorious, positively Soviet in their trancelike commitment to the letter of BBC law. Their duty is to defend the gates of Television Centre against all but those who have passes or whose names are on the Gate List. In fact only last week a story went round that Tom Jones had been refused entry because his name was not on the Gate List, even though he had got out of his Roller and sung 'It's Not Unusual', 'Delilah' and 'What's New, Pussycat?' on the pavement.

Jo Winston's radio crackled. It was the voice of the Prime Minister's driver.

INCONCEIVABLE

'They won't lift the barrier, Jo. The guard says there's no name on his Gate List.'

'Tell him it's the Prime Minister!' Jo snapped into her radio.

'I have. He says, oh yeah and he's Bruce Forsyth.'

'But it *is* the Prime Minister.'

'I know it's the Prime Minister, miss. I'm his driver, but this man says there's no name on his Gate List.'

Everyone in the reception committee twitched in horror.

The Director General turned to the Deputy Director General.

'Why has the Prime Minister's name not been forwarded to the gate?'

The Deputy Director General repeated the question to the Head of Television and Radio who asked it of the Head of Television. He asked Nigel the Channel Controller and Nigel turned to the man who was in charge on the ground, the man whose gig it was.

'Sam!' he hissed.

Before Nigel could ask me why the Prime Minister's name had not been forwarded to the gate, I pushed my way through to the front of the group and grabbed Jo's radio.

'Tell the idiot at the gate that this is Sam Bell, BBC Controller, Broken Comedy and Variety!' I barked, 'The Prime Minister is appearing on *Livin' Large* and he is to be allowed through immediately!'

After a tense moment during which we could all see the driver conveying my message to the guard, the driver radioed back.

'He says he's going to need a programme number for *Livin' Large* to check with the studio. He thinks it's a wind-up.'

Of course! Now I understood the problem in all its horror. Nobody trusts anybody in television any more. That is its curse. There has been such a plethora of shows based on practical jokes and nasty cons on TV over the past few years that everybody in the industry lives in a state of constant paranoia. They check their hotel rooms for hidden cameras, their bathrooms for tiny mikes. Nobody is safe. Impressionists ring up celebrities pretending to be other celebrities, tricking them into making appalling indiscretions which are then broadcast to the nation. Hoax current affairs programme researchers fool naive politicians into commenting on non-existent issues so as to make them look like complete idiots.

This hapless gate guard, seeing the *Livin' Large* cameras looming behind him, clearly suspected that he was the subject of what is known in the business as a 'gotcha'.

Nigel had joined me in the little cluster of people around Jo's radio.

'Give the bastard the programme number,' he hissed in my ear.

It was the obvious thing to do and I would have done it, except that I did not have the programme number. Why would I? I am a senior executive. I have people to have that type of thing for me. So does Nigel, of course, and his person is me. He was nearly in tears.

I gave Jo back her radio and set off for the barrier, which was a distance of perhaps fifty metres. For a moment I tried to maintain my dignity but trying to walk at running pace looks even more panicky than running, so I ran. At the barrier I could see that the guard was shaken but determined. For all he knew this could be a test of his guarding abilities. All in all he had clearly decided that whether it was a hoax or not the safest policy for him was to cling to the rules like a paranoid limpet.

'He hasn't got a pass. His name's not on the list and you haven't got a programme number. The rules are very clear.'

I wondered how the PM was taking all this. I thought about asking whether the Premier would mind stepping out for a moment and showing himself, but I did not have the nerve.

'Right,' I said, and grabbing the gate I attempted to lift it by brute force. This was pointless, of course. I heaved and I heaved and the guard threatened to call the police, of whom there were four in evidence.

I had to think straight. Force was not the answer. I let go of the gate and strode back to the guard.

'Ring the switchboard,' I said. 'Ask them to ring *Livin' Large* and get them to give you a programme number.'

There was an agonising wait for the switchboard to respond. It was a Saturday, after all. Eventually the guard got through, but only as far as the switchboard, who refused to put him through to *Livin' Large*.

'They're live on air at the moment,' the guard said, 'and not taking calls in the control box.'

'I know they're live on air, that's the whole . . .'

What could I do? I know these people, people at gates, people on doors, people with lists. They are immovable. They cannot be reasoned with. The mountain would have to go to Mohammed.

I set off to run back to the studio to get the programme number. As I sprinted up the car-park turning circle and back into the studio complex I could feel the eyes of every single superior I had upon me. Amazingly, I did not instantly get lost and rush into a drama studio, ruining a take, like I normally do. I pushed my way straight into *Livin' Large*, grabbed a camera script from a floor manager, noted down the programme number and charged back out towards the gates.

As I emerged from the building clutching the precious number I could see that the Daimler had been allowed through. The police, it seems, had taken charge and threatened the gate guard with immediate arrest if he did not lift his barrier and now the Prime Minister was on the red carpet being profusely apologised to by the Chairman of the Board of Governors and the Director General.

The PM laughed, he smiled, he said that these things happened and that we were not to worry about it at all. Had it not been for the flashing eyes and gritted teeth I might almost have imagined that he meant it.

As they bustled the great man off for make-up I tried to make a face at Nigel as if to say, 'Phew, got away with that, didn't we?' He would not even look at me.

Back in the studio Tazz was telling the cameras that the most mega honour in television history was about to be visited upon the kidz of *Livin' Large*, and that the Prim-o Minister-o, the Main Man UK, was already in the house!

There was cheering, there was shouting, the *Livin' Large* goblin puppets jumped up and down in front of the camera, Tazz beamed. Most of the bigwigs were watching the show in a hospitality suite on the sixth floor, but I was in the control box along with Nigel and the Head of Television.

The bank of TV monitors that faced us over the heads of the vision mixers, PAs, directors, etc., suddenly lit up with the beaming countenance of the Prime Minister. He looked great. The kids cheered. I felt that the worst of the day was behind us.

Tazz, bless her, lobbed him the first ball beautifully.

'Is it true, Prime Minister, that you play the electric guitar?'

'Perfect!' shouted Nigel in the box. 'Well done, Tazz.'

Nigel was clearly attempting to assume credit for the planting of this question, which had actually been my work. I wasn't having it.

'Yes, good girl, that's exactly what I told her to ask,' I said pointedly.

The PM smiled broadly. 'Look,' he said. 'You know a lot of kids these days think that politicians are fuddy and they're duddy but it's just not true. Yes, I do play the electric guitar and I love to surf the Internet. I'm just a regular bloke who likes pop music, comedy with proper rude bits in it and wearing fashionable trousers. Just like you, Jazz.'

We all gulped slightly at this but Tazz quite rightly let it go and threw the floor open to the assembled children. It went wonderfully. The Prime Minister was frank, open and honest. Yes, he had a pet as a child, a hamster called Pawpaw. His favourite meal was egg and chips, but there must be proper ketchup.

We could see that the PM was enjoying himself. Jo Winston had joined us in the box and she was beaming. The incident at the gate seemed to be forgotten. Then my niece Kylie asked a question.

'Mr Prime Minister. With more young people than ever living rough on the streets, with your government cutting benefits to young people more than ever before, with class sizes at record levels and with children's hospitals being forced to close, don't you think that it's an act of disgusting cynicism to come on here and pretend that you care at all about what really matters to young people?'

Oh my raving giddily diddily fuck.

The PM was absolutely not ready for it. He was stopped dead. At any other time he could easily have fielded an attack like Kylie's, but on this occasion he just wasn't ready.

He had thought himself safe. He *should* have been safe.

'Well . . . I . . . uhm . . . I do care . . . but I. . .'

Kylie pressed home her advantage.

'Do you care about the children of single mothers? Because most of them will go hungry tonight . . .'

Jo Winston's knuckles were white around the pen she clutched. The control box hot line rang. Nigel picked it up. 'Shut that fucking kid up.' I could hear the voice of the DG himself crackling on the other end.

'Shut that fucking kid up!' Nigel shouted at me and I dutifully relayed the message into the studio link, nearly blowing poor Tazz's ear off.

'No, for heaven's sake, let him answer!' Jo Winston shouted at me, but it was too late.

'Well, we're going to have to leave it there,' Tazz was saying, with a grin frozen on her face. 'So here's the new video from Sir Elton John.'

It could not have looked more terrible. Jo Winston was right. The PM needed to reply but instead Kylie was left with the last word and the Main Man UK looked like a piece of shit.

Jo Winston left the control box without a word. Her look, however, spoke volumes. She thought I'd stitched her up.

Even before Elton John had finished his song the Downing Street posse were out of the building, departing in fury, swearing revenge on the BBC and claiming loudly that the PM had been set up. The Director General had tried to tempt the great man to a glass of wine (a grand reception buffet was all waiting). He actually chased after the prime ministerial Daimler round the turning circle with a bottle of claret in his hand. But any hope of post-broadcast jollies, I'm afraid, had been dashed by the as yet unclaimed little girl in the studio.

In the control box an inquiry was under way. The Deputy Director General had arrived and also the Head of Radio and Television. They knew they were in trouble. Everybody was all too aware that publicly embarrassing the Prime Minister on live TV was not the best way to ensure the future of advert-free public service broadcasting in the UK.

400

As my various superiors spoke, contemplating the wrath that they must face from their own superiors, I was painfully aware that below us the studio was emptying. Looking down through the great glass windows onto the floor, I could see that the bulk of the audience had been escorted out and the scene-shifters were beginning to strike the set. Standing alone in the middle of all the activity and looking rather lonely and scared was my niece Kylie. The problem was that I knew that if I went anywhere near her the game would be up.

Then the game was up anyway. Nigel spotted her.

'That appalling little anarchist is still there,' he said. 'I don't believe it! That means she must belong to one of the crew!'

They all stared down. Kylie was looking more isolated than ever. The deconstruction of a TV studio after a programme has been made is a noisy, frenzied business. For a twelve-year-old child to be abandoned in the middle of it would be a pretty intimidating experience and I could see that Kylie was starting to think about having a cry. She wasn't the only one.

'If Downing Street get to hear that she belongs to an employee they'll never believe we didn't set them up,' said the Deputy Director General. 'Go and find out who the hell she's with, Bell.'

Hope! A chance! I might just get away with it! All I had to do was rush down, get Kylie out and then blame it on the friend of a friend of a scene-shifter. I was about to bound out of the box when I saw Kylie tearfully hailing a passing floor assistant. I watched in horror as the floor assistant put her microphone to her lips.

'Hello, Control.' The floor manager's voice floated out of the console loud and clear. 'I've got a little girl here called Kylie, says she's Sam Bell's niece. Is he about at all because she wants to go home.'

Dear Pen Pal

Honestly, trust Sam. Just when I want to be at my absolute most relaxed and non-tense he has gone and made a complete ass of himself at work. He tried not to tell me about it which was nice of him seeing as I'm trying to be as one with my karma, but he was writing at his book for so long that I had to ask him and it all came out. I feel awful for him, but I'm afraid I've had to tell him that I'm not going to think about it, I just can't. Every fibre of my being is currently dedicated to being in tune with the ageless rhythm of life and, however you look at it, the politics of television are simply not a part of the ageless rhythm of life. Sam doesn't mind. He never wants to talk about anything anyway, like most men I think. They don't want to touch, they don't want to talk. They just want to drink, watch TV, drink and bonk.

Dear Book

The *Livin' Large* story was in all the papers on Sunday (PM humbled by child) and they're still carrying it today. I've been named in every single article, of course. Despite me issuing a very clear statement, nobody believes that I didn't set it all up. It's just too convenient what with the girl being my niece and all.

I did not go in to work today and took the phone off the hook. I really am in very deep shit and I don't want to talk to Lucy about it because she has enough on her mind. Funny how writing this book has actually ended up as a sort of therapy for me, although it has nothing to do with having kids.

Dear Penny

I feel terribly sorry about Sam's travails but despite that I also feel curiously centred and at one, almost elated. I know I must not get my hopes up, but I do definitely feel different.

Sam seems to think he's going to lose his job but if only I could be pregnant I wouldn't mind about us being poor or anything. Sam always says, 'Ha!' when I say things like that and of course I know he's right, but if all we have would buy me a baby I'd spend it tomorrow.

Dear Book

Lucy keeps going on about not caring about being poor, only about getting pregnant. She says she'd happily see us with nothing as long as we have a child. Lucy seems very certain that it's going to work this time. She really has started to believe in the power of positive thinking. She's even said that if it's a girl she'll call it Primrose.

Actually if it does work I'll get her to do some positive thinking about me keeping my job.

Penny

My period started this morning. I just want to die.

Why did I let myself hope? How could I have been so pathetic? I don't know why, but I was. What with the crystals and the ley lines and the positive thinking and everything. I just thought for once I'd get some luck.

Why me?! Why bloody me?! Some women scarcely even want children and have them. I want nothing else!

My sister's got two. Melinda's got one. Every bloody woman in Sainsbury's seems to have about twelve. I know I shouldn't resent them but sometimes I do. It just is so unfair! Of course I know that lots of other women are in the same boat as me and all that but I just don't care about them. That's all. I don't.

Dear Self

Well, the Primrose Hill Bonk bore no fruit. Bugger.

I'm afraid to say that even I had begun to get my hopes up a bit. Poor Lucy was being so positive that she made me feel positive too. I was even having fantasies about what life would be like if we had one. Just tea-time and story-telling-type fantasies, that sort of thing. Loading up the car to go camping and . . .

I'm going to stop now.

Dear Penny

I was alone at work again today so I spent five hours on the phone trying to get through to Dr Cooper to see if I can get a referral to have a laparoscopy. Most of the 247 'getting pregnant' books that I own suggest that this will probably be the next step and Dr Cooper certainly said it would be.

I couldn't even get through to the surgery. There's some sort of flu epidemic on and it's obvious that they're a bit pushed. I'm afraid that we're going to have to consider having it done privately. I don't like to because Sam and I have always felt very strongly about the NHS, but I don't think I have any choice. The waiting lists are so long now that even though you want to do the right thing you can't. Funny, really, because these days I actually feel that because the lists are so long I should go private anyway if I can afford it, just to free up a bed. Extraordinary. I remember when Mrs Thatcher had that operation on her hand and said, 'I didn't add to the queue,' we all went potty at dinner parties all over London and now we're saying exactly the same thing.

I am so depressed.

Dear Sam

Lucy wants to have a laparoscopy done privately because she can't get through to Dr Cooper. I said *absolutely not*. I pretended that it was a matter of political principle and expressing our solidarity with the NHS. The truth is it's the money pure and simple. It's now pretty much a certainty that Nigel is going to shaft me and until I know what the future holds I can't countenance any additional expense.

I went to Oddbins today and downgraded from single malt to blended.

Dear Penny

I am really quite proud of Sam. He was absolutely immovable on the private operation bit. I had no idea he had retained such a firm grip on his political principles. Good for him.

I've booked the private operation for the end of next month.

Dear Sam

Well, I knew that it was only a matter of time before the axe fell and it fell today. I finally lost my job. I think the whole corridor knew before I did. Trevor avoided my eye and Daphne looked distinctly upset. I'm a pretty easy-going sort of boss and I think she's scared they're going to give her to some twenty-eight-year-old Armani clothes hanger who thinks only American sitcoms are funny.

Anyway, there was a warning sign in every face, so by the time I got to Nigel's office to which I'd been summoned I was ready for anything. In a way it wasn't so bad.

'Radio,' said Nigel.

'Radio,' I said.

'Radio,' said the Head of Radio and Television, who was also in attendance. 'I'm extremely keen to up our light entertainment output in sound-only situations. Your massive experience in bringing on the best of the new comedians and writers makes you the perfect person to head up this major new entertainment initiative.'

Which means that it would be more trouble and expense to sack me than to shift me to a job where it doesn't really matter what I do.

'What's the job title?' I asked.

'Chief Light Entertainment Commissioning Editor, Radio,' said the Head of Radio and Television.

'What about the money?' I said.

'The same,' Nigel replied, to my delight, 'if you go quietly and *don't* write any bitter whistle-blowing articles in the *Independent* media section or *Broadcast* magazine.'

And so the deal was done, effective immediately. I was to clear my desk that very day. One slightly dispiriting thing. I'd asked Nigel if I could take Daphne with me over to Broadcasting House (where my new office is to be). He said fine but then *she* refused! I could tell that she thought that radio was a definite step down and could see no reason why she should have to share in my reduction of status.

'No, thank you, Sam,' she said. 'It's very kind of you but I'm the personal secretary to the "BBC Controller, Broken Comedy and Variety", which is a *television* post. I am not personal secretary to the "Chief Light Entertainment Commissioning Editor, *Radio*".'

So there you go. Was it Kipling who said they were more deadly than the male? (Women, that is, not personal secretaries.)

If I thought I had a nothing job before, I don't know what I've got now. I mean, radio entertainment's fine up at the posh end, the Radio 4 clever quizzes, witty, varsity stuff and edgy alternatives, but all that's already spoken for. I've been dumped down at the Radio One 'yoof' end and they don't want comedy. They want attitude and I'm a deal too old to give them that.

Anyway, to my surprise Lucy was quite positive about the situation. She pointed out that I'd never liked my job anyway, and now I'd have the time to do what I really want to do, which is write.

Well that, of course, brought on the same old row.

'Oh yes, that's a good idea,' I said. 'I'll just bash off an award-winning script now, shall I? Except hang on, that's right, I remember, I haven't written a bloody word in years.'

'And do you know why?' she snapped. 'Because you've given up on your emotions, that's why. If you live your life entirely superficially how do you expect to write anything?'

Well, this sort of thing carried on back and forth until we went to bed, both pretty depressed. Lucy was out like a light, emotionally exhausted, poor thing, what with all that infertility about the place and having a completely useless husband. I, on the other hand, couldn't sleep. What Lucy had said kept ringing in my ears. Maybe I do avoid my writing so that I don't have to explore my emotions? Or is it the other way round? Do I ignore my feelings so that I'll be sure that I'll have nothing to write about? Either way it's a pretty sad effort. Then I began to wonder what my emotions would be if I had any. What did I feel when I wasn't avoiding my feelings? That I want to write? Who cares? That I love Lucy? Well that's not a bad subject. Love always goes down well. That I want Lucy and me to have children? I certainly feel that. I may never say it, but I want more than anything else in the world for Lucy and me to have children.

And then it struck me! It was such a shock that I went cold. It was so obvious! How could I have missed it! That's what I would write about! I sat bolt upright in bed.

'I've got it, Lucy!' I shouted and she nearly fell out of bed in shock.

'Got what?'

I could hardly form a coherent sentence I had so much to say.

'My theme. The inspiration I need! It's so obvious, darling, I can't think how I've missed it. I'll write about an infertile couple! It's a real modern drama, about life and the absence of life . . . There's jokes, too. But proper jokes. Sad jokes, which are the best kind. Sperm tests, post-coital examinations, guided fantasy sessions . . . Imagine it! The disinte-gration of this couple's sex life, the woman beginning to think about nothing but fertility . . . Adopting a gorilla . . .'

Writing it down now I admit it looks a little insensitive but I swear I didn't mean it to be. After all, I was talking about writing a *story*, a fiction, about two fictitious people, not *us* at all.

'The thing will write itself,' I said and the ideas just kept tumbling into my head and straight out of my mouth.

I would have gone further, but at that moment Lucy stopped me. She threw half a cup of cold herbal tea in my face.

'How about a scene where the woman throws her herbal tea all over the callous bastard who wants to rape her soul for a few cheap laughs,' she said.

It took me a moment to cut through the bitter irony to realise the point she was making. I was astonished.

'What!' I exclaimed. 'But you said! You said! You told me to look within!'

'I didn't tell you to try to turn our private misery into a public joke!' I've hardly ever seen her so angry. 'You don't understand anything!' she said. 'I'm thirty-four. I've been trying for a child for over five years! I may well be barren, Sam!'

Well, now I admit that I lost it a bit too. I mean, it seems to me that Lucy has developed a habit of seeing the fertility thing as being pretty much exclusively her problem. I'm in this marriage too, aren't I? I have feelings and I had thought that I was under orders to get in touch with them. I don't know, perhaps we can't have children. But if we can't, what does she want me to do about it? Weep and wail over the absence of a life that never even existed in the first place?

I'm afraid I put this point to Lucy and she took it as confirmation of her long-nurtured suspicion that I don't care whether we have a baby or not.

'And what if I don't?' I said. 'Does that make me a criminal? Have I betrayed our love because I happen to place some value on my own existence? On my career and my work? Because I have not committed my entire emotional well-being to the possibility of some abstract, nonexistent life that we may or may not be able to produce?'

Lucy was near to tears, but like the bastard that I am I pressed my advantage.

'I mean, isn't this near deification of the next generation all a bit bloody primitive? A baby is born. Its parents devote their lives to it, sacrificing everything they might have hoped to have done themselves. Then, when that baby is finally in a position to fulfil its own destiny and also the dreams its parents had for it, that baby has its own baby and the whole thing starts again. It's positively primeval.'

Lucy got up and went and made herself a cup of herbal, which I hoped she wasn't planning to throw at me. When she came back I tried to calm things down a bit, so that we could get some sleep if nothing else.

'Look, Lucy, I'm sorry . . . I don't want to upset you. Of course I want us to have a baby, it's just . . . it's just. . .'

Lucy was not in the mood to be calmed.

'It's just you want to write a comedy about it,' Lucy said. 'Well, if you *ever* even so much as *mention* the idea of exploiting our personal misery for your profit again I'll leave you. I will, Sam. I mean that.'

With that she turned her back on me and we lay there together in grim, wakeful silence.

Dear Penny

I had a pretty rotten night last night. Sam and I had a row. He thinks I'm a mawkish self-indulgent obsessive and I think he's an arrogant self-obsessed emotional retard. However, I'll write no more of that at the moment because there was dreadful news this morning that certainly puts my little worries into perspective.

Melinda rang at about nine to say that Cuthbert had been taken into hospital with suspected meningitis. Of course, it might not be. All we can do is wait. I can hardly bear to think about it. Sam, of course, seems completely unmoved by the news. I know that he isn't, but that's how he seems.

Dear Book

I don't know what Lucy wants from me. We heard horrible, horrible news from George and Melinda today. Cuthbert has suspected meningitis. Lucy's got herself very upset about it indeed, which I think is unhelpful. There's no point presuming the worst, after all, and so far it's only suspected. When we heard I said, 'Oh dear, that's absolutely terrible. Poor George and Melinda.' I could see immediately that she did not feel that this was a sufficiently emotionally charged reaction, so I said, 'Oh dear' again, but it just sounded worse. It's frustrating. Of course I'm worried about it and terribly sorry for George and Melinda but I don't know what else I can say.

Dear Penny

No news on Cuthbert. Tests still being carried out.

I went for my interview with the private doctor today. Dr James. One ten-minute appointment, one letter, one hundred pounds, that will do nicely, thank you.

Anyway, Dr James saw me promptly, which was a new experience for me, and they also offered coffee and biscuits which I did not have as I imagine that in the private sector the going rate for a custard cream is about ten quid. I told Dr James how far I'd got with investigating infertility and as expected he booked me in for a bellybutton broadcast. It makes me feel quite ill even to think about it.

Afterwards I went up to the Royal Free in Hampstead to see Melinda and Cuthbert. It was heartbreaking. Melinda is bearing up but has had very little sleep and looks pretty grim. Cuthbert was in an isolation ward and I didn't see him, but Melinda says he looks so vulnerable and fragile that she could hardly bear it. Then she started crying and I cried too, which was absolutely ridiculous as I was supposed to be comforting her. So I told her about Sam and me shagging on top of Primrose Hill, which made her laugh, but of course the story doesn't have a funny ending because it didn't work.

When I left the hospital I had to go and sit on a bench on the Heath for a while because I was too upset and emotional about poor little Cuthbert. I mean, obviously he's not mine but I know him pretty well and quite frankly any baby in torment has always broken my heart. I rang Sam on his mobile just for a chat, but he's in the process of tying up the loose ends of his old job and I could tell he was busy. 'So no news, then?' he said, which really meant, 'Why the hell are you calling me?' Sam is very practical in that respect.

Anyway, I wasn't feeling much better when I got back to work, which I'm afraid was not necessarily a very good thing. You see, when I got to the office, in, as I must point out again, a highly vulnerable and emotional state, the place was empty save for Carl Phipps!

There is no point denying that he looked handsome. Very handsome. He'd hung up his big coat and was standing there in a baggy white shirt open to the chest. What with his tight black Levi 501s and his Cuban-heeled boots all he needed was a rapier and he could have fought a duel.

'Sheila and Joanna are down at the Apollo press call,' he began to explain, but then he said, 'You've been crying.'

'No, I haven't,' I lied pathetically.

'Tell me what's wrong, Lucy. I hate to see you cry.'

Well, that was it. Suddenly I was in floods and before I knew it he had his arm around me and was comforting me. I honestly do not think that at this point he was making a move on me. At least, if he was it was a very subtle one. Anyway, first I told him all about little Cuthbert and how worried I was for George and Melinda. He was quite wonderful about that actually, genuinely concerned and in fact he knew rather a surprising amount about the symptoms.

'The majority of suspected cases turn out to be just that, suspected.'

'How do you know?' I asked into his chest.

'I played a junior doctor in three episodes of Angels a few years back. Tiny part but that's never an excuse for not doing the research.'

He was stroking my hair now, just in a comforting way.

'The symptoms in these cases are quite generalised and sometimes the real cause of the problem is never known; the baby just gets over it.'

I must say, he made me feel a lot better about things, such a change from Sam, which I know is a horrible thing to say but it's how I felt. Anyway, I ended up telling him all about myself, even all my infertility fears. He was a really good listener, which is quite rare in an actor, and really seemed concerned. Of course he came up with all the same old stories that everyone comes up with about friends and cousins who tried for years and then had ten, but somehow coming from him they seemed genuinely comforting.

Long story short. I can't put off writing it any longer. I admit it. I kissed him. Yes, I kissed him and it was fantastic. We were talking and talking and talking and then he brushed a tear from my eyelash and then he took my hand and suddenly we were kissing. And proper kissing, too, a genuinely fully charged tongue-twanging passionate clinch.

Oh my God, I go weak to think of it.

I suppose it went on for a minute or two (maybe three, no more). Just big kissing. He didn't try to push his luck, which was damn lucky really.

Anyway, in the end I pulled away. Well, it really was either that or progress further, which would have been terrible! My God, what am I even thinking of? He was ever so good and nice about me wanting to stop (not that I did want to!). He just got up, kissed my forehead gently and said, 'If ever you need someone to talk to, I'm one call away. One call.' Then he was gone.

Well, work was out of the question after that, so I just staggered home and here I am, reflecting on it all. I haven't been kissed like that in a long time. Of course I feel guilty but I can't deny I also feel very exhilarated. But then I think of Cuthbert and my own infertility and feel completely wretched about being excited by a kiss. I do wish life was easier.

It's a little bit later now and I feel worse. I got to thinking about Sam, you see, and obviously started feeling guilty. Not just about the kiss but also about last night. He suggested writing a screenplay about an infertile couple and I absolutely exploded, which I'm not sure was quite fair. After all, it's been me that's been pressing him to explore his emotions further and use his feelings in his work. Obviously I did not mean quite such specific emotions. Him exploiting our most private agonies for easy laughs and cheap emotional stings is out of the question, but I still think I should have been a bit gentler in rejecting the idea.

By the time he came home I was feeling very loyal to him, in need of his love and in need of showing him mine. I tried to hold him and to hug him and to bond in both a physical and emotional sense but, surprise, surprise, he just gave me a peck on the cheek and went to his bloody study to brood about his career. If he wants to drive me into the arms of Heathcliff style Byronic actors then he's doing a good job.

He didn't even ask if I'd heard how Cuthbert was.

Dear Sam

I got home and found Lucy all clingy and wanting to talk about the strengths in our relationship. Well, I'm sorry but I just can't do that stuff at the moment. I don't think she realises how much my life has been screwed up recently, or if she does realise she doesn't care. As far as she's concerned I'm there to offer either affection or sperm as and when she feels she needs it. My worries, my complete humiliation at work, the ignoble end to a career I've worked on since leaving university, she sees these things as selfish and unworthy obsessions.

I mean, for God's sake! The world doesn't need any more babies! Millions and millions starve every year, millions more live in a misery of deprivation and abuse. Why don't a few people start *not* having babies? Why don't a few people start living their own lives, fulfilling their own destinies? That's what I say.

I suppose the truth is that I'm lying to myself because I want us to have one too. It may not be all I care about, but it's what I care about most.

Poor Lucy. She only wanted me to show her that I love her and my God I do love her. I love her and fancy her so much. That night on Primrose Hill was just magical, even though it didn't work.

It's just that I'm not very expressive, I suppose. Bugger everything.

Dear Penny

Melinda rang at seven o'clock this morning. It's not meningitis. I'm so happy for her because it would have been almost unbearable. Cuthbert's going to have to stay in for a while under observation but he's really rallied.

I told Sam and he said, 'Oh great, that's absolutely brilliant, I mean really wonderful news, fantastic,' but after a minute he went back to looking at the media appointments section of the Guardian.

Anyway, when I got to the office today Sheila said, 'Have you been injecting Sam with monkey glands or something?'

I had no idea what she was talking about but I soon found out. On my desk there were a dozen red roses and the card attached said, 'You're beautiful and I must have you.'

I mean, it was there for all to see. No wonder Sheila presumed it must be Sam. I mean, for someone to leave a message like that, open, for all to see, he's got to be pretty confident of his ground, hasn't he? I must have gone a red so deep it would have been visible in Australia. Sheila spotted my confusion, of course.

'Unless it isn't from Sam,' she said wickedly.

'Oh no!' I said, far too loudly. 'They're from Sam. We've had a row. I expect he's trying to make up. How embarrassing.'

I'm so angry I could . . . I mean all right, yes, I kissed Carl Phipps, which was very very wrong of me, but that does not give him the right to start making public requests for intercourse, does it? Surely not? I'm a married woman! What's more, it's the appalling arrogance. The swine is so damn sure of himself.

I mean, yes, I admit it, I fancy him. But this is too much. The moment Sheila went out for her cigarettes, I phoned him at home.

'Yo,' said his answerphone (yes, 'Yo', gruesome), 'the Phipps man here. I'm either out, busy or too shagged out to pick up the phone. If it's about work then you can call my people' (my people! That's us!), 'on 0171, etc . . . Or if it's about stuff in LA you could talk to Annie on 213, etc . . . If it's about New York you could call William Morris on 212, etc . . . Otherwise, hey, do that message stuff after the beep thing.'

Well, having sat through that, I'd had plenty of time to prepare myself.

'Carl, it's Lucy from the office. Just who the hell do you think you are? I think you're horrible! Do you imagine I'm a slut? Well, let me tell you that just because you're quite good looking doesn't mean I'm going to sleep with you, all right? I'm a married woman so you can just bloody well forget it! Oh, by the way we need an answer on that soap powder ad script we sent you. Goodbye!'

I felt a lot better after that.

Dear Self

Now I really am hurt. I felt so mean this morning about everything that I sent some roses to Lucy at her office. I sent rather a saucy message too. I thought she'd be pleased. I thought when I got home tonight she'd leap on me. But no, nothing. She didn't mention it!

Anyway, then I thought perhaps the flowers didn't arrive, so I asked her if she'd had any surprises on her desk that morning.

I swear she went white.

'What?' she said. 'What do you know about it? Who told you? Have you been talking to Sheila?'

'I haven't been talking to anyone,' I said. 'I just wanted to know if you got my red roses this morning.'

Did I say that she went white before? Well, it must have only been pale because *now* she went white.

'The roses . . . you sent me?' she said.

'Yes, with the saucy note. Did you get them?'

'Oh, yes,' and her voice sounded like that of a dying hamster, a hamster dying of a sore throat. 'I got them.'

Then she became almost hysterical.

'Why?!' she shouted. 'Why did you send them?! My God, and that note! It was stupid! Stupid, stupid, stupid.'

Well, that was it. I walked out. I'm actually writing this in the pub. I mean, all the times she's gone on about me not showing her any affection and now, now I try to do something sexy and romantic and she screams at me.

I'm sorry. I know I'm not supposed to say this. I know I'm not supposed even to *think* it, but *bloody* women!

Dear Penny
I want to DIE. I JUST want to DIE.

Dear Sam
My first day in the new job today, which meant a ridiculously early 5.00am start. Lucy brought me a cup of tea, which was very nice of her although frankly I'm not sure she'd been to sleep. She kissed me and thanked me properly for the flowers. She said she was sorry about last night and it was just the tension of everything what with the looming laparoscopy and all. I told her not to worry and I think that we put the atmosphere behind us.

My new office is located at Broadcasting House, which I like. It's so old and truly BBC. It's also in town rather than miles out west and very easy for me on the tube.

My new job is awful. My principal responsibility seems to be the Radio 1 breakfast show. They have a sensational new signing at the moment, a bloke called Charlie Stone, who is supposed to be the absolute last word in postmodern youth broadcasting, which means he cracks knob gags in places where knob gags were previously considered taboo, i.e. at seven thirty in the morning on the nation's number one radio show. He's actually very good in a completely indefinable way, which is what star quality is, I suppose. Of course he gets an enormous amount of complaints. Which I believe the Channel Controller finds very encouraging.

The Controller's name is Matt Crowley and I had been emailed to meet him at the studio to 'check out' Charlie's show live.

'He's at the cutting edge of postmodern zoo radio,' my new controller assured me. 'Satirical, confrontational, anti-establishment and subversive.'

Which as always means knob gags.

When I arrived Crowley was already there (bad start) and we stood together behind the glass wall watching Charlie and his posse entertain the waking nation. I joined him at the end of a song called 'Sex My Sex' from a singer called Brenda, who is incredibly pretty and is always appearing in her bra on the cover of *Loaded*.

'All right,' said Charlie, 'that was another very sexy waxing from the very sexy Brenda. It made me want to reach for the knob . . . To turn up the volume, I mean! Tch, what are you lot like? And what a very sexy lady Brenda is. She makes my tackle taut. How could she not? She makes my luggage leap, my stonker stand. Sorry if that sounds sexist, but I'm sworn to speak only the truth.'

I was pretty astonished actually. It's so long since I listened to Radio 1 I hadn't realised how blokey it had got.

'And speaking of sex,' Charlie went on, 'tell me, lovely listeners, when did you first feel sexy? I want to hear about your first bonk. Yes, I do, and we know you're dying to tell. Did the earth move? Did you smoke afterwards or just gently steam? Think about it and give us a bell.'

Matt turned to me with a pleased proprietorial look.

'Brilliant, right?'

'Oh, right,' I assured him.

'So, here's how it is, mate,' Crowley continued. 'I may be your controller, but he's your boss, OK? *The Breakfast Show* is the station flagship. It's his show and you work for him. Your number-one occupation is to stop him getting poached by Virgin or Capital.'

Later on, alone in my new office, I made a decision.

A big and terrible decision, a decision I never imagined myself making, a decision I hate myself for even thinking about. But I've done it now and deep down, even though I know I'm wrong, I know I'm right.

Dear Penny

I've taken the week off work. After the way I've shamed myself with Carl Phipps I may never leave the house again. What must he think of me? My God! Every time I think about it I want to kill myself.

What am I to do? I'm bound to see him sooner or later. Perhaps I'll give up my job. After all, now that Sam has been transferred to radio (Sam keeps saying 'the shame of it' but I don't see what's so wrong with radio), the threat of our immediate financial ruin seems to have lifted somewhat. If I left the office I'd never have to see Carl again. I must say it's tempting.

Dear Traitor

Well, I've done it. If Lucy ever finds out, which in the end she must, I cannot bear to think what her reaction will be. But whatever the harvest, I've pitched my idea about an infertility film to George and Trevor at the BBC. I know it's terrible and madness and I'm putting at risk everything I hold dear but I am a writer. Writers write about themselves, all artists draw upon their own experiences and emotions. It's part of the job.

Reading this back, it all looks a bit like special pleading, but I think it's fair. Lucy has no right to ban me from the source of my inspiration. It may be her story but it's my story too. Anyway, I'll change the names.

I spent all last night writing a synopsis. Lucy thought I was doing this book, which I felt pretty guilty about . . . except in a way I think I'm sort of doing what we originally intended, just in a different form. Anyway, I did it and I must say I thought it looked fantastic.

I managed to get my treatment down to just under 1,000 words, which in my experience is about right. That's what I used to long for when I was reading people's treatments. God, the depression when something the size of a telephone directory lands on your desk and you're supposed to respond to it overnight. Besides, Trevor and George had agreed to meet me right away, being such good mates, and I didn't want them to have an excuse for not having read it. I biked it over to the BBC first thing this morning and we all met up at noon at Quark. I can't deny I was nervous.

When I arrived Trevor was alone. I didn't bother with any of the small talk that's normally the rule on these occasions.

'What do you think?' I asked.

'I think it's a fantastic idea, Sam,' he said with real enthusiasm. 'Dark, dramatic. Even the Controller's excited.'

I was amazed. 'You've shown it to Nigel?'

'We didn't tell him it came from you, of course.'

This was extraordinary news. Bringing in a network Controller at such an early stage was scarcely common. In fact it was unheard of.

'It's the Zeitgeist, Sam, the issue du jour,' Trevor explained to me, as if I didn't know. 'Everybody knows somebody who's doing it. That IVF documentary we ran got eight million viewers and there wasn't a laugh in it.'

Just then George came up. He was late because he'd been up at the Royal Free taking Cuthbert for a check-up. Cuthbert appears to be getting back to his old self, insomuch as George was still trying to get sick out of his breast pocket.

'Now look here, Sam,' he said. 'We've all had a gander at your idea and everyone thinks it's marvellous . . .'

'Yes, I've been telling him,' said Trevor.

And suddenly they were both talking at once.

'The scene in the restaurant where she rings up and demands her Restricted Bonking Month bonk.'

'And then the bloke can't get an erection.'

'Brilliant. Did that really happen?'

I admitted that it did.

'How's Lucy taking it, by the way? I mean, it's pretty intimate.'

This was, of course, a pretty tricky point. After all, Trevor and George are both friends of Lucy's and here I was, hoping to convince them to enable me to betray her.

'I'm amazed she's letting you do it,' said Trevor. 'I really am. I mean, I know it's a story and not about her but all the same, you've had to get your research from somewhere.'

It was time to come clean and admit that I hadn't actually told her about my plans yet. After all, I reasoned, there was no sense in getting her all excited if it came to nothing.

'Even if you do give me a commission, I'm going to keep my new job in radio and work incognito.'

I could see that George and Trevor were not entirely convinced that I was embarking on a sensible course of action, but it is not really their problem and one thing I'm sure about is that they love the treatment, as, it seems, does Nigel. Astonishingly, for the first time in as long as I can remember, I seem to be getting somewhere.

Dear Penny,

I went back to work today and there was a note in an envelope on my desk. It was from Carl. I knew it was from him because the envelope was made out of pressed rag paper and it was sealed with wax!

'You are obviously hurting in some way. Perhaps I have hurt you. I know that I never meant to. The truth is, Lucy, that I have felt drawn to you from the very first day we met. It is not just that I find you beautiful, although I do, but there is also a kind of sadness about you, a longing from within that fascinates me and makes me want to know you more. Of course I have no right to feel this way. You are a married woman and the thoughts that I have about you are entirely wrong and inappropriate. Therefore I shall not come into the office again if I can help it and I promise that I will do my best to keep out of your way from now on. Always know, though, that I am your friend and am there for you if you need me. Yours respectfully, Carl Phipps.'

Well, I mean to say! That has to be the loveliest note that anyone has ever sent me. How does he know so much about me? A longing within? I mean it's absolutely spot on. I don't think I've ever met such an intuitive man in my entire life! And it's so generous of him not to be furious about my answerphone message. I mean, for heaven's sake! I called him up and told him to forget about sleeping with me when he hadn't even asked to (well, not in words anyway).

Oh well, it's all over now, isn't it? All over before it even began, which is the best way, and I'm really pleased. But how amazing. I do believe he's actually got a crush on me.

Dear Sam

Lucy had her laparoscopy today. Superb material. I feel awful writing this because obviously it wasn't much fun for her but really, this script is going to write itself. I've never felt so motivated. I do wish I could share this sense of purpose with Lucy because it's just what she's always been wanting for me, but for obvious reasons I must keep my own counsel.

We got up at five thirty. Lucy was not allowed to have even a cup of tea because of the operation. The drive was a nightmare. Rush-hour starts at about three in the morning these days. The propaganda the car industry puts out would give Goebbels and Stalin a run for their money in terms of pure utopian disinformation. They always advertise cars by showing some smug smoothie driving at speed along a gorgeous empty road, with not another car in sight. When in the real world did anyone ever drive along an empty road? I don't think that I've once been in that position in twenty years of driving. They always tell you what the make of the car is. I don't give a toss what the car is. Why don't they tell me where the *road* is? Just once in my life I'd like to drive on a road like that.

It really was a near-surreal experience, sitting there in £15,000 worth of machinery, machinery that was supposed to liberate mankind, crawling along at a walking pace, hating every other car owner on earth. Every morning in every town in Britain virtually every adult gets into his or her tin box and starts hating. Then, having taken all day to calm down, we get back into our boxes and start hating all over again. Yet when asked the question 'Why not get on a bus?' I'm the first person to say, 'No way, they're horrible.'

Dear Penny

I'm writing this while sitting alone in a depressing, plain little hospital room waiting to be done over like a kipper.

Sam drove me to the clinic this morning, which was nice except for the fact that he insisted on doing his 'This traffic is insane' rant as if somehow we weren't as guilty as everyone else. Not easy to stomach without so much as a cup of tea inside me. On the other hand he was solicitous about my forthcoming ordeal, asking lots of questions, which I thought was good of him since I know he hates the whole ghastly business. As indeed do I, but as I say, I appreciate him showing an interest. I know what happens backwards from the 8 million books about fertility I've read in the last year or two. Sam was fascinated; he even jotted one or two things down when the car was stopped in traffic. First they feed a tube into your tummy and pump you full of gas so that they can see your insides better, then they make another hole just above your pubic triangle, and they shove a probe in to move things about a bit so that they can take their pictures. They also pump in a lot of dye which apparently will bring out the finer features. Sam actually laughed at this, but I think it was just because he was nervous.

It's amazing what women have to go through, so weird. I wonder if it would be funny to have a scene where the doctor (possibly gay) offers the woman a choice of colour dyes to see which one would go nicest with the shade of her intestines. Maybe a bit over the top. I'll have to think quite carefully about the tone of this script. I mean, is it mainly funny with a bit of emotion, or mainly emotion with a bit of funny? Somewhere in between, I think.

Anyway, once they've got everything pumped up and dyed and prodded into position they make a hole just under your bellybutton and put a long fibre-optic telescope through with a camera on the end. God, what a thought. As I was telling Sam, I was actually beginning to feel sicker and sicker. It was lucky that I didn't have anything in my stomach to throw up as we've just had the car valeted. One strange thing was that as I was telling Sam the gory details I suddenly remembered that I'd meant to have my bikini line done and I was really annoyed that I hadn't.

One brilliant thing Lucy told me was that she had wanted to have her bikini line waxed! Superb stuff! I improvised a line there and then . . . I said, 'Blimey, Lucy, it's a laparoscopy, not lap dancing,' which I think cheered her up and I'll certainly keep it for the script.

Sam just made stupid jokes, which was a bit irritating, although I know he meant well. The thing is that I don't think he really understands how demeaning and dehumanising the whole process is. You're not a woman any more, you're just a thing under a microscope, like in biology at school. I shan't write any more now because I can hear a trolley clanking in the corridor and I fear my hour has come.

Lucy was pretty zonked out when I picked her up this afternoon, so I couldn't get much out of her on the journey home. The doctor said it had all gone fine, anyway, and that they would give us the results in a few days, 'When we've got the photos back from the chemist,' he said. I hate doctors who crack glib little jokes like that. I mean, that's my wife's internal organs he's talking about! I think I'll use him in the movie, though. Stephen Fry would play him brilliantly.

When we got home Lucy went straight to bed. I'd intended to spend the evening doing some more work on my script but somehow I don't feel like it. What with Lucy in a drugged sleep upstairs, I'm feeling a bit cheap. Guilty conscience, I'm afraid. I do hope I'm not weakening. I must see this through. It's the first thing I've felt genuinely excited about in years.

Dear Penny

Well, yesterday I had the laparoscopy and today I've got a very sore throat. Sam was particularly interested in that, wondering how you could end up with a sore throat when the business was so very much down the other end. He seemed quite excited for a minute as if there might be some extraordinarily exotic reason for this phenomenon. When I explained it was just where the anaesthetist had stuck a breathing tube down my throat he actually seemed quite disappointed.

Dear Book

There really is no job for me at Broadcasting House. They just made one up to avoid a run-in with the union. Ostensibly my responsibility is to commission youth-orientated comedy, but I have absolutely no money whatsoever to do this with. The entire youth entertainment budget, and I mean all of it, has been spent on Charlie Stone's wages. I couldn't believe it when I found out. I can't spend the rest of my career pretending to laugh at Charlie Stone's knob gags, I just can't. My script development is my way out. Lucy would understand, I know she would.

Not that I'm going to tell her.

Dear Penny

Sam and I went to see Dr James, my consultant, today. Actually I think he's called Mr James. I've always found that confusing about consultants. It seems that the higher a person rises in the medical profession the less grand the title they get. Probably quite healthy, really. Stop them getting too pompous.

Anyway, the good news is that they've found nothing wrong with my innards. I do not have endometriosis, which is an enormous relief. Also I have recently ovulated.

'Tremendous news, that,' said Mr James, who is a brutally cheerful type. 'Can't make an omelette without eggs.'

There are no fibroids on the outside of the uterus and to the best of Mr James's knowledge no congenital problems in the womb ('can never be one hundred per cent sure, though'). There are also no cysts and no apparent abdominal diseases.

We were also shown some photographs of my insides, which Mr James described as 'beautiful' but which Sam and I agreed were absolutely obscene. All yellow and red and purple. Like stills from a horror movie.

'Lovely,' said Mr James. 'Absolutely lovely. You've got tip-top guts.'

After we had all admired my digestive system, Mr James got back to the subject at hand.

'So, as I say, most encouraging indeed. We didn't find a thing wrong.'

So that's all right, then. Lovely. Couldn't be better. Except for one tiny little thing, of course. I am still not fucking preg! To this I'm afraid Mr James had no answer. Sam and I remain cursed with what is described medically as 'non-specific infertility', or, to give it its full description, 'We do not have a fucking clue.'

So what now?

Well, what else? IVF, of course. Mr James said we could wait, we're relatively young, we might just have been unlucky. It might work out conventionally. Mr James says that actually quite a few previously infertile women do conceive after having a laparoscopy. Something to do with it flushing out the tubes, but nonetheless he felt it was probably time to begin some form of treatment.

Bugger. I never thought it would come to this. It would actually have been easier if he'd said, Look, the photos are the worst I've ever seen. No eggs. No tubes. No chance. Forget it for ever. Except that would have been unbearable.

Dear Sam

Today we went to see our consultant and got Lucy's lapa results. Good news and bad news. They found nothing wrong, which is good; on the other hand, they found nothing that they could 'cure', so to speak, so that's bad. Poor Lucy now faces the prospect of IVF treatment and she is pretty down about it. Well, I can't say I like the idea much myself. Of course it does mean that I'll get first-hand knowledge of the whole horrible process for my film, which will be extremely useful, but that is absolutely and completely beside the point. I'm aware that I'm secretly exploiting Lucy's misery (and my own) for our future gain, but I'd happily give it away right now. Film or no film, if there was anything on earth I could do to make Lucy pregnant, I'd do it.

Honestly. It's important that I set this down on record. The film means nothing. If tomorrow Lucy fell pregnant naturally I'd be the happiest man in the world. I can research IVF stuff without her anyway.

Dear Penny

Despite the fact that we are now definitely on the road to IVF, I've decided to make love to Sam every day this month in the hope that the laparoscopy 'tube clearing' theory will bear fruit. We started last night and I have a dreadful confession to make. About halfway through I found myself thinking about Carl Phipps.

I love Sam, of course, absolutely. But it's different.

Dear Sam

Lucy has decided to begin a cycle of IVF after her next period (presuming we don't score in the meantime with her newly flushed-out tubes). Dr Cooper, our GP, is writing to the people at Spannerfield Hospital, which is one of the top places for fertility treatment, to get us an appointment to see them.

I had a big meeting at Broadcasting House today. Infuriating, really, because I'm getting along splendidly with the script and the last thing I want to be bothered with is my actual job. The Beeb have now officially commissioned my film, by the way, which is absolutely wonderful. I am now a professional writer. It's not a bad deal at all for a first film: £40,000, but in stages. Final payment to be made on completion of principal photography, so I'm only actually guaranteed £10,000 at the moment for the first draft. I've asked Aiden Fumet to look after my business. I must say, now he's on my side I like him much better. I didn't go in with him myself when the deal was made. George and Trevor didn't feel that Nigel was quite ready yet for the news that the brilliant new writer they'd found is, in fact, the despised and sacked Sam Bell.

Anyway, as I say, I'm now a professional writer with a script fully in development at the BBC, which is an absolutely thrilling thing to be. The only fly in my professional ointment is that I still have my job at Radio which I must keep up in order to avoid making Lucy suspicious, and of course for the cash. We can't survive for the next six months on ten grand plus the minute sum Lucy makes at the agency.

So, bright and early this morning, after Lucy and I had had a three-minute quickie ('Don't worry about me, just get on with it,' were her bleary, sleepy words), I left her lying in bed trying to eat toast with three pillows under her bum and her legs propped up against the wall, and rushed off for my meeting..

The meeting was fascinating in its banality. It was a seminar pertaining to the Director General's Regional Diversity Directive (the DGRDD), which is called 'The Glory of the Quilt'. I don't know why it's called 'The Glory of the Quilt'. Somebody in the lift said they thought it related to Britain being a patchwork.

The seminar was being chaired by the Head of Youth, BBC Radio, whose name is Tom. Tom and I had already met. He called me in to impress upon me that he did not mind jokes about drugs or even anal sex. In fact he positively encouraged 'cutting edge' material, as long as it was on after nine in the evening and was in no way exploitative or offensive to minority groups.

Anyway, Tom kicked off in pretty general terms.

'Hi, yo. Welcome to this session of the ongoing series of seminars under the Director General's Regional Diversity Directive. The Glory of the Quilt. As you all know, today's ongoing subtopic is Regional Diversity and Youth.'

I hadn't known, actually, but I let it go.

'So, BBC youth radio and the regions,' said Tom. 'As you all know, the Director General is one hundred per cent committed to the BBC diversifying into the regions and I fully support him in his view . . . Bill, I asked you to formulate a comprehensive decentralisation strategy.'

I have not yet discovered what Bill's post is. Nobody I asked knew either (including Tom).

'The key to regional diversification,' said Bill, 'is accents. We need more accents about the place. Northern accents, Scottish accents, at least one Welsh accent.'

Tom leapt on this like a thirsty man hearing the bell at closing time. 'I agree,' he said. 'Accents are the key and I think we need to stress right from the word go that wherever possible those accents should be genuine.' Everyone nodded wisely at this, although Tom himself could see problems.

The problem was that a vast percentage of BBC senior staff are of course from either Oxford or Cambridge, people unlikely to possess overly strong regional accents. The choice, the meeting felt, was pretty stark. Either BBC executives stop giving jobs to their old university friends, or some of those friends will have to pretend that they come from Llandudno.

'I'm not entirely unhappy with that,' said Tom. 'If we're going to teach the kids to speak badly let's at least have people doing it who know the rules that are being broken.'

Dear Penny

I got my period today. One more infertile month to add to the long long line of them that stretch back into my distant past. Sam and I will go and see the people at Spannerfield tomorrow. He's dreading it, I know, although strangely he seems to have suddenly become a lot more interested in the process. During the last day or two he's asked me really quite a lot of questions about ovulation and LH surges and things like that. It's good that he asks, but I'm sure he's only trying to be nice.

Dear Sam

We're going to Spannerfield tomorrow. I'm pretty nervous and a bit depressed about it. I've been using some of these feelings in my script (just as Lucy always wanted me to, I might add), and it's working out rather well. Interestingly, the film is going to be less of an absolutely full-on comedy than I originally thought. Not that it won't be funny. You couldn't avoid it with that many knob gags at your disposal, but it's also going to have its serious side.

I tried a bit out on Trevor and George today. I was really nervous but I wanted to give Colin (that's the name of my lead bloke) something of what I'm feeling. I must say when I read it out to them I thought it sounded far too mawkish, but George and Trevor were very supportive. They think that a bit of emotion will really add depth to the piece and that it will play well against the comedy, which I agree with absolutely.

Dear Penny

Well, we've had our meeting at Spannerfield. Our new consultant's name is Mr Agnew and he seems very nice. He explained that there are two more tests he'd like to carry out before we commit to an IVF cycle. A hysterosalpingo-gram (HSG) for me and another sperm test for Sam. His old test is no good because apparently the Spannerfield IVF people always test the sperm them-selves. The hysterosalpingogram is an X-ray of the uterus and Fallopian tubes. This involves injecting dye into my cervix (again), which I am so look-ing forward to. Sam's test involves him having another wank. But, yet again, he is the one who's kicking up a fuss! I can't believe we're back to all that again. I said to him, I said, 'My God, Sam, it's not the end of the world! I'm asking you to have a quick one off the wrist, not fuck a hedgehog!' He laughed a lot at that and jotted it down on a piece of paper. I don't know why he did that but somehow I thought it was quite touching.

Dear Sam

Lucy says it's just a quick one off the wrist like the last time. Oh yes, just like the last time, except this time they won't let me do it at home! I have to go and masturbate at the hospital! Christ, I can't imagine a more horrible prospect. Unfortunately I made the mistake of saying this to Lucy and she said that she *could* imagine a more horrible prospect, as a matter of fact . . . having long telescopes pushed through your bellybutton, having dye injected into you, having your gut pumped full of air and photographed internally, and above all having every doctor in Britain staring up your fanny on a day-to-day basis.

She said a great line about a hedgehog which I'll definitely use.

INCONCEIVABLE

Dear Penny

Carl came into work today. He had to sign some contracts. We hardly spoke. He smiled a nice smile but then went straight into Sheila's office. It's what he said he'd do in his note and absolutely the right and proper thing, but I can't deny it gave me a jolt. A very large part of me desperately wished he'd stopped and had a chat, you know, just about inconsequential things. Of course, I must never forget that the last time we saw each other we kissed, long and hard, in fact. And Carl is right: that's a fire which must definitely not be fed. I mean, basically I've already been a bit unfaithful to Sam. I mean, not really, of course, but a bit, and that's terrible. Let's face it, if I discovered that he'd been pashing on with someone at work, even if it was only once, and totally out of character, I'd still be pretty bloody angry, to say the least.

Dear Book

Well, I must say that this morning has to rank as one of the more gruesome mornings of my life.

Communal masturbation in West London.

Actually that makes it sound better than it was. It makes it sound friendly and inclusive, like a dance or a musical.

It wasn't friendly or inclusive at all.

My God, it was grim. They say they'll see you any time between nine and twelve but Trevor told me to get there at least fifteen minutes before the place opened, as a queue develops. Trevor is an old hand at the sperm test game (ha ha ha), because when he donated to those lesbians they insisted that he have his sperm checked out first.

Anyway, there must be a lot more wankers around than in Trevor's day, because although I slunk in at eight-forty there were already four blokes ahead of me. I sat down as far away from any of them as I could. The long minutes ticked by and at nine o'clock a couple of nurses emerged from various corridors and began to take an interest in things. By this time three more men had turned up and we were being forced to sit right next to each other on the little square of chairs, which nobody liked at all. One of the nurses went to the desk and called out the first name. Up gets the bloke, goes to the desk, gets his pot and is directed down the corridor to the wanking room.

So now we all know the score. One room. One fucking room. We're going in one at a time in a slow, agonising tosser chain. Each of us realises that the amount of time that we're going to have to spend in that hellhole is entirely dependent on those in front of us in the queue. The chain moves at the speed of the slowest wanker.

After about ten minutes the door at the end of the corridor opened and the first man hurried out. He dropped his pot off at a little hatch in the wall, handed some kind of plastic-coated form back to the nurse and he was out, lucky swine. After what I considered an unnecessary minute or two of faffing about, the nurse called out the next name and up got another man, picked up his pot and the plastic-coated form and trundled down the corridor to the masturbation chamber. I must say I found this plastic-coated form a bit disconcerting. What was it? Wanking instructions? Surely most men were up to speed on that one? And *plastic-coated*. That was a bit of a gross touch, I must say.

The next bloke in took nearly fifteen minutes. *Fifteen minutes* to have a wank! I mean I've pulled them off in fifteen seconds in my time! I could see I was not the only one who thought this. Everybody was shuffling their feet a bit and looking at their watches. Eventually, of course, he emerged, and nearly ran past us to get out of the place, and so the long day wore on.

Finally at gone quarter to ten, my number came up. 'Mr Bell,' the lady said. It had to be a woman, of course. Like when you're a kid buying condoms at Boots, you could wait for hours for a lad to take over the till but he never did and you had to buy them off a teenage girl your own age. Anyway, the nurse gave me my pot and the plastic-coated instructions, and when I say plastic-coated, I don't mean neatly laminated, no, I mean a twenty-year-old form in an old plastic bag. That form has seen some sights, I bet.

'Last room on the left,' said the nurse. 'When you've finished leave your pot at the lab hatch and return the form to me.'

Well, I must say I've masturbated in pleasanter environments. Don't misunderstand me: I don't think that the NHS should be consuming its precious resources providing sensually lit boudoirs draped in red velvet and reeking of sultry scents for sad acts like me to wank in. I'm just saying it was all a bit depressing.

There was a chair, a magazine rack, a handbasin and a waste-paper basket. That was it. Apart from that it was completely bare. The plastic-coated instructions informed me that I should carefully wash my hands and knob before getting down to the business of the morning.

So I scrubbed up and viewed the chair. It was a municipal easy-chair consisting of an upright and a horizontal cushion. The sort of chair you would have found in the teachers' common room of a secondary modern school in about 1970. In the magazine rack were some old dirty mags. It's a long time since I've seen the inside of a dirty mag and for a moment I thought, 'Hello, bonus,' but really, you just couldn't get into them at all, they were so *old*. On the wall there was a sign saying, and I kid you not, that any donations of spare 'reading material' would be welcomed. Reading! We live in a world where five-year-olds can dial up snuff movies on the Internet and yet a hospital calls wank mags 'reading material'.

Then suddenly I became aware of the time!

Oh my God, I must have been in that room for two or three minutes already! Instantly I had a vision of all the men outside, shuffling their feet, looking at their watches. Suddenly I was convinced that they were all out there gnashing their teeth and muttering, 'He's reading the articles in the magazines, I'm sure of it.'

Must get down to it! Must get down to it! Don't want to hold up the queue. But how *do* you get down to it under that kind of pressure? It's impossible. I sat on the chair, I stood up, I glanced at a magazine. Panic rose within me and panic was the *only* thing that was rising!

In the end, by a supreme effort I managed to calm myself down a little. I did it by telling myself that the door was locked, that I would never have to see any of those men outside again and that I would take as long as I damn well liked.

Well, I did it. Sort of. I think there was enough. I hope so, anyway. Only time will tell. Looking at my watch I realised that I had been in there for over twenty minutes. I could feel the wave of resentment greet me as I emerged and walked past them all to hand in my pot. I was so embarrassed and flustered that I tried to walk out of the building still holding the plastic-coated form and had to be called back, which was humiliating.

Like I say, I've had better mornings.

Personally, I think it's possible that I'd rather have dye inserted into my cervix, but I'm not going to say that to Lucy, of course.

Dear Penny

Hysterosalpingogram today. It's not supposed to hurt much, but they say you should take along someone to drive you home in case you're upset or in discomfort. Sam, of course, had a very important meeting, which he did offer to cancel but I said, 'No, don't bother, I'm fine.' Drusilla came along, which was nice of her, except she seems to view all hospitals as places of unnatural torture and intrusion where nature is excluded and man insults the gods. This is slightly embarrassing when she talks about it loudly in the waiting room.

'You know half the problems they deal with here can be treated herbally,' she said so that everyone could hear. 'There's very little in life that a rose and lilac enema won't go some way towards curing.'

The hysterosalpingogram itself was all right. Legs up as per. Quick prod about, as per. Bunch of spotty students staring up me in an intense manner, as per. Then in goes the dye, they tilt it back so that the dye can flow through the tubes. Then they took a few X-rays and that was that. The doctor was in and out in ten minutes and I was in and out in twenty. It was all right, although I did feel a bit sick and faint afterwards.

Drusilla and I went for a coffee and I told her about Carl. Amazingly she thinks I should 'put the poor boy out of his misery and shag him'!

I said to Drusilla, Hang on, perhaps we're jumping the gun here, perhaps poor old Carl doesn't particularly want to shag me anyway. Perhaps he really is just a very nice guy who just wants to be my friend.

'Ha!' said Drusilla and she said it so loudly that other ladies spilt their coffee. Drusilla never minds about being noticed. I do.

Dear Sam

Lucy had her pingowhatsit today. She wanted me to go with her but for heaven's sake I have a job. The BBC pays me to sit twiddling my fingers at Broadcasting House, not Spannerfield Hospital. Besides which, today I actually had something to do, believe it or not.

The Prince's Trust are putting on a big concert in Manchester. Radio 1 is going to broadcast it live and the whole concert has been designated a Light Entertainment Brief, i.e. my responsibility. There are two reasons for this. Firstly there will be comedians on the bill (comedy, of course, being the new rock 'n' roll. Like hell). Secondly, the bill will mainly be made up of ageing old rockers, and nobody at Radio 1 who's into music wants to touch it with a bargepole. They all think that because some of the artists who are to perform have committed the cardinal sin of being over forty (and doing music that has tunes) the whole thing is terminally uncool and should be on Radio 2 anyway.

So there we are. It turns out that it is to be me who's heading up the BBC Radio side of the operation, which is why today I found myself back in Quark in Soho having lunch with Joe London. Yes, *the* Joe London, as in lead singer of the Muvvers, a man who bestrode the late sixties and early seventies rock scene like a colossus. They might sneer, back at the office, all those shaven-headed boys wearing yellow sunglasses indoors, but I was bloody excited to meet Joe London. This was my history. Joe was big when I was at school.

'We're all absolutely delighted at Radio 1 that you can do this show for us, Joe,' I said.

'Oh yeah, tasty, nice one, as it 'appens, no problem, geezer.'

'And of course the Prince's Trust are very grateful too.'

'Diamond geezer, the Prince of fahkin' Wales. Lahvly bloke, know what I fahkin' mean? Likes 'is rock does Charlie, big Supremes fan.'

Joe quaffed an alcohol-free lager.

'What's it in aid of, ven, vis concert?' he said.

'Well, Joe, principally helping young kids with drug abuse.'

Suddenly Joe's amiable manner changed.

'Well, I fink vat is fahkin' disgahstin',' he sneered. 'Lazy little sods! When we was young we 'ad to go aht and get our fahkin' drugs ourselves.'

I was just clearing up this misunderstanding and explaining that the point of the show was to help underprivileged youth, when we were joined by Joe's manager, a huge, spherical man with a cropped head and a cropped beard and no neck. His head just seemed to develop out of his shoulders like the top of an egg. He wore a black silk Nehru suit and silver slippers and he was bedecked in what must have been two or three kilos of gold jewellery. His name was Woody Monk and he greeted me with a nod before turning to whistle with approval at our waitress, whose skirt was even shorter than on the last occasion I'd seen it.

I really was dining with the old school. Joe and Woody were rock 'n' roll as it used to be, and it made me feel like a kid again. These days most pop managers look like Tintin with sunglasses.

I asked Woody Monk if it might be too much to hope that Joe would do some interviews to promote the show.

'He'll do as many as you like; we need the profile,' Monk replied, and then, as if to quell any protests that Joe might have, he showed Joe a copy of the *Sun* featuring an article about the current Rolling Stones tour.

'Look at that, Joe!' Monk said. 'Just look at it. I mean, it's obscene, disgusting. That is just a totally ridiculous figure, out of all proportion.'

Joe took off his sunglasses and had a look. 'I don't know, Woody, I like a bit of silicone myself.'

Monk tried to be patient. 'I am not talking about the bird, you divvy! I'm talking about this new Stones tour, one hundred million, they reckon! And the Eagles got the same. It's the arenas and the stadiums,' Monk explained to me, 'megabucks, these places gross in humungous proportions. In the old days when people talked about gross on tour they meant waking up with a mouthful of sick and a strange rash on your naughties.'

Basically, Monk's point was that Joe needed to tour again in the near future. His latest greatest hits album would be out for Christmas and it needed supporting.

'Are we releasing another greatest 'its album, then?' said Joe.

'Yeah, but a prestige one. Nice classy cover, all in gold, the Gold Collection . . .'

'We done the Gold Collection.'

'Orlright. The Ultimate Collection.'

'Done vat too, and the Definitive Collection and the Classic, and the Unforgettable . . .'

'Look, Joe!' Monk snapped. I could see that he was a volatile chap. 'We'll call it the Same Old Crap in a Different Cover Collection if you like, it don't matter. What we have got here is the Prince of Wales flogging your comeback.'

There, it was out, and Woody Monk did not care who knew it. As far as he was concerned this concert was a marketing exercise for Joe London and that was it. Joe, however, seemed a little embarrassed, though not, as it turned out, about the charity angle.

'Vis ain't a fahkin' comeback! To 'ave a comeback you 'ave to 'ave bin away and I 'ave not bin. So vis is not a fahkin' comeback.'

'Orlright,' said Monk. 'It's a fahkin "still here" tour, then.'

I honestly cannot remember when I have had a funnier lunch, and to think I wasted all those years lunching with comedians.

'Anyway, I gotta go,' said Monk, turning to me. 'We're all sorted, aren't we?'

I said that as far as I knew we were extremely sorted.

'Good, 'cos we don't want no fahk-ups. Vis gig is very important.'

'That's right,' said Joe. 'What with the underprivileged kiddies and all vat.'

'Bollocks to the underprivileged kids,' said Monk, hauling his massive bulk to his feet. 'They should get a bloody job, bleeding scroungers.'

So that was that.

Anyway, enough of my day job, time to get down to my script. Lucy is sitting opposite on the bed, looking lovely as she always does. She's very pleased with me at the moment because I seem to be doing so much writing. She thinks it's all for my book. I'll have to tell her soon because things are really progressing with the film. I've called it *Inconceivable* and I've been in to see Nigel to admit that the writer is none other than my despised self. He was a bit taken aback at first but then he laughed and was actually very nice about it. Ever since he commissioned my movie script I've been warming to Nigel and now consider him to be a thoroughly good bloke. Is that desperately shallow of me or evidence of my generous and forgiving nature?

Anyway, the very exciting news is that the BBC really want to get on with it. Nigel feels that the idea is very current and that everybody will be doing it soon. Besides which, the film will be extremely cheap to make, which means that the Beeb can pay for it all by themselves. The reason films usually take years to get together is because that's how long it takes to raise the money, but we're already past that hurdle and Nigel is impatient to become a film producer.

'Movies work in a yearly cycle,' he explained. 'The festival circuit is essential for a small picture. Venice, Sundance, Cannes. You need critical heat under you before the Golden Globes in February.'

He actually said 'critical heat under you'. Strange. Whereas before I would have thought he sounded like a pretentious wanker, now I think he sounds knowledgeable and cool.

Dear Penny

We went in to see Mr Agnew today at Spannerfield. He gave us our test results and everything remains clear. Sam's sperm is fine (about 90 million of them, which is enough, surely?) and a sufficient number of them heading in the right direction to pass muster. Also my pingy thingy seems to have come up normal. Mr Agnew assured me that my tubes aren't scarred, also there are no adhesions, fibroids, adenomyosis, or polyps in the womb, and that the area where the tubes join the uterus is similarly polyp-free. Quite frankly, just hearing about the 8 million things that can go wrong inside a woman's reproductive system is enough to make me ill. All Sam has to worry about is whether his sperm can swim.

Anyway, Mr Agnew was very nice and agreed with me that since we have uncovered nothing operable or treatable and yet we remain stubbornly infertile, the time may now be right to commence a course of IVF. Mr Agnew said that not only would this give us a chance of becoming pregnant (obviously) but it might also prove useful in a diagnostic sense, i.e. we might discover what, if anything, beyond the most incredible bad luck, is the problem. He explained that if we go private we can start next month, so that is what we'll do and I don't care what Sam says. If I'm going to have to do this I'll do it as soon as I possibly can and start the long horrible process of getting it over with. Quite apart from anything else, as far as I can see, the NHS is under such a strain that if we can afford to pay we ought to do so and not take the place of someone who can't. Sam says that that attitude simply reinforces the two-tier system. Well, what if it does? I have a home while other people are homeless, isn't that a two-tier system? Should I go and sit in a doorway to avoid reinforcing it?

Anyway, it's not posh at all. We all get lumped in together and all the profits that Spannerfield makes out of the private patients go straight back into the unit to fund the research programme. Personally I thought that us making a contribution to funding research sounded like a pretty good thing, but Sam says that NHS hospitals using private patients to fund their activities is the thin end of the privatisation wedge.

I couldn't be bothered to argue any further and told him to give all his food and clothes to Oxfam if he felt that strongly about it, which he doesn't.

Sam has just asked me whether hysterosalpingogram begins with 'HY' or 'HI'. He seems to have suddenly got very enthusiastic about doing his book and getting all the details right. I know I should be glad, and I am in a way. It's just that I wish he'd share some of those thoughts and feelings with me. The way we talk to each other and react to each other has become just a little bit mechanical and predictable. Is that what happens in a marriage? Is it inevitable? I'd love to talk to Sam about that sort of thing but I know he'd just try to change the subject.

I'm trying not to think too much about wanting a baby at the moment. I find it drains me. I wake up feeling all fine and then I remember that according to my life plan I ought to have a couple of five-year-olds rushing in to jump into bed with me. That's when a great wave of depression sort of descends, which I then have to fight my way out of by reminding myself how incredibly lucky I am in so many ways. Sometimes it works.

Dear Self

Long meeting with George and Trevor at Television Centre today. Nigel was there for the first hour but then he had to rush off to Heathrow (two-day seminar in Toronto: 'Children's TV: Did Bugs Bunny Win? Cartoons and our children's mental health'). *Inconceivable* is moving at a hell of a speed now. They're already talking about casting and a director. They do have some problems with the script, though. Nothing major, but it's something I'm going to have to think about very hard. It came up after we'd all been laughing at the 'communal masturbation in West London' scene. George brought up what was worrying them.

'It's too blokey, mate. Colin's stuff is really good, hilarious, in fact . . .'

'And touching in a strange sort of way,' Trevor added.

'But Rachel is a worry,' George went on. 'She's a bit two-dimensional.'

We all agreed that she has some good lines, but George and Trevor (and the ninety other BBC bods who seem to have read the thing) felt that she was clearly being drawn from a male point of view.

'You have to get inside the character of the female lead,' said Trevor. 'Maybe you should take on a woman co-writer.'

I can't even bear to write down the terrible thought that leapt immediately into my mind when Trevor said that.

This will need careful consideration.

Dear Penny

The die is cast. I'm booked in to start after my next period, presuming, that is (and I must at all times remain positive), a miracle hasn't happened naturally.

Oh God, I do so want a child. Sometimes I think about praying. Not like going-to-church praying, but just at home in the quiet. In fact, if I'm honest I do occasionally offer up a silent one, just in my head when no one's about. But then I think that that's wrong and presumptuous of me because I don't believe in God in any conventional sense so I have no right to pray to him (her? it?), do I?

I just wish I could find a little comfort because I do want a baby so very much and sometimes the feelings are so strong I don't know what to do with them.

Dear Sam

Lucy got her period today. We've drained the dregs at the last-chance saloon and now it's time to put our trust in the medical profession. Lucy asked me if I'd thought about praying and I said I hadn't but I was happy to give it a go if she wanted me to. Who knows, it might work. It seems to me that the idea of an old man with a white beard sitting on a cloud dispensing goodwill doesn't sound any more absurd than the bollocks most physicists talk. I mean really, every single bloke I know bought *A Brief History of Time* and not one of them, including me, understood a single word of it.

I went in to see Nigel today. He'd rung me twice from Toronto sounding me out about directors and co-producers. He feels we need to bring some experienced film-making talent into the mix. He's right, I think. I mean George and Trevor are great but what do they or I know about doing a distribution deal with a chain of movie houses in France? Besides which, Nigel feels that the budget will need to expand somewhat and put it outside the reach of the BBC alone. The reason for this is not because the film has got any more expensive but because Nigel feels it has such potential that we need to take it to a name director, someone with a proven track record. That, of course, means paying the going rate, which can run into a great deal of cash.

'We need someone with experience,' he said to me over the phone with the voices of Canadian TV execs crackling in the background, 'but hip. We must remember at all times that we are positioning ourselves at the cutting edge.'

I knew what was coming and I wasn't wrong. Today I had my second meeting with Justin, Petra and Ewan Proclaimer from Above The Line Productions.

I must say it was a very different affair this time. Petra actually smiled at me and Justin gripped my shoulder saying, 'On the money, pal. Kickin' ass.' Even Ewan stopped snarling and treated me with a degree of civility. It seems that he's even hotter than he was when I met him at Claridge's. He's landed a three-picture deal to direct in Hollywood.

Anyway, it seems he has a six-month 'window' before he begins pre-production 'across the big pond', and he loves my script.

'I love romantic comedy,' he explained. 'I've always liked romantic comedy but not *shite* romantic comedy. I like romantic comedy with edge, with bite, with *bollocks*! To me *Macbeth* is a romantic comedy, so's *Oedipus*. I mean what could be more romantic than a man loving his ma so much he wants to shag her? And what could be more comical?'

Slightly worrying, but I let it go.

That brought us on to the script, with which there are still two problems—one little and one big. The little problem is that I haven't given the story an end yet. I say this is a little problem because I've actually worked out two endings that would work, one happy and one sad. I haven't been able to choose which one I want to go with yet. I suppose because Lucy and I are just starting IVF ourselves I don't want to tempt fate.

The bigger problem remains the woman's voice in the film. Everyone agrees that I haven't got it right yet and that it's crucial. It's not a big thing, the story's fine, as are the jokes; it's just a matter of tone and emotional emphasis. I have to try and find a way to make the female perspective more convincing.

Time's running out. Petra and Justin are setting up auditions. Ewan is scouting for locations. I must find the woman's voice.

Dear Penny

Picked up my first sackload of drugs from Spannerfield this morning. Me and a bunch of other women, all feeling a bit self-conscious. I have to sniff the first lot, which I'll begin tonight. You sort of shove a pump up your nose and give it a blast. It doesn't sound too difficult so far.

Sam's going to Manchester for a night the day after tomorrow. It's this huge charity concert for the Prince's Trust he's involved with. The BBC are broadcasting it and for some reason it's fallen to Sam to represent them. I could go, of course, and normally I'd love to, but I've told Sam that I'm still feeling a little under the weather after the pingogram and I could use a quiet week.

This is a lie!

My God, I can scarcely believe what I'm writing, but I've decided to see Carl. He rang me at work and asked me out to dinner and I said yes! Of course there's no reason for me to feel guilty or anything, I'm just going to have a bite to eat with a friend. I'm not going to do anything with him, obviously! But nonetheless, I can't say that my conscience isn't troubling me a bit. Because let's face it, I'm not going to tell Sam about it. Well, how can I? I can't say to him, 'Oh, by the way, while you're away I'm going to have dinner with the dishiest man in England whom incidentally I have already snogged,' can I?

Dear Self

I'm writing this in my room at the Britannia Hotel opposite Piccadilly bus station in Manchester, which is, I imagine, what Kremlin Palace must have looked like at the end of October 1917. Magnificent gilt, glittering crystal, carved marble and hundreds of pissed-up yobbos wandering about looking for the bar. I love it. It's real rock 'n' roll.

Most of the BBC posse are staying at the Midland Plaza (which is a Holiday Inn but posher than most). However, Joe London and Woody Monk *always* stay at the Britannia.

'Vey understand a drinking man here,' said Joe. 'Not vat I bovver wiv all vat now, but I like ta rememba, you know wot I mean?'

'And the disco's always full of lahvly fahkin' birds,' Monk added.

On inspection Monk was proved right about this. The disco was full of lahvly fahkin' birds, but very, very tough-looking. Northern girls never cease to amaze me by how tough they look. I think it's the temperature. They seem to be impervious to cold. They never wear tights! In the middle of winter in Newcastle or Leeds you'll see them, making their way from bus station to club, groups of determined-looking girls in tiny minidresses, naked but for a square inch or two of Lycra, bare arms folded against the howling wind, translucent white legs clicking along the sodden pavement in their impossibly precarious shoes. Never mind Scott of the Antarctic, these girls would have done it in half the time and got back before the chip shop closed.

I must say I'm glad I'm married and past all that trying to pull birds business. I'd be far too terrified to talk to girls these days (actually I always was). Still, you can have a bit of a sad old look, can't you? And Monk, Joe and I have just celebrated the end of a great night by having a last drink in the Britannia Hotel disco.

And it has been a great night, I must say. A genuine rock extravaganza. Everything went brilliantly, not like on *Livin' Large*. Believe it or not my bloody sister rang and actually asked if I could take Kylie! I'm afraid the language I used was not very fraternal. I haven't sworn at her like that since we were teenagers.

The show was at the Manchester Evening News Arena, which is just vast. There must have been 15,000 fans in there.

We had an incredible bill. Representing the wrinklies was Joe London, Rod (obviously) and Bowie. We were to have had Phil Collins but there was fog at JFK. Besides this, we actually had a pretty impressive turn-out of current acts. Maybe the Prince is getting hip again. I certainly noticed that when the final bill was announced some of my fashion junkie colleagues at Broadcasting House looked quite miffed not to be involved. The biggest booking of the night was Mirage. They're colossal at the moment and being from Salford were almost local. I went along to the sound check in the afternoon and listened to Mirage's current smash, 'Get Real'.

Strawberry Lane and Penny Fields.
Norwegian Walrus yeah yeah yeah.
Who's bigger than Christ now?
I don't care.
D'ya get my meaning with your psychedelic dreaming.
I'm a Somewhere Man and we'd all love to see the plan.
Hey Maisonette Bill.
She's just a fool on the pill.
Cos getting on an E
is like having a cup of tea.
Or is it?
Get real.

Some people detect a Beatles influence.

As they left the stage I could see two familiar figures approaching across the vast acreage of the venue. It was my old lunch buddies, Dog and Fish, who were to compere the night and provide the 'comedy' element. From experience I knew that basically this would involve them coming on between each act and pretending that they did not really want to be there. The strangest aspect of modern compering (or perhaps I should say postmodern compering) is that the host of the evening invariably seems to feel the necessity to dissociate himself from the proceedings, as if it was all some sad joke they're indulging in for a laugh.

'Hello, Sam,' said Dog. 'Shag the Mrs that day, did you?'

For a moment I was at a loss but then I recalled the circumstances of my hasty retreat from One Nine Oh. I didn't know what to say, so I laughed a bit and left it at that.

'Yeah, sorry you got shafted out of telly,' added Fish. 'You were a straight geezer. Best thing that could have happened to you, though. Radio's the only truly postmodern no-bullshit medium. It's the new TV.'

'So my successor didn't give you a series, then?' I asked.

'No. Bastard,' Fish said morosely.

It wasn't my problem any more. I had this evening to worry about.

'Now, you do know you can't swear, don't you?' I said.

'No fucking problem, Sam,' said Dog and laughed as if this was a brilliant joke, and they headed for the stage.

I could see why. Brenda was starting her sound check. Brenda is a singer but her real claim to fame is that she is heart-stoppingly gorgeous. She usually performs in tiny see-through nighties and sings like she's having an orgasm.

Brenda was not doing a proper sound check because she was performing to a tape, but obviously a rehearsal was required so that the director of the concert video could ensure that Brenda's body would be well covered by the cameras if by nothing else.

It was all a bit too much for me. I wandered off to have a mooch around the hospitality section. I can't be standing about in vast empty arenas ogling young girls like that. It's not good for me. Besides, what would Lucy have thought? I always feel very close to her when I'm away, absence making the heart grow fonder and all that. I called her, but she sounded a bit distracted. She said she was tired and was going to put the answerphone on and go to bed really early.

Dear Penny

We met at Quark. I've never been there before but I know Sam goes quite often on his numerous important lunches. It's very posh and they give you little plates of nibbles the moment you arrive. I got there first (of course!) and sat there feeling like an absolute slut! I mean, I hadn't actually done anything wrong but it just seemed to me that everybody knew I was there for a clandestine dinner with a man who was not my husband.

The next thing I knew was that this dashing maître d' was opening a bottle of champagne in front of me.

'Meester Pheeepps 'e 'as call to sigh 'e will be a leetle light. 'E sigh to geeeve the liedy shompine.' Well, long story short, I'd had two and a half glasses by the time Carl turned up. I didn't want to but when one is just sitting there like a lemon, one does.

Carl looked incredible. Everybody turned to stare. He's grown his hair and sideburns again (for a part, Dick Turpin, American cable movie, silly script but fun) and what with his dark curls and big coat he looked as if he'd just come back from writing epic poetry and fighting duels in Tuscany. Anyway, he strode straight across to me and without so much as saying 'hello' or anything he kissed me on the mouth! Then he stood back, stared at me with his smouldering coal-black eyes and said that I looked absolutely ravishing, which I did not, although I must admit that I was wearing a new silk blouse with no bra (silk does rather flatter the smaller bosom like mine).

Anyway, he was full of apologies about being late, rehearsals or something. He said he already felt cheated because he knew that my husband was only away for the evening and that he'd already wasted forty precious minutes of it.

Well, that made me think, I must say.

'How did you know Sam was going to be away?' I asked.

Carl looked me in the eye. 'I'm ashamed to say that he wrote to me on behalf of His Royal Highness asking me to read a poem at the Prince's Trust Concert and instead of agreeing, as naturally I normally would have done, I . . . Well, it seemed like fate.'

I was amazed.

'This is a planned seduction!' I exclaimed and he continued to stare me in the eye and replied that he certainly hoped so.

God, I must have been the colour of a shy beetroot.

'Carl, I'm married! I . . . I love my husband. You can't possibly be serious! I shouldn't even be here.'

'Then why did you come?' he asked, and I'm afraid to say he had me there. I mean I could have protested that I had accepted his invitation entirely innocently, but after what had gone on between us before? The truth of the matter was that there was no way that this meeting could be innocent. I was just avoiding the truth because I was scared of it.

Carl answered his own question. 'You're here because you're lonely, Lucy. Because you need tenderness and passion and you're not getting it. I can see the longing in your eyes.'

I tried to protest that it wasn't true, but I'd lost the power of forming a coherent sentence, what with the champagne and the fact that in some ways . . . Oh God, he was right.

'I've tried to do the honourable thing and keep away as I said I would,' Carl said, 'but when this chance came along I couldn't fight it any longer. I've wanted you from the first day we met, Lucy. You fascinate me. I don't know any other women like you.'

This couldn't be true, surely? I mean Carl Phipps is a star, a heart-throb. He could have the pick of the bunch. I put this to him but he insisted that I was different, that he really did want me above all others. Before I knew it, there we were holding hands again. I really don't know if I encouraged this but I do know that I had left my hand lying prone between us upon the table and when he elegantly rested his hand upon it, I did not withdraw.

The hospitality backstage was really buzzing. Charlie Stone was doing some interviews to be cut into the broadcast whenever any of the old rockers got into a particularly long guitar solo.

I found myself in Joe London's dressing room. Woody Monk was there, of course, and Wally, the drug-addled lead guitarist of the Muvvers and Joe's sidekick for nearly thirty years. Wally looked quite extraordinary, like a mummified corpse. He reminded me of that Stone

Age hunter they found after he'd been frozen for 20,000 years in the Alps. They were rehearsing one of the Muvvers' early hits and Joe and Wally seemed to be having a little trouble remembering exactly how the song went. Joe said, 'Nah, man, you go fahkin' da da da dum after the second line when I sing, "Youngest gun, dream won't stop", orlright?'

This threw Wally completely. 'Is that the lyric?' he mumbled with apparent surprise.

'Of course it's the fahkin' lyric. I mean we've only done it eight trillion fahkin' times, geezer!'

'Well, that's amazing, man,' said Wally. 'I always thought you were singing "Currant bun, cream on top". In't that amazing?'

Then Joe saw me. It took a moment for him to focus, but he recognised me, and he seemed genuinely pleased to see me. I told him how proud and happy the BBC were that he and the band had graced us with their presence and he couldn't have been sweeter about it.

'I larve a big gig, me. A nice big charity gig. 'Ere, Wally, you remember that one we done for RockAid with Mark Knopfler and the Straits?'

'Nah,' said Wally. Silly question really because it was quite obvious that Wally did not really remember anything at all.

Just then Rod Stewart puts his head round the door to say hello. I must admit it was all pretty exciting.

'Rod! 'Ow's it going, you old bastard? Orlright?' Joe said. 'Nice one. 'Ow's Britt? Sorry Alana. 'Ow's Alana?'

This was, of course, something of a *faux pas*.

'Not Alana, you pillock,' said Monk. 'He moved on.'

'Oh, yeah, sorry. 'Ow's Rachel?' Joe corrected himself.

'I don't fink it's 'er any more eiver,' said Monk.

'Well, whatever, ven, the new one, 'ow is she?' Joe seemed impervious to social embarrassment.

Rod having gone on his way, Joe turned back to me.

'Lovely bloke, top geezer. Diamond. 'Asn't changed at all. Still loves his soccer. That's what I like abaht gigs like this. They bring out the best in all of us. We're here to support starvation abroad and drug abuse at home. Just a bunch of top geezers and stunning birds coming together to help uvver people. No ego. No attitude. Just cats wot care.'

I left just as the show was about to start. I really wanted to ring Lucy but I knew she wanted a quiet night and was probably already in bed.

Three bottles of wine between us, a quick 'Perhaps we should have coffee somewhere quieter,' and suddenly I'm in a taxi heading for his place. Yes, we were snogging and, yes, he was using his hands, upstairs and outside only, but when all you're wearing is a silk blouse, it might as well have been inside.

Before I knew it we were in his flat. Carl was being wonderfully provoca-tive. I mean he didn't just leap or anything. He was, well, 'sensitive' is the best way of putting it. After the initial pash in the taxi he really held back and I didn't feel at all pressurised. So how did I end up on the couch with him? With six-year-old brandy being ignored on the coffee table while we writhed together? Because I wanted to, that's why. The booze had knocked out my inhi-bitions and I wanted to be there, with Carl breathing sensual nothings into my ear and expertly removing my shoes as if he'd been doing it all his life.

And then suddenly I'm floating through the air as he swept me up into his arms with hardly a jolt or a shudder and carried me through to his bedroom, beautifully neat with a vast kingsize bed covered in crisp fresh white linen. This is a man who has a woman who does, no doubt about that. He laid me on the bed and we kissed a little more and then he began to unbutton my blouse.

That was when I stopped it. His other hand was beginning to work its way up under my skirt, beautifully and gently but under my skirt nonetheless. Somehow I managed to find a voice and against every desire and hormone in my body I asked him to stop.

He did so, immediately. I mean he was still half on top of me but he sus-pended his exploratory hand actions, even going to the effort of doing up the button he had just undone. On the other hand, he did not remove his lips from my ear into which he whispered, 'Lucy, please. I want to make love to you all night, tenderly and gently and completely. I want to massage your body and touch every inch of your beautiful skin. I want to be a part of you, as one.'

Oh God, I wanted it. How many years is it since Sam wanted to touch every inch of my skin? And massage! Christ, it takes me all evening to get Sam to give me even the most perfunctory shoulder rub and here was this gorgeous man . . . Except all that has nothing to do with anything. I'm married and I love my husband.

Did I mention that he'd taken his shirt off? He did that after he'd laid me on the bed. He looked absolutely superb, more muscular than I'd expected but not too much. I think saying no was the hardest thing I've ever done.

'Carl. I can't. You're wonderful, beautiful, and I could fall in love with you in an instant, perhaps I already have. But I'm married. I love my husband, it's not exciting like this, but then nothing is exciting for ever, is it?'

'Isn't it? That's a rather bleak view to have of life, Lucy.'

And of course he was right. Oh God, he was right. What an appalling thing to have to say. I want it, I crave it, I need it, but I'm going to deny myself because I believe that life is better lived sensibly and unexcitingly. You can't just go doing exactly what you like the whole time. Not if you want to look after the things that really matter to you.

'Please, I have to go now,' I said. 'I can't be strong for much longer. Will you call for a cab? Please?'

And to his great credit he did not try to persuade me further. He just said, 'Of course,' and rang for a taxi. I could see that he was as upset as I was.

'This time I really won't call you again, Lucy,' Carl said as he kissed me goodbye (on the cheek). 'It wouldn't be fair on either of us.'

The gig was pretty dreadful. I don't think I've ever heard anything so loud in my life. The engineers assured me that it sounded better on the radio, but it was rough going for the audience. Anyway, the kids seemed to enjoy themselves, or at least they acted as though they did. Then again, if you've paid twenty quid you're going to make the effort, aren't you?

Afterwards there was a line-up to meet the Prince, but I was excluded because the Head of BBC Manchester had muscled his way in and nicked my place. I didn't really mind. I imagine you'd feel a bit of an idiot in one of those royal line-ups. I'm sure the royals do.

Anyway, as I say, me and Joe and Woody Monk ended up in the bar at the Britannia. Joe kept getting the rounds in. I've noticed that about people who've given up the booze. They're always very anxious to buy other people drinks. After Joe had got me my fifth bottle of Pils I had to explain that I was taking it easy as I was likely to be called upon to provide sperm samples in the near future.

'Oh, blimey,' he said. 'Paternity suit, eh? I get one of vose a veek. Fahking DNA, ruined the art of the casual shag.'

Well, I'm home now, drunk and feeling very strange. Angry with myself for so nearly doing something very stupid, and angry with myself for not doing it. I know I'll feel terrible in the morning, even without the appalling hangover that I'm definitely due. But the main thing is that in the end I resisted temptation. Whatever I may have thought or desired, I did not actually do anything. Well, almost nothing anyway, and that's what matters.

One thing I do feel is that I'm very much in love with Sam. I hope that's not the booze and the guilt talking because I do feel it, perhaps not often, and not in the way Carl excited me tonight, but I do still fancy him. I mean it. It's not just because I'm drunk. He does still turn me on, and that's because I love him. If you want the love and the security that a proper relationship brings then you have to go for the long haul. Even if you do really really really want to shag another bloke.

Anyway, what I really want to say is that I feel very close to Sam now. I rang him at his hotel and told him so. I hope I didn't sound too drunk because I have specifically asked him to cut down on the booze because of our IVF business, which I did not give a thought to tonight like the disgusting slapper that I am. Also I hope I didn't make him suspicious. I mean I do sometimes ring up to tell him I love him.

Actually I think I'm going to be sick.

I just spoke to Lucy, which I'm really glad about. I'd just been thinking how much I missed her when she phoned. It was so nice. I haven't heard her as affectionate in ages.

I really am a lucky man. A lucky, lucky man. I just don't deserve a girl like Lucy, she's beautiful and funny and interesting and I'm just a git. In fact I'm worse than a git. I'm a bastard, a deceiving bastard, because I've already betrayed her trust over my movie script, and now I'm planning a second and even greater betrayal that I can hardly bear to think about, let alone write.

I hope I didn't sound like I'd had a drink.

Dear Penny

Well, it's been a week since the night I choose not to mention and I feel a bit better about it all. I'm absolutely committed to my love for Sam and there's an end to it. In fact we're really getting on at the moment.

I think it's partly Sam, actually. He seems very positive about things and about himself, which is quite a change from the way he's been, well, for years really. It's very nice.

I've been sniffing my drugs every night. This way of pumping them up your nose is all right, but it does mean that you go to bed making the most appalling honking snorts. I can't believe Sam can still fancy me, although he assures me he does.

Dear Self

Lucy is snorting and honking like a pig in bed, poor thing. It's these drugs she's taking up her nose. I've had to come through into the spare room, which is where I'm writing this. To be honest I don't think I'll get much sleep anyway. You see, I've finally made my big decision.

I'm going to read Lucy's book.

I have to if I want this script to be as good as it can be. If I want to have any chance at all of it having genuine heart and soul then the heroine's voice must be authentic. I mean Lucy would want me to get the woman right, wouldn't she? Of course she would.

I tried taking a look tonight while she was in the bath. I felt like a thief, which of course is what I am. The damn thing was locked, of course. She's got one of those leatherbound journals from WH Smith.

What I must do is go and buy another one. I'm certain that all the keys are the same. They only cost about a fiver.

I feel terrible about this, but what can I do? If I don't blow it, within six months or so I could have my own movie. The ultimate dream of every wannabe writer on the planet. Courage, Sam. You have no choice.

Dear Penny

I went into Spannerfield today for a check-up. It seems the sniffing business is not moving fast enough, so they're going to switch me over to injections. Just shallow ones in the leg, which I can do myself, but I can't say I'm looking forward to it.

There was a lady waiting there who's on her sixth cycle! I felt so sorry for her. She's from the Middle East and it's terribly important to her to have a child. I think the pressure on women is greater in some cultures. At least I don't have to put up with that!

In so many ways I'm lucky with Sam, apart from loving him, that is, which goes without saying. He really is very gentle and supportive in his own way and he certainly never puts me under any pressure. I've asked him to give up the booze completely, by the way, in order to get his sperm into tip-top condition. I thought he'd sulk but he's been very nice about it. He said it didn't bother him at all.

Dear etc.

Damn, blast and bollocks. I hate being off the booze. Somebody had a leaving do today and I had to drink Coke. It's surprisingly difficult to kick the sauce. You say to yourself, 'It can't be so hard, I'll just take a month off,' but then suddenly Trevor's having a dinner party and you *have* to drink for that. Then there's the pub dominos team reunion coming up and you *have* to drink for that.

Ah well. I'm going to stick with it. I love Lucy and I'm not going to let her down, particularly now that I'm actively planning to deceive her. My local Smith's was out of Lucy's type of journal today and I didn't have time to go further afield, but I'll do it tomorrow. My resolve is hardening. Lucy is being ever so nice to me at the moment as well, which doesn't make betraying her any easier. We seem to have entered a new stage of affection. Perhaps it's the treatment. Also I imagine Lucy is feeling quite emotional because there is now the actual, real possibility that the treatment will work and in a couple of months' time we'll be on our way to becoming parents. And what then?

I got a taste of it today, actually. George and Melinda brought Cuthbert round for tea. He's crawling now, that is when he can find a moment in his busy shrieking, shitting and vomiting schedule. My God, that lad can puke. There seems to be a constant flow of milky vom emanating from his mouth. He doesn't *hurl* it, not often anyway. It's not as if he's coating the furniture or anything, it's just always *there*, sort of falling from his toothless gums. I've seen it on George's shoulder many a time. It's as if a large and angry seagull hovers permanently above him, waiting for him to put on a decent suit.

Penny

I'll probably be writing to you a bit less from now on. The original intention of the letters was, as you know, in order to become a partner with my emotions and to avoid feeling like a cork bobbing about on the sea of fate. Well, I no longer feel like a cork because by beginning this cycle of IVF, gruesome though it is, I really feel a lot better and that I've taken control of my destiny. I don't like to admit it, but I feel very slightly confident. I mean, although the chances are reckoned at about a fifth, I'm top of the list in terms of the perfect patient. I don't even feel strange about trying to get a baby this way, which I thought I might. In fact just the reverse.

I was talking to Joanna at work about it and she said something I hear quite a lot. She sort of shook her head in disbelief and said, 'Wow, isn't it amazing? I mean we really are playing God these days, aren't we?' Now she wasn't trying to be mean, quite the opposite. She's very supportive, but nonetheless I bridled. People do still seem to see IVF as a deeply unnatural process and so it is, but no more unnatural than taking antibiotics or flying in an aeroplane. All IVF is, when you get right down to it, is the process of getting the sperm and the egg to meet outside the body. That's it. It's my egg. It's Sam's sperm. If it works it'll develop inside me. All they do is create more ideal conditions for the moment of conception than the inside of my plumbing. As far as I'm concerned, it's like a Caesarean but in reverse. Millions of women have their babies removed by the hand of man. I'm just going to have mine inserted, that's all.

I just took a moment out to inject my leg. Sam hates this and turns away (as if I enjoy it!). Actually, he probably turned away because my legs look so horrible. These injections leave awful bruises (maybe I'm not doing it very well). I look as though I've been beaten up by a midget.

Dear Sam

Nigel and Justin have been asking again about the ending. I've told them that I'll do it soon, but I'm not sure when. Lucy's and my IVF cycle will last a few weeks and I can't decide whether to commit myself to saying how my story ends before I know our result or after. Surprisingly, Ewan is being tremendously good about it. He says it's only one out of a hundred scenes and since the whole story is one of doubt, hope and unanswered questions he rather likes the idea of leaving the ending ambiguous for as long as possible. He says it'll be very healthy for the actors to discover their parts in the same ignorance and confusion that the characters are in themselves. I find myself warming to Ewan.

I've now bought four diaries from WH Smith identical to the one Lucy uses for her journal. One of them is bound to have a key that fits hers. Tomorrow, when she's gone off to work, I intend to return to the house and read her story.

Dear Penny

I wasn't going to write to you tonight but then I thought I would because Sam's been acting very strangely this evening. From the moment I got back from work it's all seemed rather odd. He's been alternately offhand and angry-looking and then suddenly very huggy and affectionate. Perhaps it's his hormones. I've heard that when women are pregnant their partners some-times react in sympathy with them, experiencing the same symptoms. Who knows, maybe it's the same with IVF?

I must say I'm feeling pretty strange myself, in fact. I've started having hot flushes, so the injections must be working. Their purpose is to sort of shut down my reproductive system so that the hospital can take over. Basically they induce a sort of premature menopause. That's nice, isn't it?

Dear Sam

Well, I'm devastated. I just don't know what I think any more. They do say that eavesdroppers never hear good of themselves. Well, nor do diary readers.

Lucy very nearly had an affair.

I'm stunned. It is the absolute last thing I would have expected of her. What's more, I have to seethe in silence. I can't say anything about it, because the way I found out is unforgivable. And what would I say, anyway? I don't really know what I think about it at all. Of course part of me is riven with jealousy. The thought of that *fucking shit* Carl Phipps sneaking about trying to screw my wife and actually managing to get his hands on her, albeit briefly, makes my blood boil. I'm furious. I'm livid. I want to punch him and give her the biggest piece of my mind in history.

On the other hand, she was pissed, and she didn't do it, did she? She pulled back because she loved me. Would I have done the same? Me, who is capable of sneaking about and invading the private diary of the woman I love? I mean, if I honestly ask myself, if I was drunk, on Winona Ryder's bed, and she'd taken her top off and offered to kiss me all over and shag me all night, would I have held back the way Lucy did?

That's why I feel so confused. Part of me is angry and hurt and jealous and part of me is thrilled. Thrilled that after all these years, and with me being such a grump most of the time (plenty about that in her book), Lucy still loves me the way she does, loves me enough to walk away from a fantasy when the crunch came.

Of course one positive thing is that now I know she nearly betrayed me it makes me feel slightly better about betraying her.

Dear Penny

I feel pretty awful, I must say. Now I know how Mum felt a couple of years ago. Sam's not himself either. He seems emotionally confused. He kisses me a lot, but then I catch him glaring at me.

Dear Sam

I've read the rest of Lucy's book now and it's wonderful. Just what I'd hoped for and exactly what I need. It's stuffed with really funny thoughts and poignant bits. I felt very guilty reading it and not just because it's so wrong to be doing so but also because it's clear that I haven't always been as attentive to Lucy as I should have been. I'll definitely try to be more sensitive to her needs from now on. I'm not one for fatalism but perhaps I was meant to find out about what so nearly happened so that I can work harder on my marriage before it's too late.

Anyway, I've copied out loads of good stuff from Lucy's book and really feel that I can get down to finishing the script. Obviously I'll give Lucy some kind of co-writing credit, depending on how much of her stuff I use. That'll of course mean telling her, which clearly I shall have to do anyway in the end. Oh Christ, how am I going to do that?

Dear Penny

Sam came with me to the hospital today to pick up all the needles and drugs for the next series of injections. He's really making an effort, for which I'm very grateful as IVF does make me feel low. The fact that it seems to be bringing out the best in Sam is a great help. He's also got very enthusiastic about his work, which is a huge relief for me as his negativity had got very wearing. I must say I can't quite see what the enthusiasm is based on. We listened to a bit of Charlie Stone's show this morning on our way to Spannerfield and it struck me as being about the most puerile thing I've ever heard. I said so and Sam agreed with me, so I asked him how he'd managed to get so absorbed in it. He said that he had things in the pipeline. I definitely get the impression that there's something Sam isn't telling me, but I don't mind. He's allowed his secrets. After all, I have mine. Looking back I can scarcely believe that episode with Carl ever happened. How could I have been so stupid? To so nearly throw away everything I have. I feel particularly strongly about that now that we're really moving on with the IVF. Could it work? I try not to let myself hope too much, but I can't help it.

Sam

I'm filling in the final details on the IVF part of the script now. Well not the *final* detail—I still can't decide about the ending—but I'm very pleased with the way I've dramatised the process. Ewan is delighted, too, as are the rest of the team. We had an excellent meeting at his house this evening. His wife Morag made us a fabulous dinner and was very interesting about the script. She's one of those uniquely Scottish beauties, almost eerily white with green eyes, a hint of pale freckles and a great mane of strawberry-blonde hair. Quite gorgeous. Not a patch on Lucy, though. Well, let's face it, no woman is. It's probably an awful thing to admit, but I think the terrible shock about Phipps has sort of *reminded* me of how beautiful Lucy is. I mean of course I knew anyway, but maybe I'd begun to take it for granted.

I really really do love Lucy. More than ever, I think. And that's not because of how much she's improved my script.

Ewan laughed and laughed at the new stuff. Particularly the business about the injections. The surprising thing was how excited he was at the thought of being able to put a needle on the screen that wasn't full of heroin. He seems to think that this in itself is an incredibly original idea.

'So liberating,' he said. 'Hasn't been done in years.'

Dear Penny

Well, Sam administered his first injection into my bum this evening. He had his last practice try on an orange and then prepared to go for the real thing. All I could say was what I had been saying ever since we first saw the bloody things at the hospital, which was, 'That fucking needle is four inches long.' I mean honestly the damn things are not needles at all, not in any normal sense. More like spears or lances. The doctor explained that they have to be like that because the purpose is to administer an intermuscular injection.

Ewan is anxious to know all the details about the process, which I think is healthy. I explained to him that the intermuscular injection introduces a hormonal drug, which provokes the female subject into a sort of hyperovulation, producing far more eggs than is natural. It is, of course, physically intrusive and rather upsetting. Quite aside from having a four-inch-long needle stuck into your arse by your partner.

'Exactly,' said Ewan. 'This is a crucial scene, a crucial image. Actually, I think we should call the picture *My Arse Is an Orange*.'

To my dismay there was a lot of enthusiastic nodding at this from Nigel, Justin and Petra. I felt rather alone but nonetheless tried to fight my corner.

'Yes, brilliant idea, except that the film is called *Inconceivable*.'

'Oh, aye, at the moment,' said Ewan casually.

I turned to George and Trevor for support, but they just stared at the bowl of Kettle Chips.

Anyway, the deed had to be done. Sam looked as nervous as I was as he filled up the ghastly weapon with the ampoules of hormone solution, tapping the damn thing to make sure all the air was out.

'Are you ready?' he said.

'That fucking needle is four inches long.'

'And it's not going to get any shorter,' Sam said. 'Drop 'em.'

And so that was it. Up went the skirt, down came the knickers and there I was bent over the bed like a condemned woman with Sam hovering at my arse end with a spear in his hand. Most undignified. I could feel Sam drawing an imaginary cross on my right buttock with his sterilising swab. Upper outside quarter is the rule. That way there is less chance of skewering a major nerve centre and rendering the patient paralysed. One, two, three, and in he plunged. You have to do it all in one easy movement, holding the needle like a pen or a dart. I must say he did it very well, I hardly felt a thing, until he depressed the plunger and pumped in the hormone solution.

I must say Sam looked quite pale when I came up for air. He said he felt he'd earned a drink, but that of course he wouldn't have one. He said it nicely, as a joke. I really think this whole business is bringing us closer together.

Later on, after we'd all left the Proclaimers' house, I turned on Trevor and George for not helping me defend my title.

'Oh, come on, Sam,' said George. '*Inconceivable* is just a rather poor pun. Surely after all the years we've spent at TV Centre deleting crap puns you don't expect me to defend one now.'

George can be a hurtful bastard when he wants to be.

'You liked it before,' I said.

'Oh yes, before,' he said airily. Yes, before a fashionable young director with a three-picture deal in Los Angeles said he didn't like it. God, I never thought George could be so spineless. We're all caught in the headlights of fashion and fame.

I'm going to sleep now. Sam's still at the dressing table doing his book. It's amazing the way he's come round to the whole thing. I wonder if he'll ever let me read it. Of course I could never let Sam read mine, not unless I removed the Carl Phipps entries. Like Stalin rewriting history.

I must be sure to lock my journal very carefully. I found it open in the drawer today, so I must have forgotten to lock it last night, although I can't think how, I always check. Oh well, lucky Sam didn't find it open. He might not have been able to resist a read. Actually I think that's unfair. I think he'd do the right thing. I'm not sure if I would.

After the disagreement over the title, which I think I won, we got back to discussing the hypodermic scene. Nigel was not sure about the 'You might feel a bit of a prick' line, which I was appalled at because it's one of my favourite lines.

Anyway, I was just getting all heated and defensive as we writers do, when Ewan really alarmed me by saying, 'It doesn't matter, anyway, we won't be hearing the dialogue. I always play thrash metal music over my injection scenes. It's a personal motif. I'm known for it. Have you ever heard of a Boston grunge band called One-Eyed Trouser Snake? They'd be perfect.'

A bit worrying, that, but there's nothing I can do about it. Everyone knows that in movies the writer is lower than the make-up girl's cat.

Anyway, then Nigel asked Ewan if he'd given any thought to casting.

'Well, the girl's what? Twenty-two? Twenty-three?' Ewan replied.

I quickly interjected that in fact I'd been thinking early thirties and unbelievably Ewan just laughed!

'Look, Sam. I think we'll need to be pretty non-specific about the girl's age. I mean obviously we're not looking at teenage waifs but she's got to be vaguely shaggable, for Christ's sake. I'll tell you what I'll do. I'll accept anything from an old-looking twenty-one-year-old to a young-looking twenty-eight.'

I couldn't reply. His pragmatism (I might almost say cynicism) had temporarily rendered me speechless. There was worse to come.

'What about the man?' Nigel asked.

'I was thinking in terms of Carl Phipps,' Ewan replied.

I can't write any more tonight. All I can say is that it'll be over my dead body.

Dear Penny

I saw Carl Phipps again today for the first time since what I think we must describe as 'that night'. It was a bit of a shock. I don't know if he was as flustered as I was because we avoided each other's eye. He'd come in to talk to Sheila about a movie script that's come through. It's small-budget, mainly BBC money, but Sheila thinks it's interesting.

'It's a pretty funny script,' she said, 'although it hasn't got an end yet for some reason. I've never heard of the author, but Ewan Proclaimer's slated to direct and you can't get any hotter than him.'

Carl enquired what the theme was and you could have knocked me down with a feather when Sheila said infertility.

'It's absolutely the theme of the moment,' she said. 'Lucy, you're our expert on the subject. Would you like to cast an eye over this script for us? Tell Carl what you think.'

'No thanks,' I replied with as much dignity as I could. 'I get all that at home.'

Dear Sam

We held auditions today for Rachel, which was very exciting and also most disconcerting since the casting director has definitely erred on the lower end of Ewan's age range. The venue was a church hall near Goodge Street on the Tottenham Court Road. Ewan sat behind a long trestle table with Petra, also a PA with blue hair and an earnest-looking young man with a ponytail who is to be the second assistant director. George and I slunk around at the back trying not to ogle the actresses too much.

Ewan was getting the girls to read one of Rachel's speeches, which I had basically lifted straight out of Lucy's book. It's from the bit where she tried a guided fantasy. Wonderful stuff. There were a couple of actresses who made it sound absolutely marvellous.

'"I mean, why the hell should I have to *imagine* a baby? Why can't I just *have* one! Far less nice people than me have lots. I'd be a better mum than half the women I see letting their children put sweets in the trolley at Sainsbury's . . ."'

Listening to it was both exhilarating and excruciating. I mean it works so well and yet of course it's Lucy's voice, Lucy's feelings. I really have done a terrible thing. Standing there watching all these gorgeous young women, all ten years younger than Lucy, mouthing her thoughts, made me feel very awkward about myself indeed. But what's done is done. It'll be worth it for us both in the end. George was thrilled.

'Very nice speech, Sam,' he said. 'The woman's voice is so much more clearly defined. You've obviously really unlocked something.'

That made me feel both better and worse.

Perhaps I should just tell Lucy, make a clean breast of it. But I can't. Not while she's all hormonally messed up with IVF. Besides, supposing she stopped me? This is my big break, my chance, and the BBC would probably sue me for the money they've already spent. Anyway, Lucy said to me that if I did this thing that I have done she'd leave me, so I can't tell her, can I? Not yet.

Dear Penny

Drusilla has come up with another plan. I blush even to report it. She rushed into the office at lunch today with a map of Dorset and the train times from Paddington. She says that Sam and I have to go to the West Country, walk to the village of Cerne Abbas, go out onto the hillside and prostrate our-selves naked upon the penis of the great chalk man that is set upon the slope. Then, well, you guessed it, we have to have it off! It seems that this is an even more fertile and spiritual place than Primrose Hill, far far more so, in fact. Drusilla says that hundreds of couples use it and the conception rates are con-siderably higher than with IVF. On summer nights apparently there's a queue and the local druid has to bless one of the big toes as a sort of back-up bonking area. Drusilla says that in reflexology the feet are connected to the genitalia so doing it on the foot is nearly as good.

I must say the idea of standing in a queue of hippies waiting to have it off on an ancient penis which would no doubt be still warm from the last lot did not appeal to me much, but Drusilla claims that there's actually a colossal sense of community. She says people who meet there often become lifelong pals, going off to India together in their camper vans and swapping partners. The very least they do is exchange cards at the winter solstice.

Well, I told her that I was committed to the IVF cycle and that I certainly did not intend to interrupt it now. I told her I'd think about it for future refer-ence. I've kept the train timetable, just in case. Not that it'll be of any remote use in a month or two. These new railway companies keep changing them and they don't even mean much in the first place.

I will say this, though. If this cycle doesn't work (which statistically I know it won't, although I can't help feeling sort of hopeful), I might give Dorset a go. Sam and I could use a bit of a holiday and I do love him particularly at the moment. We had such a good time on Primrose Hill (until the arrival of the squirrel) that I think it would be fun to do a little tour of the fertile spots of Britain and shag on all of them.

Dear Sam

Rather an unpleasant day on the movie. We were back in the church hall near Goodge Street looking at men, and of course that complete fucking bastard Carl Phipps was reading for the part of Colin! I have to tell you that it was excruciating sitting there being quiet while the smug, philandering, wife-snogging rat was saying *my lines*. I know that I've no right to get on my high horse. All the same, I wanted to punch him.

We were seeing the men one at a time instead of bringing in a crowd like we did for the women. This is because Ewan wants a 'name' for the bloke and so they have to be handled a bit more carefully. Actually, I've begun to notice that there's quite a lot of casual sexism in the film industry, which is surprising considering that they're all supposed to be so right-on. It's the old rules of the market. There are far fewer decent roles for women than there are for men and so even the talented women are more desperate, hence they can be paid less and treated worse.

Ewan was using the scene where Colin gets his sperm test results to hear the actors read, and I must say it was quite exciting to see the scene come to life. The little blue-haired PA was reading in the part of Rachel.

'"Forty-one per cent swimming in the wrong direction,"' she read out in that peculiarly depressed delivery that only people who 'read in' can achieve.

Carl Phipps brushed her aside and addressed Ewan directly.

'I've got stupid sperm!' he shouted, far too loudly in my opinion. Anyone can shout. 'What is it with sperm! It's lazy, it's sluggish, it's got no idea where it's going. It sounds like a pub full of blokes!'

Ewan laughed heartily, which was fair enough because it's actually a bloody good line, but I thought the delivery was abysmal. A performance hewn from solid mahogany. Personally I thought that what with the disappearance of the rainforests it was ecologically unsound of him to produce such a wooden performance and I whispered as much to George.

'Actually, I thought it was pretty good,' said George. 'The line's a bit obvious, though. You don't need to spoonfeed us the gags, you know. Trust the audience.'

I hadn't really noticed before quite what a pompous arse George can be when he wants.

'Superb, Carl, absolutely superb,' Ewan was saying.

'Yes, and so good of you to agree to come in and read for us,' Justin added.

This was a reference to the fact that Carl is a star and hence should not really have to do such a mundane thing as actually audition for a part because we should all be aware of how brilliant he is anyway.

'No actor is too big to read for a part, Ewan,' Carl crawled.

After the low snake had slithered off we all gathered round to discuss his paltry efforts. I had expected an instant and resounding raspberry, and was bitterly disappointed when Ewan announced happily that he felt we'd found our Colin and everybody readily agreed. I was horrified and protested loudly.

'Oh no, hang on,' I said. 'I mean, hang on! I completely disagree. He's wrong for it. I mean, everything he did was wrong for Colin.'

'How's that, then?' Ewan enquired.

'Well, he was anal, uptight, repressed and terminally stiff.'

'Exactly,' said Ewan happily. 'A completely convincing Englishman.'

Dear Penny

Sam, who has been very good up until now, made a bit of a mess of tonight's injection and it really hurt. He didn't mean to, I know, and he was really apologetic. I was telling him about the script we had in at the office about infertility and IVF. It's called Inconceivable *and is to be a co-production between the BBC and Above The Line Films. I've been feeling a bit bad about it ever since I heard, having stopped Sam from developing exactly the same idea. He told me not to worry about it, but I do worry. I mean I've always been on at Sam to search within himself for his writing and the one time he did, I banned it. What's more, I actually think that it's quite a good idea that they're doing the film. Sam seemed surprised at this—eager, almost. I wonder whether he still harbours dreams of persuading me to change my mind. Not much point, I'd have thought, now that someone else has had the idea. Anyway, I'm not going to change my mind, I'm afraid.*

I explained to Sam that whereas I shall definitely go and see Inconceivable *when it comes out I just couldn't have borne for it to be based on our story directly. I mean it would all go just too deep. The pain and all.*

Dear Sam

I got a bit of a shock tonight. I'd just been getting ready to give Lucy her nightly injection when she started talking about *Inconceivable*. I should have expected it, of course. I knew that the Phipps fucker was on Sheila's books or how could he have stalked Lucy in the way he did. Nonetheless, it was still a shock. For a little while I was thrilled, actually, because Lucy was being very positive about the whole idea. She seems to think that bringing the subject of infertility into the realms of normality via the medium of comedy is a very empowering thing. I could not agree more, of course, especially if I win a BAFTA.

I was soon to be disappointed, though. She still hasn't relented about her own privacy and I can see that it'll be a little while before I can even think about telling her.

Anyway, I was just getting the needle ready for the plunge, when she brought up the subject of casting. She said that there'd been an offer put in on Carl Phipps to play the husband. I gritted my teeth and resolved to change the subject when she started to eulogise about the bastard. Saying that she thought he would be superb, being such a nice man and a truly sensitive actor and of course so good-looking. I swear I did not mean to jab the needle in so clumsily, well obviously I didn't, I'm not a thug. I just jerked involuntarily, hearing her being so nice about the snake.

Anyway, I feel terrible now for being such a clod with the needle and have just brought her Horlicks and some toast in bed. God, she looks gorgeous, sitting there under the duvet cupping her mug in both hands. I resolve this night to look after her for ever and never let her be hurt. After, that is, I've broken her heart by revealing my black treachery.

Dear Penny

I did something today that I swore I wouldn't do. I went to Mothercare. Only for a few minutes at lunchtime, but it was probably not a good idea. Everything looks so lovely. The clothes, the toys, all these amazing buggies with their great big fat wheels. I bought some things too. Just a couple of baby-gros and a fluffy ball with a bell inside it. I don't see how it can do any harm to have a positive attitude and if the IVF does fail then my cousin's just had one and I can send it all to her.

Dear Sam

Things are moving at an incredible pace on the film. One of the good things about it being produced by a television company is that they're not afraid of tight schedules. And with Ewan set to begin pre-production on his first US feature in only five months, the schedule could not be tighter. It's all cast now; Carl Phipps as Colin (fate has a sick sense of humour) and Nimnh Tubbs as Rachel. Nimnh is not as big a star as Carl but she's highly regarded, having played most of the younger Shakespeare totty at the RSC and recently a *'Hedda Gabler for the Millennium generation'* (*Daily Telegraph*) at the National. I have not yet discovered how to pronounce Nimnh but I must make sure I do before rehearsals begin, which, believe it or not, is at the beginning of next week.

Dear Penny

I went to the Disney store in Regent Street in my lunch break today. I really must stop this. Except actually I've always wanted to own the video of Snow White, which is a genuine movie classic. As for the other toys and videos and the little Pocahontas outfit I bought, well, they'll be useful to have around when friends come over with their children, even if I don't have one of my own.

Look, Penny, I know what you're thinking, or what you would be thinking if you existed, in fact I know what I'm thinking and you're wrong. I mean I'm wrong. There's nothing sad or unhealthy about me occasionally buying toys. Why shouldn't I dream? Why shouldn't I indulge in a few delicious fantasies? Supposing they come true, eh? Oh dear, it would be so wonderful I can hardly bear to think about it.

Dear Sam

Whatever I may think about Ewan casting Carl Phipps, I can't fault him with Nimnh Tubbs. She's wonderful. Beautiful and heart-breaking. She was going through some of the stuff I pinched from Lucy's book today and you could have heard a pin drop. She manages to make it funny and sad at the same time. When she read out that stuff about praying and feeling guilty for only believing in God when she wants something, people clapped, as indeed did I.

And I suppose, if I'm absolutely honest, Carl Phipps isn't bad either. He does seem to have a kind of natural intensity which doesn't look forced or anything. When he does the lines it's possible for me to almost forget it's me talking. They were looking at the part where Colin tries to explain to Rachel about what she thinks is his indifference towards the idea of kids and he admits that in the abstract sense he doesn't want children . . .

'"But as a part of you, as an extension and expression of our love, that I do want and if it happened, I'd be delighted. No, I'd be more than delighted. I'd be in Heaven."' Phipps sort of paused here and looked into Nimnh's eyes. I swear they'd both gone a bit teary, both the actors, that is, not both Nimnh's eyes, although that as well, obviously. I'd heard that actors achieve the watery-eyed look by pulling at the hairs in their noses but if they did that they did it bloody slyly because I didn't notice.

Even George, who's a tough, thick-skinned bastard, seemed quite emotional. He told me that it was good stuff and I told him that I'd meant every word of it.

After that Ewan called a short break. All the actors and crew made a beeline for the tea and biscuit table as actors and crew always do. I decided to introduce myself to Nimnh who, being an actress, was holding a cup of hot water into which she was jiggling some noxious herbal teabag or other.

'Hi, I'm the writer. I'm so glad you've decided to do this, Nimnn . . . Nhimmn . . . Nmnhm. . .'

Of course it was only then that I realised I'd forgotten to check up on how to pronounce the woman's name and that I had absolutely no idea.

'It's pronounced Nahvé. It's ancient Celtic,' she said and there was a delightful hint of Irish in her voice which I could tell she was rather proud of. 'I feel my Celtic roots very deeply. My family hail from the bleak and beautiful Western Isles of the Isle of Ireland.'

Well there's no answer to that. As it happens, I didn't need one because just then Carl came up, all blokey and matey.

'I'm Carl. You're Sam, aren't you? I know your wife slightly. She works at my agency.'

Yes, you know her slightly, mate, I thought, and slightly is as much as you're ever going to know her, you lying sneaking bastard.

'Tremendous script, mate,' Carl continued. 'Really tremendous.'

I thanked him and then when his back was turned managed to sur-reptitiously put ketchup in his tea. A small but important victory. Then the PA called the company back to rehearse. As Nimnh passed me she pointed to the script and the speech Ewan wanted to look at.

'I cried when I first read it,' she said.

The terrible thing is, so did I.

I'd only just put it into the script that morning. I couldn't put it in earlier because Lucy hadn't written it. She takes her book to Spannerfield and if the queue's long, which it normally is, she some-times jots down her thoughts.

Nimnh sat on a chair in the middle of the rehearsal room, with a pen and a book in her hand, and read the speech.

'"I don't know. As we get closer to the day that will either see me reborn or on which I'll just die a bit more, the longing inside me seems to become almost physical, as if I've swallowed something heavy and very slightly poisonous. A sort of morning sickness for the barren and unfulfilled. Do I dare to hope that perhaps soon the longing will end?"'

I could hardly bear it. Nimnh was reading the speech (and reading it very well), but all I could hear was Lucy. All I could see was Lucy, sitting in a crowded waiting room all alone. Scribbling down her thoughts, thoughts I was now making public.

Everyone was very positive about the speech. Ewan loves the way I'm 'building the script in layers', as he calls it. George said that he really felt I'd cracked the female protagonist.

'Nothing to do with me, mate,' I told him. 'Didn't I tell you? I took on a woman co-writer.'

Dear Penny

I've just re-read some of the stuff I've been writing recently and quite frankly I'm a bit embarrassed. Mawkish, self-pitying drivel. I'm sorry I bored you with it. All that stuff about the 'longing within' and 'morning sickness for the barren'. Great Christ, three-quarters of the world is starving! How can I be so self-indulgent? All I can say is thank GOD no one will ever, ever read it. Still, it does help to get it all out, even if I do sound like an absolute whinger.

I went for another blood test today as per. That's about it. Nothing else to tell.

Dear Sam

I've now officially handed in my notice at BBC Radio. It'll mean going into debt because the advance they've given me for my film is nothing like enough to keep us, but it has to be done. I've taken so many days off in the last couple of months that they'd even begun to notice at Broadcasting House. Normally, if you don't push your luck they'll let you bumble on until you retire but even they have limits so I thought I'd better go before I was pushed.

I dropped in on Charlie Stone's studio on my last morning, to say goodbye.

'Right, OK, nice one,' he said. 'Who are you?'

Which is, I think, a fitting epitaph for my career in broadcasting.

I haven't told Lucy about me chucking my job. How can I? She hasn't got the faintest idea what I'm up to.

There was a big script conference today prior to commencement of principal photography. It was held at Above The Line in Soho because Ewan didn't want to schlep all the way out to White City. Therefore George and Trevor and even Nigel had to schlep into town. Interesting, that. It strikes me that Nigel's not as tough as he'd like to think he is. The BBC are putting up most of the money but Nigel lets the Corporation get treated like junior partners to three haircuts with half a rented floor in Soho.

And why?

Film, that's why. The whole world is bewitched by film, the inimitable glamour of the silver screen. Or at least the whole of the London media world, which is the whole world as far as we who live in it are concerned. Novels, theatre, TV? All right in their way, but in the final analysis boring. If a novelist writes a novel the first question his first interviewer will ask is, 'Will it be made into a movie?' If an actor gets a part in a £10 million TV mini-series they'll say to their friends, 'Of course it's only telly.' It's Hollywood, you see. After ninety years we're all still mesmerised. We still want to get there. Nobody working at the BBC is going to get to Hollywood but somebody from Above The Line might and in Ewan's case will. Which is why we come to him.

Fortunately for me it was a very positive meeting indeed. Everybody agreed that the current draft of the script is good. Ewan made it clear that he was very happy.

Then came the inevitable caveat. This is a thing that always happens to writers in script discussions, no matter how enthusiastic those discussions might be. Somebody says 'except for'. I've done it to hundreds myself: 'Everybody is absolutely delighted, except for . . .'

'The ending,' Nigel said, and they all nodded.

It was a fair call, I had to admit.

'Vis-à-vis the absence thereof,' said Petra putting the unspoken doubt into words.

I knew I would have to stick to my guns. It turns out that Lucy was right all along. You do need to write from the heart. It does have to come from within, and at the moment I don't have the heart to decide on the fate of my characters. I don't know how I'll feel when the news comes through, so I don't know how they'll feel.

'It's only the last page,' I said. 'The last few lines, in fact. I'll hand it in when I said, in a few days.'

'But, Sam,' Nigel protested. 'Ewan starts filming next week.'

'Well, he doesn't need to start with the end, does he?' I said, looking at Ewan, who stared into his Aqua Libra in a suitable 'I shall pronounce my conclusions in my own time' manner.

'With respect,' Petra said—in fact very nearly snapped—'it's a bit difficult keeping the American distributors *and* their money in place when we don't know how the story comes out.'

'Well, I don't know how the story comes out,' I protested. 'I'm sorry but I don't.'

Ewan hauled himself from the depths of his futon and reached for an olive. 'Look, it's my movie, you ken?' he said, which is directors all over for you. I'd written it. Various people were paying for it. Hundreds of people were going to be involved in making it. But it would, of course, be 'his' movie, a 'Ewan Proclaimer Film'.

'As I've made clear before,' he continued, 'if Sam wants to hold back on the ending then that's fine. It's good motivation for the actors and it keeps us all on our toes. They're playing two people over whom hangs a life or no-life situation. I'm very happy to help them to maintain that ambiguity. Improvisation is the life blood of creative endeavour.'

Well, that shut them up, let me tell you.

There's a church in Hammersmith next to the flyover which I call 'the lonely church'. I call it that because it's been almost completely cut off by roads from the community it was built to serve. Millions of people see it every year but

*only at fifty miles an hour. Its spire pokes up beside the flyover as the M4
starts to turn back into the A4. It's a beautiful church, although you wouldn't
know it until you were about ten feet away from it. I found myself there today.
I'd just sort of wandered off after my appointment at the hospital and I must
have walked two or three miles because suddenly there I was standing outside
the lonely church of St Paul's as I now know it to be called. I didn't go in, but I
sat in the grounds trying to find the faith to pray. I don't know whether I managed it. I don't know what it would feel like to really believe in a prayer. I do
know that I concentrated very hard and tried to think why I deserved a child
and came up with the answer that I deserved one because it was the thing that
I wanted more than anything else on earth. I suppose in a way that was a
prayer, whatever that means.*

Not long now. A couple of weeks at most and then we'll know.

George and Trevor took me out to lunch today. We begin shooting
tomorrow and they absolutely insisted that I join them for a final conference. I was delighted to. Now that I'm no longer a BBC exec and on a
budget to boot I don't get to dine at Quark quite as regularly as I used to
and I thought it would be almost like old times.

They were both already seated when I arrived and looking very serious. George didn't even bother to stare at the waitress's backside, which
must have been a first for him. All in all, it was not like old times one
bit. They got straight to the point.

'Sam,' said George, but I could see that he spoke for both of them.
'You're going to have to tell Lucy about this.'

It took me completely aback. Silly, really. George and Trevor are both
good friends of Lucy and it should have occurred to me that they would
be worrying about the obvious autobiographical details that I was
exploiting even if they were ignorant about the depths of my betrayal.

'I can't,' I said. 'Not now. We're just about to complete a cycle of IVF.'

They were both genuinely concerned. It was as obvious to them as it
was to me that a pseudonym would not disguise me for ever.

'People are very excited about this project,' George insisted. 'What are
you going to do if it's a hit? You won't be able to hide from the media,
you know. My God! Imagine if they found out before she did and she
read it in the papers, or, worse, got doorstepped by a hack?'

'Even if it's a flop you can't possibly keep the fact that you've written a
movie a secret,' Trevor insisted. 'She's your wife, for heaven's sake.'

They're right, of course, and I certainly didn't need a fifty-quid lunch
(courtesy of the licence payer) for anybody to tell me.

I told them that I'd tell her when I know how the story ends.

Dear Penny

Sam gave me the last injection tonight before egg collection, which we go in for at 7.00am the day after tomorrow. Rather dramatically, the injection had to be done at midnight. It's now 12.15 but I know I shall have trouble sleeping. Sam's been very good about the injections. Apart from that one time, they haven't hurt at all. Talking to some of the women at the hospital, it seems that some husbands (partners, I should say) can't bring themselves to do it at all, so the poor women have to go in at seven every morning for weeks. Sam's given me a lot of strength. Taking such an interest and always being around when I need him. Some husbands hate it all so much that they try to pretend it isn't happening. Sam hasn't been like that at all. Quite the opposite. He's been fascinated, which has made things much easier for me. I tried to thank him a bit tonight because I know he's never really, really wanted children. Not really.

She's wrong about me not really wanting children and I told her so. I told her I really do want us to have children, that I want it with all my heart, and I do. I told her I wanted it because I love her and that our children would be an extension and expression of that love. Another part of us. But if it doesn't happen then we'll still have us, and our love will be no less whole . . . and then I realised that I was quoting the bloody script! And I couldn't remember whether I'd said it before, or written it in my book, or made it up for the film, or nicked it from Lucy's book! I suddenly realised that I no longer knew whose emotions were whose. I thought I've got to tell her, right now. And I did try. I started to, but I couldn't. Not now. She's having her eggs collected tomorrow.

Sam was a bit distracted, actually. Probably the fact that he's got to have another hospital wank tomorrow. He hates that so much. Anyway, he didn't say much. I think he wanted to but he didn't and I didn't press him. We just held each other. I feel incredibly close to Sam tonight. I told him that I love him and that it gives me strength to know that, whatever happens, I'm safe in that love.

I thought he was going to cry. Then I thought he was going to tell me something. Then he didn't say anything.

Dear Sam

This morning Lucy and I went to Spannerfield for the big day of egg and sperm collection. We got there at 6.50am for 7.00 as instructed, to find a lengthy queue of cold, sheepish-looking people already there. Most of them were women in for injections because they don't have husbands like me who have the sheer iron guts to do it themselves. Some of us, however, about ten couples, were in for the full business and we were duly led off to a ward with a row of curtained-off beds in it.

There was a rather nice nurse called Charles. Lucy knew him already but it was all new for us husbands (or partners).

'All right, Lucy,' said Charles. 'We'll just pop this on and hop into bo-bos and, Sam, we'll be wanting a little deposit from you for the sperm bank, so I'll just leave a paying-in pot here and I'll call you when there's a service till free.'

Lucy had to put on a sort of nightie-smock that was entirely open at the back.

'Dignified little number,' she said. 'Think I'll wear it to a première.'

For a moment I was completely thrown.

'Première?' I said with what could only have been incriminating alarm. 'Première of what?'

'Nothing, just any old première,' she replied, looking at me rather strangely. 'I was joking.'

Just then Charles returned and summoned me to do my duty.

'Your chamber awaits,' he said. And with grim resignation I took up my pot and went.

There are at least two rooms at the actual unit so the pressure of the queue was somewhat alleviated. In fact Charles told me that I had as much time as I liked because we were all in for the whole day anyway.

Well, that was some small comfort, but having said it you've said everything, because this was the most pressurised visit of them all. As I sat there alone, in the little room, trousers round my ankles (having duly washed my knob as instructed), I contemplated the awesome nature of my responsibilities. My wife, whom I love very very much, has just gone through six weeks of the most appallingly intrusive therapy. Drugs have been pumped into her at every hour of the day, forcing her body to shut down in a premature menopause prior to it being taken over and coerced into a grotesque fertility, overproducing eggs until her ovaries have become heavy, bloated and painful. Every other day for weeks she has traipsed across London to sit in queues with other desperate women, waiting to have various body fluids taken from her and to have her most intimate womanly self probed and manipulated.

Now if at this point I fail to ejaculate successfully into a pot, making absolutely sure that I catch the first spurt, this whole dreadful business will have been a total waste of time.

Sam looked quite pale when he returned from doing his duty. He said he thought he'd got enough. I said I damn well hoped so. They only need one.

The egg extraction was a rather weird experience. Being there with Lucy while the doctors take over makes you feel like an awkward guest at your own party.

I sat up at the non-business end and Lucy was soon snoring rather fitfully, having been put out for the count. They had her legs up in stirrups and a doctor lost no time in getting down to business. There was a little television screen on which he could see what he was doing through some ultrasound technique or other and he talked me through it.

'Now we're removing the fluid from inside the follicle, within which should be the eggs.'

Sure enough, they were siphoning out test tube after test tube of pale red liquid and then handing them through a little kitchen hatch into what I presumed was the lab.

It was extraordinary. The lady through the hatch kept shouting, 'One egg . . . two more eggs . . . another egg,' like a dinner lady. Anyway, in the end the doctor had got the lot and so he backed up the Pickford's removal van between Lucy's legs and started to dismantle the scaffolding rig he'd put up her.

On the way home in the car Sam told me all about it. I was feeling pretty woozy anyway and I can't say that stories of doctors sucking eggs out of my vagina made me feel much better. Still, at least it's over. Sam says they told him they got twelve eggs, which was about what they wanted.

It was so strange to think that at that very moment, as we drove home, back in the hospital his sperm were being whirled round in a centrifuge prior to being shaken up in a tube with my eggs.

We both agreed that the whole experience was one that we were not anxious to repeat. I said that perhaps we wouldn't have to. I just have this funny feeling that it's going to work.

'I feel good inside,' I told him, and then I was sick into the glove compartment, but it's all right, the doctors said that might happen. All right for me, that is, not Sam, who had to clear it out.

Dear Sam

We began principal photography today. God, it was exciting. We're filming in an old warehouse in Docklands, which they've done out as the hospital. I took the light railway, which is not a bad service. They offered to send a car for me but I said no. Lucy might have wondered why commissioning editors of Radio were suddenly being treated so grandly. When I left she was still in bed. I took her a cup of herbal and longed to tell her where I was going. It would have been so wonderful.

It's the thing I've dreamt of all my life. What's more, Lucy has shared so many of those dreams, and now they've come true I can't even share it with her. How cruel is that? Fate can be an absolute bugger.

I'll tell her soon, I swear it. The moment we're through this IVF cycle. George says it's pointless to put it off and that there'll never be a good time, but I can't possibly tell her now, she's too fragile. She's taken the week off work (although they say you don't have to) and seems to be in a world of her own. Sort of serene, but very delicate. She says she's trying to be entirely relaxed and meditative. Well, I don't think she'd be very calm within if I said to her, 'Oh, by the way, darling, I've turned our mutual agony into a movie and what's more you've unwittingly written half of it.'

How did I get into this? I'm sure I had no choice. Didn't I? I definitely seem to remember having no choice, but it's all gone a bit hazy.

I must say, though, that the day was wonderful. Incredibly exciting. Just seeing all the cameras and cables and trucks and catering and actors and crew, and all because of me. It felt fantastic.

Ewan was starting with Rachel's laparoscopy and at first I thought he must have sacked Nimnh because an entirely different actress was on set in the operation smock. I was just getting up the courage to protest to Ewan, because I think Nimnh is wonderful, when I noticed Nimnh sitting in a folding chair smoking a cigarette. On further investigation it turned out that the new actress was a bottom double! Imagine it!

It seems there'd been a row earlier that morning when despite Nimnh's protests Ewan had been adamant about filming Rachel from behind, getting into bed with the open-backed smock on.

'For Christ's sake, it's not about perving on her arse! It's about her vulnerability! Can't you see that?' he exclaimed. 'This woman is a piece of meat, stripped of dignity. Her arse is *quite literally* on the line and we need to see it!'

Well, Nimnh had simply folded her arms and refused point blank. She said she did not do two Desdemonas and a Rosalind at the RSC in order to have her bum used to sell videos. I thought she was absolutely right, actually, although like every man on the set I would have loved to see the bum under discussion. Thinking about it, that's probably another good reason why she shouldn't have to show it.

Dear Penny
It's three days now since the egg extraction and today was the day to have it put back in. That is, if there's anything to put back, which was the first anxiety.
Well, it turned out all right, in that we had managed to create seven

embryos, which they said was good. A doctor explained that some of the embryos are good and some are not so good but, the long and the short of it was that we had two very good and two pretty good. The doctor said that they were prepared to insert three if we insisted, but she strongly recommended that we do only two, which I was very happy to go along with. I mean the possibility of triplets is pretty daunting. Anyway, although the consultation was presented as a series of choices for us, in the long run, let's face it, you do what you're told, don't you? We agreed that two embryos be reinserted and the rest would be donated to the hospital for research, which apparently is their usual procedure if the donors have no objections, which we didn't.

The reinsertion was very quick indeed. No anaesthetic or anything. They just wheel you in, spread your legs, and squirt them up. It's incredibly low tech really when you consider the dazzling medical science that has led up to it.

It's a hell of a lot easier than the egg extraction. The only real discomfort is that they make you do it with a full bladder because for some reason this makes for a clearer ultrasound picture. Afterwards they won't let you wee for about three-quarters of an hour, which is absolutely excruciating, and you keep feeling that the terrible pressure must be crushing the life out of your poor embryos.

Then they let you go home. As we were getting ready to leave, Charles, the nurse, came in with a printout of the computer image of our two embryos, both of which were already dividing into further cells.

'This is them,' he said. 'Good luck.'

When we got home Sam made some tea and I just sat in the sitting room staring at the photo, thinking that this could be the first photo in an album of our children's lives. It's not many kids who get to see themselves when they were only two or three cells big.

Sam reminded me that the chances are that these ones won't either and I know that, of course, but I'm sure that mental attitude has an effect on the physical self. I know I can't will it to happen, but the least I can do is give Dick and Debbie the most positive start in life that I can.

Yes, all right, I've given them names! And I'm not embarrassed about it either. They're mine, aren't they? They exist, don't they? At least they did when the picture was taken. And now? Who knows? I could see that Sam was not at all sure about personalising things in this way. But why not? They're fertilised embryos! That's a huge step for us. We have to be positive.

Sam reminded me yet again that it's only a one-in-five chance. Well, I know! Of course the odds are long, but they're not impossible. Twenty per cent isn't a bad shot. When my photo was taken they were alive.

'Think about that, Sam,' I said. 'Two living entities created from you and me. All they have to do now is hang on inside for a few days.'

It's funny, but Lucy's enthusiasm, the strength of her will, is infectious. Because the more I looked at that photo, the more real those two little translucent splodges became. They are, after all, already embryos. They've already passed the beginning of life. And I couldn't deny that in a way they looked pretty tough, I mean for three-celled organisms, that is, obviously.

'Of course they're tough,' said Lucy. 'Think what they've been through already! Sucked out of me by vacuum cleaner, pumped out of you into a cold plastic pot. Whirled around in a centrifuge, shaken up until they bash into each other, smeared on a microscope slide then sucked up again and squirted through a syringe. It's a positive assault course. Dick and Debbie are SAS material!'

And they might make it. They could make it. I mean, why the hell shouldn't they? If they can just hang on for a few more days while they grow a few more cells.

Then Lucy whispered at her stomach.

'Come on, Dick and Debbie,' she said. It was sort of as a joke, but I could see that she meant it, so I said it too but louder.

'Come on, Dick and Debbie!'

Then we started shouting it.

Funny, really, the two of us sitting there, laughing and shouting at Lucy's stomach.

Whatever happens now, that was a good thing to do.

Dear Penny

I wonder if this will be the last sad letter that I ever write you? The long wait is coming to an end. One more vaginal suppository is all I have to take (there's been nine, plus three more spikes in the bum). I hope Dick and Debbie realise what I'm going through for them. I hope we're not hoping too much. It's only a one-in-five chance, after all.

Sam said that any child of mine would be one in a million.

Then we kissed for ages.

I can't deny that I feel good. I'm not even slightly periodic and normally I can feel my period coming for a week.

After we had kissed, Sam got very serious and said that when it's all over, for better or . . . well, hopefully for better, he wants to talk. I said fine and he said, 'No, really talk, about the last few months, and all that we've been feeling and going through together.' This is a very encouraging sign for me because, as I've said before, Sam is not always the most communicative of people. He says he wants to talk about where he wants to go as a writer and what sacrifices we would both have to make for it and, well, lots of other things.

He says he wants to go away this weekend. Whatever the news is and . . . well, talk.

I said that I thought it was a great idea. We can take Dick and Debbie on their first trip.

We thought about that for a while and then we kissed again and then he said he loved me and I said I love him. One thing is for sure: whatever happens, whether Dick and Debbie make it or not, IVF has been good for Sam and me. It's really brought us closer together.

It's twelve thirty at night. Lucy and I have had a lovely evening together and we've agreed to go away together next weekend. I'll tell her everything then.

She's been asleep for an hour now. But I couldn't sleep because as I lay there thinking about Dick and Debbie I decided on the way my film is going to end. I've just written it up and faxed it to Ewan.

INT. DAY. COLIN AND RACHEL'S HOUSE.
The news comes in the afternoon. Colin and Rachel are sitting, anxiously awaiting a phone call. They hold hands. The phone rings. Colin tries to answer it but Rachel is holding his hands too tightly. There's a moment of comedy and emotion as Colin has to remove a hand from Rachel's traumatised grip in order to pick up the receiver. He listens for a moment. In Rachel's eyes we see the hope and the fear of her entire life. Colin smiles. He says, 'Thank you,' and puts the phone down. He looks at Rachel, she looks at him, he says, 'They made it.' The End.

That's it. Whatever happens to Lucy and me, that's the end of my movie. It's the ending I felt tonight, the ending I want.

Ewan just phoned. I hope he didn't wake Lucy.

'It's mawkish, oversentimental, middle-class,' he said. 'I love it.'

Petra called as well. She was hugely relieved. 'The right decision, Sam,' she said. 'I might as well tell you now. If I'd gone to LA with anything other than a developing foetus, they'd have withdrawn their funding.'

Somehow I think that now everything will be all right.

Dear Penny

Today I got my period.

It started at about eleven this morning. It came without warning but it's a heavy one and it means that all my dreams are dead.

I'm not pregnant. I've never been pregnant. The two embryos I called Dick and Debbie died a week ago.

I don't believe I've ever cried as much in my whole life as I did today. I wasn't just crying for the loss of the babies that never existed. That was only the beginning of my trouble, the beginning of the nightmare that was today. I've been crying for the loss of my whole life, a life I thought I knew but it turns out I didn't know at all.

I'm writing this alone in bed. Sam isn't here and he won't be coming back. I don't know where he is and I don't care. I've left him.

I'm going to write down what happened so that I never forget.

After I'd cried so much that I thought I would dehydrate I knew that I should tell Sam. We'd been through it all together and I felt that he'd want to be with me at the end of it. Besides, I needed him. Having gone about for a week half-believing that I had a child inside me, or even two, I suddenly felt more desperately alone than I could have imagined possible.

But when I spoke to his office at Broadcasting House I was amazed to discover that Sam no longer worked there. The woman I was speaking to said that he'd left weeks ago. She didn't want to tell me where he was, either, as she said it was very private. I told her that I was his wife and I was ill and that she had to tell me where he was. She gave in in the end but she didn't want to. I could tell that she was wondering why Sam's wife didn't know that he'd changed his job. I was wondering that too.

When I was riding in the taxi I think I believed he was having an affair. That's what I expected to find at the address the woman had given me. Sam in the arms of another woman. I wish that that's what I had found.

The address was a film location. A big warehouse in Docklands with the usual trucks and trailers and generators outside and inside. There were people everywhere. I passed a group dressed as nurses and as I walked in I could see immediately that one of the sets was a hospital operating room for women, with stirrups and that sort of thing. I stood there for a while, hidden in the shadows, not knowing what to think. Everything was so confused, and I felt scared. I could see that all the lights and the attention were concentrated on what was a bedroom set, a bedroom very like my own, in fact. There were two actors on the set, one of them, to my astonishment, Carl Phipps. The other was a woman I recognised as Nimnh Tubbs from the RSC. Someone called for quiet and the two of them began to play out a scene. It was a rehearsal. I knew that because I could see that the camera was not being operated. Carl sat at a desk and pretended to type into a laptop.

'What the hell do you find to write about?' he said. 'What an emotionally retarded shit I am, I suppose. I know you secretly think I'm holding my sperm back. You think their refusal to leap like wild salmon up the river of your fertility and headbutt great holes in your eggs is down to a belligerently slack attitude which they've caught off me.'

I could feel myself going cold. Surely that was exactly the sort of thing that

Sam always used to say to me? What was going on? Why was Nimnh Tubbs sitting on the bed holding a journal just like I do every night? Just like I'm doing now, in fact.

Then a young Scottish man who was clearly the director stepped into the scene.

'Obviously we'll pick up a reaction from you there, Nimnh,' he said. 'Semi-distraught, emotionally dysfunctional, pathetic little woman stuff, OK?'

Nimnh nodded wisely. She knew that type.

Perhaps I'm stupid, but at this point I still didn't know what was going on. I just stood there, convinced that I was in some horrible dream. They started rehearsing again, more words I knew.

'I just happen to believe that when God made me he made me for a purpose beyond that of devoting my entire life to reproducing myself.'

And she replied, 'When God made you he made a million other people on the same day. He probably doesn't even remember your name.'

Then I knew. Those were my words! My actual verbatim words! Just then I saw Sam. I don't know whether I'd realised what was going on before or after he appeared, but either way I was no longer confused. I knew what had been done to me.

The director had called Sam over. Nimnh was having trouble with the motivation behind the scene and the director wanted her to hear it from the writer.

The writer. I was the bloody writer. He'd read my book.

Sam wittered on, posing importantly, loving himself.

'Don't forget that this woman is beginning a journey that will see her lose all dignity and sense of previous self,' he said. 'Before she knows it she'll be making a fool of herself at hippy visualisation classes, adopting a baby gorilla and claiming it's got nothing to do with her infertility. She'll have reduced her sex life to a series of joyless, soulless, cynically calculated servicings, treating her poor, hapless hubby as some kind of farmyard animal, brutally milked for its sperm . . .'

It was then that I walked forward onto the set. Some young woman with blue hair and a walkie-talkie tried to stop me, but I was not to be stopped. I don't know what Sam thought.

But I knew what I thought. One word.

'Bastard,' I said. It was all I could say. 'Bastard.'

Carl was nearly as surprised as Sam was, but I had no time for him.

'You bastard, Sam, you utter, fucking bastard.'

He tried to speak, but I wouldn't let him.

'I got my period, if you're interested,' I said. 'We failed. Dick and Debbie didn't make it.'

I didn't care that the director and Carl and Nimnh and the woman with blue hair could hear me. I didn't care about anything. They all began to turn away with embarrassment, but I told them to stay. I told them that they might as well listen now because they'd hear it all soon anyway, that Nimnh would be saying it all tomorrow.

George ran up. My God, George! They were all in on it.

Carl seized the moment to ask me what I was doing, what was going on.

'Ask him!' I said, and all eyes turned to Sam. 'He's told you everything else about me . . . My God, Sam, you've been stealing my book. Stealing my thoughts and feelings, like a thief!'

I don't know whether I actually said all that. I do know that I was crying. I'm certainly not a person who makes scenes in front of strangers lightly. I think that failing IVF had already pretty much destroyed what emotional defences I had. And then all this.

Then both Sam and Carl tried to lead me away. Carl was trying to get me to calm down and explain. Then Sam rounded on Carl.

'You keep out of this!' he said, and he looked like he was going to cry too. 'I know all about you!'

Carl was astonished. It was the last thing he expected.

'Now look here . . .' he started to say, but I didn't let him get the chance, I just went for Sam.

'Yes, that's right, Sam!' I shouted. Everyone really was backing away now, even the Scottish director, who did not look like a man who would embarrass easily. 'You know all about Carl! That he took me out and that I kissed him. You know everything about me, don't you? Because you've stolen my bloody thoughts! Well, here's another little piece of me and you can have it for nothing. You won't have to sneak about picking locks on people's diaries for this! I hate you! I hate you more than I ever believed I could hate anyone and I never want to see or speak to you again.' Then I ran out of the building with both Carl and Sam running after me. If it wasn't the worst thing that has ever happened to me it would be funny.

We stood there, the three of us, on a pavement in the Docklands, Sam desperately protesting that he'd never meant it to be like this, Carl hanging back wondering whether to intervene or not.

'I meant it, Sam, what I said,' I told him. I was calmer by this time, calm enough to look him in the eye. 'I told you once that if you did this thing I'd leave you and that's what I'm going to do.'

He tried to say that I wasn't myself, that I was over-reacting because we'd failed IVF. Over-reacting. That's a phrase I won't forget in a hurry.

'You've read my book, Sam,' I told him. 'You know that having a child with you was the thing I wanted most in the world. Well, it isn't any more, it's the thing I want least. I'm glad Dick and Debbie are dead!'

He looked at me for a moment. He was numb, I could see that. Then he started to cry.

He knew he'd lost me.

Tonight is the first time I've opened this 'book' document on my computer since that night when I finished my script and Lucy and I held each other for the last time and I was happy for the last time.

That was three months ago and not one minute has gone by since then, waking or sleeping, when I haven't missed Lucy with all my soul.

I don't know why I've decided to write something in this book now, I just thought I would. I suppose the truth is that I've bored my friends enough with how unhappy I am and the only person left whom I can safely bore without risk of further increasing my solitude and isolation is myself.

I made the biggest mistake of my life when I did what I did to Lucy. Every day I've asked myself how I could have been so stupid and I still don't have an answer. I suppose that I just never thought Lucy really meant it when she said that she'd leave me. I keep going over it all in my mind and I still think that if she hadn't found out about it in such a terrible, brutal way she might not have reacted quite as she did. Either way it's academic now, and one thing's for sure: it's all my fault.

The film is finished, or at least what's known as principal photography is finished, and the editing process has begun. I take no interest in it, of course. In fact I've had nothing at all to do with the project since the day I ran out of the studio chasing vainly after Lucy in an effort to persuade her to forgive the unforgivable. George and Trevor keep me informed. They say that everybody remains very excited. Funny, this is the fulfilment of a lifetime's ambition and I don't care. After the full extent of my appalling behaviour was so ruthlessly exposed I felt that the only honourable action I could take was to put an end to the film immediately. It turned out that it was no longer mine to stop. The BBC own it in partnership with Above The Line and having already spent over £2 million on it they were reluctant to cancel. Saving my marriage was not number one on their list of priorities.

I told Lucy what I'd tried to do and she wrote me a pretty caustic note about it saying that she didn't care whether the film progressed or not, that what I had stolen from her she didn't want back anyway.

I've given her all the money I got from the film. Half of it's Lucy's anyway and the rest is to go towards me buying her out of her half of the house. She doesn't want to live in it any more. She couldn't even bear to enter it. She got her sister and her mother to organise her things. That nearly broke my heart. In fact it did break my heart.

The final level of my torment is that she and Carl Phipps have become an item. Lucy hasn't told me this herself, of course, because as I say we don't speak, but she knows I know because she tells Melinda and Melinda tells George. It's not a very satisfactory line of communication but it's all I have. I torture myself trying to find out more, begging George for every gruelling snippet. I think about Lucy all the time. Apparently the relationship between her and Phipps is all very perky and positive and keen at the moment, which of course I'm very happy about and which of course I loathe and despise.

I've started writing another script. I'm doing what Lucy told me to do, drawing it from within. It's about a stupid, lonely, pathetic, weak, useless bastard who deserves everything he gets. It's a comedy.

Another six weeks gone by. Six miserable weeks.

I've discovered that despite what they say, time is not a great healer. Every morning I wake up hoping that the simple fact that a few more restless empty hours have elapsed will in itself provide me with some relief from the pain of my self-inflicted wounds, and every morning I'm disappointed. I still loathe myself and I still love Lucy, who is at this very moment in bed with Carl Phipps (it's two in the morning).

I'm afraid to say that I'm in danger of turning into a very sad act indeed. I get pissed every night and I haven't washed my sheets in a month.

I'm writing this entry in my book, by the way, because I got a letter from Lucy today and I don't know what else to do with myself. Actually it's not a letter, it's an email. This amazed me, incidentally. When we lived together Lucy couldn't even work the timer on the cooker. I suppose the bastard has taught her.

I'd written to her asking if she wanted a divorce and also if she knew where the key to the garden shed was, because the lawn is now about a foot high. I'll download Lucy's reply into this file.

Dear Sam

The key to the garden shed is under the second fuchsia pot on the right of the door. If this is the first time your thoughts have turned to the garden then I imagine that all the plants will be dead. If they are not, please give them TLC immediately. There is plant food in the shed. If greenfly or similar is in evidence fill the hand spray with soapy water and administer a gentle soaking. Do NOT use chemicals as the garden is entirely organic. Actually I should imagine that it's entirely cat shit by now because you have to go round and trowel it up once a week.

I suppose that I want a divorce in that we're clearly not married any more and perhaps it's time to formalise that. However, I don't think it's fair that it's me who has to say to you that I want a divorce. After all, I clearly don't want a divorce in that I never wanted our marriage to come to an end. The only reason I want a divorce is because of what you did and I wouldn't want a divorce if you hadn't done it, therefore in a real sense it's you that wants a divorce. Having said that, I suppose I do want a divorce. But I just don't think I could face it at the moment.

I can't believe it's come to this, Sam. How could you have been so stupid?

Yours, etc., etc. Lucy.

Dear Sam

Four more months have passed and once again I find that I feel the need to collect my thoughts.

Next week is the première of *Inconceivable*. Everyone is very excited about the film and the opening is to be rather a grand affair. We're promised television cameras and the presence of celebrities. The film is already being spoken of as *the* new British movie. I must say, there seems to be a *the* new British movie about once a week these days. I don't want to be cynical about my own film, but the phoenix of British cinema has risen from the ashes so often it must be getting quite dizzy.

Lucy is going to attend the première.

I didn't think that she would, but the publicist has just confirmed that she's coming, and will of course be on the arm of Carl Phipps. The publicist assures me that she expects them to be very much the golden couple of the night and to attract a lot of press.

The première is of course a real emotional issue for me. At first I thought I'd stay away, not knowing if I could face seeing Lucy with Phipps. George and Trevor, however, say that I have to come. They point out that the film is very good and that this should be celebrated. I've seen a tape and I think that it's good too. Ewan Proclaimer may be an arrogant bastard, but he certainly deserves his reputation as a hot director. George and Trevor also point out that the story is mine (and Lucy's) and that if anyone should be present at the moment of triumph it should be me. After all, George argued with his customary brutal honesty, I've sacrificed the only thing I had that was worth having in order to write this movie. I might as well go to the party.

Dear Penny

I never expected to open this book again. It ended so sadly I imagined I'd want nothing more to do with it. Now, however, I have something to say that should be recorded here because it's the end of the story and also the beginning. I don't want to talk to Carl because it might be nothing and if it is nothing I'd prefer never to have to think of it again, and if it isn't nothing then I don't want to speak until I know for sure.

You see, I think I might be pregnant. I'm three weeks late and the tester from Boots has proved positive. I've made an appointment to see Dr Cooper tomorrow.

I can hardly allow myself to believe that it might finally have happened.

PENNY!

Dr Cooper has confirmed it. This is the single happiest moment of my life. I am numb with joy.

I must stay calm, however. These are very early days; it could all still go wrong.

I've been concentrating very hard on my breathing.

A baby, Penny! Imagine it. It's all I've ever wanted from life.

It's now a little later. I've been making some camomile tea and attempting to centre myself. My heart has been pounding so mightily since I got back from the surgery that I'm scared I'm going to shake everything right out of me. Perhaps it'll help if I confess to you, Penny, that this joy is also tinged with one tiny element of sadness. You know what it is, of course. I've written to you so often about my love for Sam that you will not have expected the passing of that love to leave no mark on me at all. It is very sad that Sam, whom I loved so much and for so long and with whom I shared so many disappointments, can be no part of this wonderful moment.

It's not that I wish that the baby was his, not at all. I loved Sam with all my heart but love when it is not reciprocated is a pretty useless thing and I walked away. I thought that Sam loved me and I'm quite sure that he thought he did too, but he didn't. What he did to me proved that. Love has to include respect and consideration and trust. It's a partnership in which one partner protects the other. Sam didn't protect me and he didn't love me. He didn't love anyone, certainly not himself. Poor Sam.

It wasn't easy getting over him or coming to terms with what happened to me, but thank goodness I had Carl. I don't think I could have got through without him.

He wrote to me the day after the awful scene on the film set and asked if he could see me. I admit I flew to him, I was so upset and confused about *everything that I was happy to get comfort and affection wherever I could find it. I'm very glad I did.*

We didn't sleep together that first night, or the next, but I admit that it was not long afterwards.

My God, Penny, it was wonderful!

Perhaps it was the rawness of my emotions and also the rather defunct nature of my sex life in the preceding months that made me so receptive, but credit must also go to Carl. Some men just have a knack, that's all. He made love to me as if it was the only thing that he wanted to do on earth at that moment.

It went on for weeks, Penny, that first glorious fling. Sheila issued all sorts of dire warnings about being caught on the rebound and displacement of unhappiness and things like that but Drusilla said that passion is its own reward and she was right!

Carl is the first man I have ever been with (there have not been exactly many) who really seems to relish massaging a woman. He still does it (although perhaps not quite as often). We lie together naked on his bed and he's happy to work at my neck and shoulders for an hour or more. One thing I did notice is that he likes to watch himself while he does it. He has a large mirror at the end of his bed and I often catch him drinking in the rippling muscles of his image as he massages me. Fair enough, I suppose. No reason why he should be watching me. I can assure you he has a lot better muscle definition than I have.

I love the weekends. Carl is very big on Sunday mornings, lots of croissants and real coffee, big dressing gowns and the papers, just like being in a hotel, which is lovely. That and occasional trips to a little cottage he has in the Cotswolds, all log fires and stone walls, very Wuthering Heights. I can't say it's been perfect, of course. I've had my low moments, as, no doubt, has he. Carl also carries baggage with him. It's not another girl, it's more . . . well, Carl loves himself rather a lot, not in a horrid way, don't get me wrong, in fact it's quite charming. It's just I sometimes feel that simply being Carl Phipps is often enough for Carl. He doesn't need anyone else.

That's why I must be very careful about this business of our baby. Carl often says he loves me and how much he regrets the fact that I seem to be unable to have kids, but I don't know how he'll feel when confronted with the fact that I'm having one. I shan't force him.

I do love Carl, I know I do. It is not the same as my love for Sam was, of course. I don't think that any two loves can ever be the same. If they were they'd be interchangeable and what would be the point of that? I must say it's very strange living with a man who likes to talk so much. By rights I should love it. Sam, of course, was famously the man hidden behind the newspaper

*and I hated that. It's just that Carl's preferred topic of conversation is himself.
I'm constantly astonished at the skill with which he seems able to bring the
most unlikely topics back to the subject of Carl Phipps. Mention metaphysics
and Carl will tell you that he has for a number of years been working on a
verse play about John Donne; mention Schleswig Holstein and Carl has made
a toothpaste commercial in Flensburg. It's his work, really. It possesses him.
Basically Carl is and always will be a very very dedicated actor.*

*Perhaps I just attract men who are obsessed with their work. At least Carl is
enthusiastic about his, unlike gloomy old Sam. At least Carl believes in himself.*

*I want to tell him the wonderful news as soon as I possibly can. I tried his
mobile but he's on set and mobiles are banned. Not the* Inconceivable *set.
That was finished months ago. He's guesting on an ITV detective thing, playing a charming killer. I'm sure he's wonderful in it (he says he isn't but I can
see he knows he is).* Inconceivable *is about to be released and there seems to
be rather a lot of excitement about it. In fact, I've agreed to go to the première,
which is the day after tomorrow. At first I was adamant that I wouldn't, but in
the end I was persuaded. The whole thing is still sort of unfinished business,
and I think that seeing the film might finally draw a line under it all.*

*Also I do want to see Sam again and perhaps at his moment of triumph
(our moment of triumph; I'm a credited and paid-up writer, ha!) will be a good
time.*

I can hear Carl letting himself in. Time to tell him the news.

*I've told Carl and he's absolutely thrilled. He went all misty-eyed and talked a
lot about fatherhood and his own father and the circle of time and the scheme
of things and replacing himself on earth. Then he put on his big coat and went
for a very long walk, returning looking windswept and very serious. I suggested that we should go out and celebrate but he didn't want to. He says that
creating a life is a huge responsibility and he wants to spend some time in
meditation. Each to their own, of course, but nonetheless it would have been
nice to chink glasses for a moment even if I can only drink water.*

Dear Sam

I'm writing this on the evening of the première of *Inconceivable*. I
should be tying my bow tie because it's all going to be rather a posh do,
but I can't find it. I can't find my trousers either. I can never find anything in the house any more. This is because everything is on the floor,
which also happens to be where I keep my pizza boxes and my empty
bottles and cans. George is in the other room waiting for me. He's kindly
agreed to be my date for the night but only if I wash my hair and trim
my beard. This I've done.

I don't know how I'll be able to bear it when I see her, particularly when she arrives with another man. I love her so much, you see. When I think of all the evenings when I turned down the chance to hold her and to touch her because I wanted to work or read the paper. My God, if I had my time again.

Actually, I've finally finished my next script and it's about just that. It's called *Don't It Always Seem to Go* and it's about a bloke fucking up his life and then realising what he's lost. Amazingly, I've got it commissioned. George and Trevor think it's even better than *Inconceivable*. Lucy was right. All I needed to do was draw from within.

Dear Penny

Tonight has been very strange. I hardly know what to think.

This evening I attended the première of Inconceivable, *which, first of all, I must say I thought was wonderful. Sam really did do a marvellous job. I always knew what a good writer he is. I won't say that it was easy seeing all that pain played out again on screen (and revisiting my own thoughts), but it was done very sensitively and also extremely amusingly.*

The whole evening was much more glamorous than I expected and also more exciting. Well, I suppose it's a pretty exciting thing, going to the première of a movie you didn't even know you'd half written. I went with Carl and it was a very strange experience to be at the centre of all that attention. Cameras flashed, microphones appeared from nowhere, and people with autograph books shouted 'Carl! Carl!' I had on a new dress from Liberty's, which I was quite pleased with, very posh and rather daring at the front. The Wonderbra has of course done wonders for the smaller bosom, and now I'm pregnant perhaps I'll grow my own.

Of course a great deal of the excitement that surrounded Carl and me was that it was our first time out at a big event as 'an item'. Lots of journalists wanted to know about our future plans but we just smiled gaily and said how thrilled we were about the film.

Tonight has been the most extraordinary and may just possibly turn out to be the happiest of my life.

And not because the film was a great success, although it was, which was wonderful. They cheered at the end and I don't think they were just being nice. We had a real star-studded première with lots of celebs. Quite a few that I used to know had rallied round which I was touched by. There was a real crush in the foyer with TV and radio people grabbing interviews from anyone they recognised. I was trying to fight my way through to the booze and I heard Dog and Fish being very nice about the film.

'Brilliant,' said Dog. 'If you like your comedy with big laughs, this is it.'

'Personally we prefer our comedy with a small side salad,' Fish added. I think they're improving.

Charlie Stone turned up, which was very nice of him because he really is hip at the moment, and the press went mad. Particularly because he had the gorgeous Brenda on his arm as well, which guaranteed pictures.

Even Joe London was there with his wife Toni, and also Wally the guitarist. Joe was positive about the movie if a little faint in his praise.

'Not bad,' he said. 'Fort it was a bit of a bird's film myself.'

The interviewer asked Wally what he thought of the film.

'What film?' he said.

Anyway, all this is beside the point. I've only written it down because it was exciting and I don't want to forget it. The main event of the evening was about to happen, and it was not the film at all. It was Lucy.

Well, now comes the crunch, Penny. There are no future plans. Carl and I are not an item. I've left him and I think that he was mightily relieved.

Well, let's face it. From the first moment I told Carl about me being pregnant I knew in my heart that he doesn't want to have a baby. He said he was delighted, but he was lying. I finally tackled him about it in the limo on the way to the première. As good a time as any, I thought. I asked if he really was genuinely happy that I was pregnant.

'Happy? Of course I'm happy, darling, I'm delirious.'

Oh dear, Penny. He's a better actor on screen than he is off. There was a long and uncomfortable pause before he added, 'I'm happy because you're happy. That's what matters.'

Which is as much as to say, I'm devastated, my beautiful little life is about to be completely ruined by your bloody baby.

'But you have to be happy too, Carl,' I said, 'or it won't work.'

He sat quietly for another minute, trying to find the courage to start to wriggle out of it. He looked magnificently tortured in his beautiful dinner jacket.

'It's a shock, that's all,' he said finally. 'I mean, you said you couldn't have kids, that's why I didn't use protection.'

'Well, I thought I couldn't, but now it seems I can.'

'And that's great,' said Carl, not looking at me. 'Really great.'

And that's when I realised, finally realised, what I'd known all along, but was afraid to admit to myself.

He doesn't want a child, Penny, why the hell would he? He's happy. He has everything he wants, except to be big in the States, and a mewling, puking infant won't get him that. The truth is, Carl doesn't want to be tied down at all.

We suddenly found ourselves facing each other in the crush at the bar.

Oh my God, she looked lovely. So glamorous, so sexy, so beautiful. I was crushed by her presence, I just wanted to stand there and worship her. I did stand there and worship her.

I think it was the saddest moment yet. Here I was on the greatest night of my life, standing before the woman of my dreams. We'd written a hit movie together, and yet I knew I'd lost her, that she hated me.

We made small talk for a moment and then she told me her news. It came absolutely out of the blue. Lucy's pregnant.

I really was happy for her, honestly I was, although I also just wanted to die. I told her that I was thrilled and delighted and that Carl is the luckiest man on earth. I meant it too, I really did.

Then the evening began to take an unexpected turn.

'I've left Carl,' Lucy said, and my heart lurched. 'This evening, in fact, just before the film started. He doesn't want a child, so I'm going to go it alone. It's the modern way, and at least I'll have a bit of money, thanks to you and our film.'

Well, I was aghast. Was this my chance? After all, he'd caught her on the rebound, why shouldn't I? The second bounce, the double whammy. The possibilities of the situation were only just beginning to sink in when a publicist came over to get Lucy for an interview. She was in far more demand than I was this evening, by the way, even though I was the top-billed writer.

Suddenly she was leaving.

'Well . . . goodbye, Sam,' she said.

I made my decision. Well, it was more of an impulse than a decision.

'Lucy,' I said. 'Come back to me! Please, please come back. I'll do anything. I made the stupidest mistake of my life, but I didn't mean it. Tell me how I can make it up! Please, I love you. . .'

'Sam,' she said. 'Don't be absurd. We can't go back. I'm pregnant with another man's baby.'

'I'll look after it!' I blurted. 'I'll help bring it up. I'll be its father.'

And I meant it too. I'd love to bring up Lucy's child. I don't care who else's it would be. Lucy's child would be part of her and there's nothing about Lucy that I would not love.

It was a stunning thing to say. I felt winded, suddenly everything seemed to be in slow motion, like I wasn't actually there but was sort of hovering above it all, watching. The publicist kept tugging at my arm. She can't have heard what Sam said, or if she had she didn't care. Publicists at premières have to be very single-minded.

'Sam,' I said. 'You didn't even want children of your own, let alone somebody else's.'

Perhaps it was just the noise of the crowd but my voice sounded very strange to me. Sam looked absolutely desperate, wild even, like Rasputin, although I think that was mainly the beard.

'Can't a man make a mistake, for fuck's sake?!' Sam shouted, inevitably choosing the very moment when the room went quiet.

It was fate's favourite practical joke. Kill the volume just when the idiot with long hair and a beard is shouting obscenities. Everybody turned to look. Lucy went red. God, I wanted to ravish her there and then.

I thought she was going to hit me. Instead she just stared at me for a moment and then left, with the publicist scuttling after her.

Dear Penny

This morning when I woke (I hadn't thought I'd been asleep at all but I must have been, I suppose) there was a huge bunch of flowers on my doorstep. This is what the card said:

If I have to serve a life sentence for what I did, can't I at least serve it with you?

Which is not a bad line, I must say, and I swear if he ever uses it in a script I'll kill him.

I am of course very confused. I do love Sam, of course I love Sam, but I can't just pick things up as if nothing has happened. Can I?

Except of course something has happened. Something really extraordinary. Sam has offered to help me bring up my child. He loves me, there can be no better proof of that. I do believe that my joy is complete.

I've just received an email from Lucy. She will have me back. We are to be a family. I have never in my entire life been so happy as I am now.

Dear Penny

Today has been a very upsetting day, although now that it's over I feel curiously strong. I'm not pregnant. Dr Cooper says that I was pregnant, at least he thinks I was, but I'm not any more. He says that I've suffered a very early miscarriage, which is very common, if indeed I was pregnant at all. Whatever the problem is with me and fertility, it's not yet solved. Sam came with me to the doctor and afterwards we sat in the car and cried a little together. After that we went and got pissed.

Dear Sam

Lucy and I have been back together for six months. The happiest six months of my life, despite the fact that we've just been through our second IVF cycle and failed it. Lucy was very upset, of course, we both were, but we're OK. We had a wonderful holiday in India afterwards, no replacement, of course, but still absolutely fantastic.

I'm writing this sitting on the bed in a lovely little room in a country hotel in Dorset. Lucy is wearing nothing but a silk slip and is making my heart ache with love and desire. She's packing up a knapsack with champagne, chocolates and a big rug. It's a beautiful warm summer evening. In an hour or so we'll creep out into the night and make our way up the hill to the great and ancient chalk giant's penis. It might work, it might not. Either way, I can't wait.

BEN ELTON

Ben Elton has created some of the most popular television over the past twenty years, with such series as *The Young Ones*, *Blackadder* and *The Thin Blue Line*. His career as a writer goes from strength to strength, with five previous bestselling novels to his credit and three hit West End plays. Most recently, he has made his debut in the world of film, writing the screenplay and directing *Maybe Baby*, based on his novel, *Inconceivable,* and starring Hugh Laurie, Joely Richardson, Dawn French, Rowan Atkinson, Joanna Lumley and Emma Thompson. All this, and his success as a stand-up comedian, make Ben Elton one of today's most important comic voices.

In his novel, *Inconceivable*, Ben Elton drew upon the experiences and emotions he and his wife Sophie shared as they went through three cycles of IVF treatment at London's Hammersmith and Lister hospitals, although Elton is keen to point out that the story is 'not autobiographical in any sense. There's a lot of real emotion in there, they're thinking things I thought, or versions of things I noticed. But as a comedian I exaggerate the horrors of it all.'

In fact, unlike his fictitious couple, Elton showed the first thirty pages of his novel to his wife as they were embarking on their first IVF

treatment. 'She laughed a lot and said, "This is fun, but you're going to have to work on the woman's voice because she sounds like a bloke."' Ben Elton heeded this advice and admits that he had great support from his wife throughout the writing of the book. 'If she hadn't liked the idea I wouldn't have done what Sam did under any circumstances.'

So how does the comedian, who is renowned for his left-wing principles, feel about having to go private to get IVF treatment in the first place? 'There were no NHS places available for us anyway, and if there had been one it was logically absurd for someone as wealthy as me to be taking it with the pressure the system is under. In fact, at Hammersmith Hospital all the private money goes straight back into the unit and is necessary for its very survival.'

After two failed IVF cycles, Sophie became pregnant third time lucky and the Eltons are now proud parents of twins, Charlotte and Albert (Lottie and Bert), who will be one in August. 'It's been an astonishing year for me,' says Ben Elton. 'If you are fortunate enough to have love in your life, any time is a good time to become a father. But, speaking entirely personally, I feel very fortunate, in some ways, that it took us so long. Obviously I wish that Sophie hadn't had to go through what she went through and that I hadn't had to go through it with her, but, here we are, with two adorable children. I can't think of any ambitions that I haven't fulfilled, so I'll never need to tell my kids that they stopped me from doing anything. Some happy fate has delivered me great good fortune.'

Jane Eastgate

601-006-1